summer breal

AST
AC

WRIT

DA

WITH COLOR B

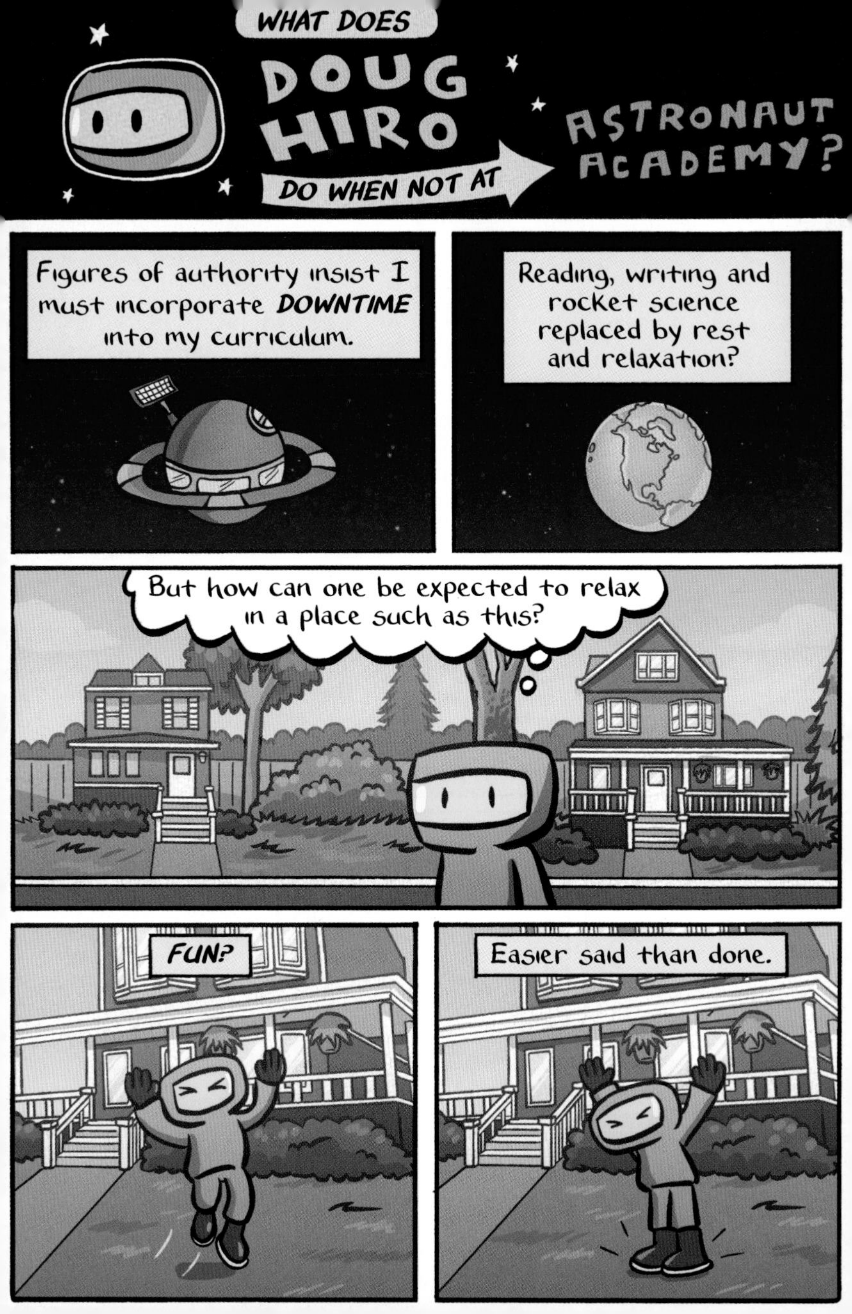
WHAT DOES
DOUG HIRO
DO WHEN NOT AT
ASTRONAUT ACADEMY?
Figures of authority insist I must incorporate DOWNTIME into my curriculum.
Reading, writing and rocket science replaced by rest and relaxation?
But how can one be expected to relax in a place such as this?
FUN?
Easier said than done.

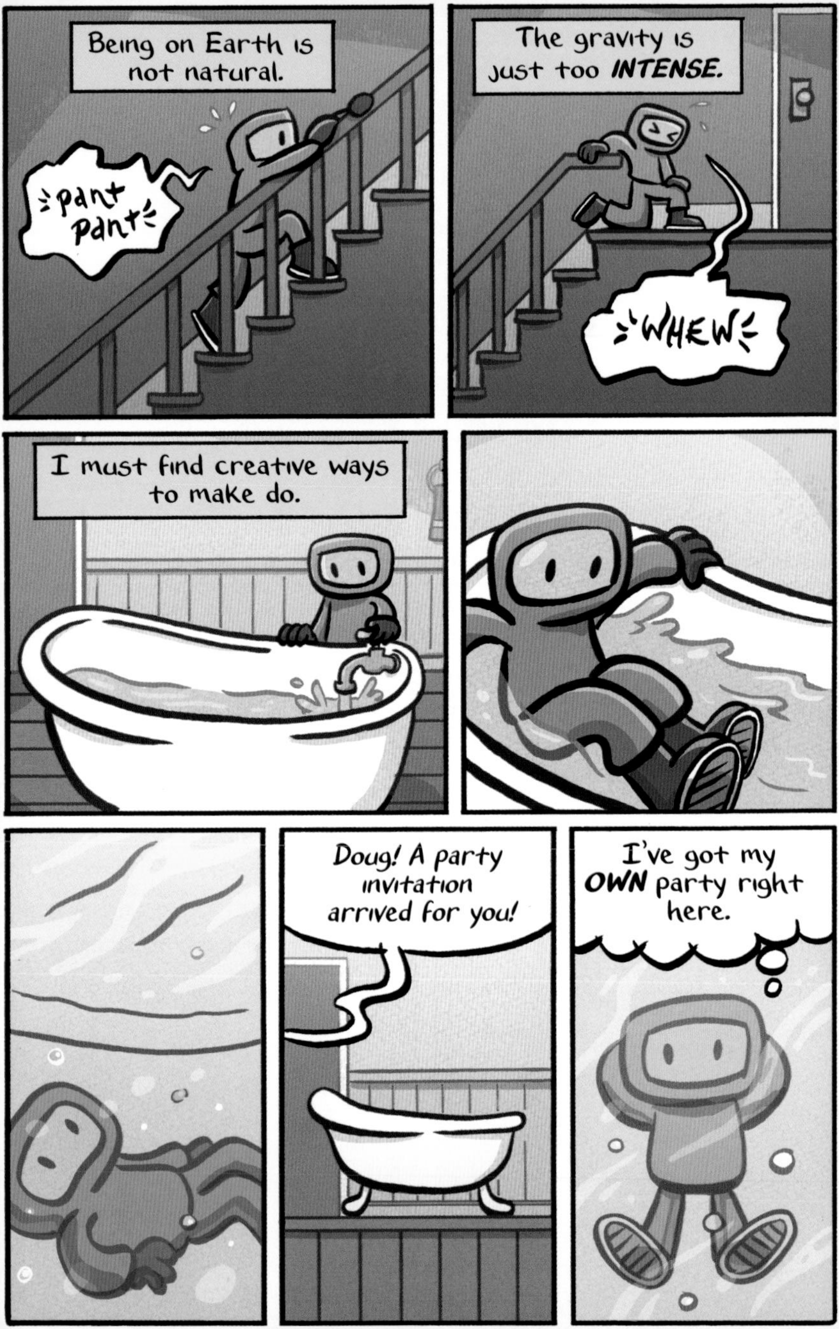
Being on Earth is not natural.
pant pant
The gravity is just too INTENSE.
WHEW
I must find creative ways to make do.
Doug! A party invitation arrived for you!
I've got my OWN party right here.

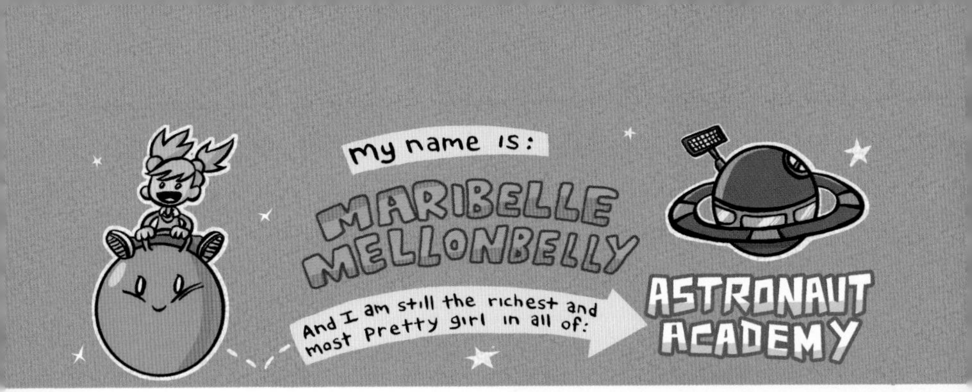
my name is:
MARIBELLE MELLONBELLY
And I am still the richest and most pretty girl in all of:
ASTRONAUT ACADEMY

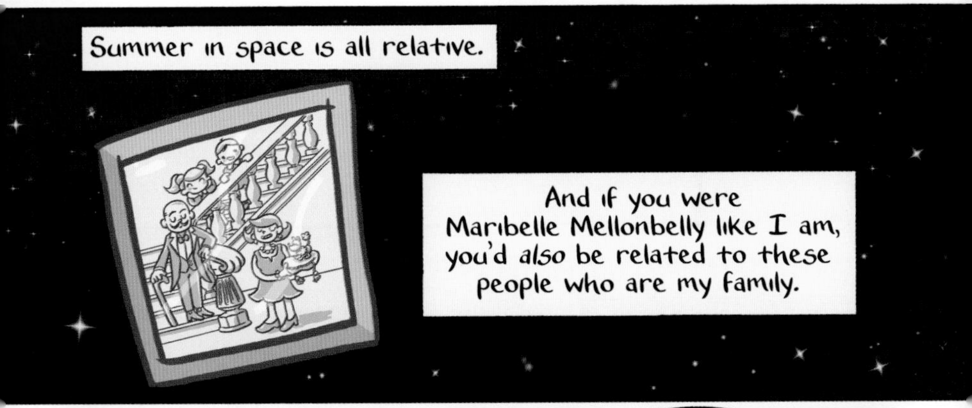
Summer in space is all relative.
And if you were Maribelle Mellonbelly like I am, you'd *also* be related to these people who are my family.

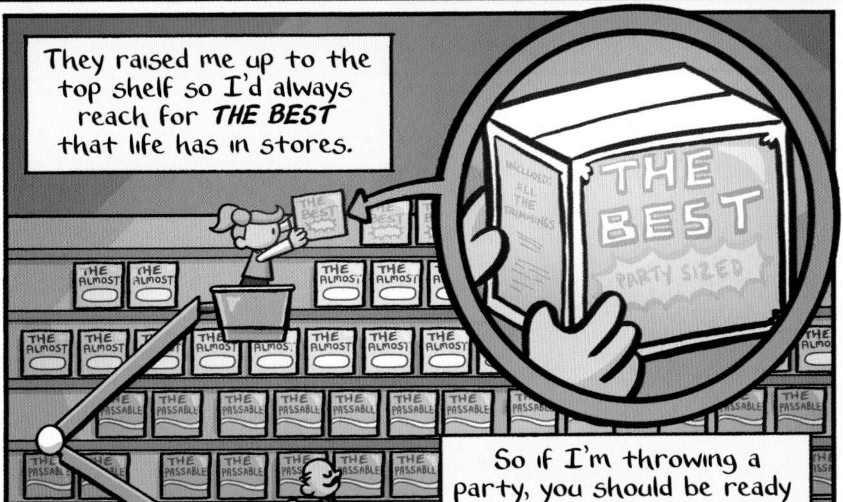
They raised me up to the top shelf so I'd always reach for ***THE BEST*** that life has in stores.
THE BEST
INCLUDED: ALL THE TRIMMINGS
PARTY SIZED
THE ALMOST
THE PASSABLE
THE WHATEVER
So if I'm throwing a party, you should be ready to catch on to the subtle selling points in an invitation that will be heading your way.

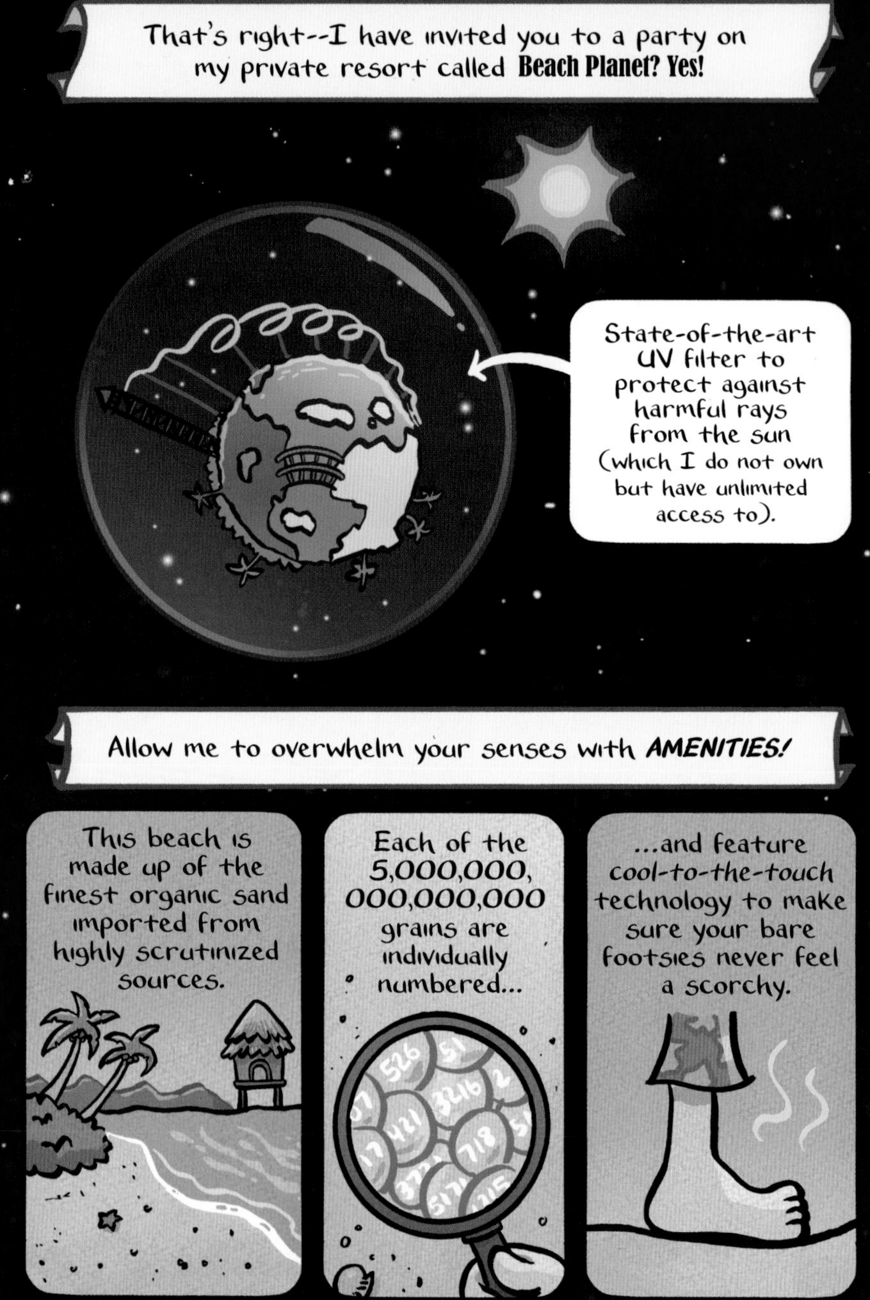
That's right--I have invited you to a party on my private resort called **Beach Planet? Yes!**
State-of-the-art UV filter to protect against harmful rays from the sun (which I do not own but have unlimited access to).
Allow me to overwhelm your senses with ***AMENITIES!***
This beach is made up of the finest organic sand imported from highly scrutinized sources.
Each of the 5,000,000,000,000,000 grains are individually numbered...
...and feature cool-to-the-touch technology to make sure your bare footsies never feel a scorchy.

The water is exactly the shade of blue-green that 90% of trained eyeballs agree is *OCULARLY APPEALING!*

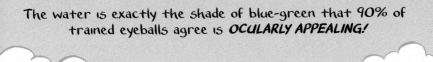

An army of manservants are at the ready. All of whom are *VERY SHADY* with their umbrella technique.

A volleyball net made from *TIGHTLY INTERWOVEN* fibers was donated by generous stallion philanthropists.

COMPLIMENTARY BEACH TOWELS!!!

Honor and a privilege!

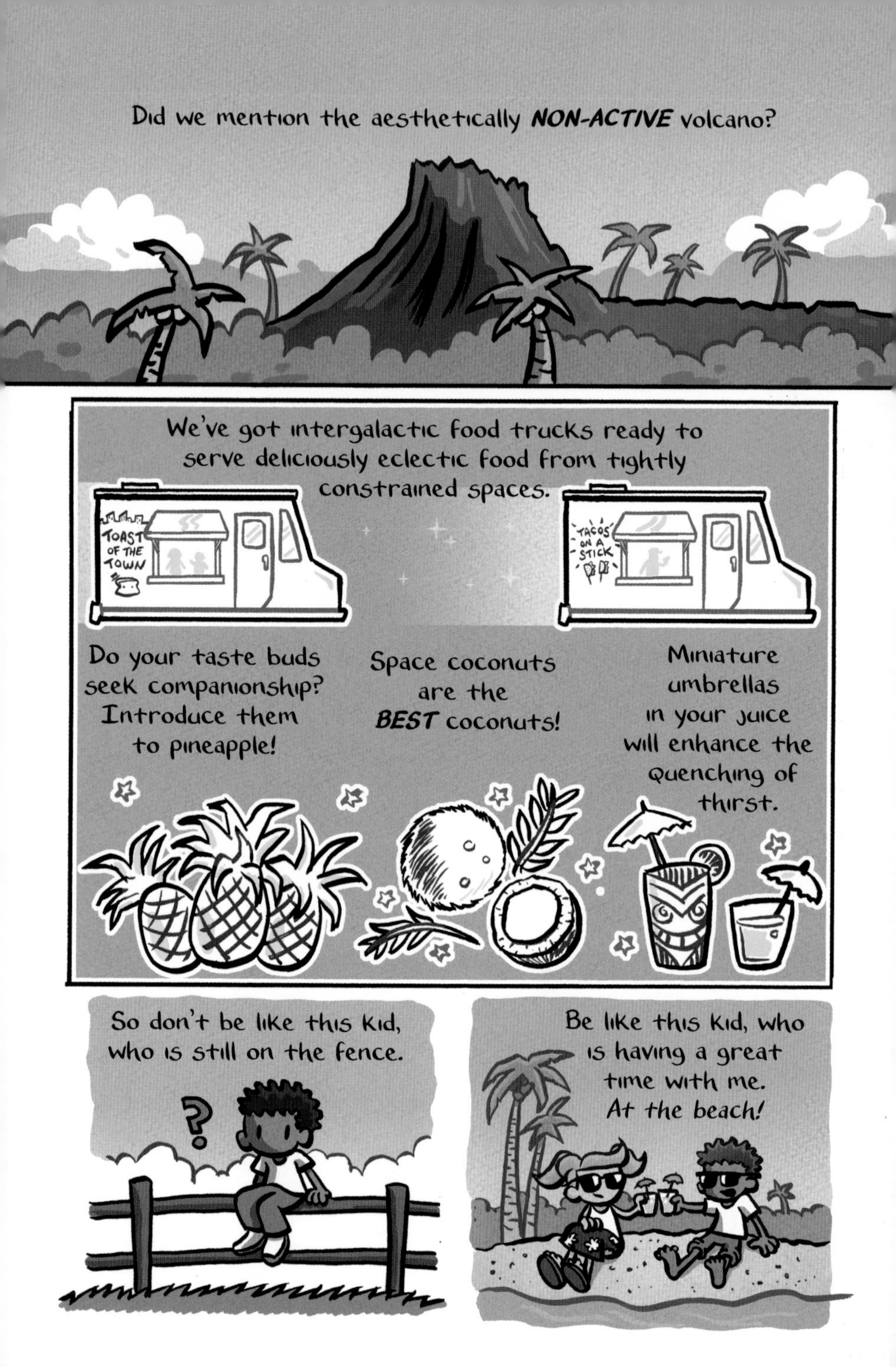
Did we mention the aesthetically **NON-ACTIVE** volcano?
We've got intergalactic food trucks ready to serve deliciously eclectic food from tightly constrained spaces.
TOAST OF THE TOWN
TACOS ON A STICK
Do your taste buds seek companionship? Introduce them to pineapple!
Space coconuts are the **BEST** coconuts!
Miniature umbrellas in your juice will enhance the quenching of thirst.
So don't be like this kid, who is still on the fence.
?
Be like this kid, who is having a great time with me. At the beach!

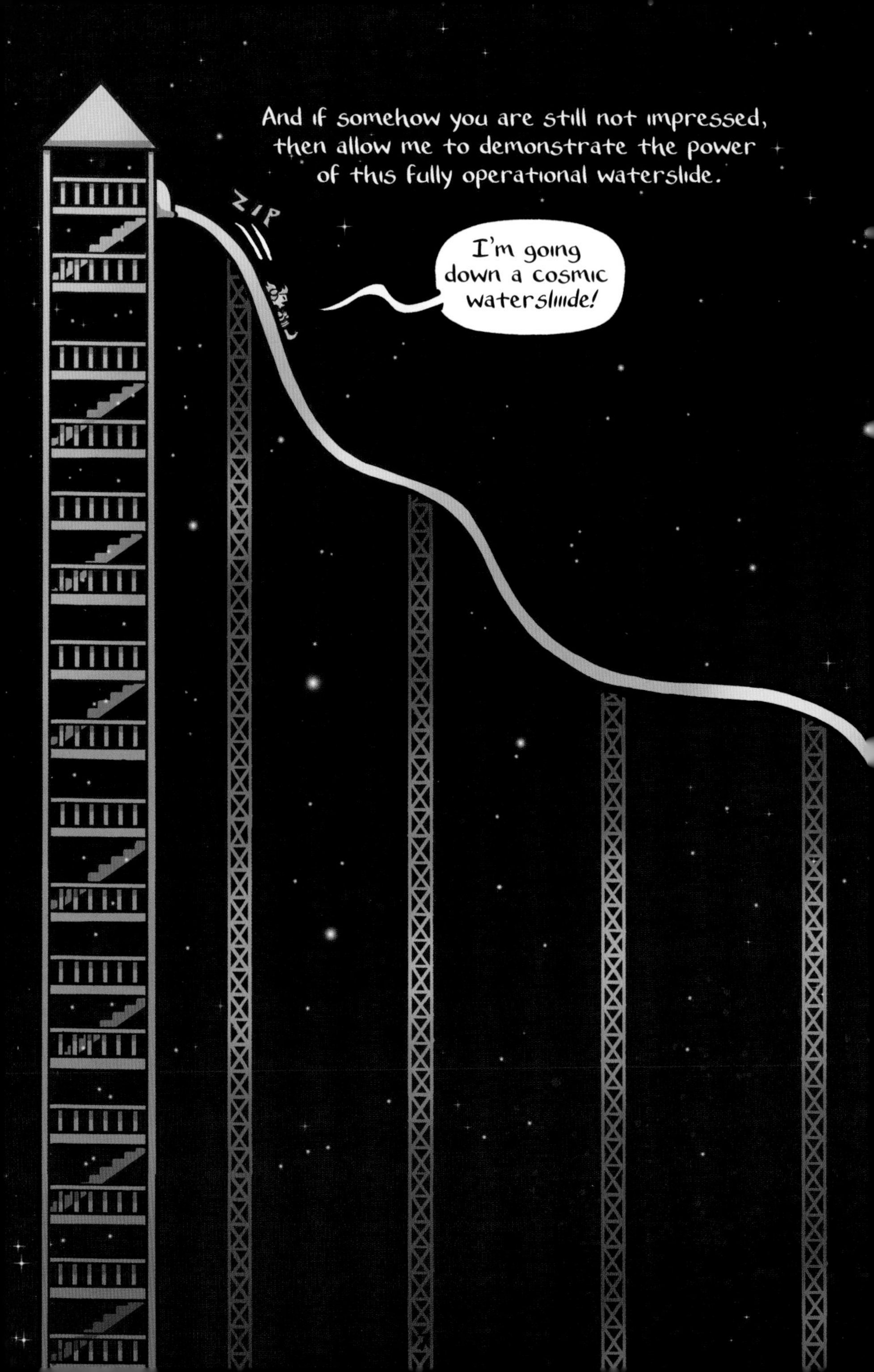
And if somehow you are still not impressed, then allow me to demonstrate the power of this fully operational waterslide.
ZIP
I'm going down a cosmic waterslide!

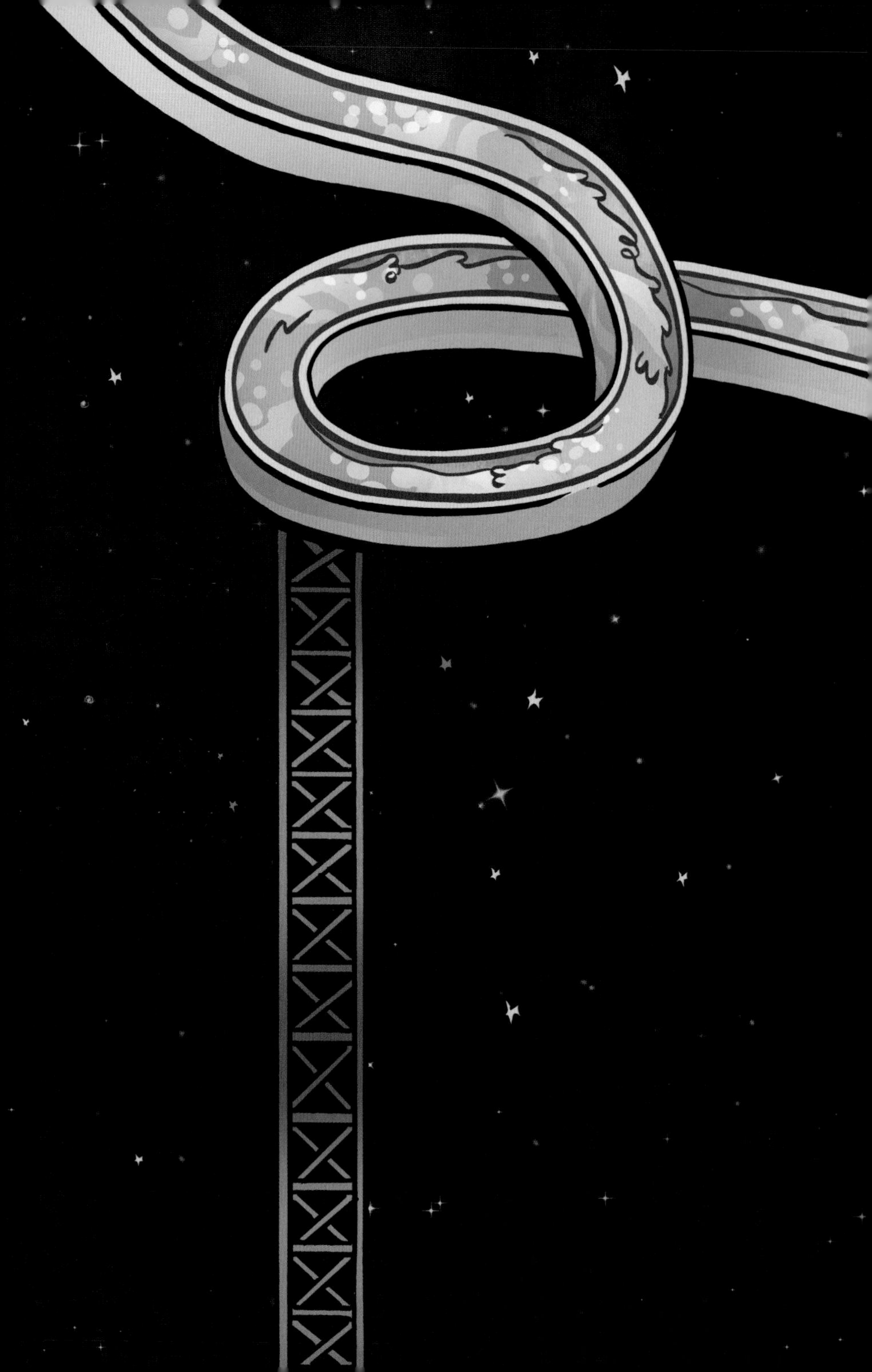

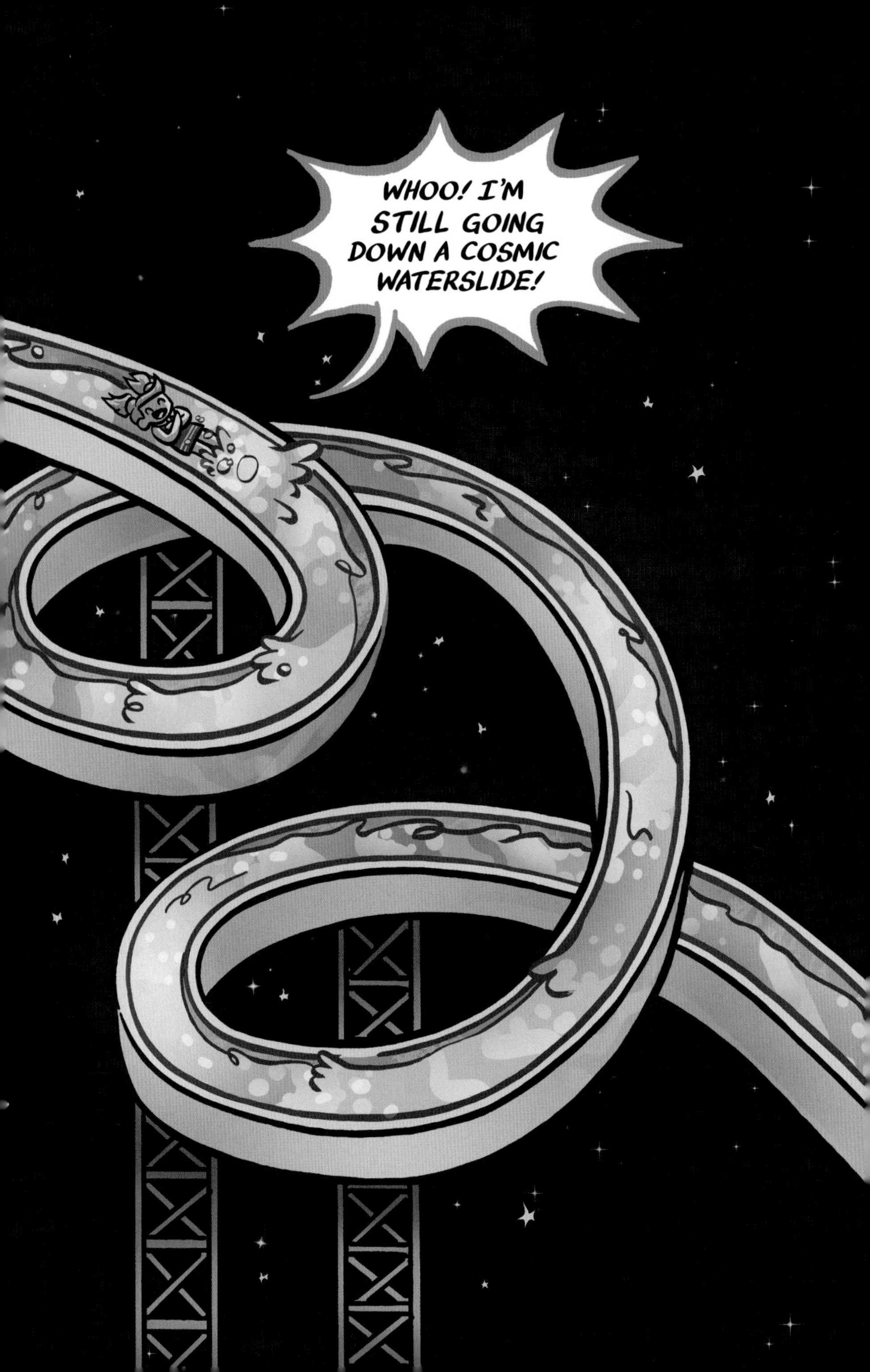
WHOO! I'M STILL GOING DOWN A COSMIC WATERSLIDE!

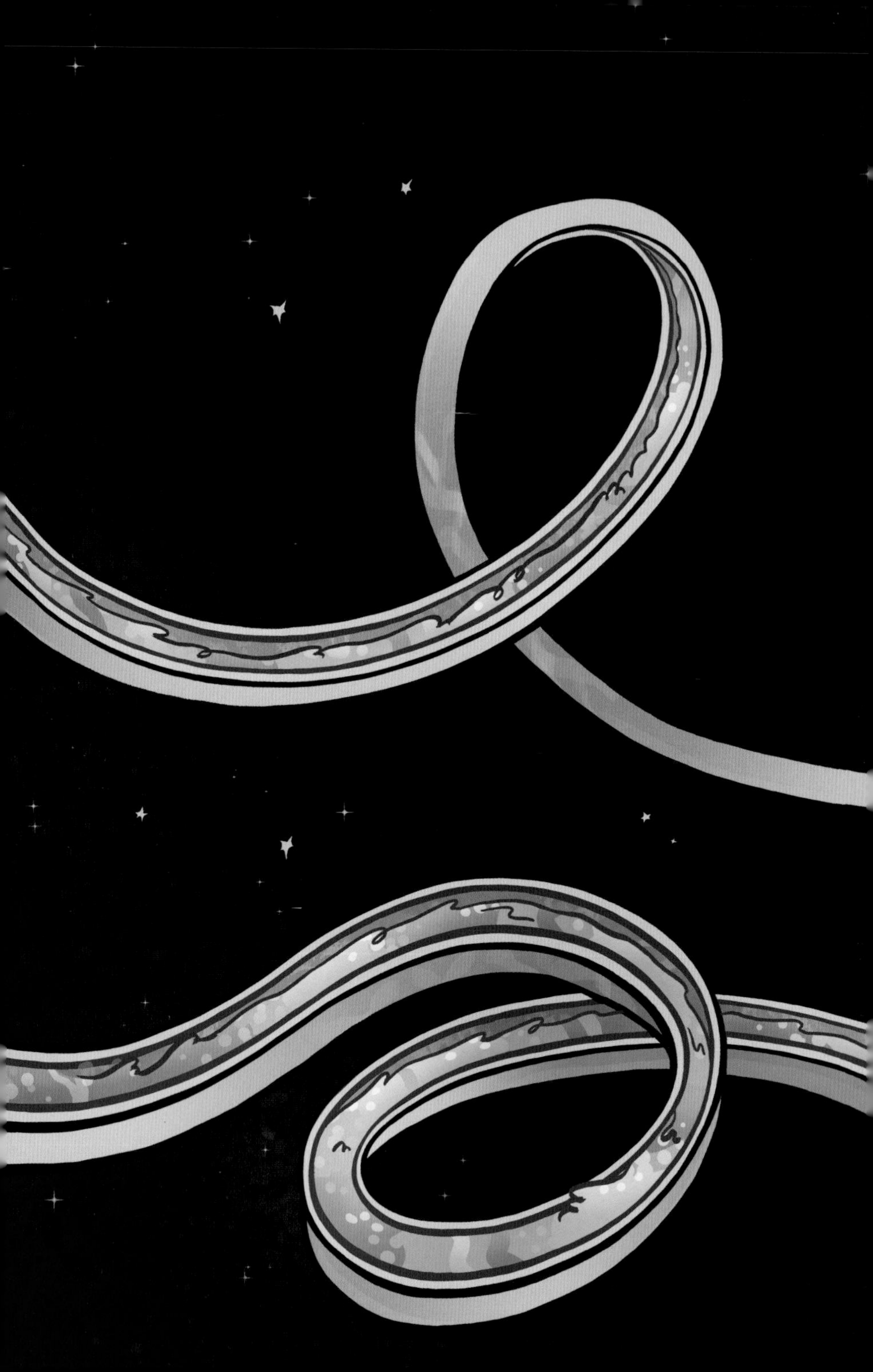

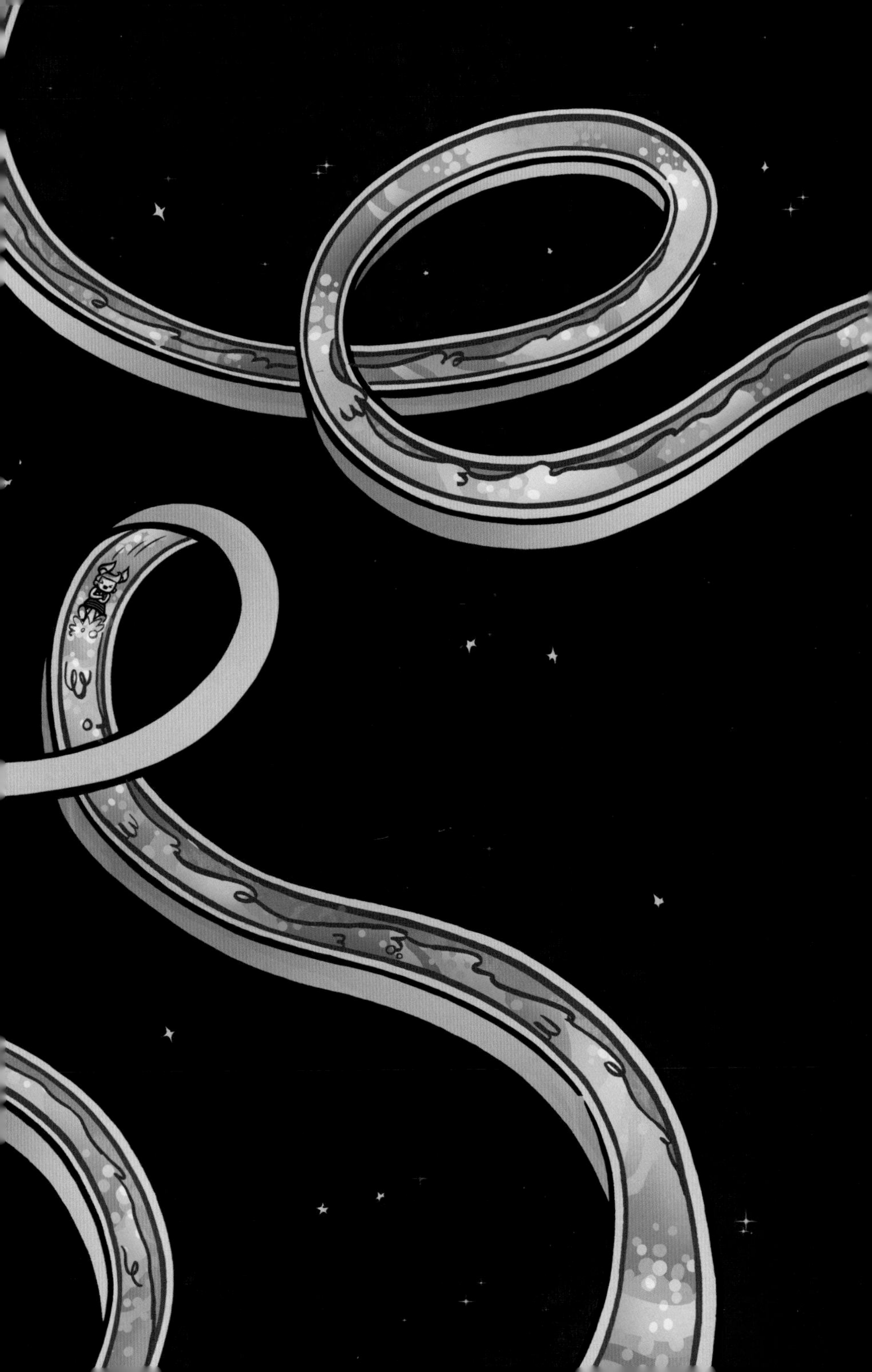

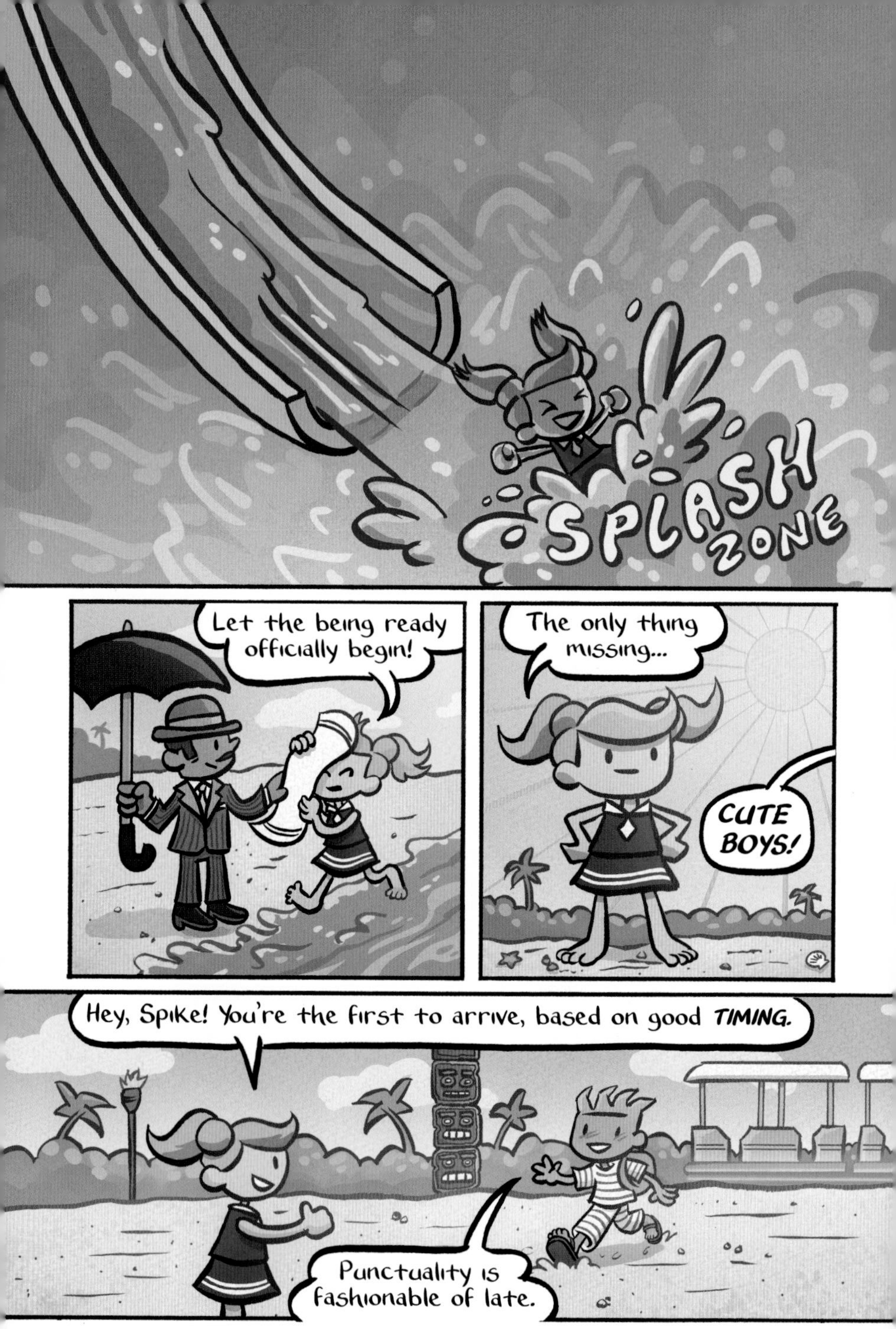
SPLASH
ZONE
Let the being ready officially begin!
The only thing missing...
CUTE BOYS!
Hey, Spike! You're the first to arrive, based on good TIMING.
Punctuality is fashionable of late.

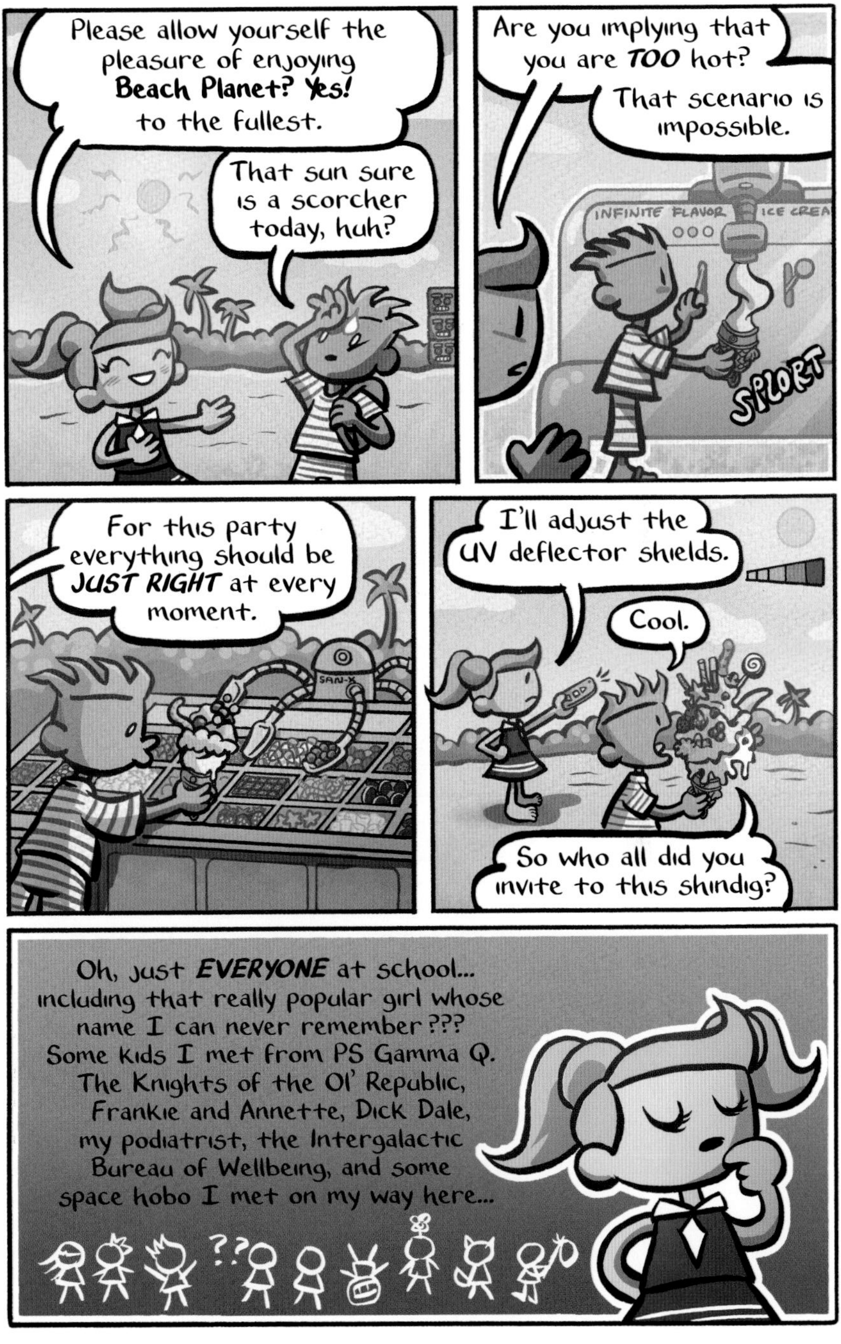

Please allow yourself the pleasure of enjoying Beach Planet? Yes! to the fullest.
That sun sure is a scorcher today, huh?
Are you implying that you are TOO hot?
That scenario is impossible.
INFINITE FLAVOR ICE CREA
SPLORT
For this party everything should be JUST RIGHT at every moment.
SAN-X
I'll adjust the UV deflector shields.
Cool.
So who all did you invite to this shindig?
Oh, just EVERYONE at school... including that really popular girl whose name I can never remember??? Some kids I met from PS Gamma Q. The Knights of the Ol' Republic, Frankie and Annette, Dick Dale, my podiatrist, the Intergalactic Bureau of Wellbeing, and some space hobo I met on my way here...
???

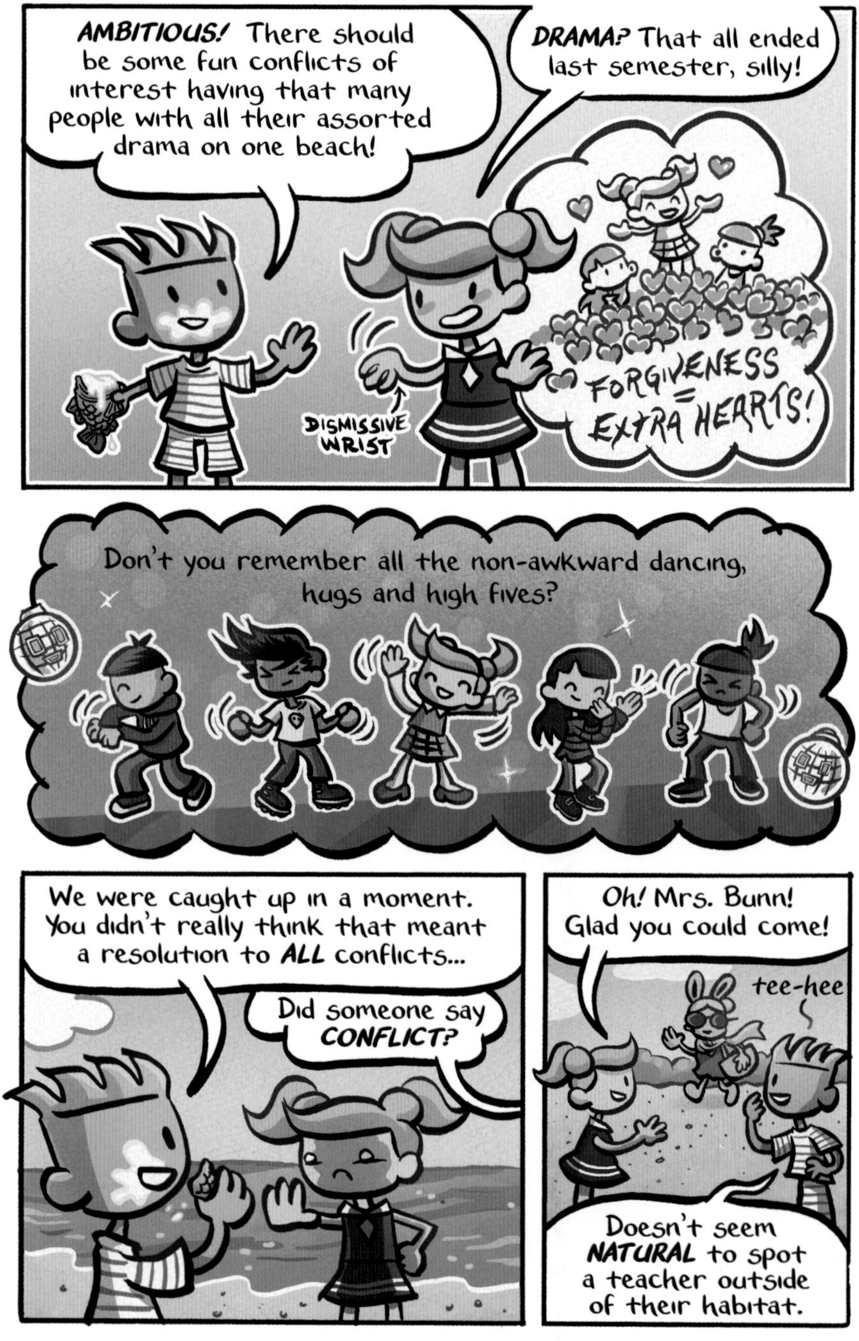
AMBITIOUS! There should be some fun conflicts of interest having that many people with all their assorted drama on one beach!
DRAMA? That all ended last semester, silly!
FORGIVENESS = EXTRA HEARTS!
DISMISSIVE WRIST
Don't you remember all the non-awkward dancing, hugs and high fives?
We were caught up in a moment. You didn't really think that meant a resolution to ALL conflicts...
Did someone say CONFLICT?
Oh! Mrs. Bunn! Glad you could come!
tee-hee
Doesn't seem NATURAL to spot a teacher outside of their habitat.

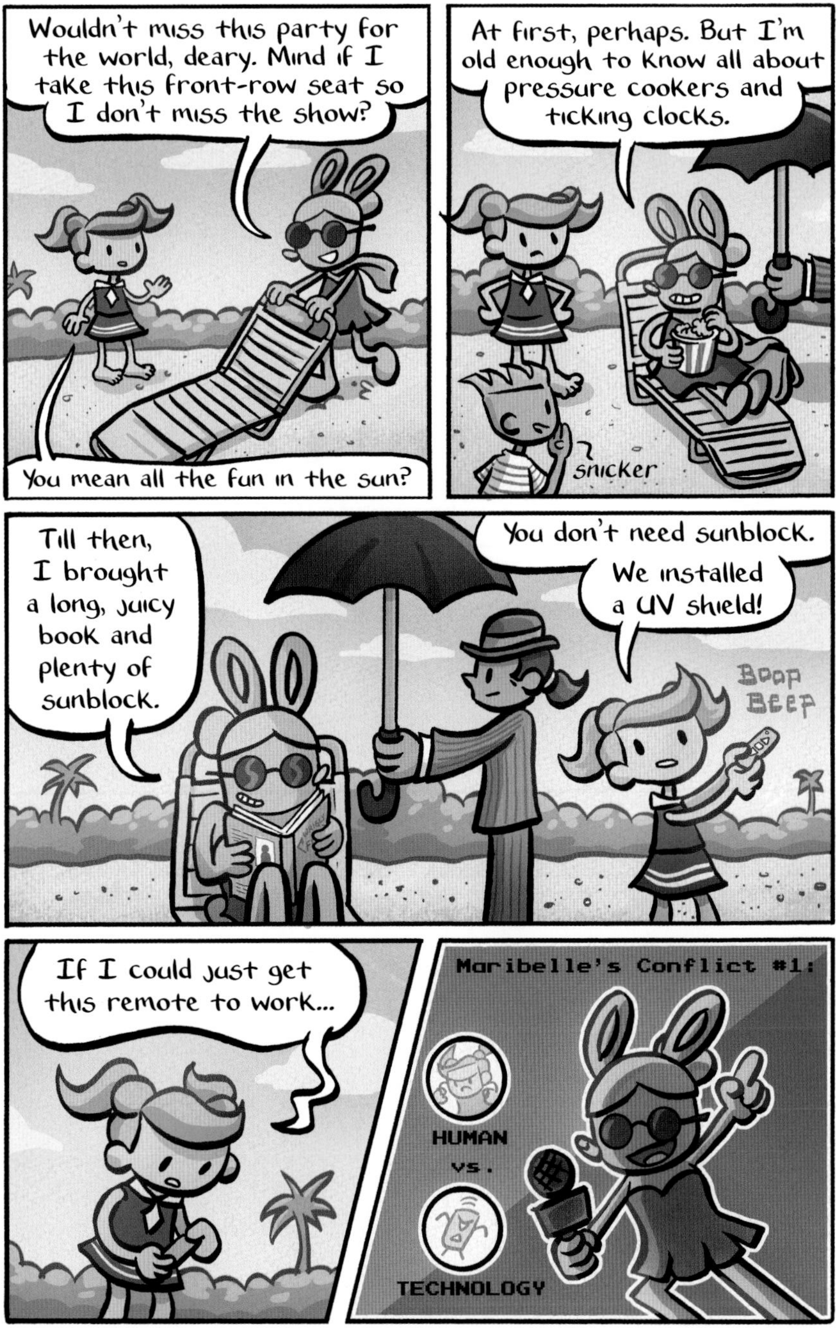
Wouldn't miss this party for the world, deary. Mind if I take this front-row seat so I don't miss the show?
You mean all the fun in the sun?
At first, perhaps. But I'm old enough to know all about pressure cookers and ticking clocks.
snicker
Till then, I brought a long, juicy book and plenty of sunblock.
You don't need sunblock.
We installed a UV shield!
BOOP BEEP
If I could just get this remote to work...
Maribelle's Conflict #1:
HUMAN
VS.
TECHNOLOGY

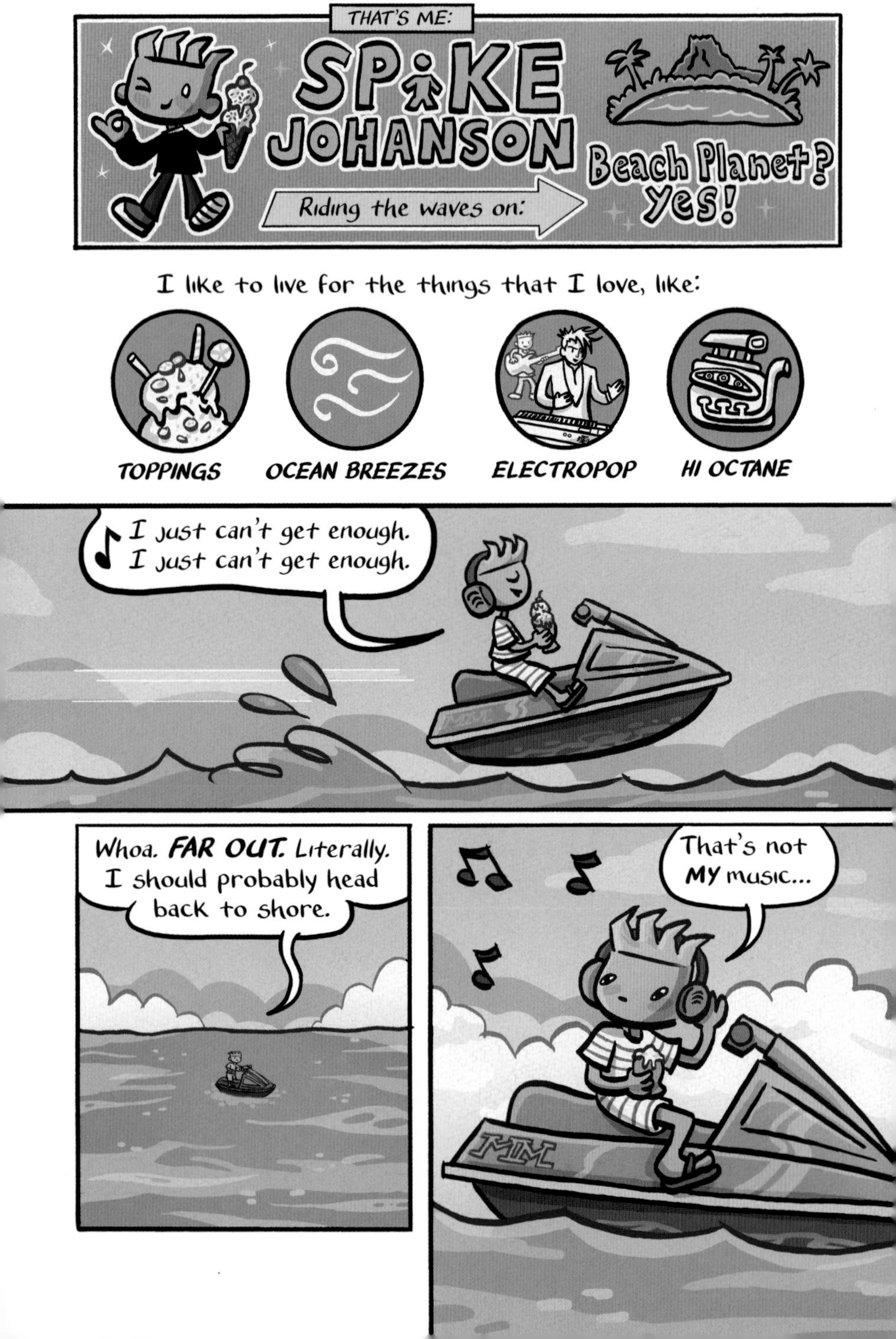
THAT'S ME:
SPIKE JOHANSON
Riding the waves on:
Beach Planet? yes!
I like to live for the things that I love, like:
TOPPINGS
OCEAN BREEZES
ELECTROPOP
HI OCTANE
I just can't get enough. I just can't get enough.
Whoa. FAR OUT. Literally. I should probably head back to shore.
That's not MY music...
MM

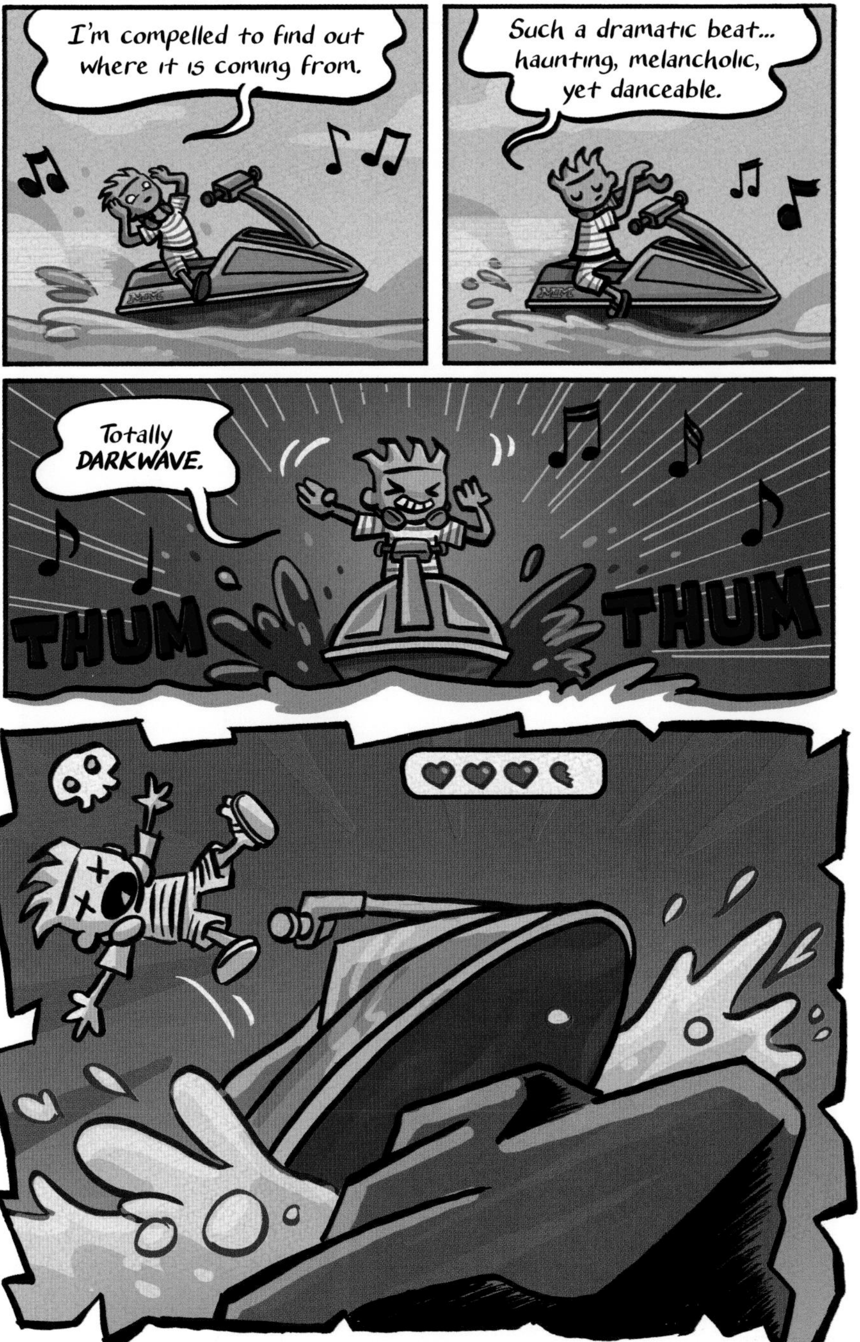
I'm compelled to find out where it is coming from.
Such a dramatic beat... haunting, melancholic, yet danceable.
Totally DARKWAVE.
THUM
THUM

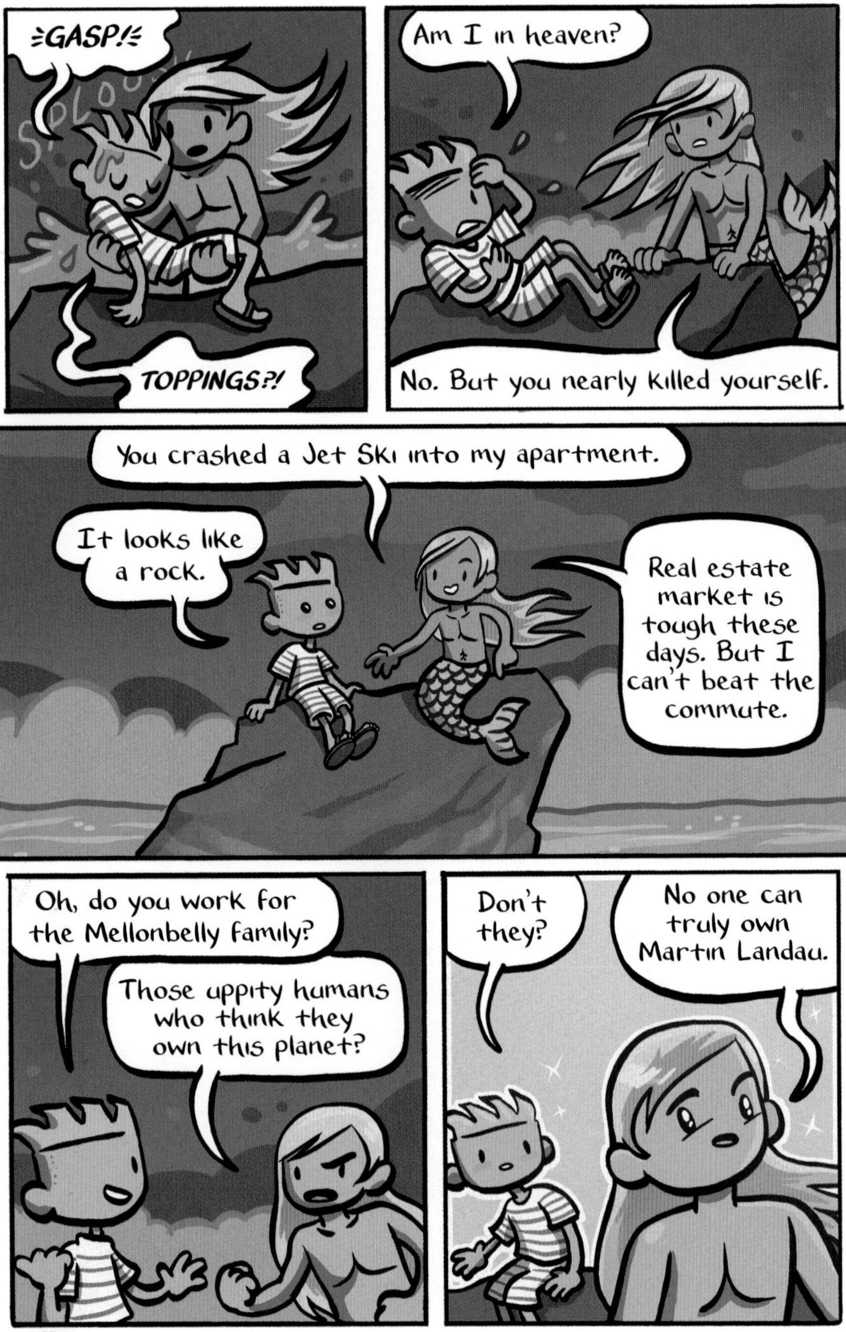

GASP!
SPLOOSH
TOPPINGS?!
Am I in heaven?
No. But you nearly killed yourself.
You crashed a Jet Ski into my apartment.
It looks like a rock.
Real estate market is tough these days. But I can't beat the commute.
Oh, do you work for the Mellonbelly family?
Those uppity humans who think they own this planet?
No one can truly own Martin Landau.
Don't they?

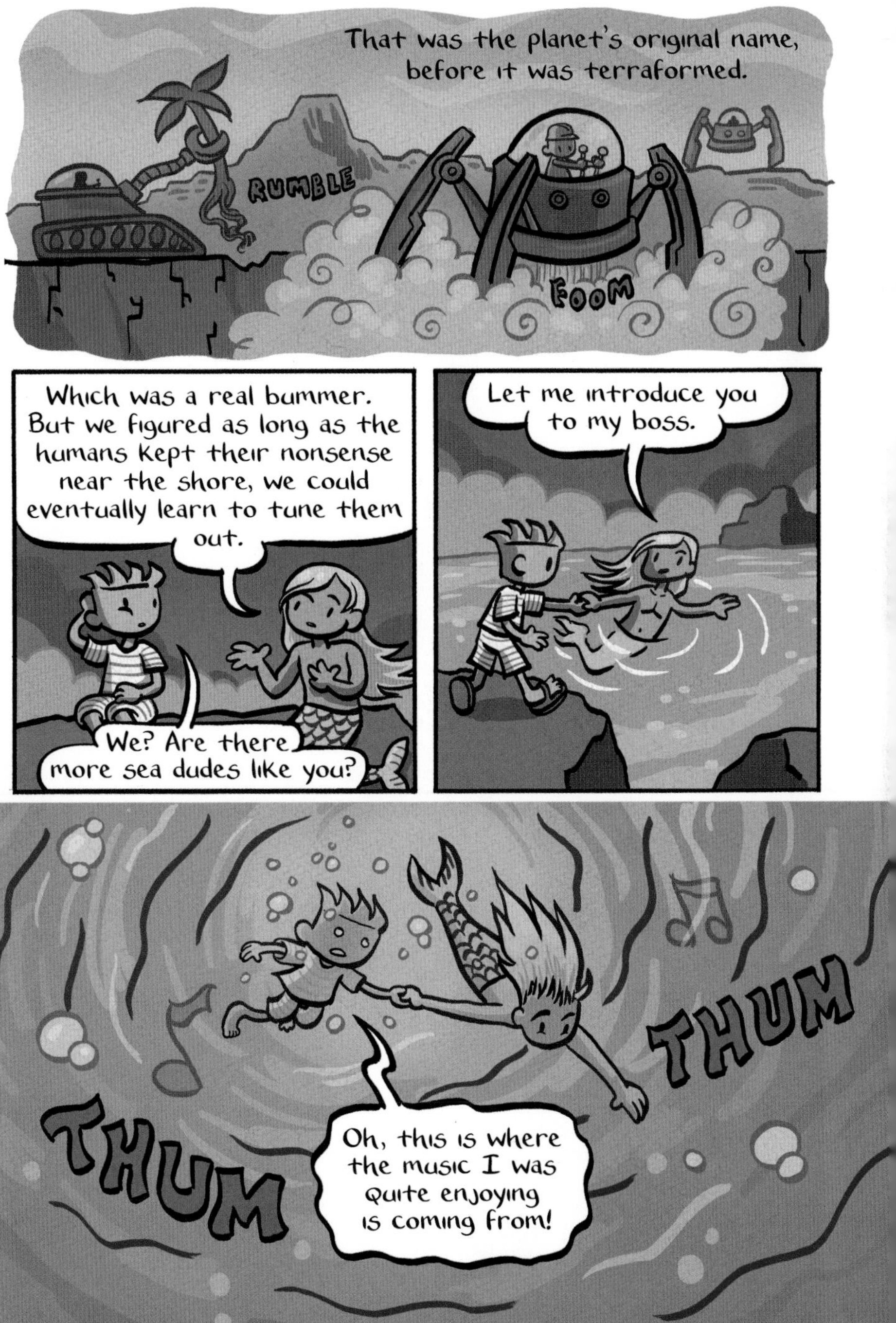

That was the planet's original name, before it was terraformed.
RUMBLE
FOOM
Which was a real bummer. But we figured as long as the humans kept their nonsense near the shore, we could eventually learn to tune them out.
We? Are there more sea dudes like you?
Let me introduce you to my boss.
THUM
THUM
Oh, this is where the music I was quite enjoying is coming from!

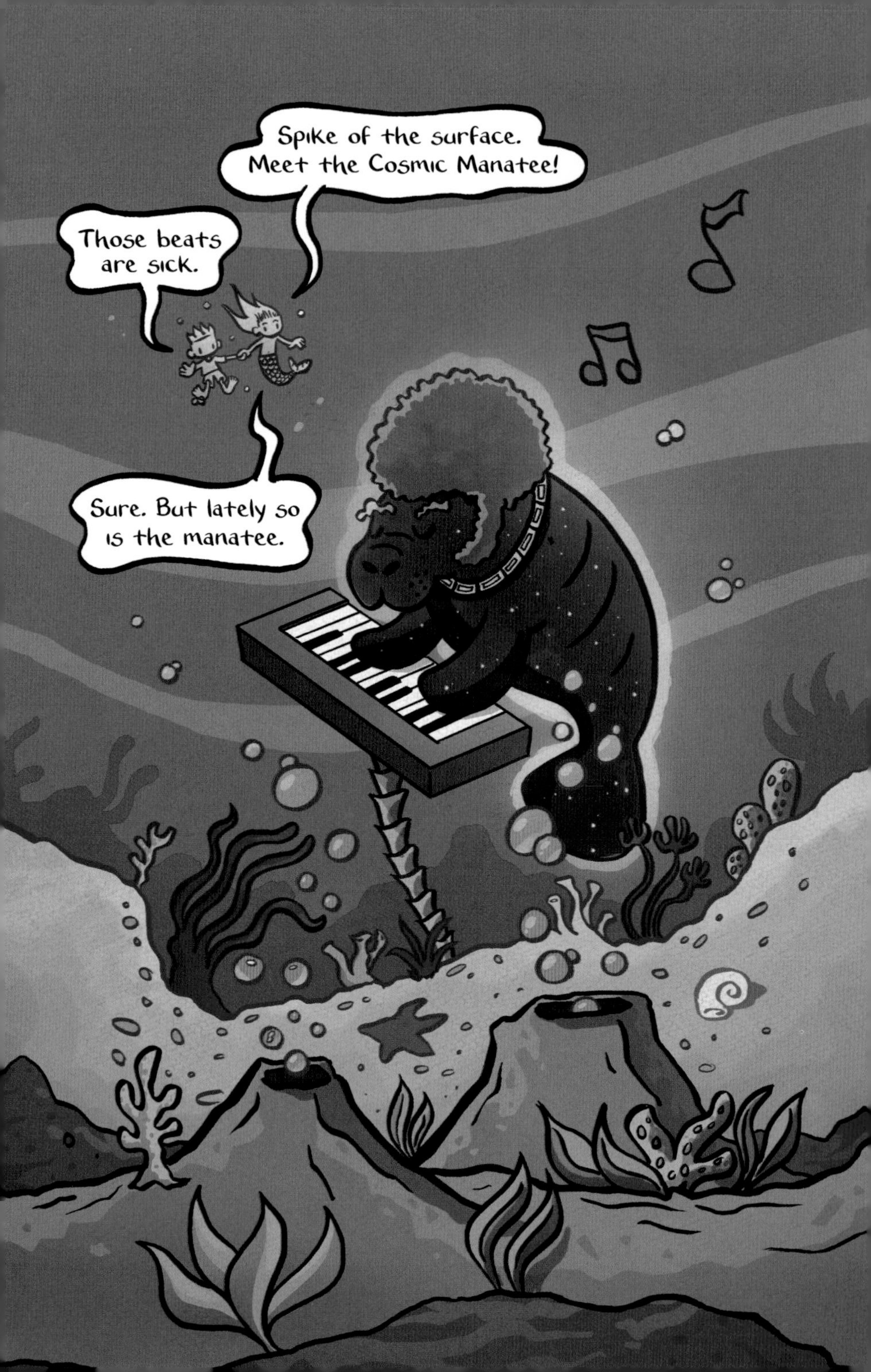
Spike of the surface. Meet the Cosmic Manatee!
Those beats are sick.
Sure. But lately so is the manatee.

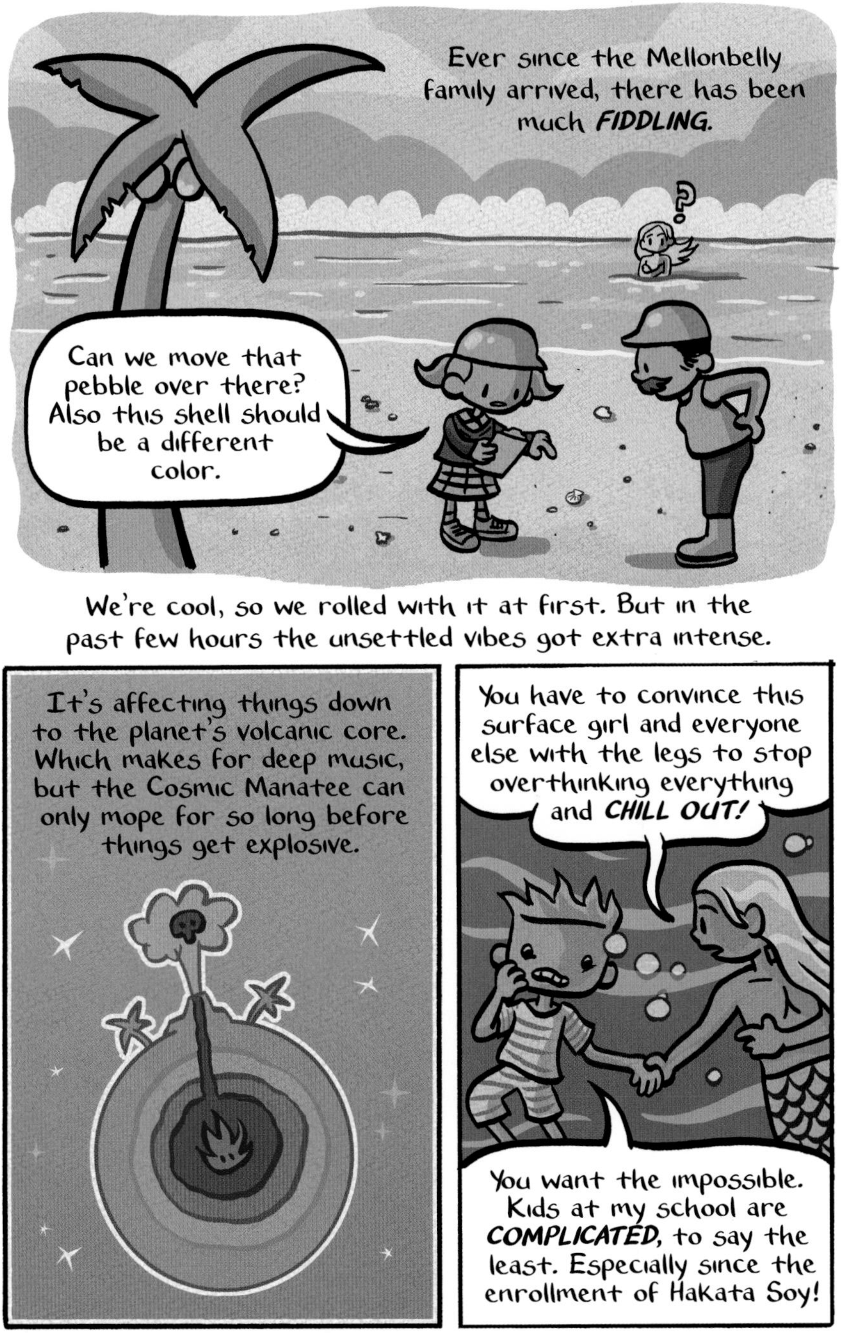
Ever since the Mellonbelly family arrived, there has been much *FIDDLING.*
?
Can we move that pebble over there? Also this shell should be a different color.
We're cool, so we rolled with it at first. But in the past few hours the unsettled vibes got extra intense.
It's affecting things down to the planet's volcanic core. Which makes for deep music, but the Cosmic Manatee can only mope for so long before things get explosive.
You have to convince this surface girl and everyone else with the legs to stop overthinking everything and *CHILL OUT!*
You want the impossible. Kids at my school are *COMPLICATED,* to say the least. Especially since the enrollment of Hakata Soy!

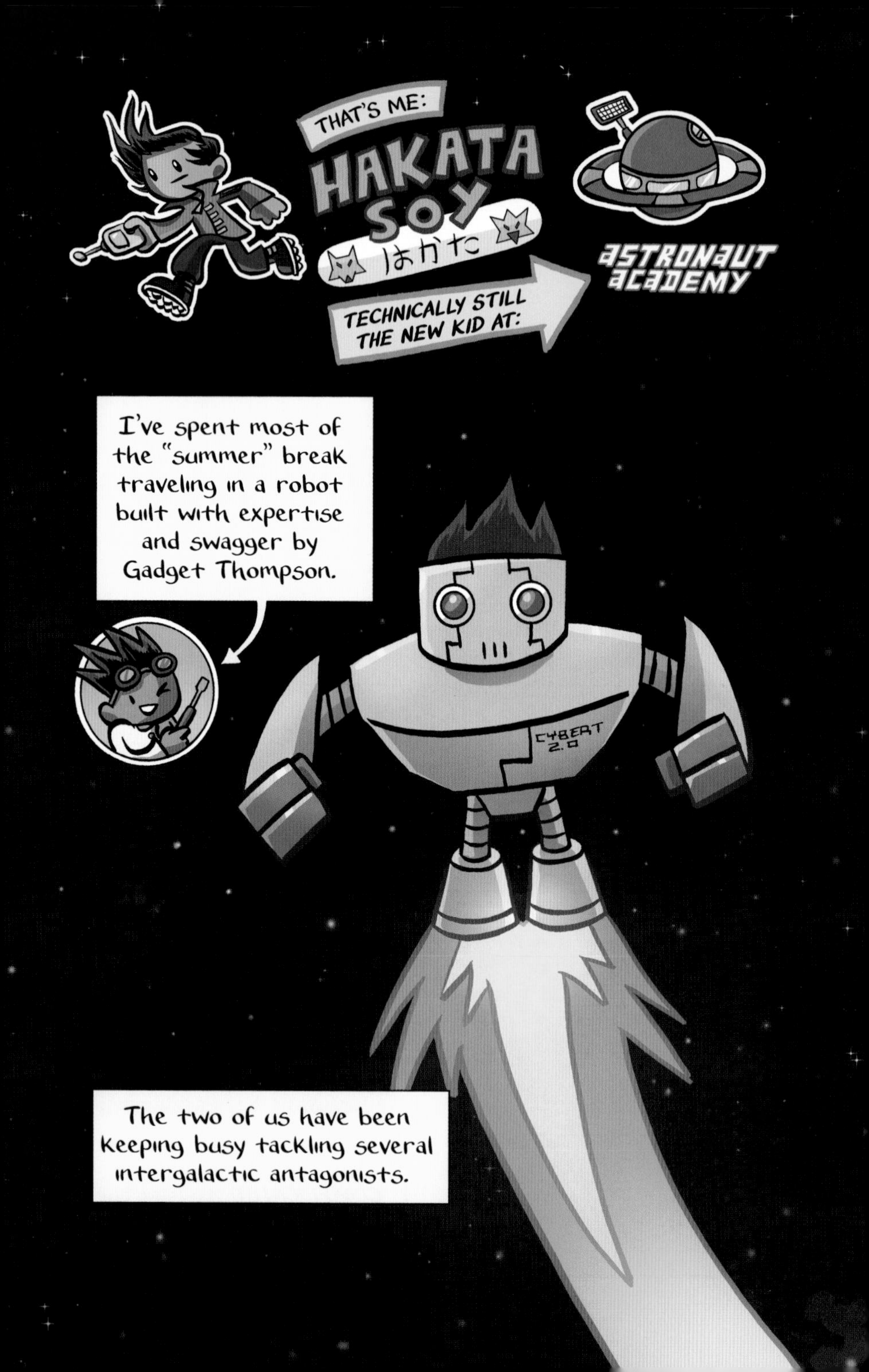
THAT'S ME:
HAKATA SOY
はかた
TECHNICALLY STILL THE NEW KID AT:
ASTRONAUT ACADEMY
I've spent most of the "summer" break traveling in a robot built with expertise and swagger by Gadget Thompson.
CYBERT 2.0
The two of us have been keeping busy tackling several intergalactic antagonists.

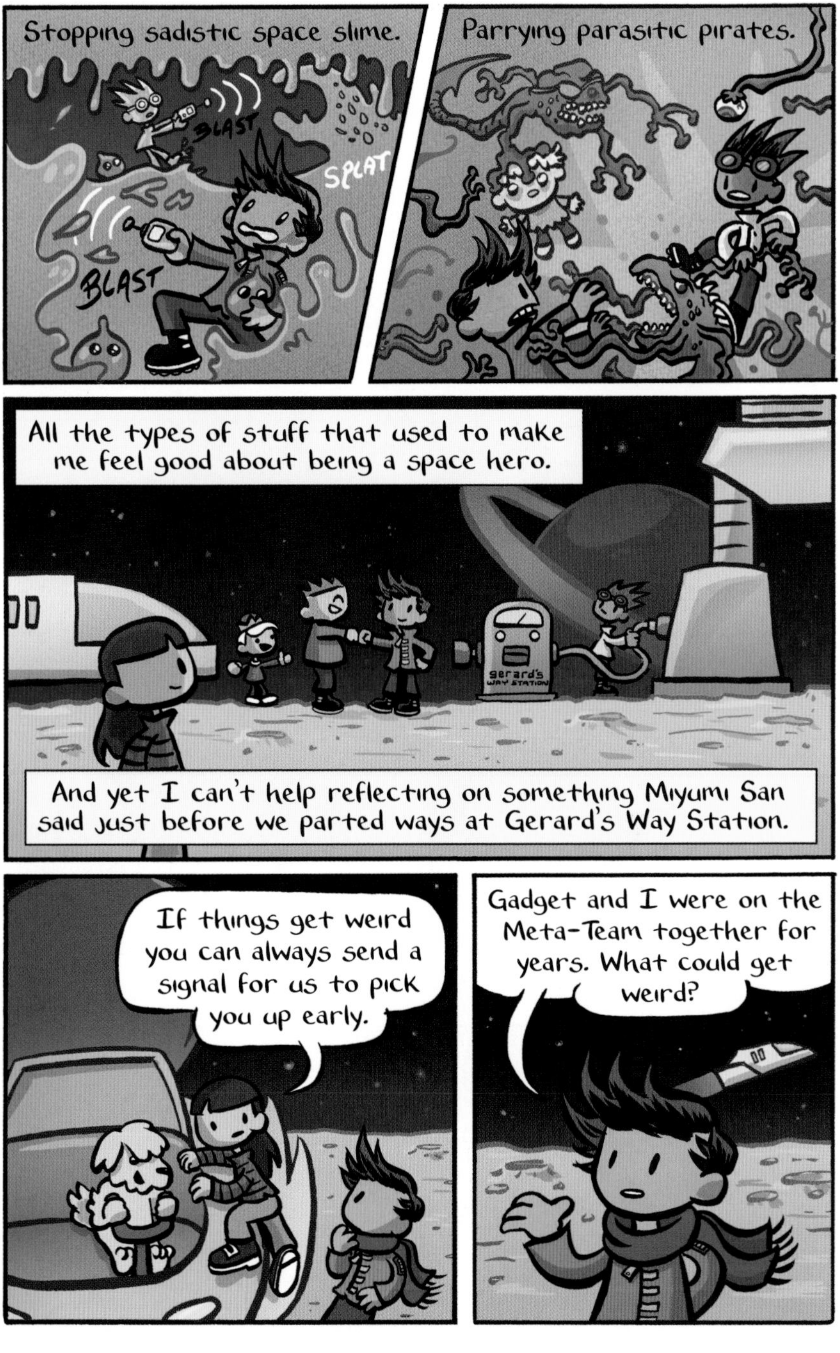
Stopping sadistic space slime.
BLAST
SPLAT
BLAST
Parrying parasitic pirates.
All the types of stuff that used to make me feel good about being a space hero.
gerard's WAY STATION
And yet I can't help reflecting on something Miyumi San said just before we parted ways at Gerard's Way Station.
If things get weird you can always send a signal for us to pick you up early.
Gadget and I were on the Meta-Team together for years. What could get weird?

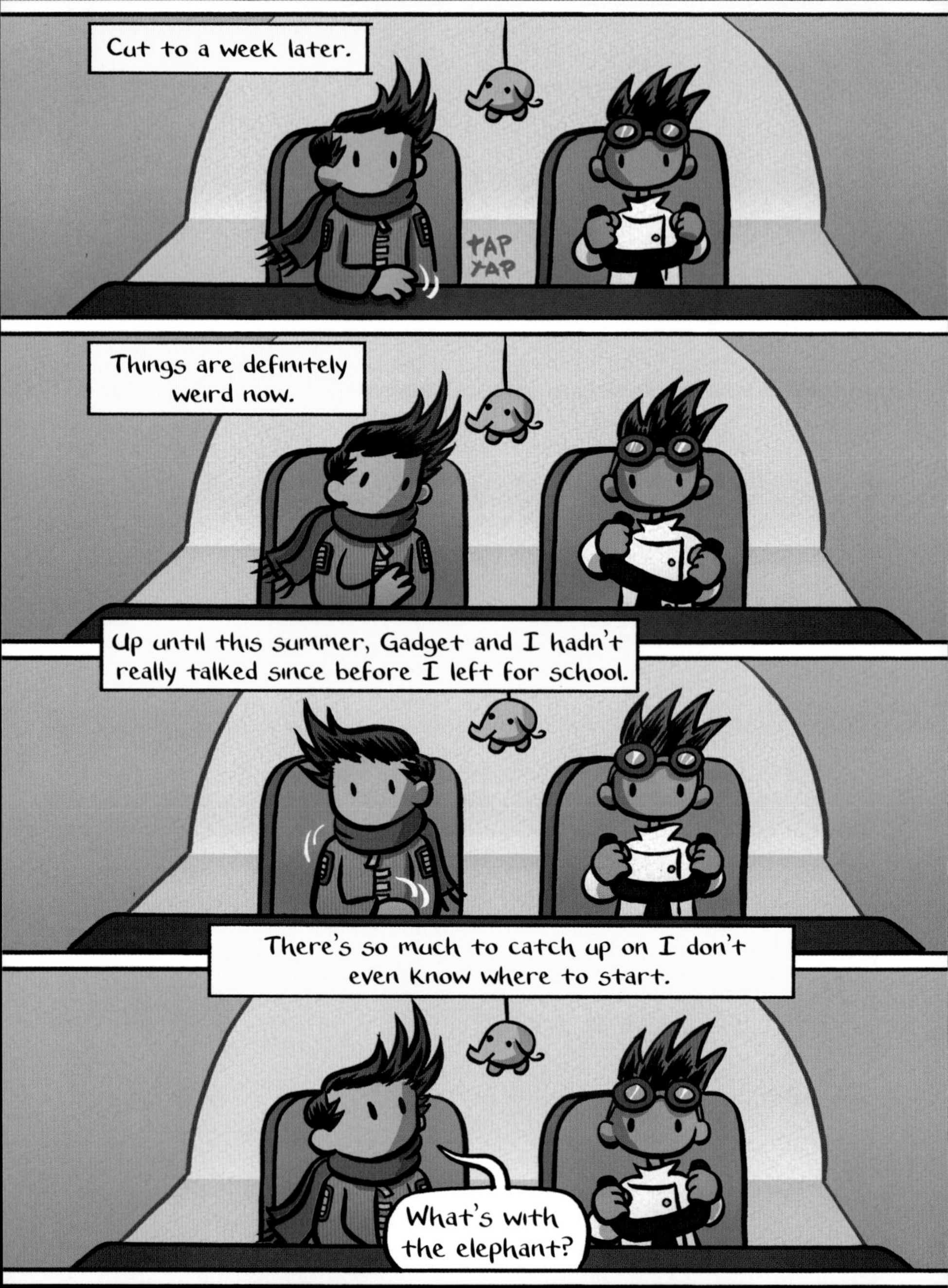
Cut to a week later.
TAP TAP
Things are definitely weird now.
Up until this summer, Gadget and I hadn't really talked since before I left for school.
There's so much to catch up on I don't even know where to start.
What's with the elephant?

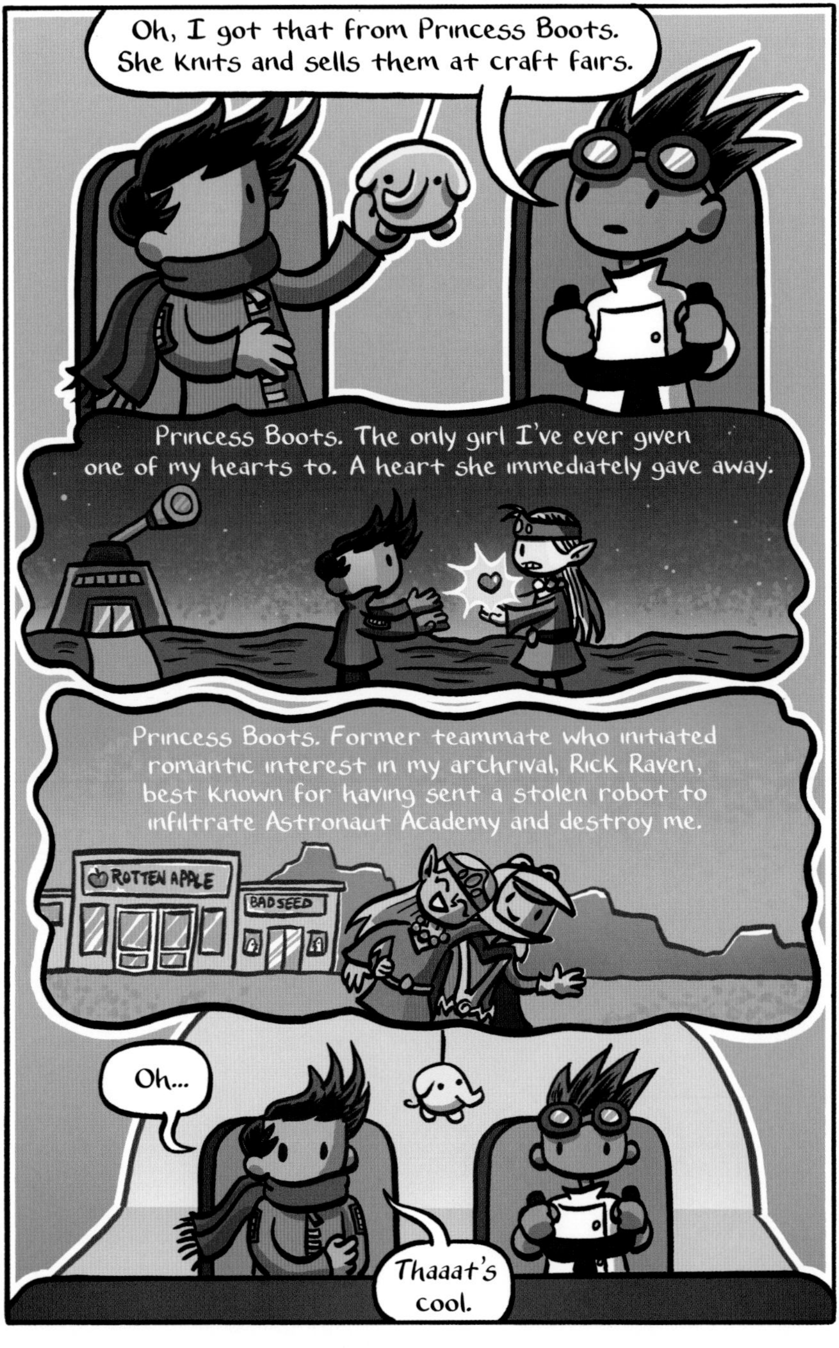
Oh, I got that from Princess Boots. She knits and sells them at craft fairs.
Princess Boots. The only girl I've ever given one of my hearts to. A heart she immediately gave away.
Princess Boots. Former teammate who initiated romantic interest in my archrival, Rick Raven, best known for having sent a stolen robot to infiltrate Astronaut Academy and destroy me.
ROTTEN APPLE
BAD SEED
Oh...
Thaaat's cool.

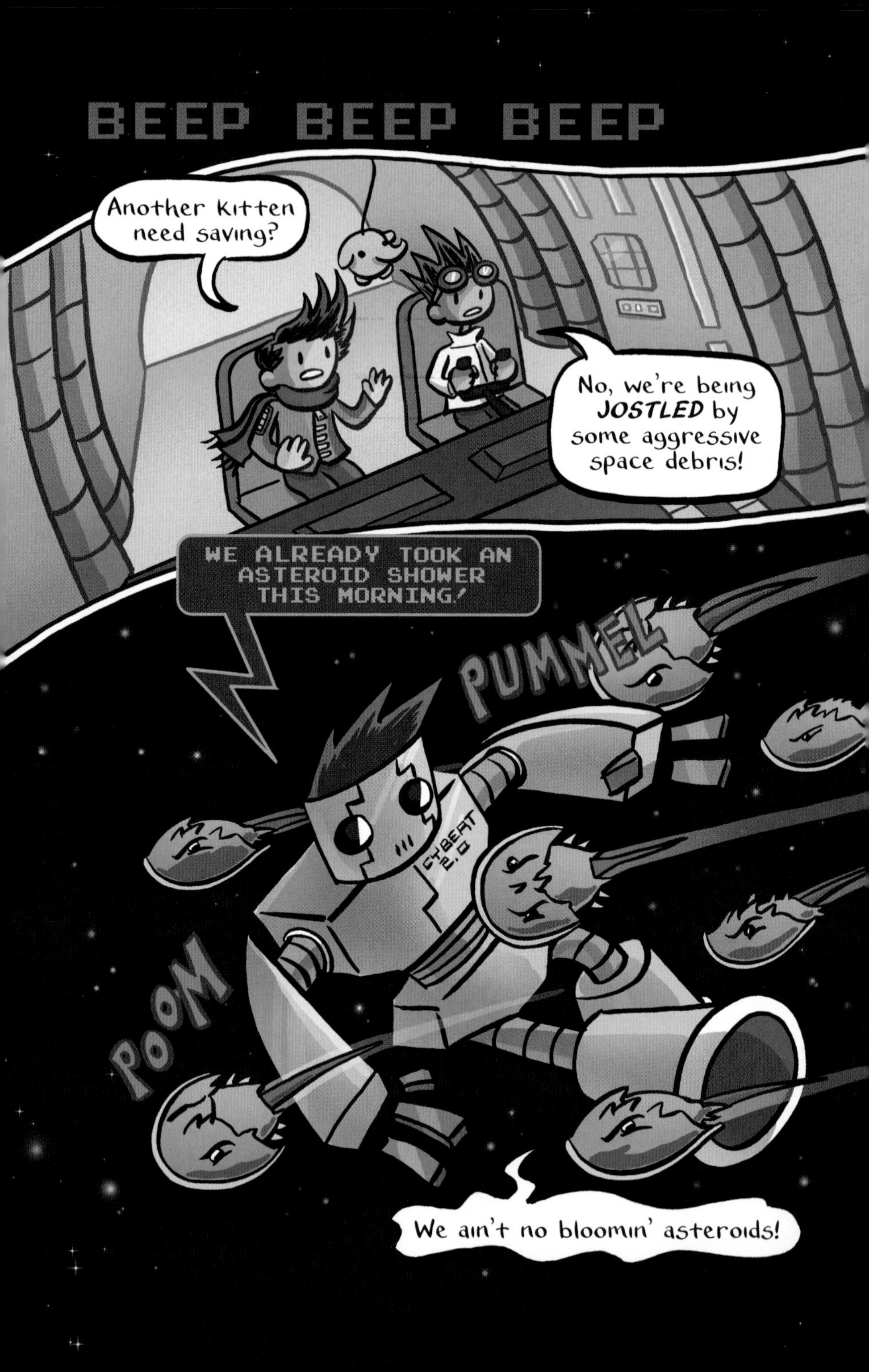
BEEP BEEP BEEP
Another kitten need saving?
No, we're being JOSTLED by some aggressive space debris!
WE ALREADY TOOK AN ASTEROID SHOWER THIS MORNING!
PUMMEL
CYBEAT 2.0
POOM
We ain't no bloomin' asteroids!

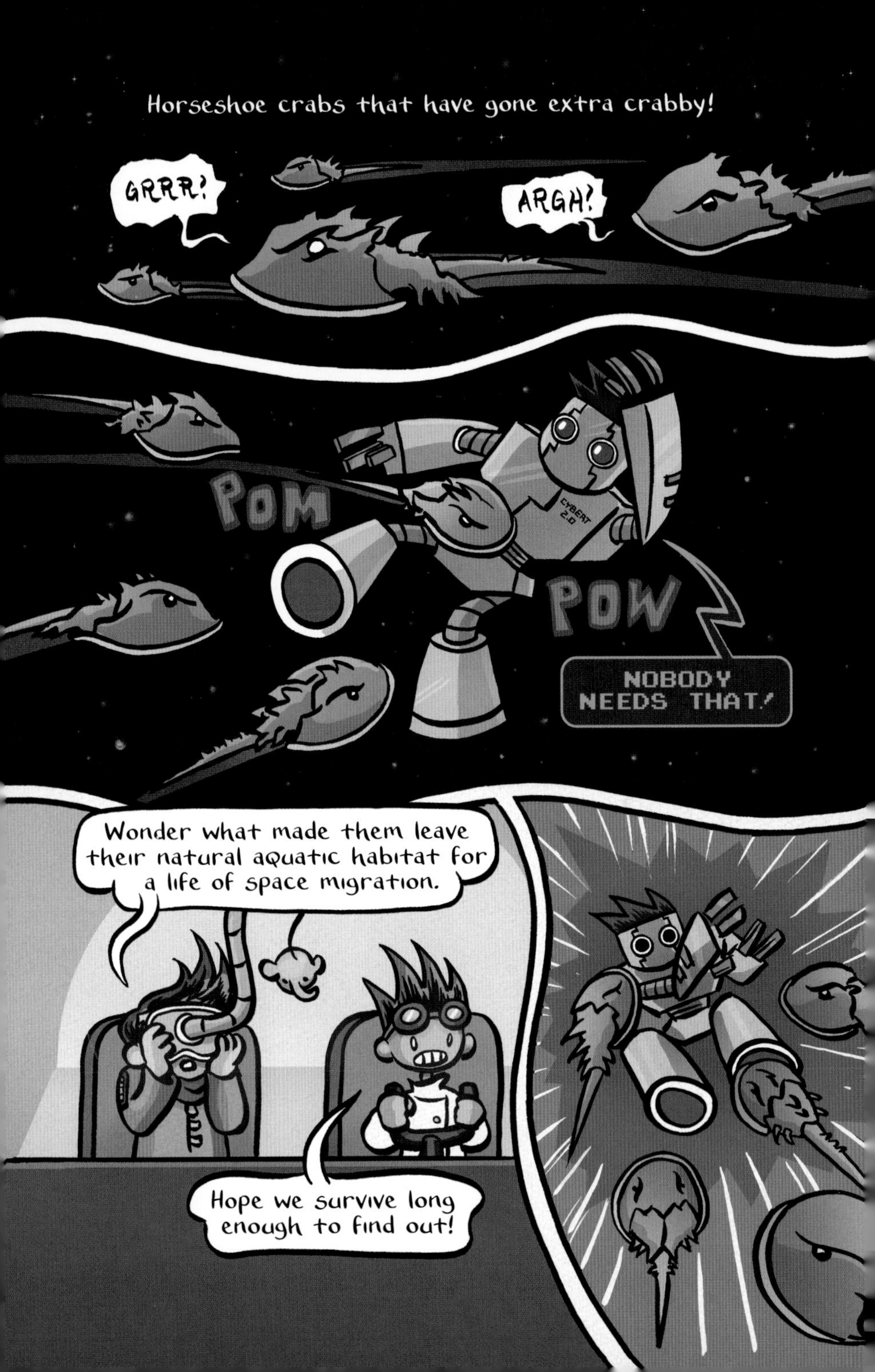
Horseshoe crabs that have gone extra crabby!
GRRR?
ARGH?
POM
POW
NOBODY NEEDS THAT!
CYBERT 2.0
Wonder what made them leave their natural aquatic habitat for a life of space migration.
Hope we survive long enough to find out!

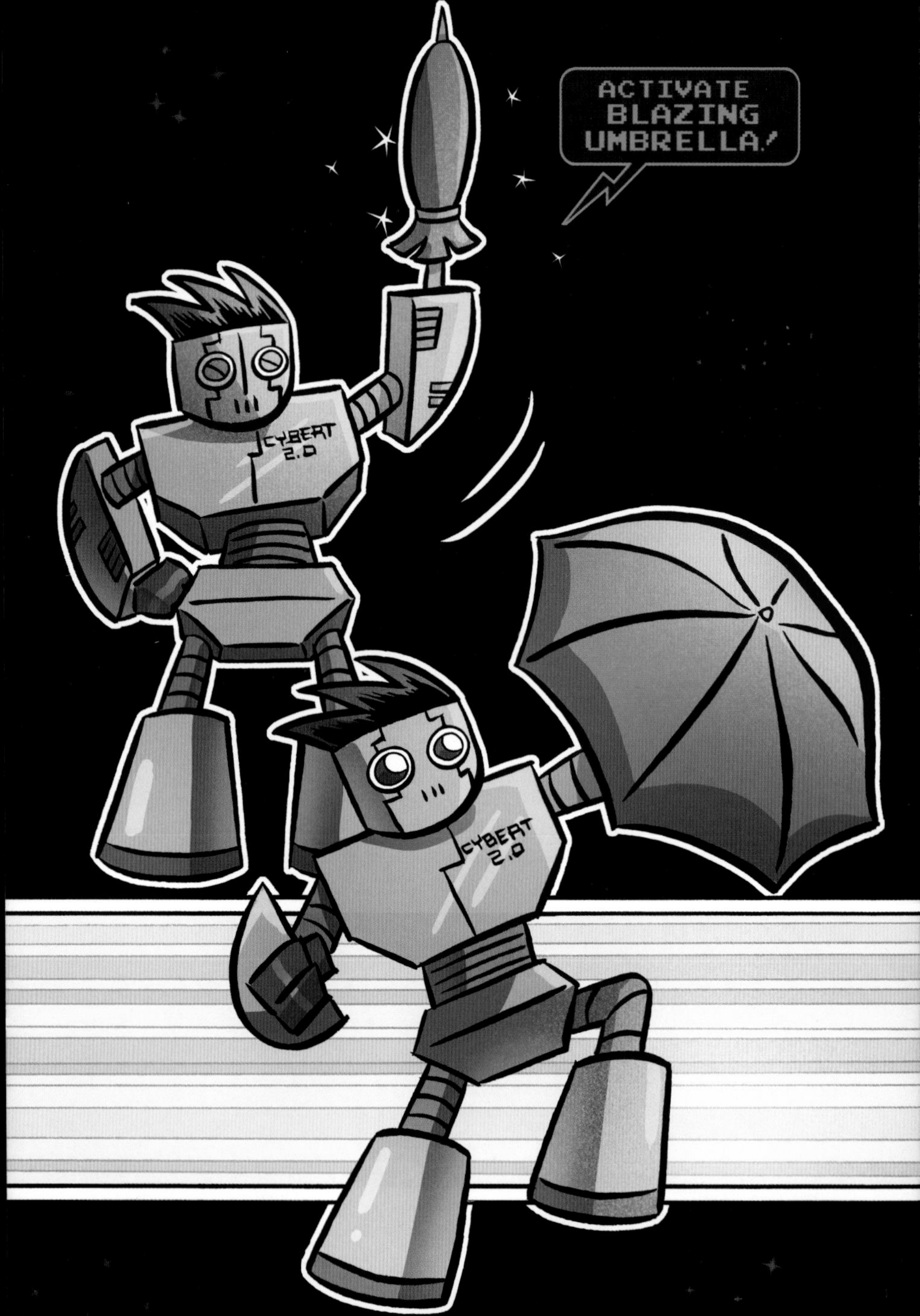
ACTIVATE BLAZING UMBRELLA!
CYBERT 2.0
CYBERT 2.0

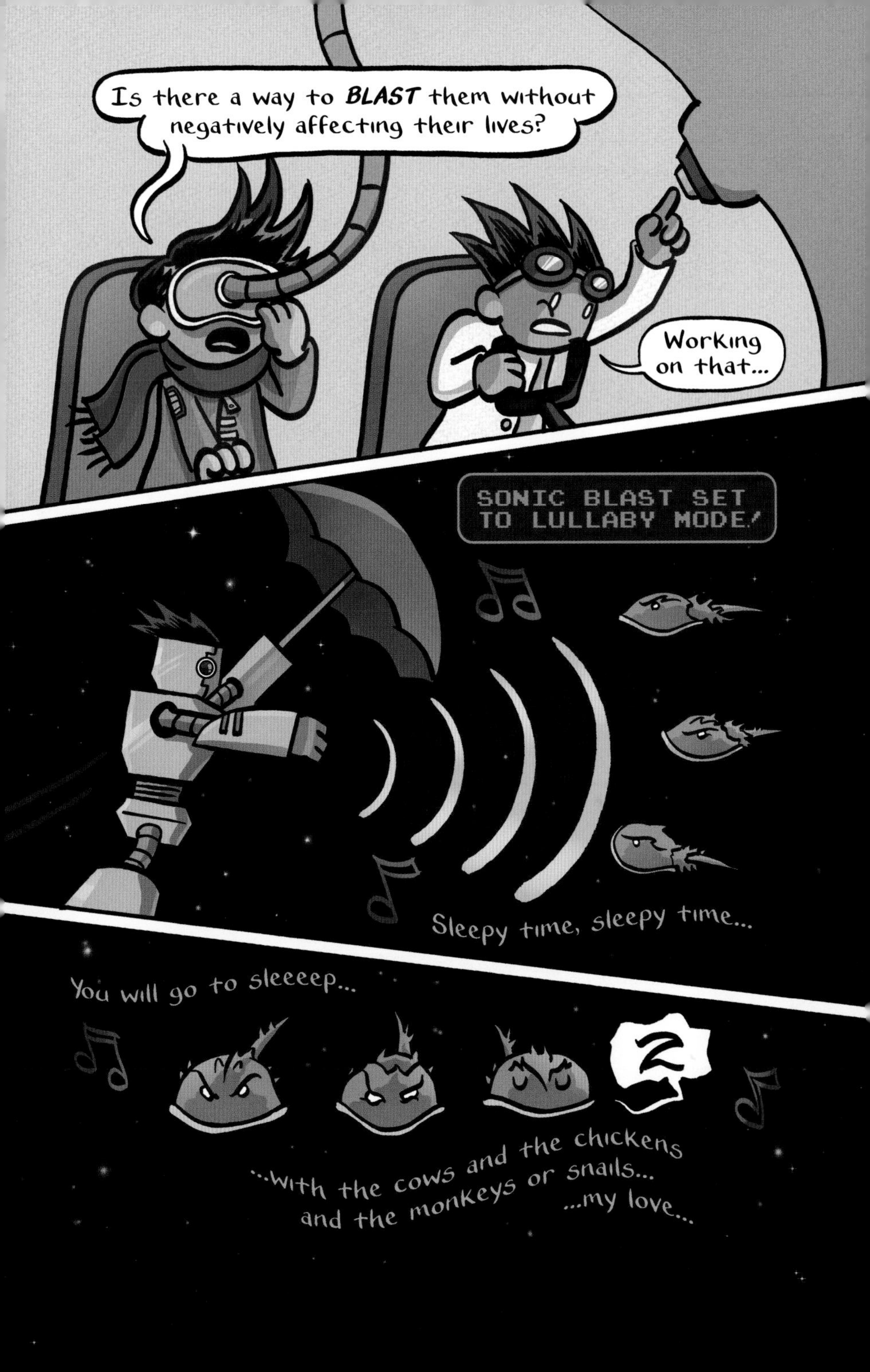
Is there a way to BLAST them without negatively affecting their lives?
Working on that...
SONIC BLAST SET TO LULLABY MODE!
Sleepy time, sleepy time...
You will go to sleeeep...
Z
...with the cows and the chickens and the monkeys or snails...
...my love...

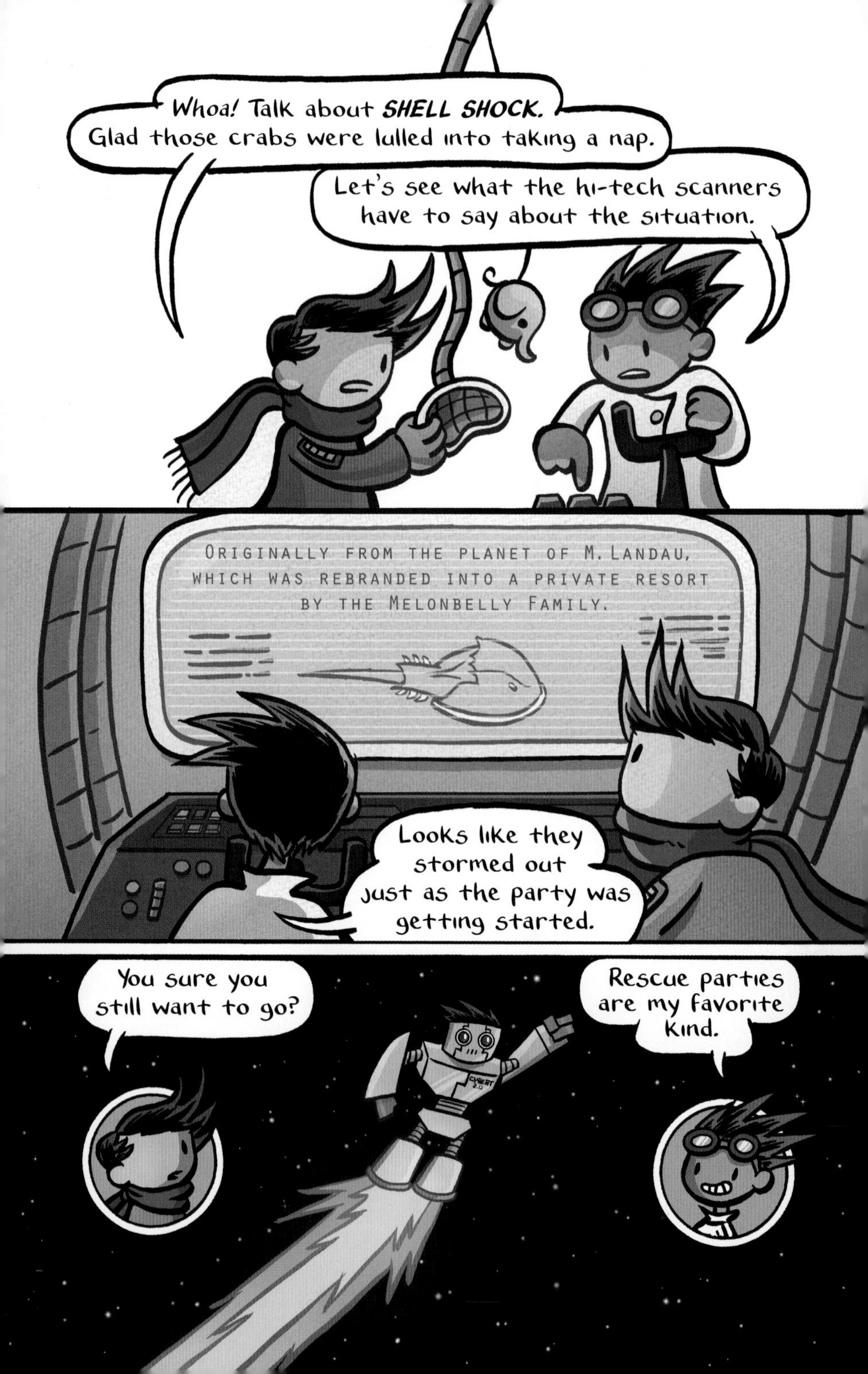
Whoa! Talk about SHELL SHOCK. Glad those crabs were lulled into taking a nap.
Let's see what the hi-tech scanners have to say about the situation.
ORIGINALLY FROM THE PLANET OF M. LANDAU, WHICH WAS REBRANDED INTO A PRIVATE RESORT BY THE MELONBELLY FAMILY.
Looks like they stormed out just as the party was getting started.
You sure you still want to go?
Rescue parties are my favorite kind.

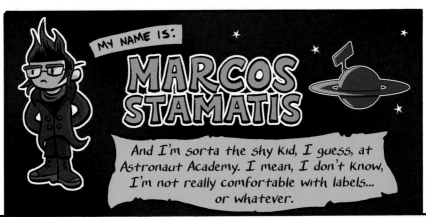

MY NAME IS:

MARCOS STAMATIS

And I'm sorta the shy kid, I guess, at Astronaut Academy. I mean, I don't know, I'm not really comfortable with labels... or whatever.

Are you sure you want to go to this beach party, honey? There are going to be other people there.

It's my first invitation. It could also be my last...

Okay, but it's on a beach planet. Which probably means sunlight.

I **KNOW!** You don't have to remind me for the billionth time.

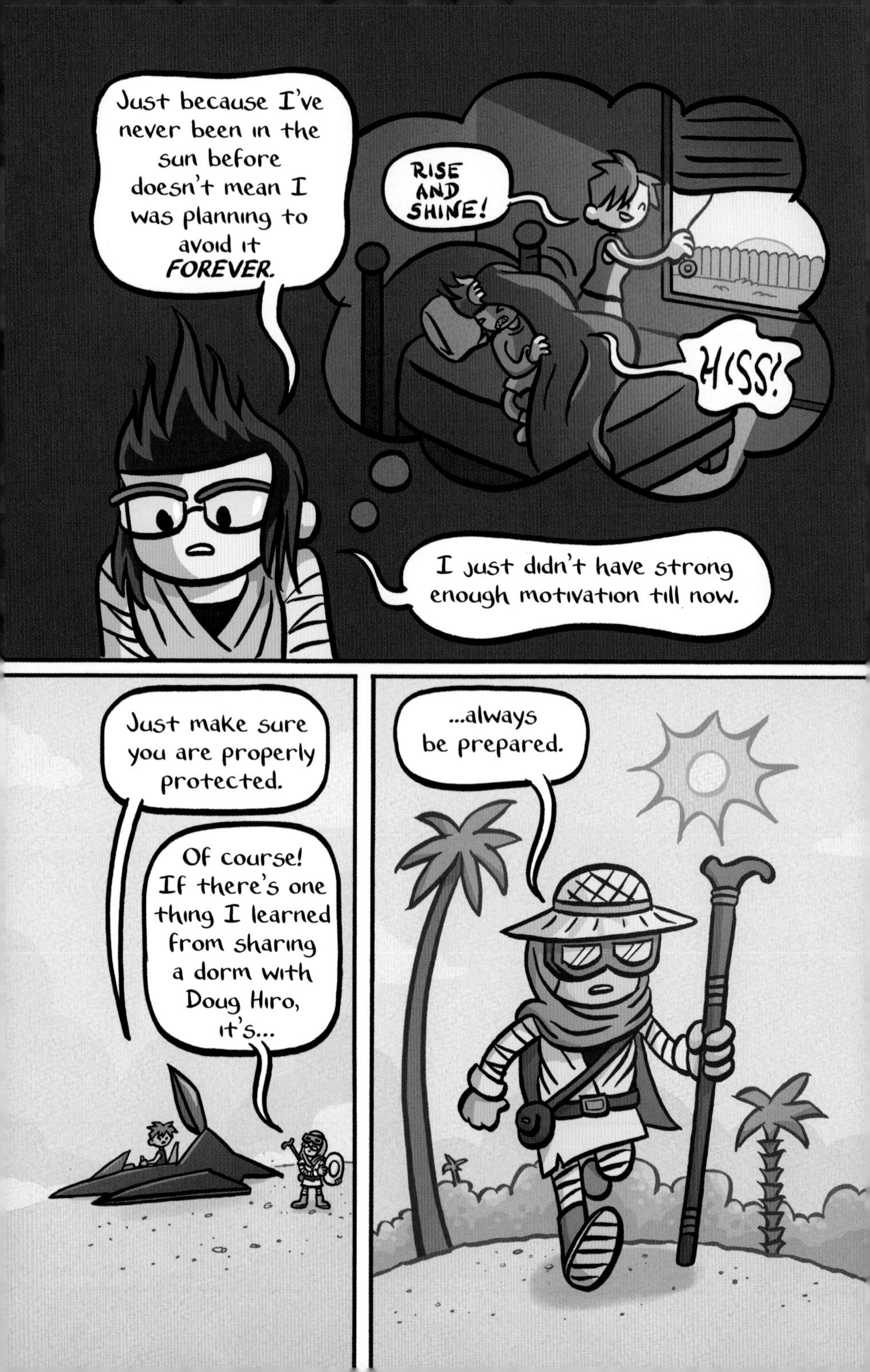

Just because I've never been in the sun before doesn't mean I was planning to avoid it FOREVER.
RISE AND SHINE!
HISS!
I just didn't have strong enough motivation till now.
Just make sure you are properly protected.
Of course! If there's one thing I learned from sharing a dorm with Doug Hiro, it's...
...always be prepared.

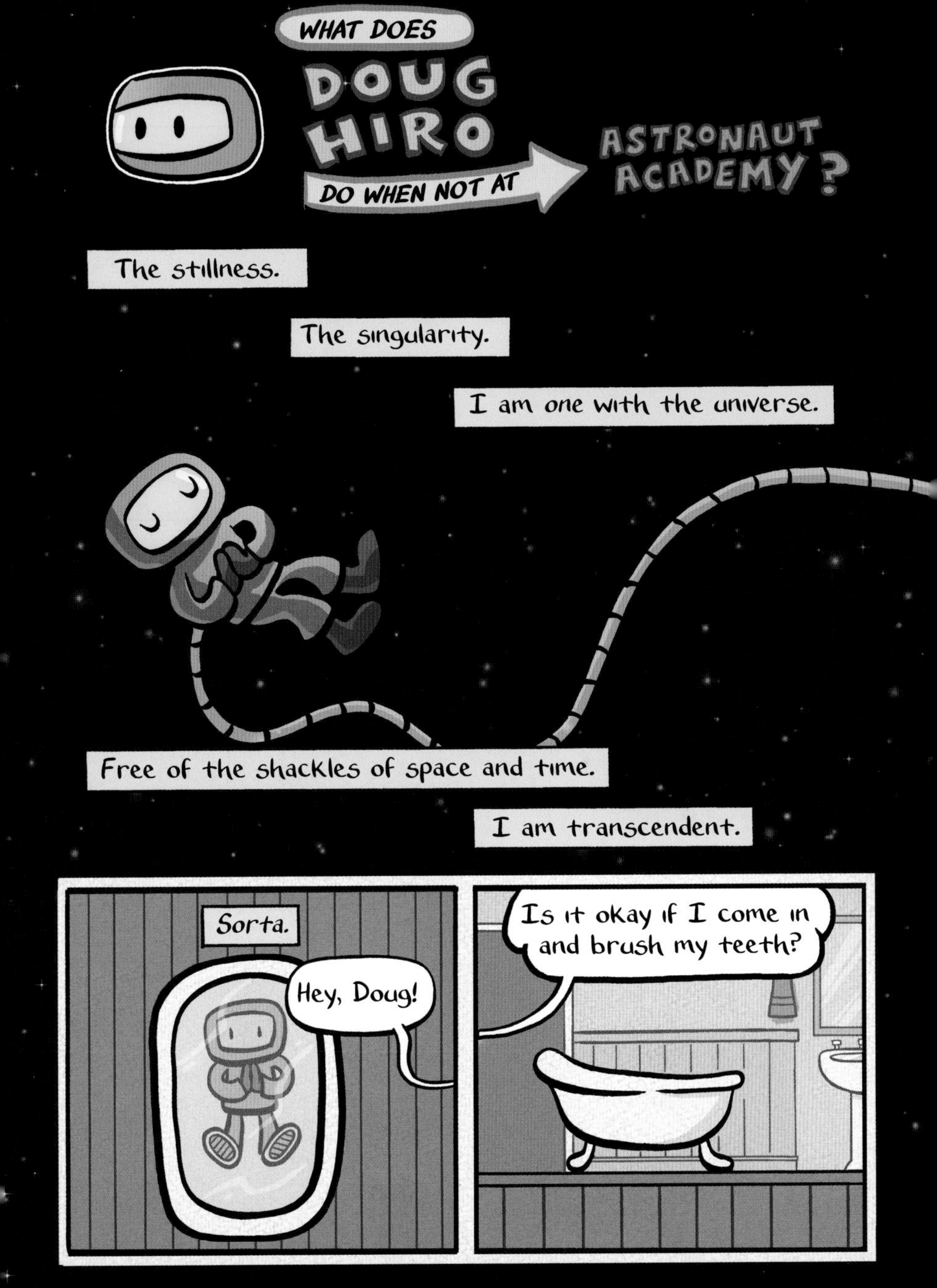
WHAT DOES
DOUG HIRO
DO WHEN NOT AT
ASTRONAUT ACADEMY?
The stillness.
The singularity.
I am one with the universe.
Free of the shackles of space and time.
I am transcendent.
Sorta.
Hey, Doug!
Is it okay if I come in and brush my teeth?

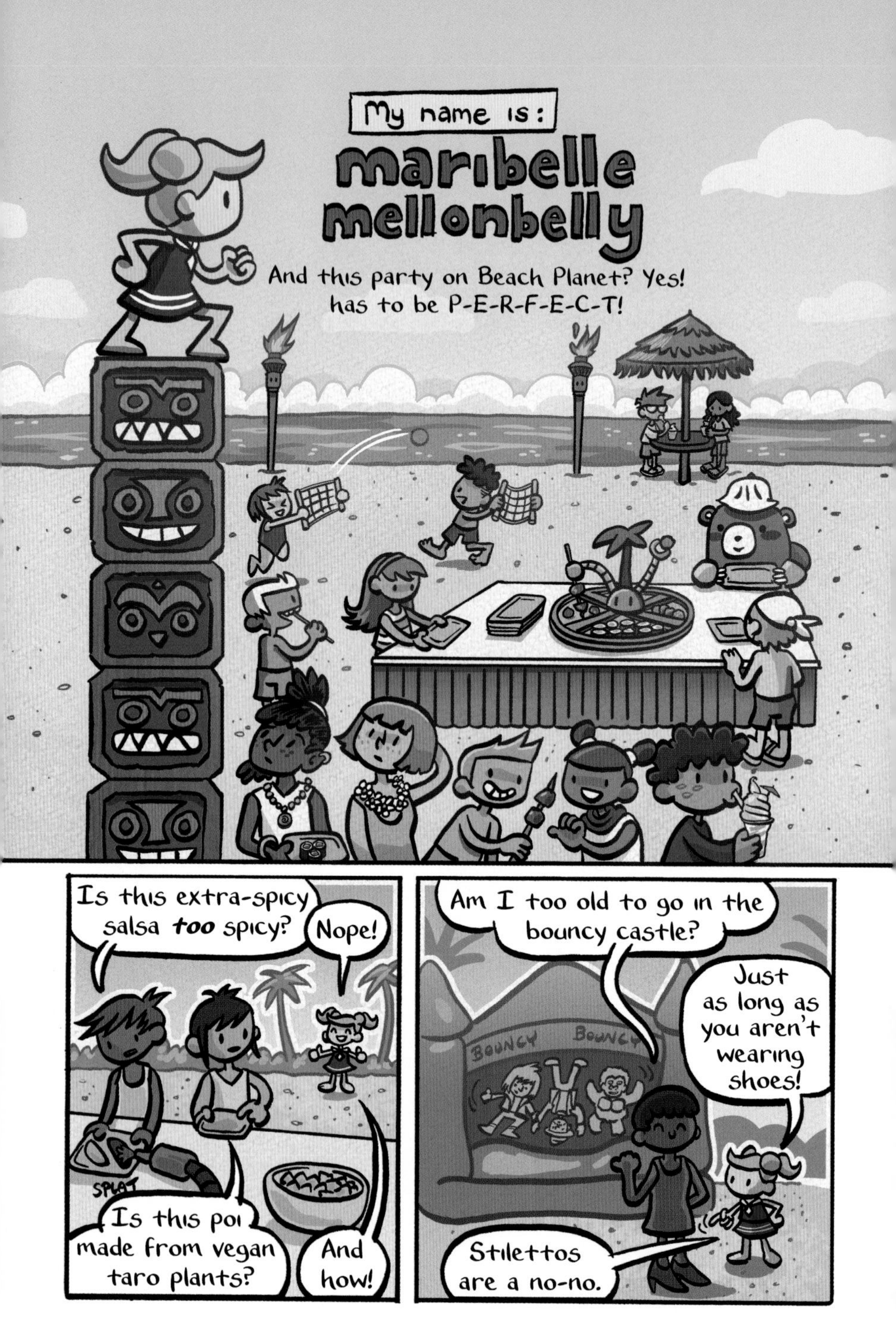

My name is:
maribelle mellonbelly
And this party on Beach Planet? Yes! has to be P-E-R-F-E-C-T!
Is this extra-spicy salsa ***too*** spicy?
Nope!
SPLAT
Is this poi made from vegan taro plants?
And how!
Am I too old to go in the bouncy castle?
BOUNCY
Just as long as you aren't wearing shoes!
Stilettos are a no-no.

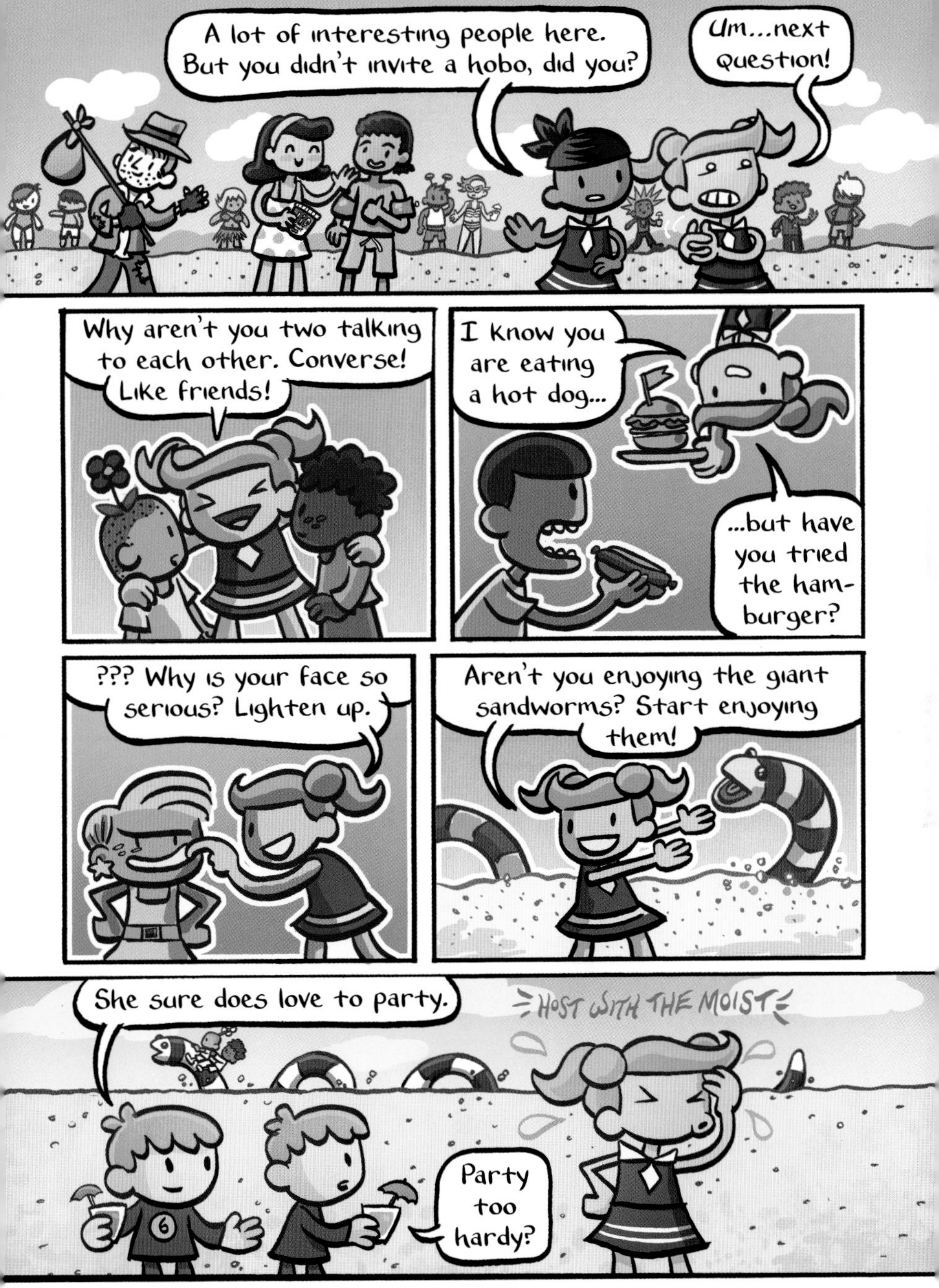

A lot of interesting people here. But you didn't invite a hobo, did you?
Um...next question!
Why aren't you two talking to each other. Converse! Like friends!
I know you are eating a hot dog...
...but have you tried the hamburger?
??? Why is your face so serious? Lighten up.
Aren't you enjoying the giant sandworms? Start enjoying them!
She sure does love to party.
HOST WITH THE MOIST
Party too hardy?

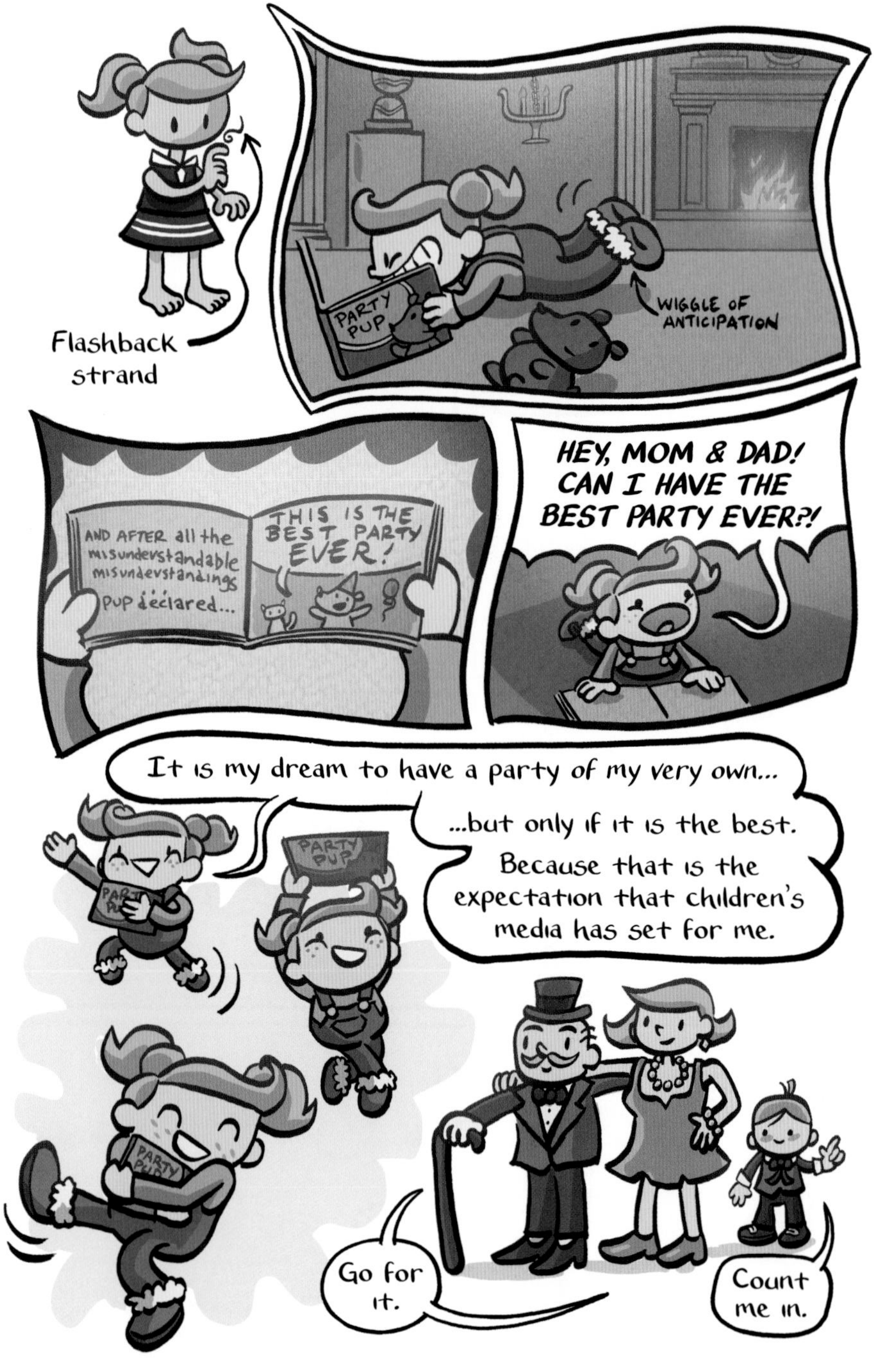
Flashback strand
PARTY PUP
WIGGLE OF ANTICIPATION
AND AFTER all the misunderstandable misunderstandings pup declared...
THIS IS THE BEST PARTY EVER!
HEY, MOM & DAD! CAN I HAVE THE BEST PARTY EVER?!
It is my dream to have a party of my very own...
...but only if it is the best.
Because that is the expectation that children's media has set for me.
PARTY PUP
Go for it.
Count me in.

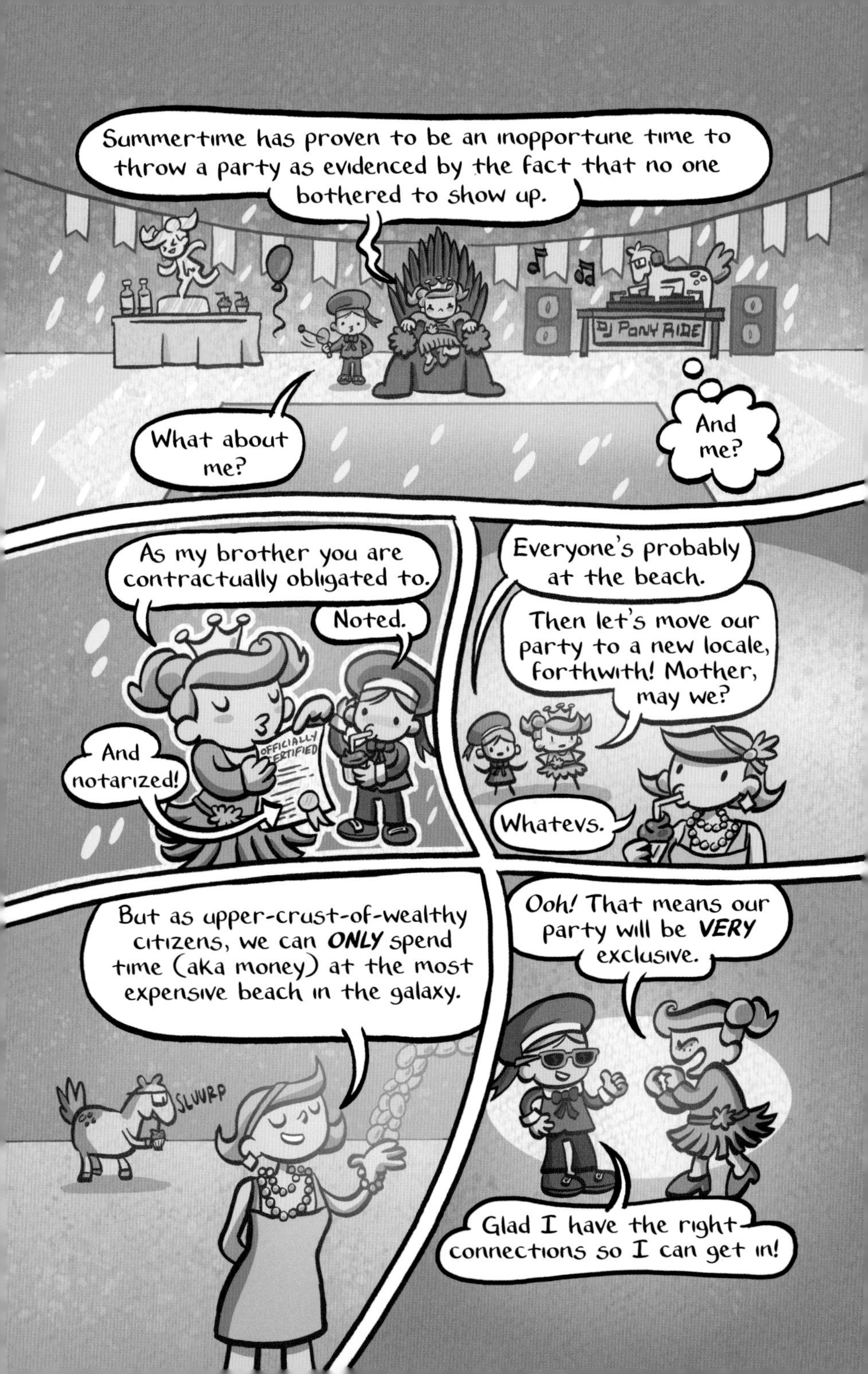
Summertime has proven to be an inopportune time to throw a party as evidenced by the fact that no one bothered to show up.
DJ PONY RIDE
What about me?
And me?
As my brother you are contractually obligated to.
Noted.
OFFICIALLY CERTIFIED
And notarized!
Everyone's probably at the beach.
Then let's move our party to a new locale, forthwith! Mother, may we?
Whatevs.
But as upper-crust-of-wealthy citizens, we can ONLY spend time (aka money) at the most expensive beach in the galaxy.
SLUURP
Ooh! That means our party will be VERY exclusive.
Glad I have the right connections so I can get in!

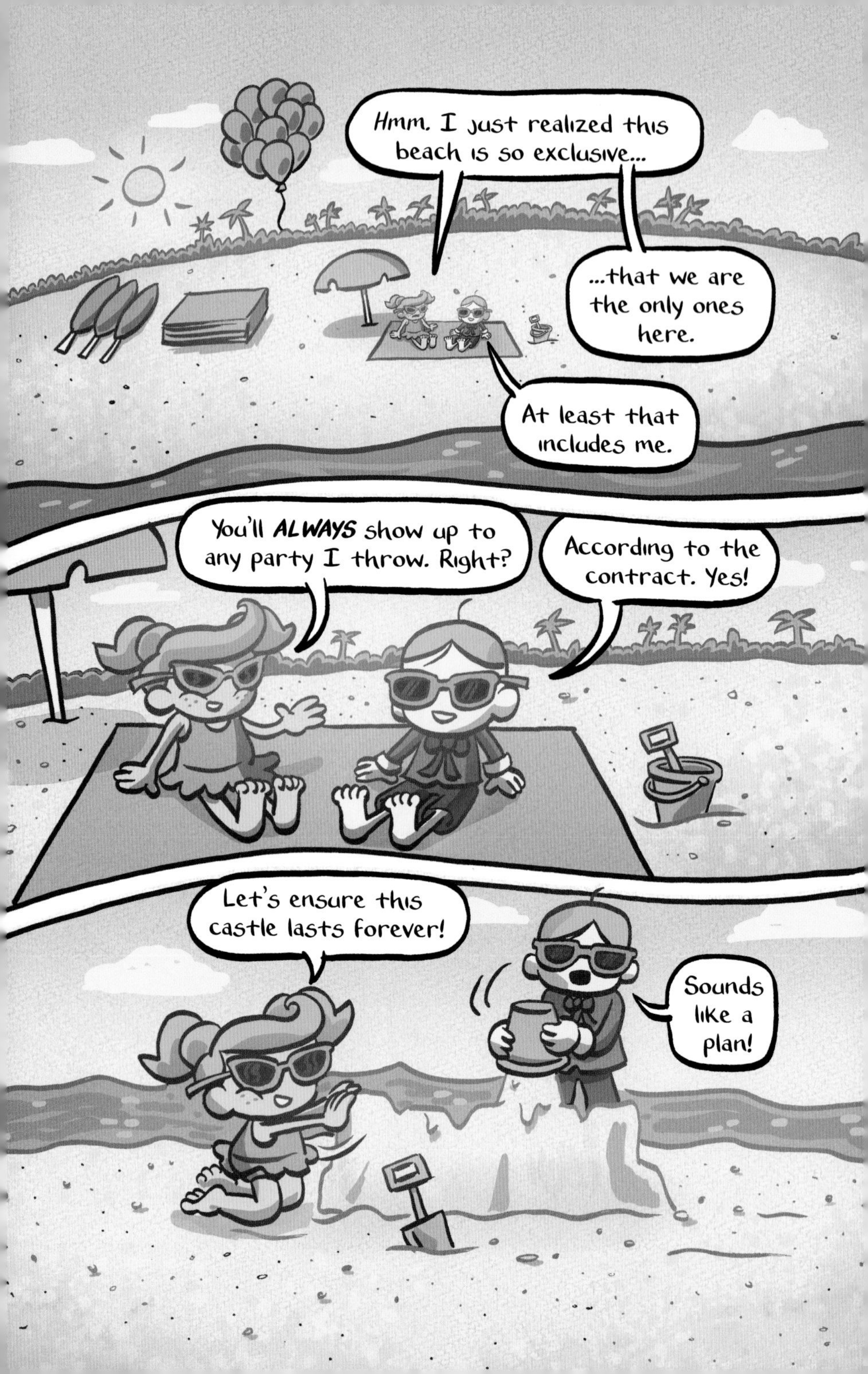
Hmm. I just realized this beach is so exclusive...
...that we are the only ones here.
At least that includes me.
You'll **ALWAYS** show up to any party I throw. Right?
According to the contract. Yes!
Let's ensure this castle lasts forever!
Sounds like a plan!

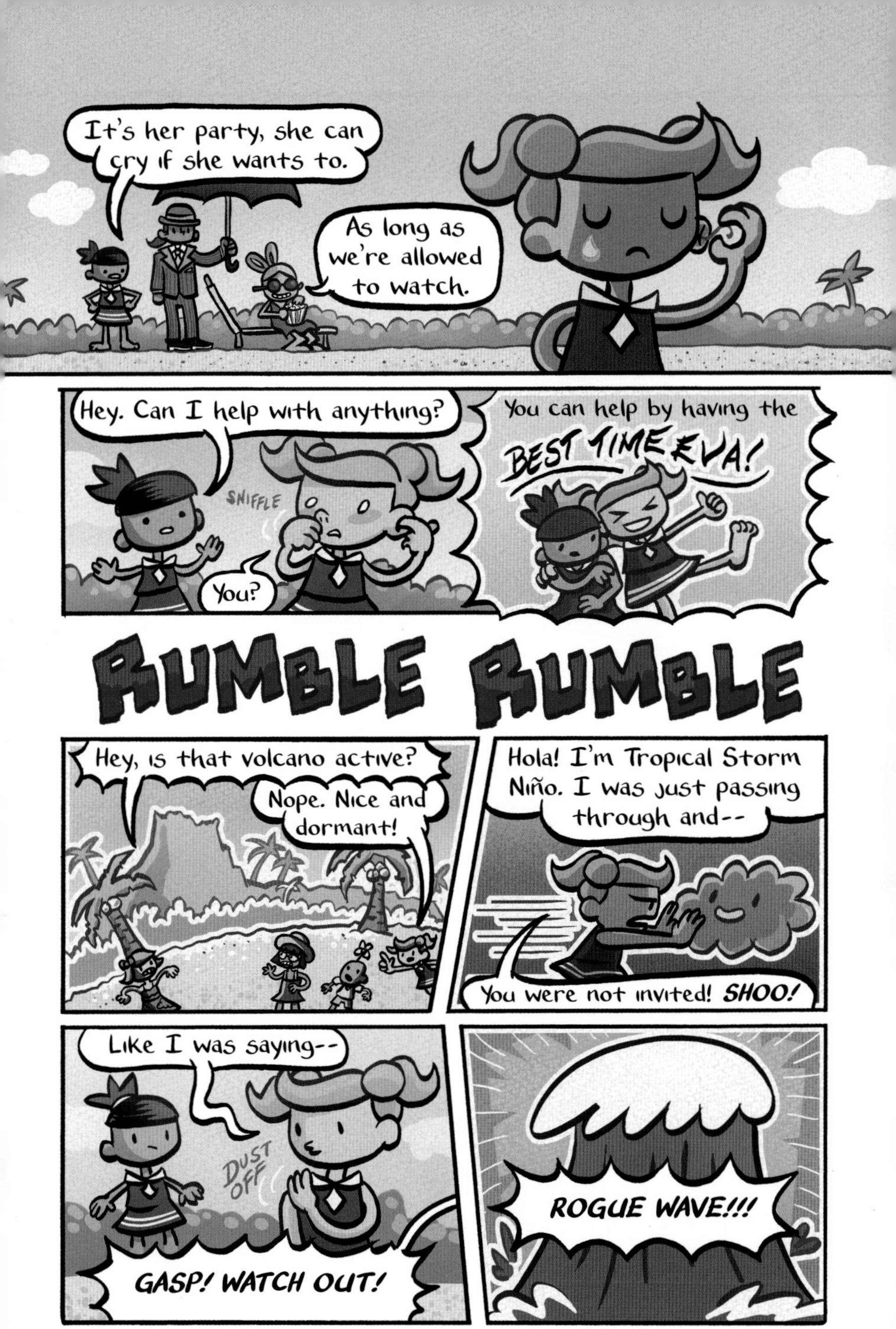

It's her party, she can cry if she wants to.
As long as we're allowed to watch.
Hey. Can I help with anything?
SNIFFLE
You?
You can help by having the
BEST TIME EVA!
RUMBLE RUMBLE
Hey, is that volcano active?
Nope. Nice and dormant!
Hola! I'm Tropical Storm Niño. I was just passing through and--
You were not invited! SHOO!
Like I was saying--
DUST OFF
GASP! WATCH OUT!
ROGUE WAVE!!!

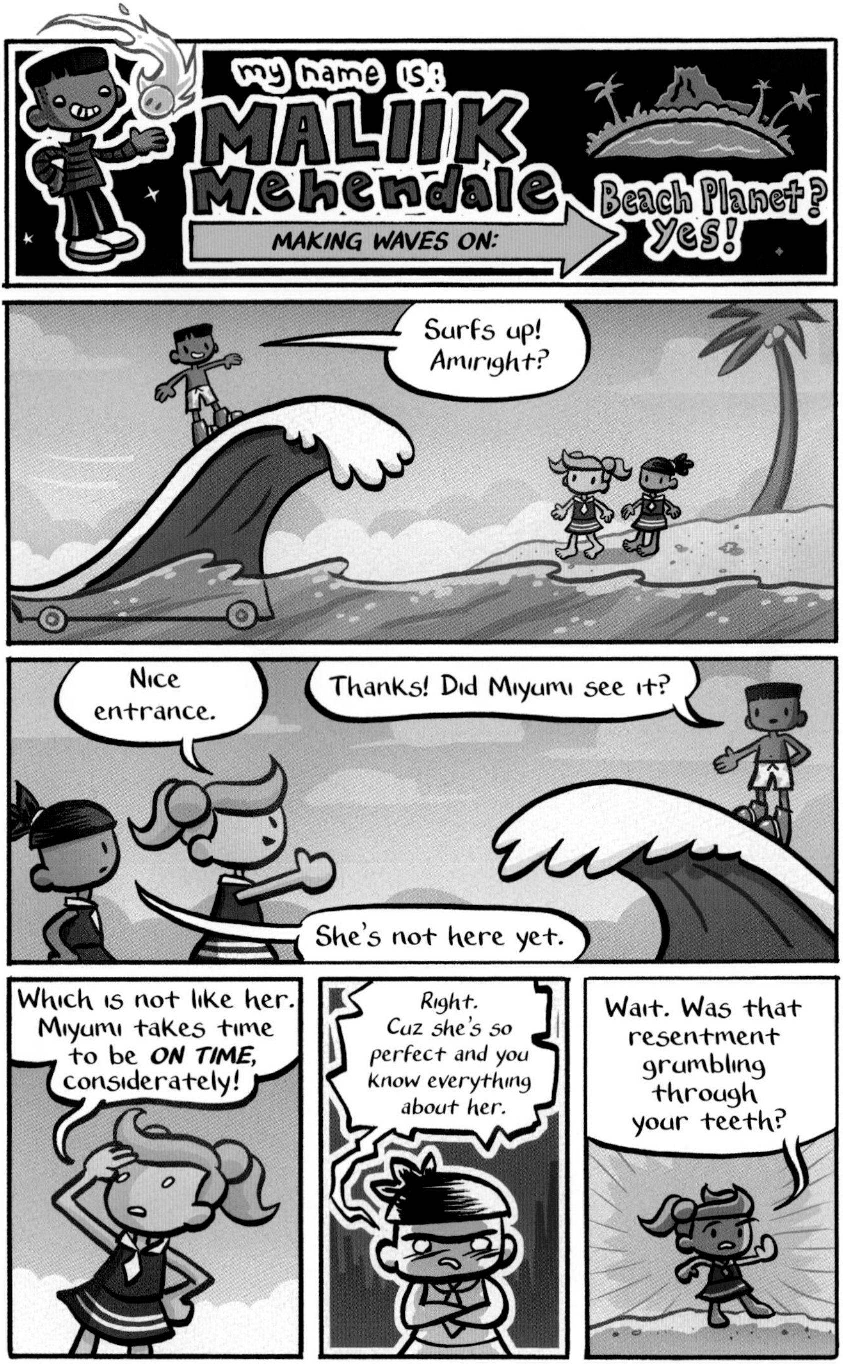
my name is:
MALIIK Mehendale
MAKING WAVES ON:
Beach Planet? yes!
Surfs up! Amiright?
Nice entrance.
Thanks! Did Miyumi see it?
She's not here yet.
Which is not like her. Miyumi takes time to be ON TIME, considerately!
Right. Cuz she's so perfect and you know everything about her.
Wait. Was that resentment grumbling through your teeth?

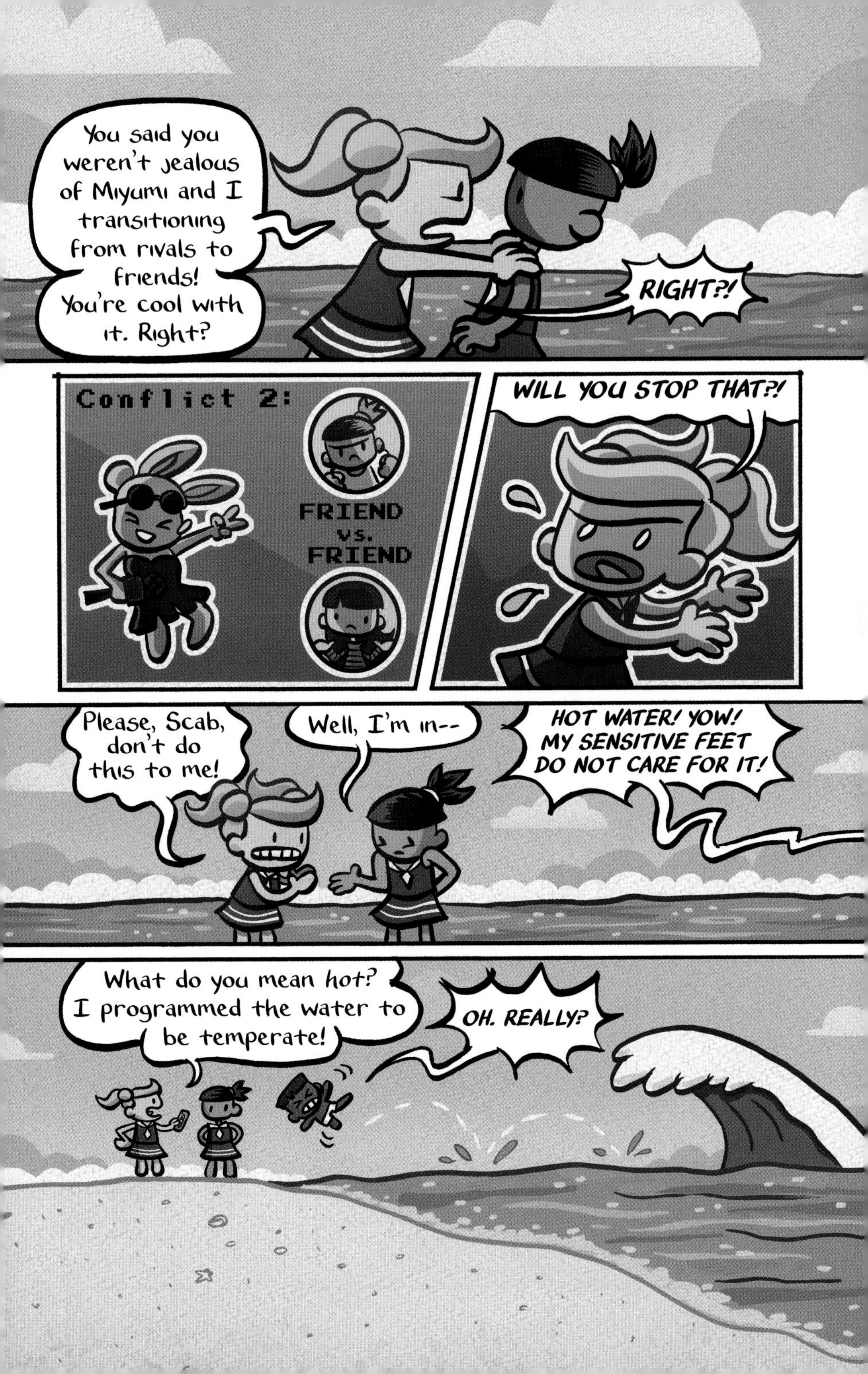
You said you weren't jealous of Miyumi and I transitioning from rivals to friends! You're cool with it. Right?
RIGHT?!
Conflict 2:
FRIEND vs. FRIEND
WILL YOU STOP THAT?!
Please, Scab, don't do this to me!
Well, I'm in--
HOT WATER! YOW! MY SENSITIVE FEET DO NOT CARE FOR IT!
What do you mean hot? I programmed the water to be temperate!
OH. REALLY?

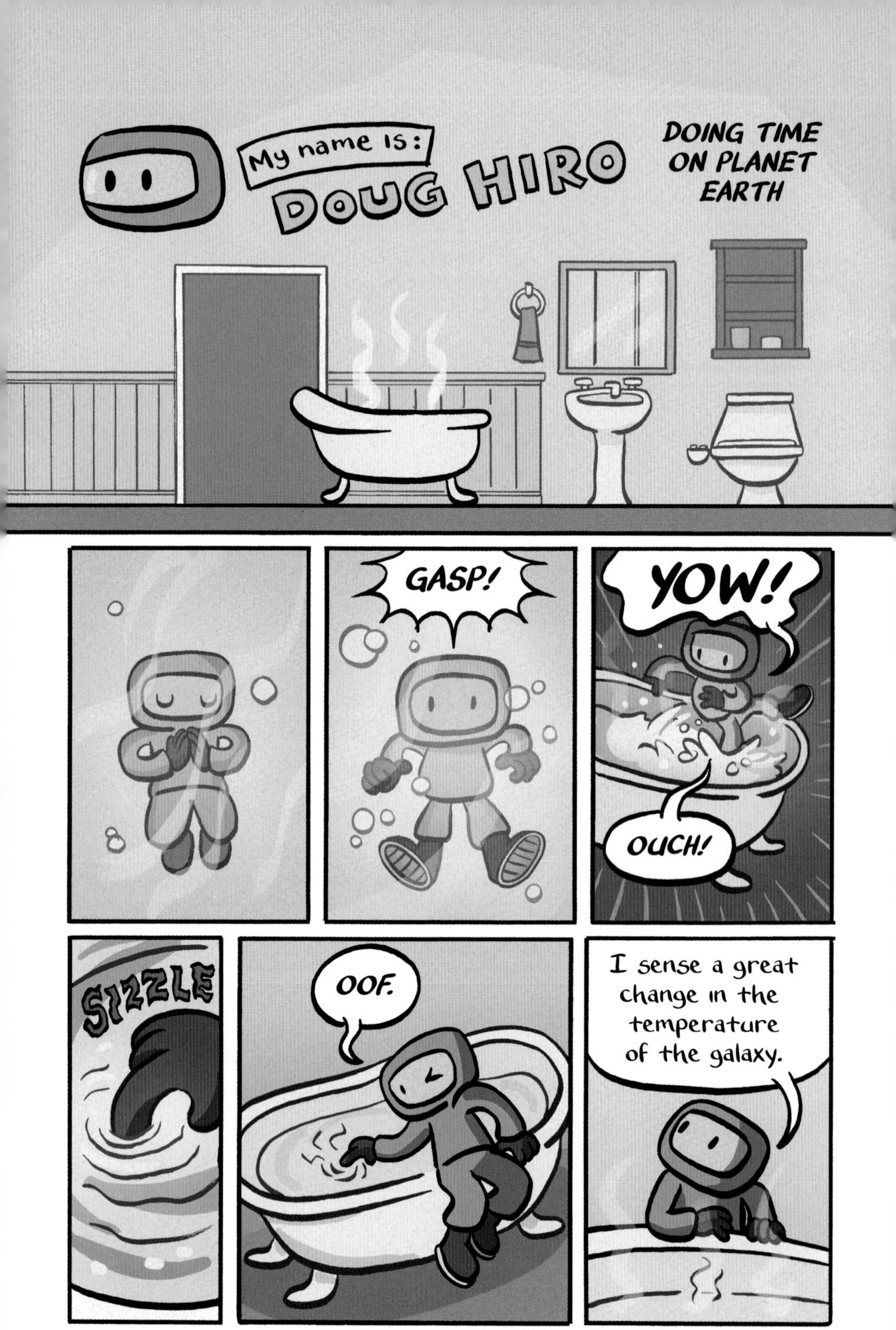
My name is:
DOUG HIRO
DOING TIME ON PLANET EARTH
GASP!
YOW!
OUCH!
SIZZLE
OOF.
I sense a great change in the temperature of the galaxy.

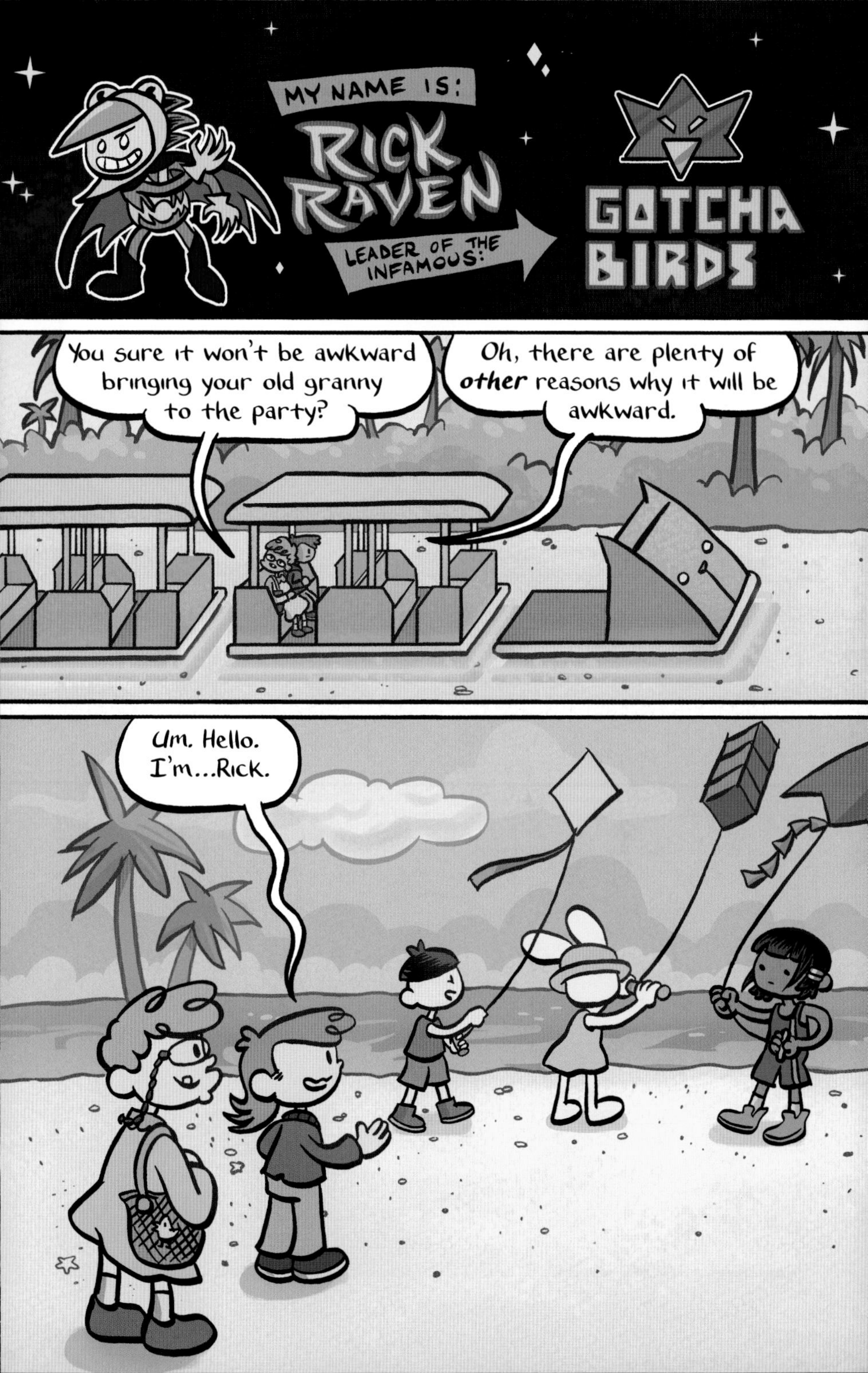
MY NAME IS:
RICK RAVEN
LEADER OF THE INFAMOUS:
GOTCHA BIRDS
You sure it won't be awkward bringing your old granny to the party?
Oh, there are plenty of *other* reasons why it will be awkward.
Um. Hello. I'm...Rick.

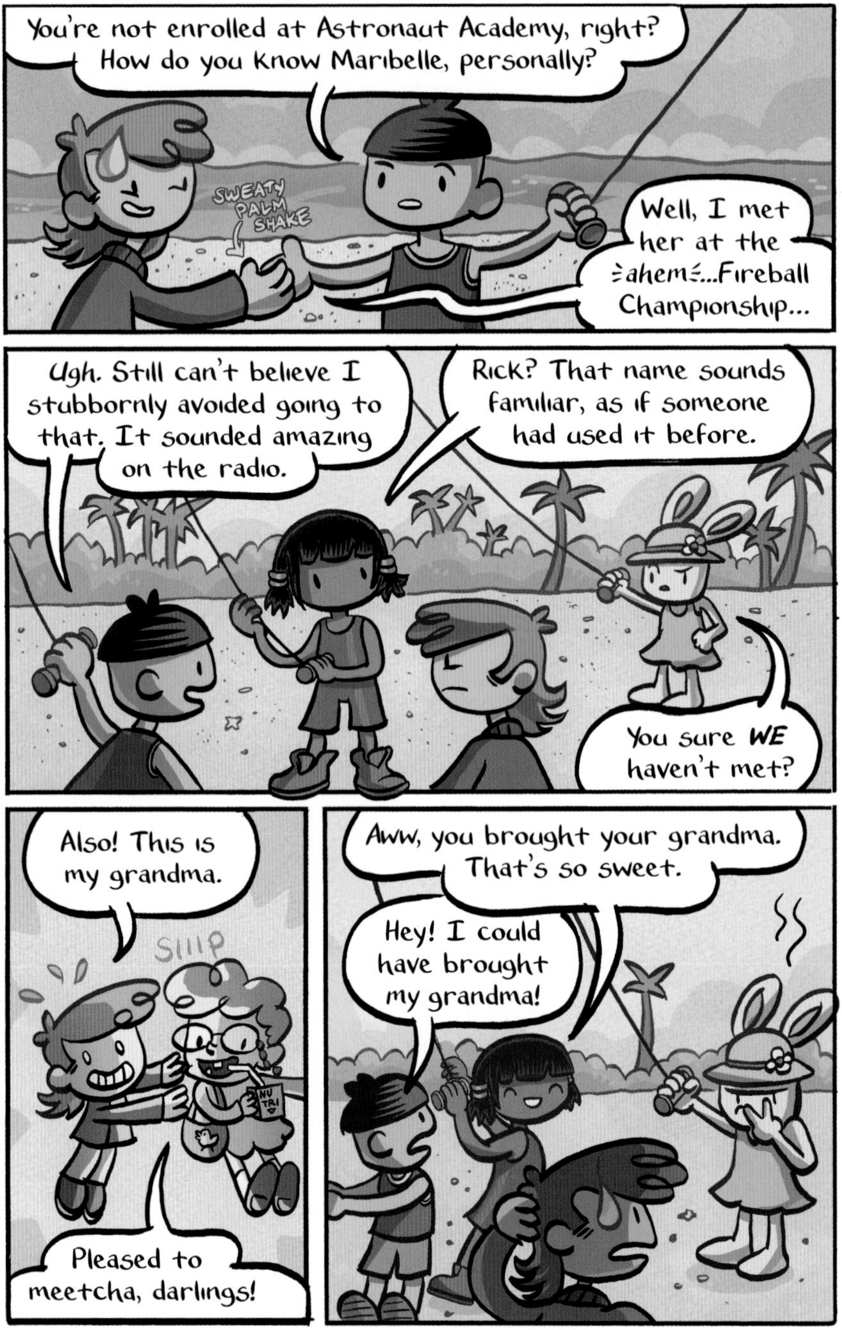
You're not enrolled at Astronaut Academy, right? How do you know Maribelle, personally?
SWEATY PALM SHAKE
Well, I met her at the *ahem*...Fireball Championship...
Ugh. Still can't believe I stubbornly avoided going to that. It sounded amazing on the radio.
Rick? That name sounds familiar, as if someone had used it before.
You sure ***WE*** haven't met?
Also! This is my grandma.
SIIIP
NU TRI
Pleased to meetcha, darlings!
Aww, you brought your grandma. That's so sweet.
Hey! I could have brought my grandma!

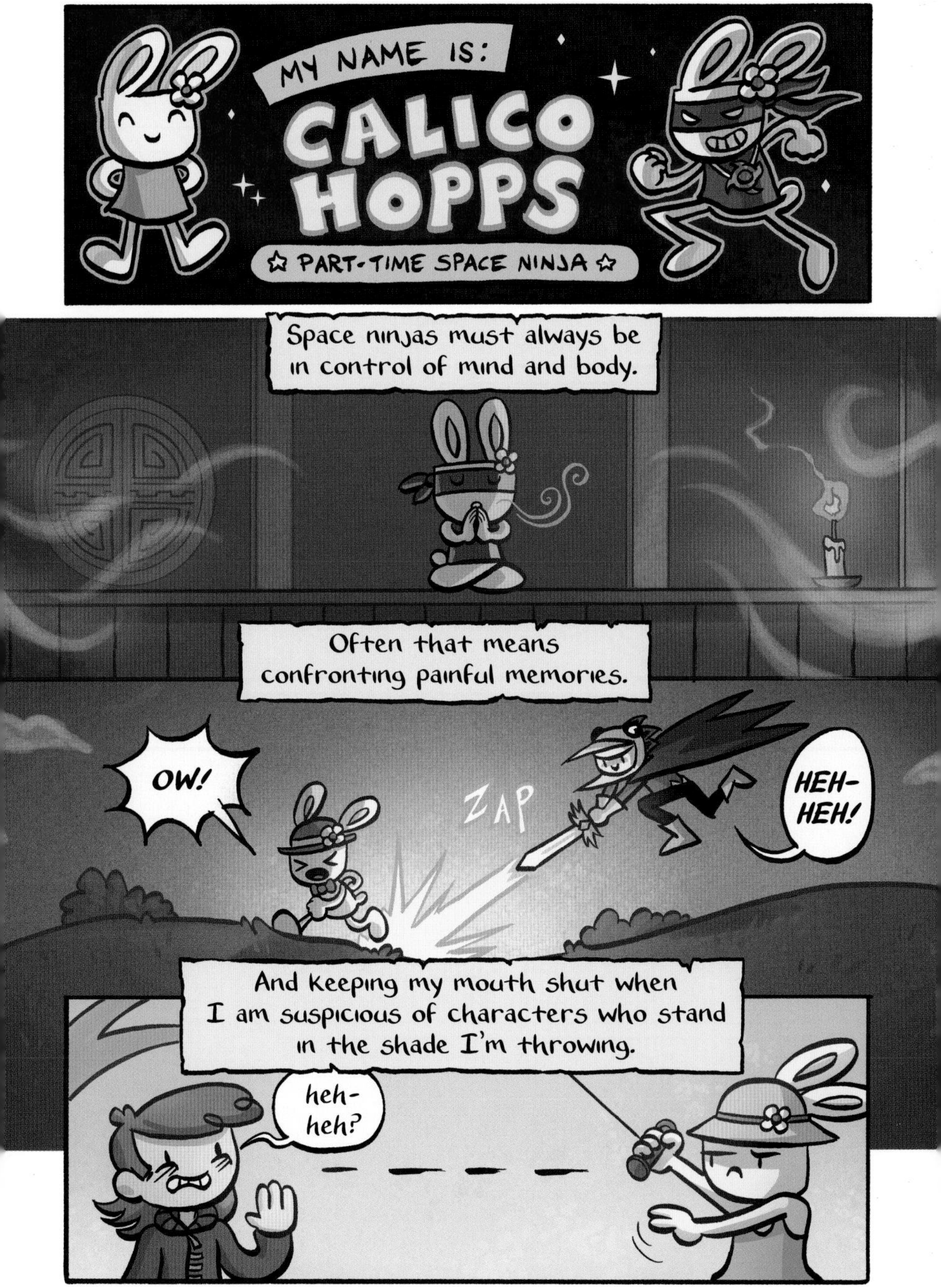
MY NAME IS:
CALICO HOPPS
PART-TIME SPACE NINJA
Space ninjas must always be in control of mind and body.
Often that means confronting painful memories.
OW!
ZAP
HEH-HEH!
And keeping my mouth shut when I am suspicious of characters who stand in the shade I'm throwing.
heh-heh?

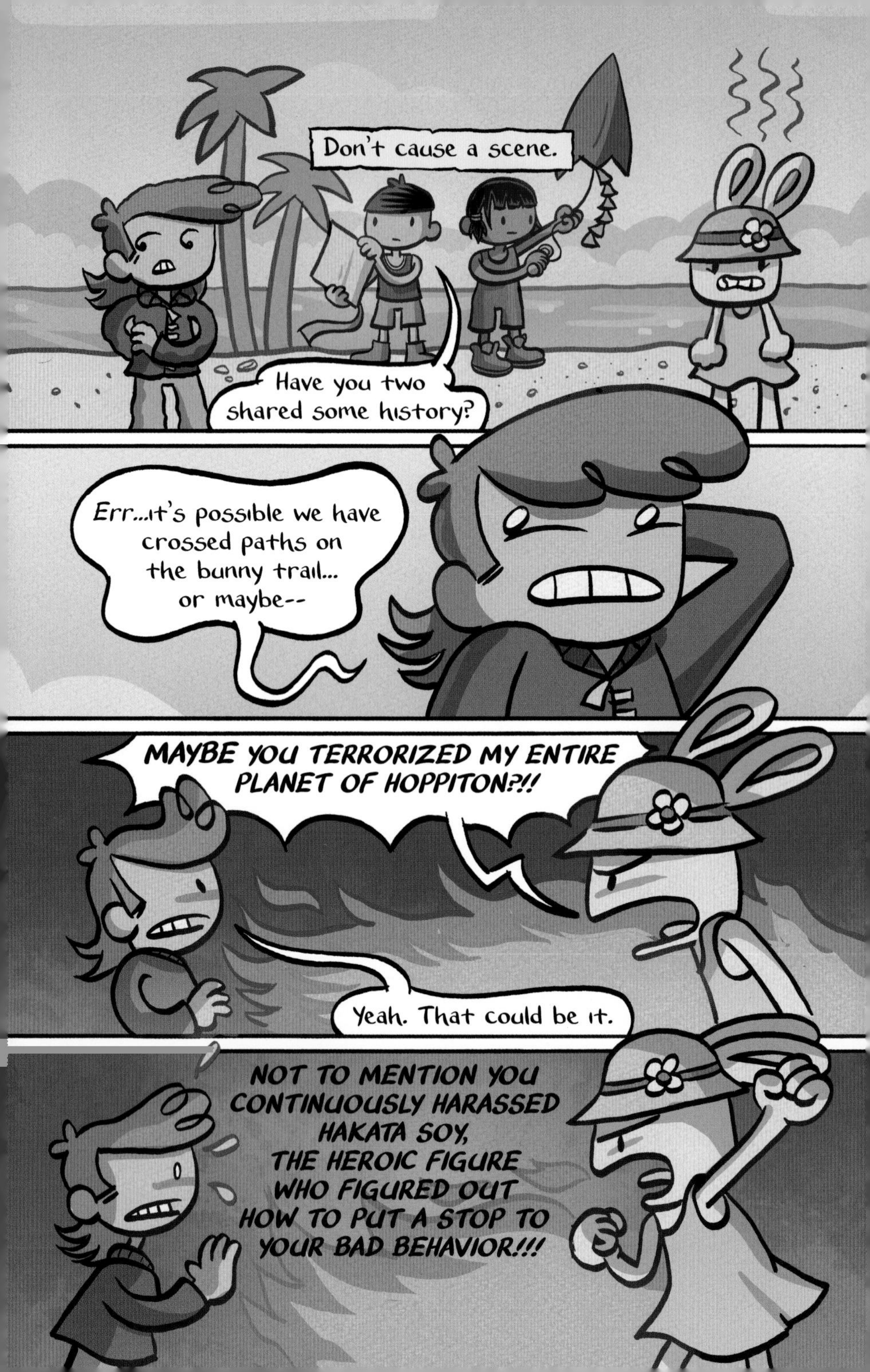
Don't cause a scene.
Have you two shared some history?
Err...it's possible we have crossed paths on the bunny trail... or maybe--
MAYBE YOU TERRORIZED MY ENTIRE PLANET OF HOPPITON?!!
Yeah. That could be it.
NOT TO MENTION YOU CONTINUOUSLY HARASSED HAKATA SOY, THE HEROIC FIGURE WHO FIGURED OUT HOW TO PUT A STOP TO YOUR BAD BEHAVIOR!!!

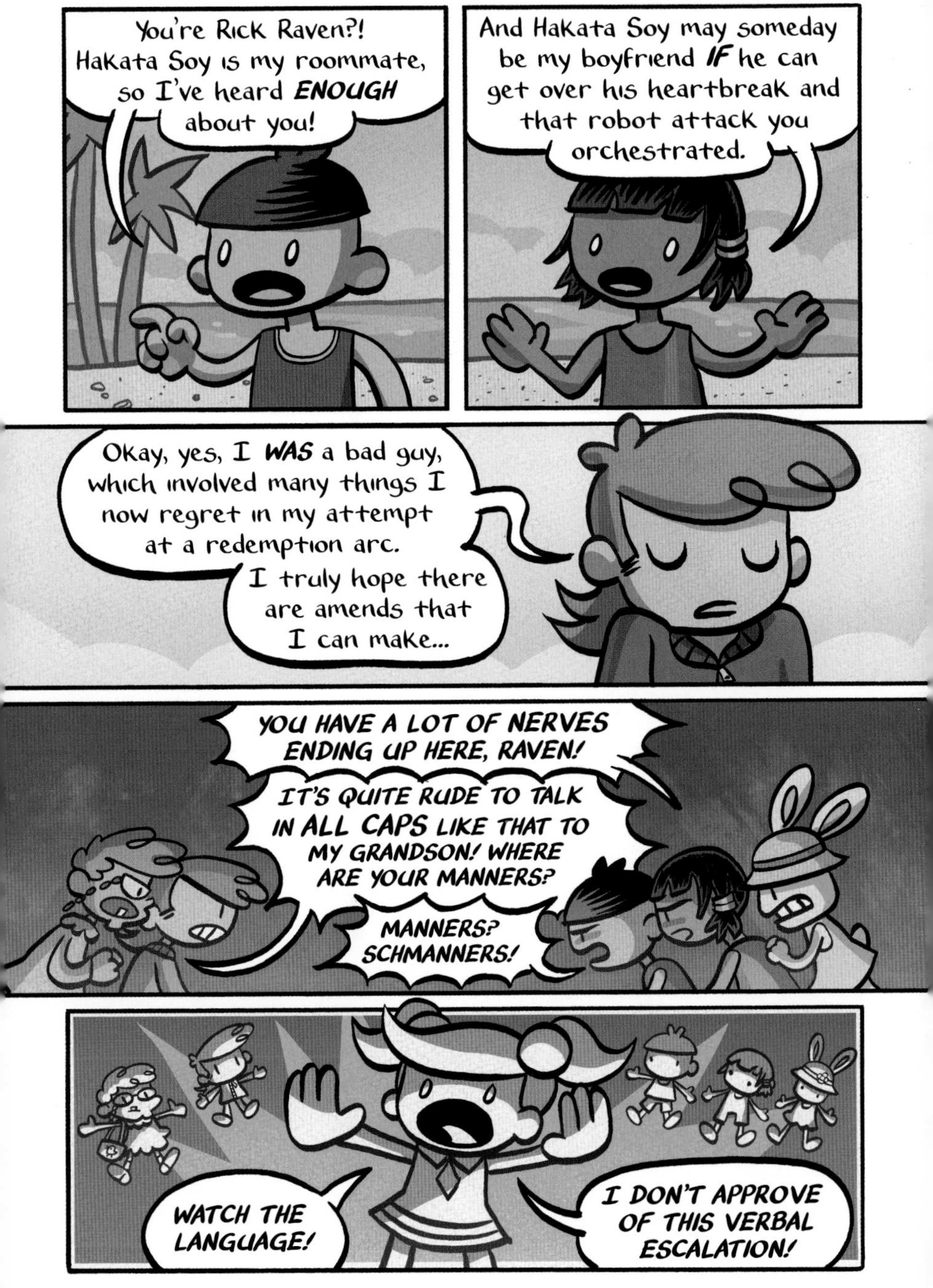
You're Rick Raven?! Hakata Soy is my roommate, so I've heard ENOUGH about you!
And Hakata Soy may someday be my boyfriend IF he can get over his heartbreak and that robot attack you orchestrated.
Okay, yes, I WAS a bad guy, which involved many things I now regret in my attempt at a redemption arc.
I truly hope there are amends that I can make...
YOU HAVE A LOT OF NERVES ENDING UP HERE, RAVEN!
IT'S QUITE RUDE TO TALK IN ALL CAPS LIKE THAT TO MY GRANDSON! WHERE ARE YOUR MANNERS?
MANNERS? SCHMANNERS!
WATCH THE LANGUAGE!
I DON'T APPROVE OF THIS VERBAL ESCALATION!

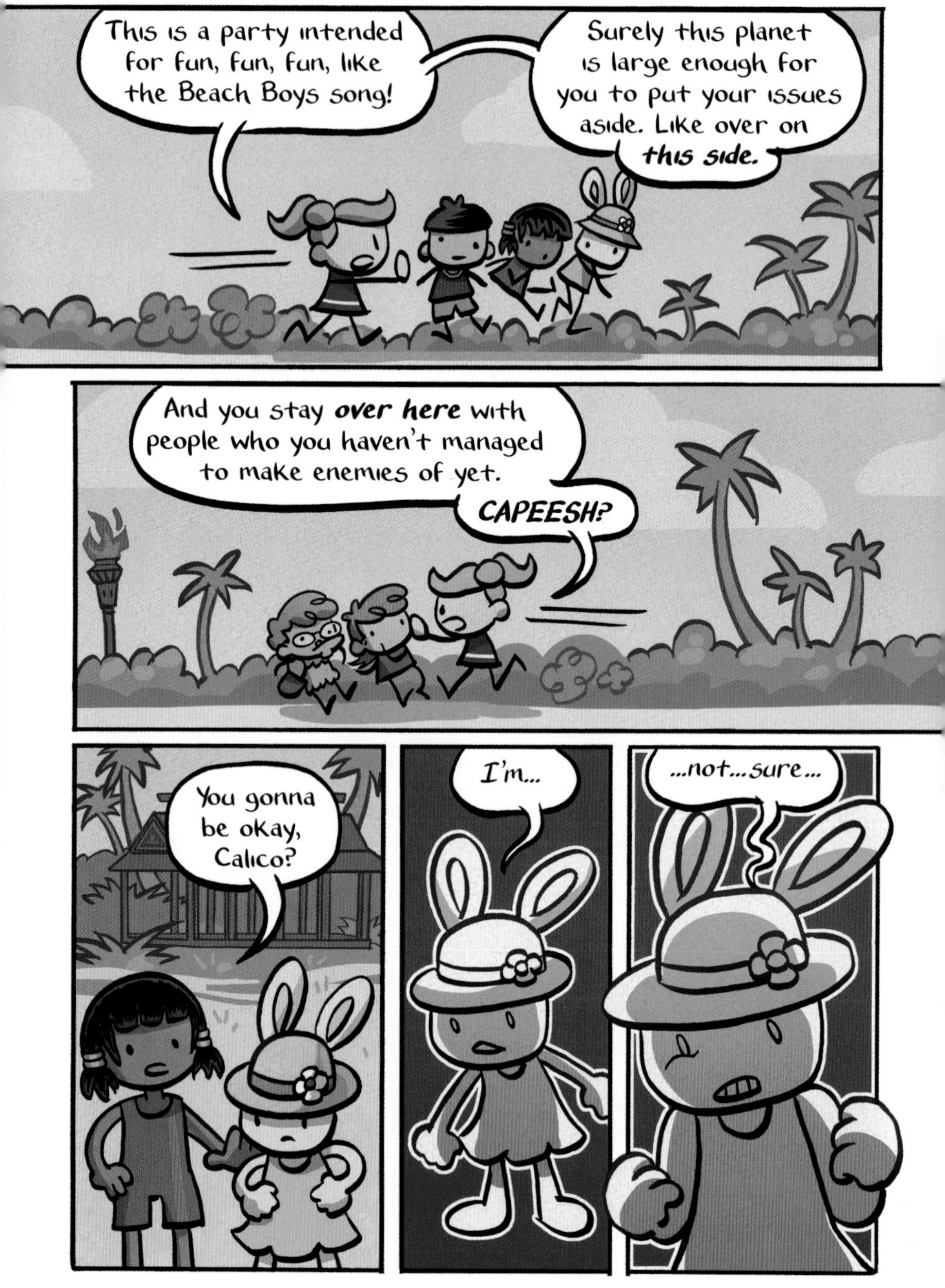
This is a party intended for fun, fun, fun, like the Beach Boys song!
Surely this planet is large enough for you to put your issues aside. Like over on **this side.**
And you stay **over here** with people who you haven't managed to make enemies of yet.
CAPEESH?
You gonna be okay, Calico?
I'm...
...not...sure...

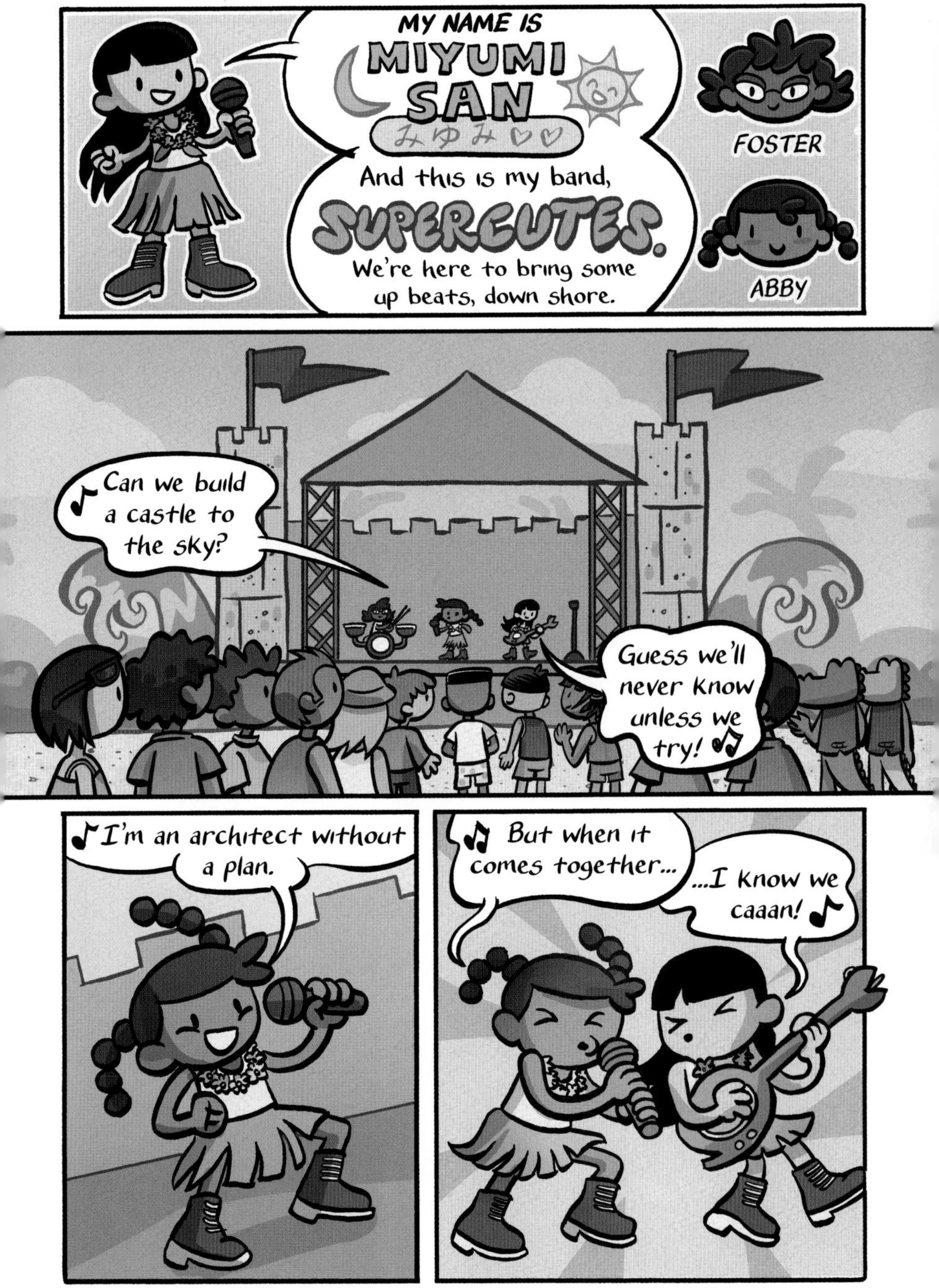
MY NAME IS
MIYUMI SAN
みゆみ♡♡
And this is my band,
SUPERCUTES.
We're here to bring some up beats, down shore.
FOSTER
ABBY
Can we build a castle to the sky?
Guess we'll never know unless we try!
I'm an architect without a plan.
But when it comes together...
...I know we caaan!

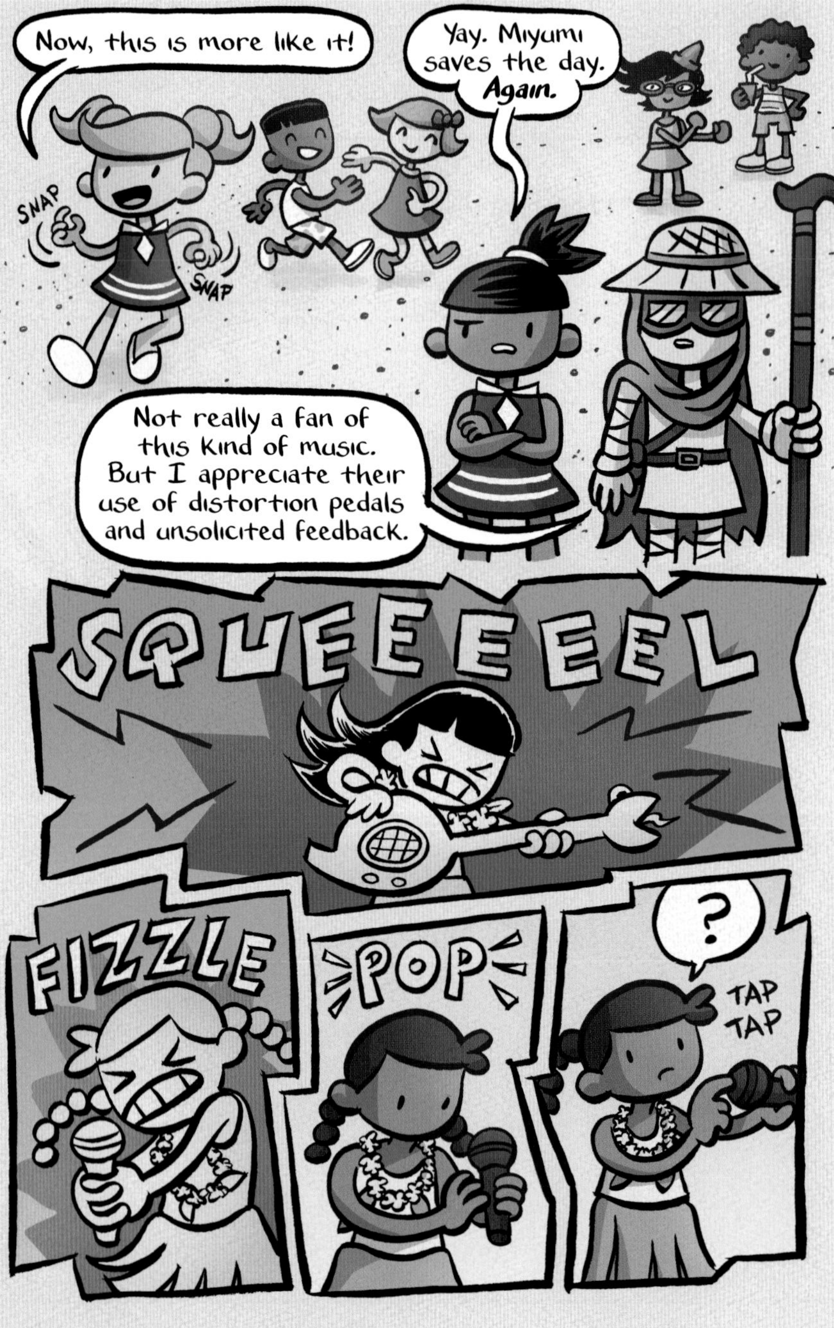
Now, this is more like it!
SNAP
SNAP
Yay. Miyumi saves the day. **Again.**
Not really a fan of this kind of music. But I appreciate their use of distortion pedals and unsolicited feedback.
SQUEEEEEL
FIZZLE
POP
?
TAP TAP

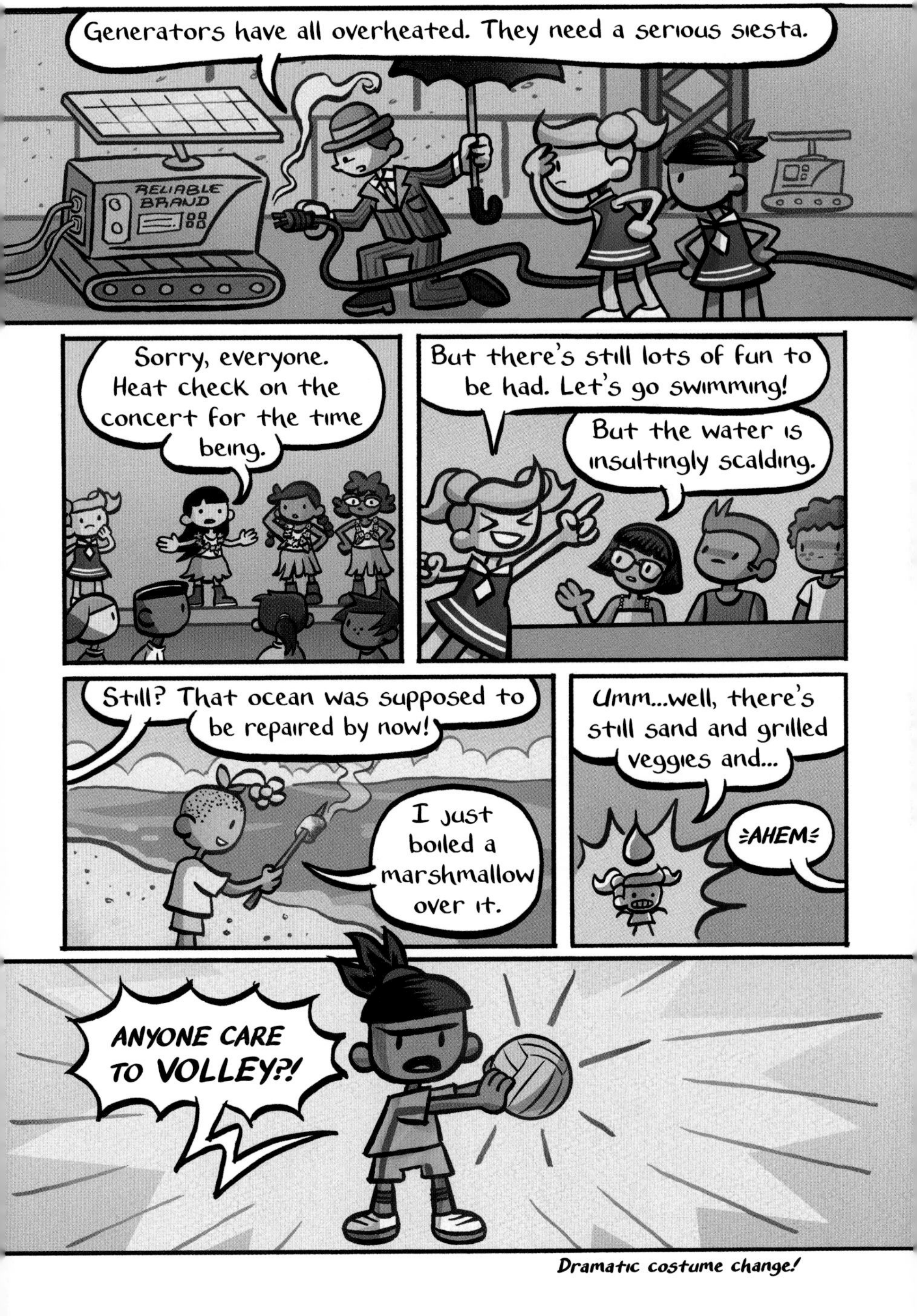

Generators have all overheated. They need a serious siesta.
RELIABLE BRAND
Sorry, everyone. Heat check on the concert for the time being.
But there's still lots of fun to be had. Let's go swimming!
But the water is insultingly scalding.
Still? That ocean was supposed to be repaired by now!
I just boiled a marshmallow over it.
Umm...well, there's still sand and grilled veggies and...
AHEM
ANYONE CARE TO VOLLEY?!

Dramatic costume change!

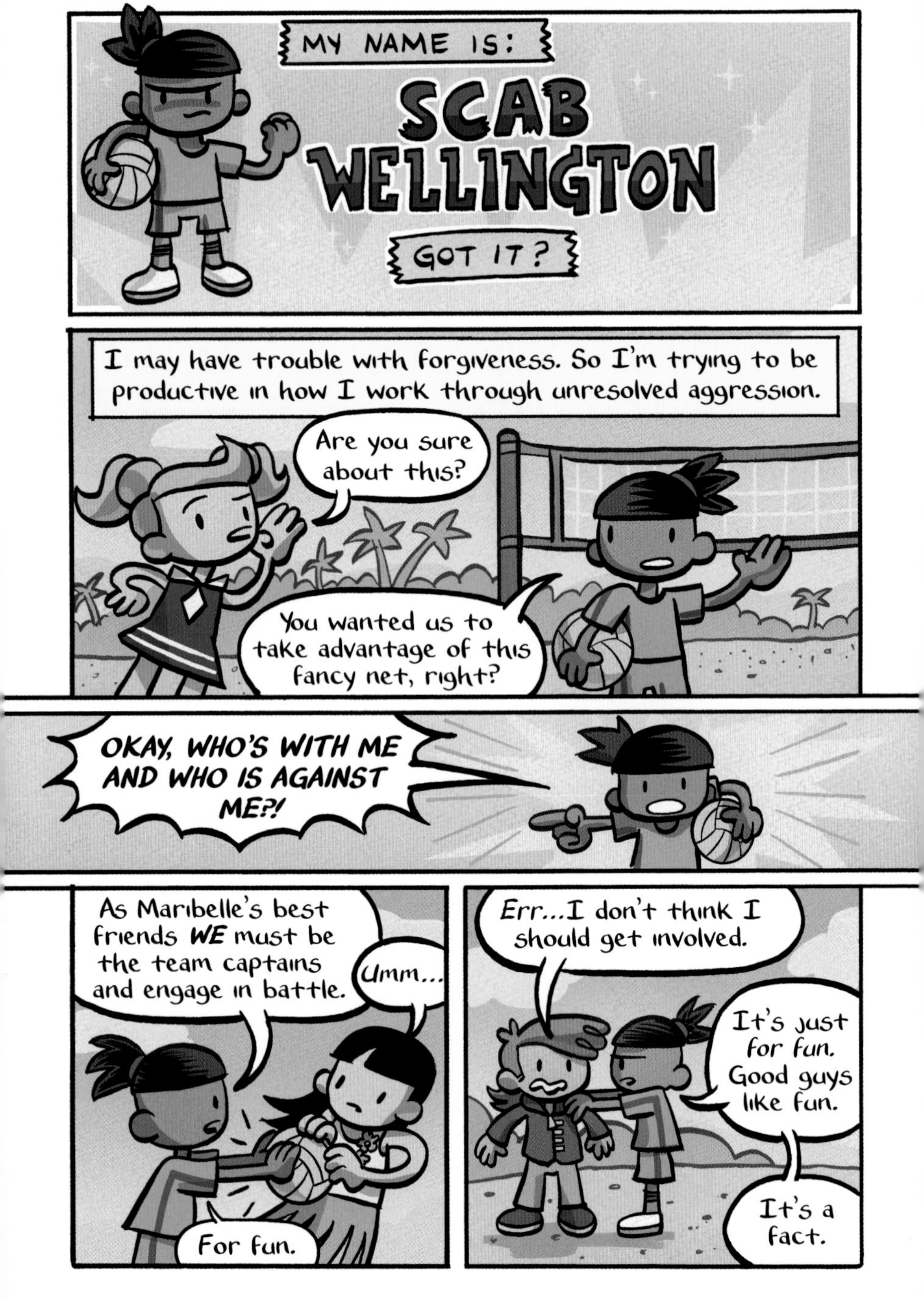
MY NAME IS:
SCAB WELLINGTON
GOT IT?
I may have trouble with forgiveness. So I'm trying to be productive in how I work through unresolved aggression.
Are you sure about this?
You wanted us to take advantage of this fancy net, right?
OKAY, WHO'S WITH ME AND WHO IS AGAINST ME?!
As Maribelle's best friends WE must be the team captains and engage in battle.
Umm...
For fun.
Err...I don't think I should get involved.
It's just for fun. Good guys like fun.
It's a fact.

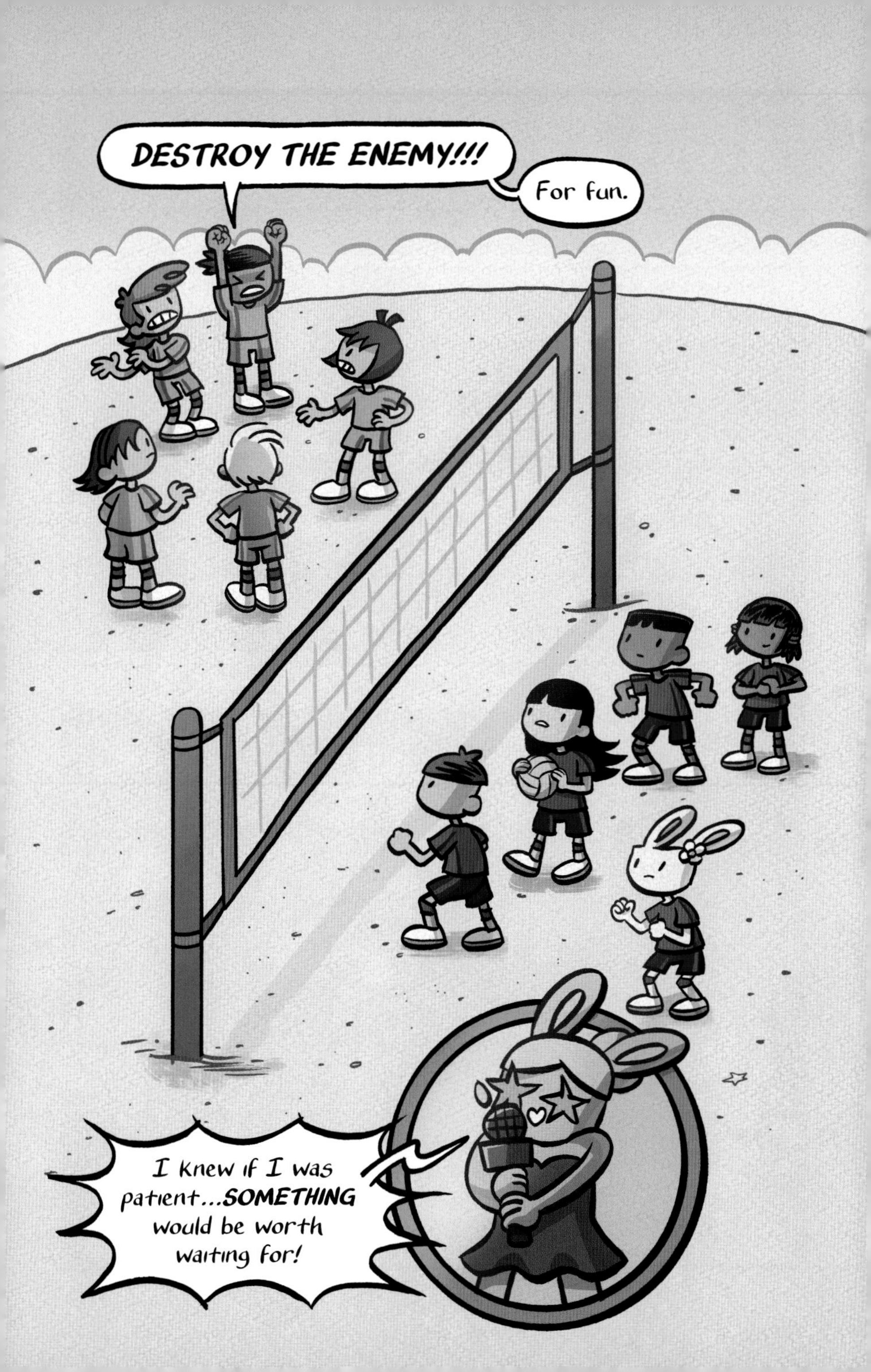
DESTROY THE ENEMY!!!
For fun.
I knew if I was patient...SOMETHING would be worth waiting for!

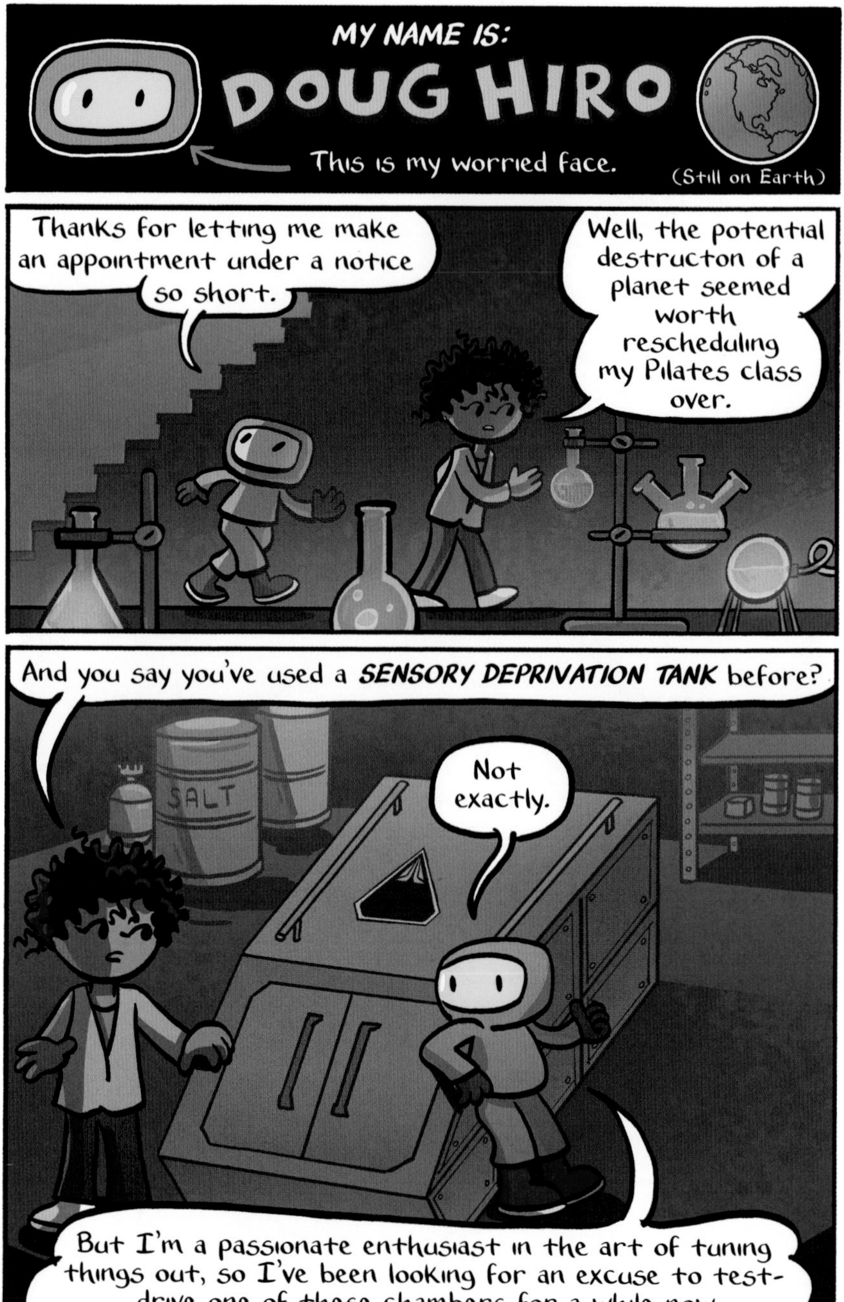
MY NAME IS:
DOUG HIRO
This is my worried face.
(Still on Earth)
Thanks for letting me make an appointment under a notice so short.
Well, the potential destructon of a planet seemed worth rescheduling my Pilates class over.
And you say you've used a SENSORY DEPRIVATION TANK before?
SALT
Not exactly.
But I'm a passionate enthusiast in the art of tuning things out, so I've been looking for an excuse to test-drive one of these chambers for a while now.

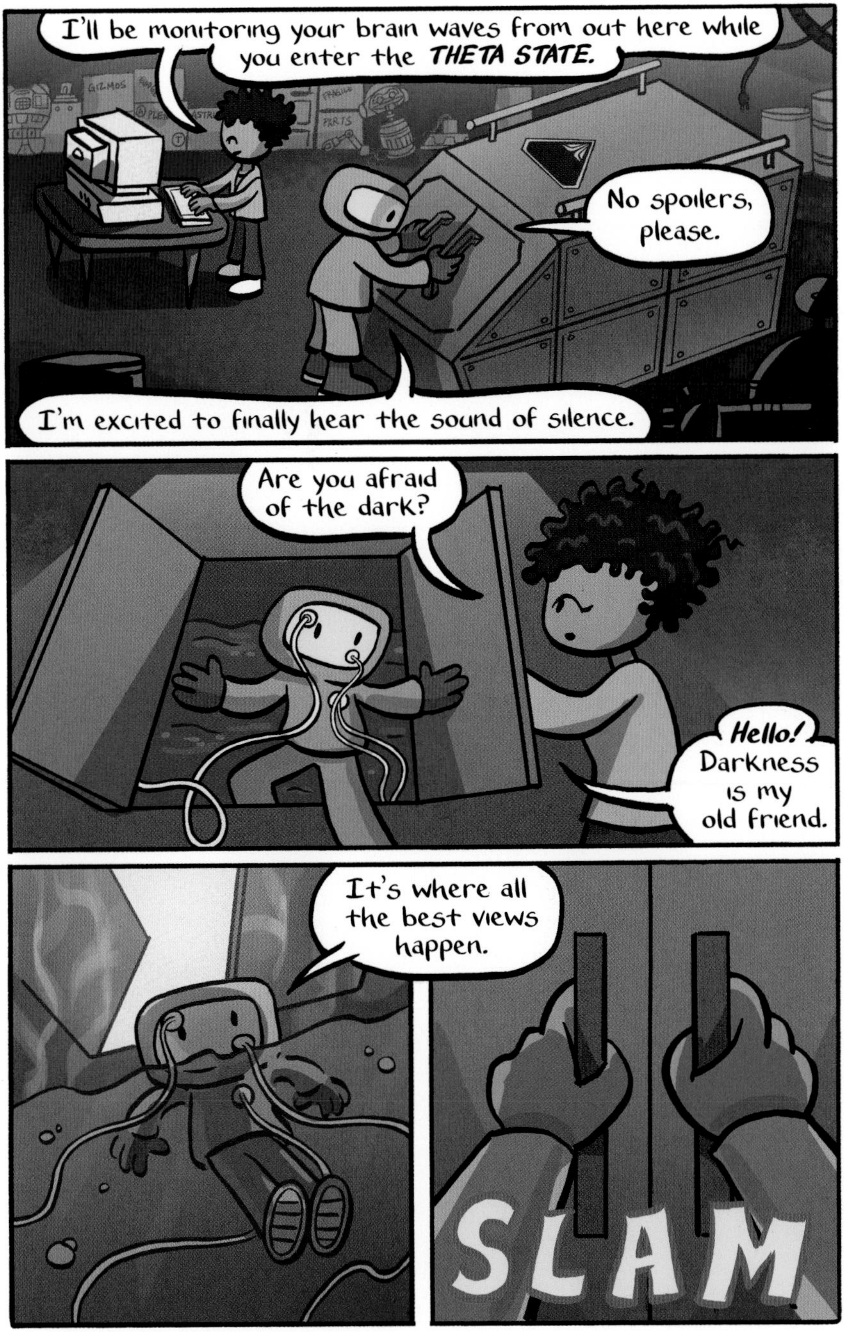
I'll be monitoring your brain waves from out here while you enter the THETA STATE.
No spoilers, please.
I'm excited to finally hear the sound of silence.
Are you afraid of the dark?
Hello! Darkness is my old friend.
It's where all the best views happen.
SLAM

Okay.

This is some *legit* vacuum.

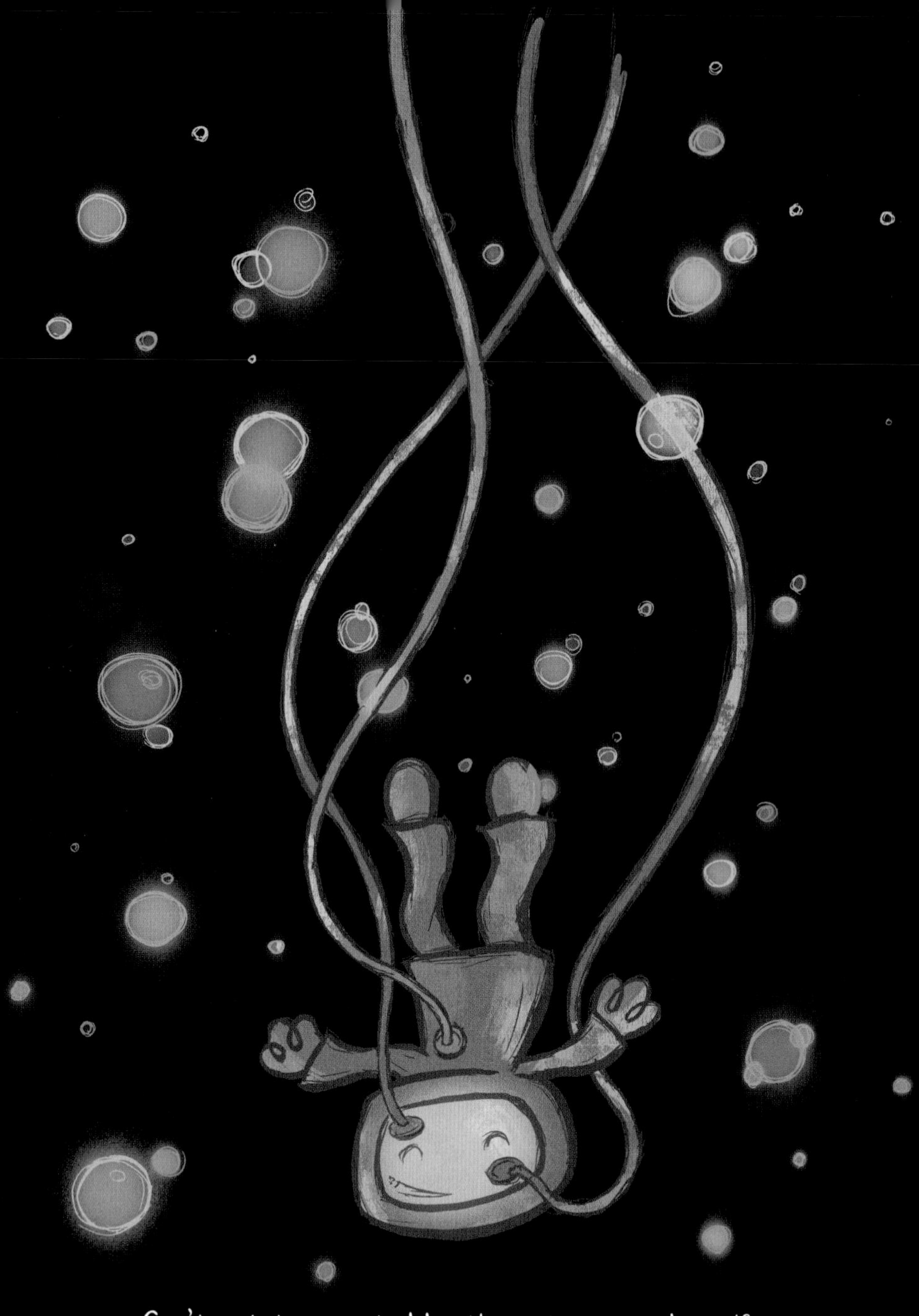

Can't get too excited by the exterior void itself.
Need to focus ***INWARD.***

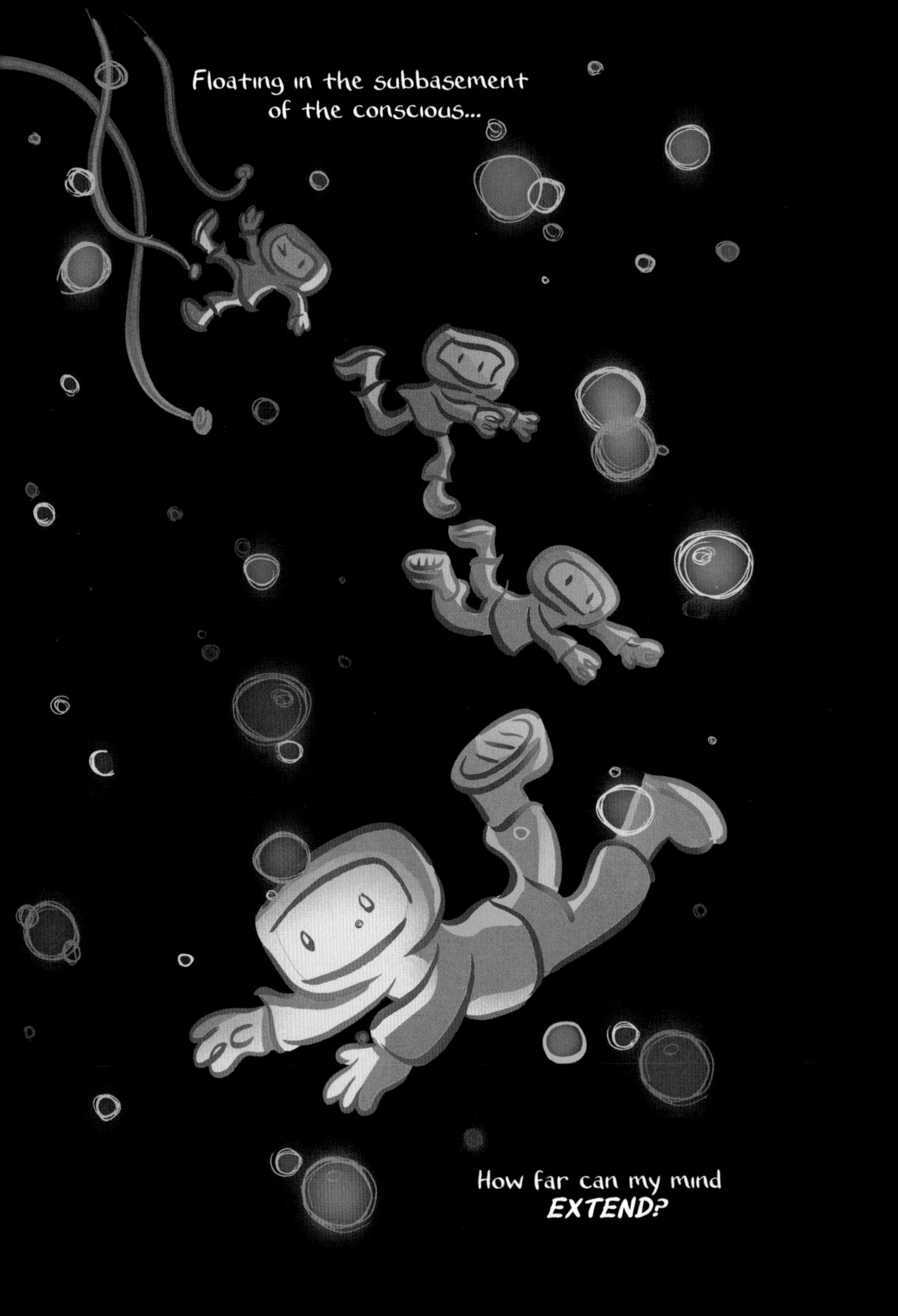
Floating in the subbasement of the conscious...
How far can my mind EXTEND?

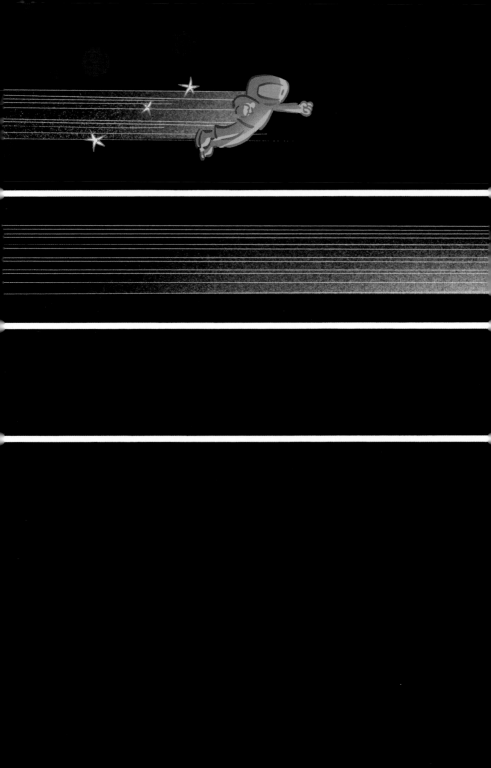

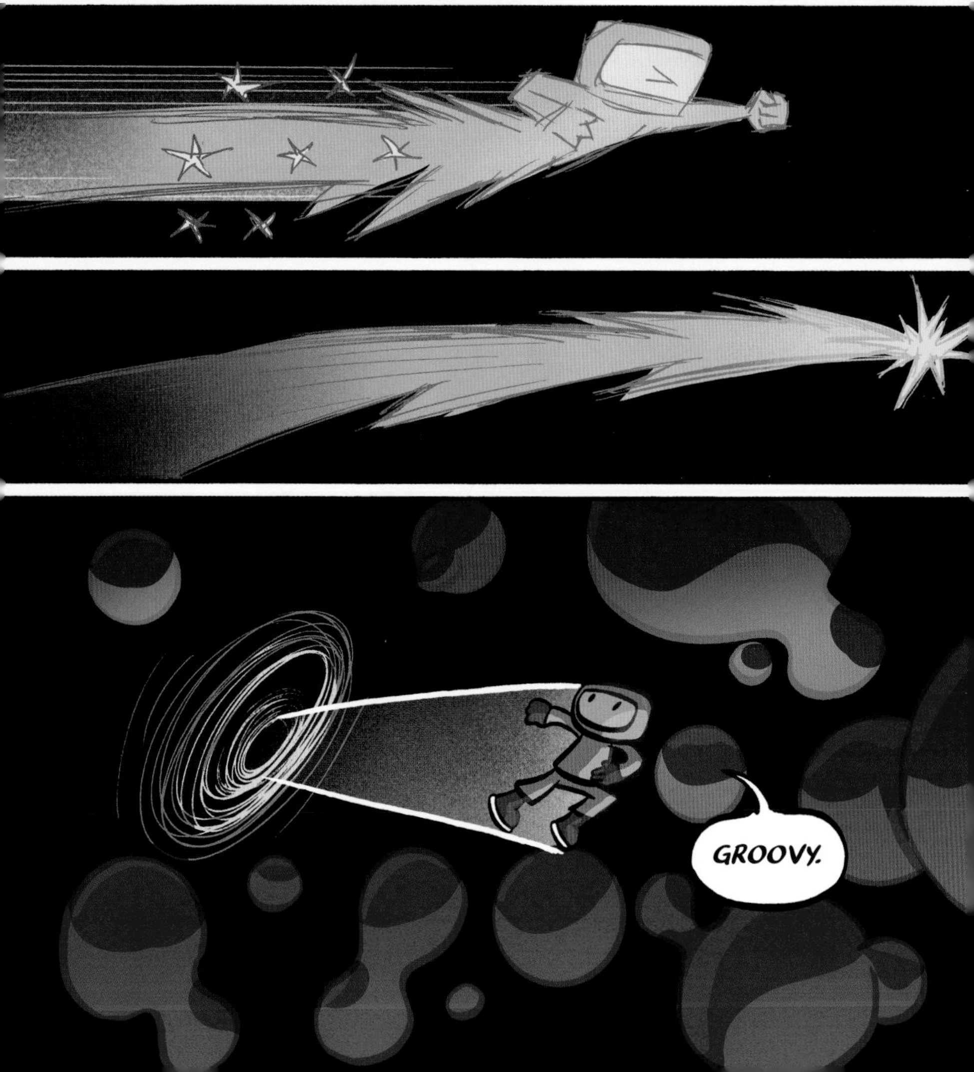
GROOVY.

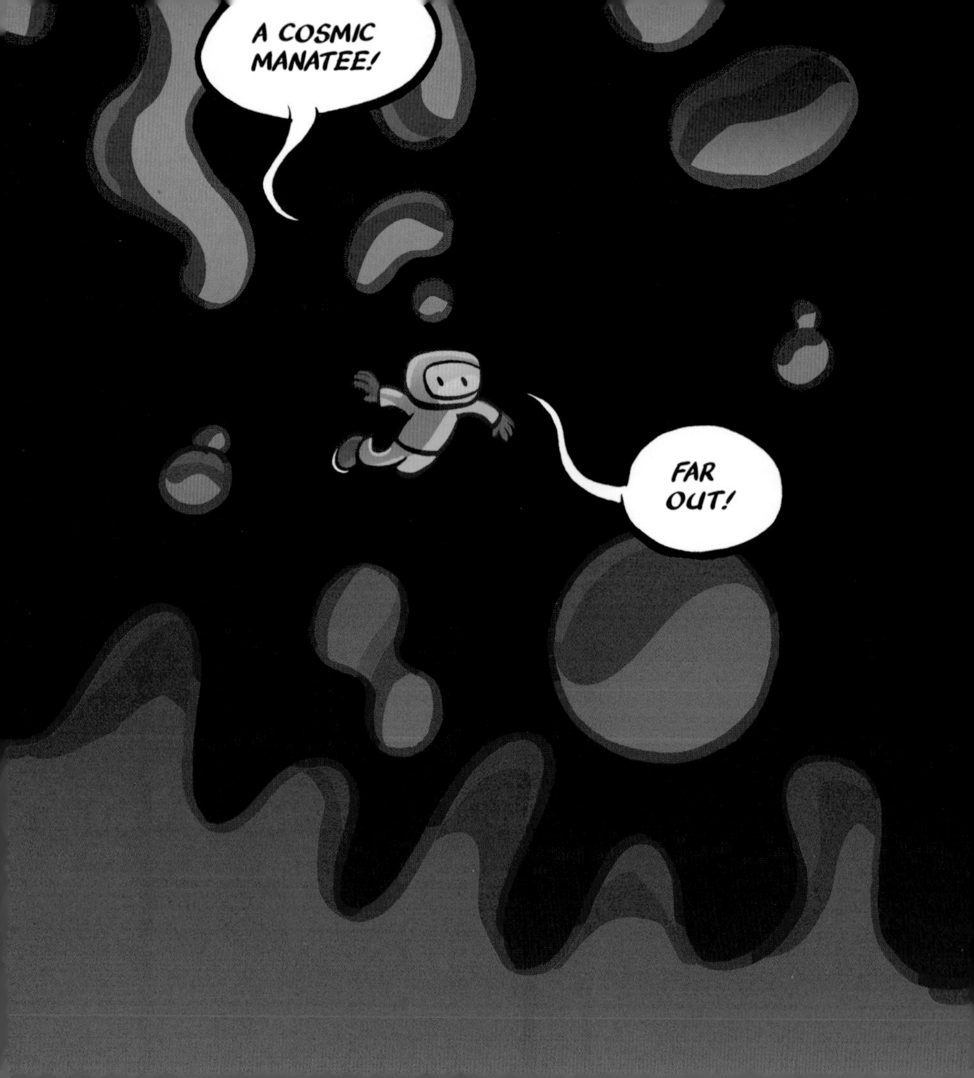
A COSMIC MANATEE!
FAR OUT!

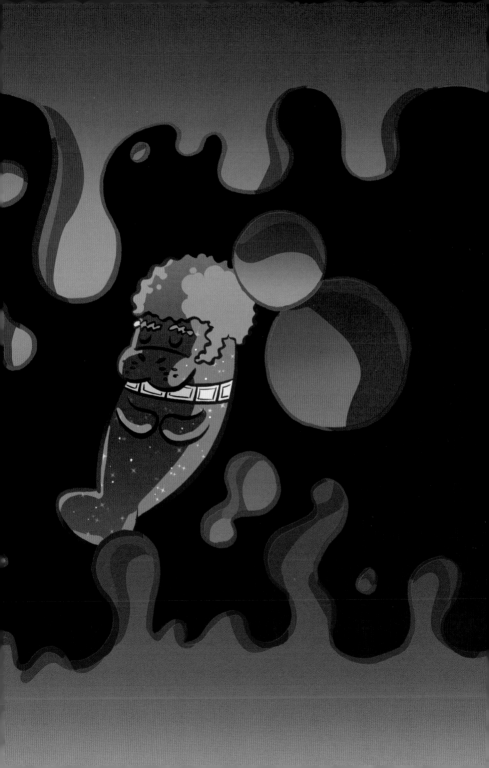

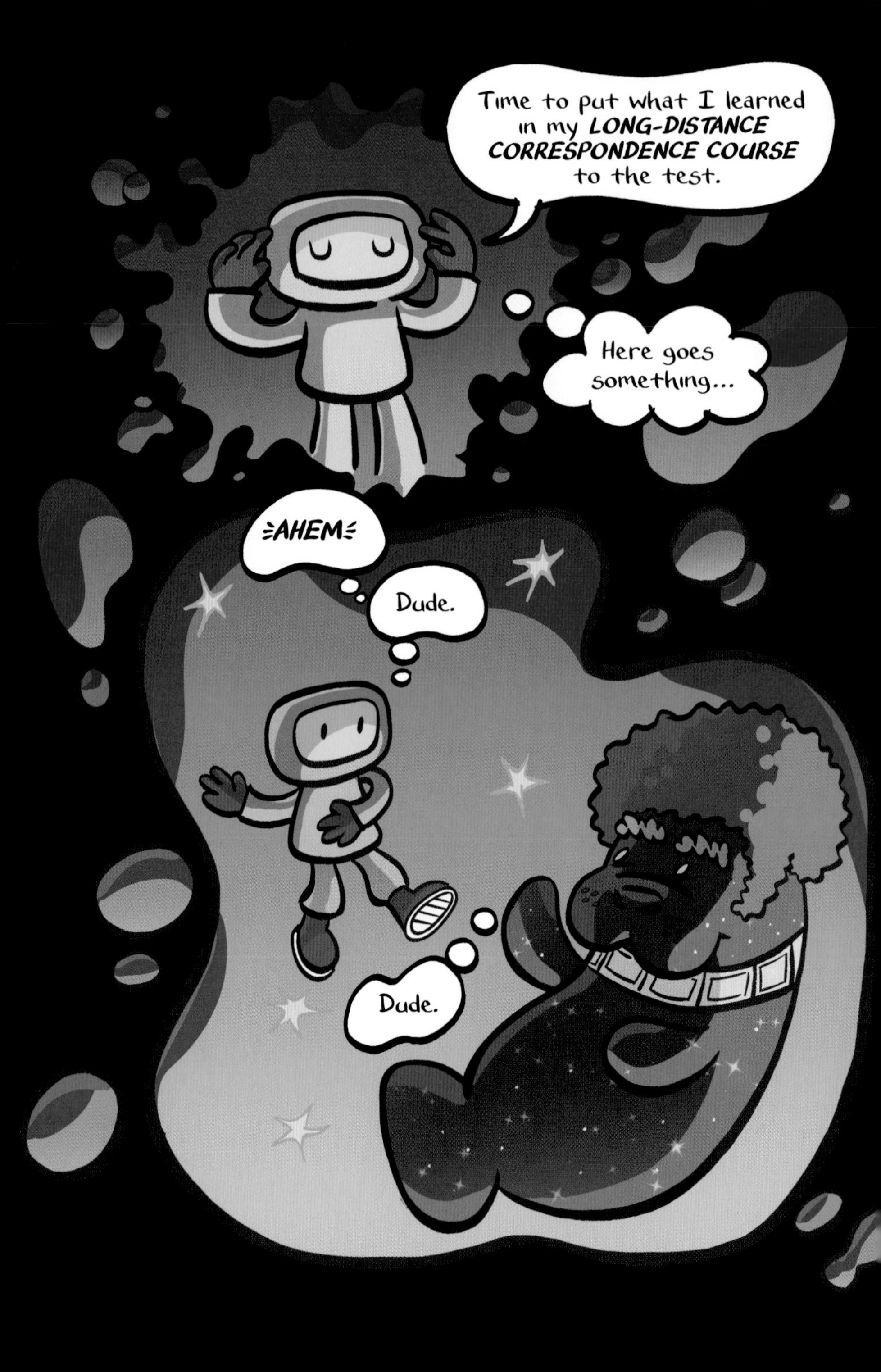
Time to put what I learned in my **LONG-DISTANCE CORRESPONDENCE COURSE** to the test.
Here goes something...
AHEM
Dude.
Dude.

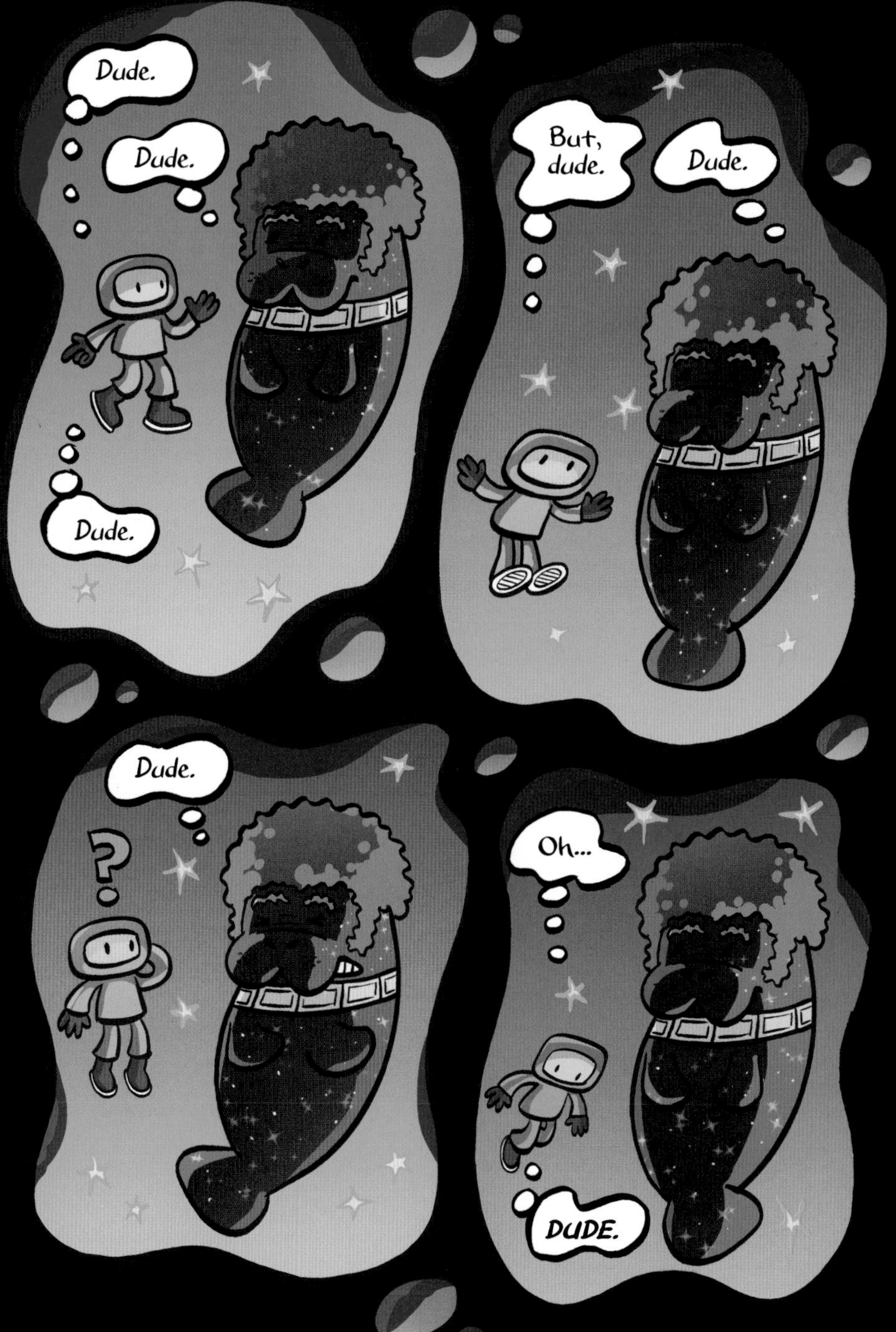
Dude.
Dude.
Dude.
But, dude.
Dude.
Dude.
?
Oh...
DUDE.

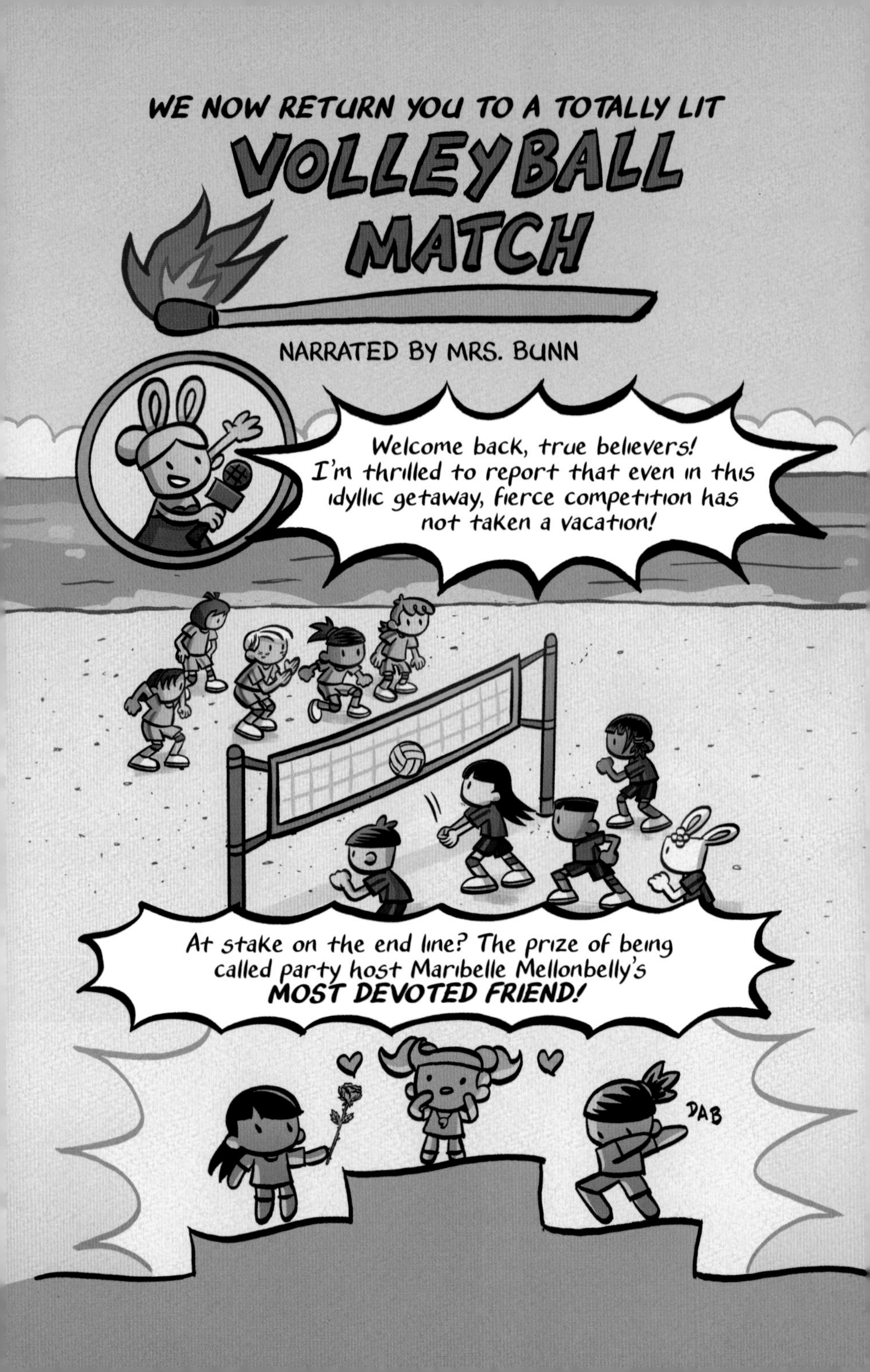
WE NOW RETURN YOU TO A TOTALLY LIT
VOLLEYBALL MATCH
NARRATED BY MRS. BUNN
Welcome back, true believers! I'm thrilled to report that even in this idyllic getaway, fierce competition has not taken a vacation!
At stake on the end line? The prize of being called party host Maribelle Mellonbelly's MOST DEVOTED FRIEND!
DAB

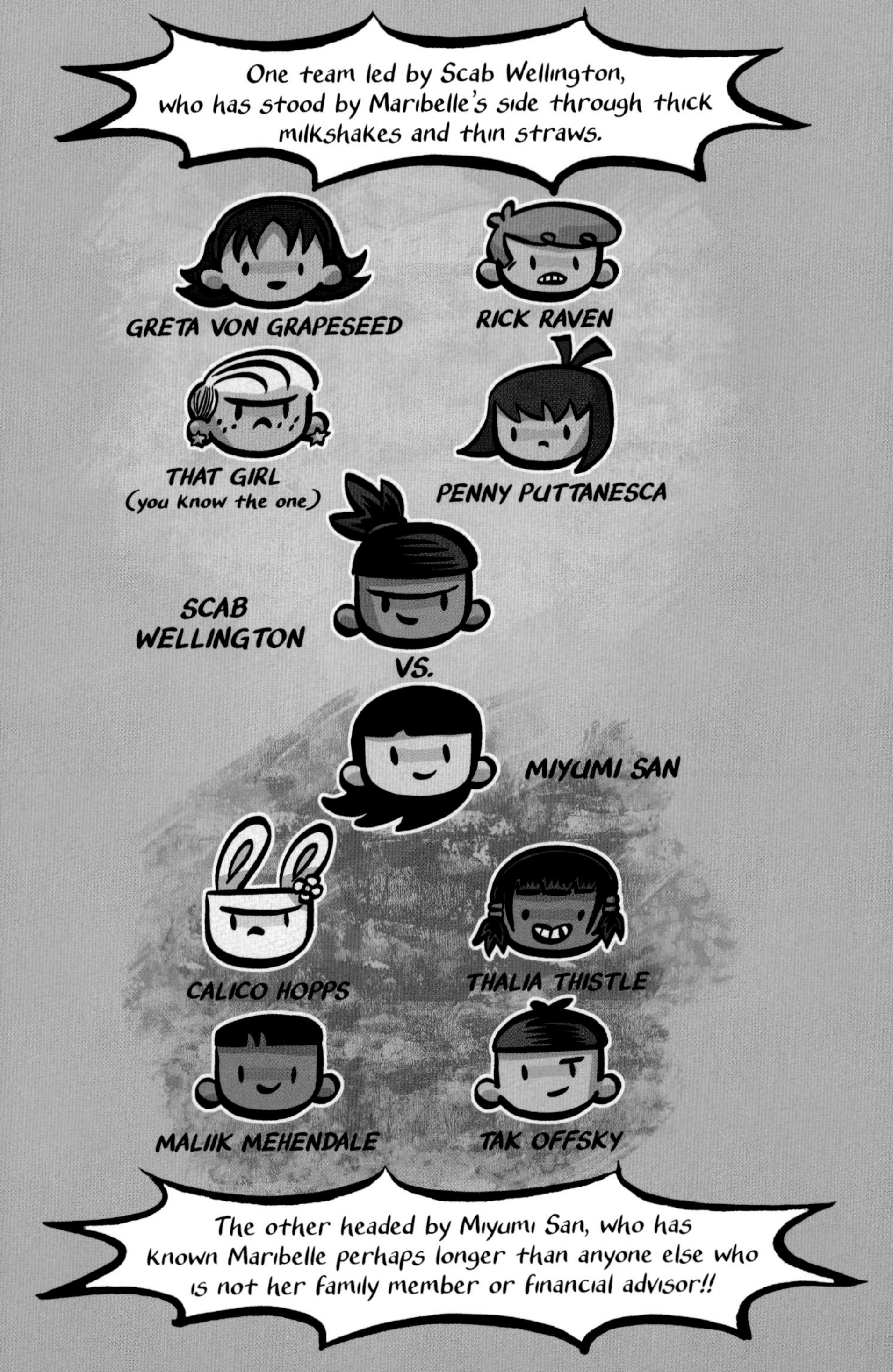
One team led by Scab Wellington, who has stood by Maribelle's side through thick milkshakes and thin straws.
GRETA VON GRAPESEED
RICK RAVEN
THAT GIRL (you know the one)
PENNY PUTTANESCA
SCAB WELLINGTON
VS.
MIYUMI SAN
CALICO HOPPS
THALIA THISTLE
MALIIK MEHENDALE
TAK OFFSKY
The other headed by Miyumi San, who has known Maribelle perhaps longer than anyone else who is not her family member or financial advisor!!

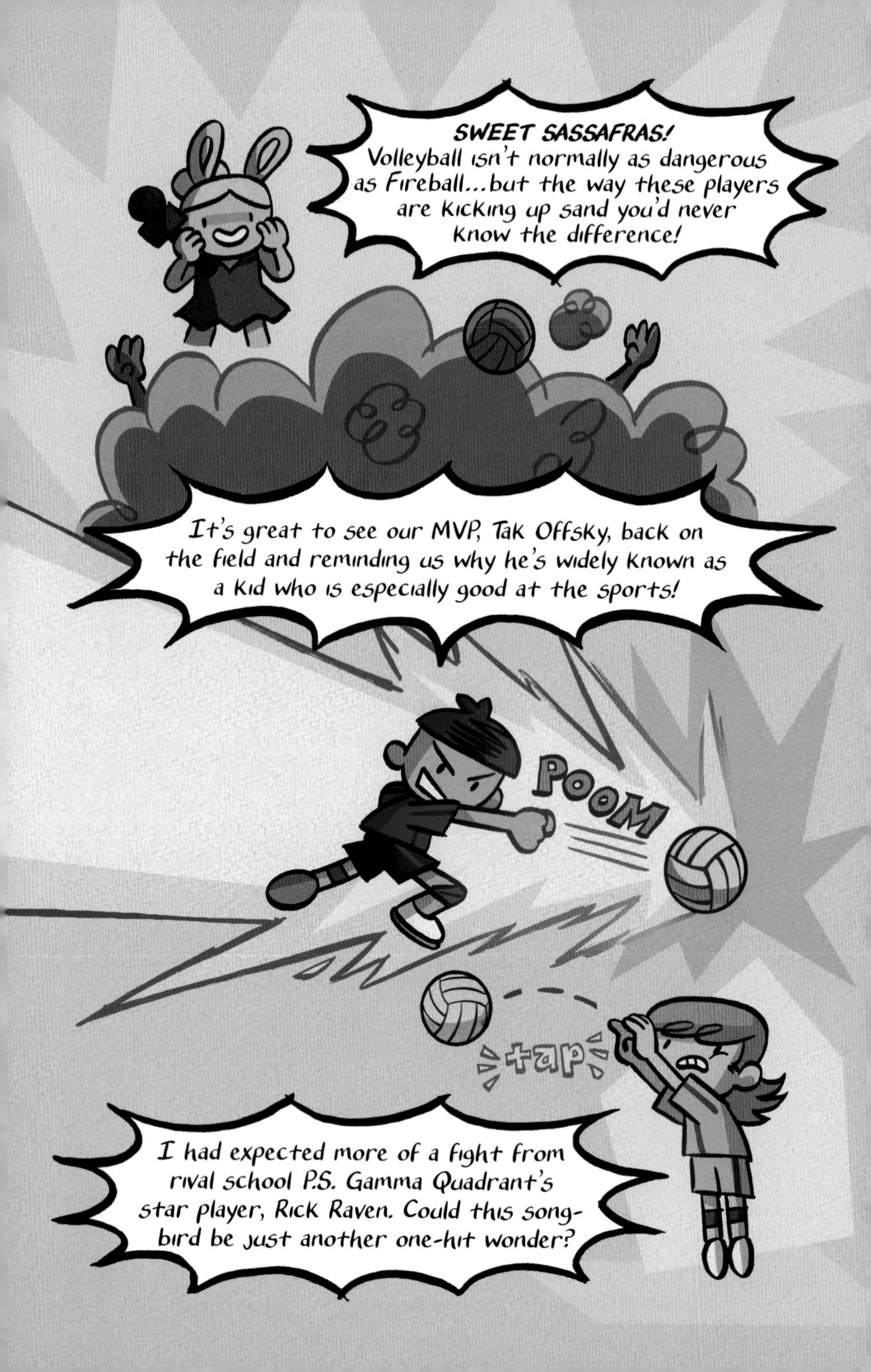
SWEET SASSAFRAS! Volleyball isn't normally as dangerous as Fireball...but the way these players are kicking up sand you'd never know the difference!
It's great to see our MVP, Tak Offsky, back on the field and reminding us why he's widely known as a kid who is especially good at the sports!
POOM
tap
I had expected more of a fight from rival school P.S. Gamma Quadrant's star player, Rick Raven. Could this song-bird be just another one-hit wonder?

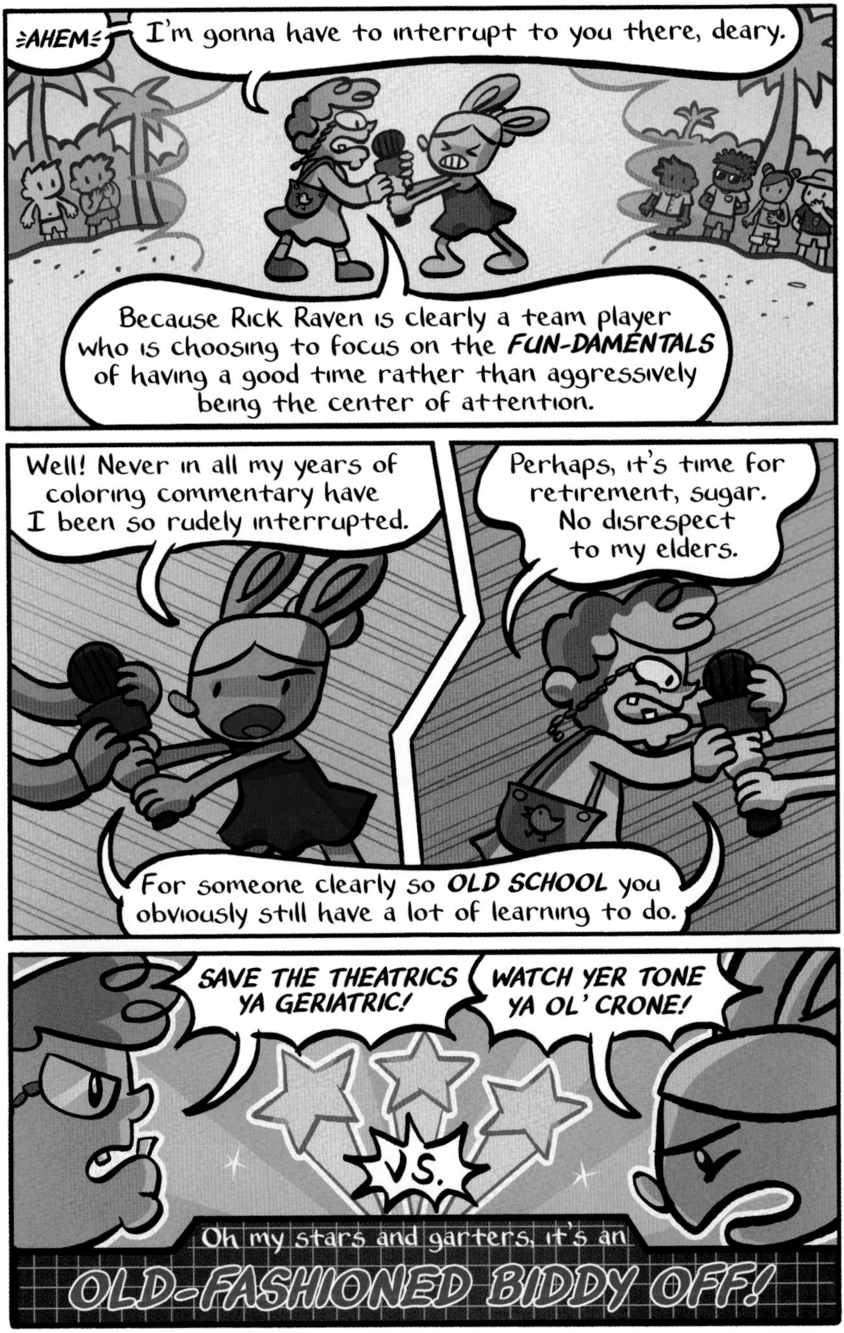
AHEM
I'm gonna have to interrupt to you there, deary.
Because Rick Raven is clearly a team player who is choosing to focus on the FUN-DAMENTALS of having a good time rather than aggressively being the center of attention.
Well! Never in all my years of coloring commentary have I been so rudely interrupted.
Perhaps, it's time for retirement, sugar. No disrespect to my elders.
For someone clearly so OLD SCHOOL you obviously still have a lot of learning to do.
SAVE THE THEATRICS YA GERIATRIC!
WATCH YER TONE YA OL' CRONE!
VS.
Oh my stars and garters, it's an
OLD-FASHIONED BIDDY OFF!

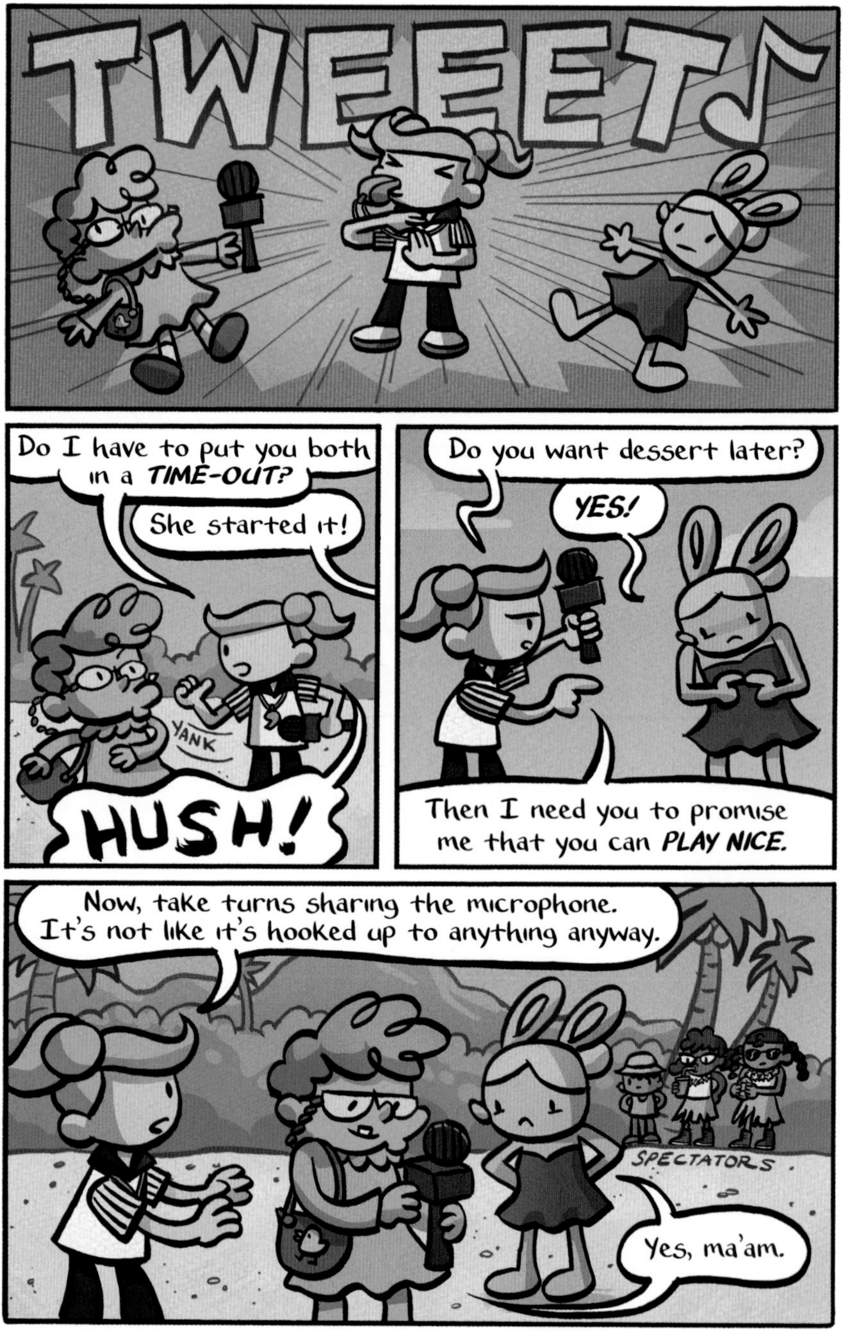
TWEEET♪
Do I have to put you both in a TIME-OUT?
She started it!
YANK
HUSH!
Do you want dessert later?
YES!
Then I need you to promise me that you can PLAY NICE.
Now, take turns sharing the microphone. It's not like it's hooked up to anything anyway.
SPECTATORS
Yes, ma'am.

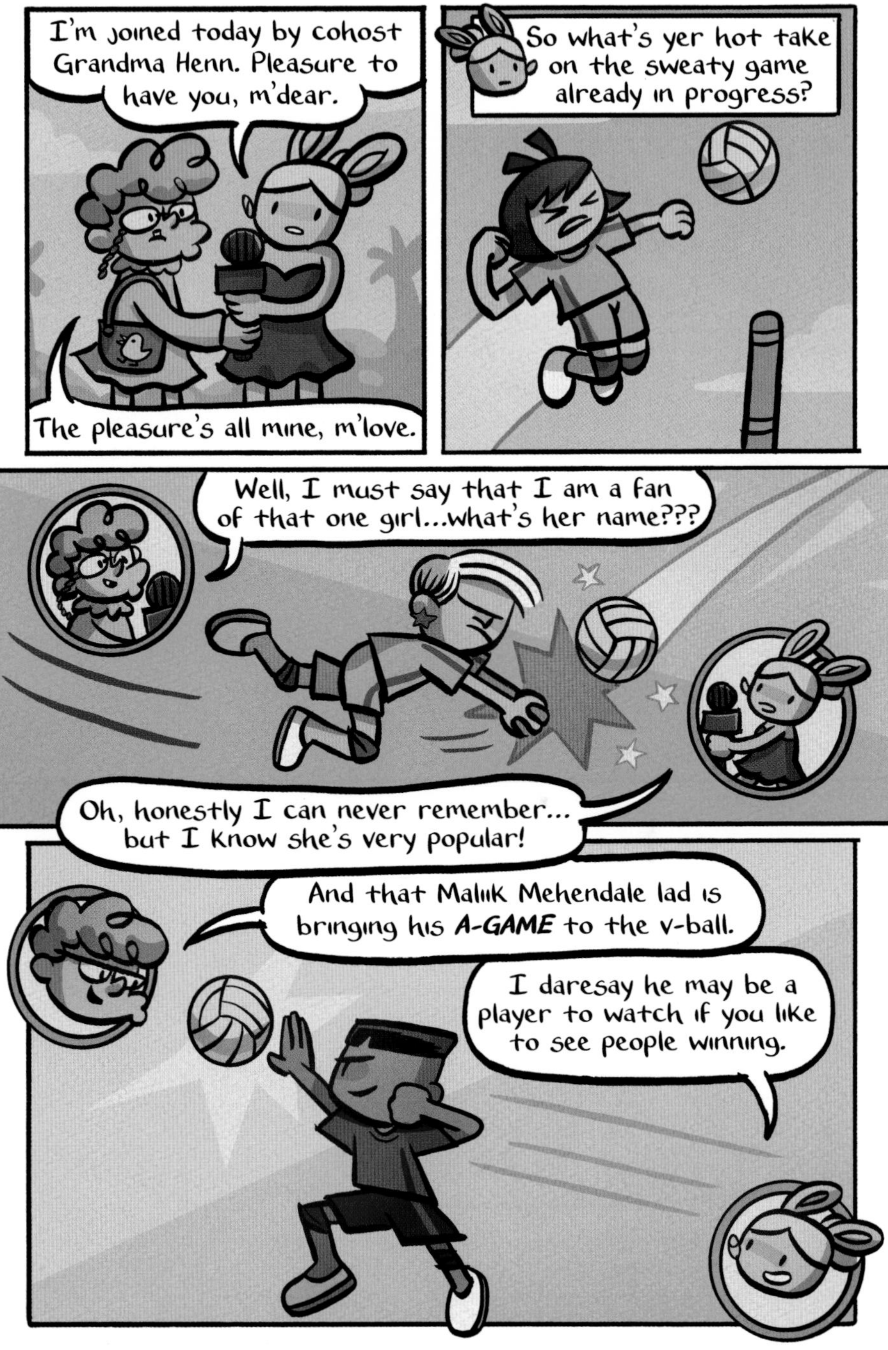
I'm joined today by cohost Grandma Henn. Pleasure to have you, m'dear.
The pleasure's all mine, m'love.
So what's yer hot take on the sweaty game already in progress?
Well, I must say that I am a fan of that one girl...what's her name???
Oh, honestly I can never remember... but I know she's very popular!
And that Malik Mehendale lad is bringing his **A-GAME** to the v-ball.
I daresay he may be a player to watch if you like to see people winning.

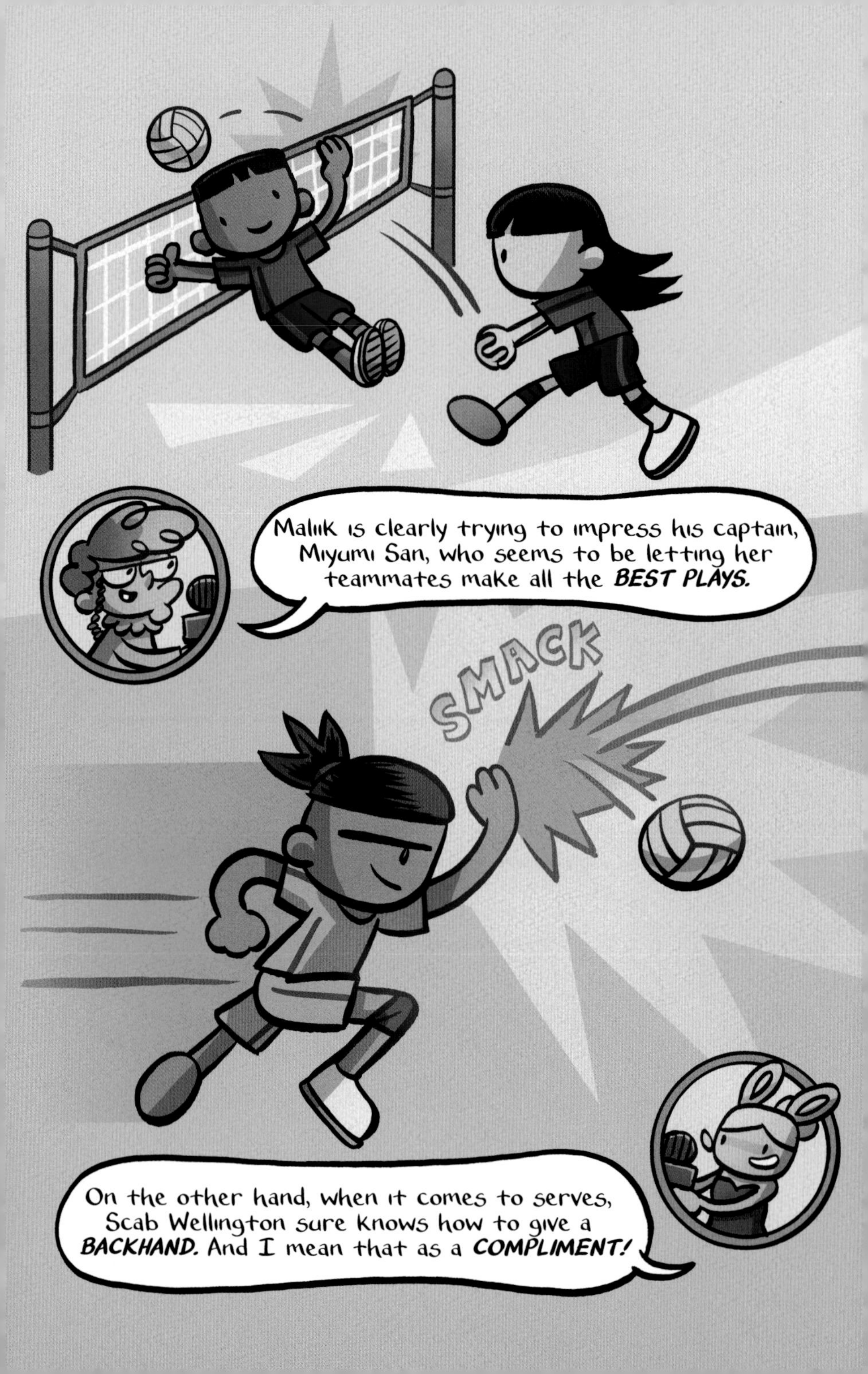
Malik is clearly trying to impress his captain, Miyumi San, who seems to be letting her teammates make all the BEST PLAYS.
SMACK
On the other hand, when it comes to serves, Scab Wellington sure knows how to give a BACKHAND. And I mean that as a COMPLIMENT!

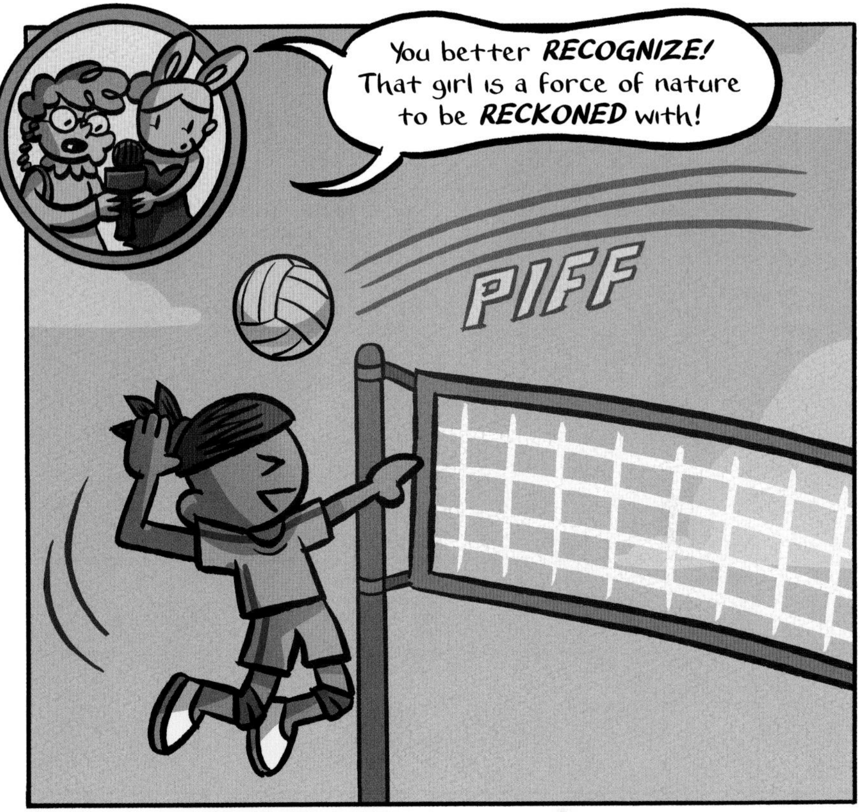
You better RECOGNIZE! That girl is a force of nature to be RECKONED with!
PIFF

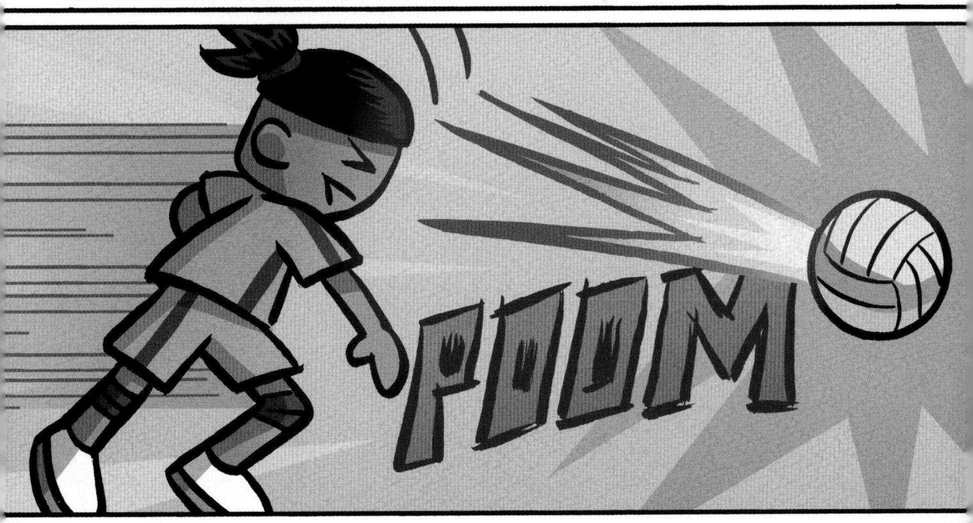
FOOM

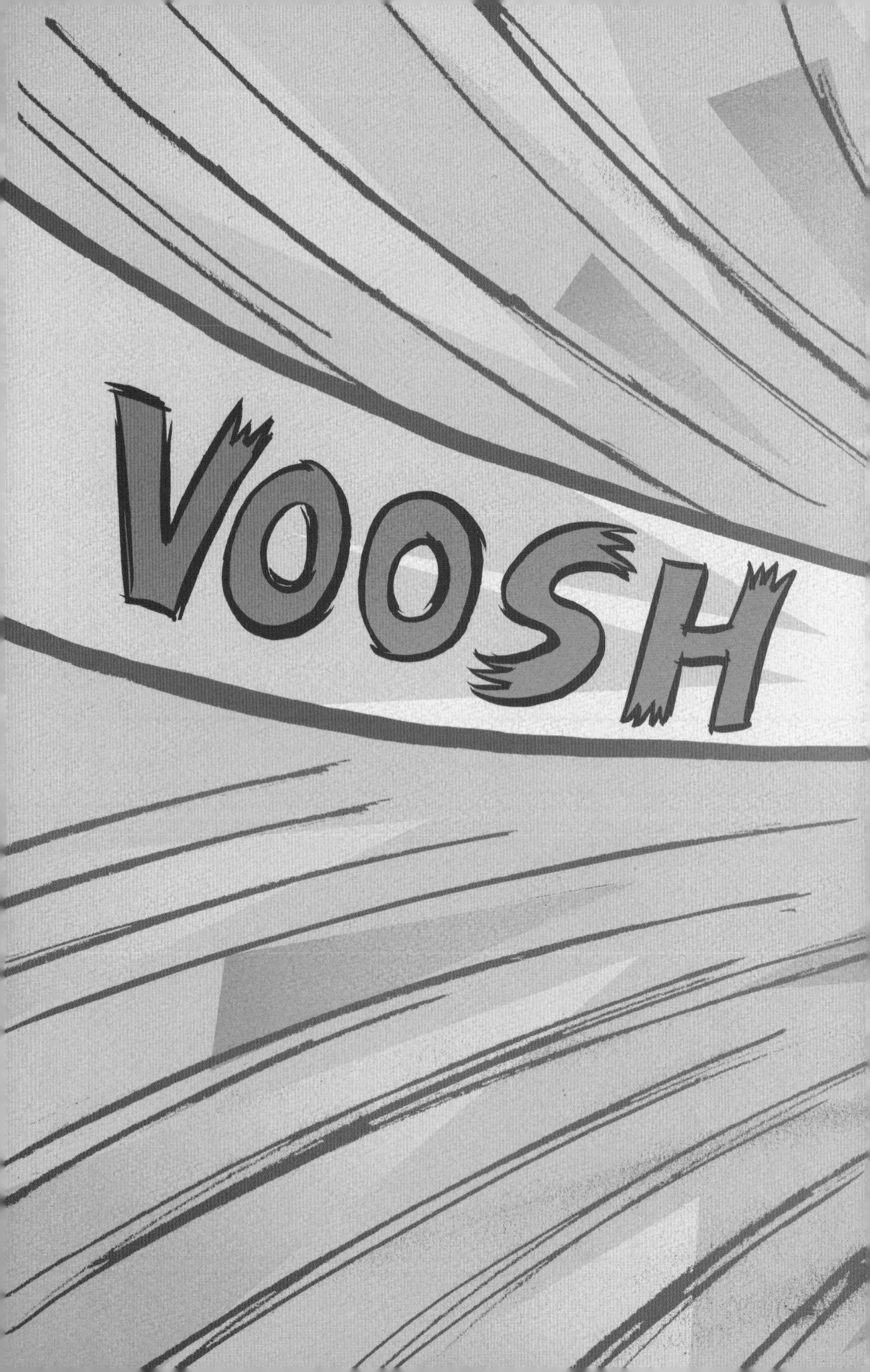
VOOSH

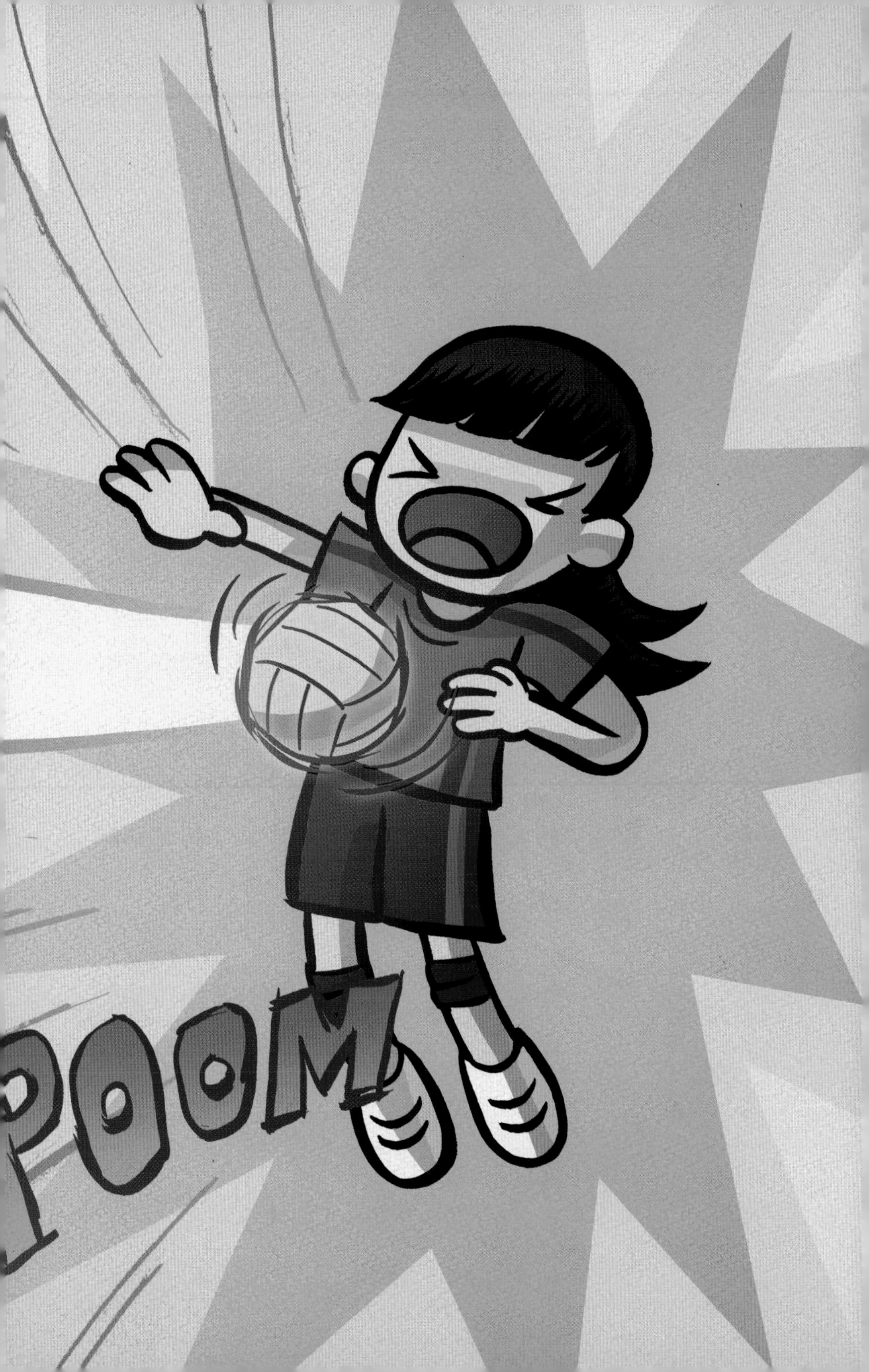
POOM

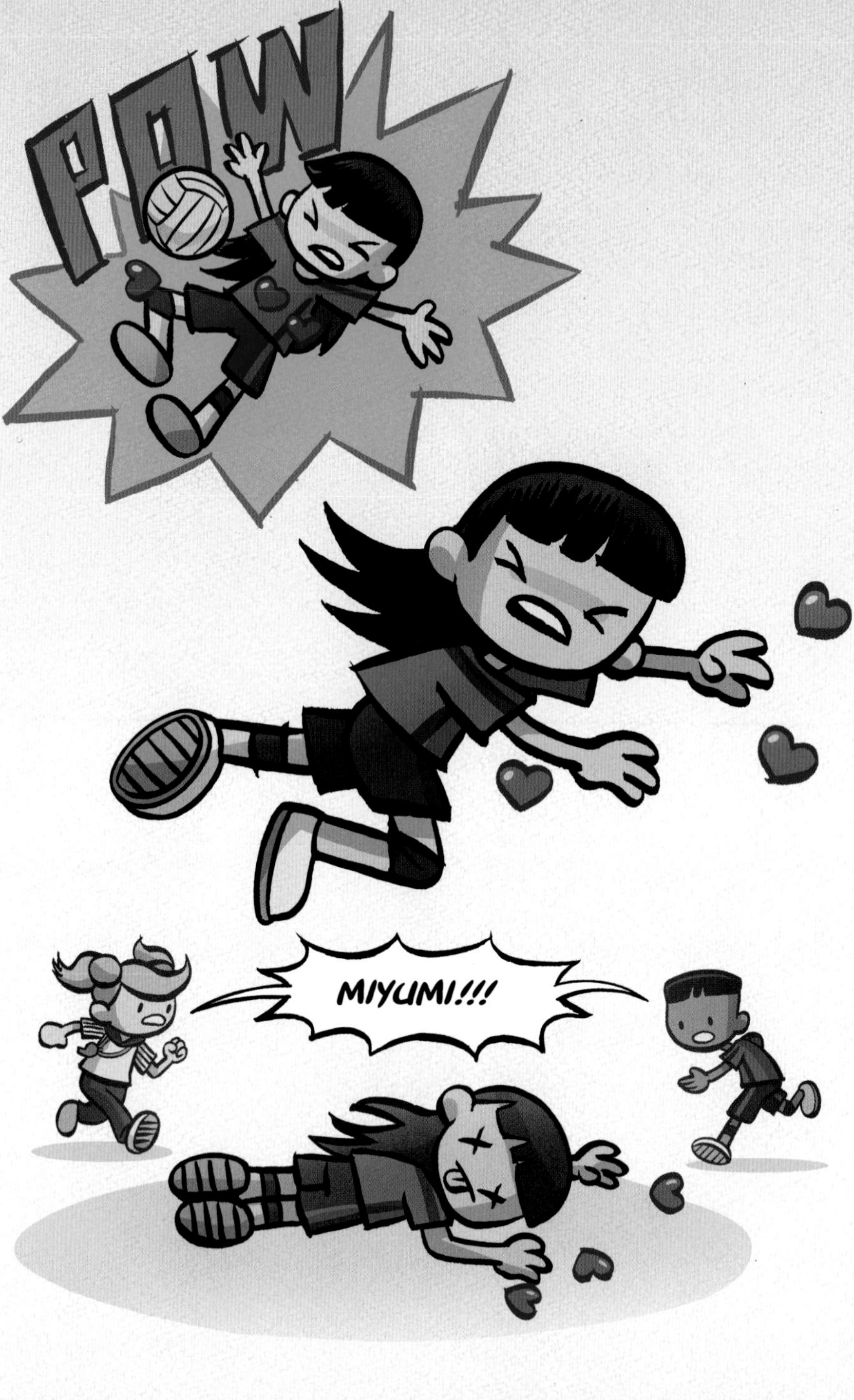
POW
MIYUMI!!!

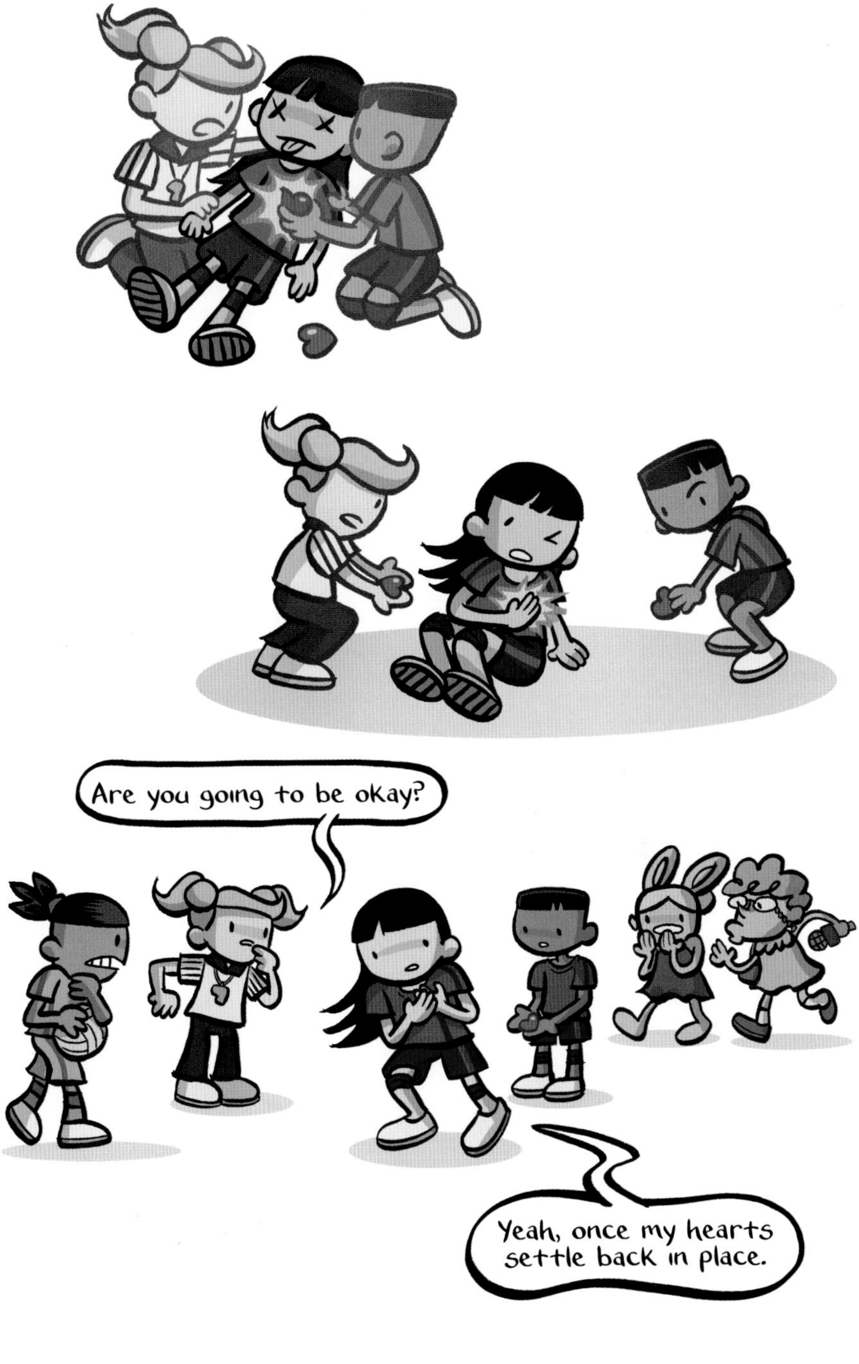
Are you going to be okay?
Yeah, once my hearts settle back in place.

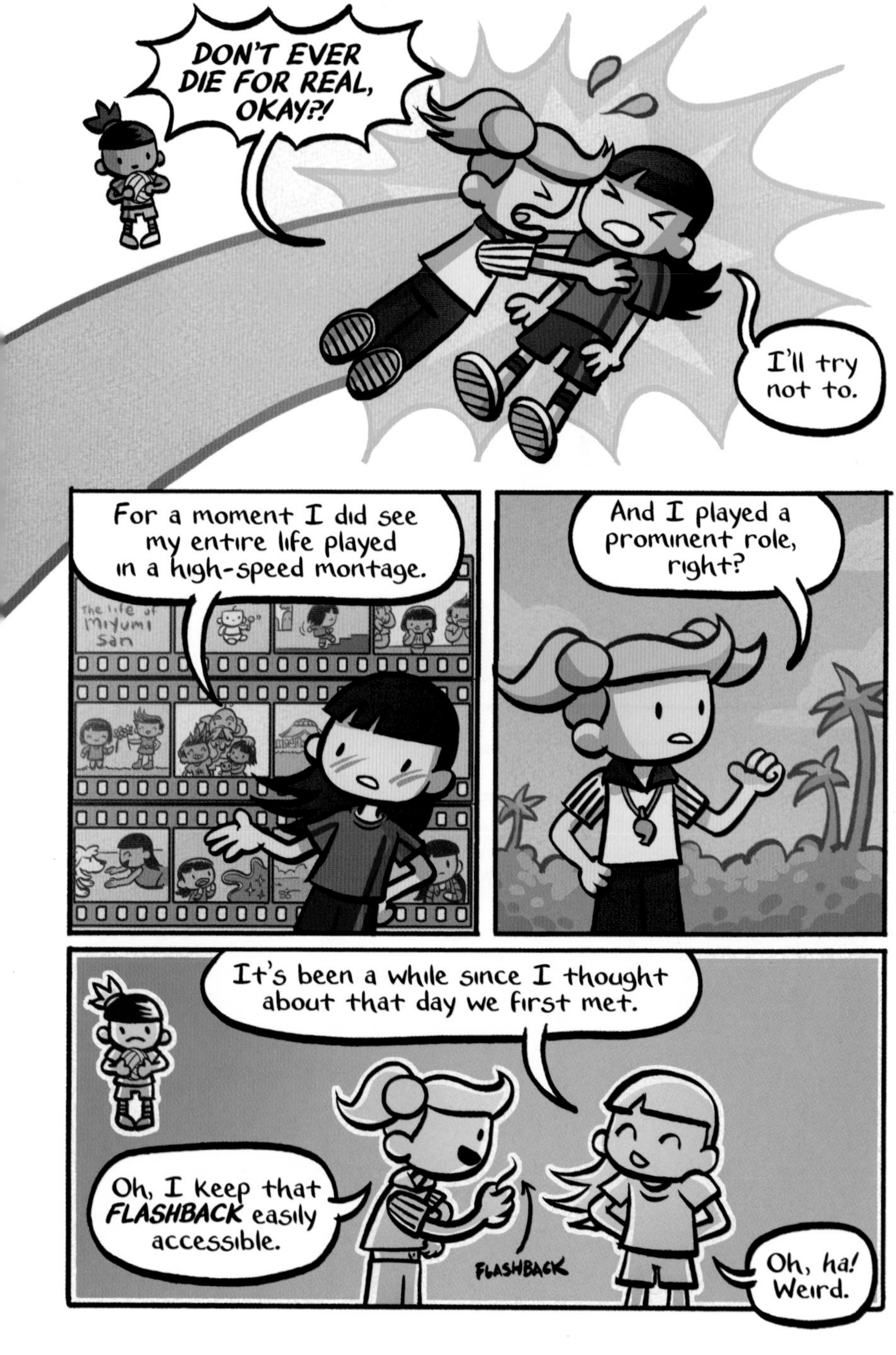
DON'T EVER DIE FOR REAL, OKAY?!
I'll try not to.
For a moment I did see my entire life played in a high-speed montage.
The life of Miyumi san
And I played a prominent role, right?
It's been a while since I thought about that day we first met.
Oh, I keep that FLASHBACK easily accessible.
FLASHBACK
Oh, ha! Weird.

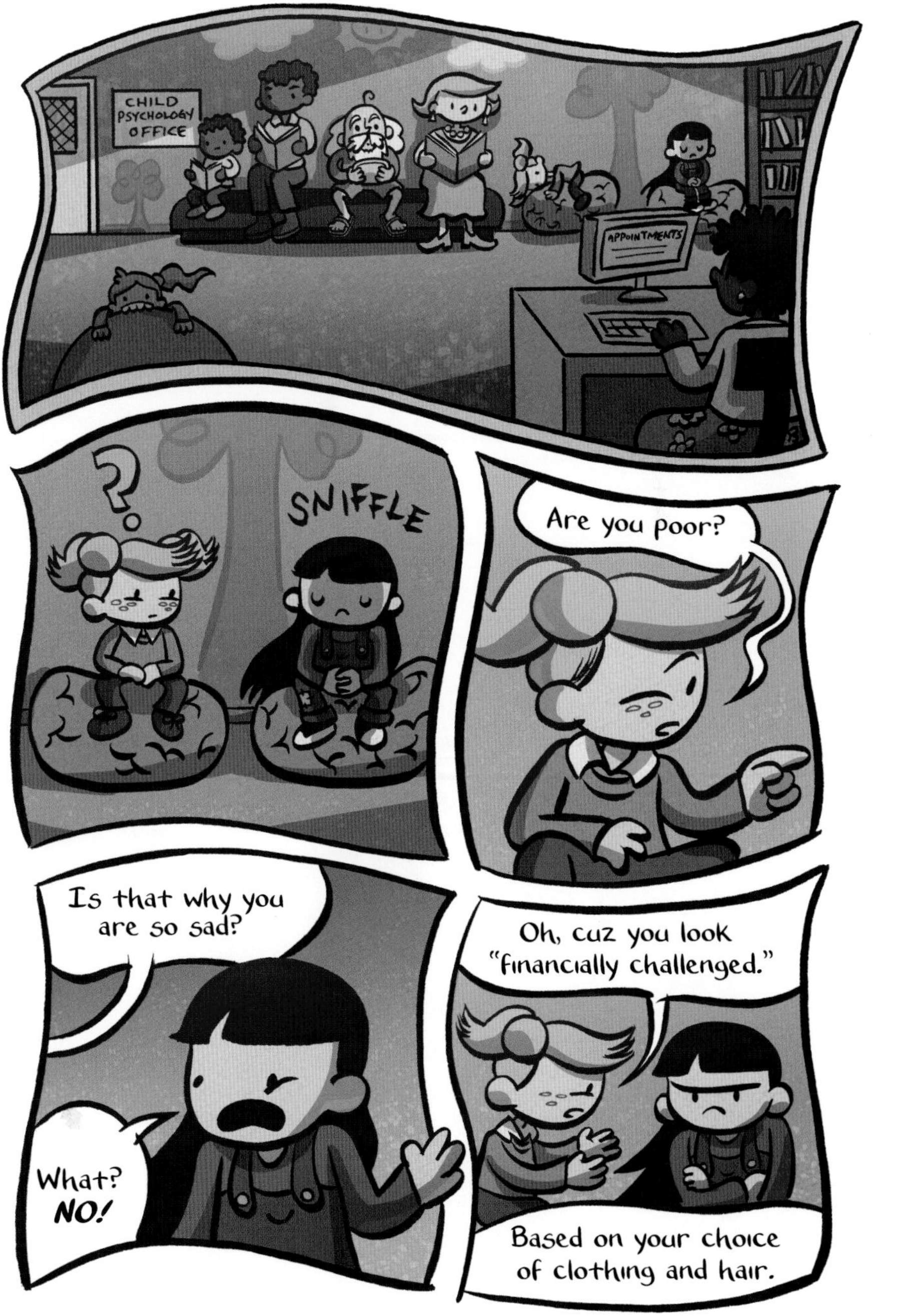
CHILD PSYCHOLOGY OFFICE
APPOINTMENTS
SNIFFLE
Are you poor?
Is that why you are so sad?
What? NO!
Oh, cuz you look "financially challenged."
Based on your choice of clothing and hair.

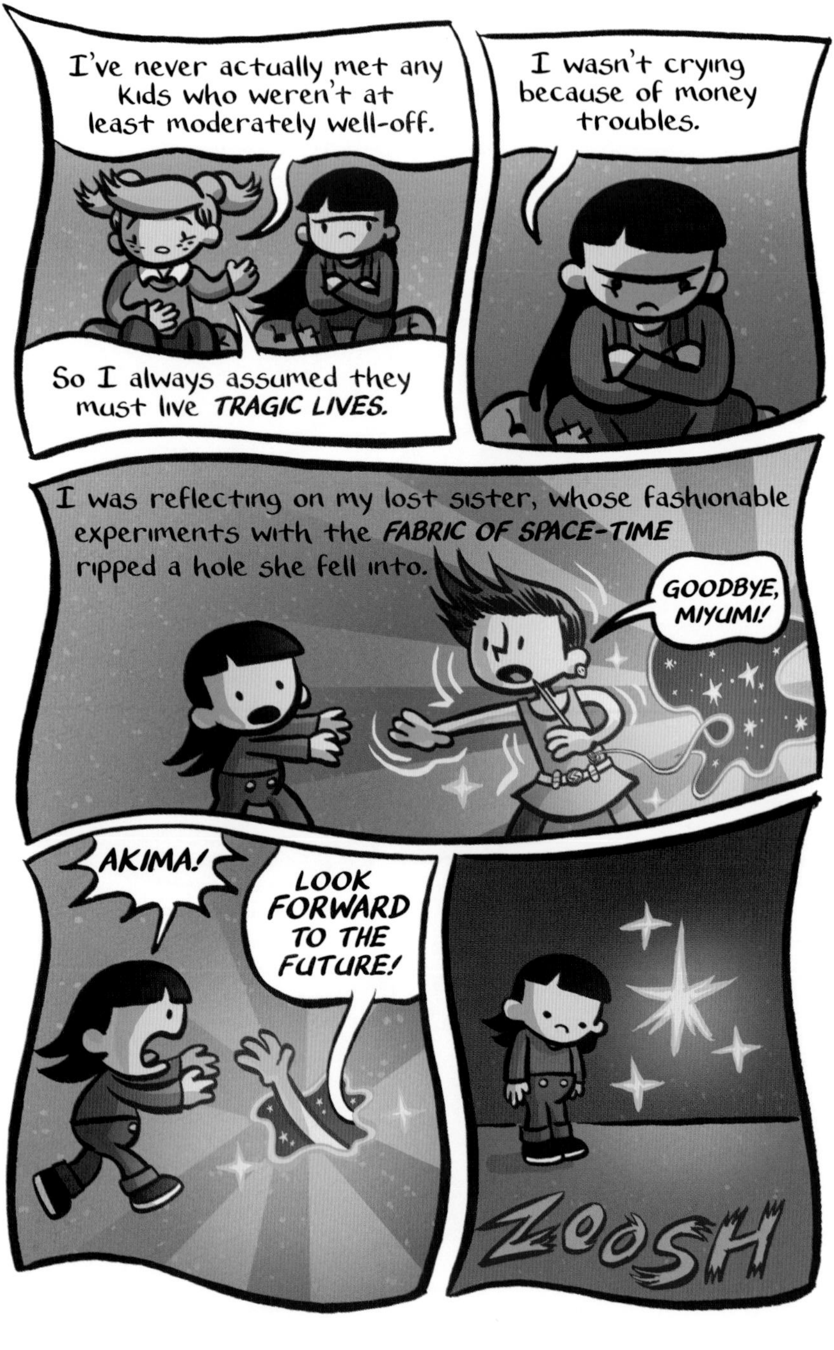
I've never actually met any kids who weren't at least moderately well-off.
So I always assumed they must live TRAGIC LIVES.
I wasn't crying because of money troubles.
I was reflecting on my lost sister, whose fashionable experiments with the FABRIC OF SPACE-TIME ripped a hole she fell into.
GOODBYE, MIYUMI!
AKIMA!
LOOK FORWARD TO THE FUTURE!
ZOOSH

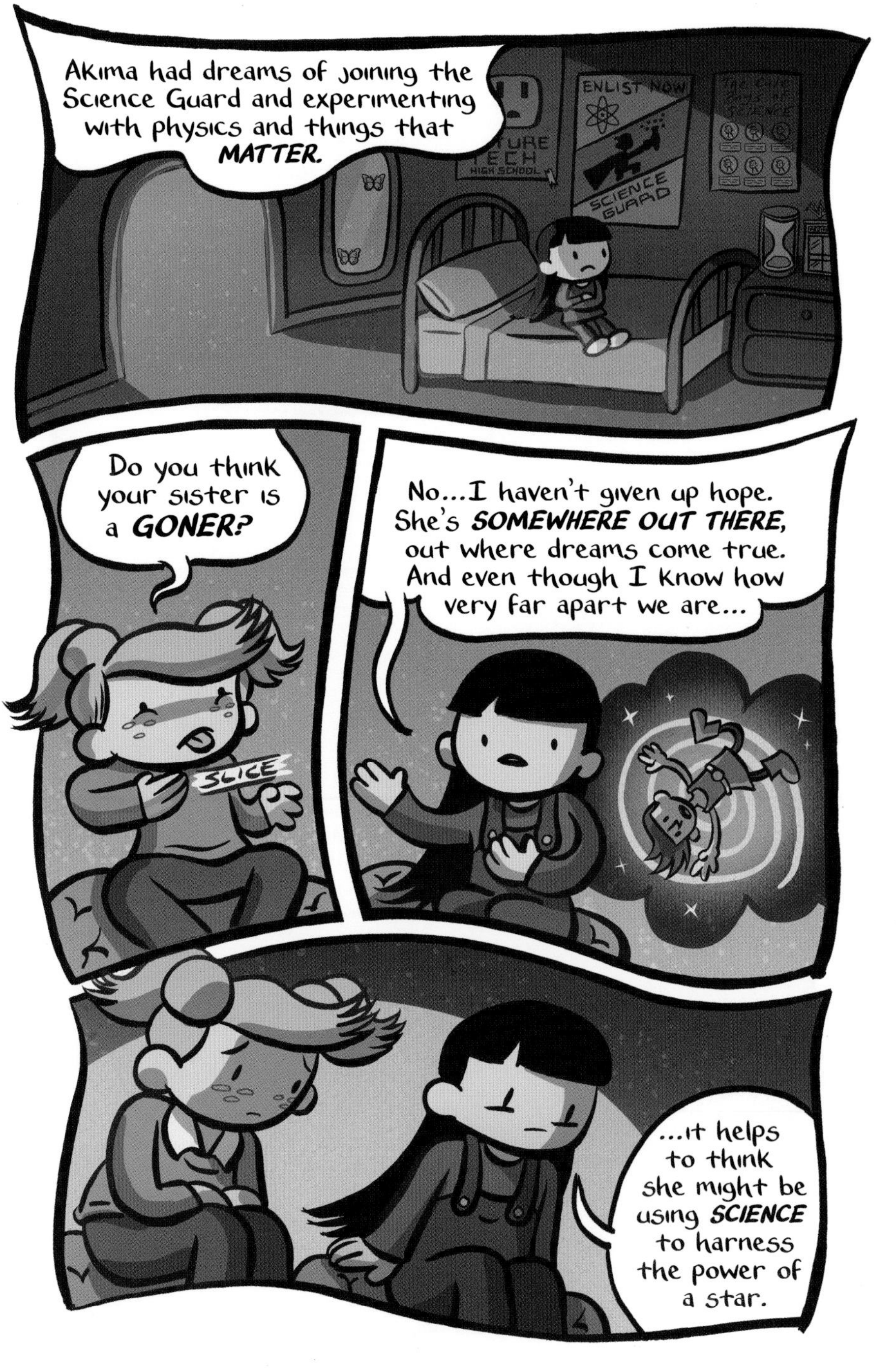
Akima had dreams of joining the Science Guard and experimenting with physics and things that MATTER.
ENLIST NOW
SCIENCE GUARD
HIGH SCHOOL
Do you think your sister is a GONER?
SLICE
No...I haven't given up hope. She's SOMEWHERE OUT THERE, out where dreams come true. And even though I know how very far apart we are...
...it helps to think she might be using SCIENCE to harness the power of a star.

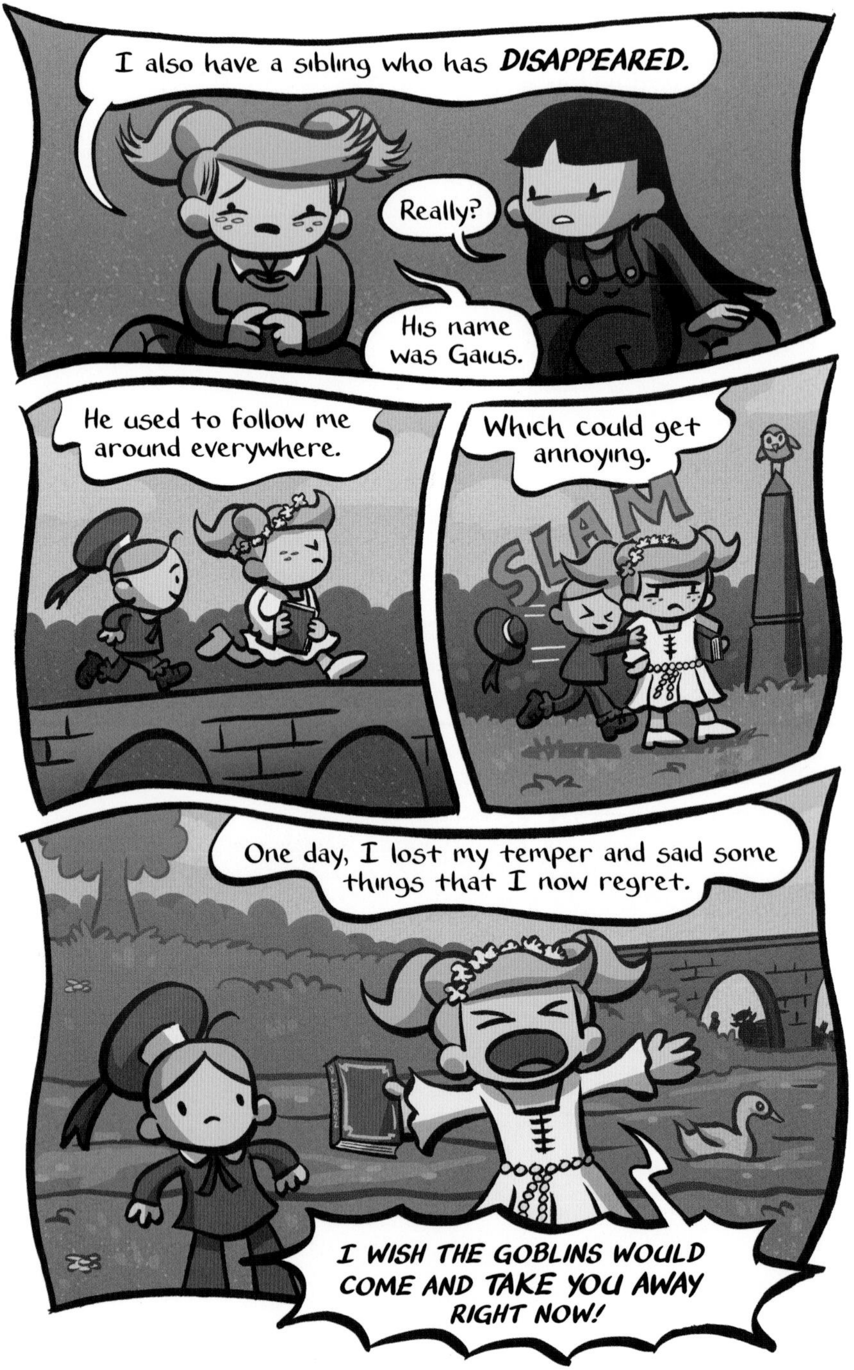
I also have a sibling who has DISAPPEARED.
Really?
His name was Gaius.
He used to follow me around everywhere.
Which could get annoying.
SLAM
One day, I lost my temper and said some things that I now regret.
I WISH THE GOBLINS WOULD COME AND TAKE YOU AWAY RIGHT NOW!

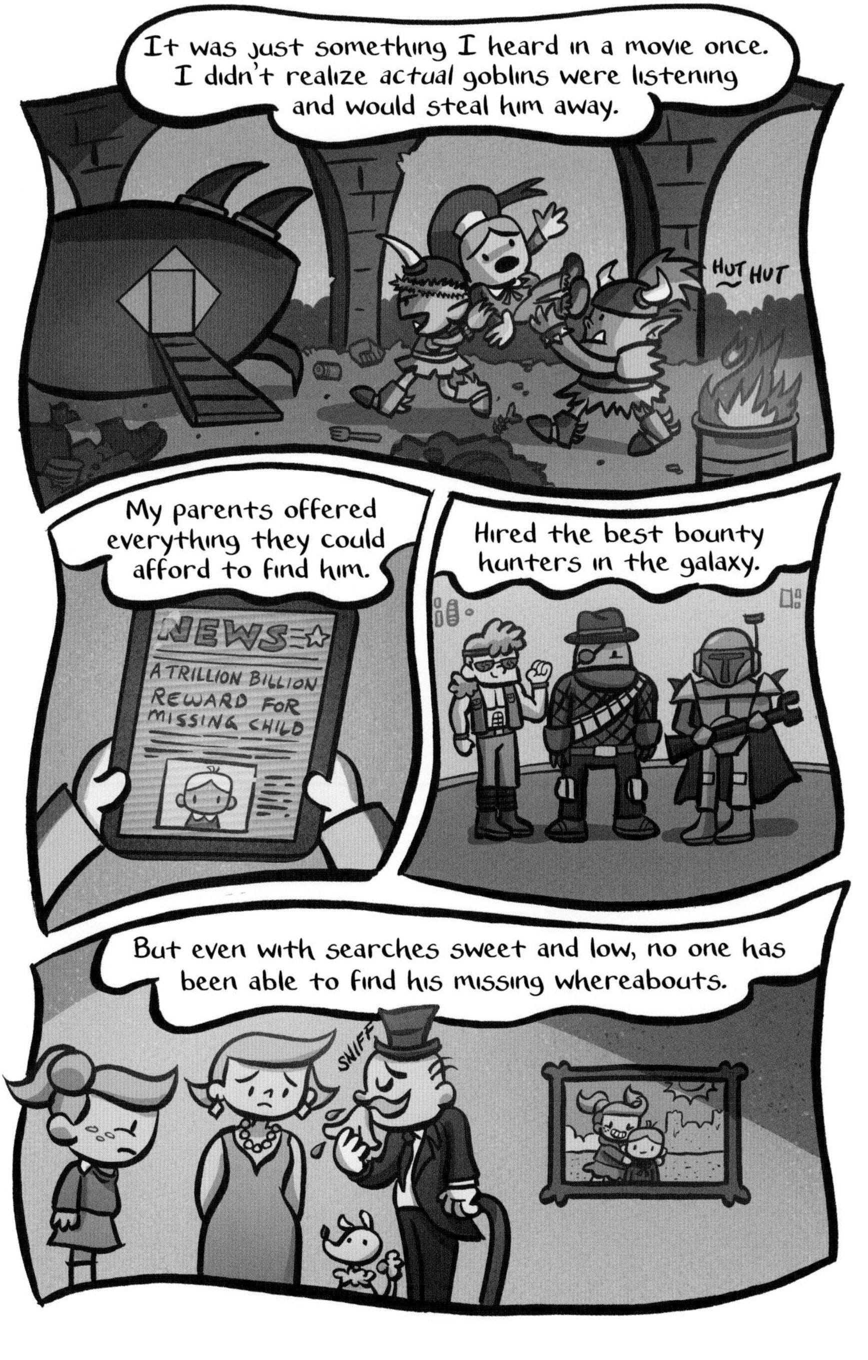
It was just something I heard in a movie once. I didn't realize actual goblins were listening and would steal him away.
HUT HUT
My parents offered everything they could afford to find him.
NEWS
A TRILLION BILLION REWARD FOR MISSING CHILD
Hired the best bounty hunters in the galaxy.
But even with searches sweet and low, no one has been able to find his missing whereabouts.
SNIFF

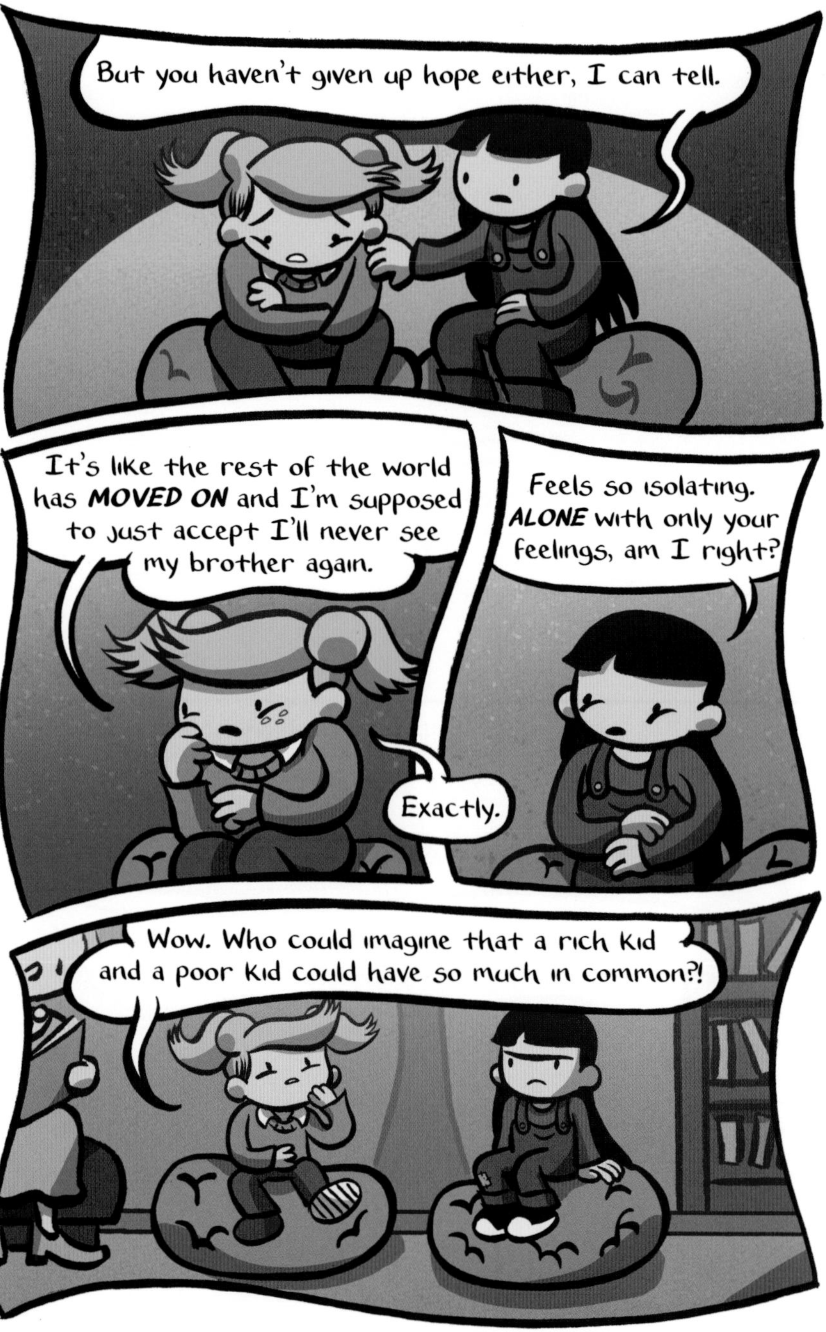
But you haven't given up hope either, I can tell.
It's like the rest of the world has **MOVED ON** and I'm supposed to just accept I'll never see my brother again.
Feels so isolating. **ALONE** with only your feelings, am I right?
Exactly.
Wow. Who could imagine that a rich kid and a poor kid could have so much in common?!

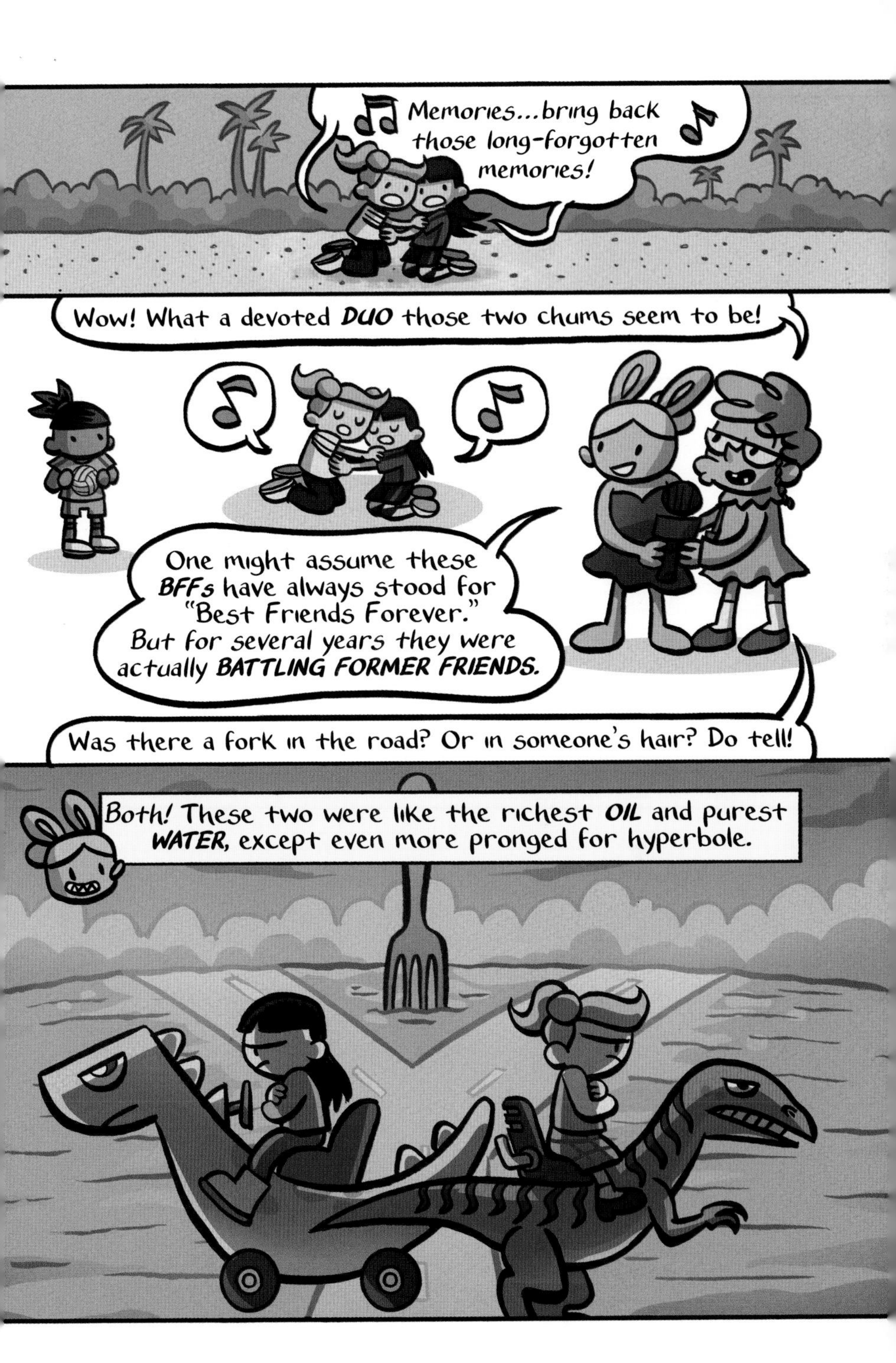
Memories...bring back those long-forgotten memories!
Wow! What a devoted DUO those two chums seem to be!
One might assume these BFFs have always stood for "Best Friends Forever." But for several years they were actually BATTLING FORMER FRIENDS.
Was there a fork in the road? Or in someone's hair? Do tell!
Both! These two were like the richest OIL and purest WATER, except even more pronged for hyperbole.

EVERY TIME I SEE MARIBELLE IT MAKES MY EYES VOMIT!

MIYUMI'S GOODY TWO-SHOES ARE SO PHONY THEY ARE CLEARLY KNOCKOFFS.

BRAVA!

I may not teach drama, but I sure enjoyed watching theirs play out.

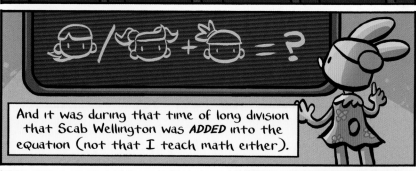

And it was during that time of long division that Scab Wellington was ADDED into the equation (not that I teach math either).

Scab would have done anything to protect her friendship with Maribelle.

ANY ENEMY OF MARIBELLE IS AN ENEMY OF MINE!

INTERGALACTIC BUREAU OF WELLBEING
CONTAINMENT CENTER

Whoops.

CELLBLOCK 4

Sorry. I get that the plastic fork was a bit much.

86

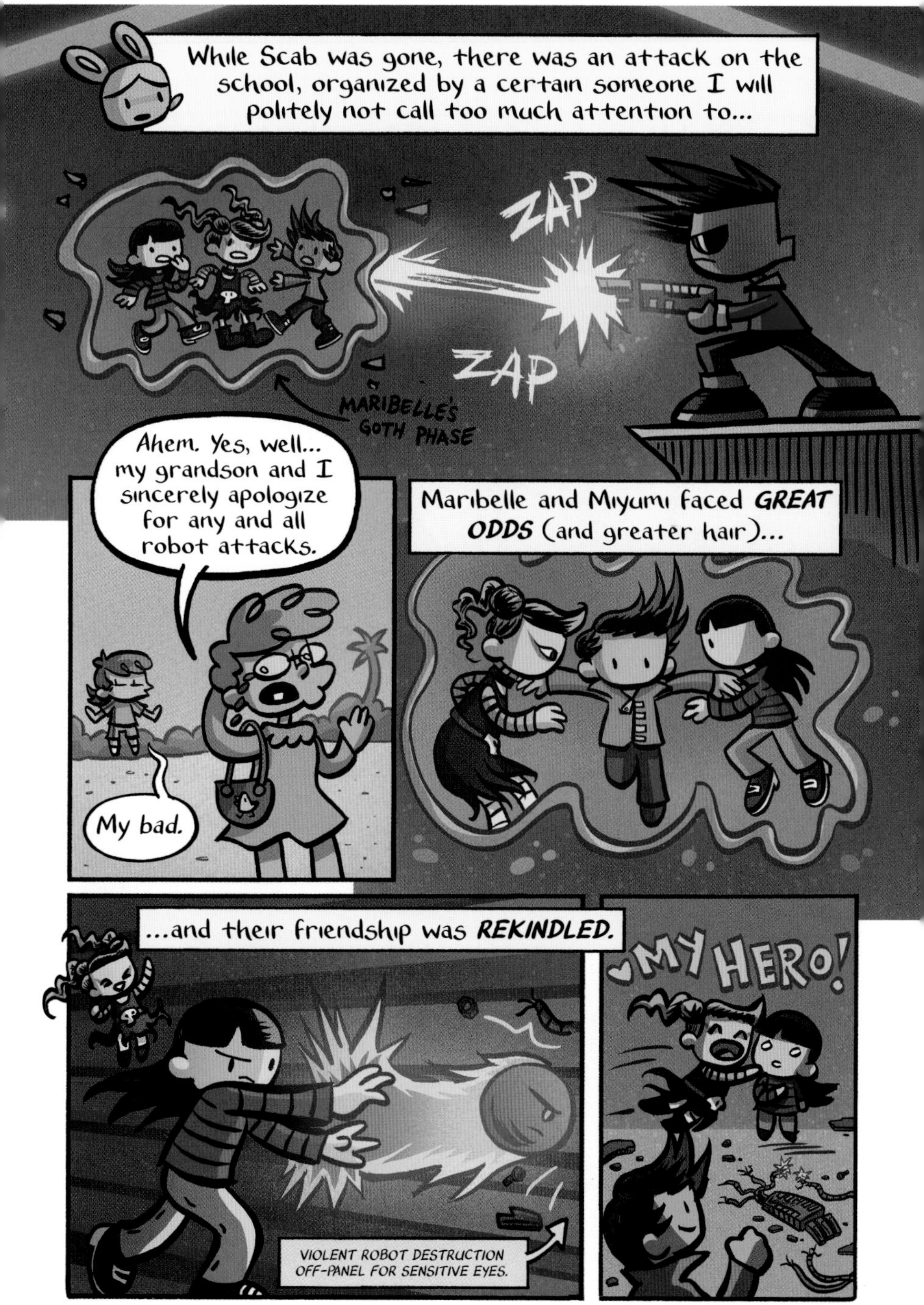

While Scab was gone, there was an attack on the school, organized by a certain someone I will politely not call too much attention to...
ZAP
ZAP
MARIBELLE'S GOTH PHASE
Ahem. Yes, well... my grandson and I sincerely apologize for any and all robot attacks.
My bad.
Maribelle and Miyumi faced GREAT ODDS (and greater hair)...
...and their friendship was REKINDLED.
VIOLENT ROBOT DESTRUCTION OFF-PANEL FOR SENSITIVE EYES.
MY HERO!

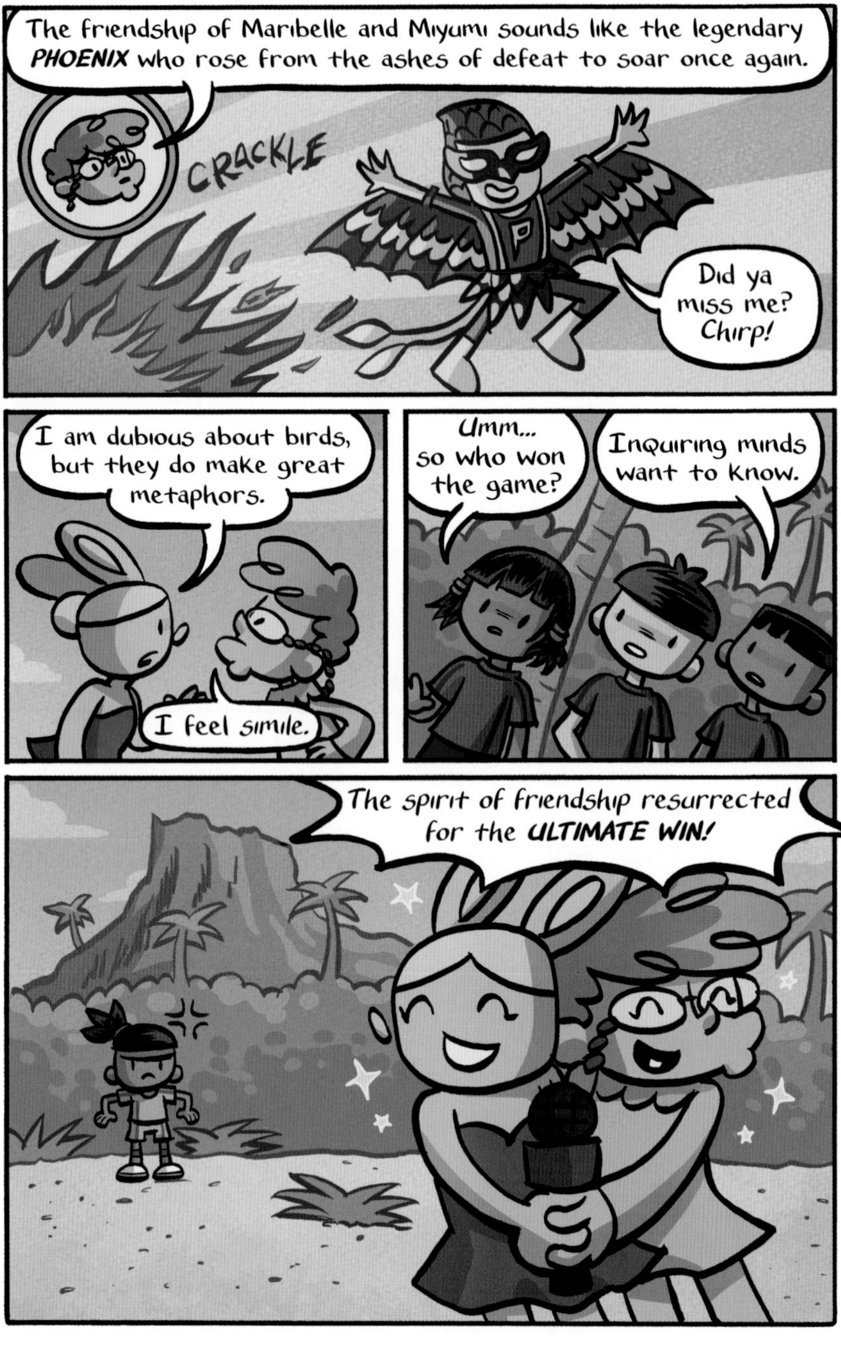
The friendship of Maribelle and Miyumi sounds like the legendary PHOENIX who rose from the ashes of defeat to soar once again.
CRACKLE
Did ya miss me? Chirp!
I am dubious about birds, but they do make great metaphors.
I feel simile.
Umm... so who won the game?
Inquiring minds want to know.
The spirit of friendship resurrected for the ULTIMATE WIN!

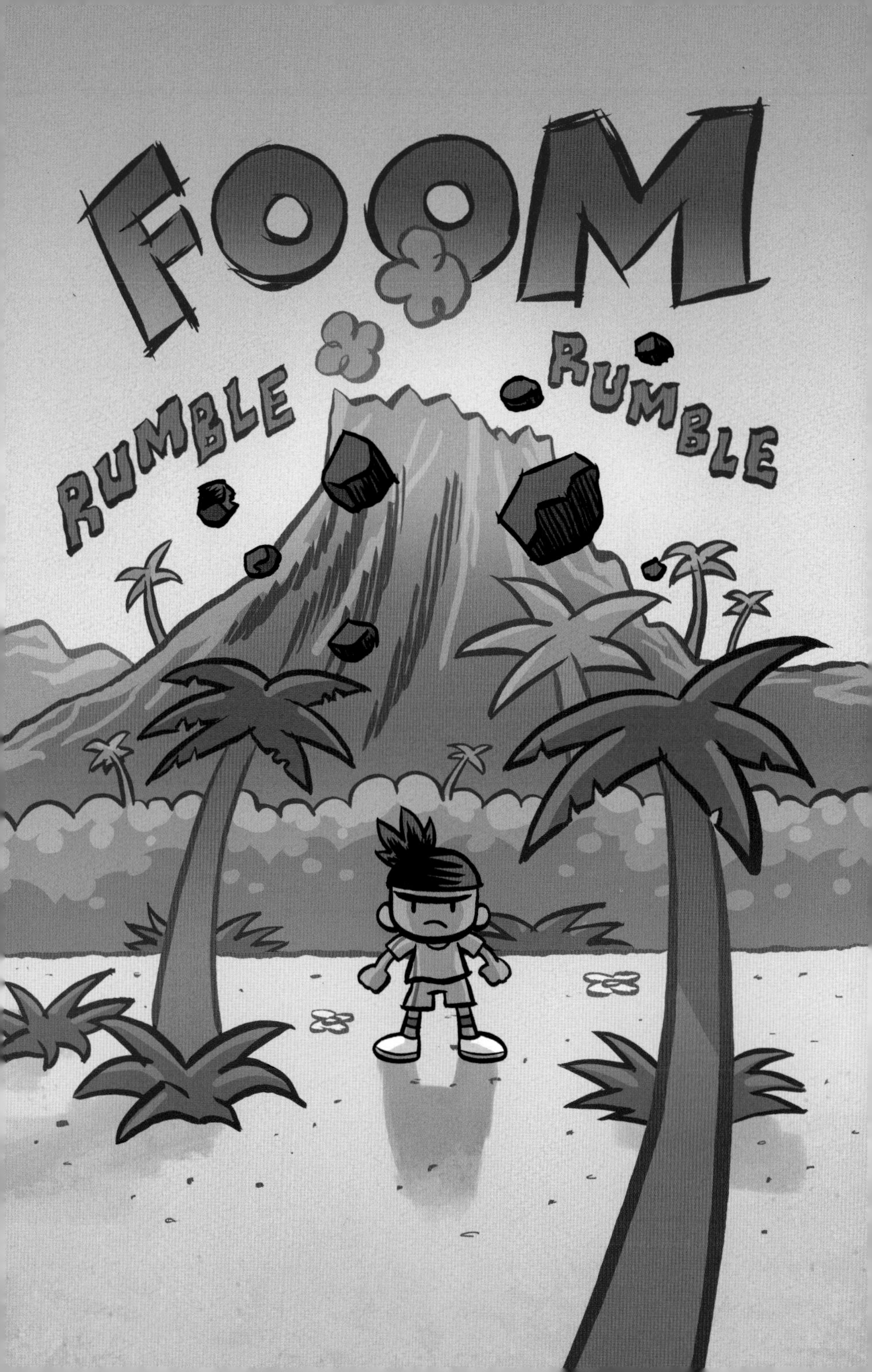
FOOM
RUMBLE
RUMBLE

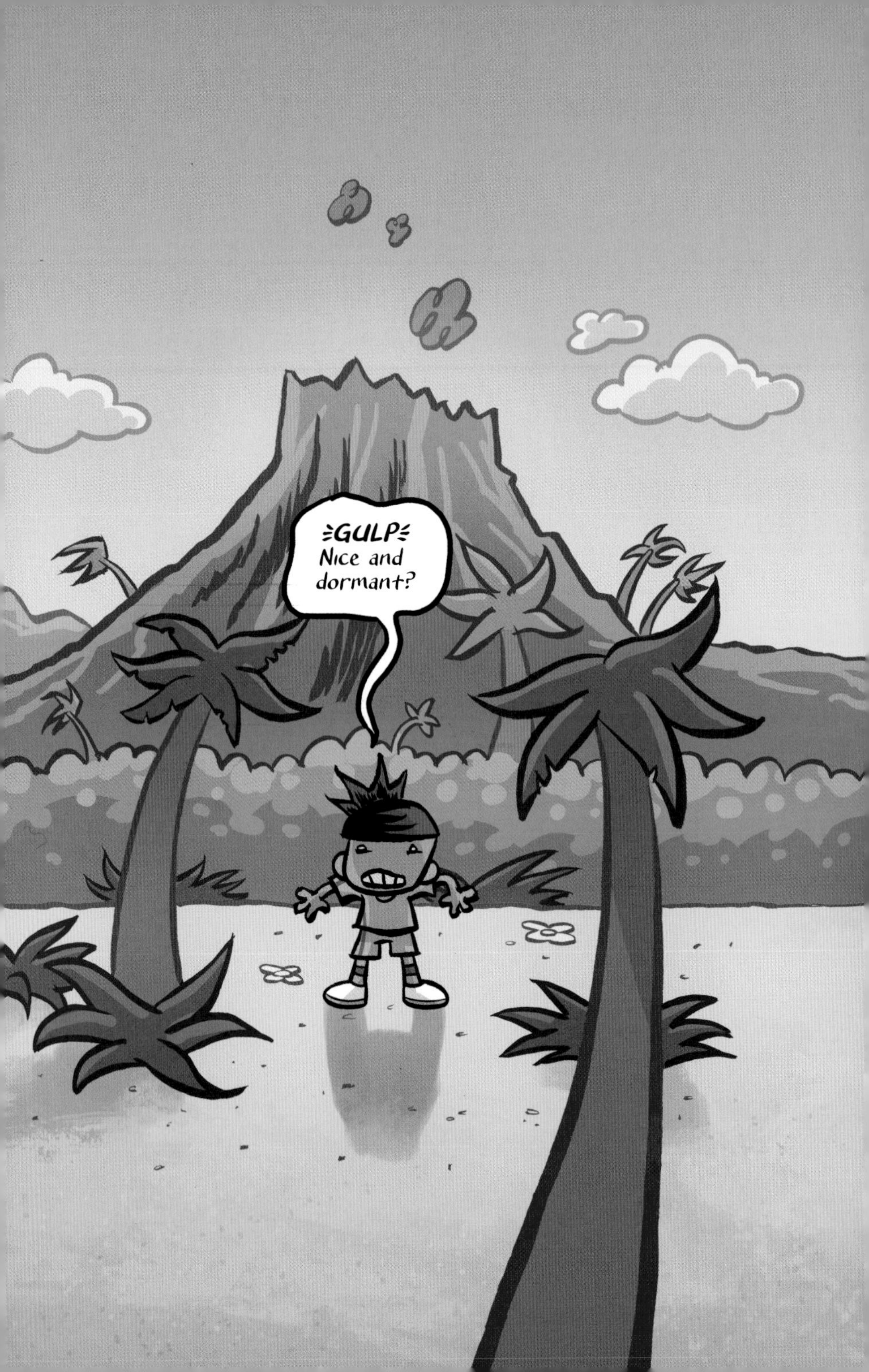
GULP
Nice and dormant?

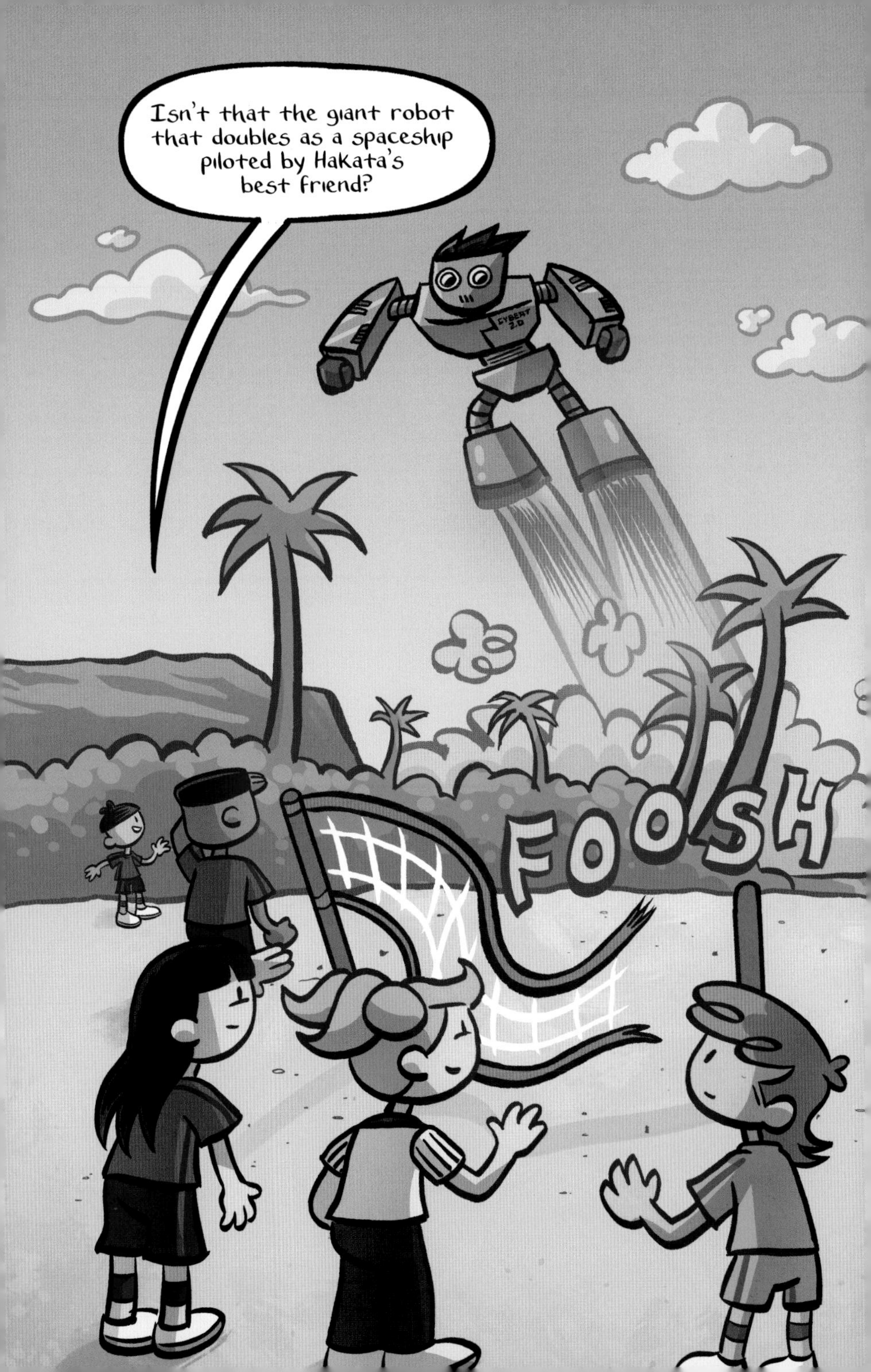
Isn't that the giant robot that doubles as a spaceship piloted by HaKata's best friend?
CYBERT 2.0
FOOSH

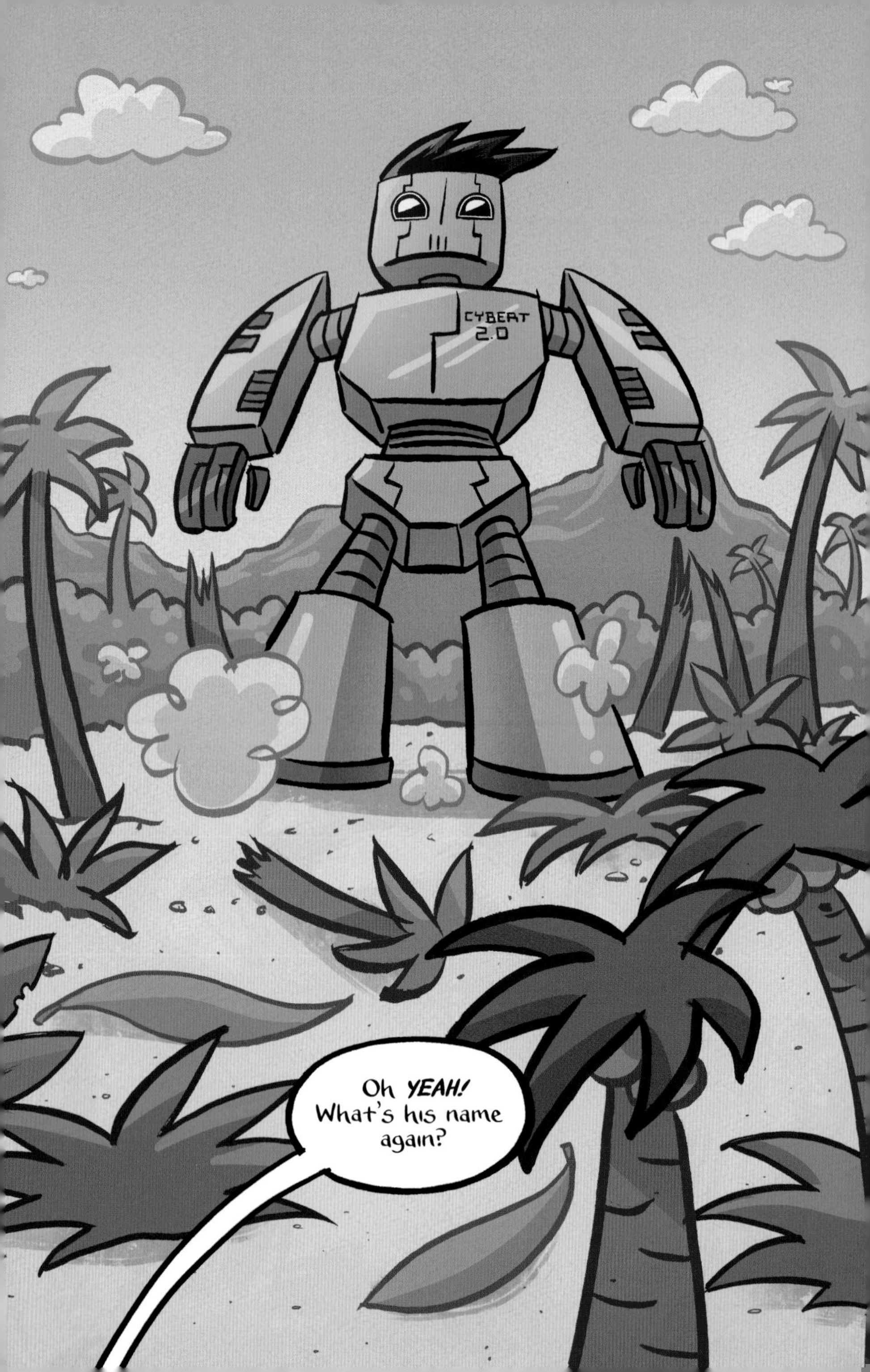
CYBERT 2.0
Oh *YEAH!* What's his name again?

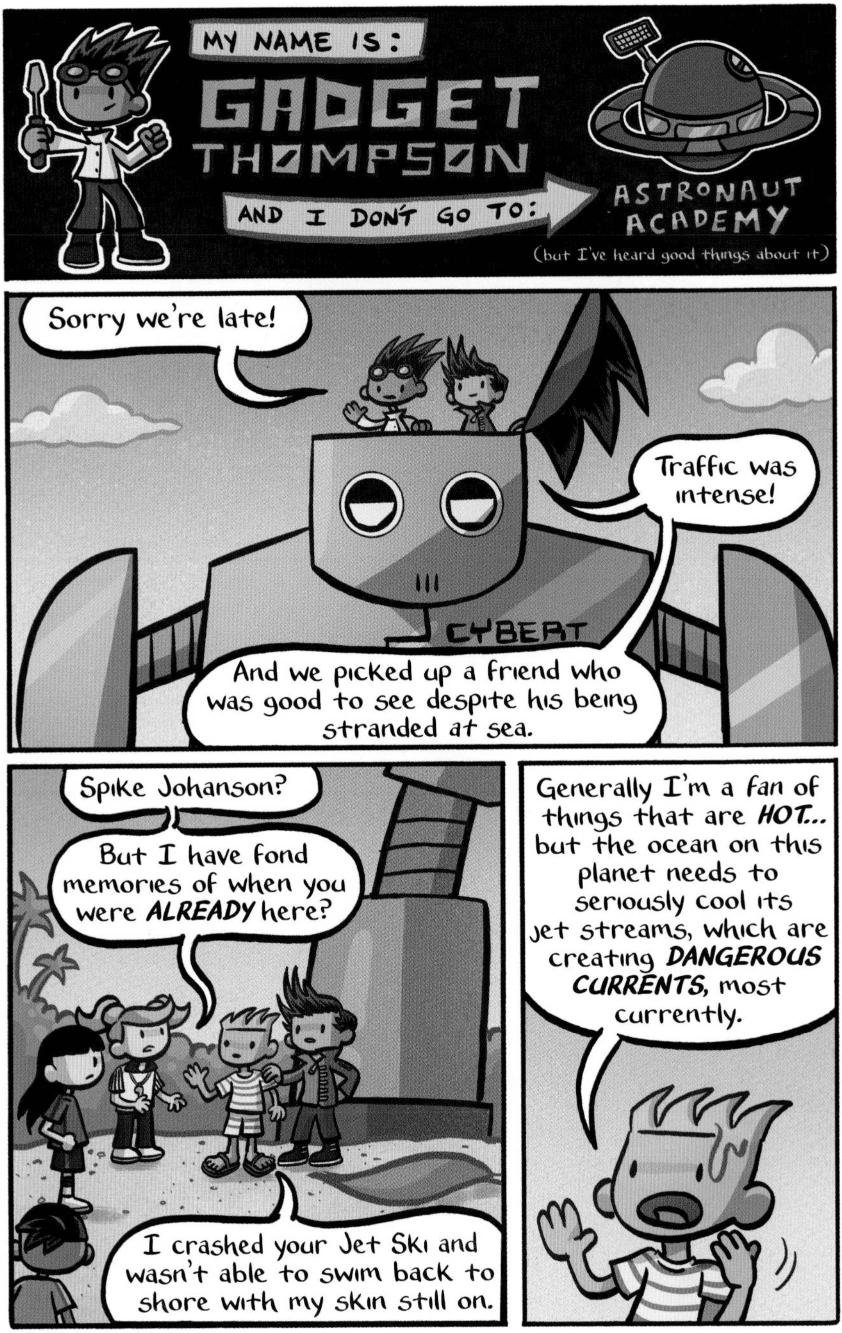
MY NAME IS:
GADGET THOMPSON
AND I DON'T GO TO:
ASTRONAUT ACADEMY
(but I've heard good things about it)
Sorry we're late!
Traffic was intense!
CYBERT
And we picked up a friend who was good to see despite his being stranded at sea.
Spike Johanson?
But I have fond memories of when you were ALREADY here?
I crashed your Jet Ski and wasn't able to swim back to shore with my skin still on.
Generally I'm a fan of things that are HOT... but the ocean on this planet needs to seriously cool its jet streams, which are creating DANGEROUS CURRENTS, most currently.

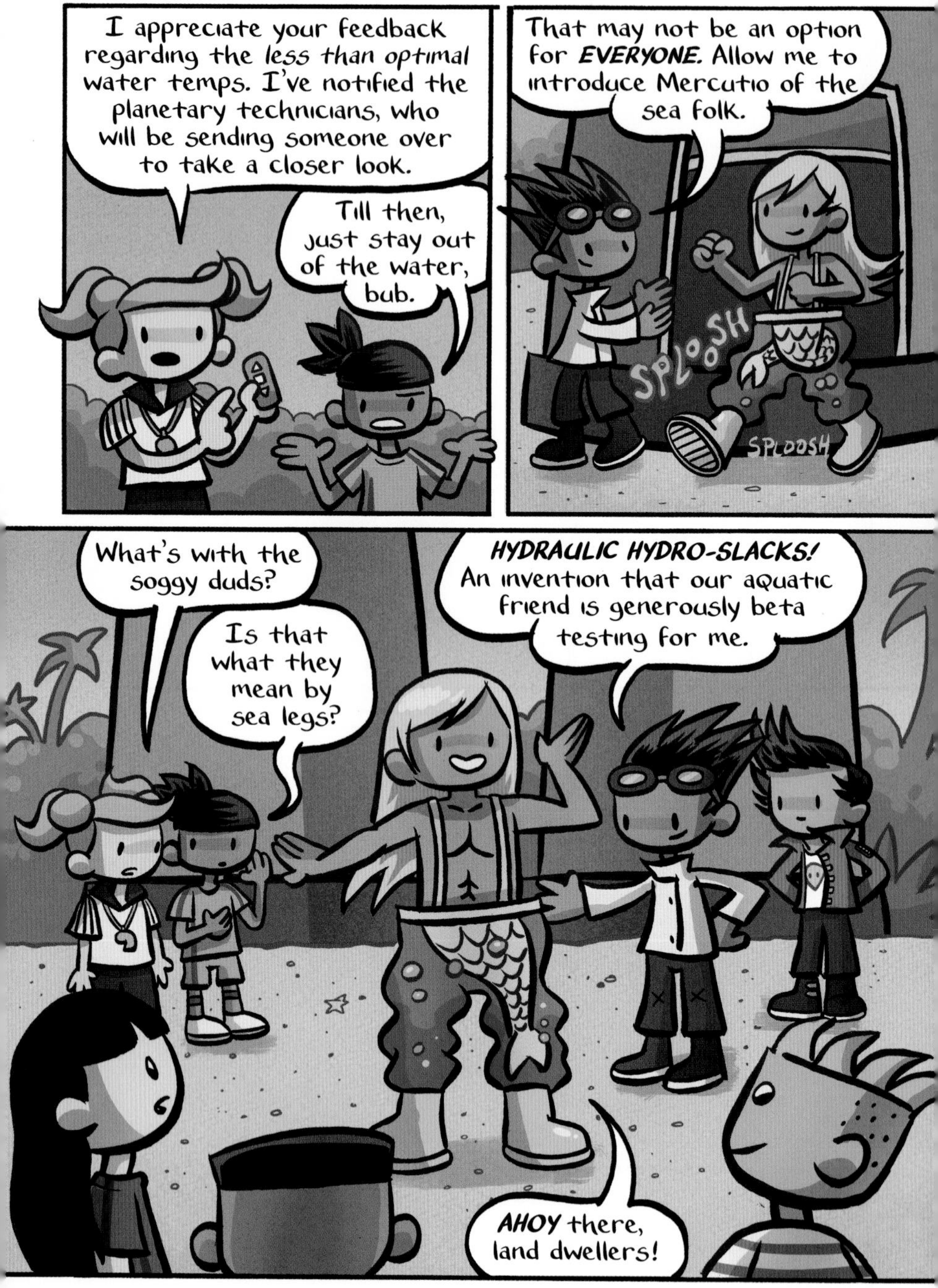
I appreciate your feedback regarding the *less than optimal* water temps. I've notified the planetary technicians, who will be sending someone over to take a closer look.
Till then, just stay out of the water, bub.
That may not be an option for ***EVERYONE.*** Allow me to introduce Mercutio of the sea folk.
SPLOOSH
SPLOOSH
What's with the soggy duds?
Is that what they mean by sea legs?
HYDRAULIC HYDRO-SLACKS! An invention that our aquatic friend is generously beta testing for me.
AHOY there, land dwellers!

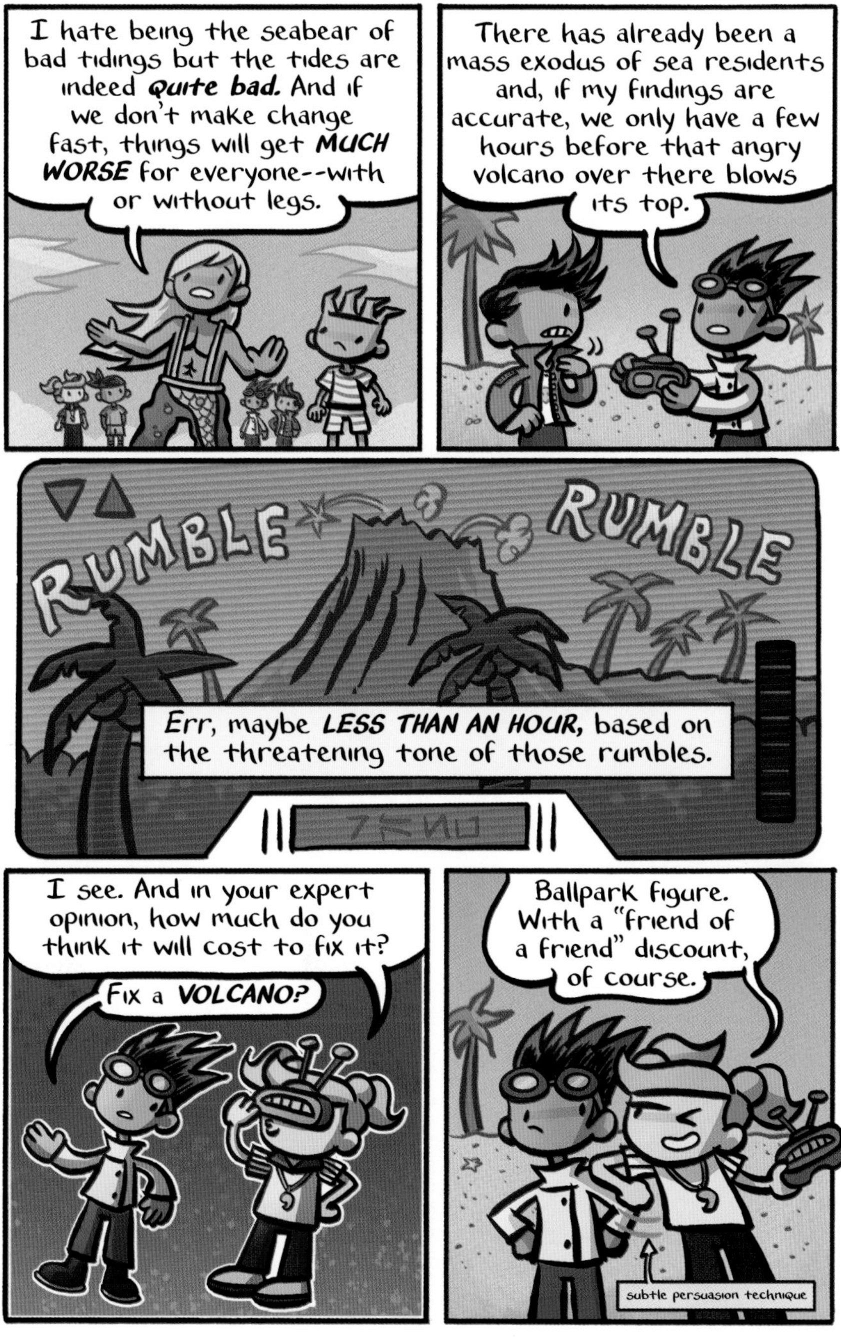
I hate being the seabear of bad tidings but the tides are indeed **QUITE BAD.** And if we don't make change fast, things will get **MUCH WORSE** for everyone--with or without legs.
There has already been a mass exodus of sea residents and, if my findings are accurate, we only have a few hours before that angry volcano over there blows its top.
RUMBLE
RUMBLE
Err, maybe **LESS THAN AN HOUR,** based on the threatening tone of those rumbles.
I see. And in your expert opinion, how much do you think it will cost to fix it?
Fix a **VOLCANO?**
Ballpark figure. With a "friend of a friend" discount, of course.
subtle persuasion technique

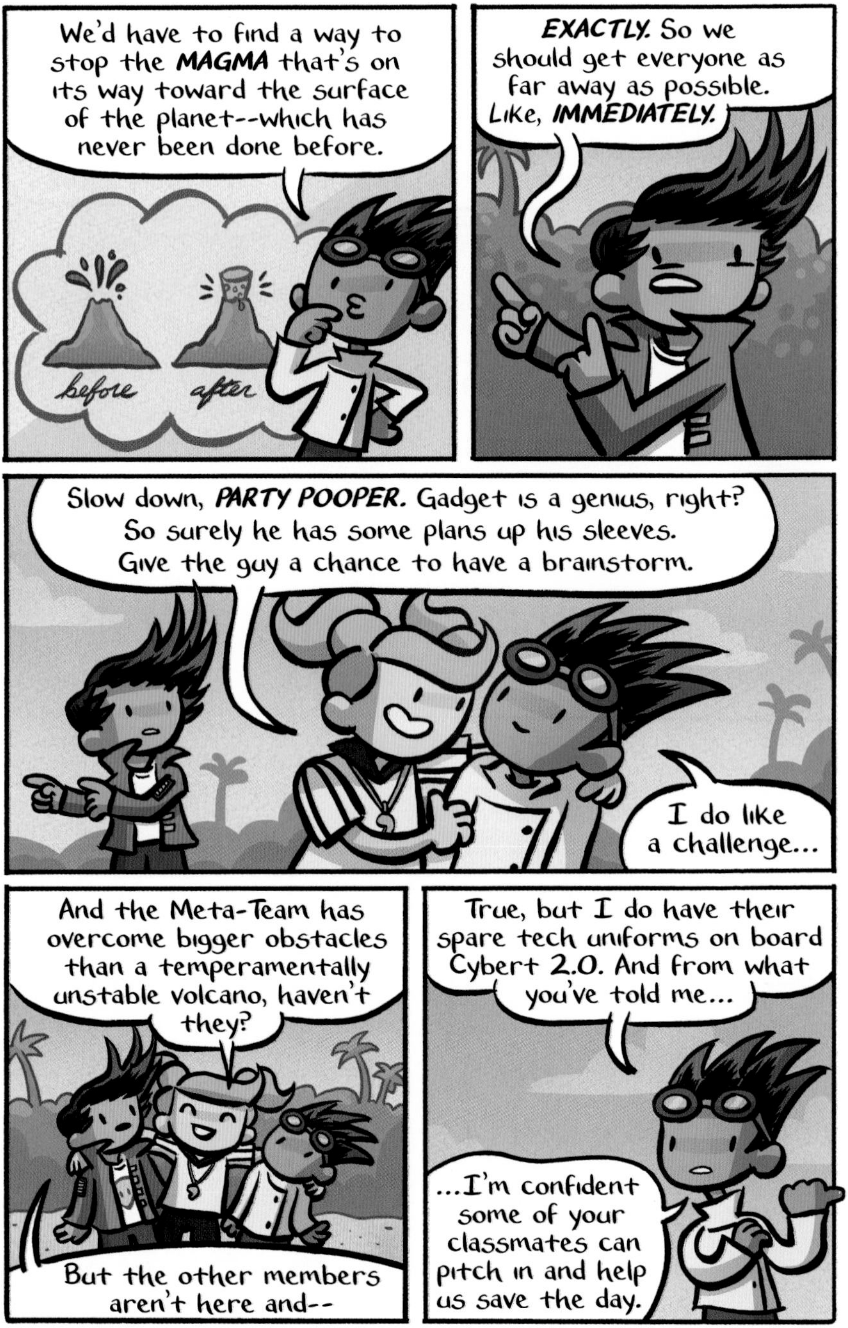
We'd have to find a way to stop the MAGMA that's on its way toward the surface of the planet--which has never been done before.
before
after
EXACTLY. So we should get everyone as far away as possible. Like, IMMEDIATELY.
Slow down, PARTY POOPER. Gadget is a genius, right? So surely he has some plans up his sleeves. Give the guy a chance to have a brainstorm.
I do like a challenge...
And the Meta-Team has overcome bigger obstacles than a temperamentally unstable volcano, haven't they?
But the other members aren't here and--
True, but I do have their spare tech uniforms on board Cybert 2.0. And from what you've told me...
...I'm confident some of your classmates can pitch in and help us save the day.

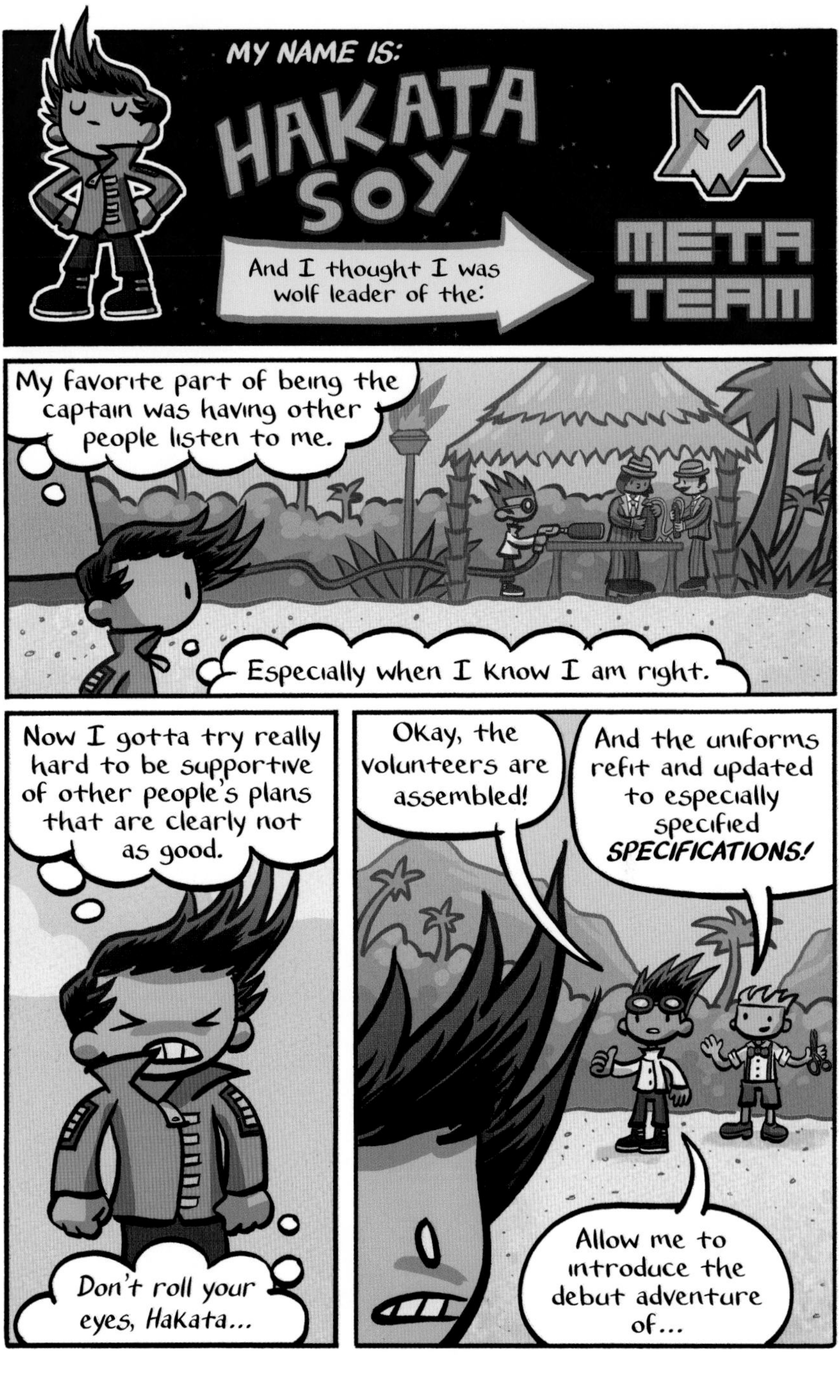

MY NAME IS:
HAKATA SOY
And I thought I was wolf leader of the:
META TEAM
My favorite part of being the captain was having other people listen to me.
Especially when I know I am right.
Now I gotta try really hard to be supportive of other people's plans that are clearly not as good.
Don't roll your eyes, Hakata...
Okay, the volunteers are assembled!
And the uniforms refit and updated to especially specified SPECIFICATIONS!
Allow me to introduce the debut adventure of...

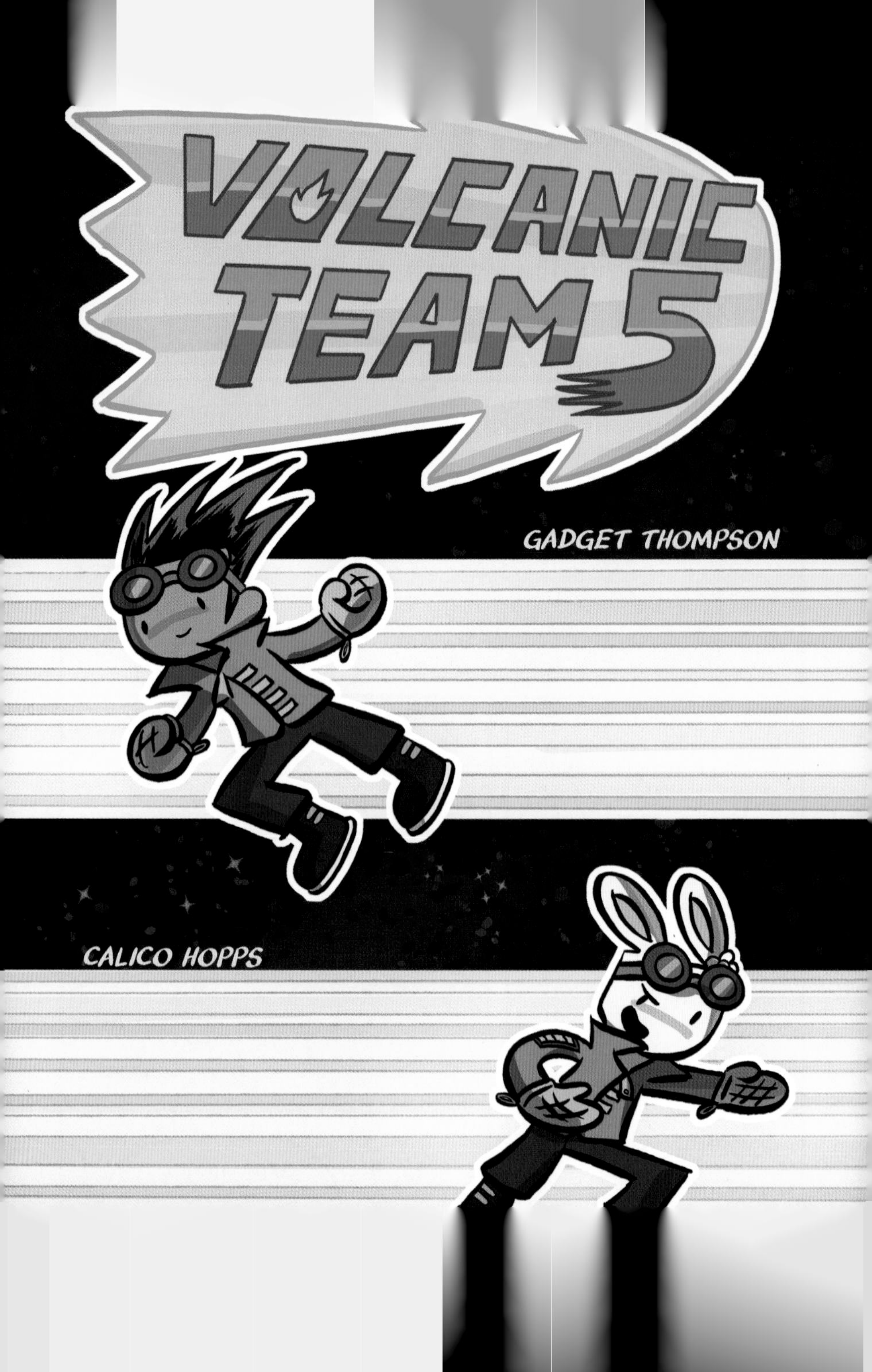
VOLCANIC TEAM 5
GADGET THOMPSON
CALICO HOPPS

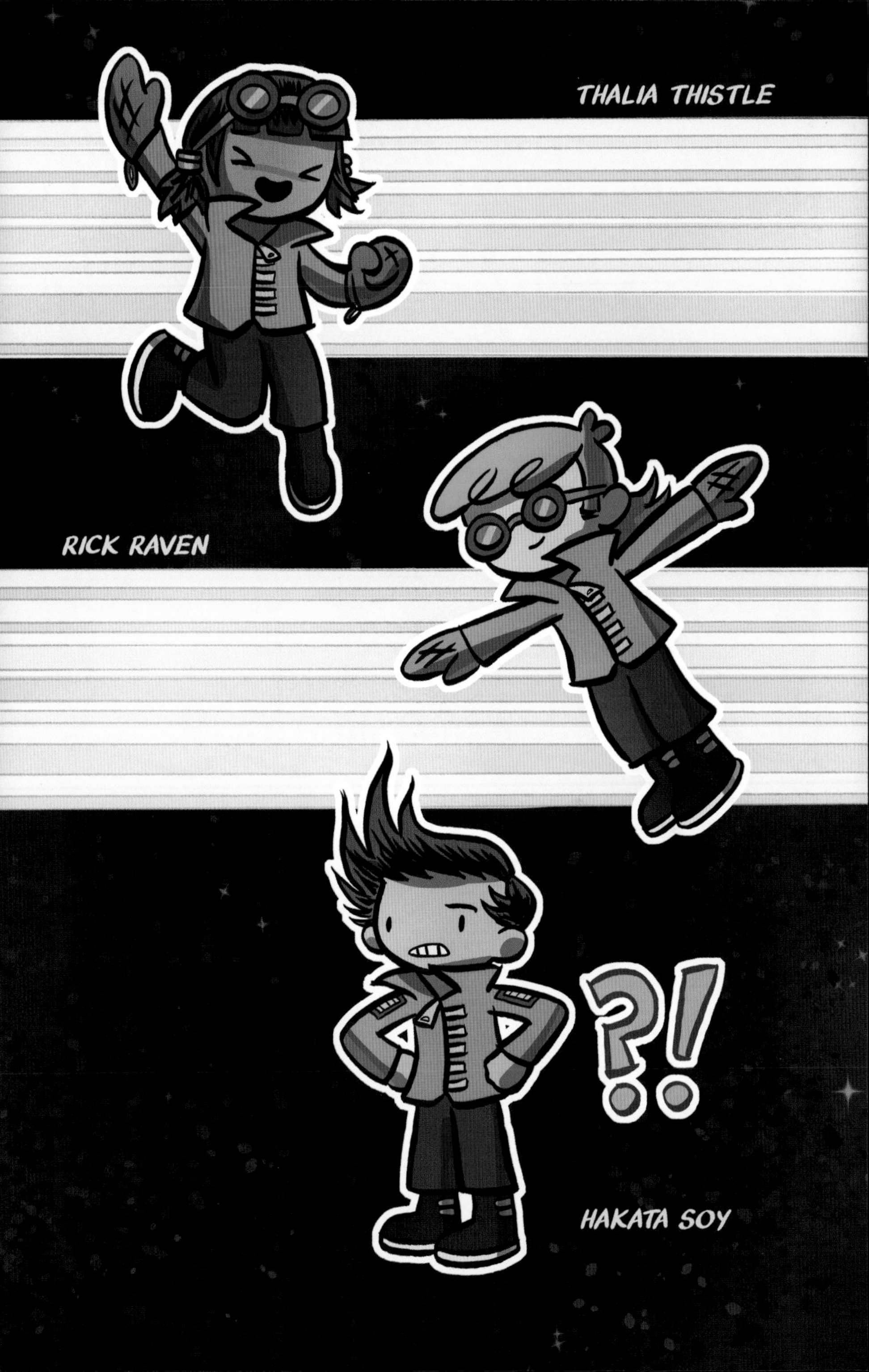
THALIA THISTLE
RICK RAVEN
HAKATA SOY
?!

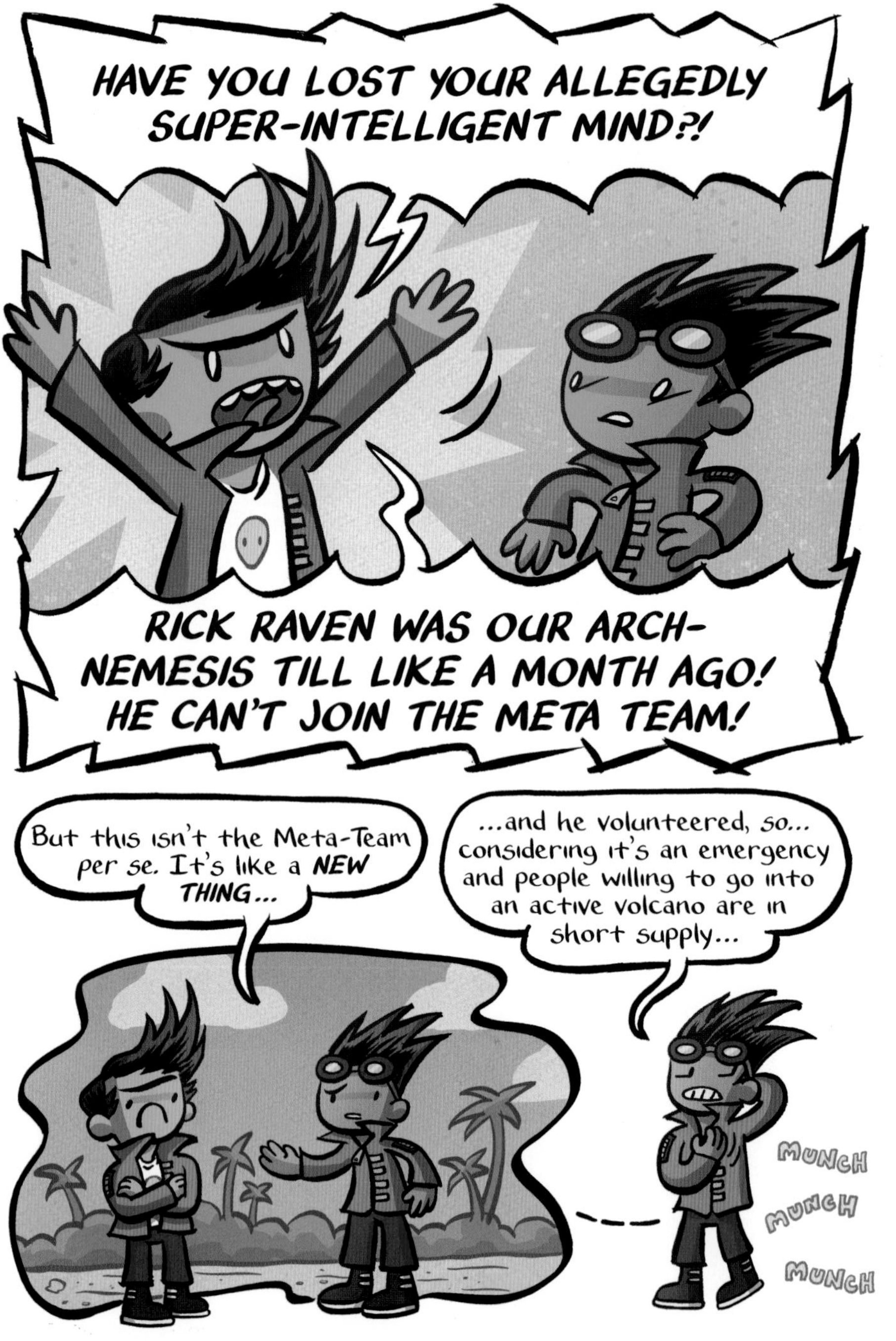
HAVE YOU LOST YOUR ALLEGEDLY SUPER-INTELLIGENT MIND?!
RICK RAVEN WAS OUR ARCH-NEMESIS TILL LIKE A MONTH AGO! HE CAN'T JOIN THE META TEAM!
But this isn't the Meta-Team per se. It's like a NEW THING...
...and he volunteered, so... considering it's an emergency and people willing to go into an active volcano are in short supply...
MUNCH
MUNCH
MUNCH

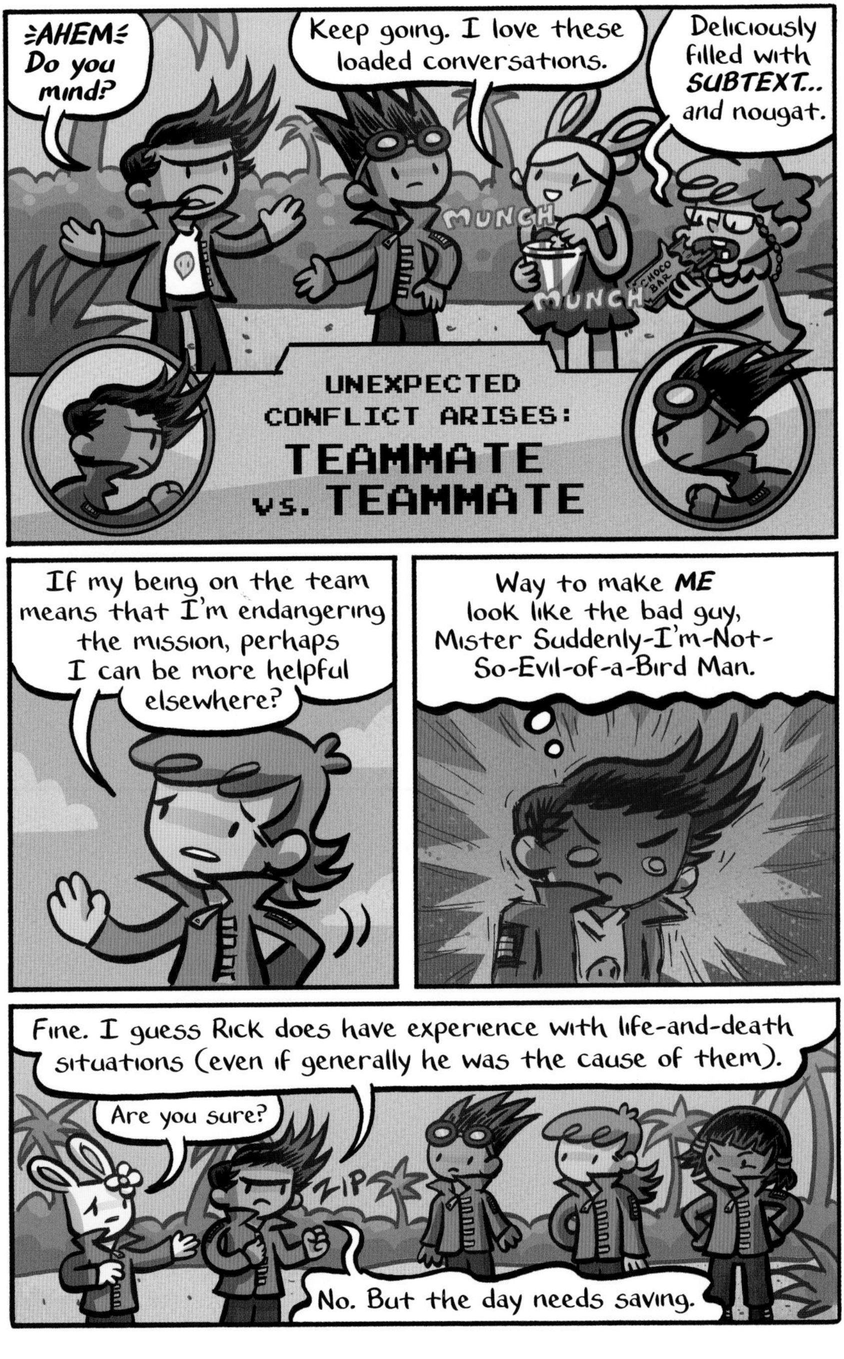

AHEM Do you mind?
Keep going. I love these loaded conversations.
Deliciously filled with SUBTEXT... and nougat.
MUNCH
MUNCH
CHOCO BAR
UNEXPECTED CONFLICT ARISES:
TEAMMATE vs. TEAMMATE
If my being on the team means that I'm endangering the mission, perhaps I can be more helpful elsewhere?
Way to make ME look like the bad guy, Mister Suddenly-I'm-Not-So-Evil-of-a-Bird Man.
Fine. I guess Rick does have experience with life-and-death situations (even if generally he was the cause of them).
Are you sure?
ZIP
No. But the day needs saving.

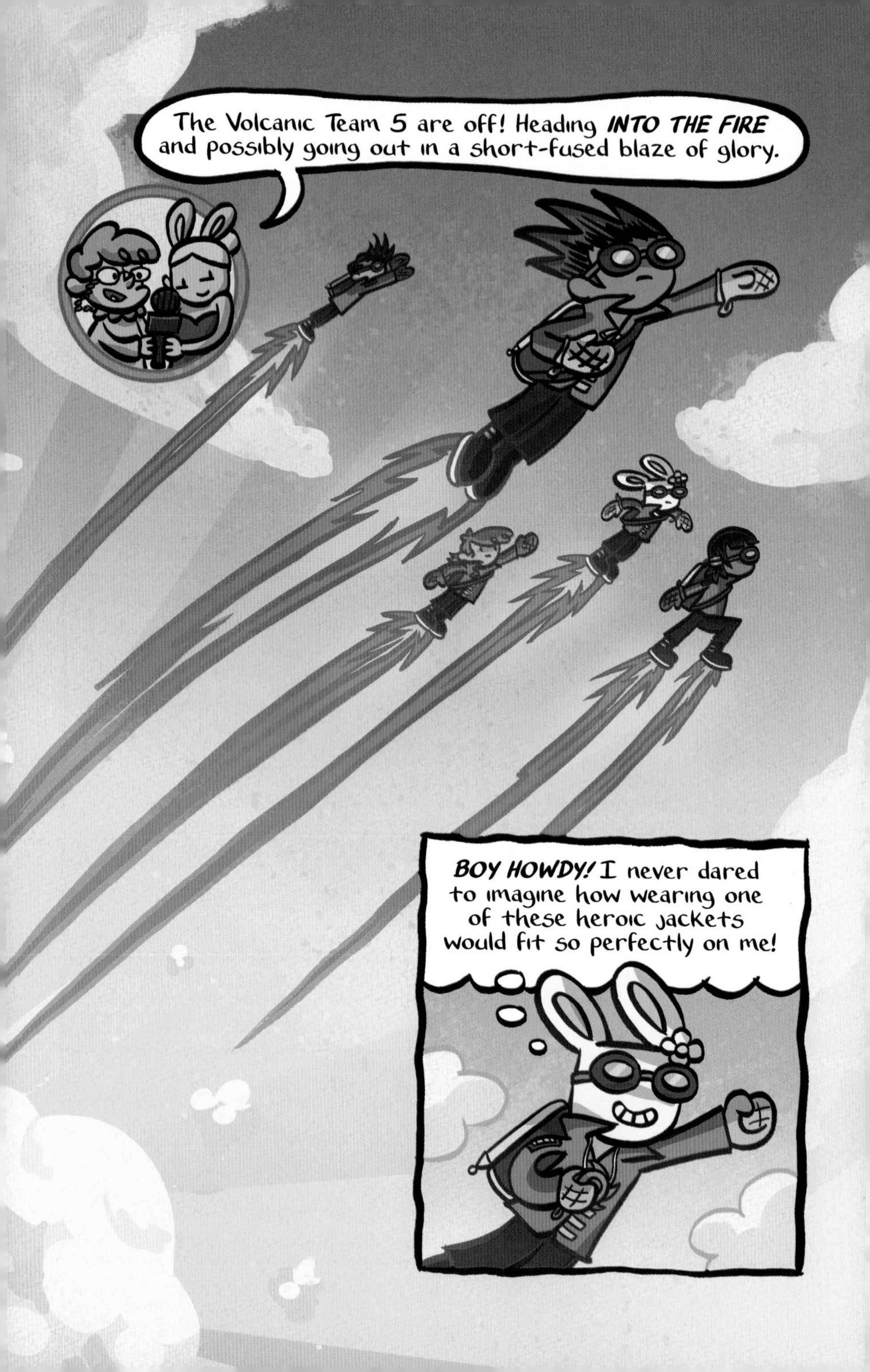
The Volcanic Team 5 are off! Heading **INTO THE FIRE** and possibly going out in a short-fused blaze of glory.
BOY HOWDY! I never dared to imagine how wearing one of these heroic jackets would fit so perfectly on me!

Freeze rays charged and ready?
Just follow my lead and we should get out of here in a non-liquefied state.
CLICK
TROUBLE RUMBLE

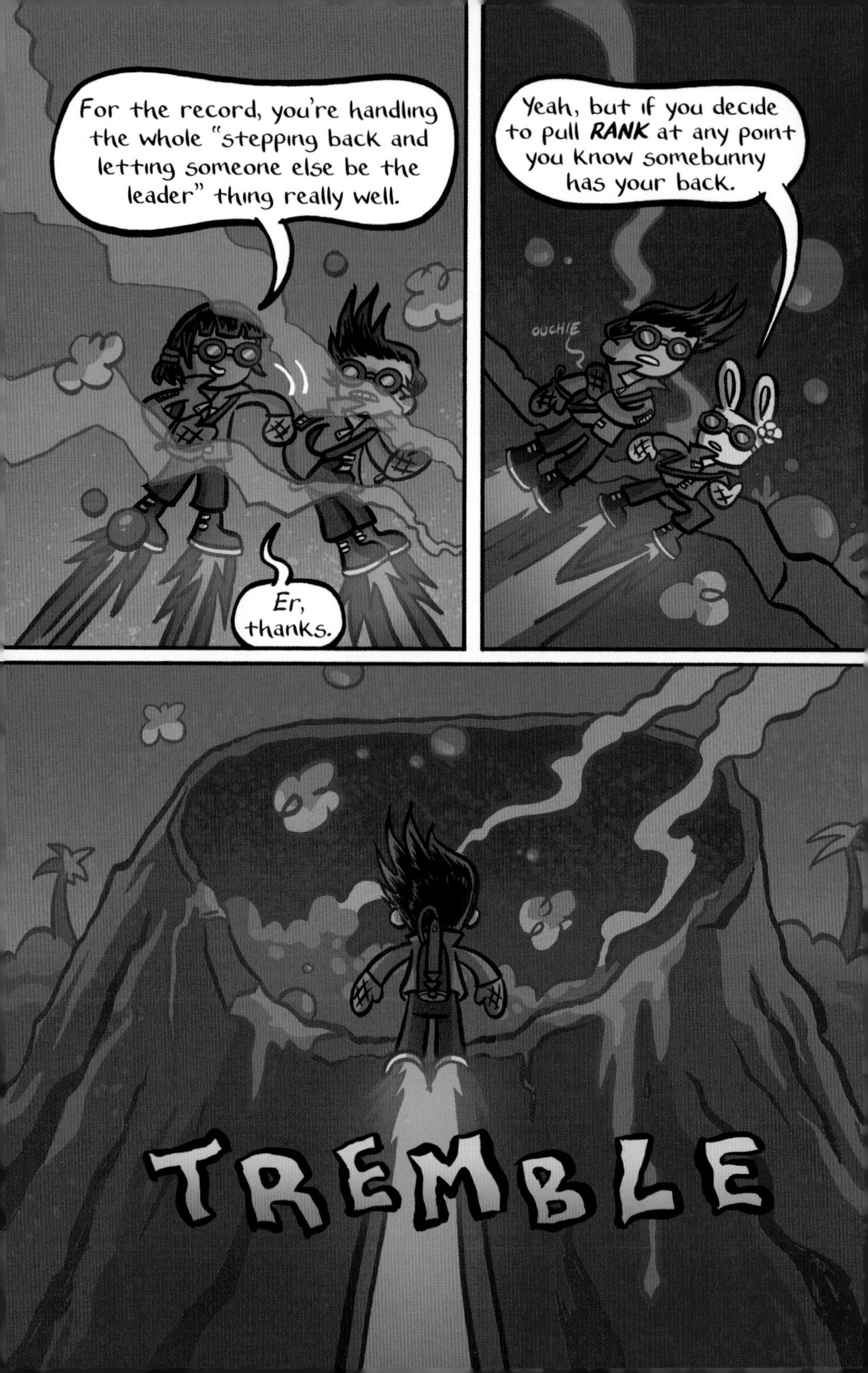
For the record, you're handling the whole "stepping back and letting someone else be the leader" thing really well.
Er, thanks.
Yeah, but if you decide to pull **RANK** at any point you know somebunny has your back.
OUCHIE
TREMBLE

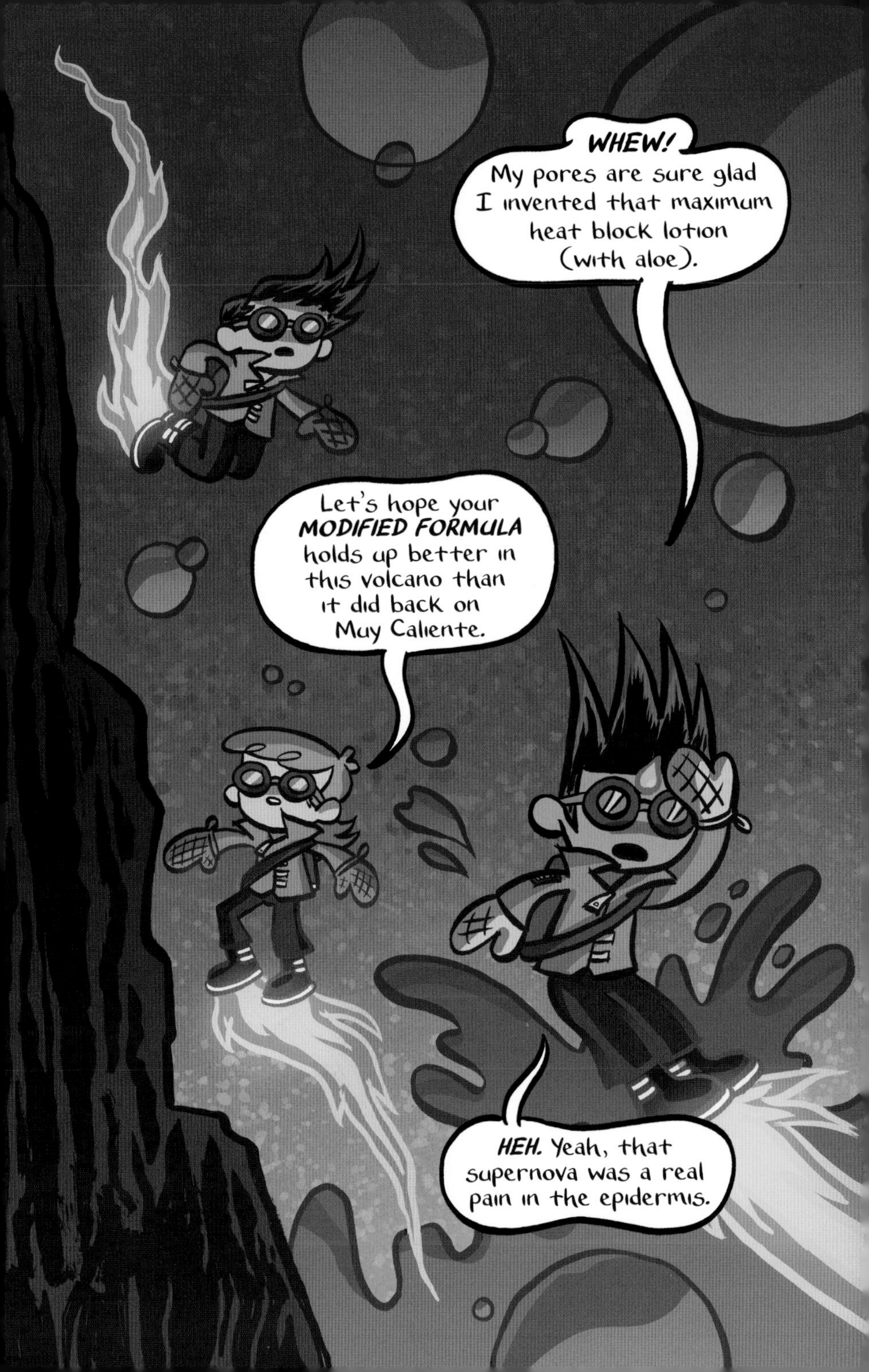
WHEW! My pores are sure glad I invented that maximum heat block lotion (with aloe).
Let's hope your MODIFIED FORMULA holds up better in this volcano than it did back on Muy Caliente.
HEH. Yeah, that supernova was a real pain in the epidermis.

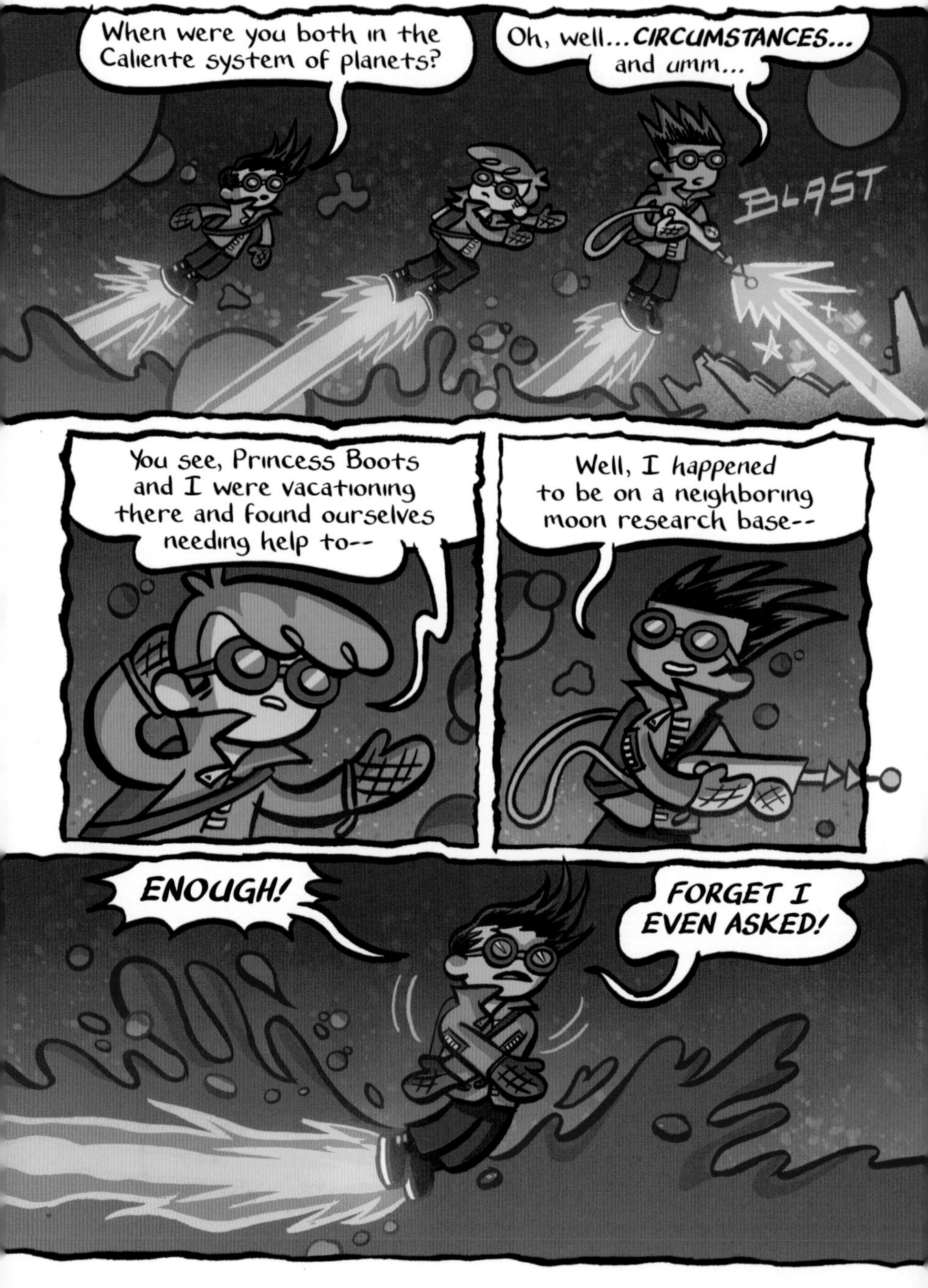
When were you both in the Caliente system of planets?
Oh, well... CIRCUMSTANCES... and umm...
BLAST
You see, Princess Boots and I were vacationing there and found ourselves needing help to--
Well, I happened to be on a neighboring moon research base--
ENOUGH!
FORGET I EVEN ASKED!

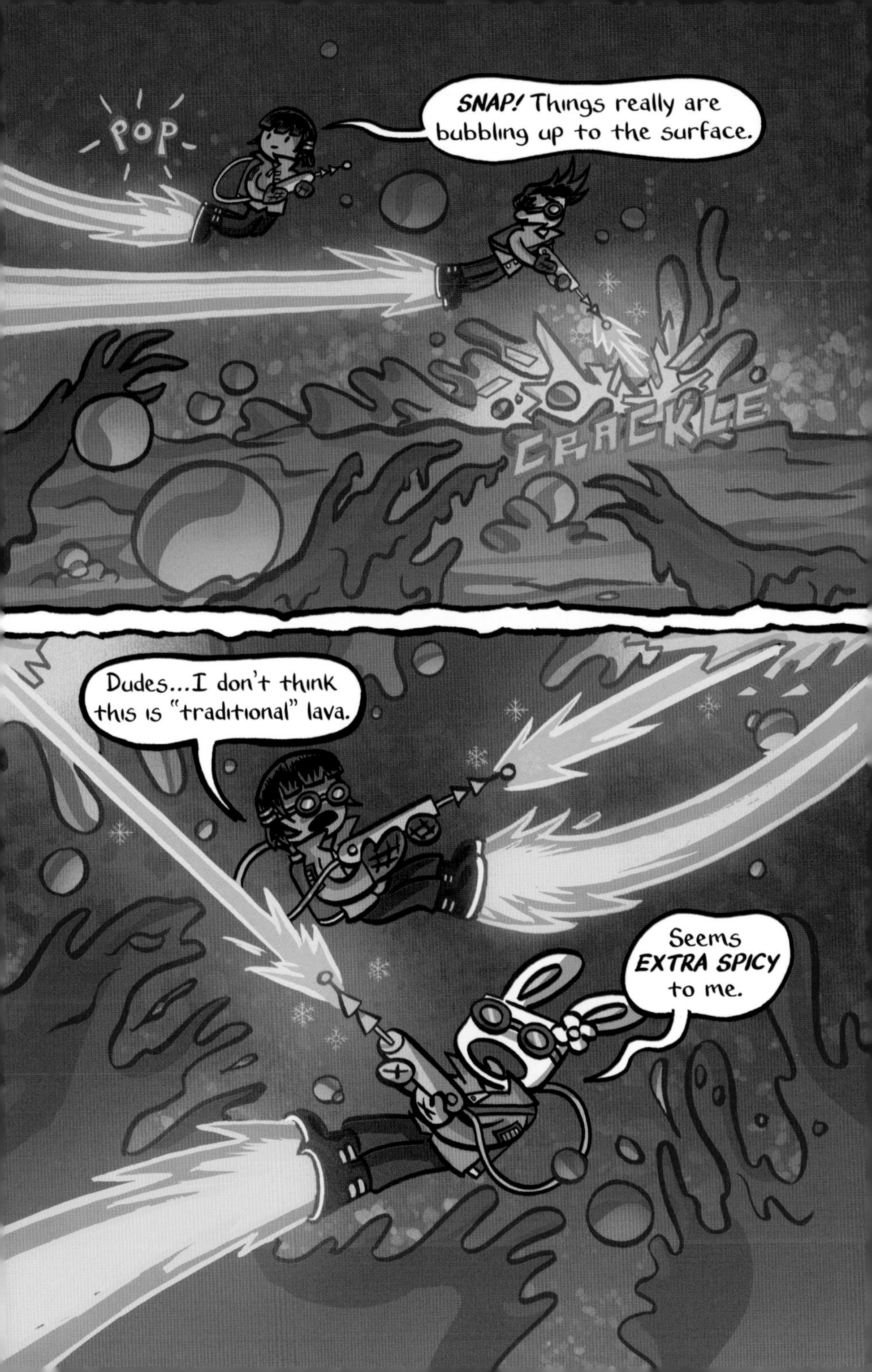

POP
SNAP! Things really are bubbling up to the surface.
CRACKLE
Dudes...I don't think this is "traditional" lava.
Seems **EXTRA SPICY** to me.

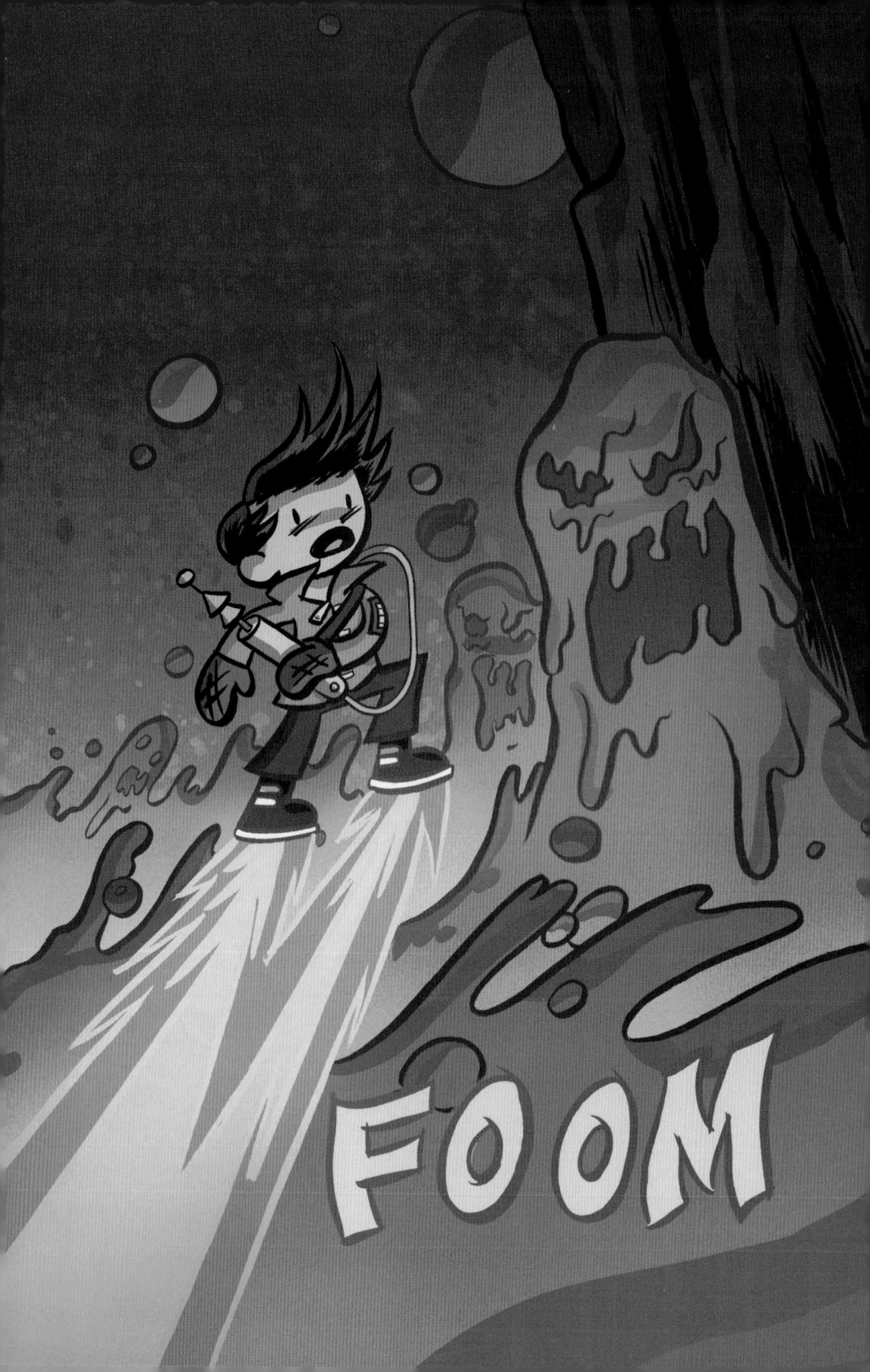
FOOM

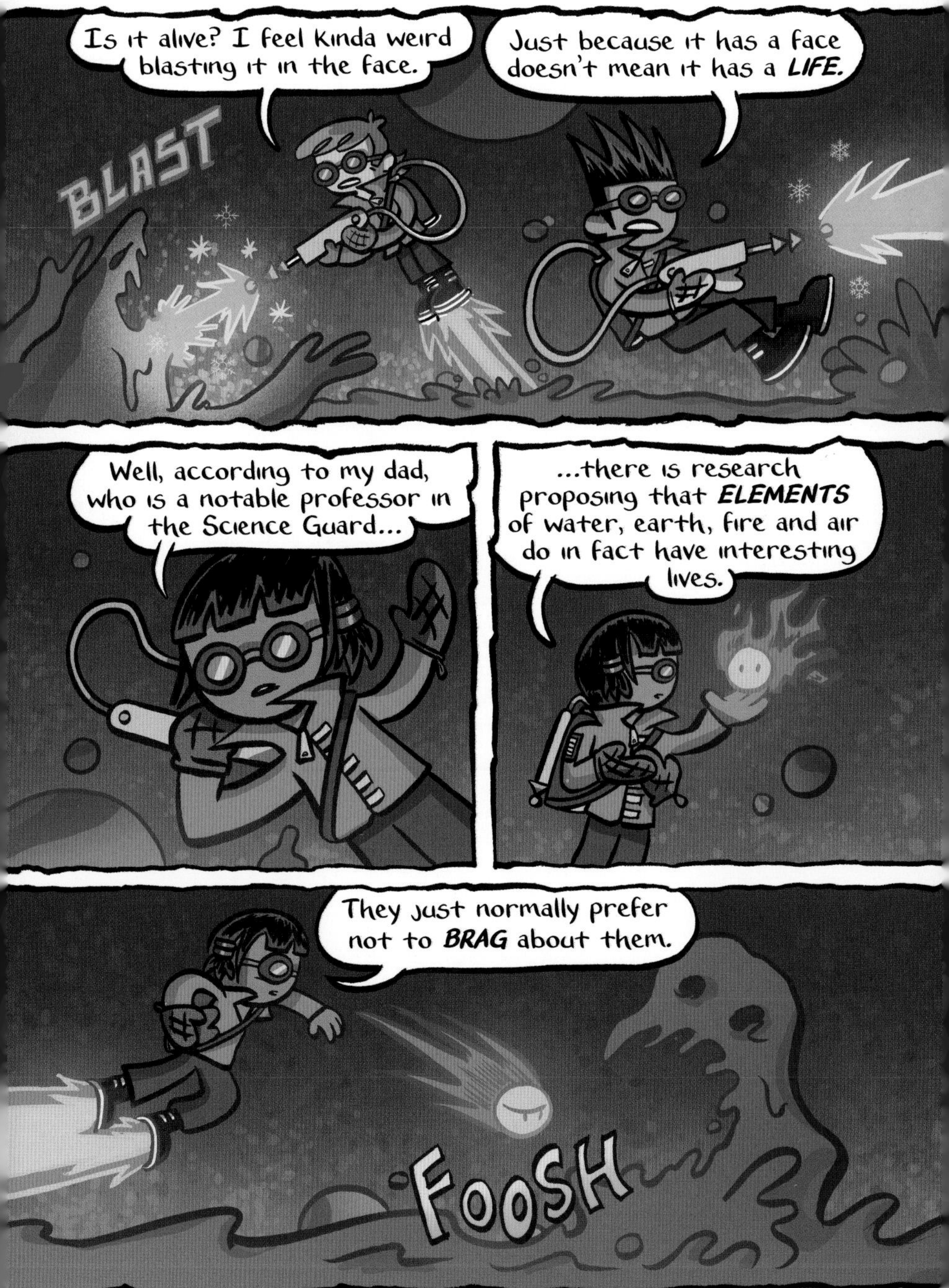
Is it alive? I feel kinda weird blasting it in the face.
BLAST
Just because it has a face doesn't mean it has a LIFE.
Well, according to my dad, who is a notable professor in the Science Guard...
...there is research proposing that ELEMENTS of water, earth, fire and air do in fact have interesting lives.
They just normally prefer not to BRAG about them.
FOOSH

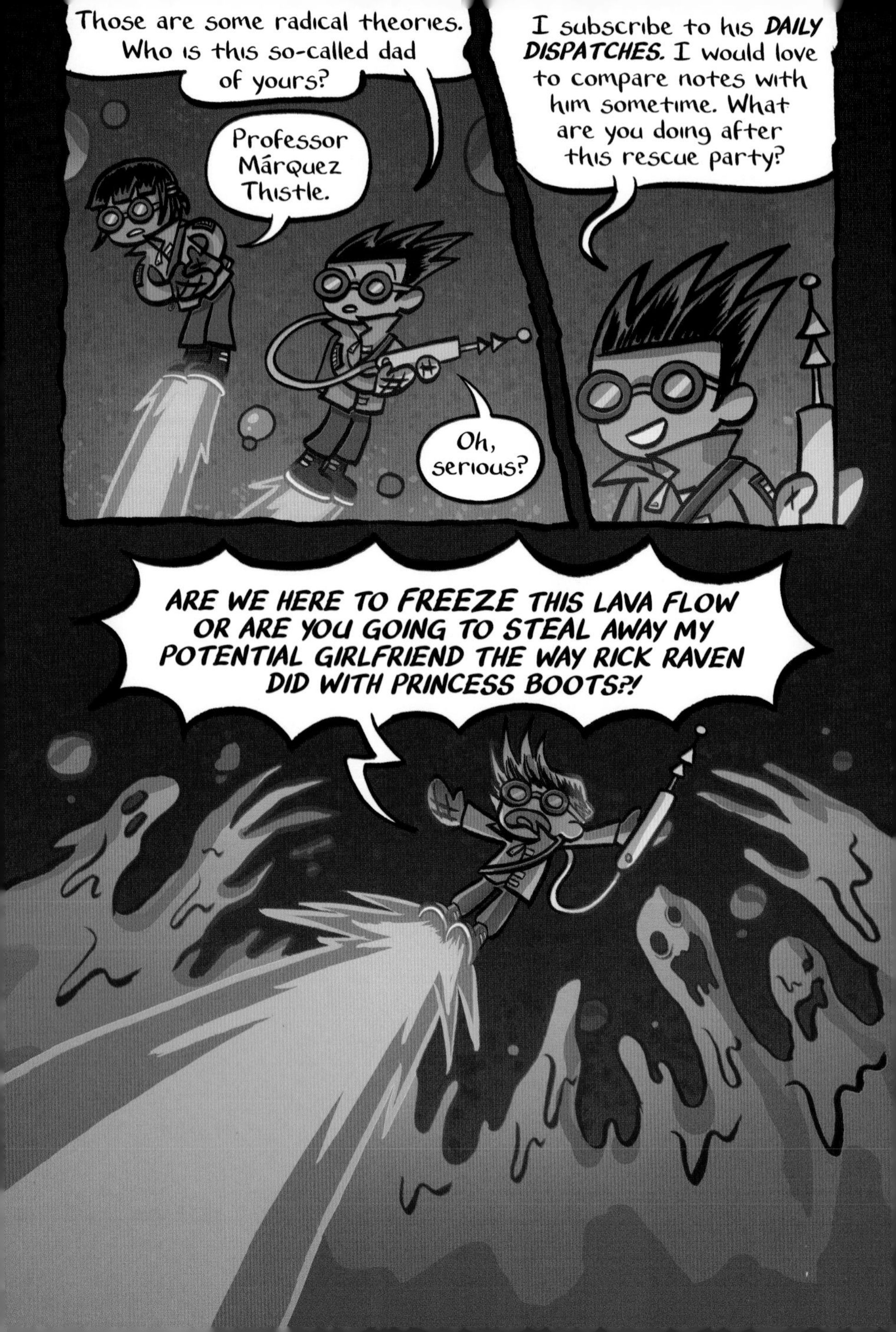

Those are some radical theories. Who is this so-called dad of yours?
Professor Márquez Thistle.
Oh, serious?
I subscribe to his DAILY DISPATCHES. I would love to compare notes with him sometime. What are you doing after this rescue party?
ARE WE HERE TO FREEZE THIS LAVA FLOW OR ARE YOU GOING TO STEAL AWAY MY POTENTIAL GIRLFRIEND THE WAY RICK RAVEN DID WITH PRINCESS BOOTS?!

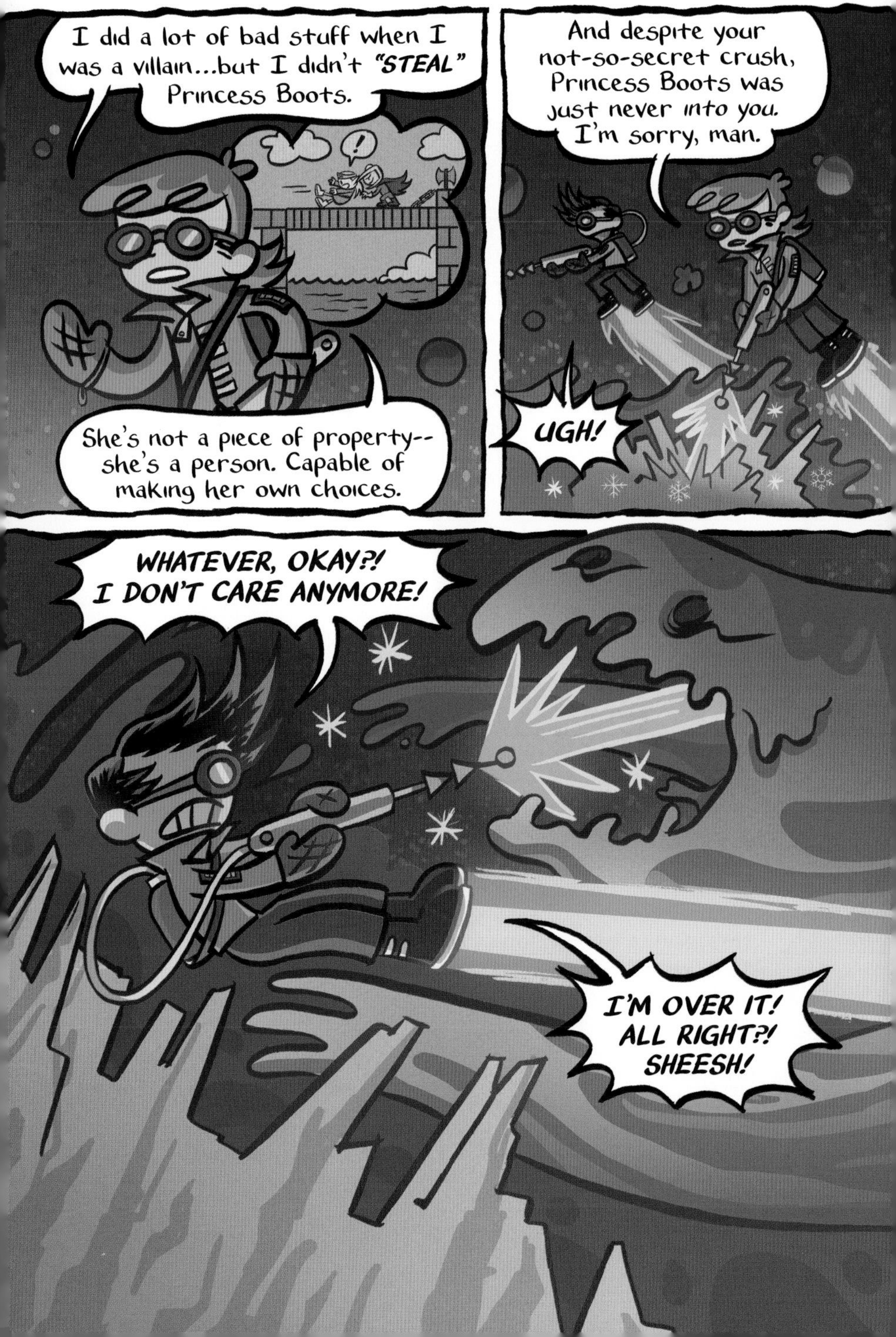

I did a lot of bad stuff when I was a villain...but I didn't "STEAL" Princess Boots.
She's not a piece of property--she's a person. Capable of making her own choices.
And despite your not-so-secret crush, Princess Boots was just never into you. I'm sorry, man.
UGH!
WHATEVER, OKAY?! I DON'T CARE ANYMORE!
I'M OVER IT! ALL RIGHT?! SHEESH!

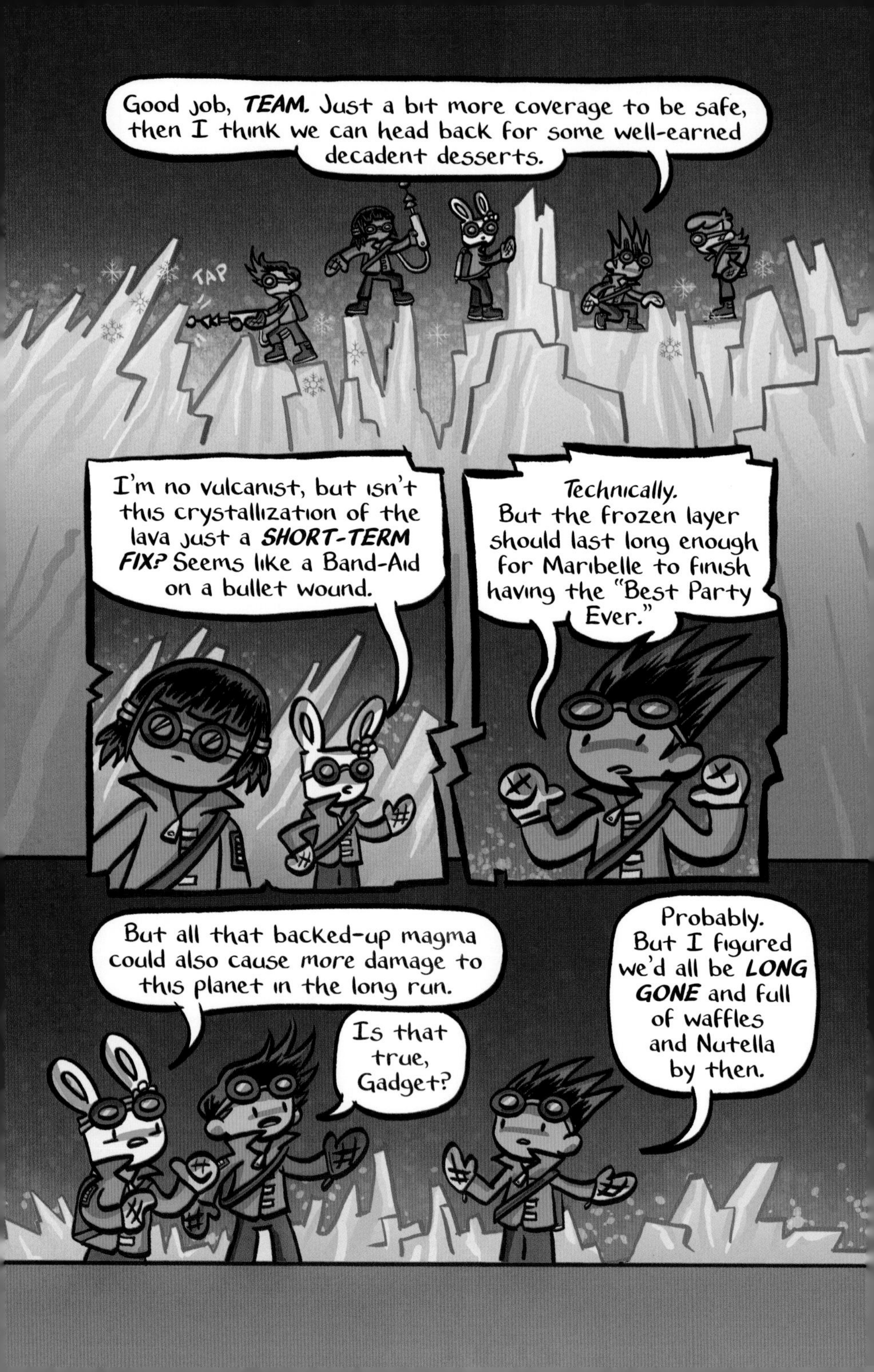
Good job, TEAM. Just a bit more coverage to be safe, then I think we can head back for some well-earned decadent desserts.
TAP
I'm no vulcanist, but isn't this crystallization of the lava just a SHORT-TERM FIX? Seems like a Band-Aid on a bullet wound.
Technically. But the frozen layer should last long enough for Maribelle to finish having the "Best Party Ever."
But all that backed-up magma could also cause more damage to this planet in the long run.
Is that true, Gadget?
Probably. But I figured we'd all be LONG GONE and full of waffles and Nutella by then.

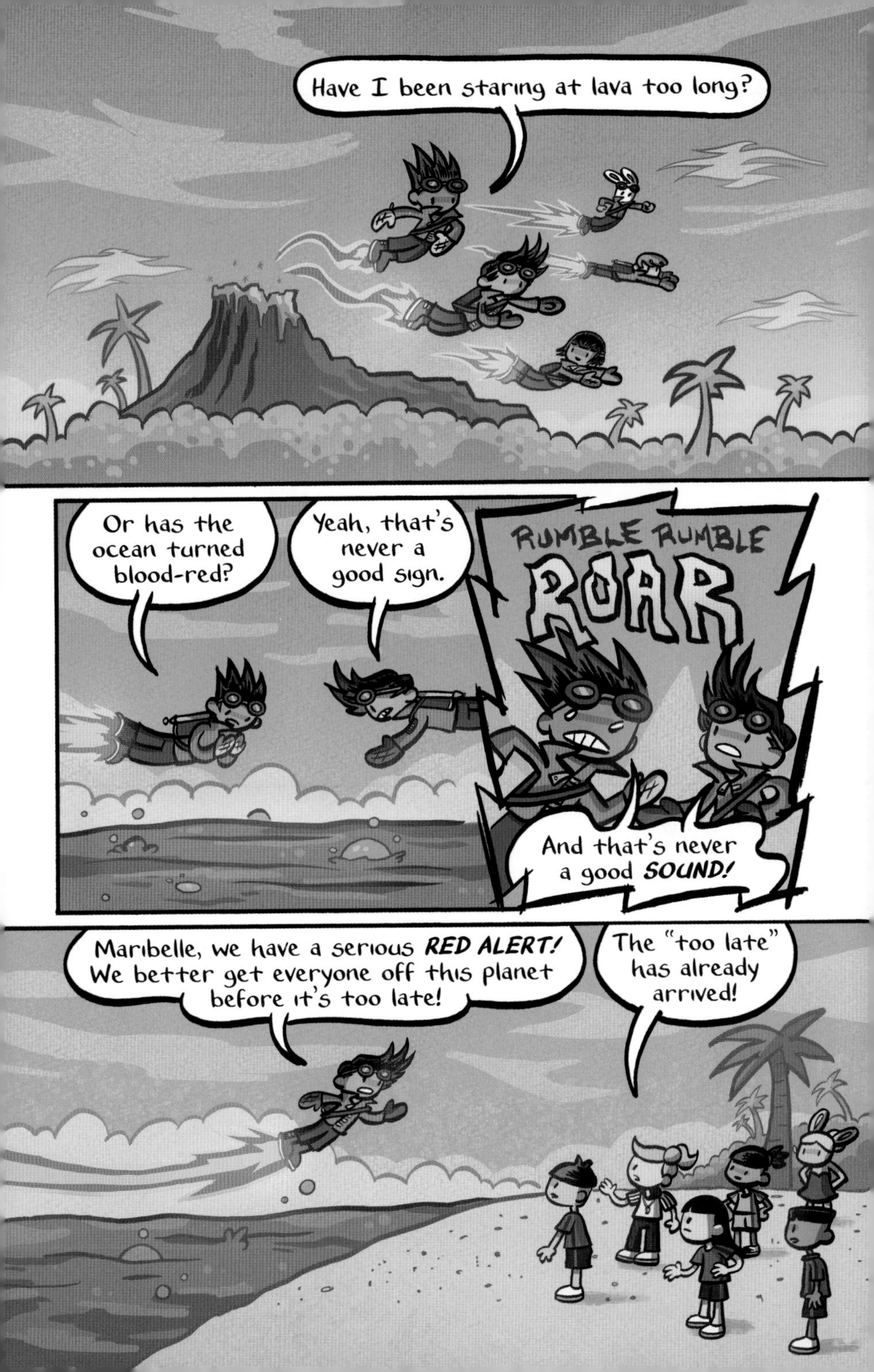
Have I been staring at lava too long?
Or has the ocean turned blood-red?
Yeah, that's never a good sign.
RUMBLE RUMBLE
ROAR
And that's never a good SOUND!
Maribelle, we have a serious RED ALERT! We better get everyone off this planet before it's too late!
The "too late" has already arrived!

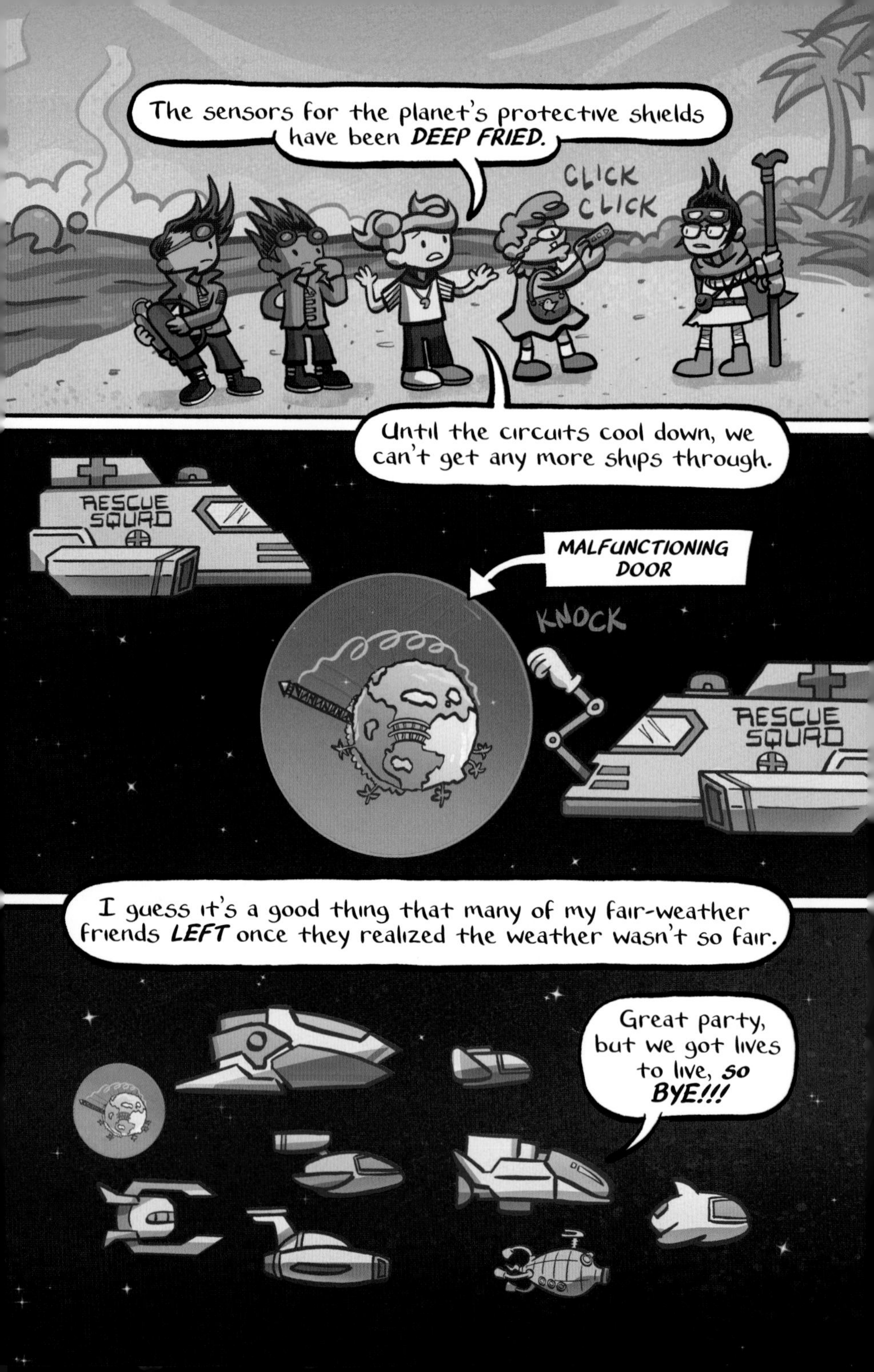
The sensors for the planet's protective shields have been DEEP FRIED.
CLICK CLICK
Until the circuits cool down, we can't get any more ships through.
RESCUE SQUAD
MALFUNCTIONING DOOR
KNOCK
RESCUE SQUAD
I guess it's a good thing that many of my fair-weather friends LEFT once they realized the weather wasn't so fair.
Great party, but we got lives to live, SO BYE!!!

So, like...

We're totally *TRAPPED?*

FLAIL   FLAIL

No! Because your tech skills are gonna find a work-around!

That's a lot of *PRESSURE.*

On top of what's already a lot of volcanic pressure.

What happened to that *CAN-DO* spirit? You can rise to this challenge before that lava rises to the surface.

I'm just gonna leave this in your capable hands, okay?

THANKS!

Go Volcanic Team 5! *Whoo!*

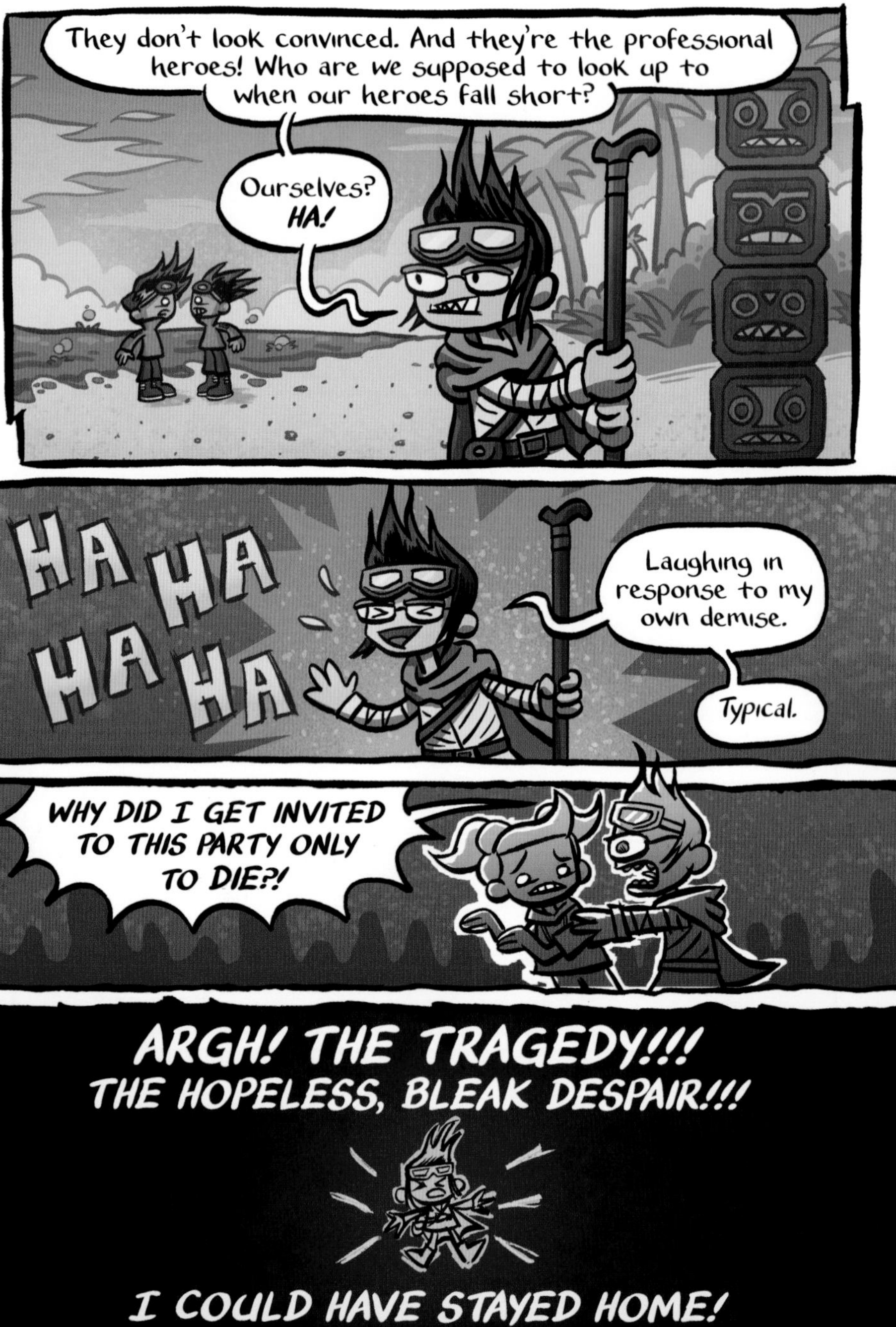
They don't look convinced. And they're the professional heroes! Who are we supposed to look up to when our heroes fall short?
Ourselves? HA!
HA HA HA HA HA HA
Laughing in response to my own demise.
Typical.
WHY DID I GET INVITED TO THIS PARTY ONLY TO DIE?!
ARGH! THE TRAGEDY!!!
THE HOPELESS, BLEAK DESPAIR!!!
I COULD HAVE STAYED HOME!

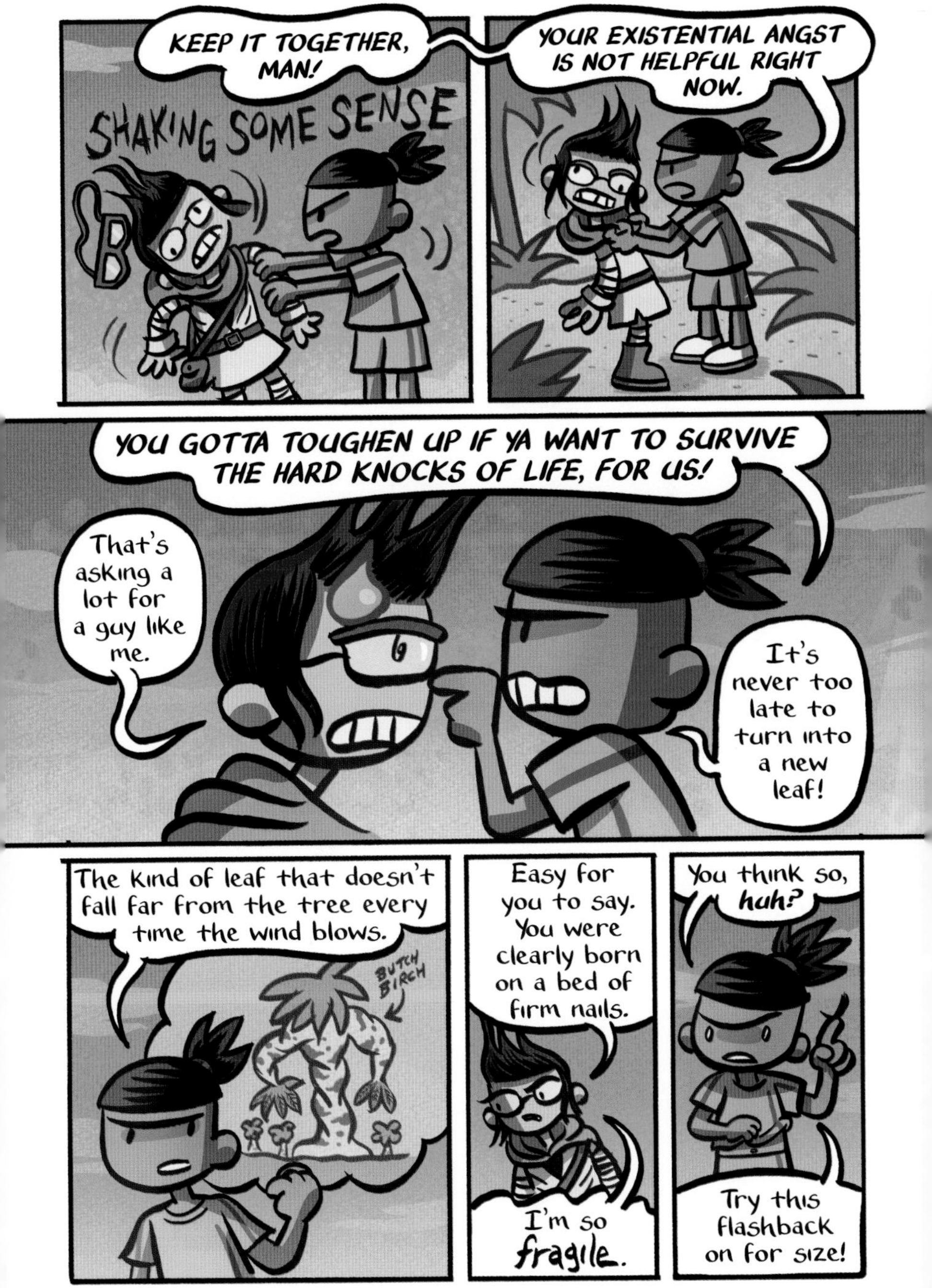
KEEP IT TOGETHER, MAN!
SHAKING SOME SENSE
YOUR EXISTENTIAL ANGST IS NOT HELPFUL RIGHT NOW.
YOU GOTTA TOUGHEN UP IF YA WANT TO SURVIVE THE HARD KNOCKS OF LIFE, FOR US!
That's asking a lot for a guy like me.
It's never too late to turn into a new leaf!
The kind of leaf that doesn't fall far from the tree every time the wind blows.
BUTCH BIRCH
Easy for you to say. You were clearly born on a bed of firm nails.
I'm so fragile.
You think so, huh?
Try this flashback on for size!

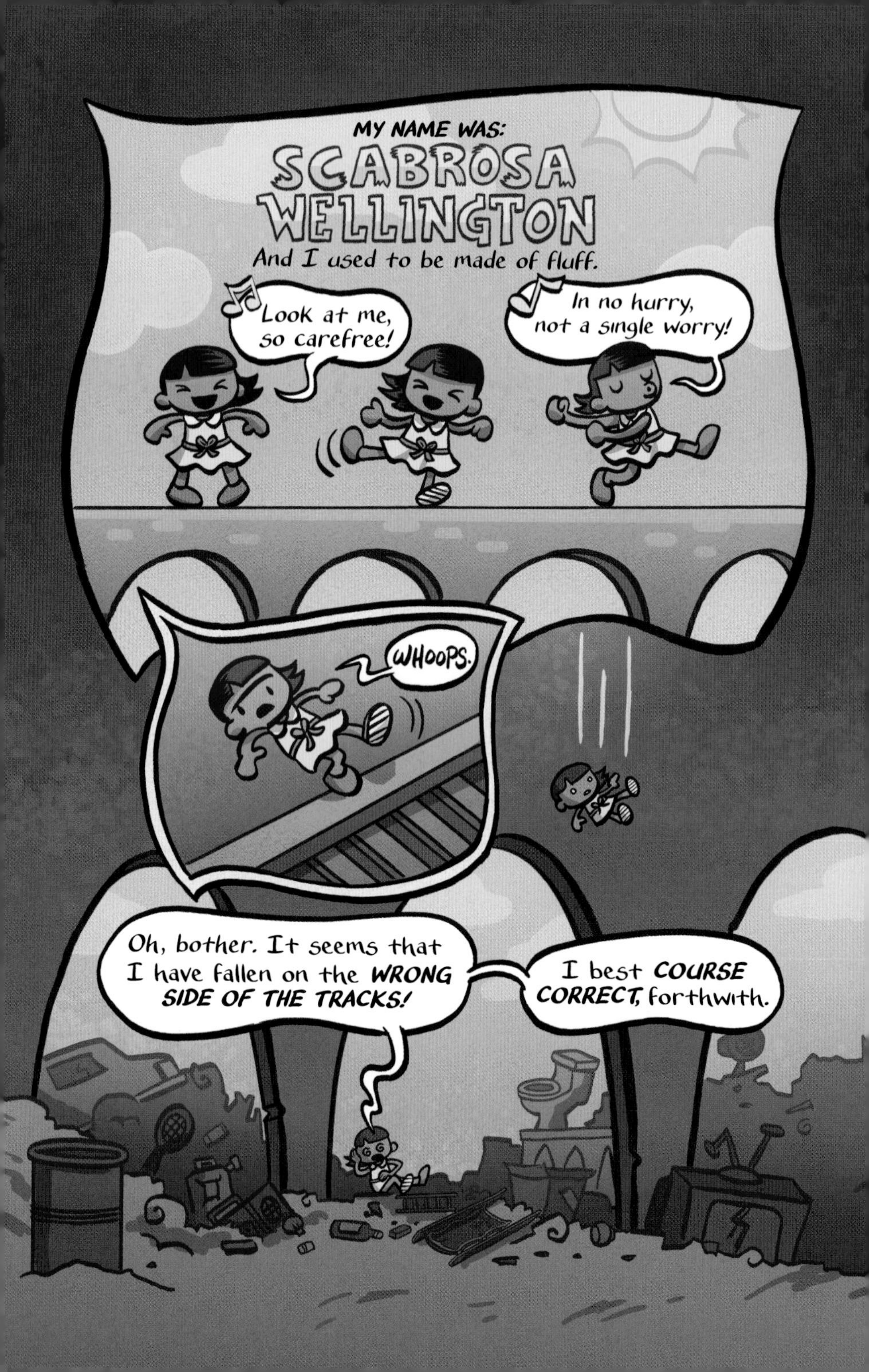
MY NAME WAS:
SCABROSA WELLINGTON
And I used to be made of fluff.
Look at me, so carefree!
In no hurry, not a single worry!
WHOOPS.
Oh, bother. It seems that I have fallen on the WRONG SIDE OF THE TRACKS!
I best COURSE CORRECT, forthwith.

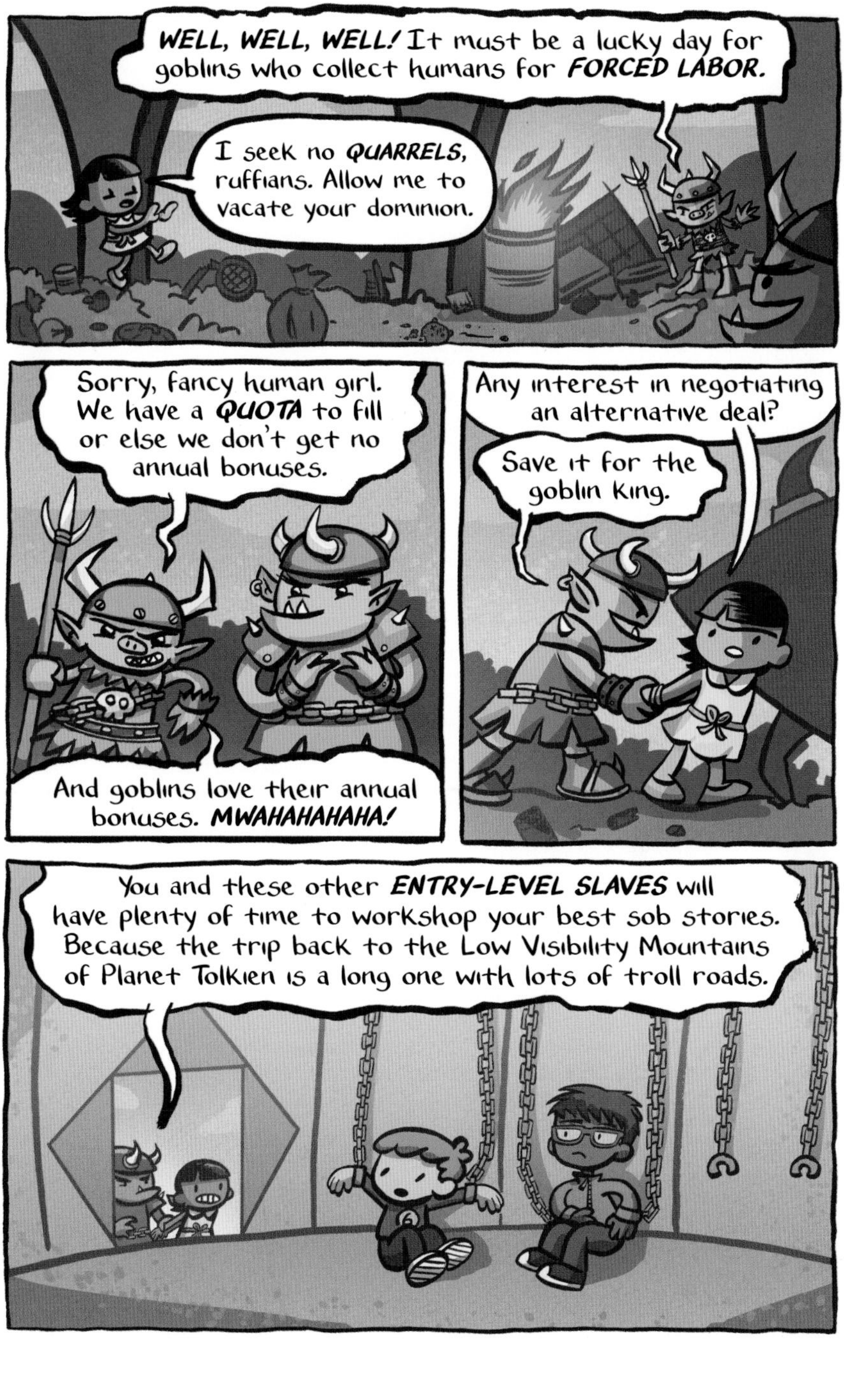
WELL, WELL, WELL! It must be a lucky day for goblins who collect humans for FORCED LABOR.
I seek no QUARRELS, ruffians. Allow me to vacate your dominion.
Sorry, fancy human girl. We have a QUOTA to fill or else we don't get no annual bonuses.
And goblins love their annual bonuses. MWAHAHAHAHA!
Any interest in negotiating an alternative deal?
Save it for the goblin King.
You and these other ENTRY-LEVEL SLAVES will have plenty of time to workshop your best sob stories. Because the trip back to the Low Visibility Mountains of Planet Tolkien is a long one with lots of troll roads.

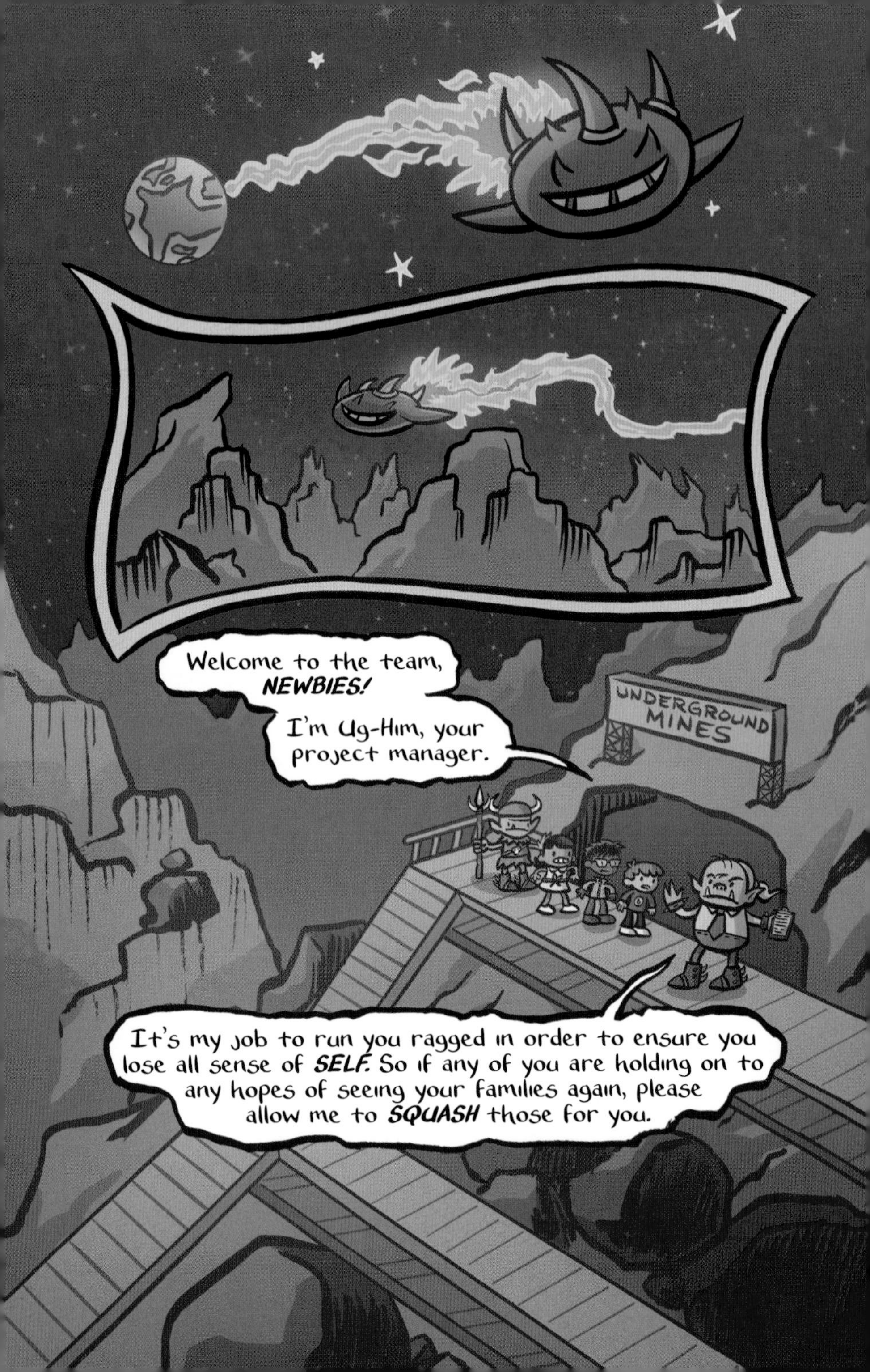
Welcome to the team, NEWBIES!
I'm Ug-Him, your project manager.
UNDERGROUND MINES
It's my job to run you ragged in order to ensure you lose all sense of SELF. So if any of you are holding on to any hopes of seeing your families again, please allow me to SQUASH those for you.

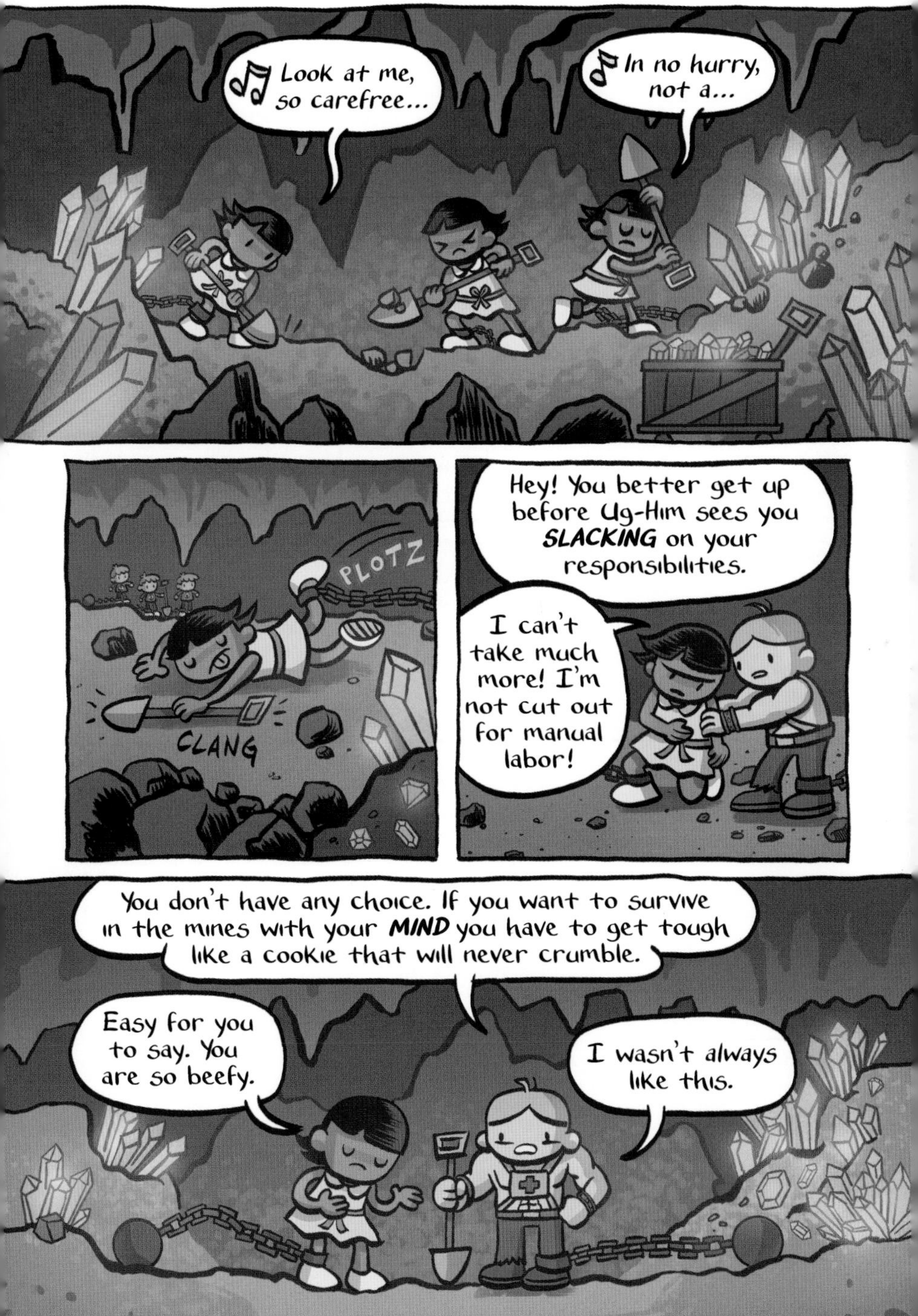
Look at me, so carefree...
In no hurry, not a...
PLOTZ
CLANG
Hey! You better get up before Ug-Him sees you SLACKING on your responsibilities.
I can't take much more! I'm not cut out for manual labor!
You don't have any choice. If you want to survive in the mines with your MIND you have to get tough like a cookie that will never crumble.
Easy for you to say. You are so beefy.
I wasn't always like this.

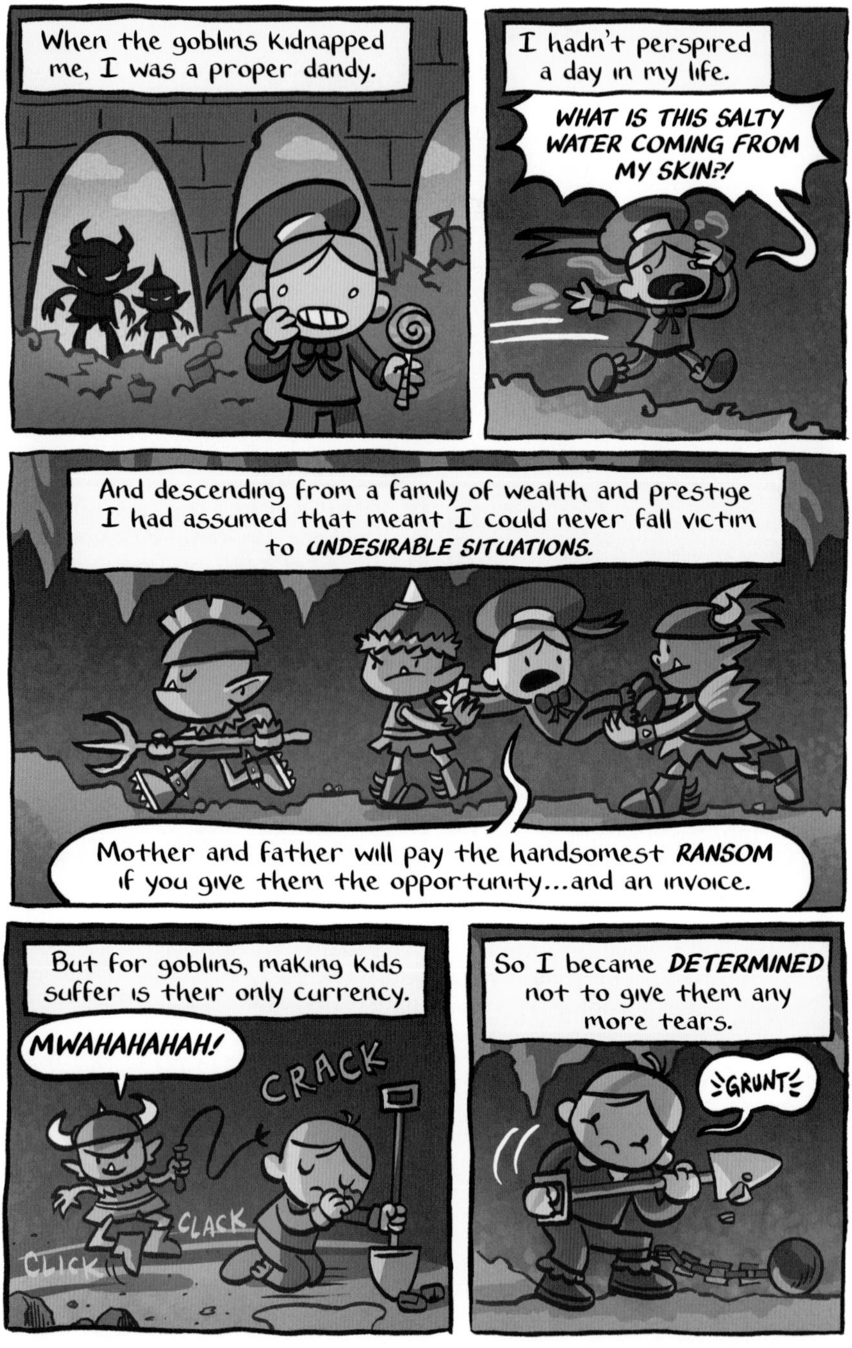
When the goblins kidnapped me, I was a proper dandy.
I hadn't perspired a day in my life.
WHAT IS THIS SALTY WATER COMING FROM MY SKIN?!
And descending from a family of wealth and prestige I had assumed that meant I could never fall victim to UNDESIRABLE SITUATIONS.
Mother and father will pay the handsomest RANSOM if you give them the opportunity...and an invoice.
But for goblins, making kids suffer is their only currency.
MWAHAHAHAH!
CRACK
CLACK
CLICK
So I became DETERMINED not to give them any more tears.
GRUNT

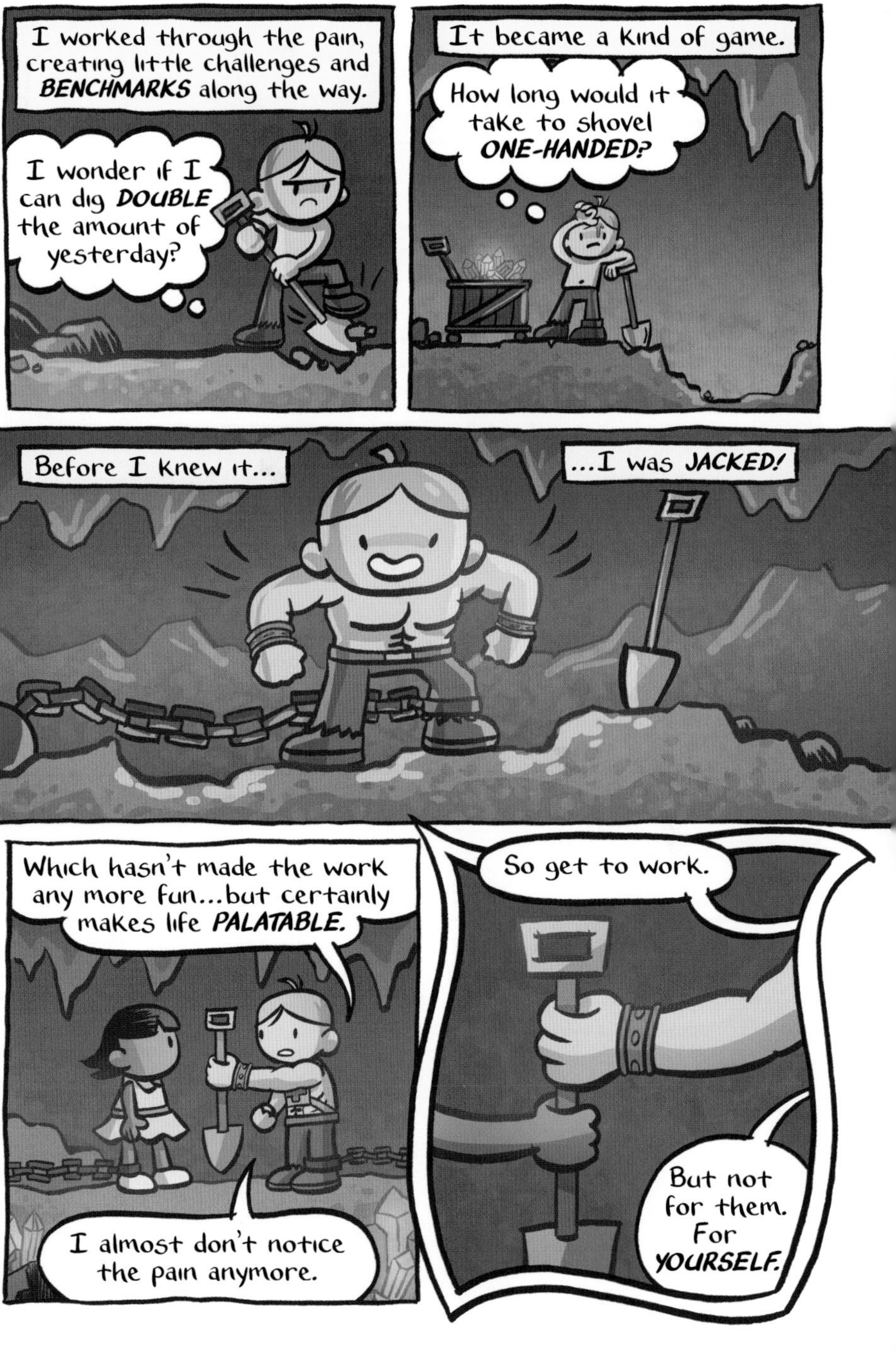

I worked through the pain, creating little challenges and **BENCHMARKS** along the way.
I wonder if I can dig **DOUBLE** the amount of yesterday?
It became a kind of game.
How long would it take to shovel **ONE-HANDED?**
Before I knew it...
...I was **JACKED!**
Which hasn't made the work any more fun...but certainly makes life **PALATABLE.**
I almost don't notice the pain anymore.
So get to work.
But not for them. For **YOURSELF.**

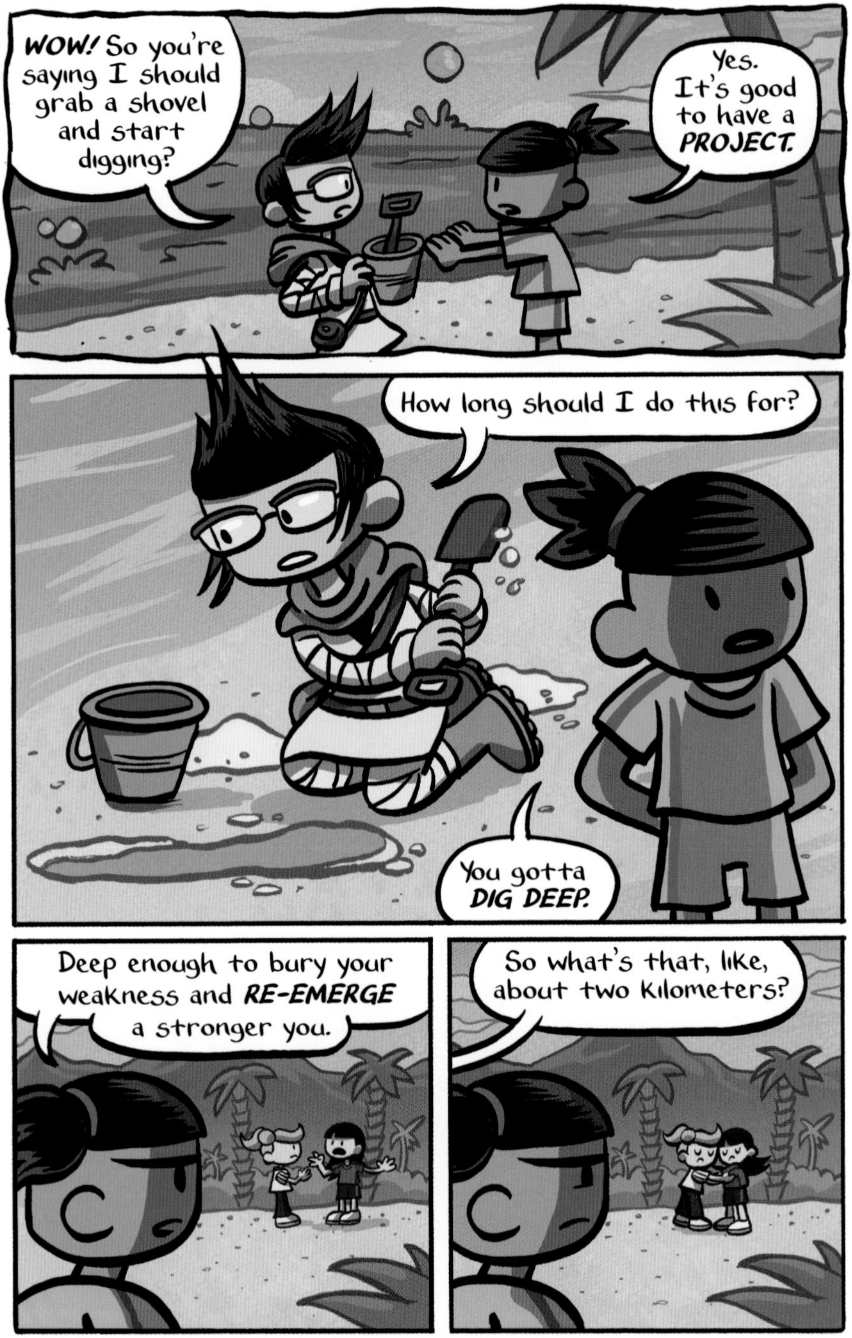
WOW! So you're saying I should grab a shovel and start digging?
Yes. It's good to have a PROJECT.
How long should I do this for?
You gotta DIG DEEP.
Deep enough to bury your weakness and RE-EMERGE a stronger you.
So what's that, like, about two kilometers?

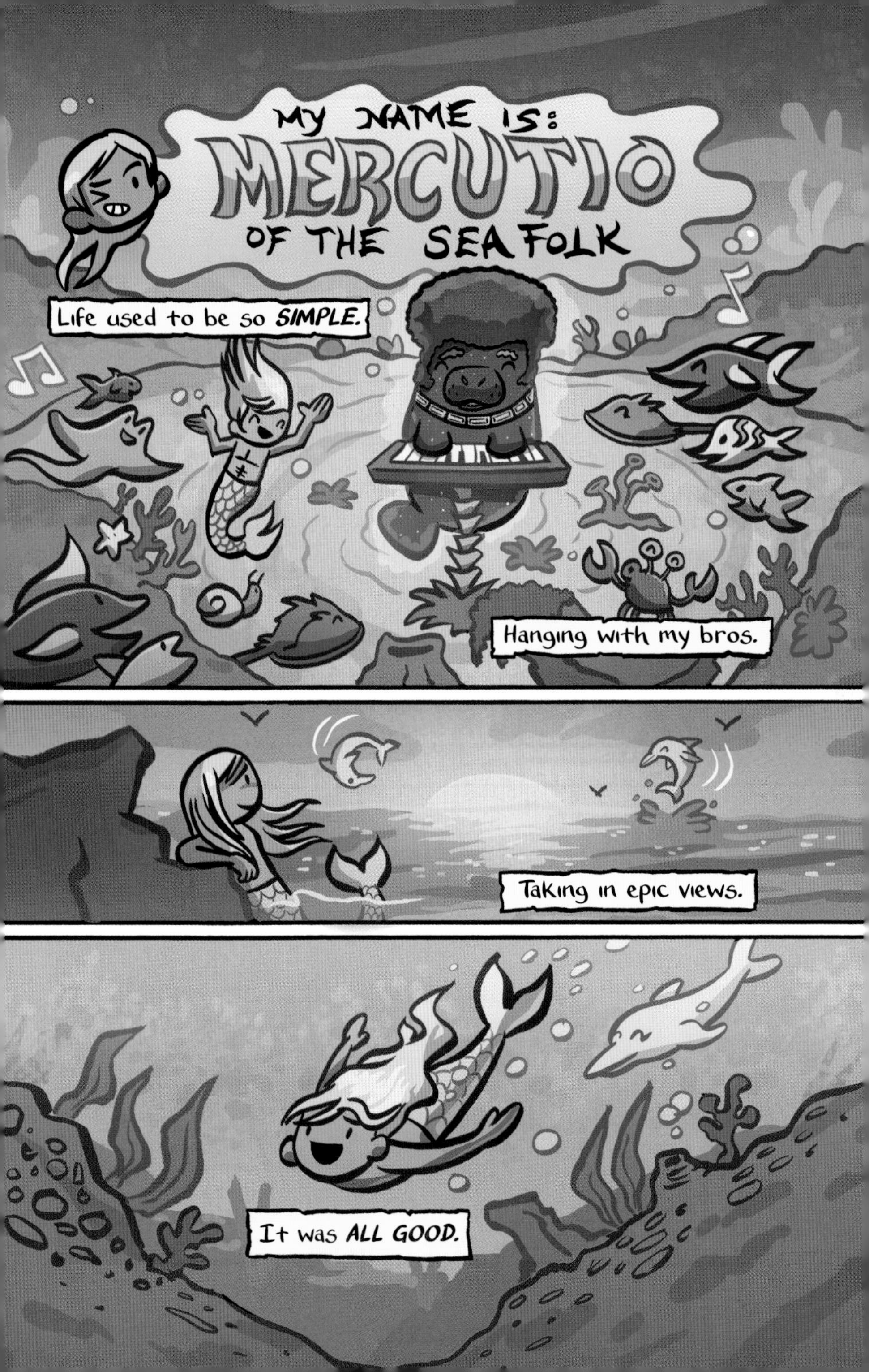
MY NAME IS:
MERCUTIO
OF THE SEA FOLK
Life used to be so SIMPLE.
Hanging with my bros.
Taking in epic views.
It was ALL GOOD.

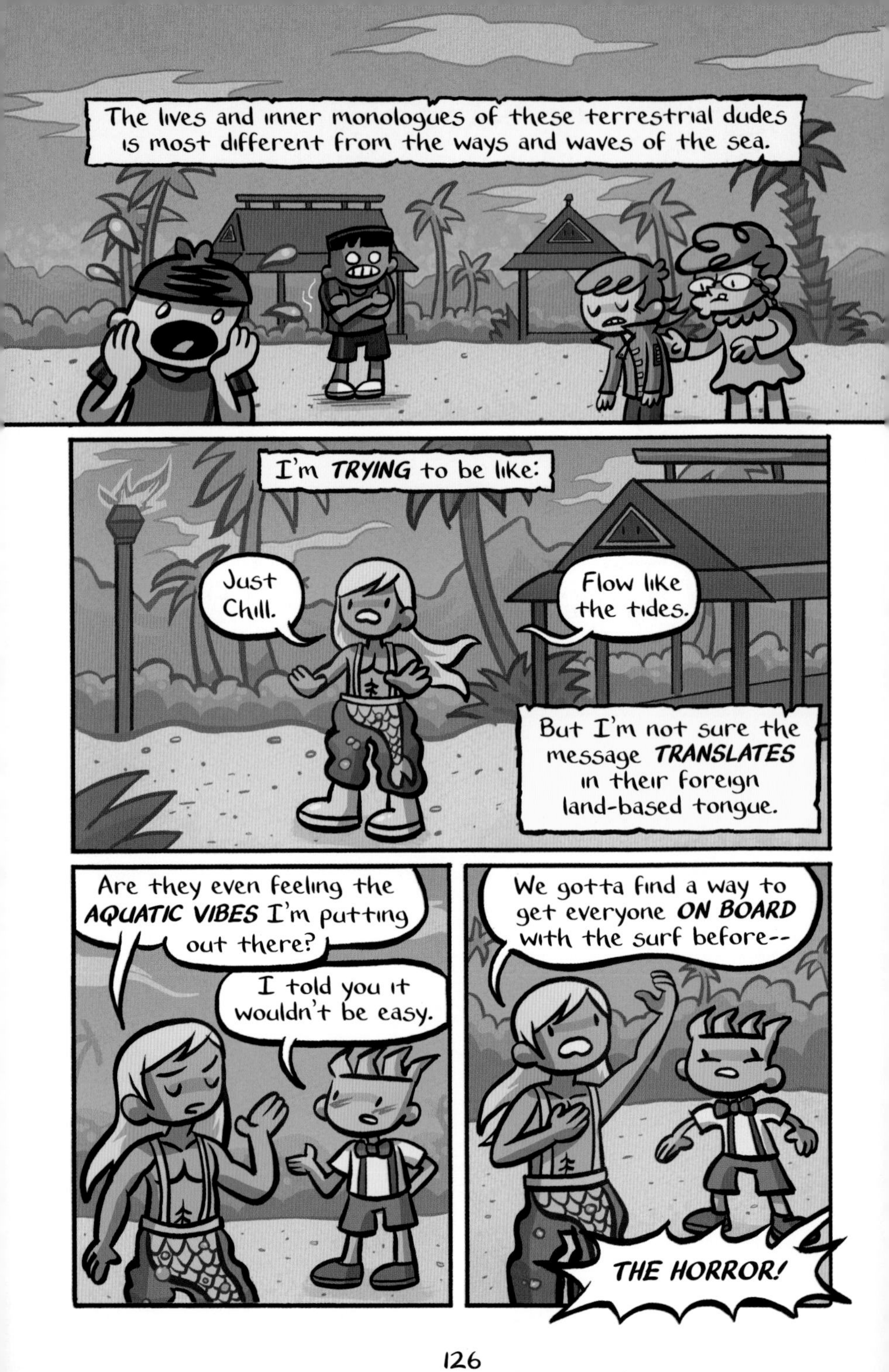
The lives and inner monologues of these terrestrial dudes is most different from the ways and waves of the sea.
I'm **TRYING** to be like:
Just Chill.
Flow like the tides.
But I'm not sure the message **TRANSLATES** in their foreign land-based tongue.
Are they even feeling the **AQUATIC VIBES** I'm putting out there?
I told you it wouldn't be easy.
We gotta find a way to get everyone **ON BOARD** with the surf before--
THE HORROR!

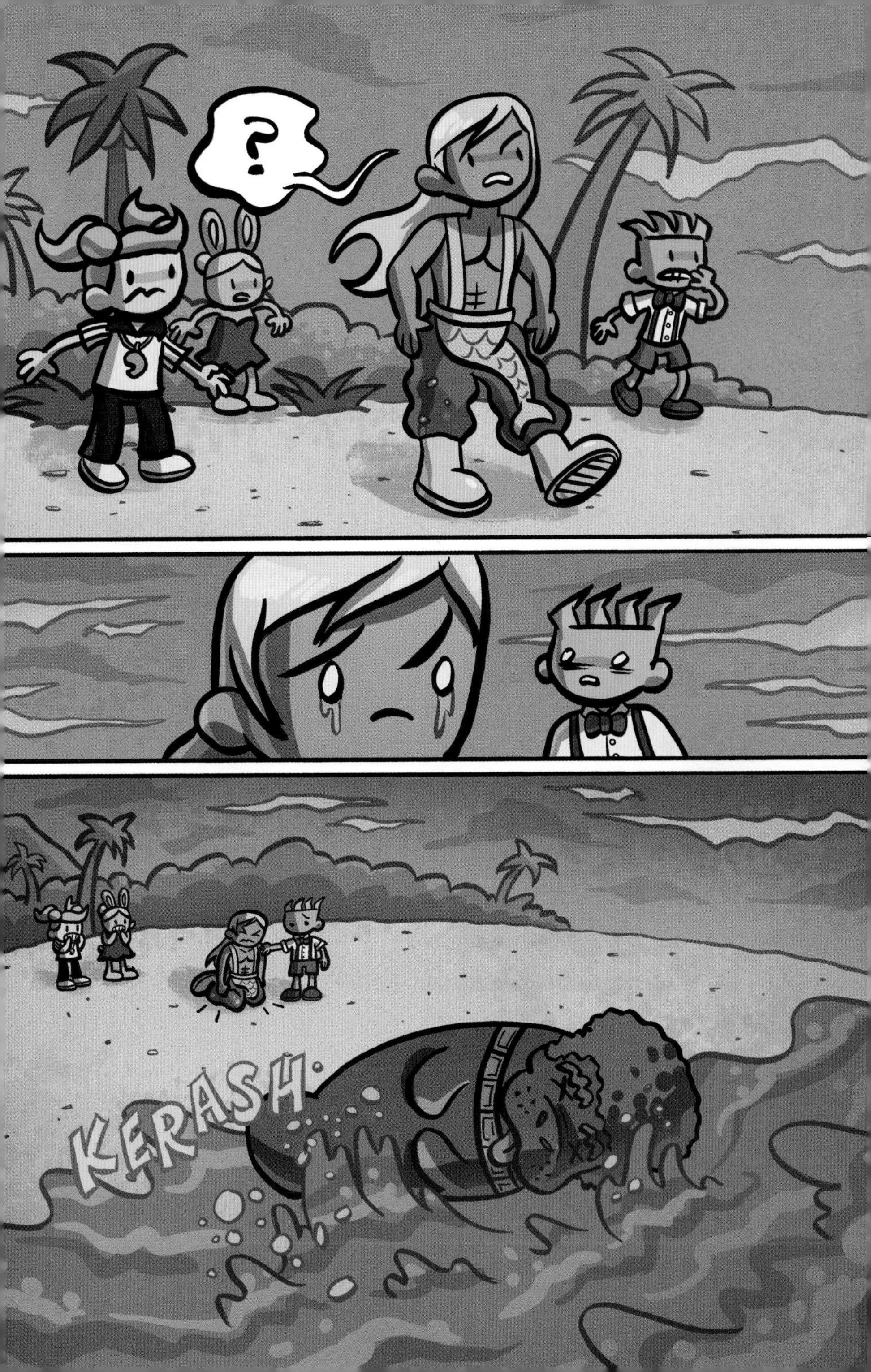
?
KERASH

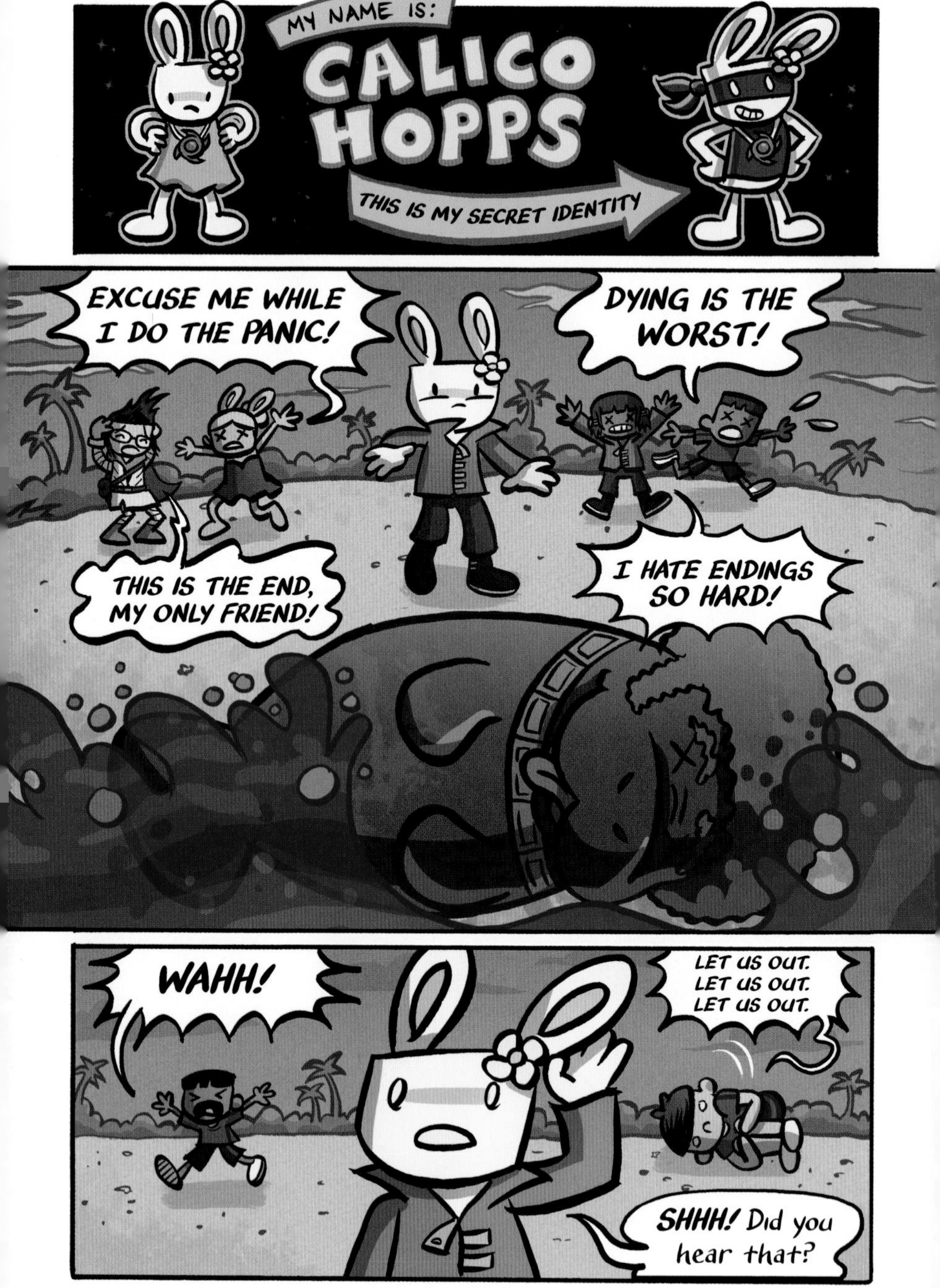
MY NAME IS:
CALICO HOPPS
THIS IS MY SECRET IDENTITY
EXCUSE ME WHILE I DO THE PANIC!
DYING IS THE WORST!
THIS IS THE END, MY ONLY FRIEND!
I HATE ENDINGS SO HARD!
WAHH!
LET US OUT. LET US OUT. LET US OUT.
SHHH! Did you hear that?

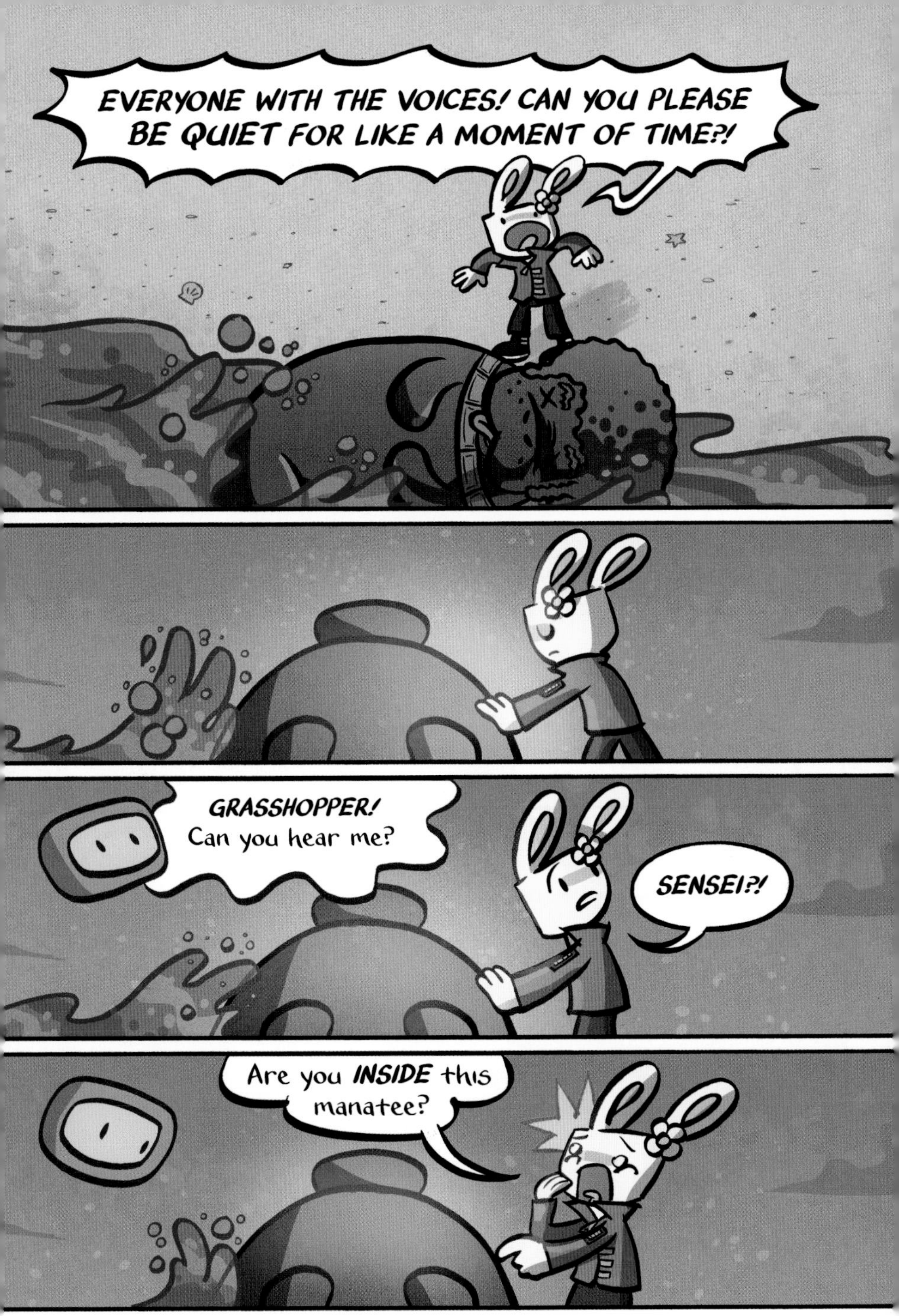
EVERYONE WITH THE VOICES! CAN YOU PLEASE BE QUIET FOR LIKE A MOMENT OF TIME?!
GRASSHOPPER! Can you hear me?
SENSEI?!
Are you INSIDE this manatee?

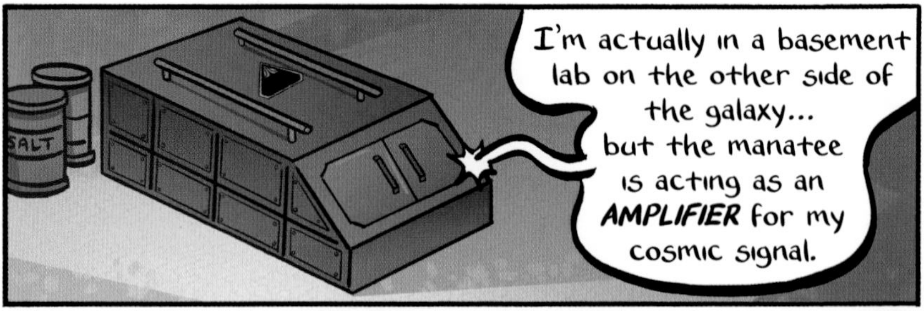
I'm actually in a basement lab on the other side of the galaxy... but the manatee is acting as an AMPLIFIER for my cosmic signal.
SALT

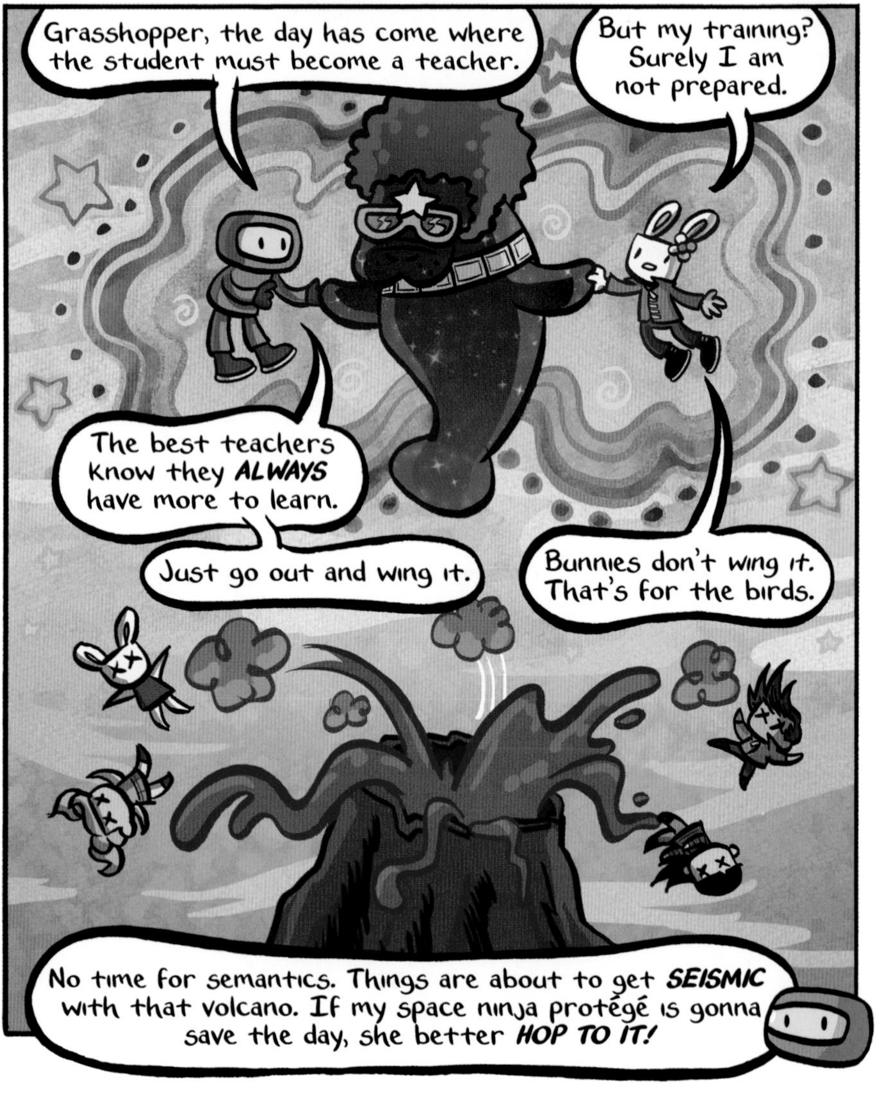
Grasshopper, the day has come where the student must become a teacher.
But my training? Surely I am not prepared.
The best teachers know they ALWAYS have more to learn.
Just go out and wing it.
Bunnies don't wing it. That's for the birds.
No time for semantics. Things are about to get SEISMIC with that volcano. If my space ninja protégé is gonna save the day, she better HOP TO IT!

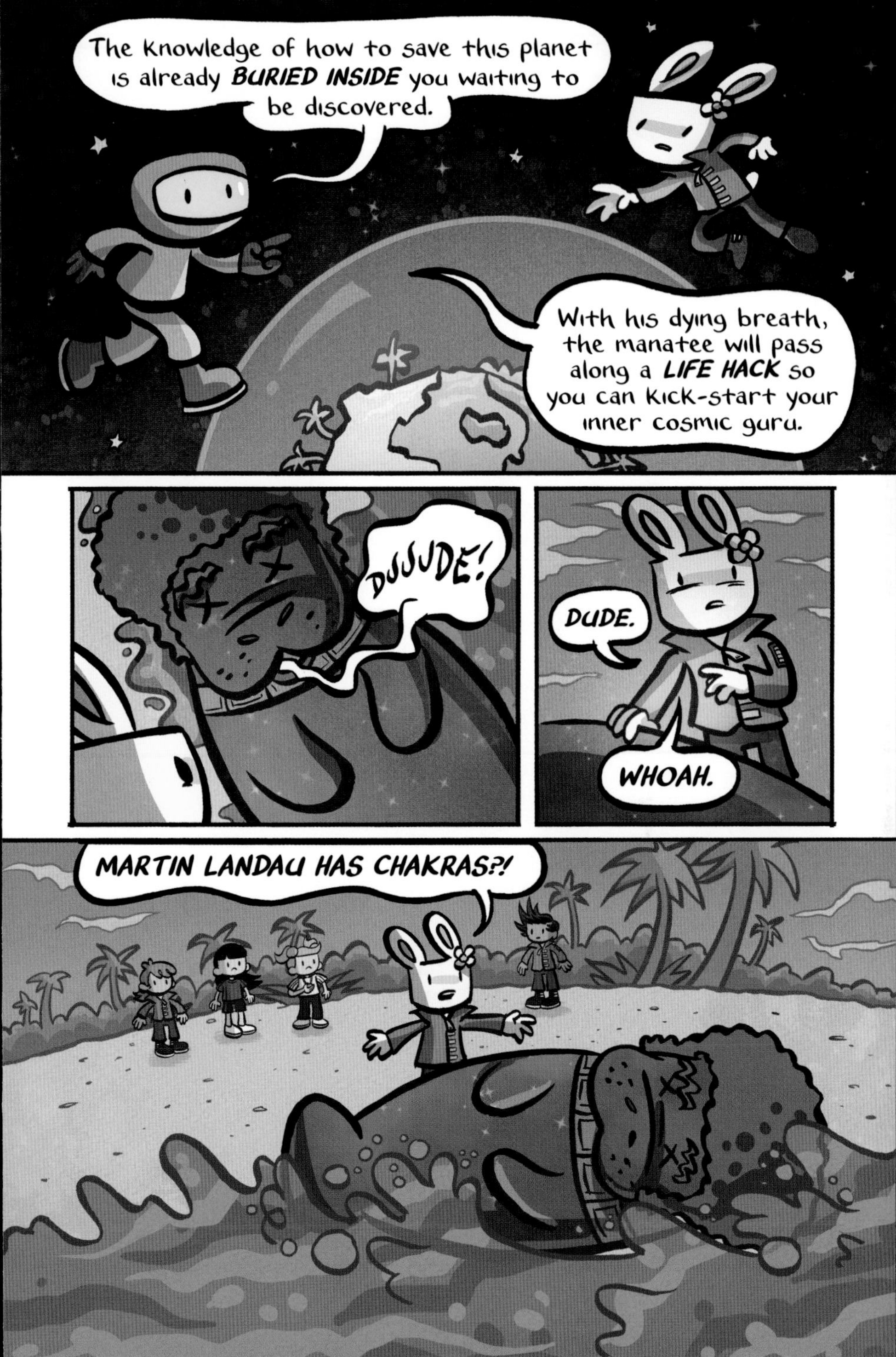
The knowledge of how to save this planet is already BURIED INSIDE you waiting to be discovered.
With his dying breath, the manatee will pass along a LIFE HACK so you can kick-start your inner cosmic guru.
DUUUDE!
DUDE.
WHOAH.
MARTIN LANDAU HAS CHAKRAS?!

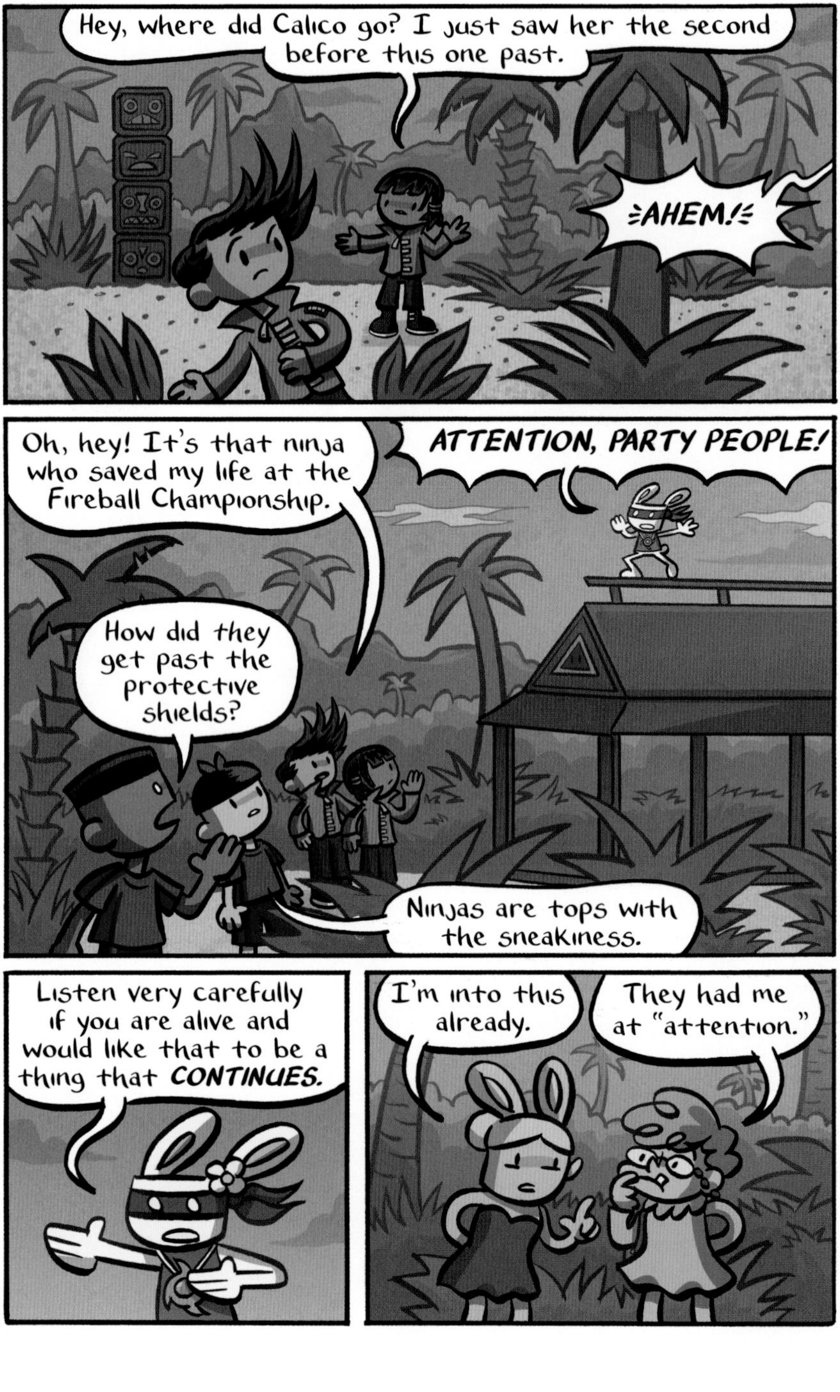
Hey, where did Calico go? I just saw her the second before this one past.
AHEM!
Oh, hey! It's that ninja who saved my life at the Fireball Championship.
ATTENTION, PARTY PEOPLE!
How did they get past the protective shields?
Ninjas are tops with the sneakiness.
Listen very carefully if you are alive and would like that to be a thing that CONTINUES.
I'm into this already.
They had me at "attention."

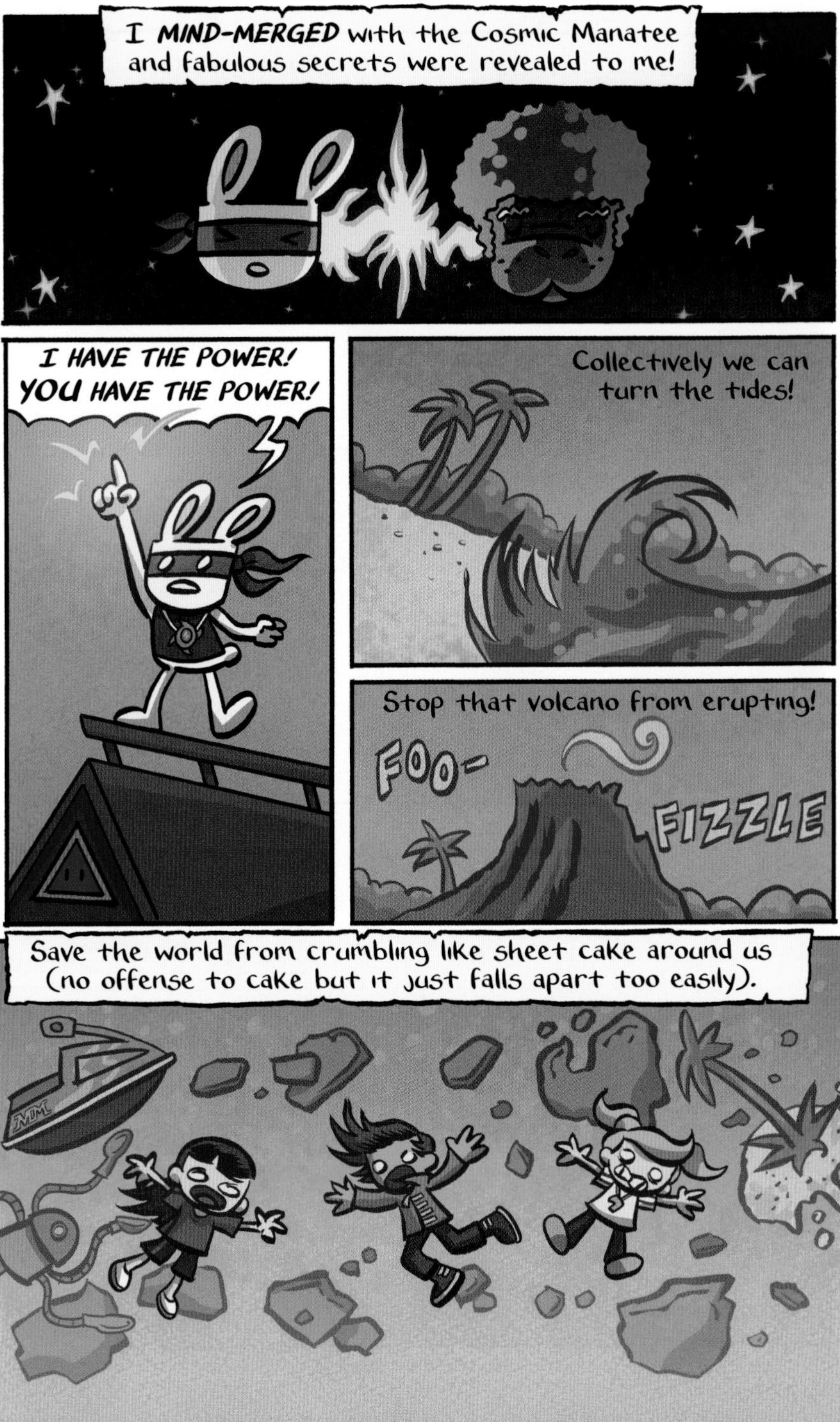
I MIND-MERGED with the Cosmic Manatee and fabulous secrets were revealed to me!
I HAVE THE POWER! YOU HAVE THE POWER!
Collectively we can turn the tides!
Stop that volcano from erupting!
FOO-
FIZZLE
Save the world from crumbling like sheet cake around us (no offense to cake but it just falls apart too easily).
NM

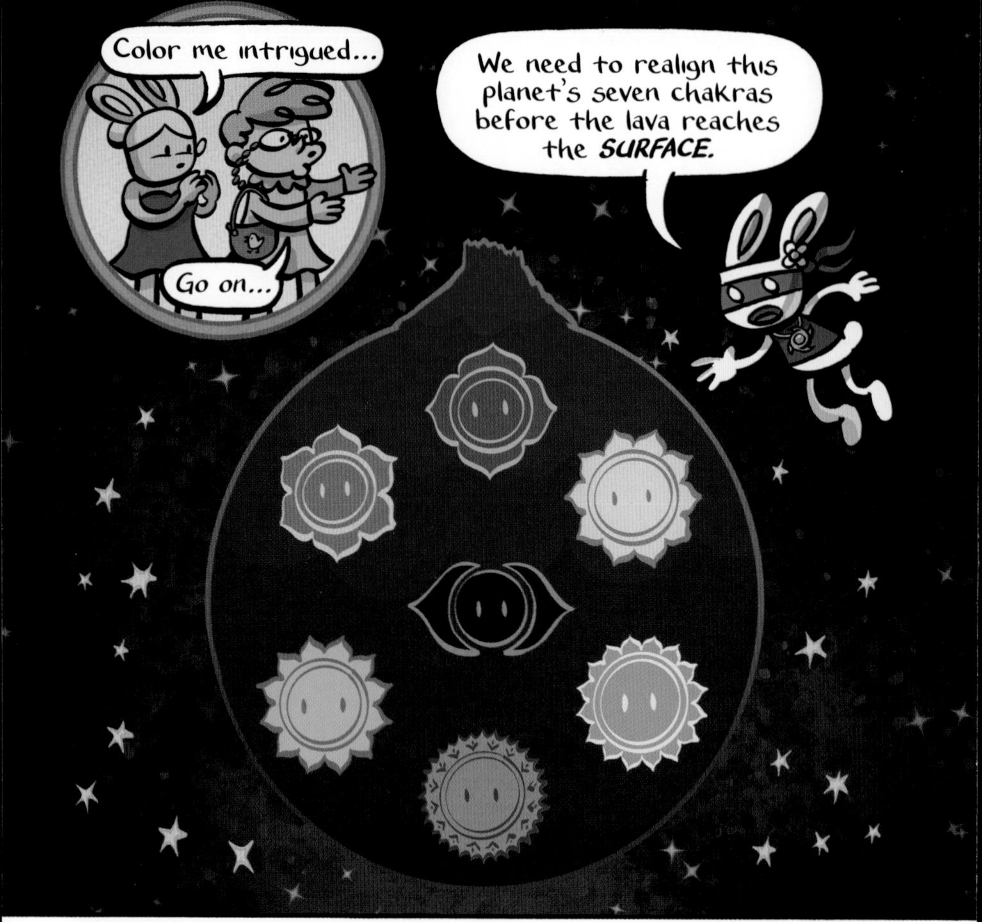
Color me intrigued...
Go on...
We need to realign this planet's seven chakras before the lava reaches the SURFACE.

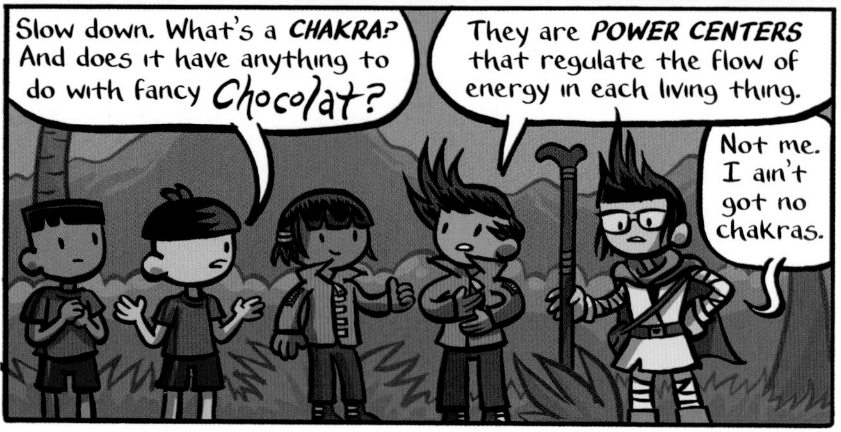
Slow down. What's a CHAKRA? And does it have anything to do with fancy Chocolat?
They are POWER CENTERS that regulate the flow of energy in each living thing.
Not me. I ain't got no chakras.

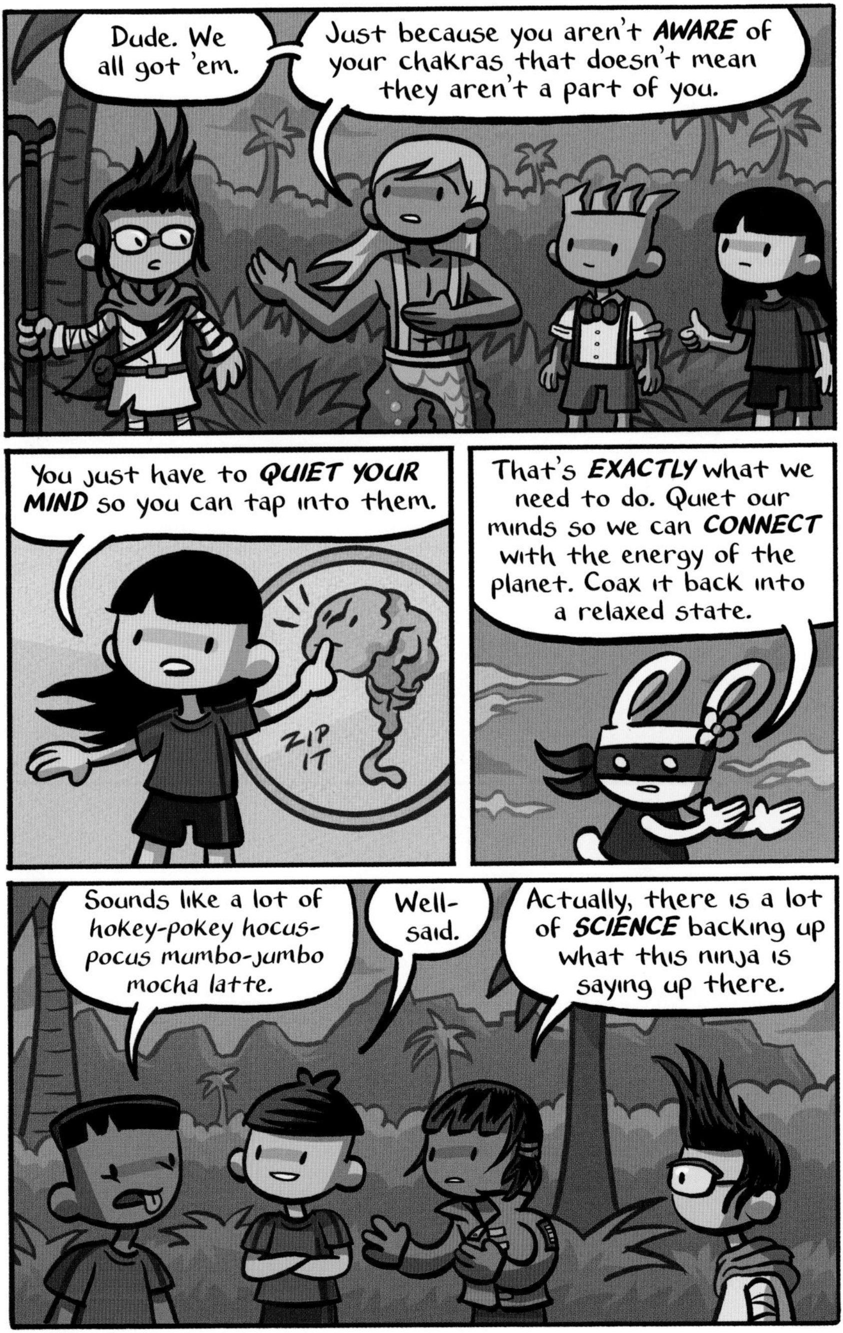
Dude. We all got 'em.
Just because you aren't AWARE of your chakras that doesn't mean they aren't a part of you.
You just have to QUIET YOUR MIND so you can tap into them.
ZIP IT
That's EXACTLY what we need to do. Quiet our minds so we can CONNECT with the energy of the planet. Coax it back into a relaxed state.
Sounds like a lot of hokey-pokey hocus-pocus mumbo-jumbo mocha latte.
Well-said.
Actually, there is a lot of SCIENCE backing up what this ninja is saying up there.

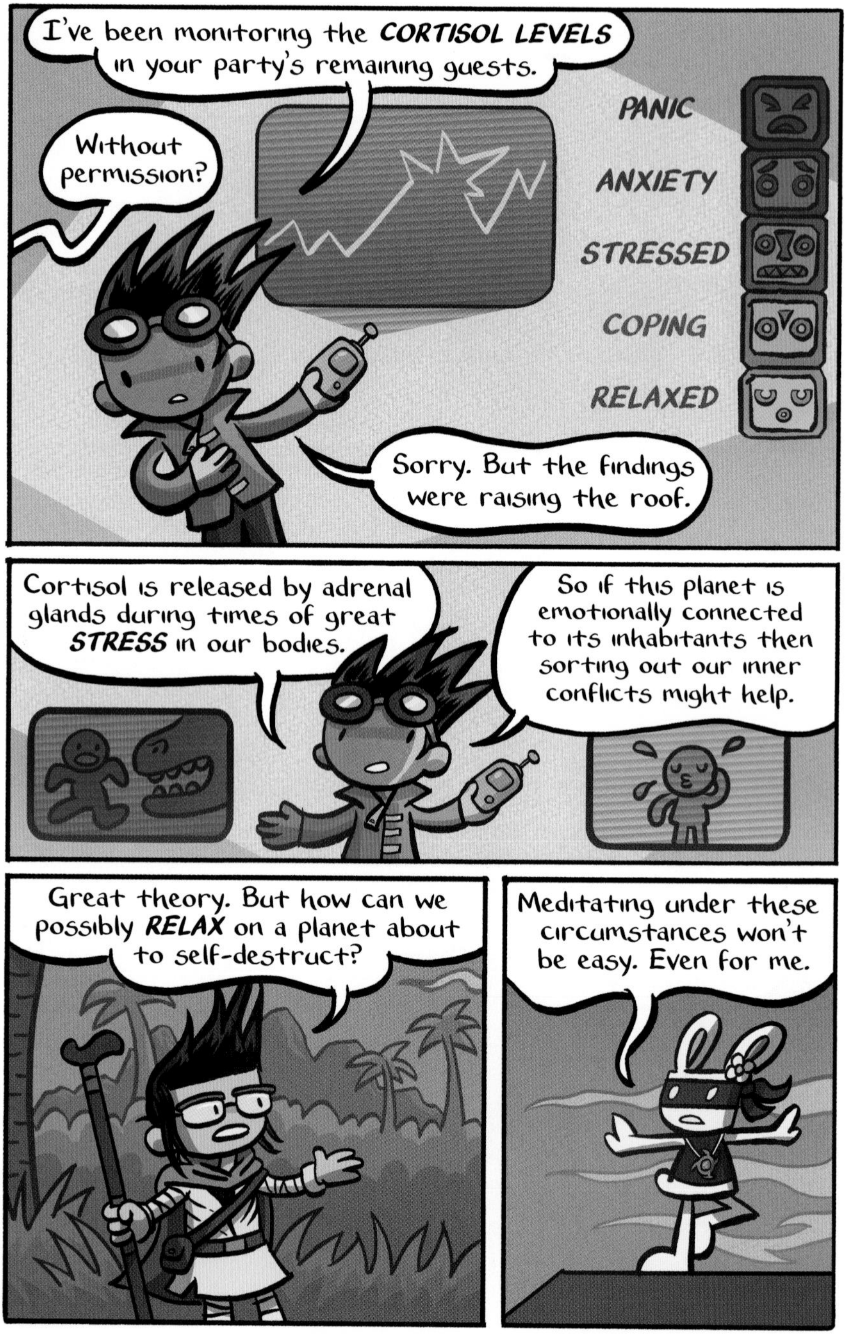
I've been monitoring the CORTISOL LEVELS in your party's remaining guests.
Without permission?
PANIC
ANXIETY
STRESSED
COPING
RELAXED
Sorry. But the findings were raising the roof.
Cortisol is released by adrenal glands during times of great STRESS in our bodies.
So if this planet is emotionally connected to its inhabitants then sorting out our inner conflicts might help.
Great theory. But how can we possibly RELAX on a planet about to self-destruct?
Meditating under these circumstances won't be easy. Even for me.

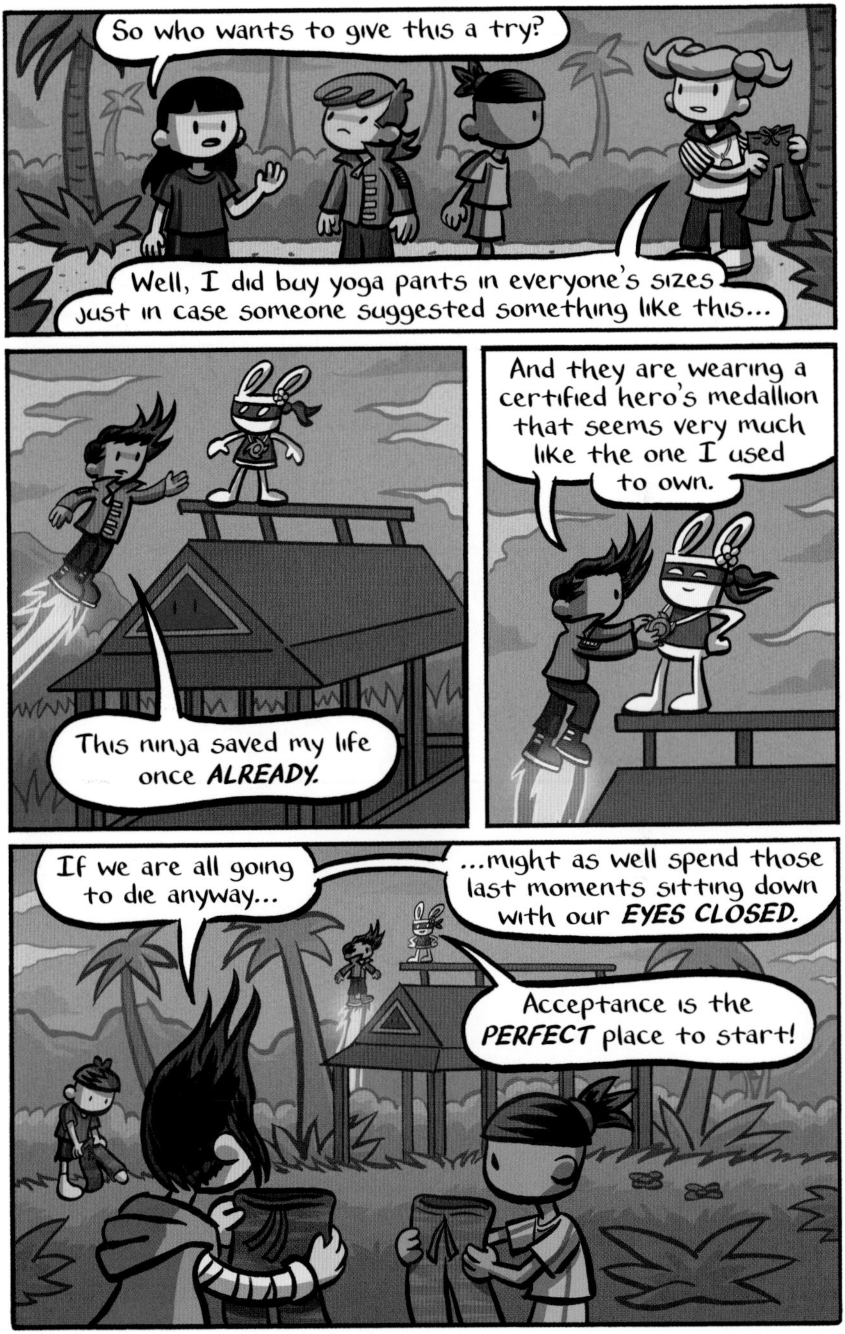
So who wants to give this a try?
Well, I did buy yoga pants in everyone's sizes just in case someone suggested something like this...
This ninja saved my life once ALREADY.
And they are wearing a certified hero's medallion that seems very much like the one I used to own.
If we are all going to die anyway...
...might as well spend those last moments sitting down with our EYES CLOSED.
Acceptance is the PERFECT place to start!

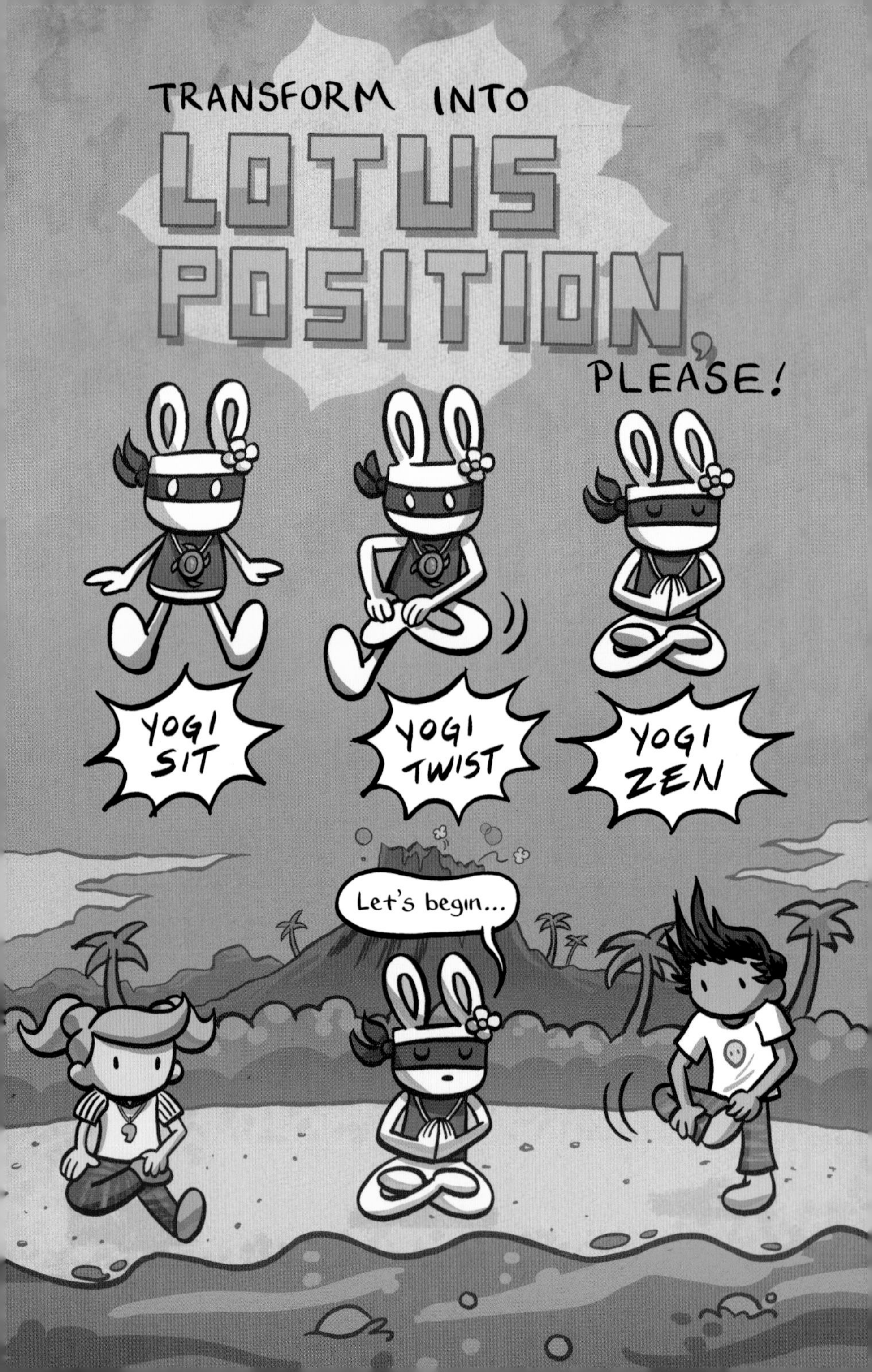
TRANSFORM INTO
LOTUS POSITION,
PLEASE!
YOGI SIT
YOGI TWIST
YOGI ZEN
Let's begin...

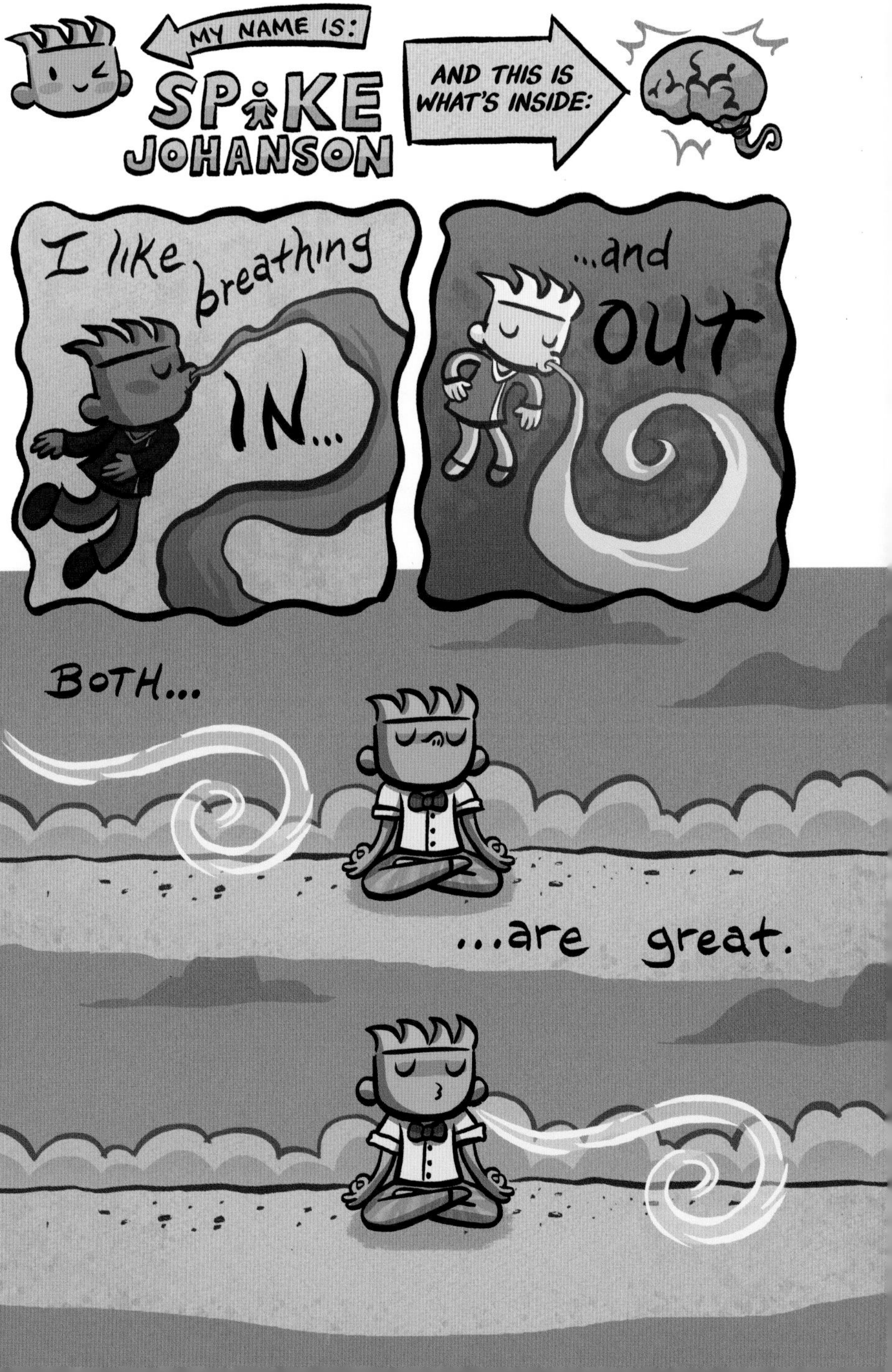
MY NAME IS:
SPIKE JOHANSON
AND THIS IS WHAT'S INSIDE:
I like breathing
IN...
...and
OUT
BOTH...
...are great.

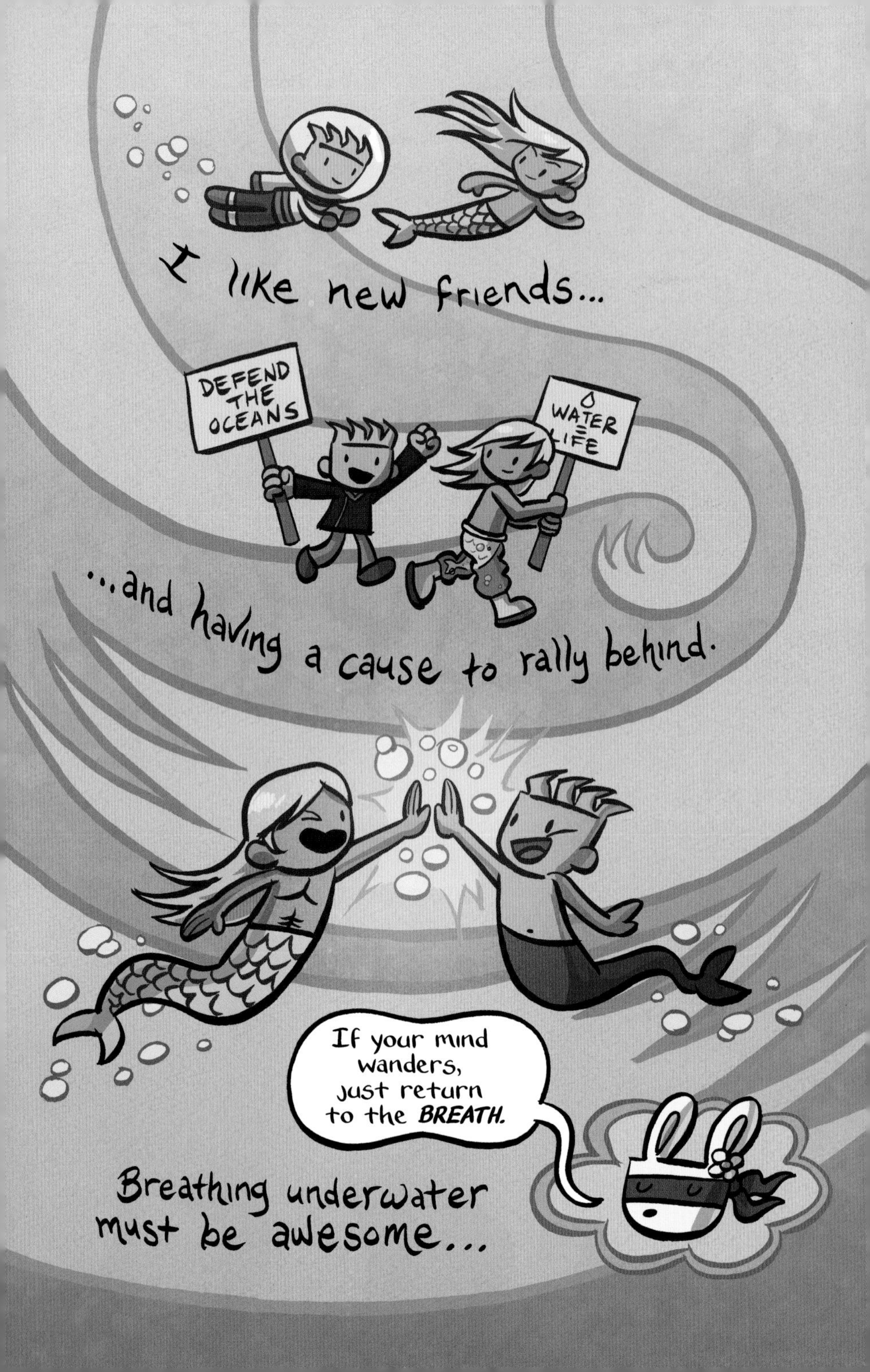
I like new friends...
DEFEND THE OCEANS
WATER = LIFE
...and having a cause to rally behind.
If your mind wanders, just return to the BREATH.
Breathing underwater must be awesome...

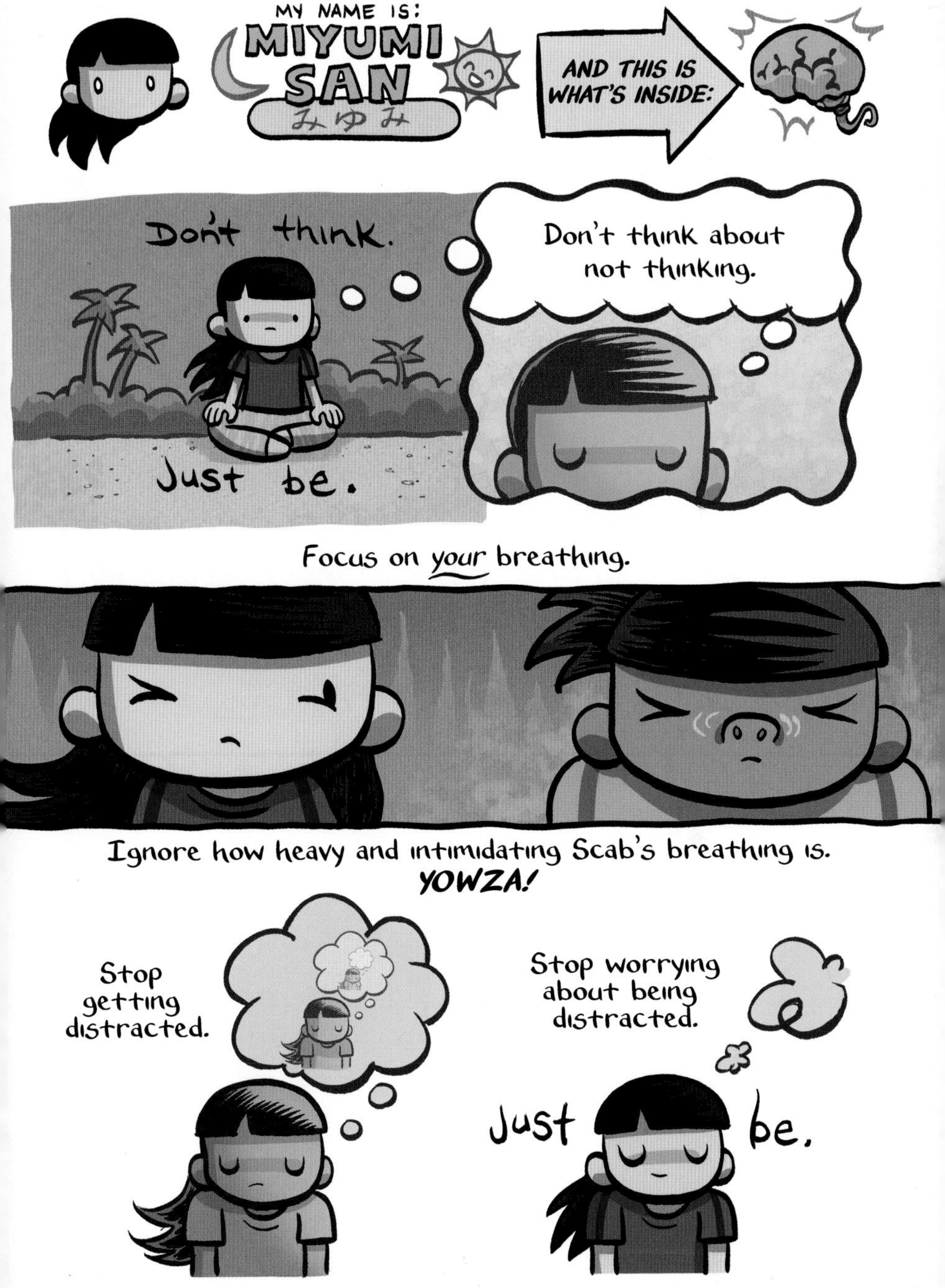

MY NAME IS:
MIYUMI SAN
みゆみ
AND THIS IS WHAT'S INSIDE:
Don't think.
Just be.
Don't think about not thinking.
Focus on your breathing.
Ignore how heavy and intimidating Scab's breathing is.
YOWZA!
Stop getting distracted.
Stop worrying about being distracted.
Just be.

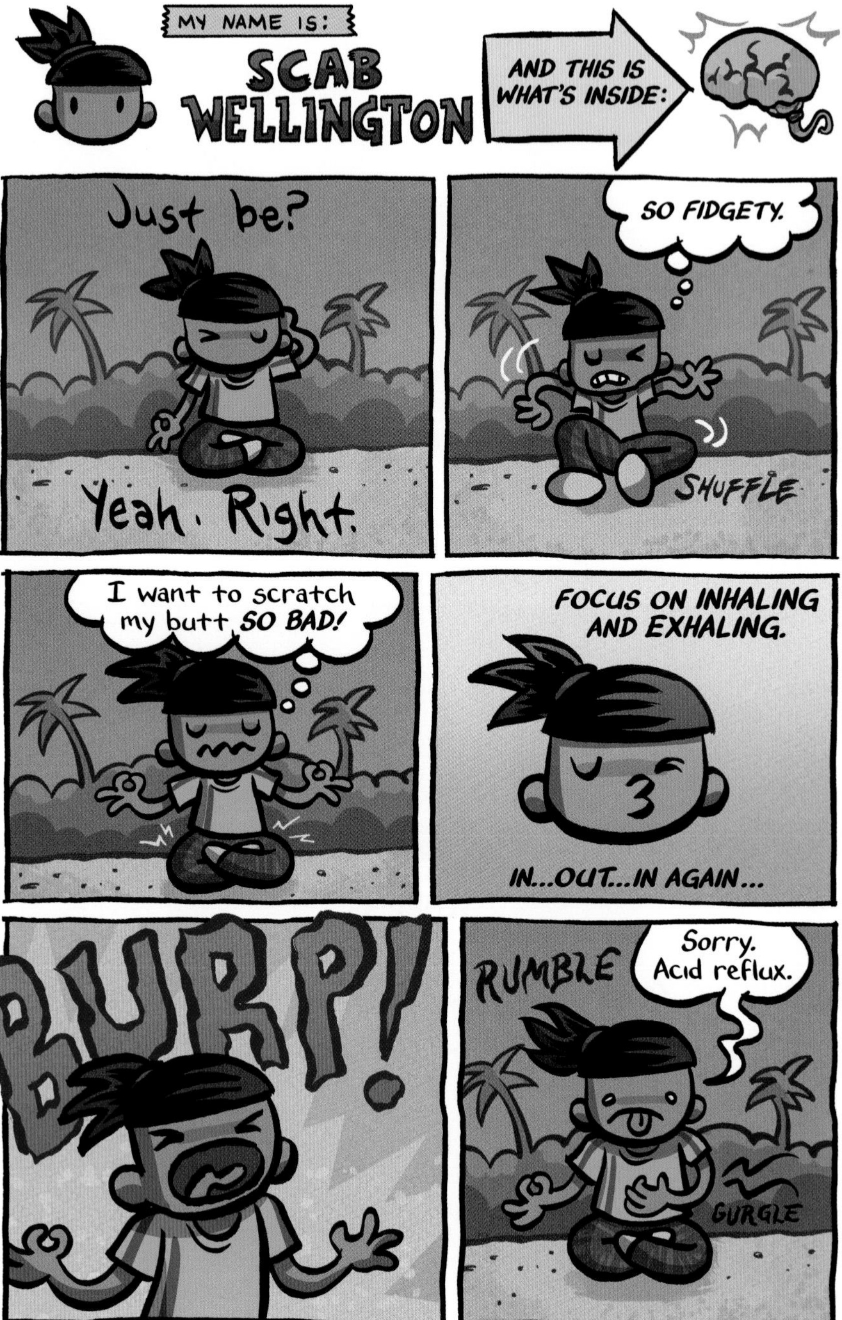
MY NAME IS:
SCAB WELLINGTON
AND THIS IS WHAT'S INSIDE:
Just be?
Yeah. Right.
SO FIDGETY.
SHUFFLE
I want to scratch my butt SO BAD!
FOCUS ON INHALING AND EXHALING.
IN...OUT...IN AGAIN...
BURP!
RUMBLE
Sorry. Acid reflux.
GURGLE

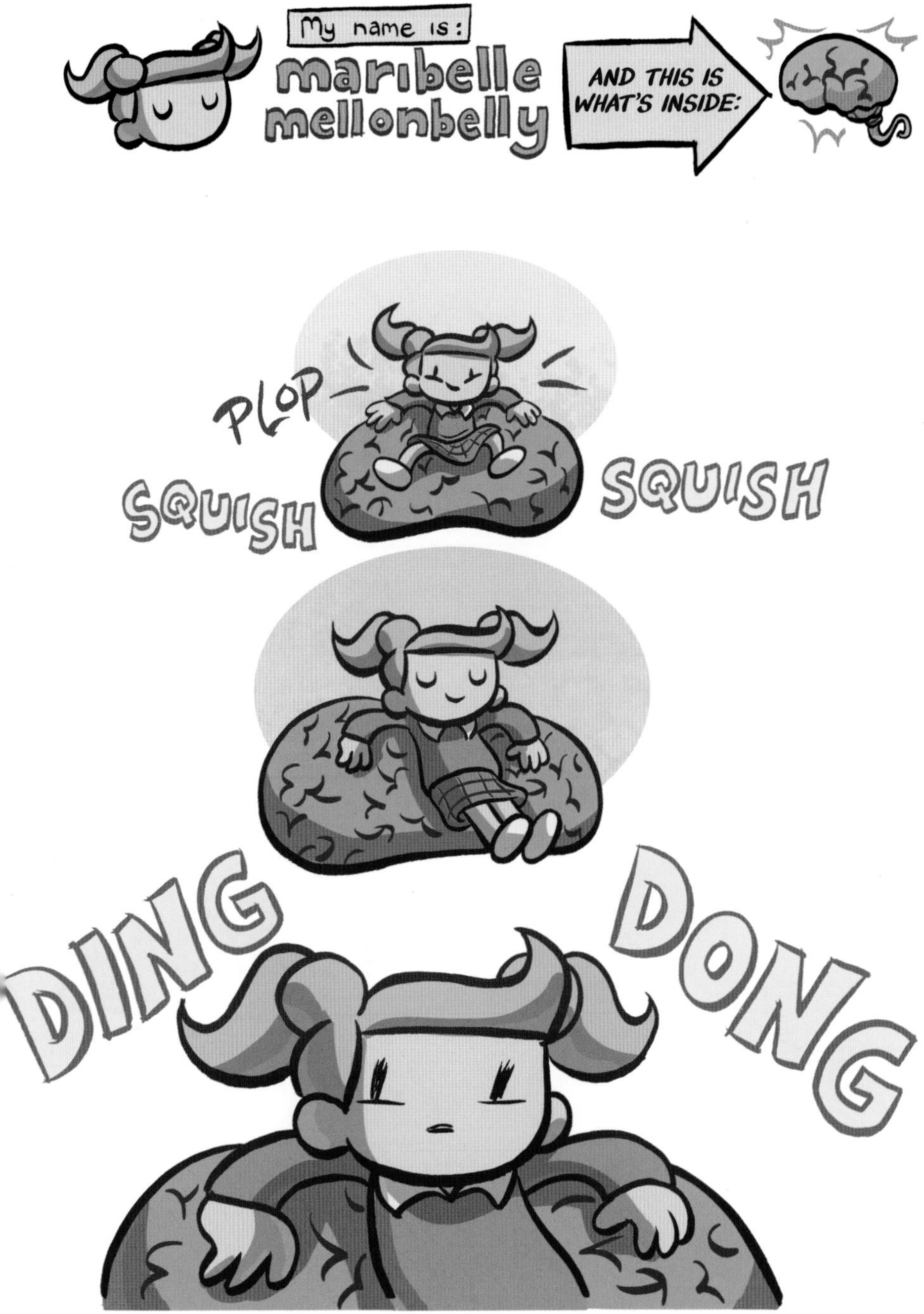
My name is:
maribelle mellonbelly
AND THIS IS WHAT'S INSIDE:
PLOP
SQUISH
SQUISH
DING
DONG

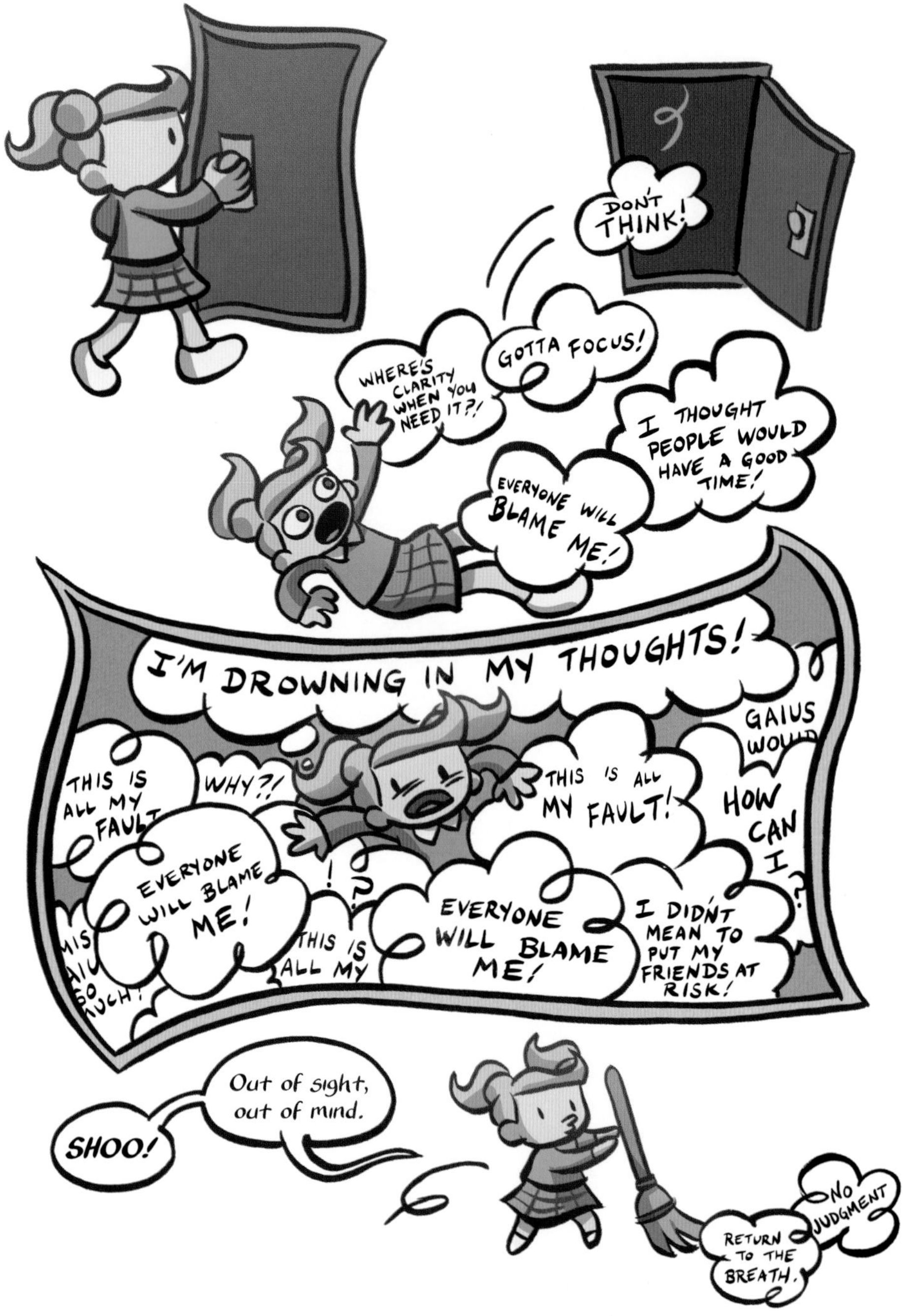
DON'T THINK!
WHERE'S CLARITY WHEN YOU NEED IT?!
GOTTA FOCUS!
I THOUGHT PEOPLE WOULD HAVE A GOOD TIME!
EVERYONE WILL BLAME ME!
I'M DROWNING IN MY THOUGHTS!
GAIUS WOULD
THIS IS ALL MY FAULT
WHY?!
THIS IS ALL MY FAULT!
HOW CAN I
EVERYONE WILL BLAME ME!
!
?
EVERYONE WILL BLAME ME!
I DIDN'T MEAN TO PUT MY FRIENDS AT RISK!
THIS IS ALL MY
?
SHOO!
Out of sight, out of mind.
NO JUDGMENT
RETURN TO THE BREATH.

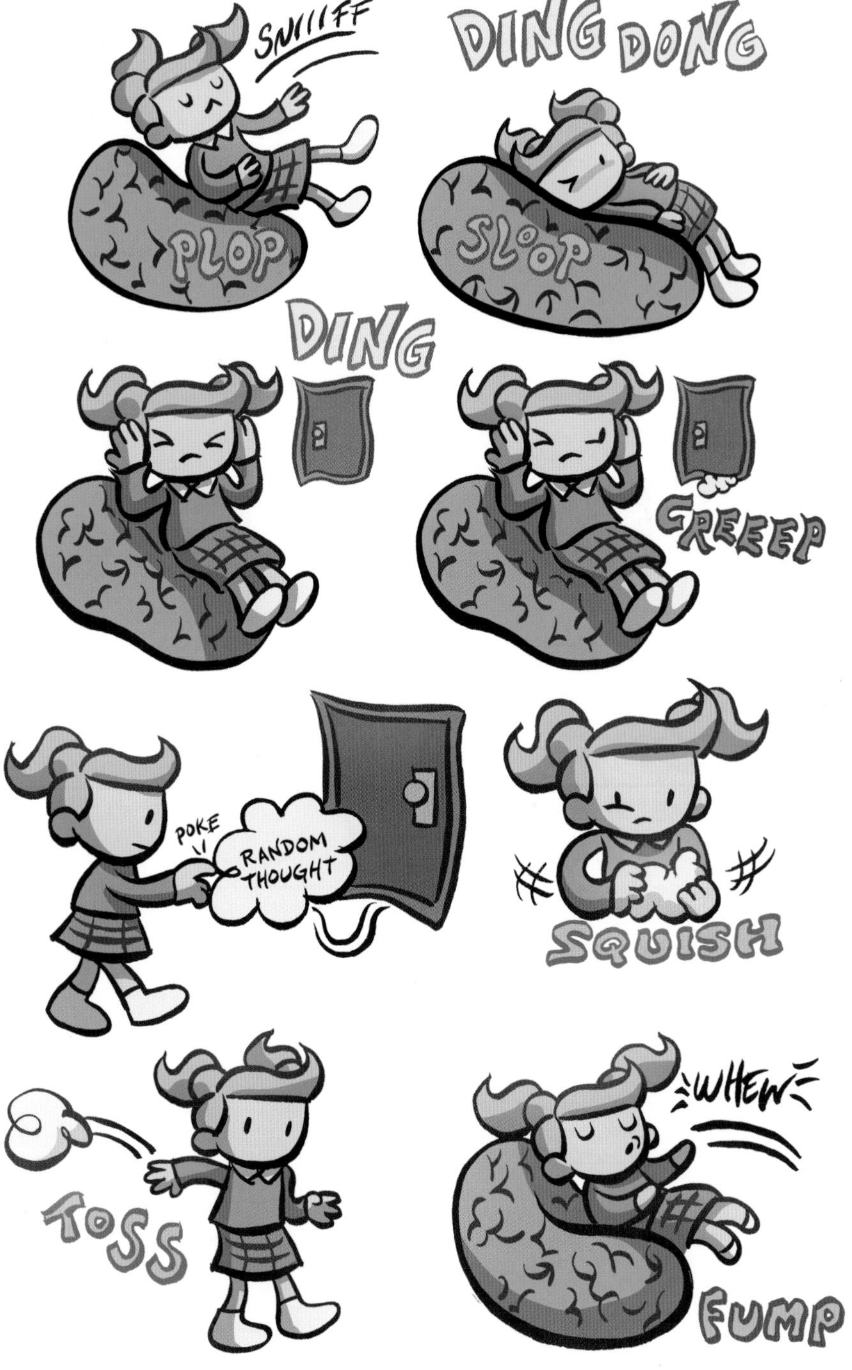
SNIIIFF
PLOP
DING DONG
SLOOP
DING
CREEEP
POKE
RANDOM THOUGHT
SQUISH
TOSS
WHEW
FUMP

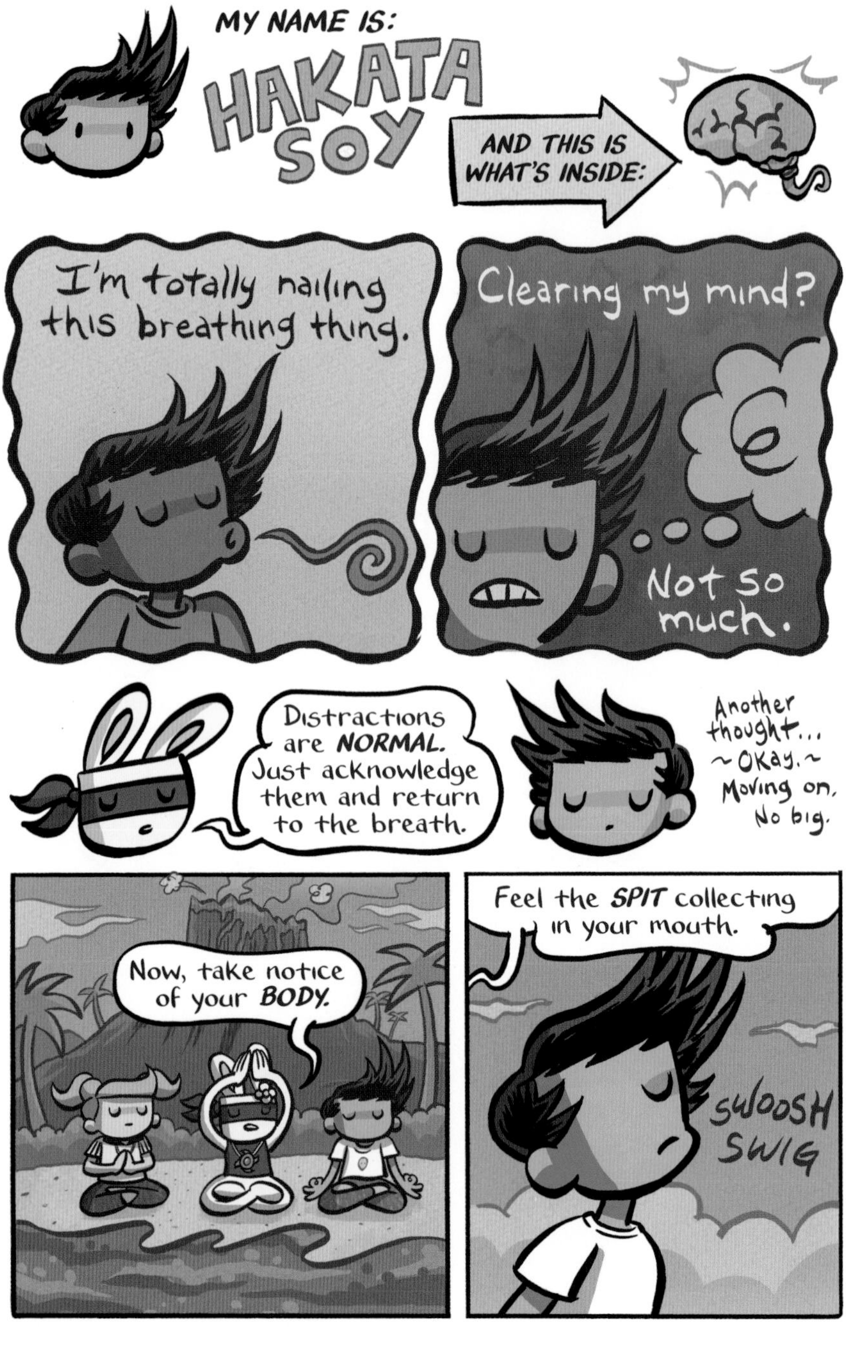
MY NAME IS:
HAKATA SOY
AND THIS IS WHAT'S INSIDE:
I'm totally nailing this breathing thing.
Clearing my mind?
Not so much.
Distractions are NORMAL. Just acknowledge them and return to the breath.
Another thought... ~Okay.~ Moving on. No big.
Now, take notice of your BODY.
Feel the SPIT collecting in your mouth.
SWOOSH
SWIG

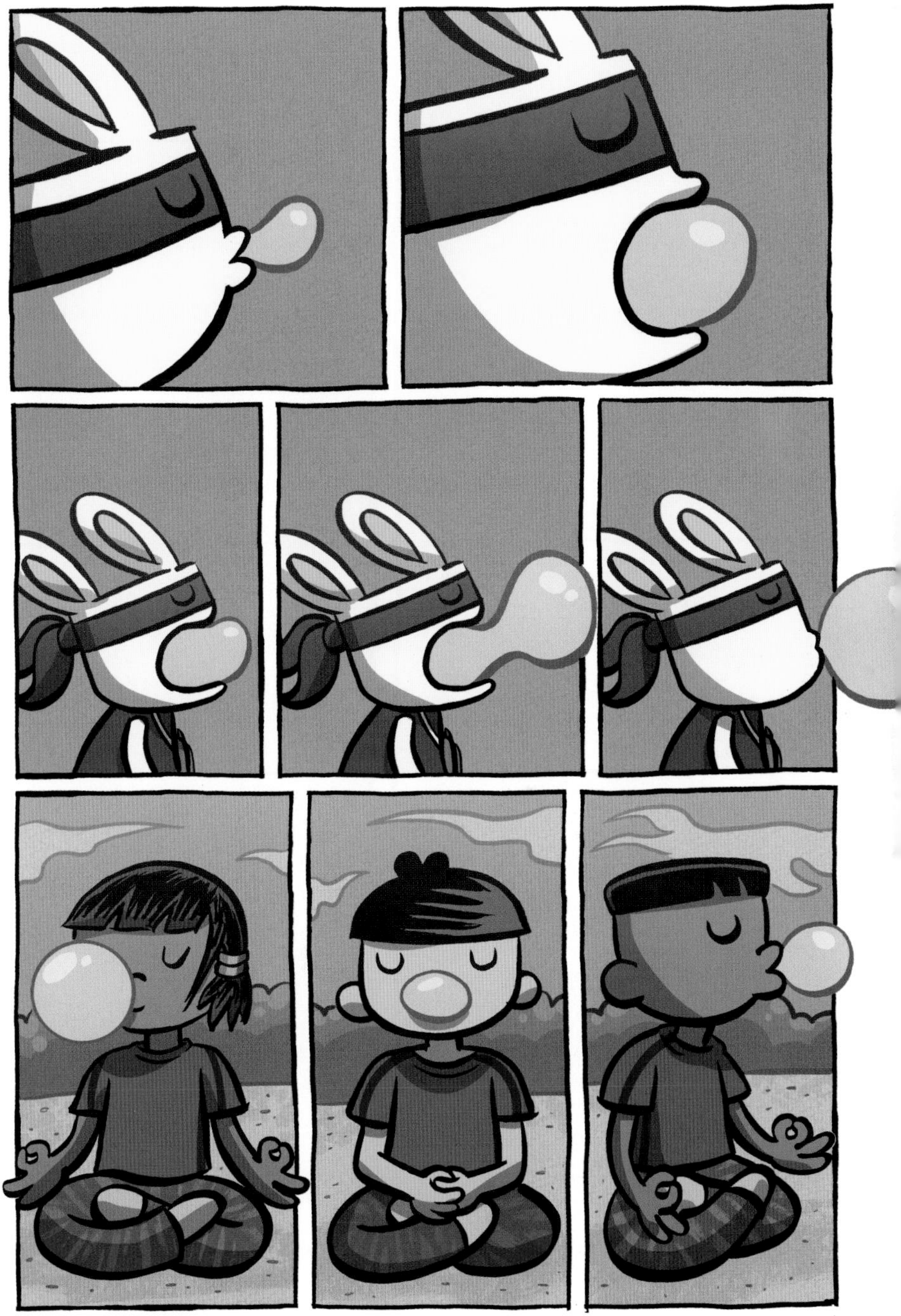

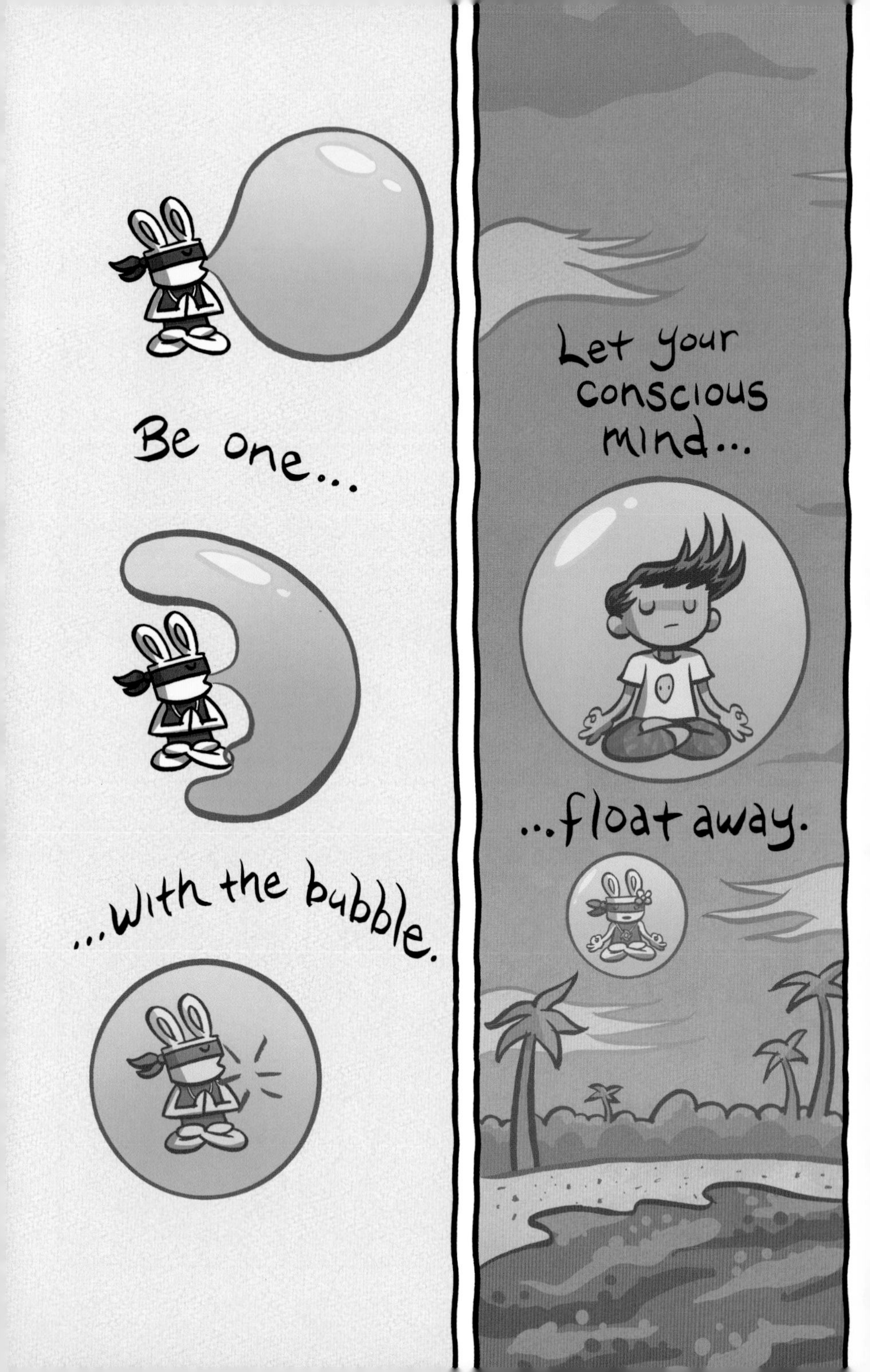

Be one...
...with the bubble.
Let your conscious mind...
...float away.

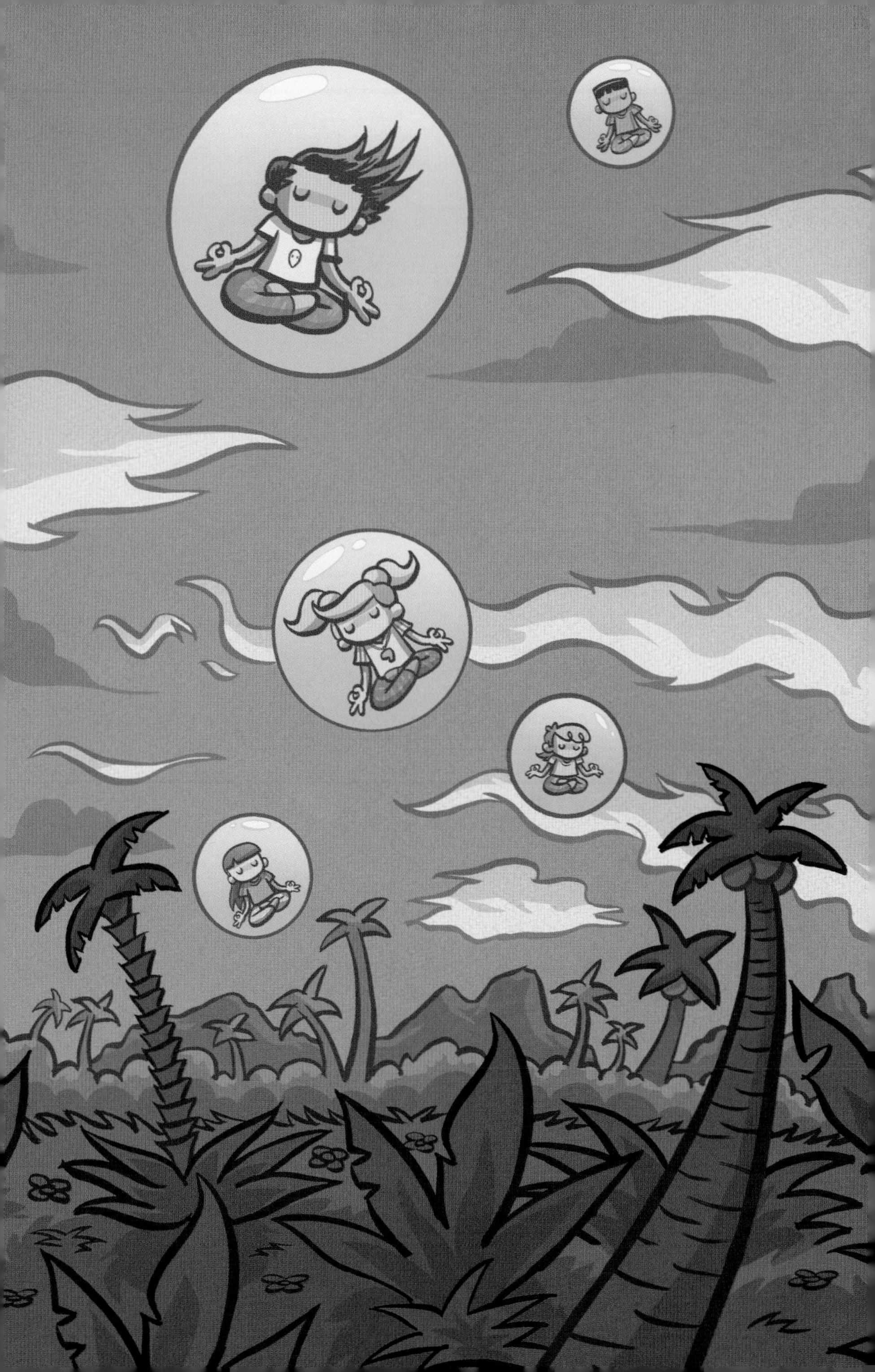

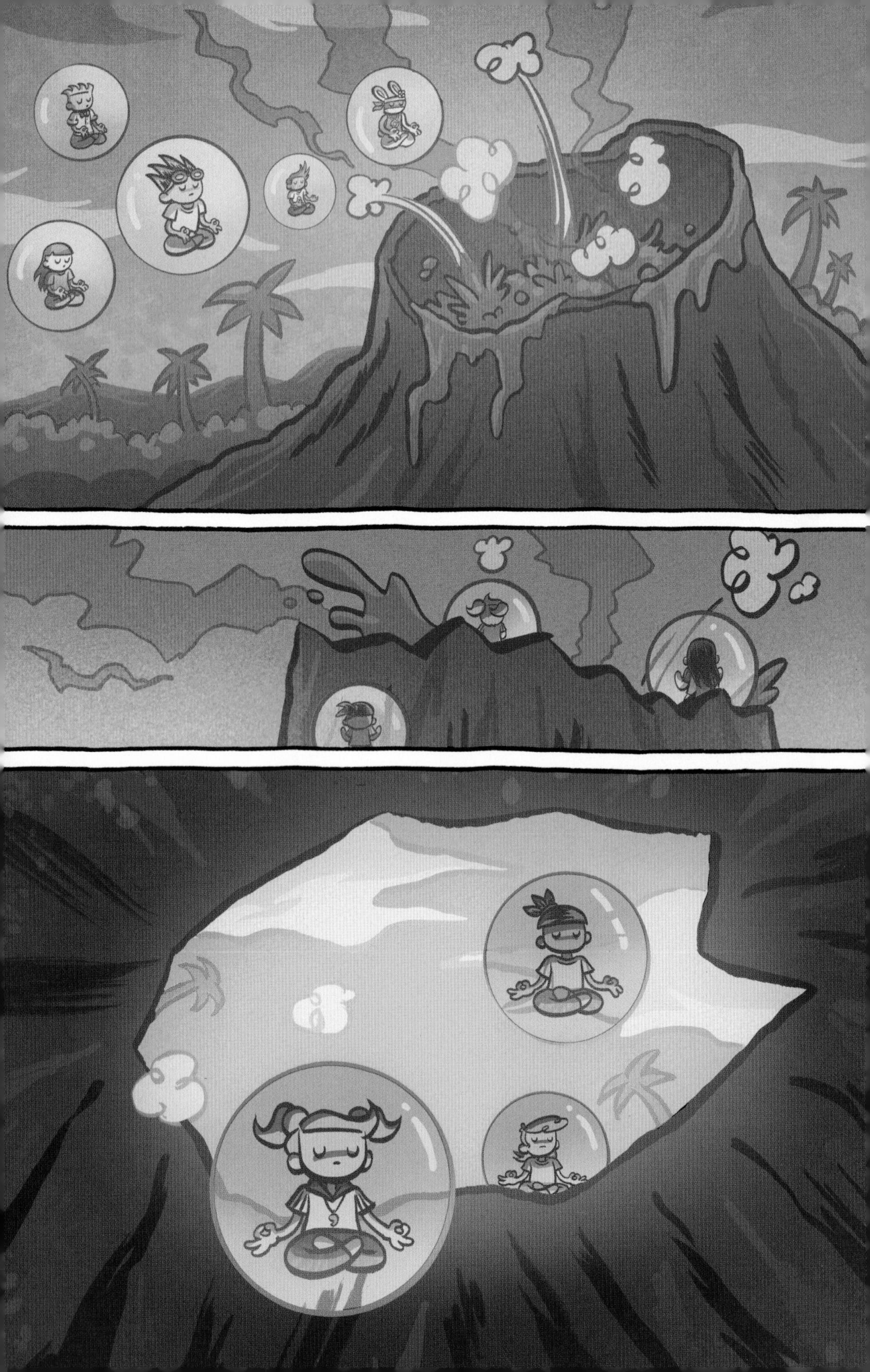

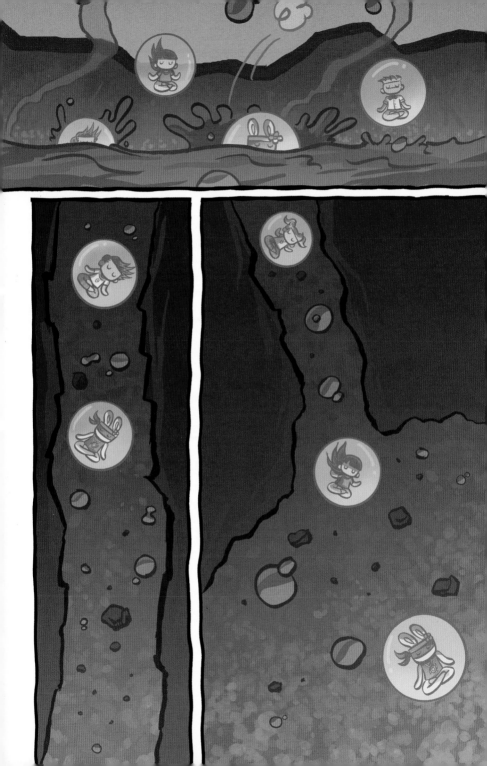

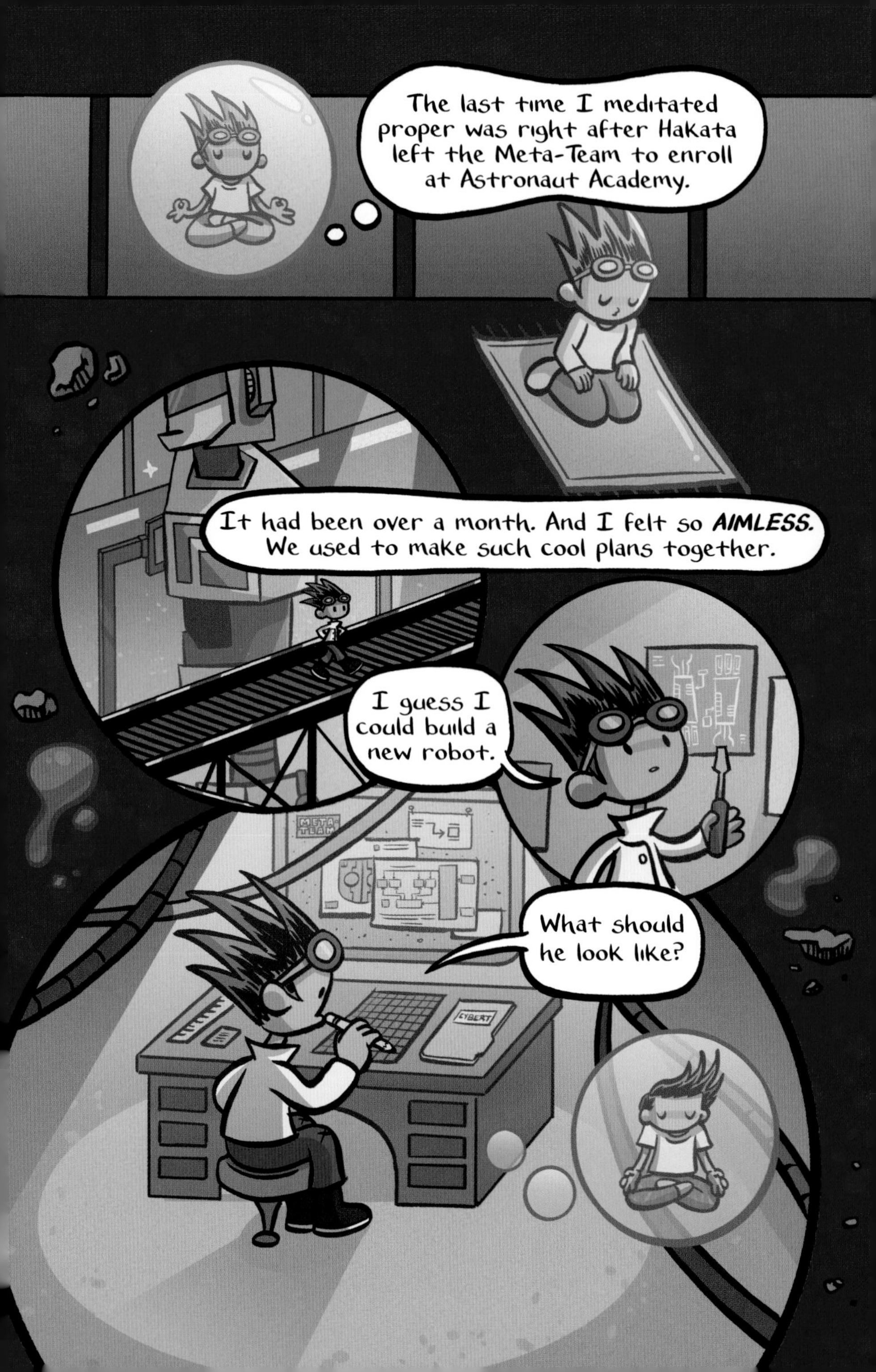
The last time I meditated proper was right after Hakata left the Meta-Team to enroll at Astronaut Academy.
It had been over a month. And I felt so AIMLESS. We used to make such cool plans together.
I guess I could build a new robot.
What should he look like?
META TEAM
CYBERT

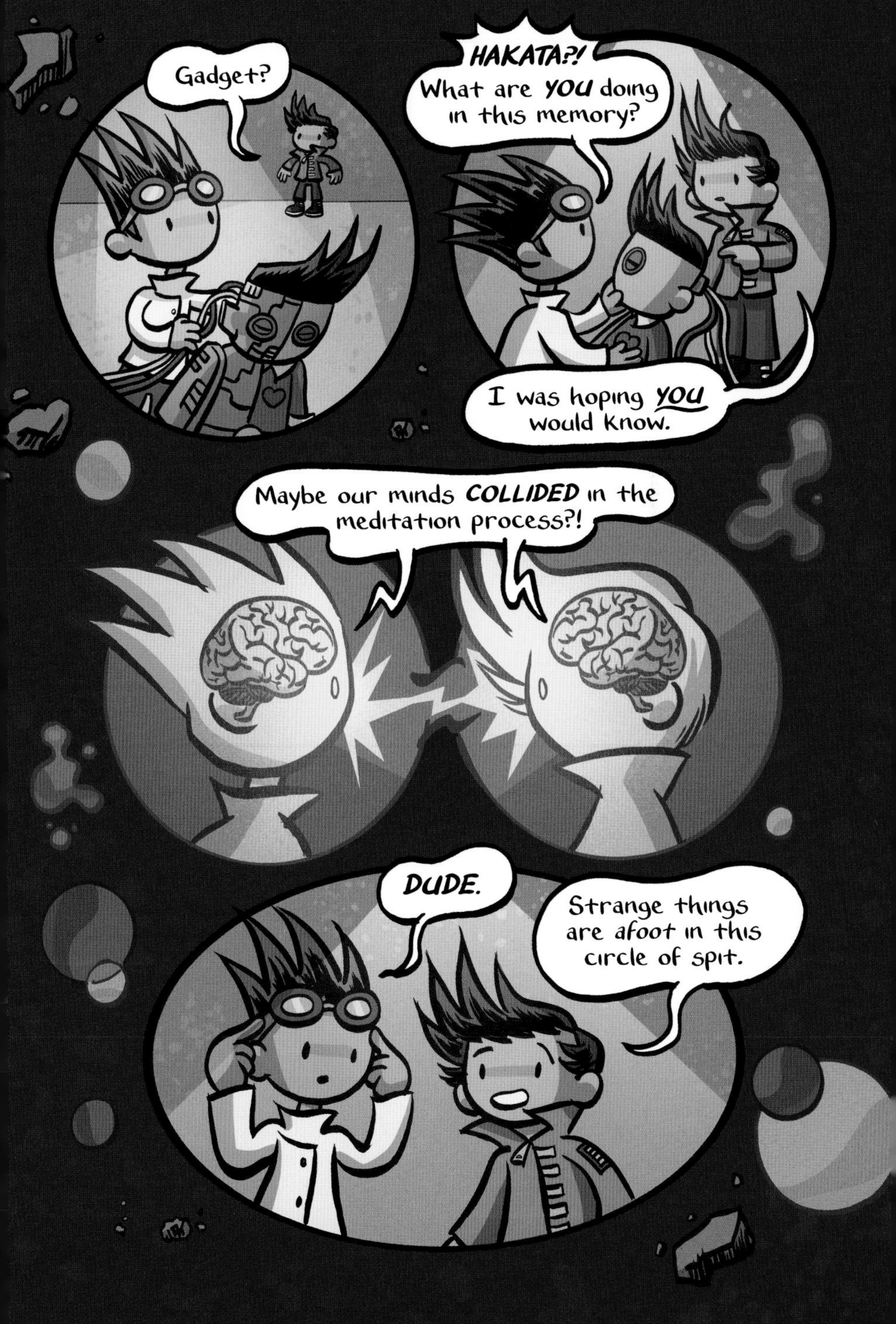
Gadget?
HAKATA?! What are YOU doing in this memory?
I was hoping YOU would know.
Maybe our minds COLLIDED in the meditation process?!
DUDE.
Strange things are afoot in this circle of spit.

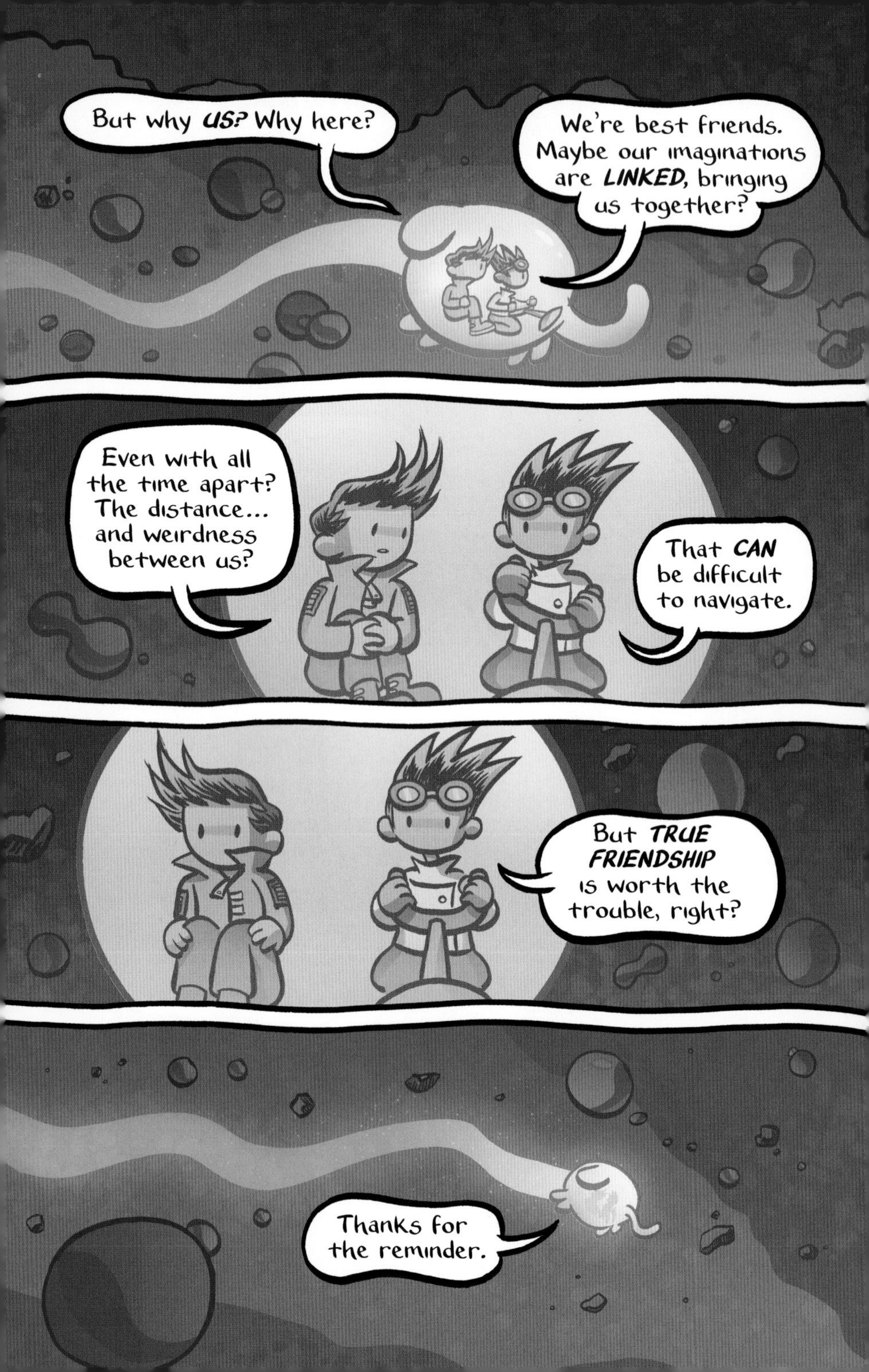
But why US? Why here?
We're best friends. Maybe our imaginations are LINKED, bringing us together?
Even with all the time apart? The distance... and weirdness between us?
That CAN be difficult to navigate.
But TRUE FRIENDSHIP is worth the trouble, right?
Thanks for the reminder.

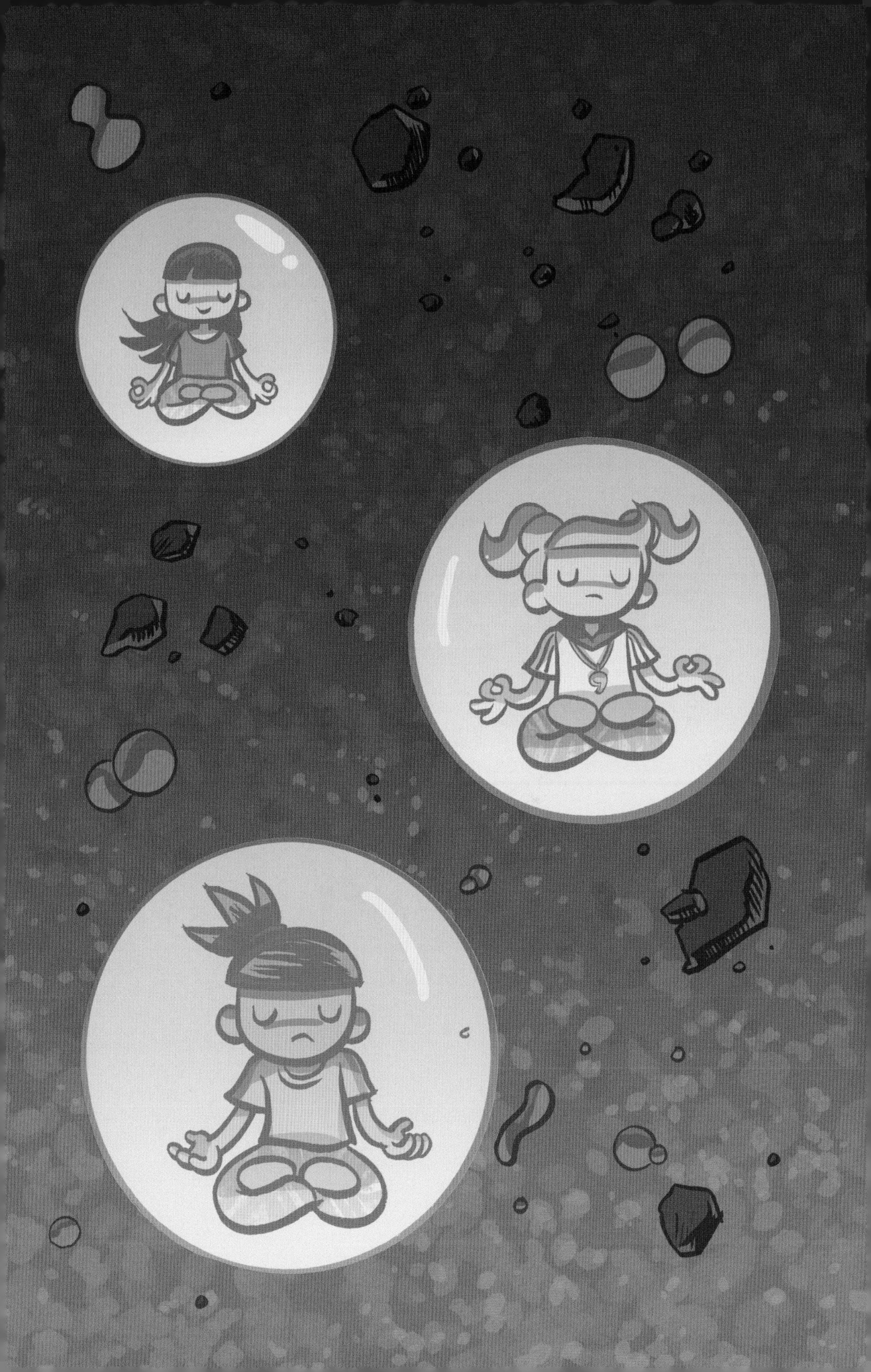

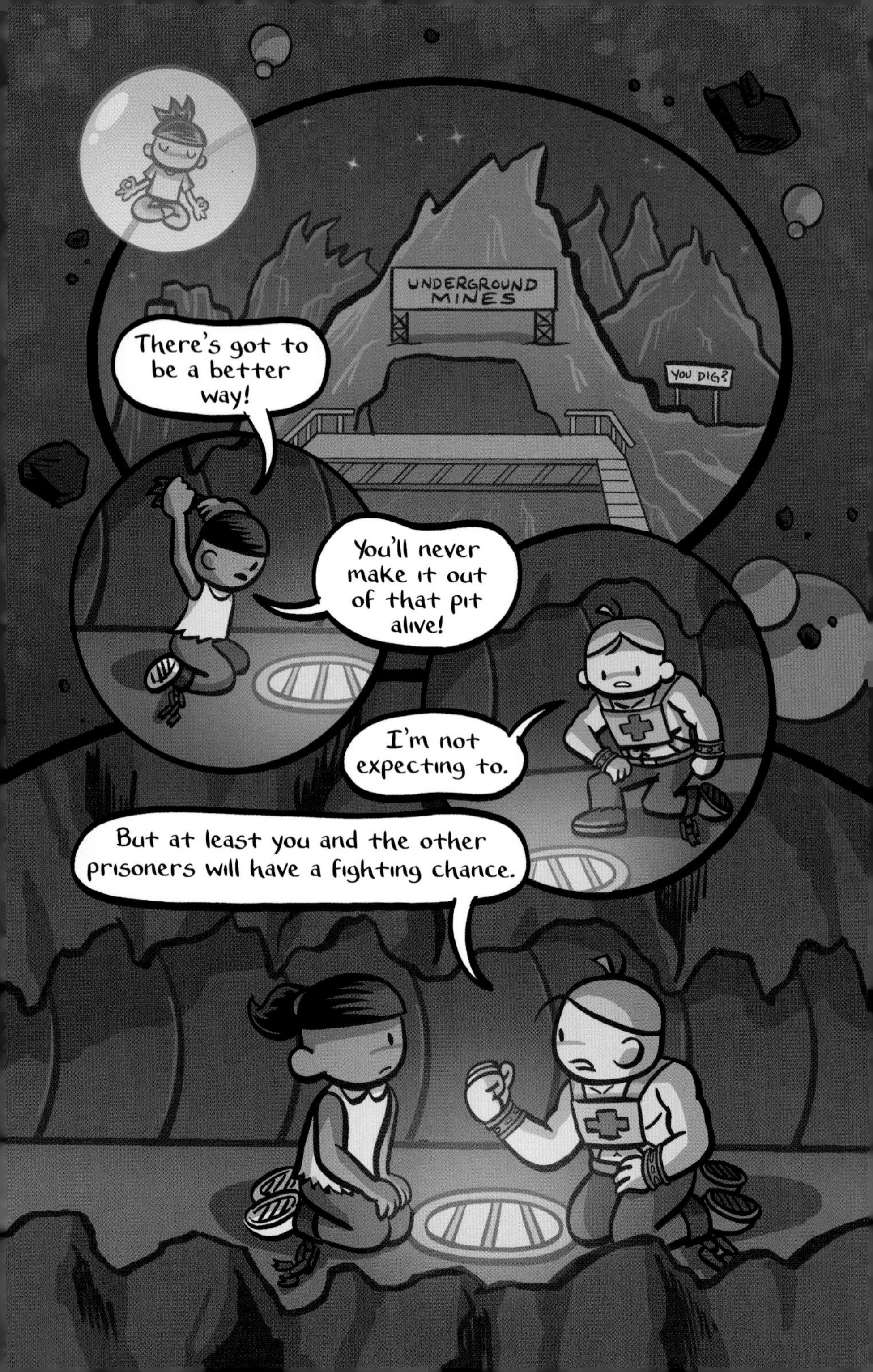
UNDERGROUND MINES
YOU DIG?
There's got to be a better way!
You'll never make it out of that pit alive!
I'm not expecting to.
But at least you and the other prisoners will have a fighting chance.

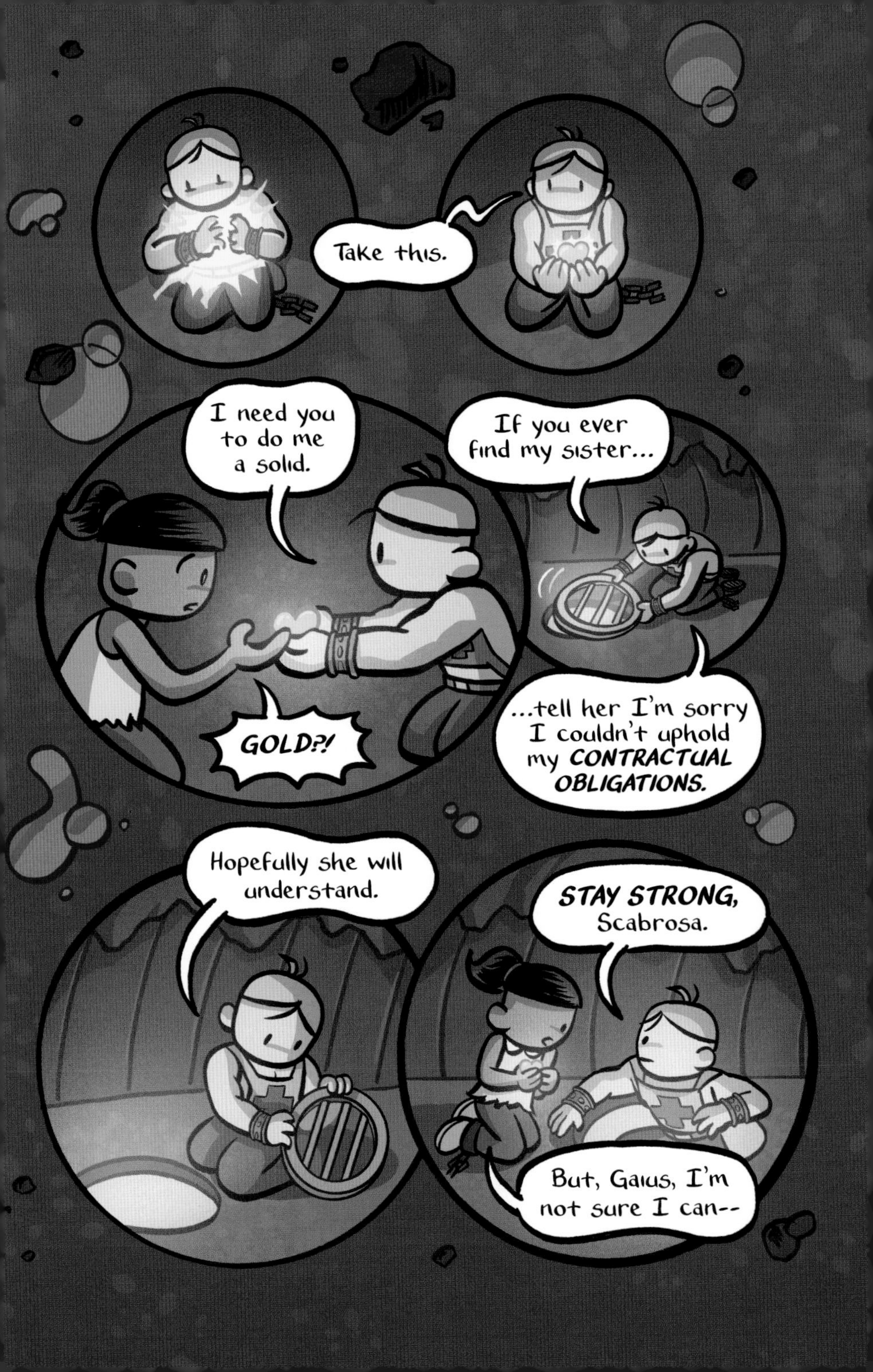
Take this.
I need you to do me a solid.
GOLD?!
If you ever find my sister...
...tell her I'm sorry I couldn't uphold my CONTRACTUAL OBLIGATIONS.
Hopefully she will understand.
STAY STRONG, Scabrosa.
But, Gaius, I'm not sure I can--

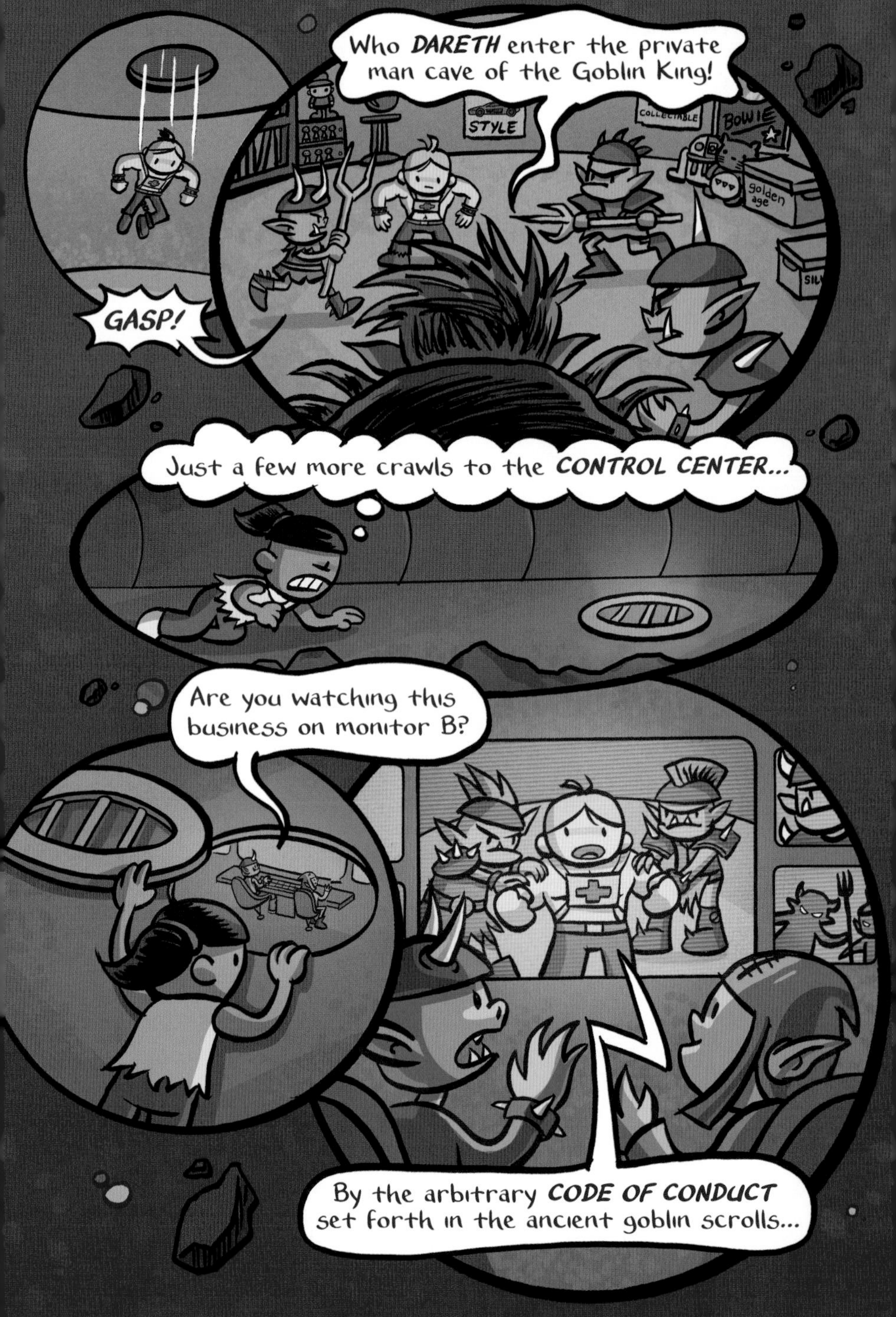
Who DARETH enter the private man cave of the Goblin King!
STYLE
COLLECTABLE
BOWIE
golden age
GASP!
Just a few more crawls to the CONTROL CENTER...
Are you watching this business on monitor B?
By the arbitrary CODE OF CONDUCT set forth in the ancient goblin scrolls...

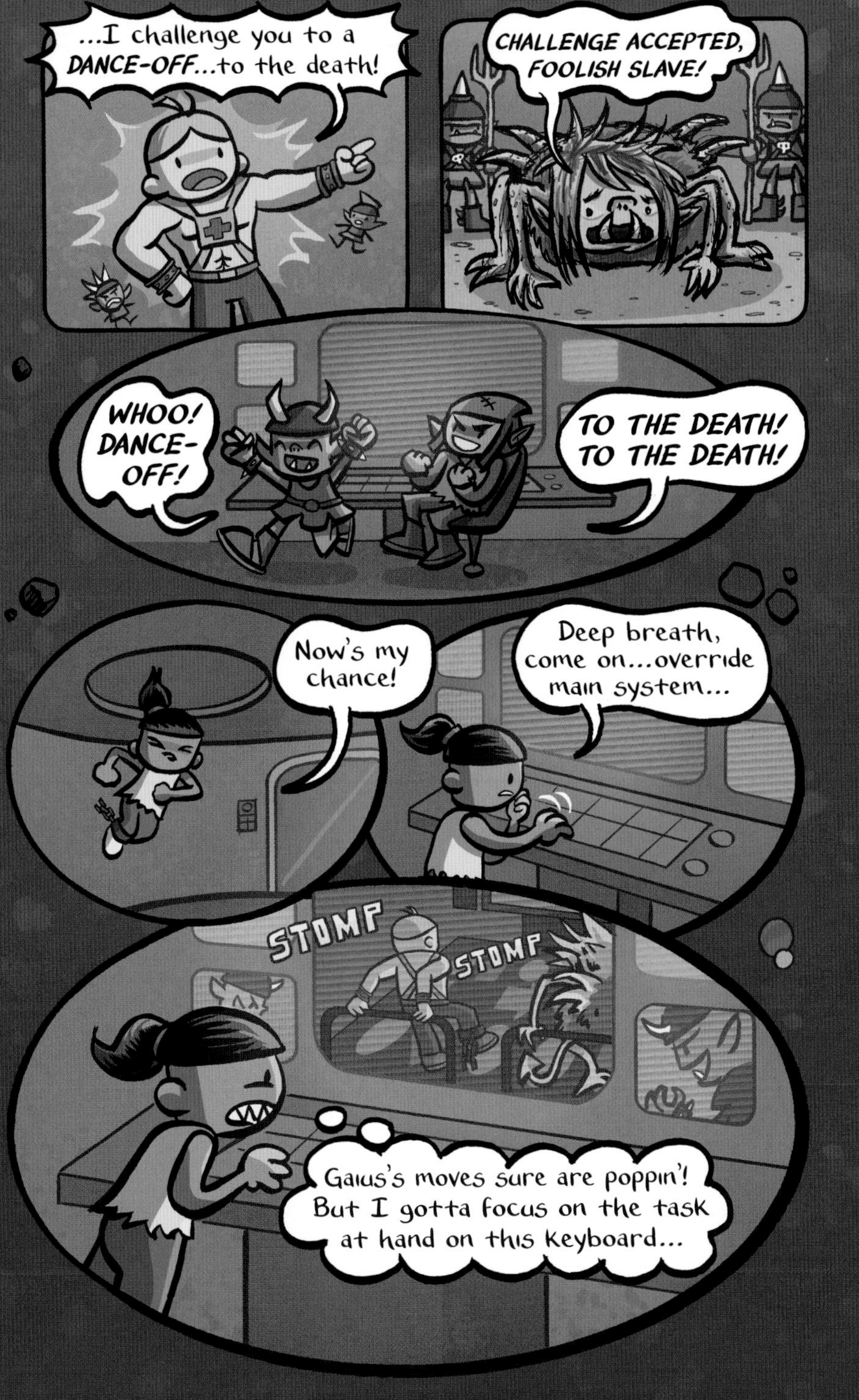
...I challenge you to a DANCE-OFF...to the death!
CHALLENGE ACCEPTED, FOOLISH SLAVE!
WHOO! DANCE-OFF!
TO THE DEATH! TO THE DEATH!
Now's my chance!
Deep breath, come on...override main system...
STOMP
STOMP
Gaius's moves sure are poppin'! But I gotta focus on the task at hand on this keyboard...

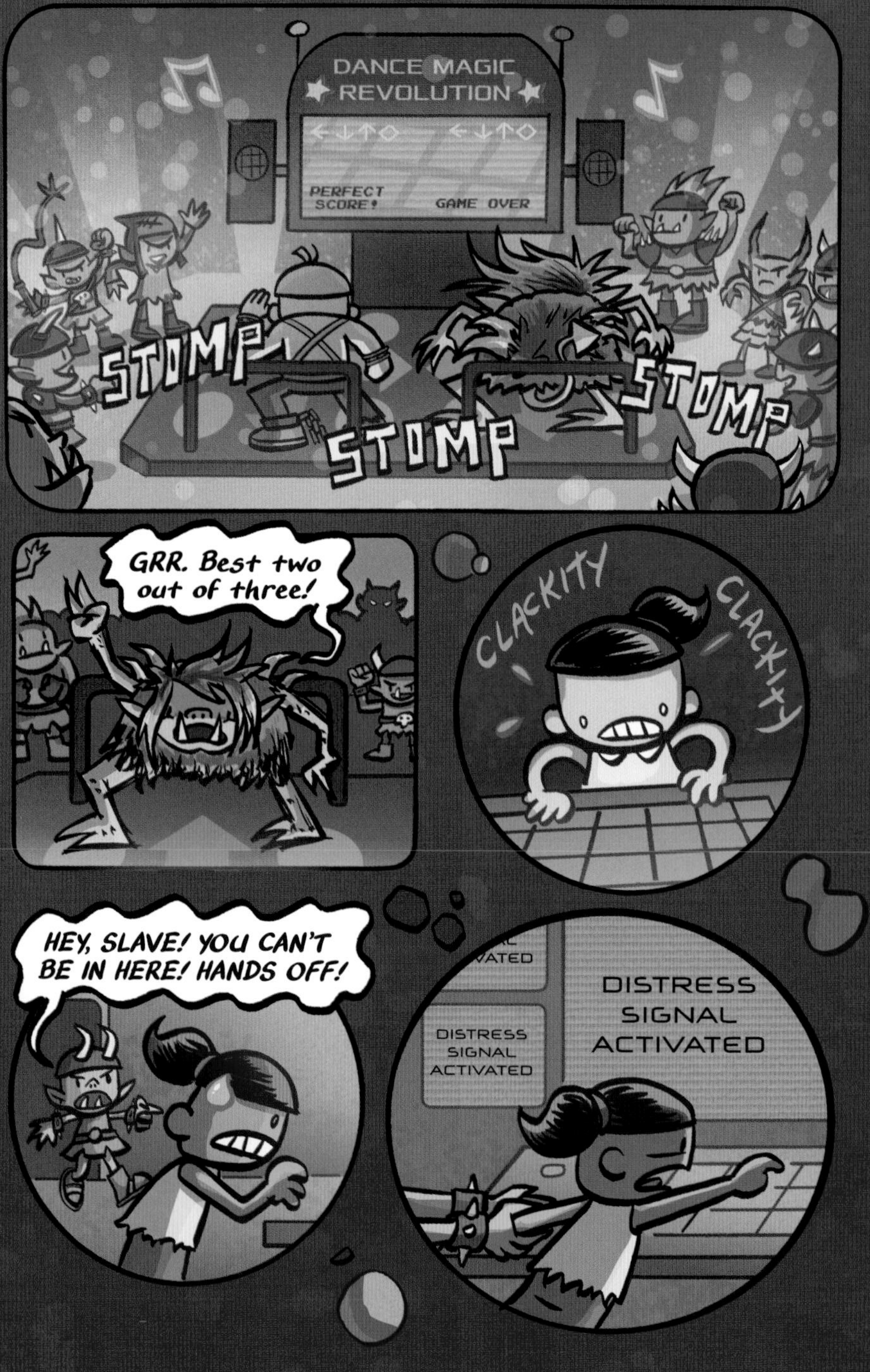
DANCE MAGIC
REVOLUTION
PERFECT
SCORE!
GAME OVER
STOMP
STOMP
STOMP
GRR. Best two out of three!
CLACKITY
CLACKITY
HEY, SLAVE! YOU CAN'T BE IN HERE! HANDS OFF!
DISTRESS
SIGNAL
ACTIVATED
DISTRESS
SIGNAL
ACTIVATED

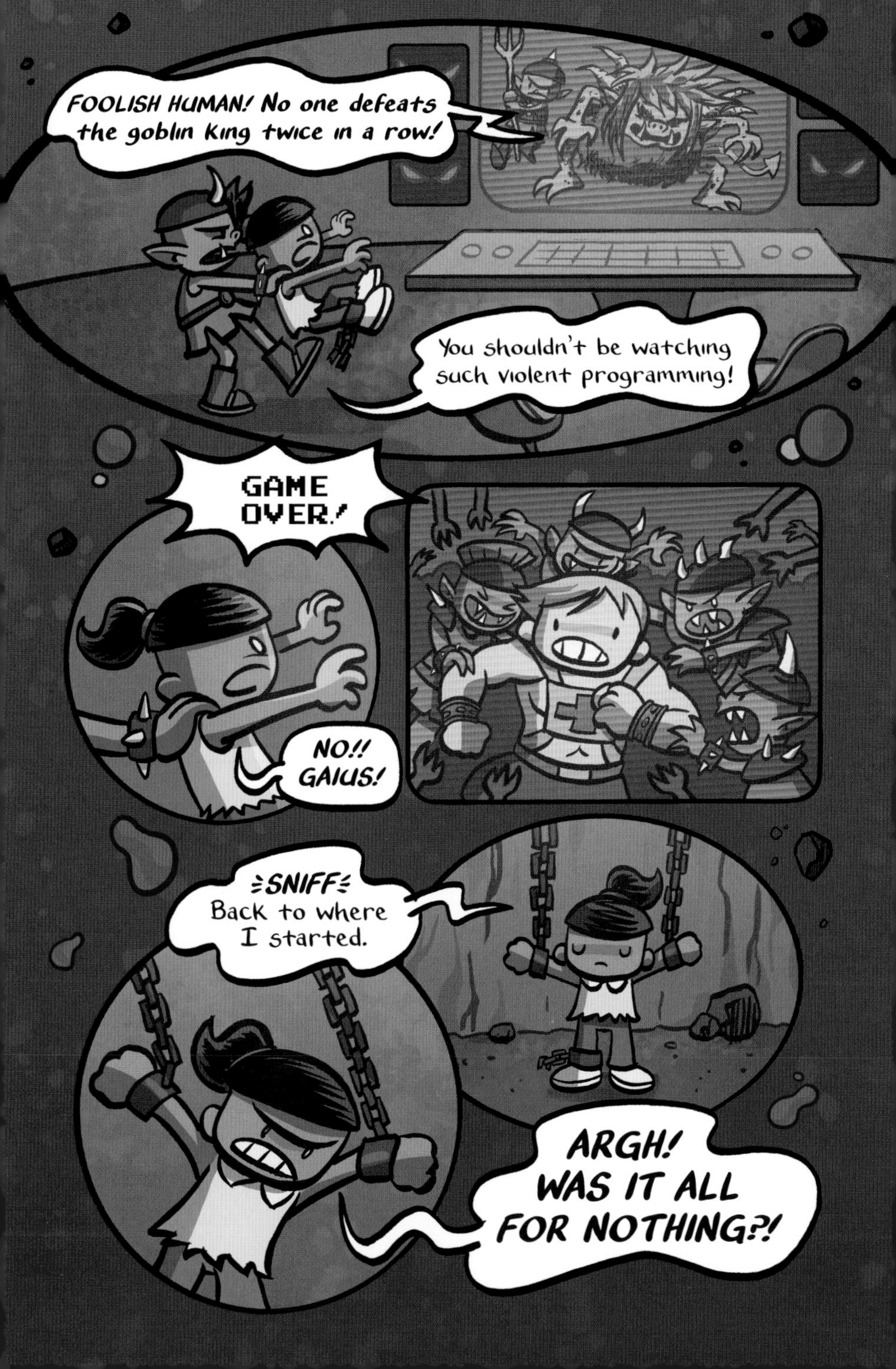
FOOLISH HUMAN! No one defeats the goblin king twice in a row!
You shouldn't be watching such violent programming!
GAME OVER!
NO!! GAIUS!
SNIFF
Back to where I started.
ARGH! WAS IT ALL FOR NOTHING?!

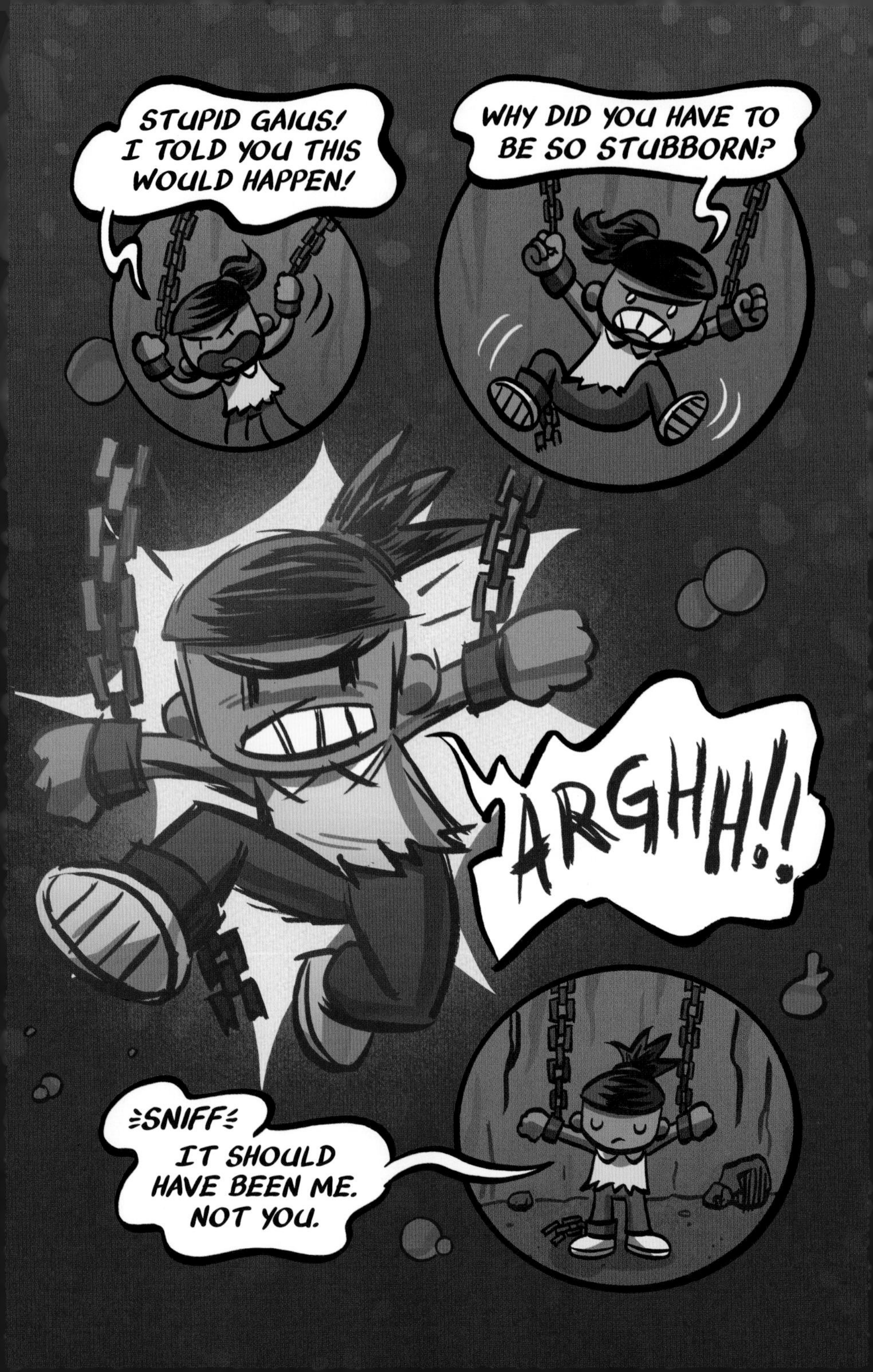
STUPID GAIUS! I TOLD YOU THIS WOULD HAPPEN!
WHY DID YOU HAVE TO BE SO STUBBORN?
ARGHH!!
SNIFF
IT SHOULD HAVE BEEN ME. NOT YOU.

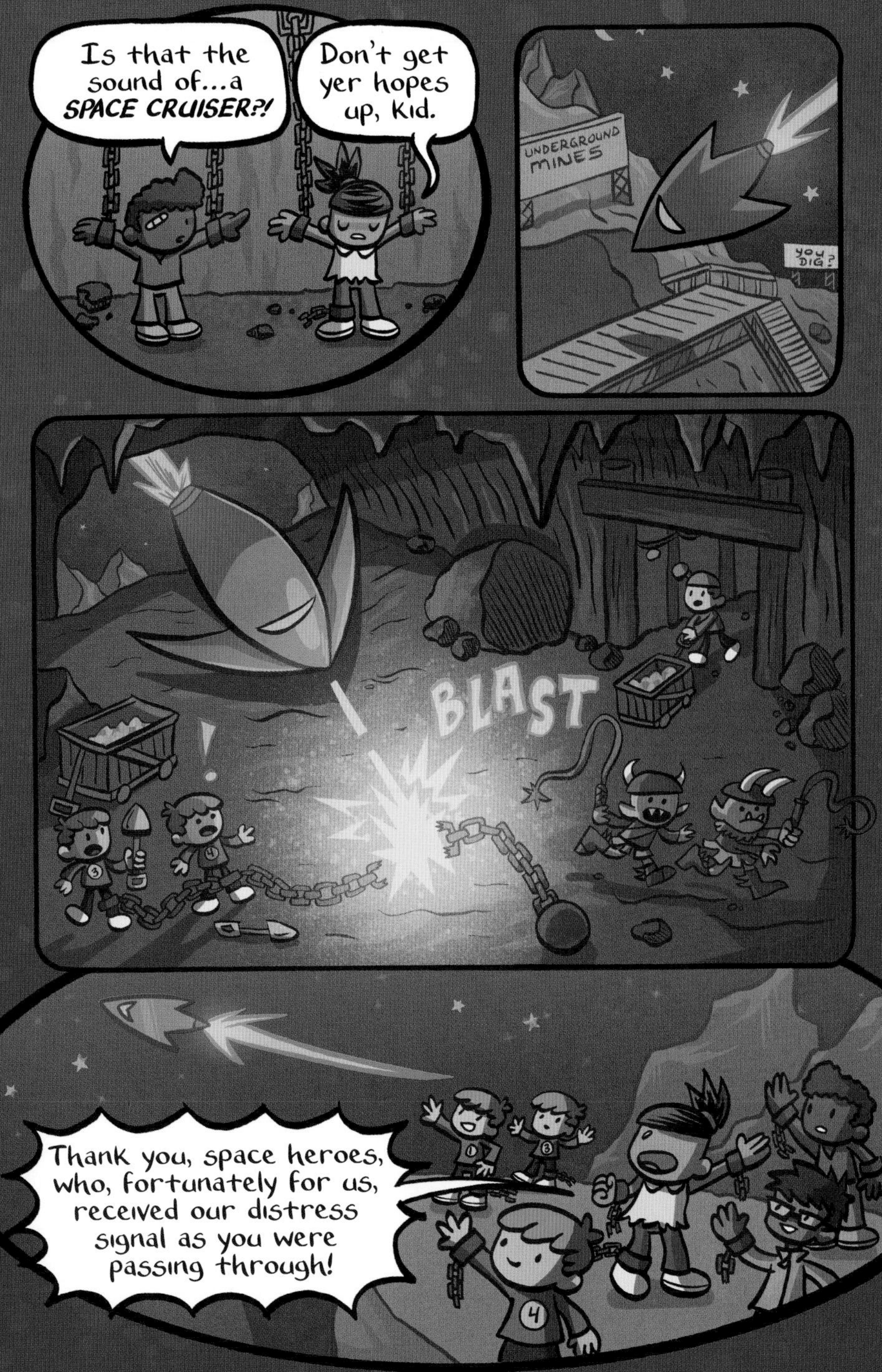
Is that the sound of...a SPACE CRUISER?!
Don't get yer hopes up, kid.
UNDERGROUND MINES
YOU DIG?
BLAST
Thank you, space heroes, who, fortunately for us, received our distress signal as you were passing through!

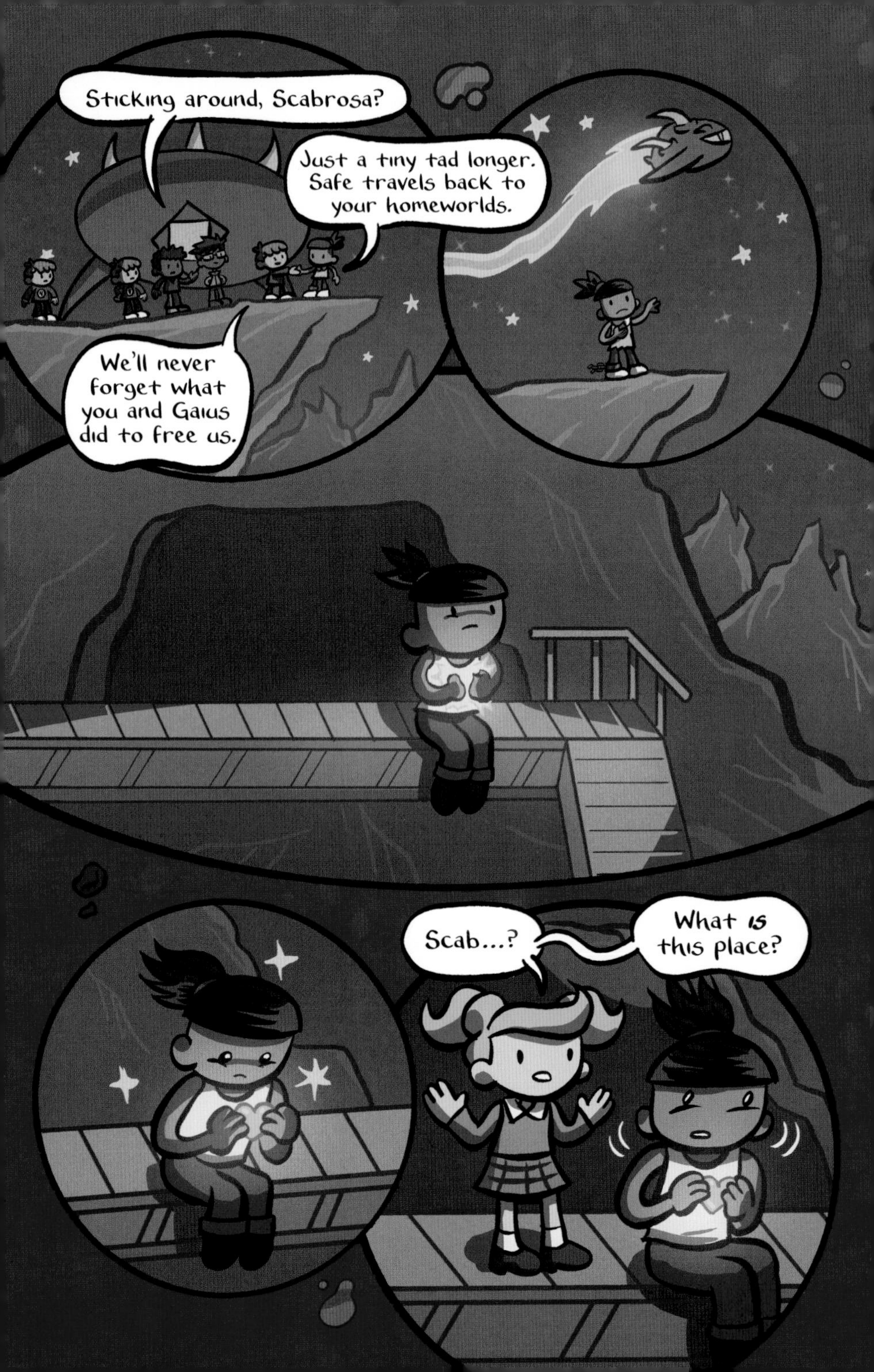
Sticking around, Scabrosa?
Just a tiny tad longer. Safe travels back to your homeworlds.
We'll never forget what you and Gaius did to free us.
Scab...?
What IS this place?

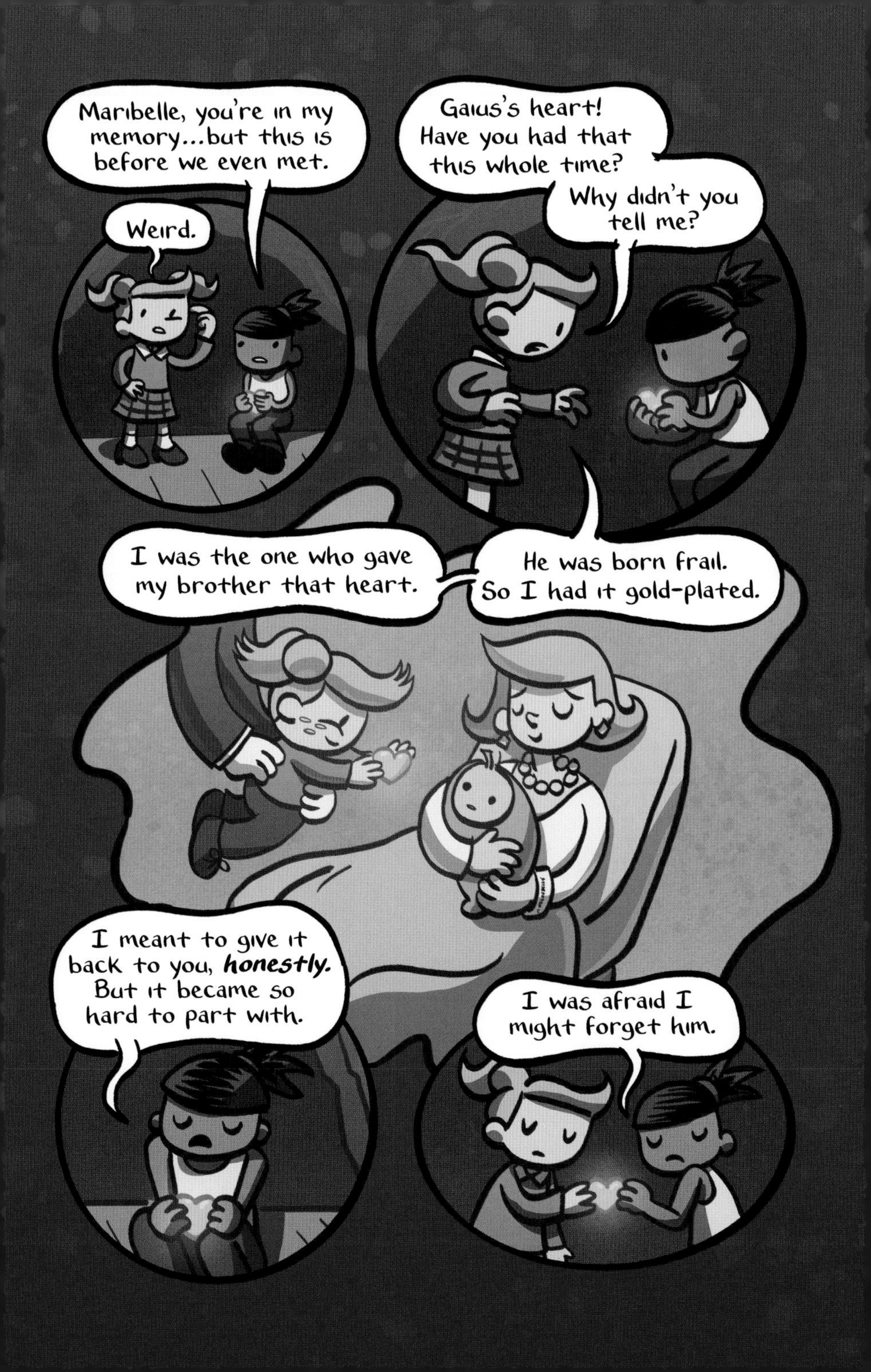
Maribelle, you're in my memory...but this is before we even met.
Weird.
Gaius's heart! Have you had that this whole time?
Why didn't you tell me?
I was the one who gave my brother that heart.
He was born frail. So I had it gold-plated.
I meant to give it back to you, *honestly.* But it became so hard to part with.
I was afraid I might forget him.

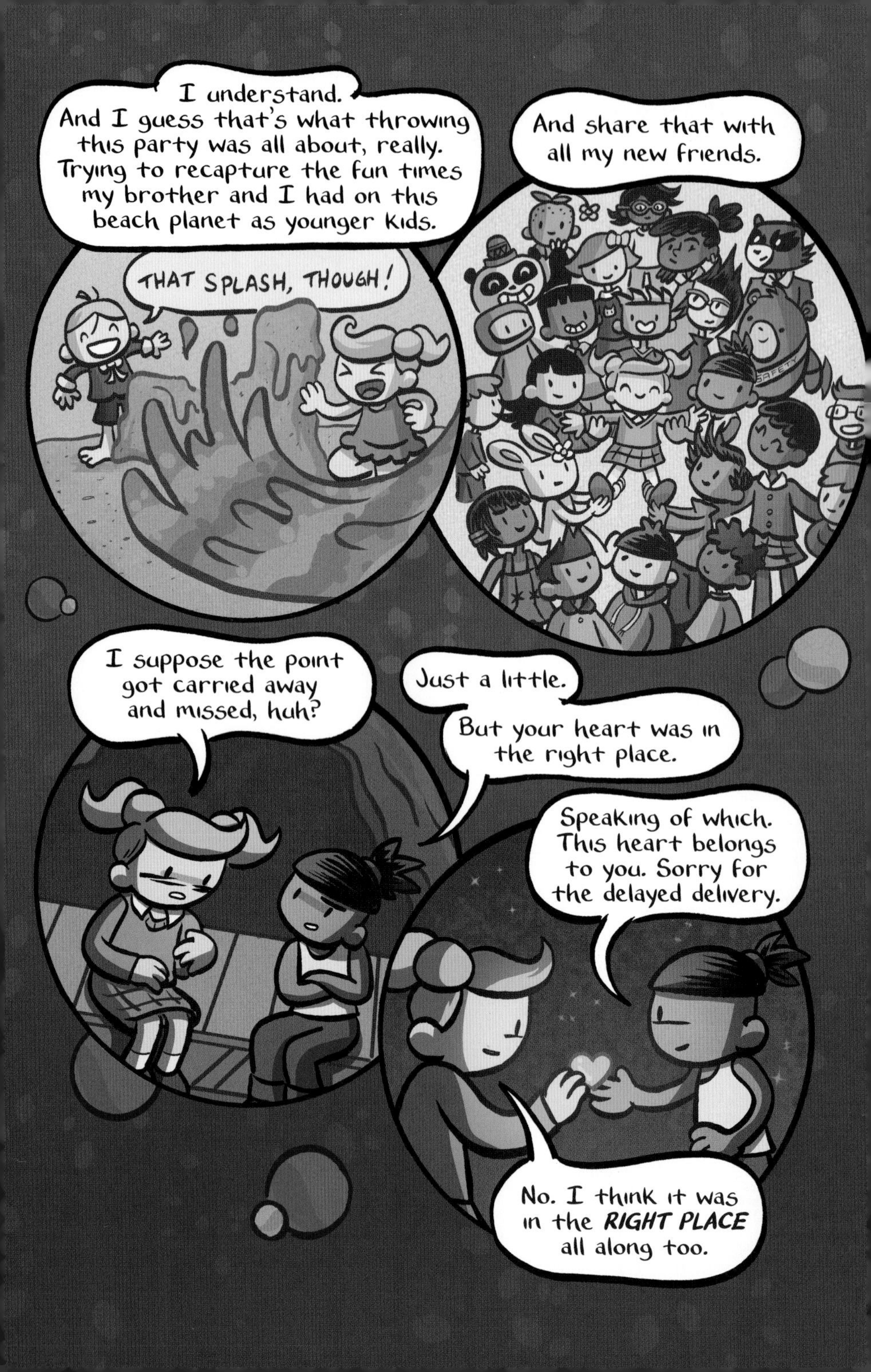
I understand. And I guess that's what throwing this party was all about, really. Trying to recapture the fun times my brother and I had on this beach planet as younger kids.
And share that with all my new friends.
THAT SPLASH, THOUGH!
SAFETY
I suppose the point got carried away and missed, huh?
Just a little.
But your heart was in the right place.
Speaking of which. This heart belongs to you. Sorry for the delayed delivery.
No. I think it was in the ***RIGHT PLACE*** all along too.

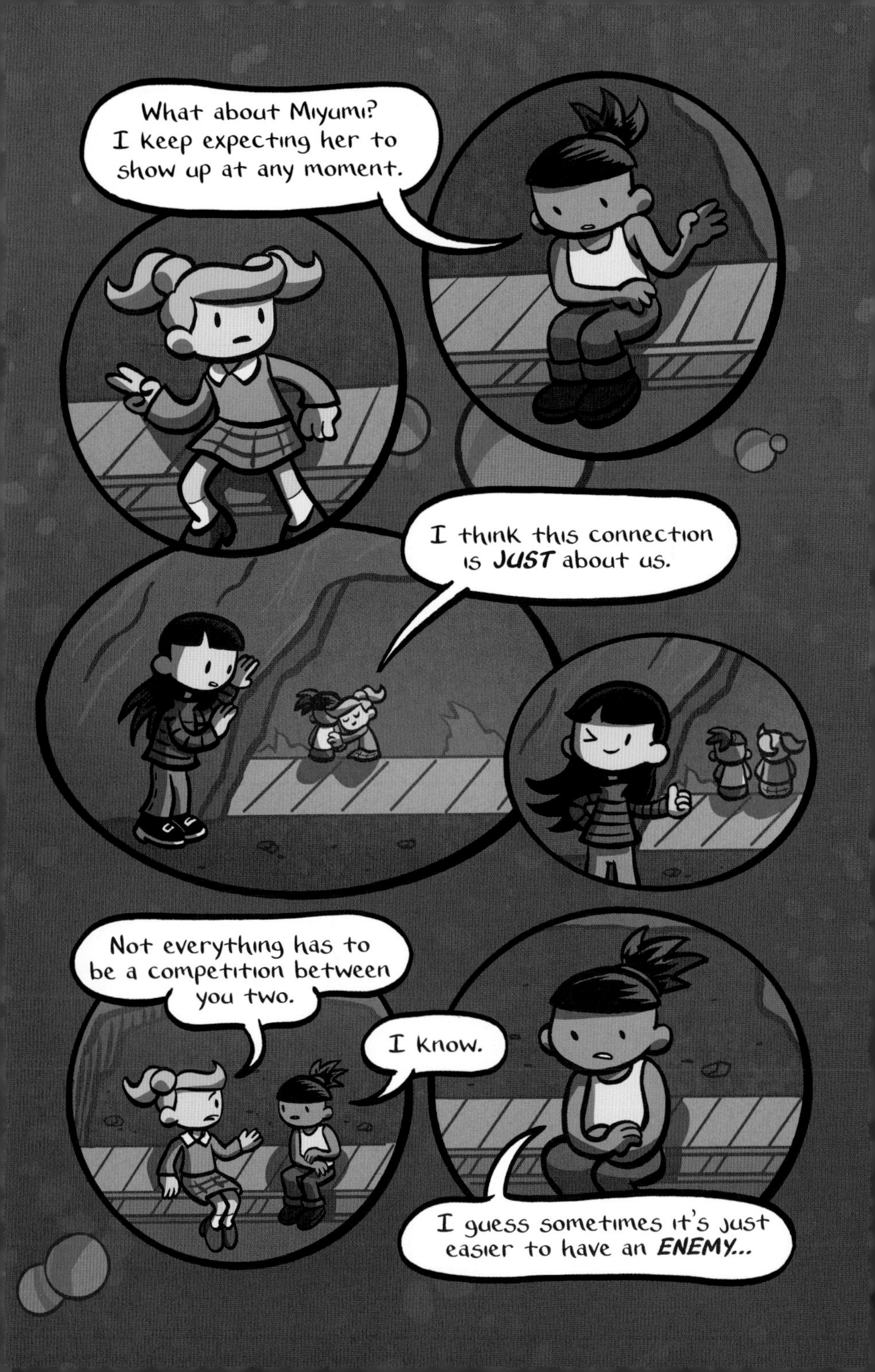
What about Miyumi? I keep expecting her to show up at any moment.
I think this connection is JUST about us.
Not everything has to be a competition between you two.
I know.
I guess sometimes it's just easier to have an ENEMY...

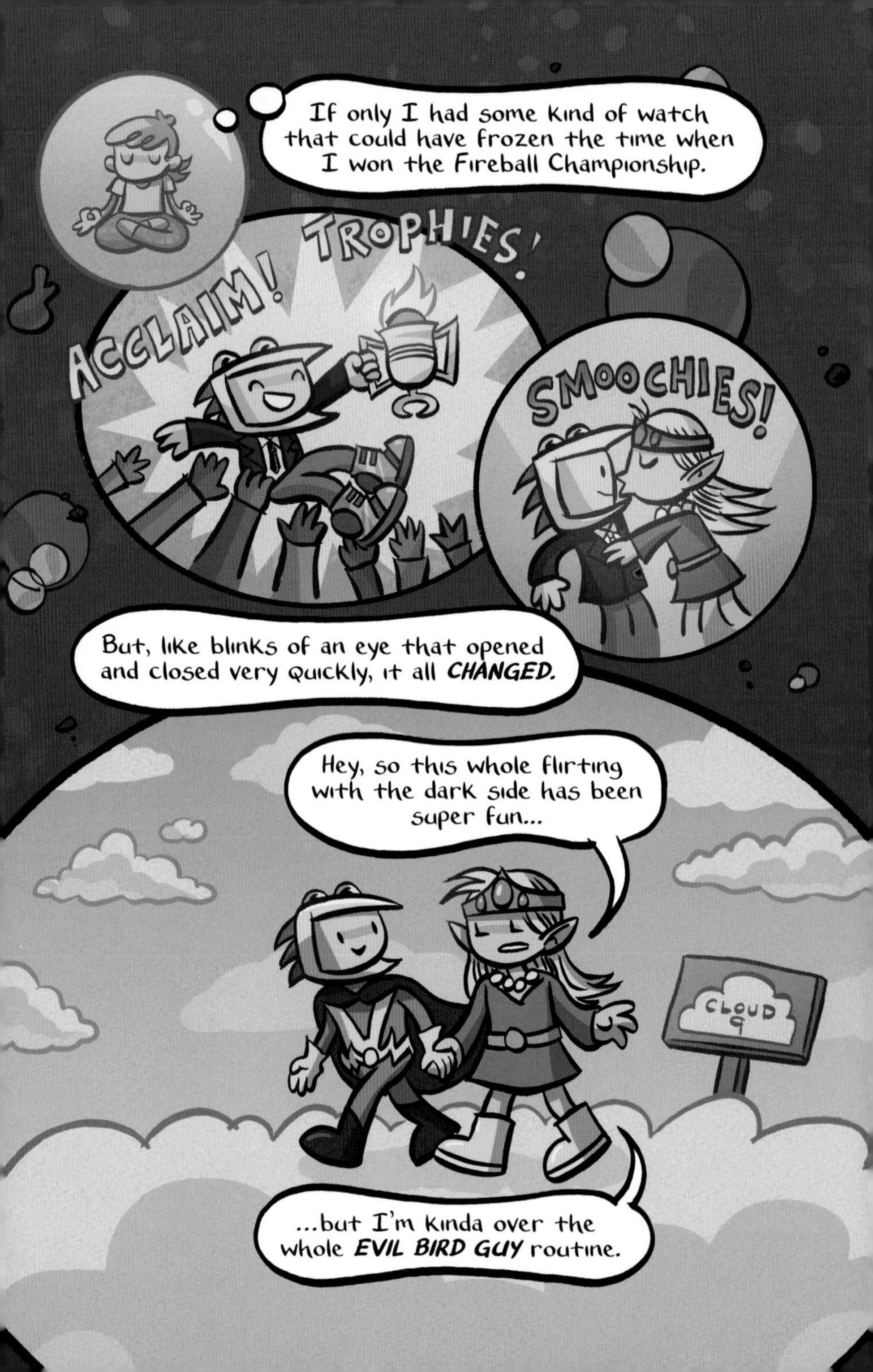
If only I had some kind of watch that could have frozen the time when I won the Fireball Championship.
TROPHIES!
ACCLAIM!
SMOOCHIES!
But, like blinks of an eye that opened and closed very quickly, it all *CHANGED.*
Hey, so this whole flirting with the dark side has been super fun...
CLOUD 9
...but I'm kinda over the whole *EVIL BIRD GUY* routine.

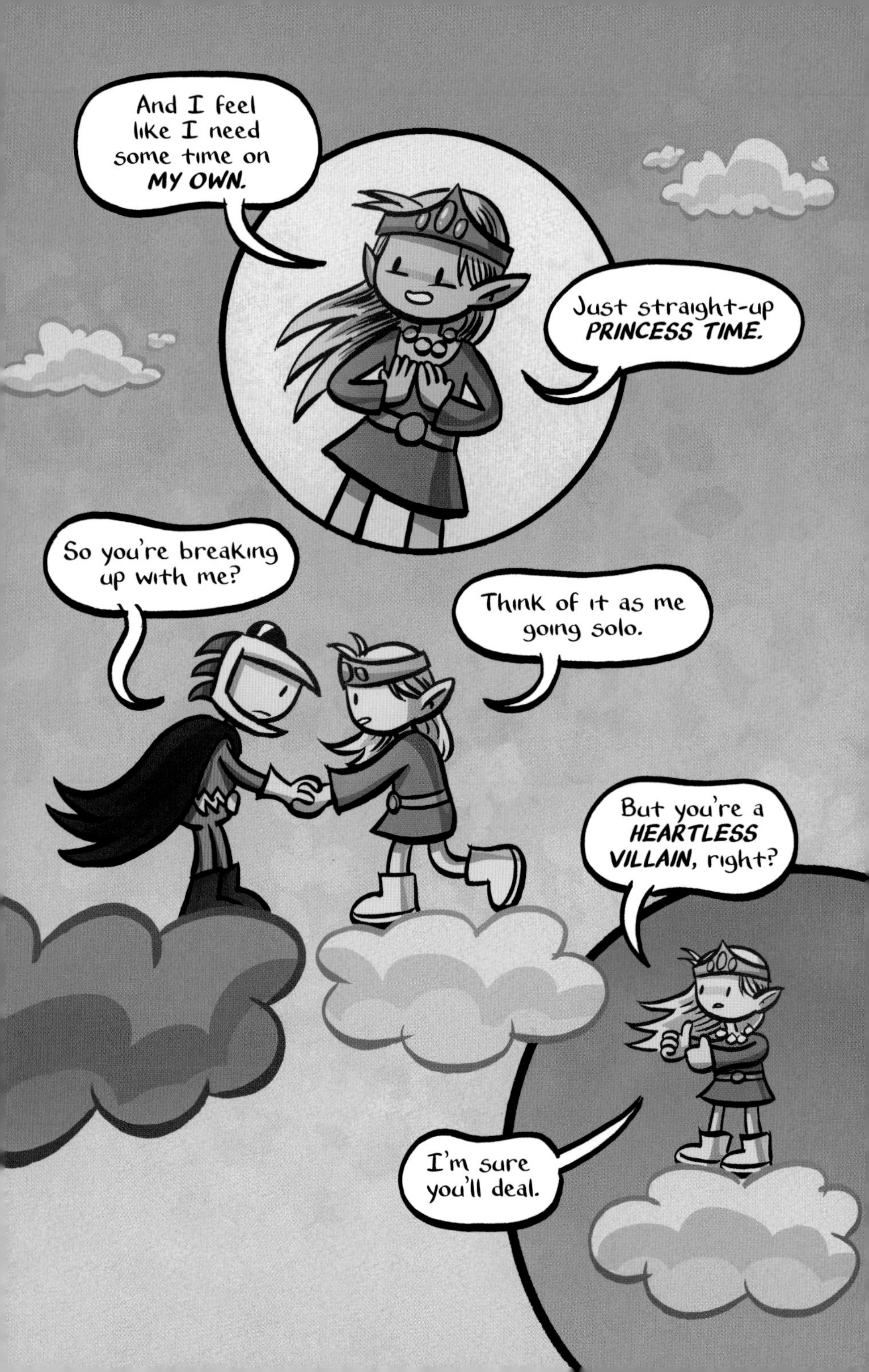
And I feel like I need some time on **MY OWN.**
Just straight-up ***PRINCESS TIME.***
So you're breaking up with me?
Think of it as me going solo.
But you're a ***HEARTLESS VILLAIN***, right?
I'm sure you'll deal.

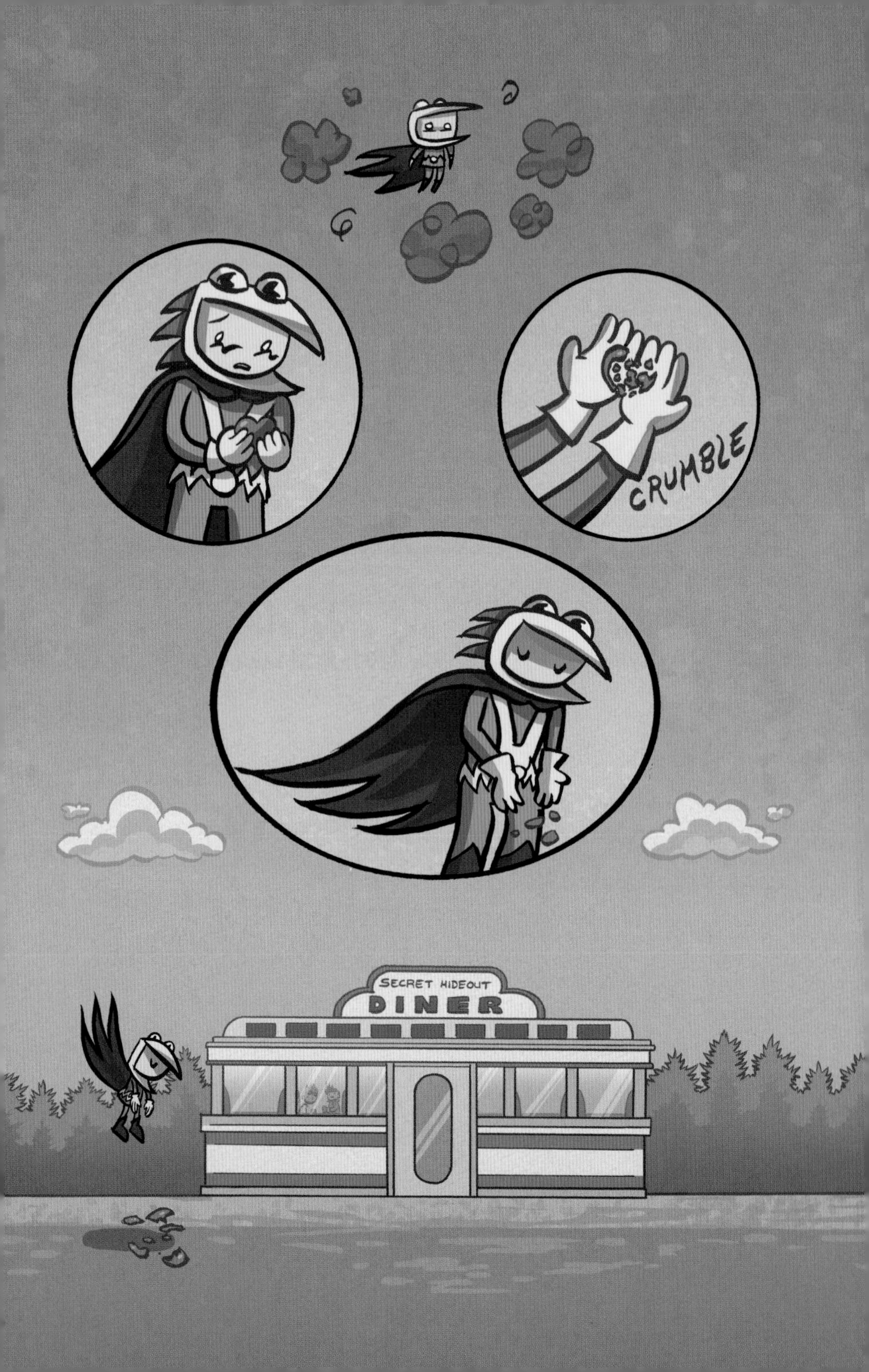
CRUMBLE
SECRET HIDEOUT
DINER

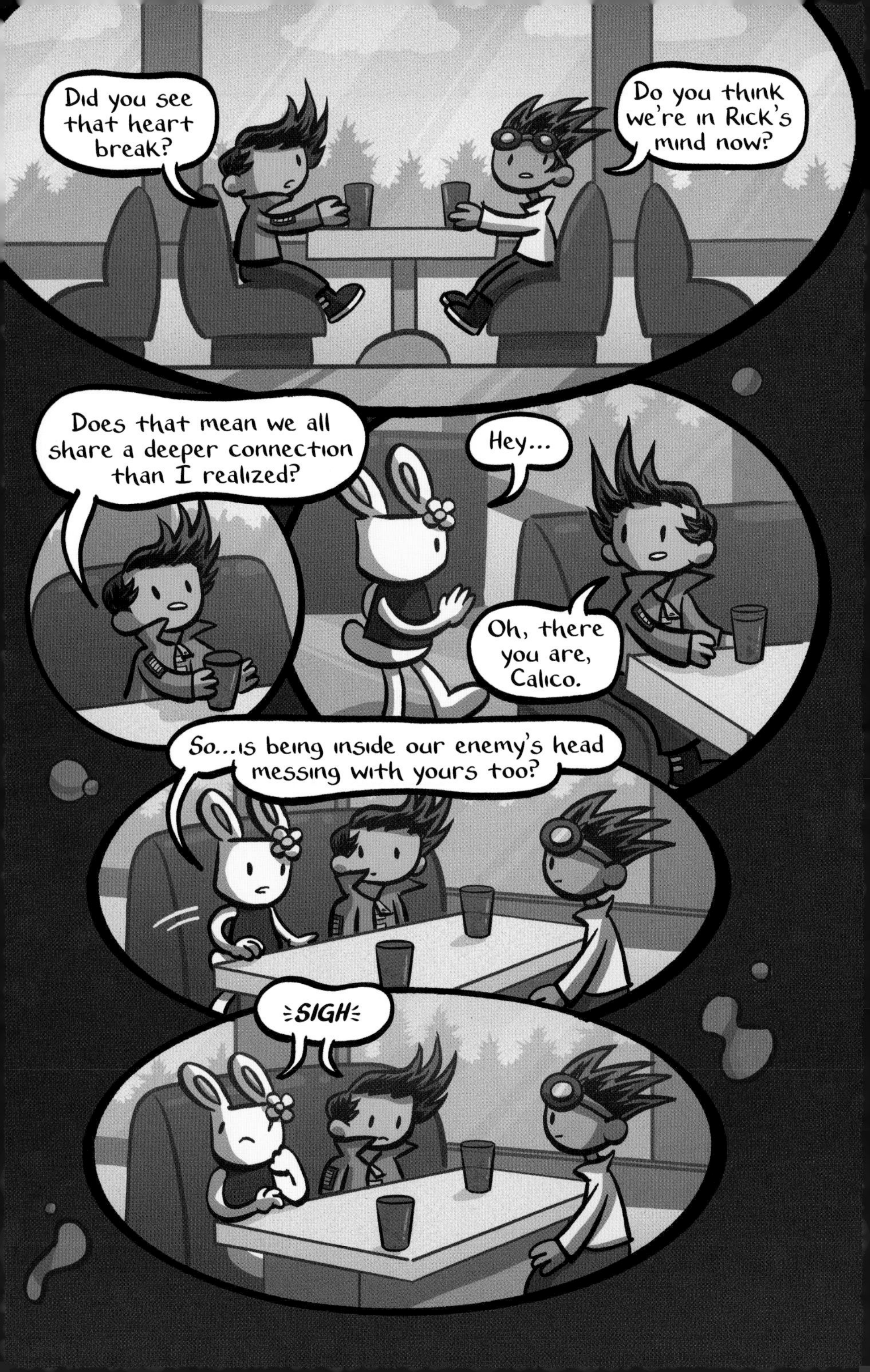
Did you see that heart break?
Do you think we're in Rick's mind now?
Does that mean we all share a deeper connection than I realized?
Hey...
Oh, there you are, Calico.
So...is being inside our enemy's head messing with yours too?
SIGH

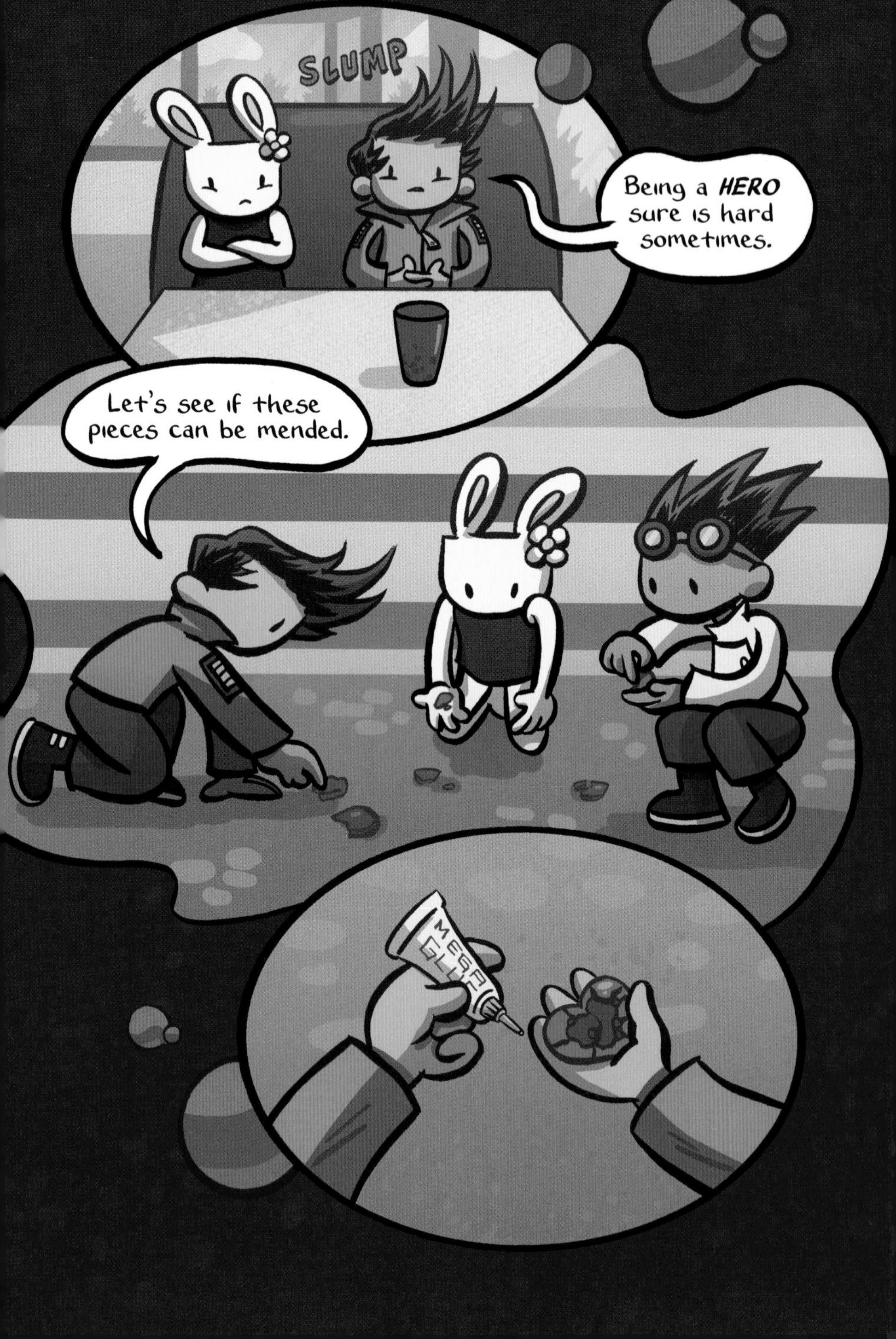
SLUMP
Being a HERO sure is hard sometimes.
Let's see if these pieces can be mended.
MEGA GLUE

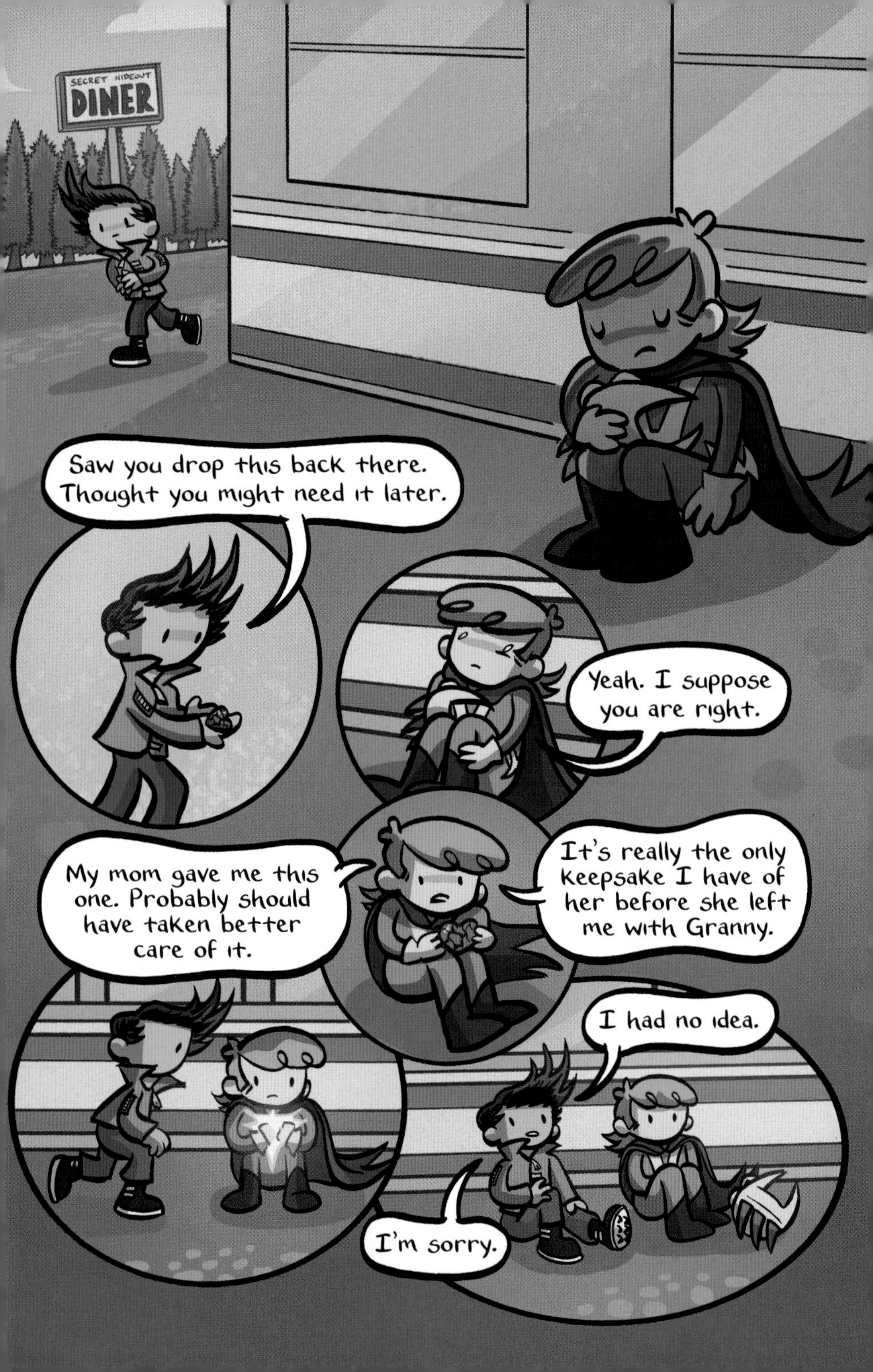
SECRET HIDEOUT DINER
Saw you drop this back there. Thought you might need it later.
Yeah. I suppose you are right.
My mom gave me this one. Probably should have taken better care of it.
It's really the only keepsake I have of her before she left me with Granny.
I had no idea.
I'm sorry.

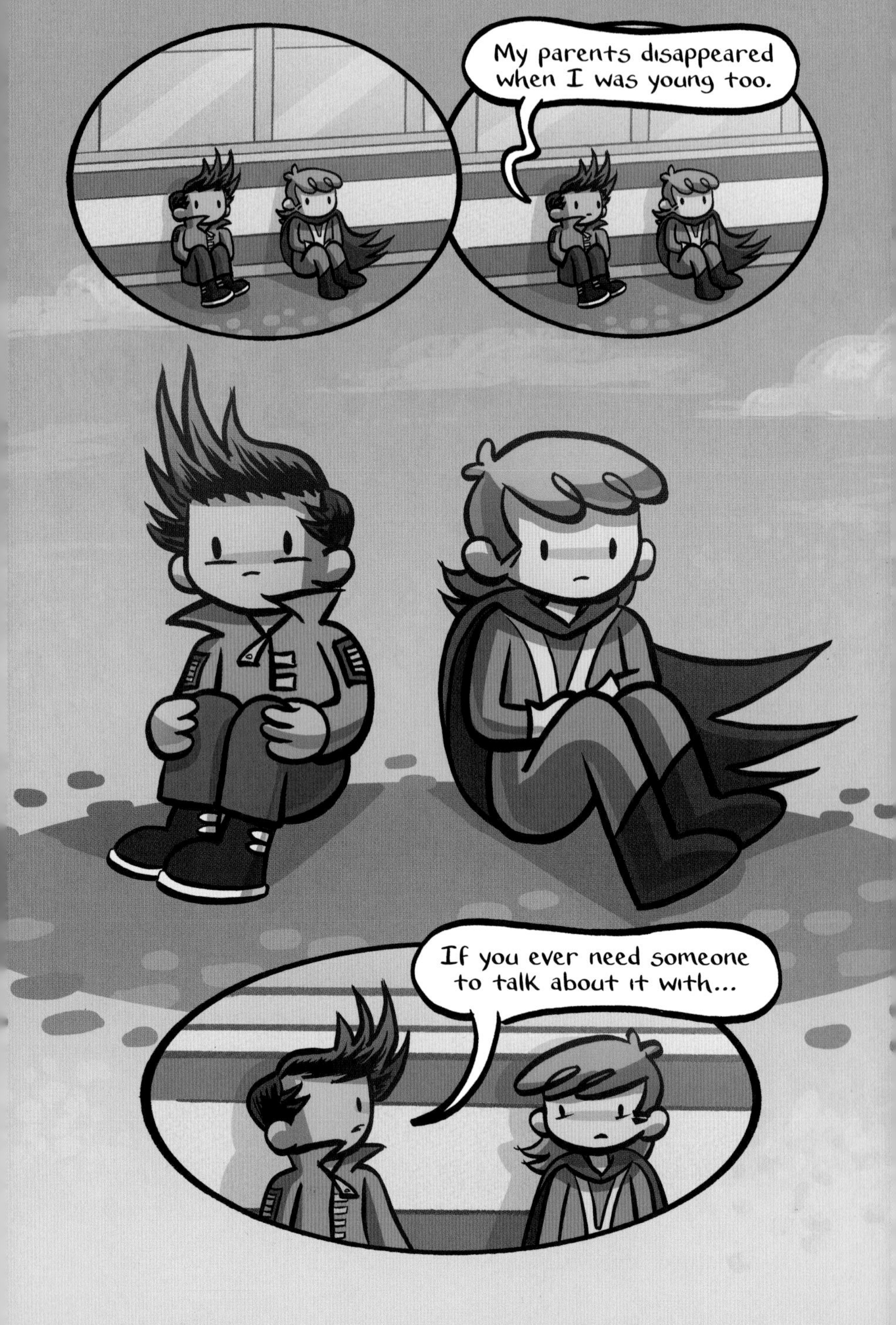
My parents disappeared when I was young too.
If you ever need someone to talk about it with...

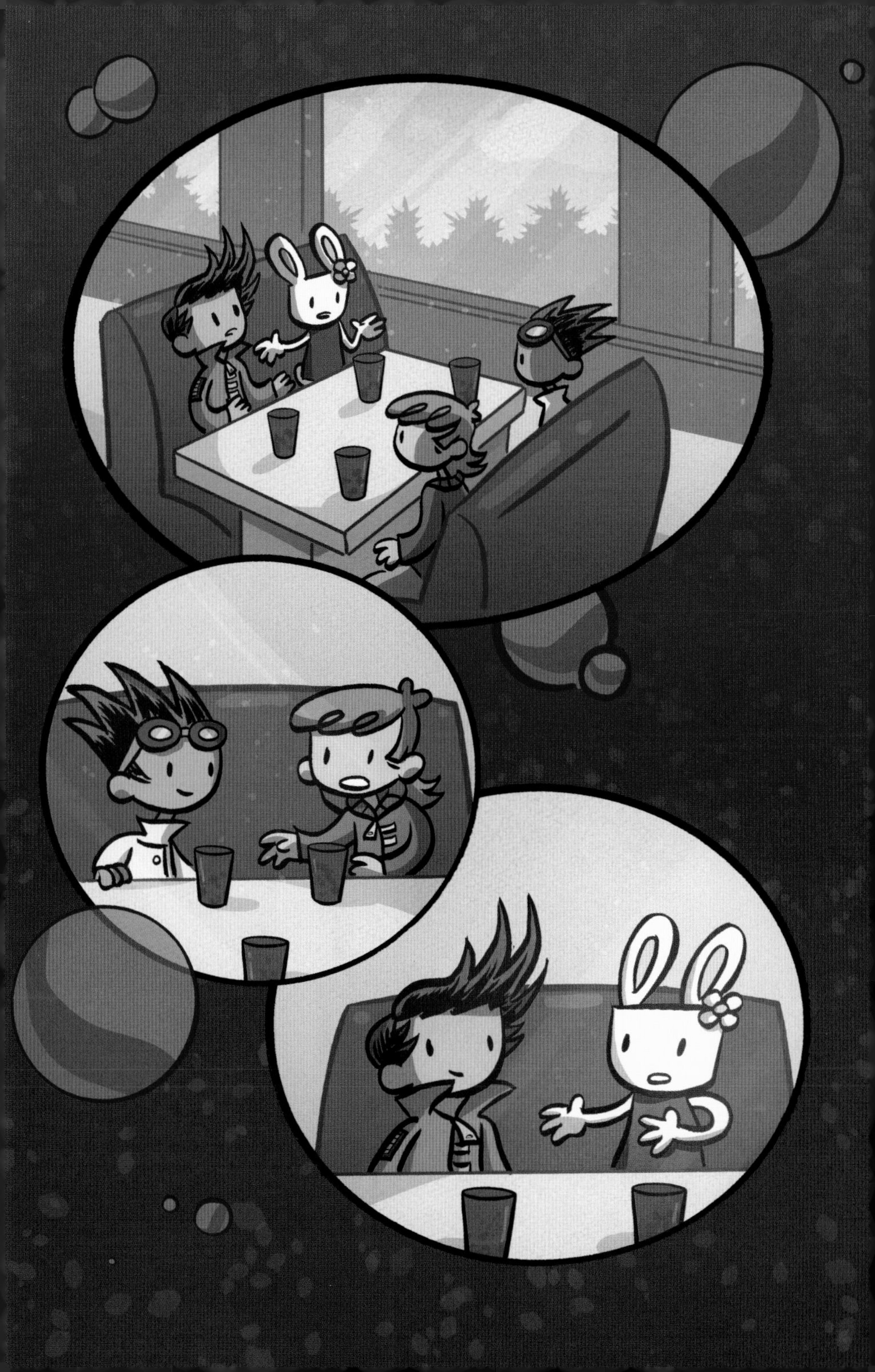

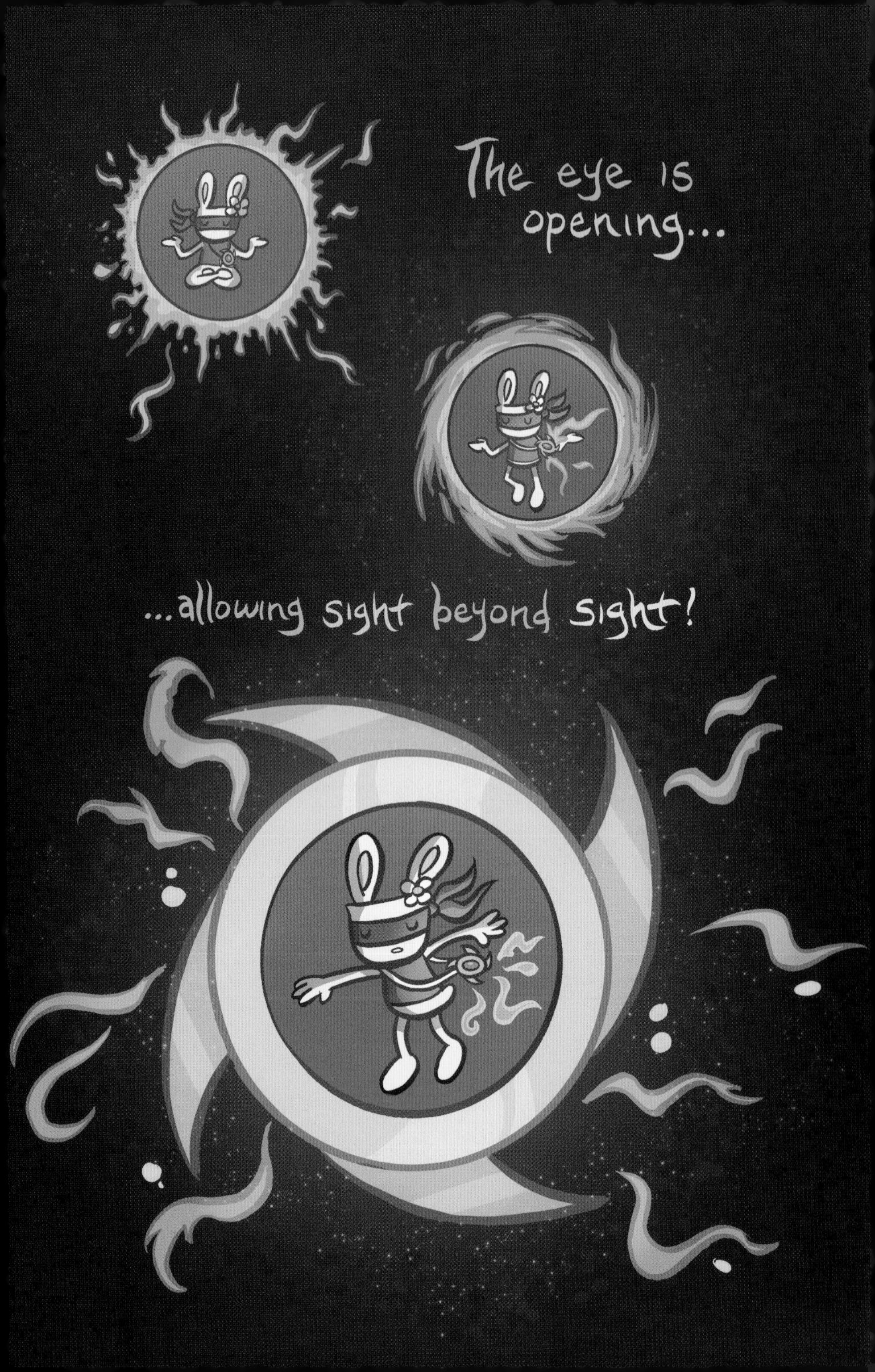
The eye is opening...
...allowing sight beyond sight!

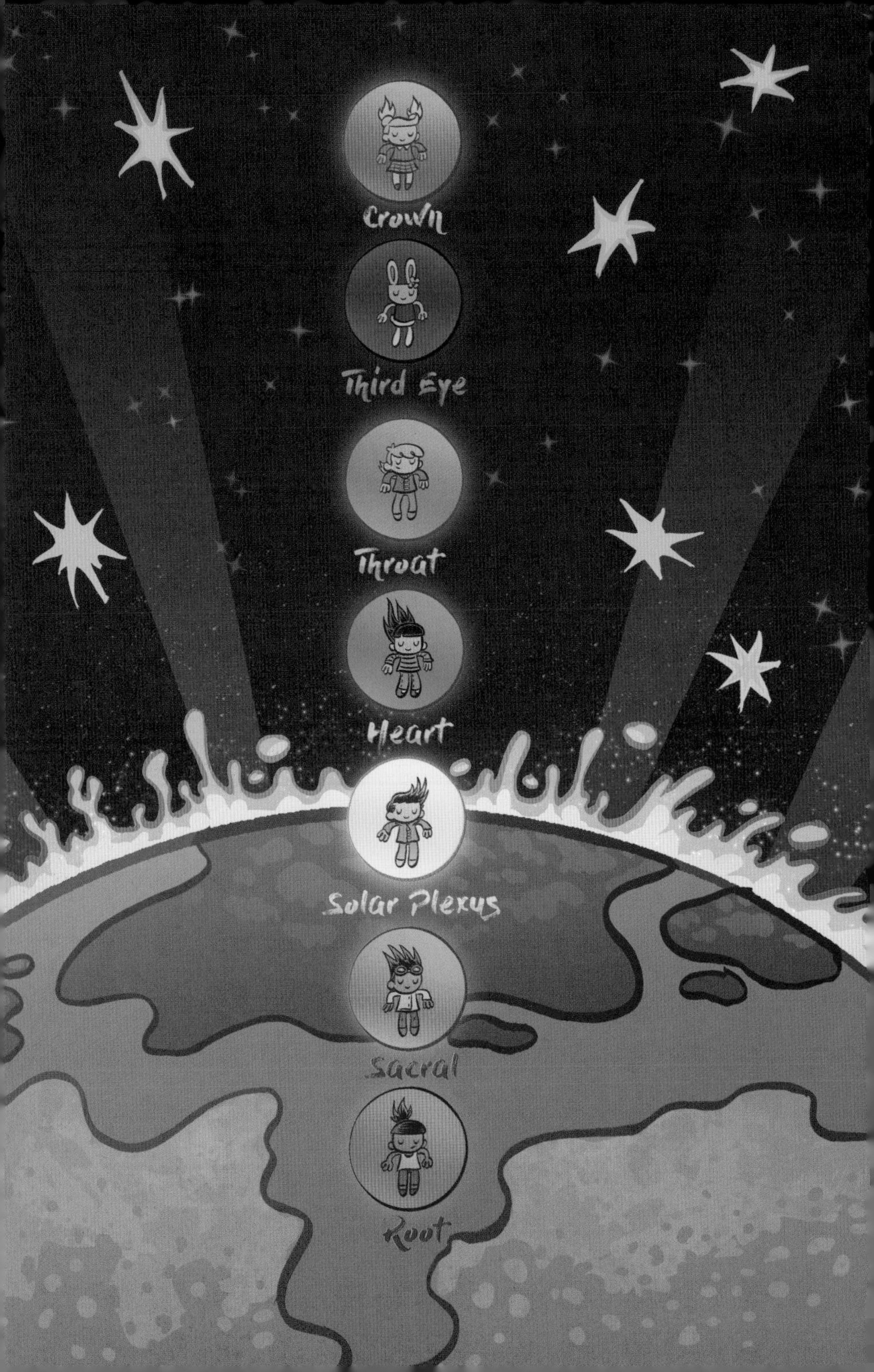
Crown
Third Eye
Throat
Heart
Solar Plexus
Sacral
Root

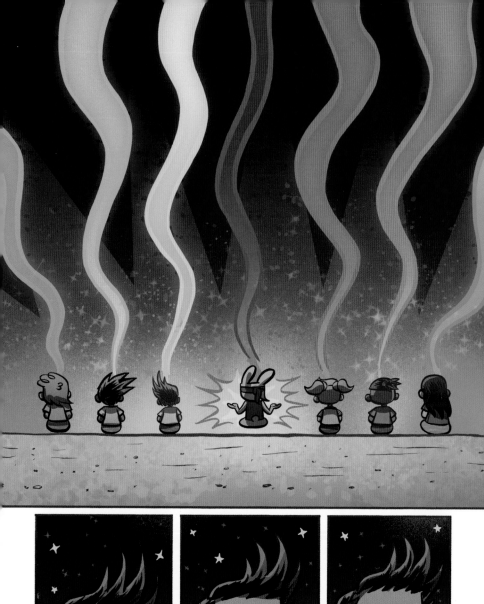

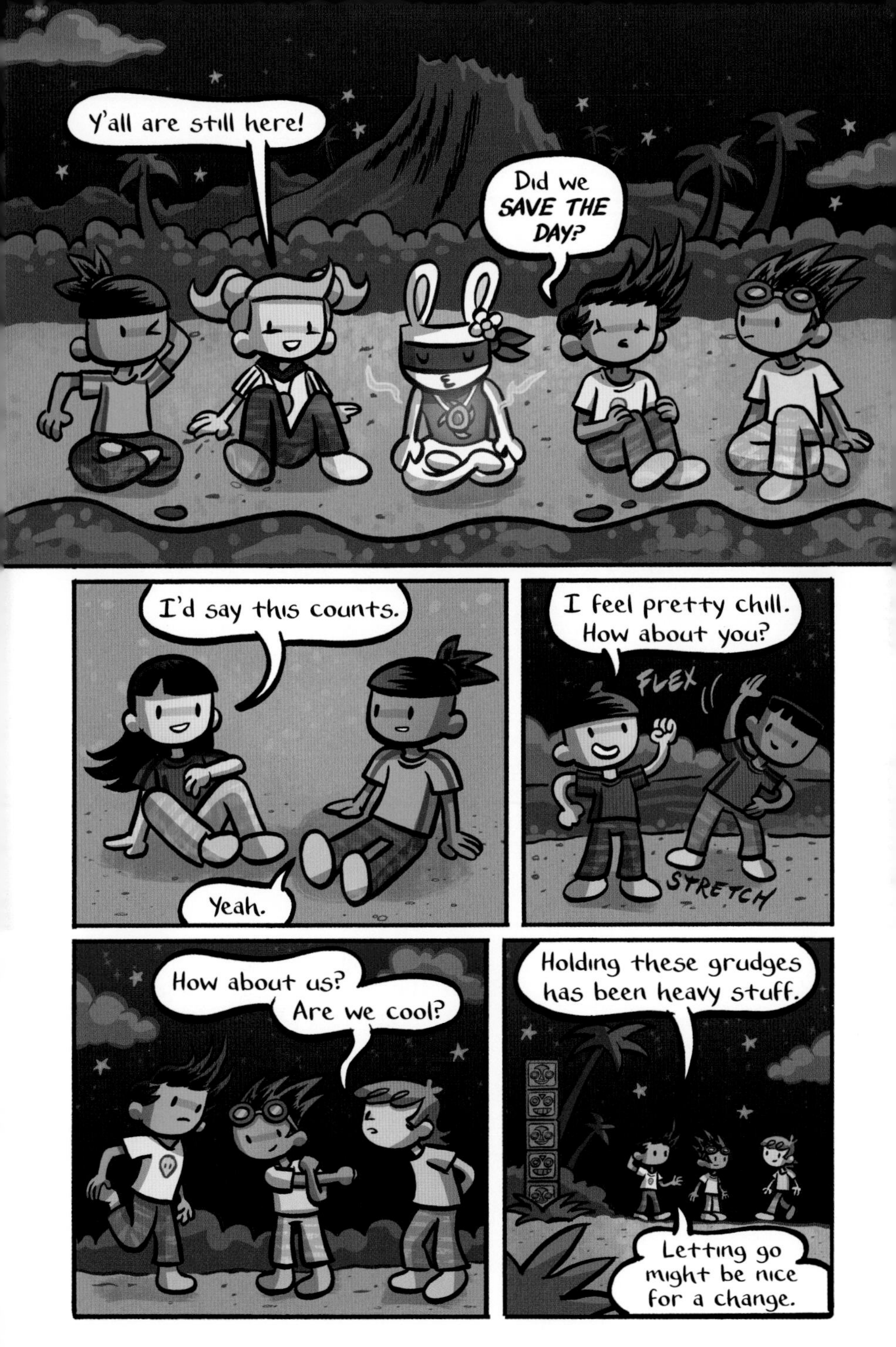
Y'all are still here!
Did we SAVE THE DAY?
I'd say this counts.
Yeah.
I feel pretty chill. How about you?
FLEX
STRETCH
How about us? Are we cool?
Holding these grudges has been heavy stuff.
Letting go might be nice for a change.

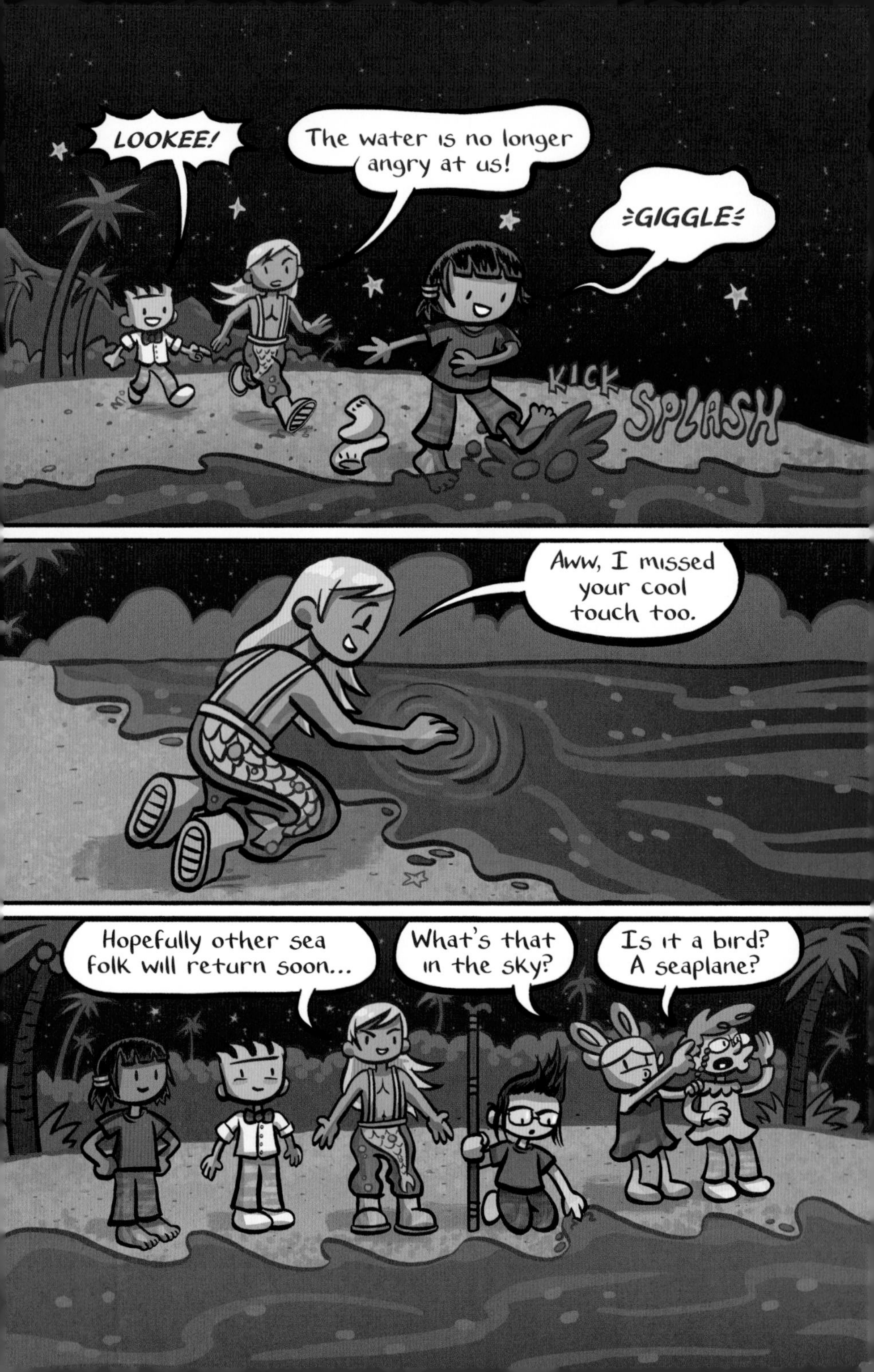
LOOKEE!
The water is no longer angry at us!
GIGGLE
KICK
SPLASH
Aww, I missed your cool touch too.
Hopefully other sea folk will return soon...
What's that in the sky?
Is it a bird? A seaplane?

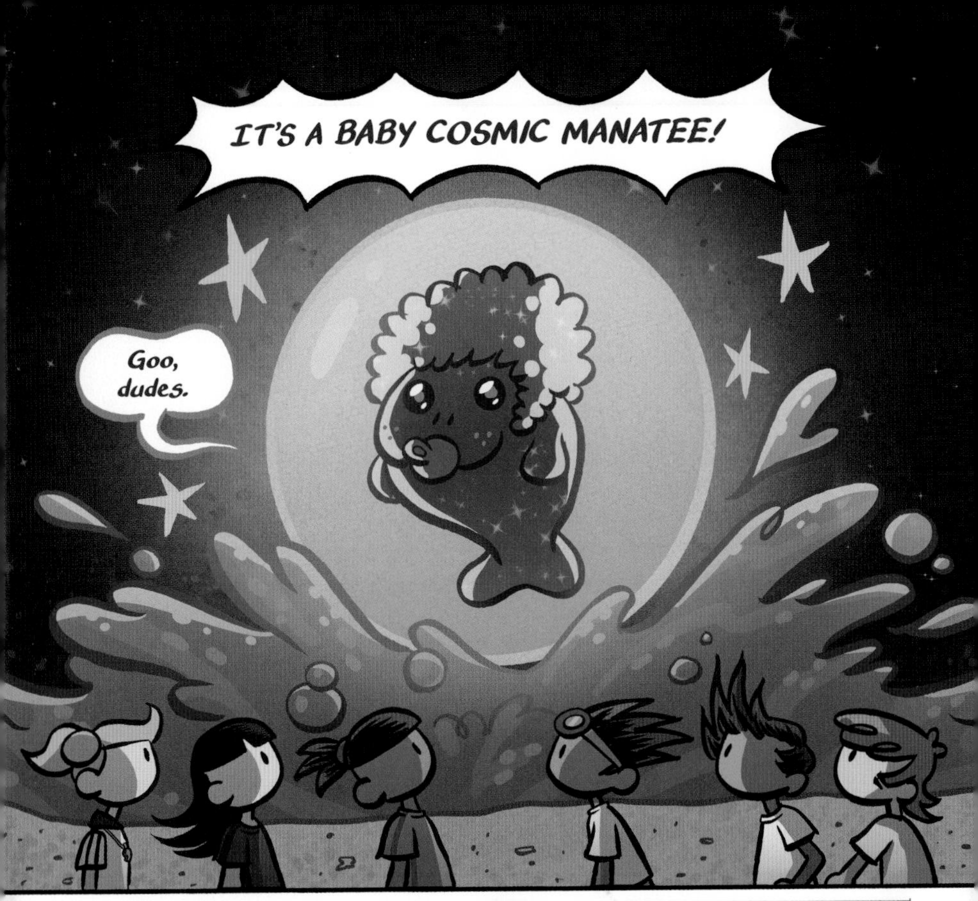
IT'S A BABY COSMIC MANATEE!
Goo, dudes.

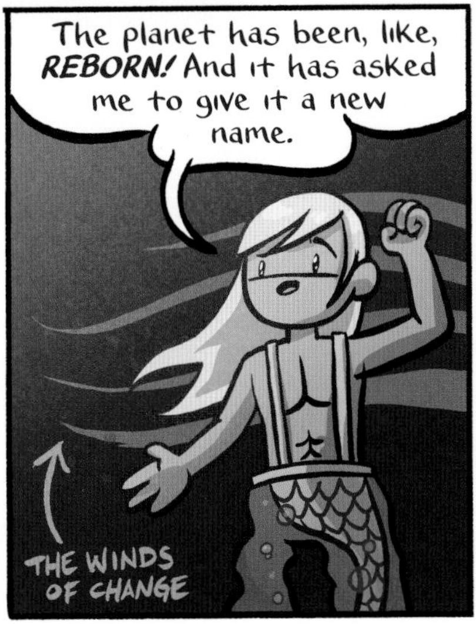
The planet has been, like, REBORN! And it has asked me to give it a new name.
THE WINDS OF CHANGE

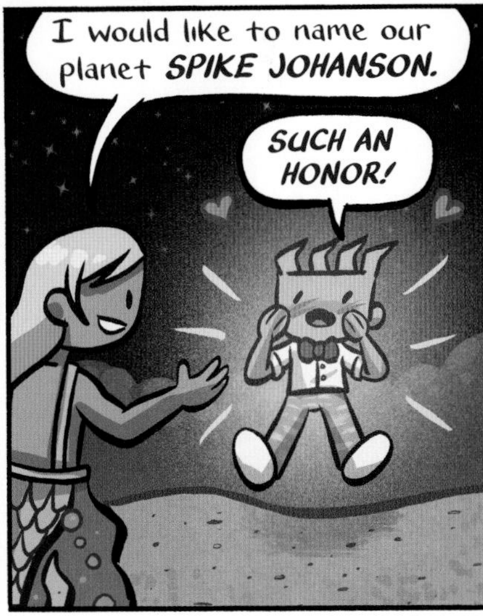
I would like to name our planet SPIKE JOHANSON.
SUCH AN HONOR!

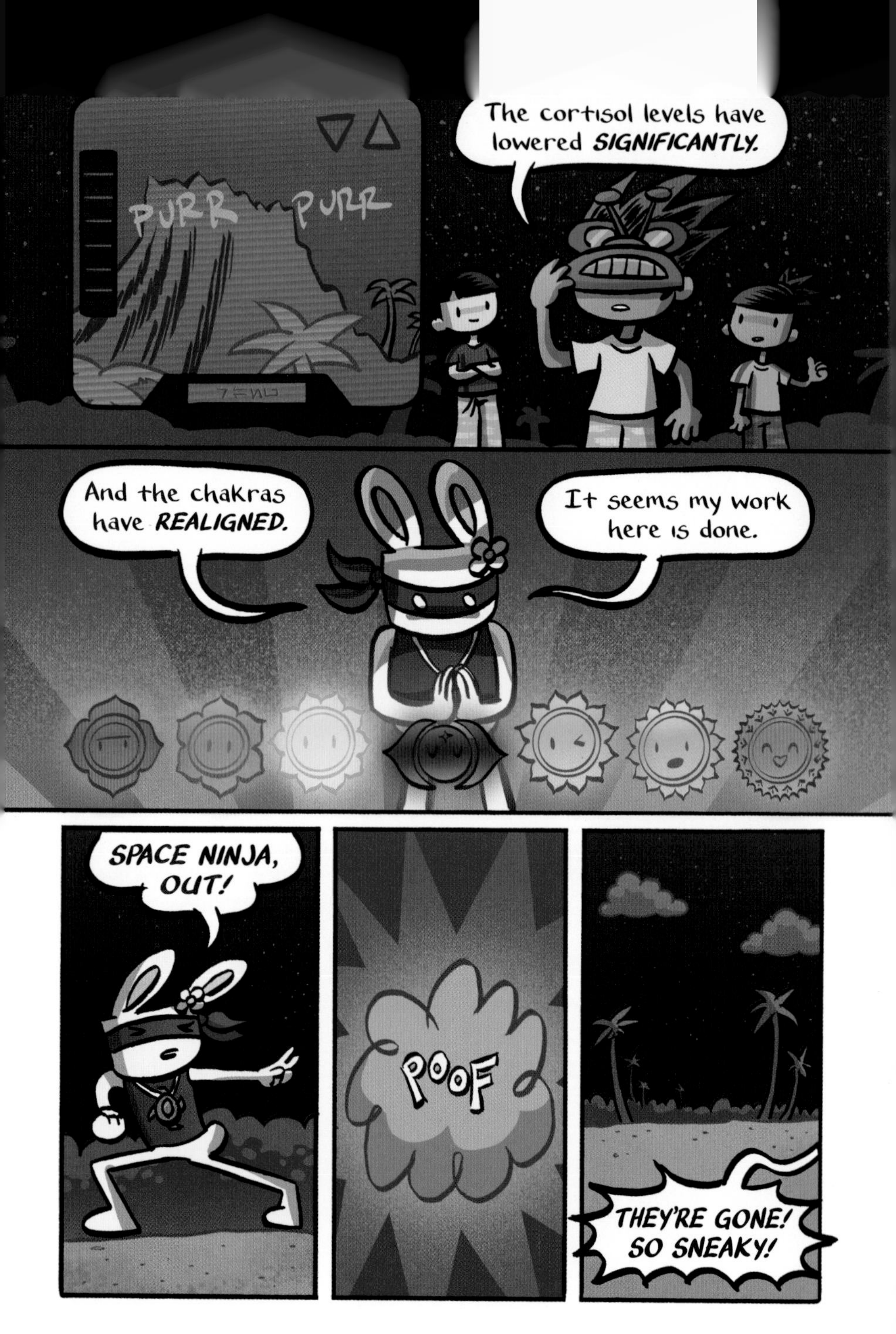
PURR PURR
The cortisol levels have lowered SIGNIFICANTLY.
And the chakras have REALIGNED.
It seems my work here is done.
SPACE NINJA, OUT!
POOF
THEY'RE GONE! SO SNEAKY!

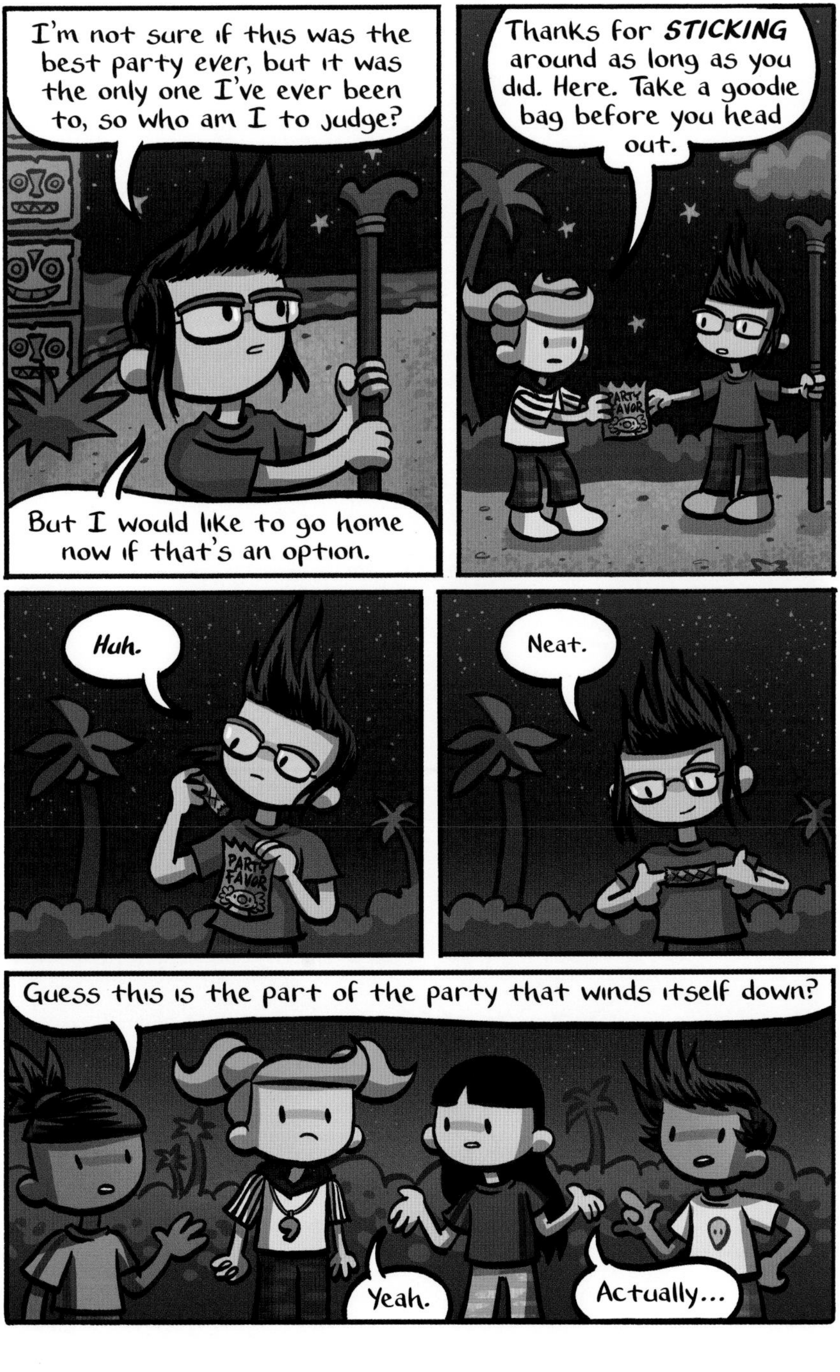
I'm not sure if this was the best party ever, but it was the only one I've ever been to, so who am I to judge?
But I would like to go home now if that's an option.
Thanks for **STICKING** around as long as you did. Here. Take a goodie bag before you head out.
PARTY FAVOR
Huh.
PARTY FAVOR
Neat.
Guess this is the part of the party that winds itself down?
Yeah.
Actually...

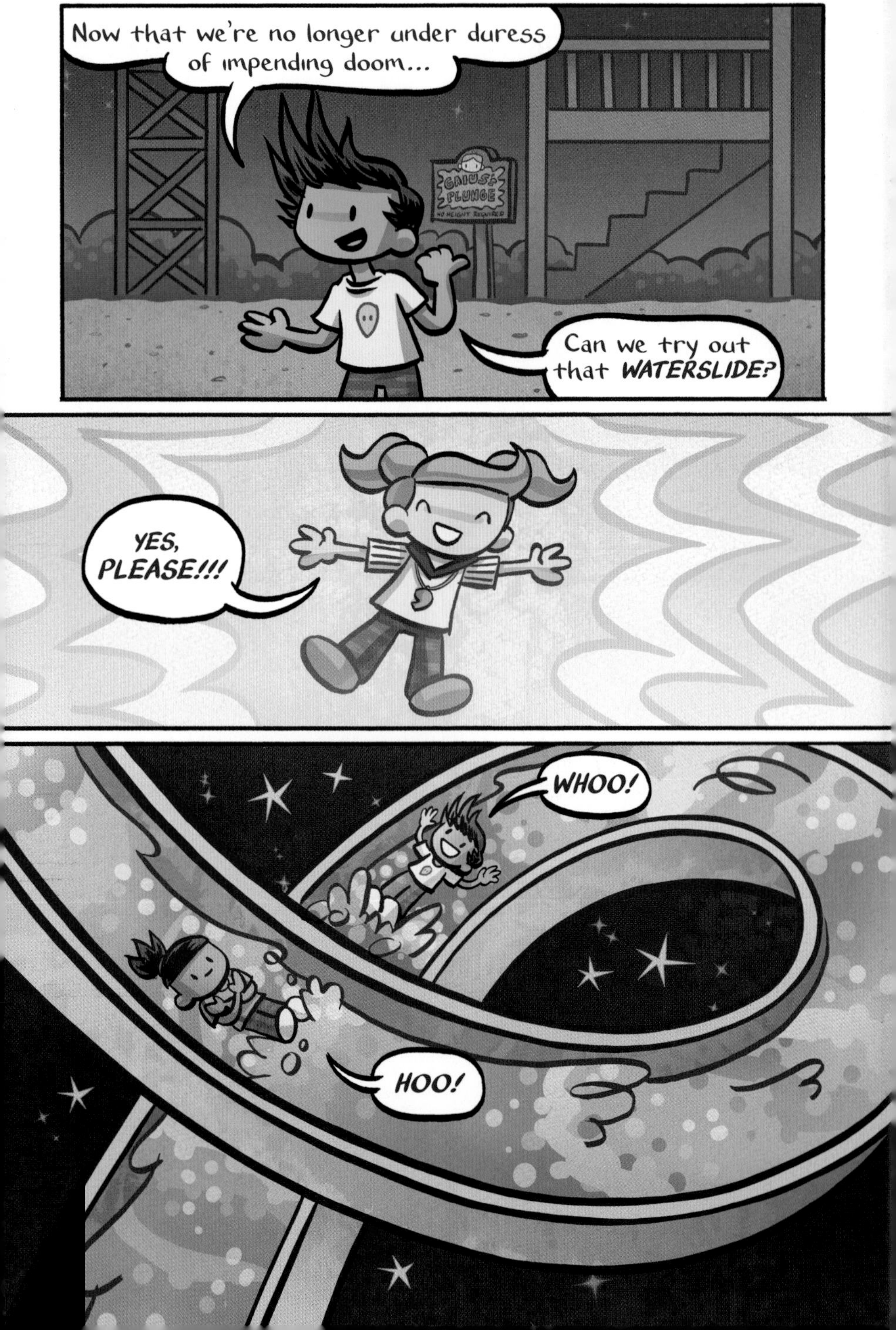
Now that we're no longer under duress of impending doom...
Can we try out that WATERSLIDE?
YES, PLEASE!!!
WHOO!
HOO!

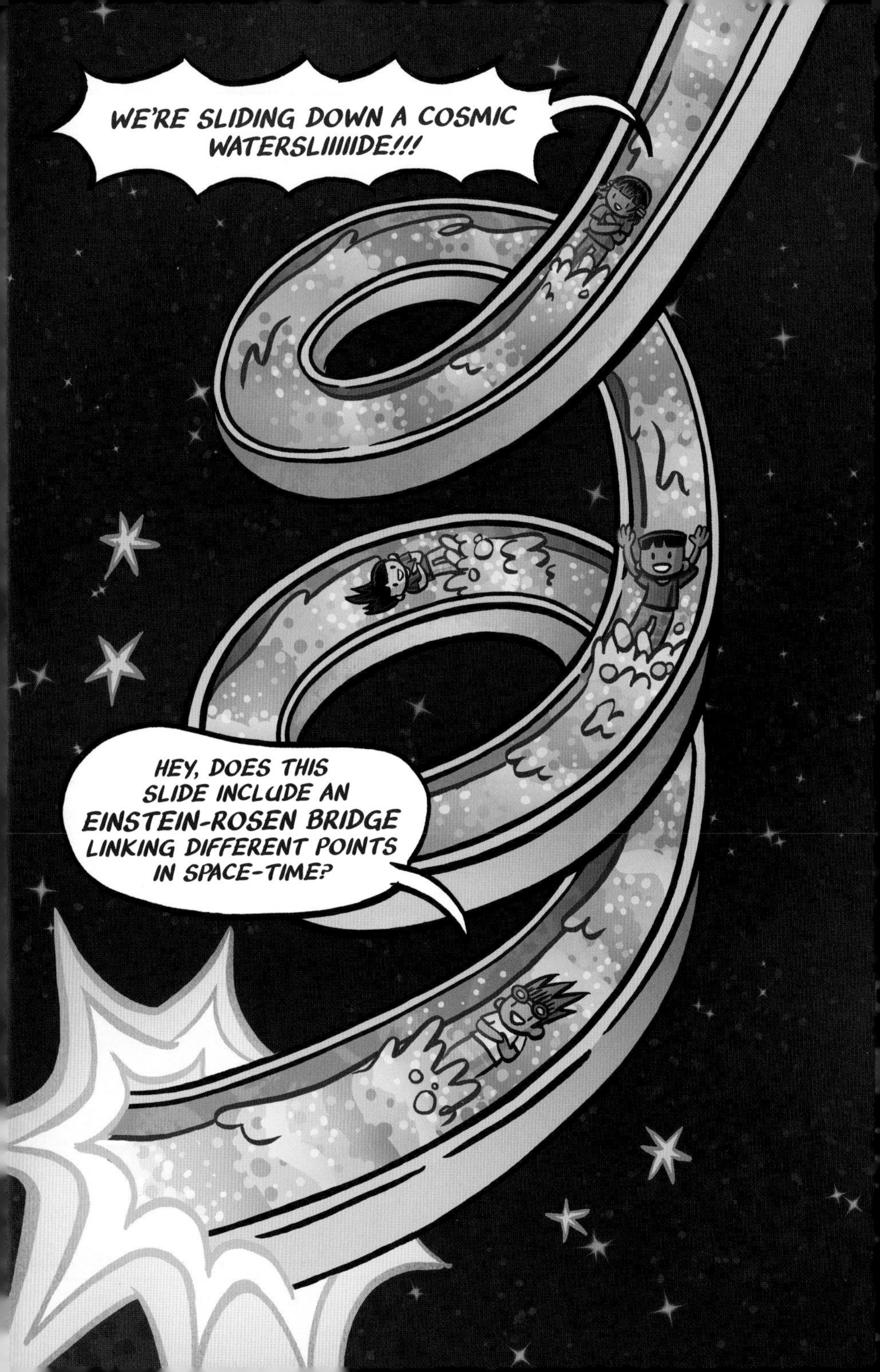
WE'RE SLIDING DOWN A COSMIC WATERSLIIIIIDE!!!
HEY, DOES THIS SLIDE INCLUDE AN EINSTEIN-ROSEN BRIDGE LINKING DIFFERENT POINTS IN SPACE-TIME?

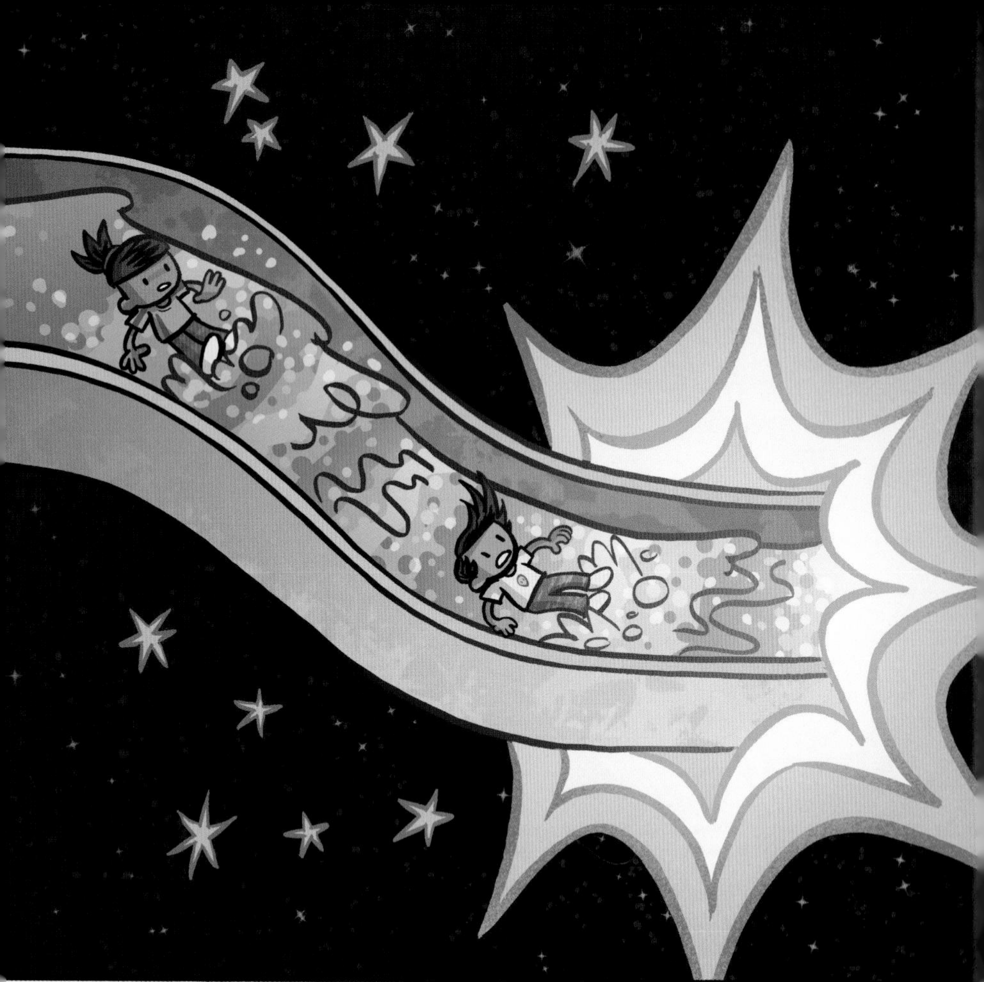

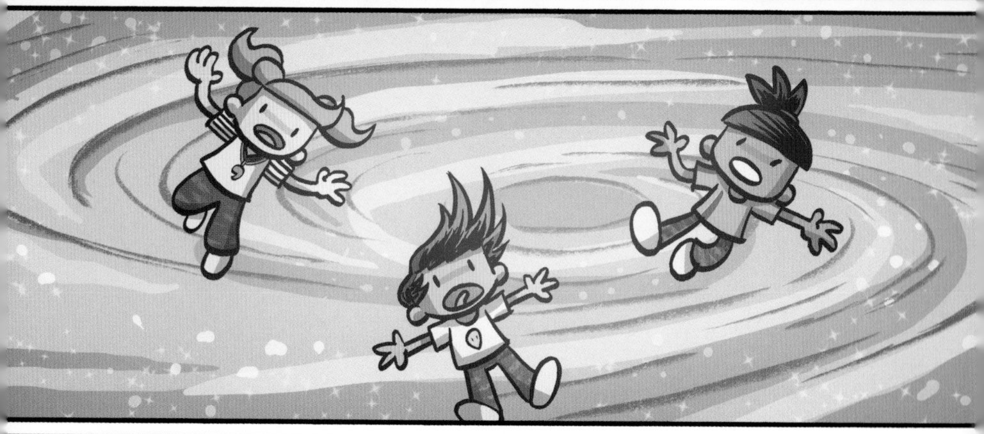

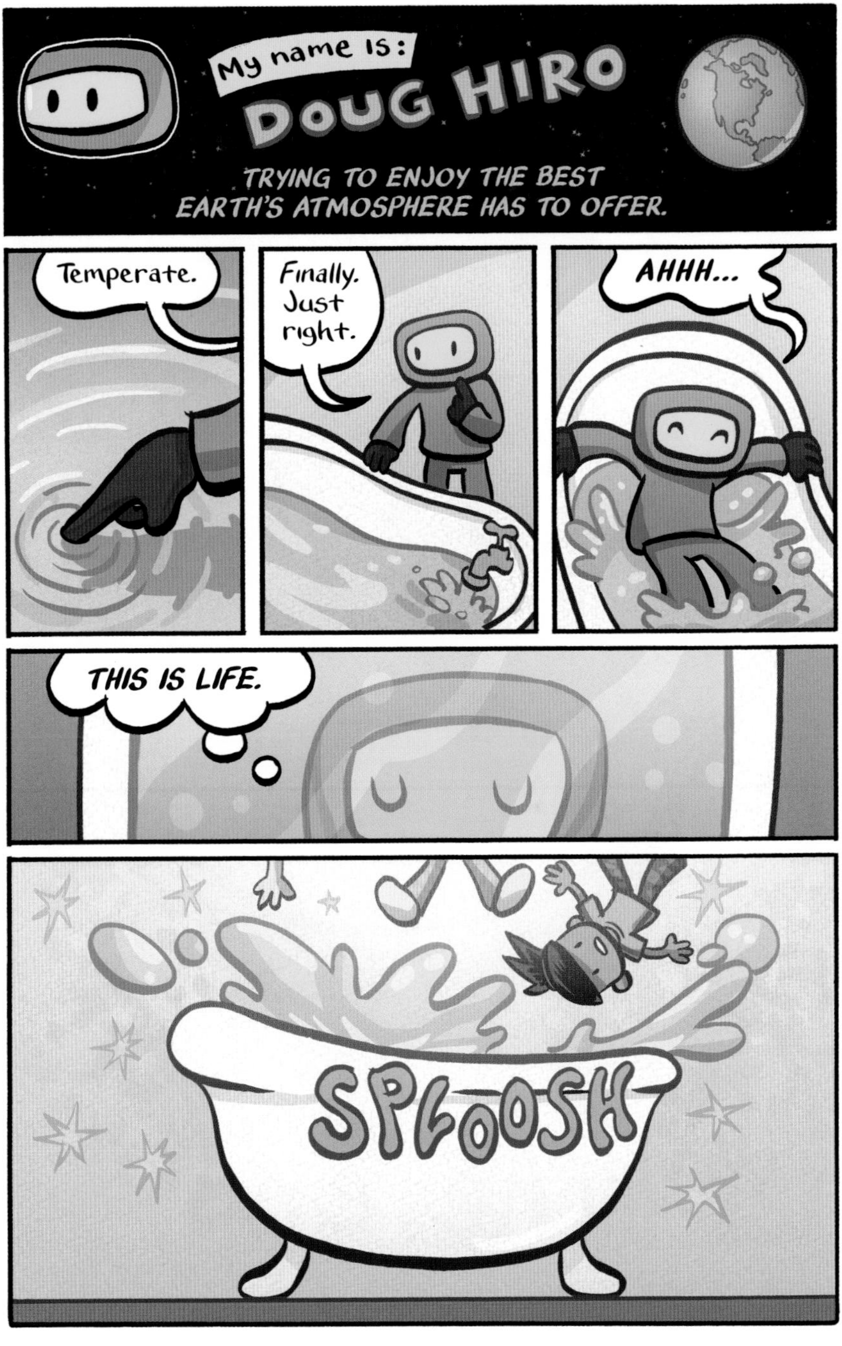
My name is:
DOUG HIRO
TRYING TO ENJOY THE BEST EARTH'S ATMOSPHERE HAS TO OFFER.
Temperate.
Finally. Just right.
AHHH...
THIS IS LIFE.
SPLOOSH

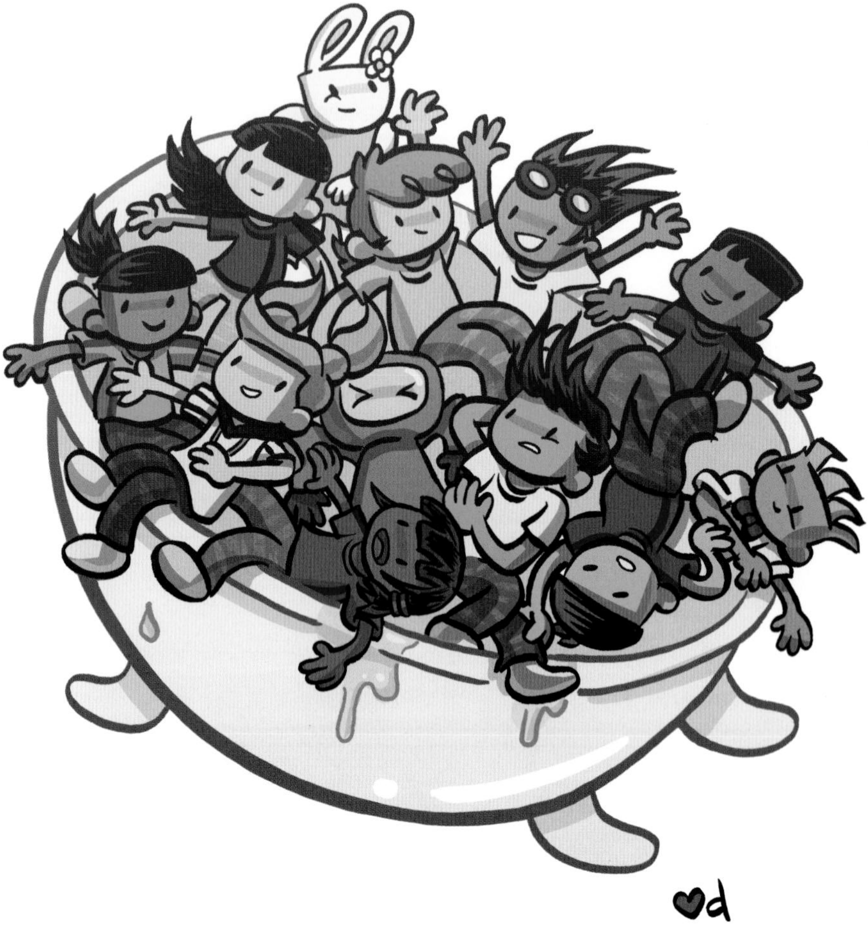

The end

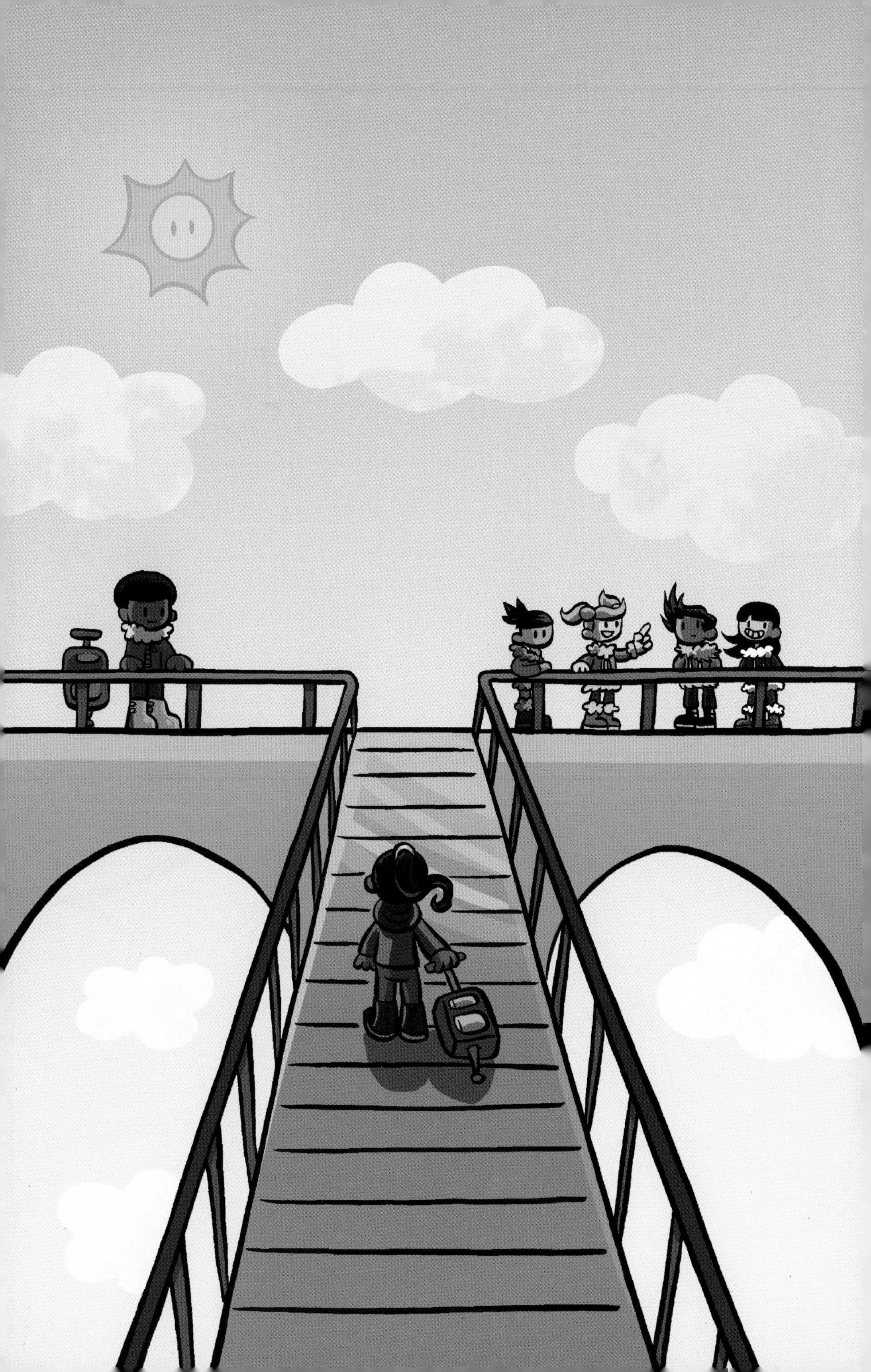

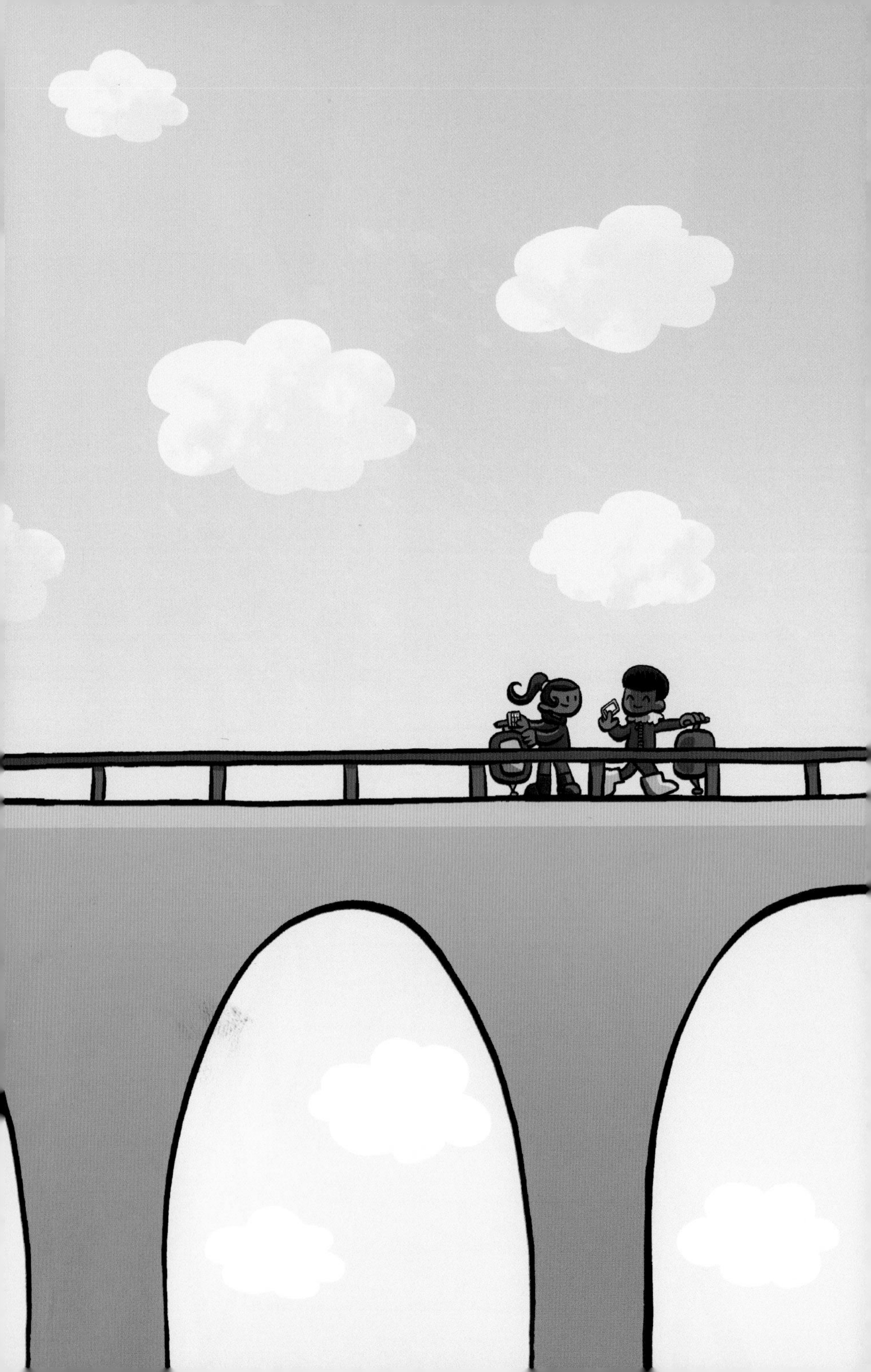

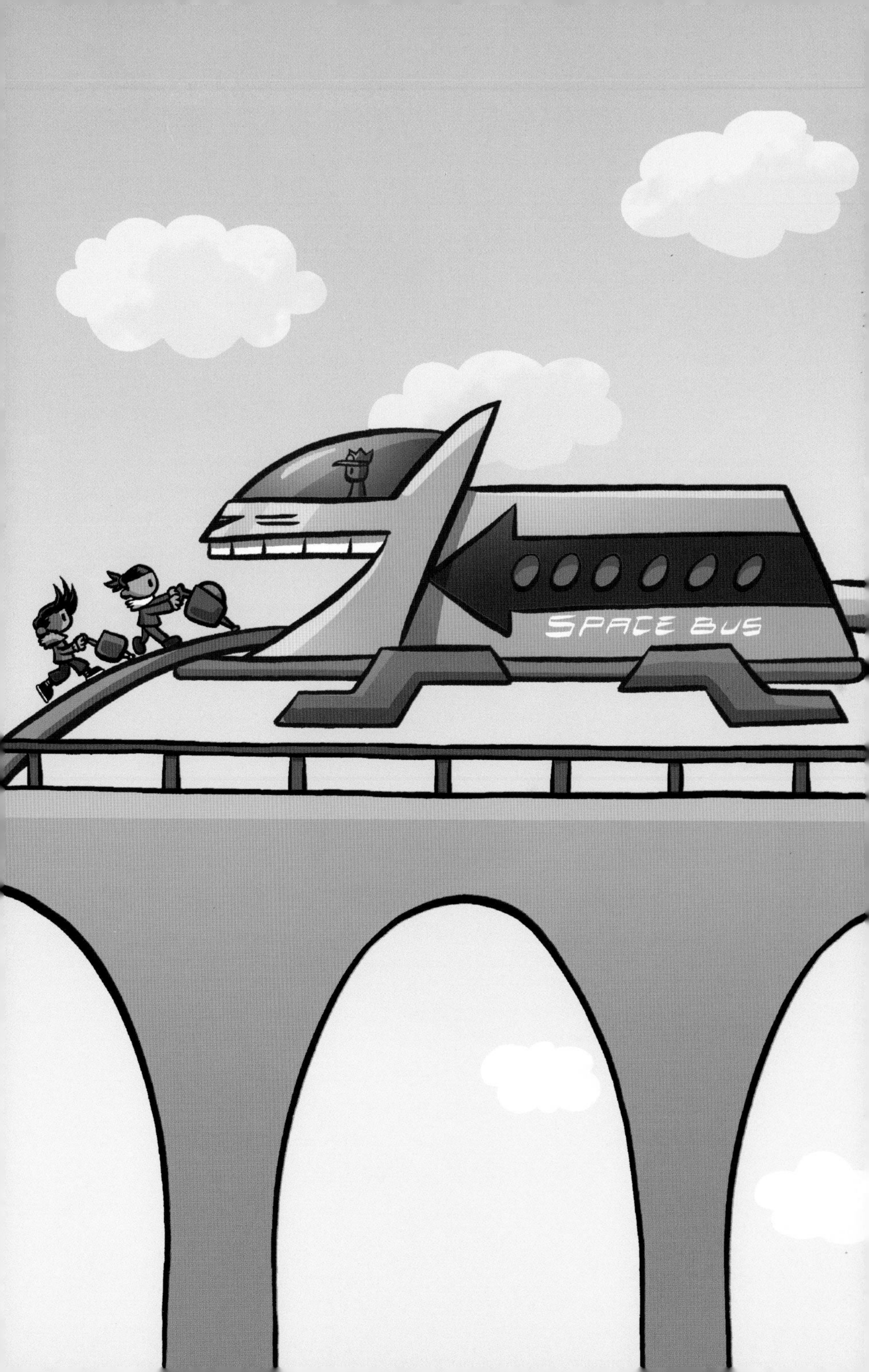
SPACE BUS

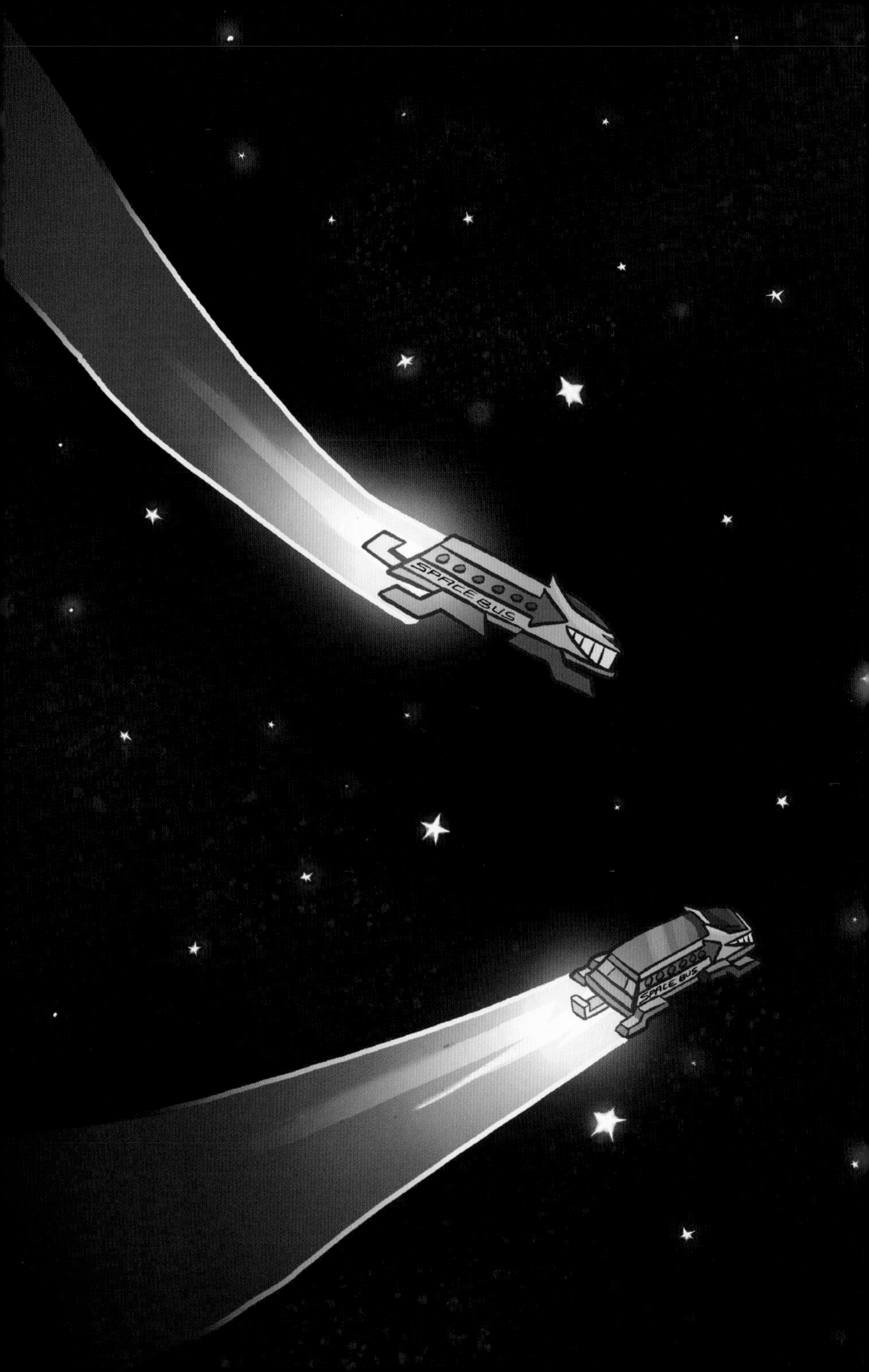
SPACE BUS
SPACE BUS

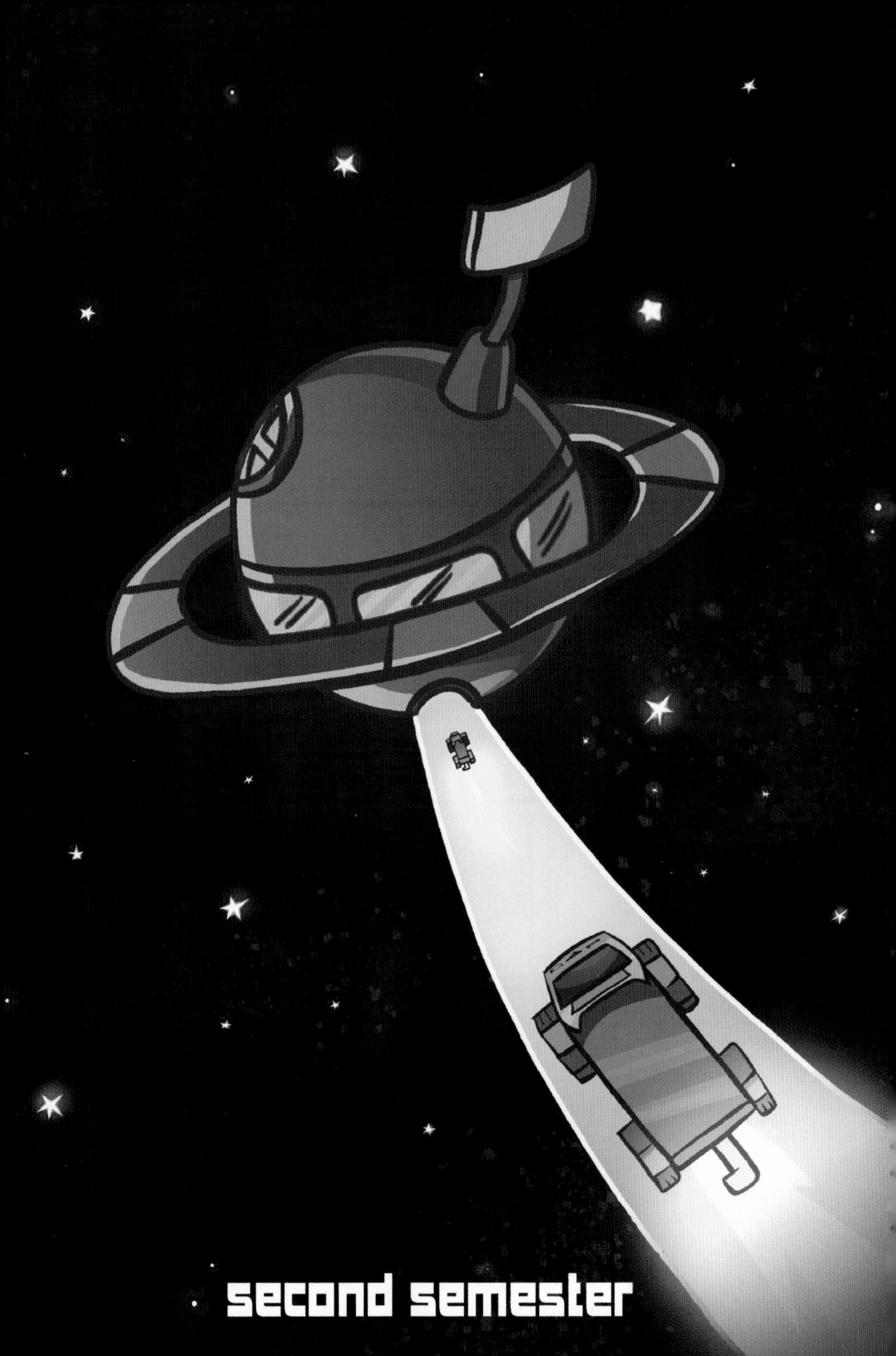

second semester

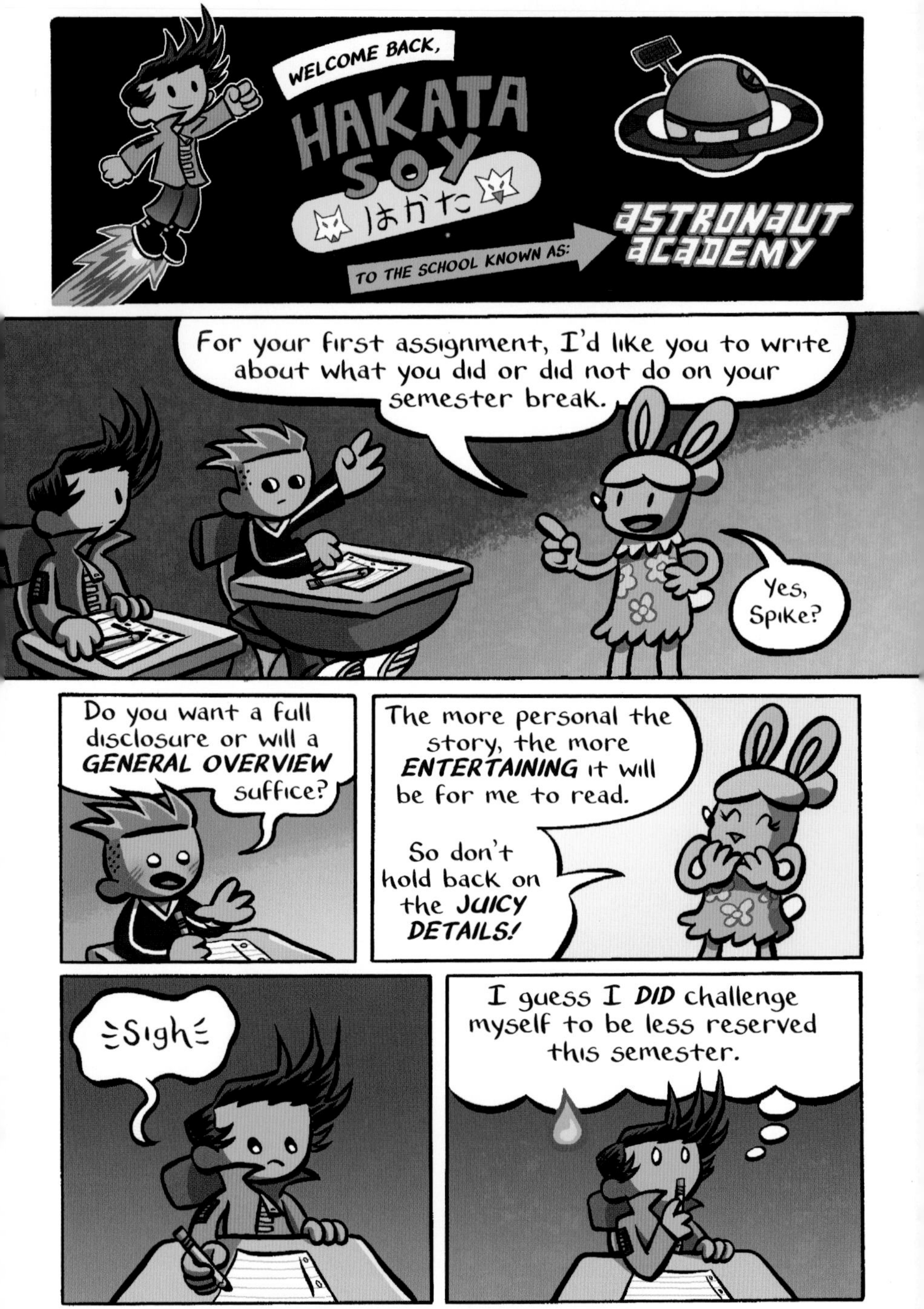
WELCOME BACK,
HAKATA SOY
はかた
TO THE SCHOOL KNOWN AS:
ASTRONAUT ACADEMY
For your first assignment, I'd like you to write about what you did or did not do on your semester break.
Yes, Spike?
Do you want a full disclosure or will a GENERAL OVERVIEW suffice?
The more personal the story, the more ENTERTAINING it will be for me to read.
So don't hold back on the JUICY DETAILS!
Sigh
I guess I DID challenge myself to be less reserved this semester.

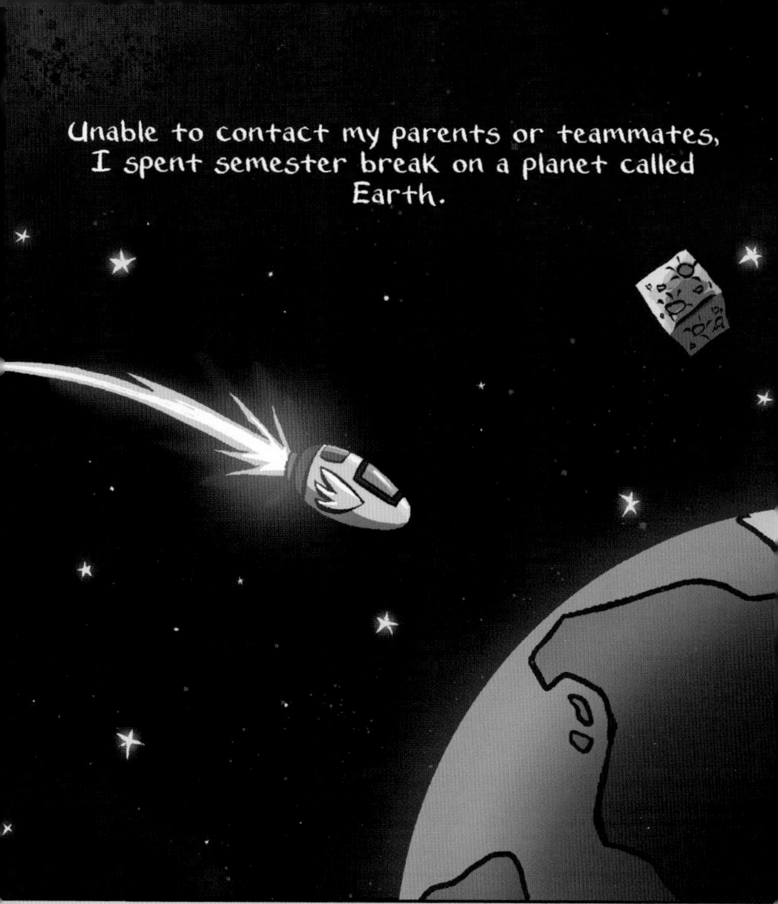
Unable to contact my parents or teammates, I spent semester break on a planet called Earth.

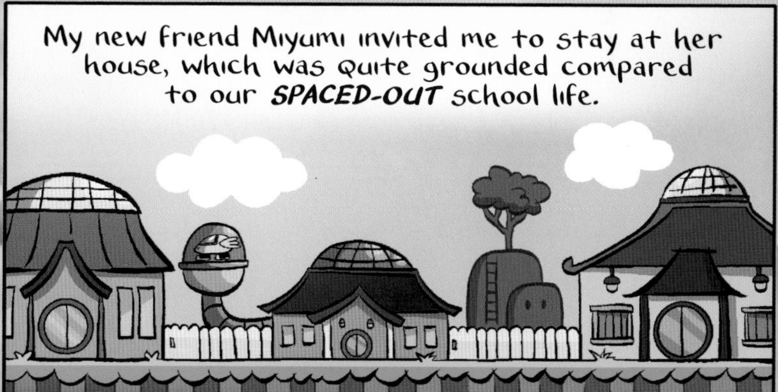
My new friend Miyumi invited me to stay at her house, which was quite grounded compared to our SPACED-OUT school life.

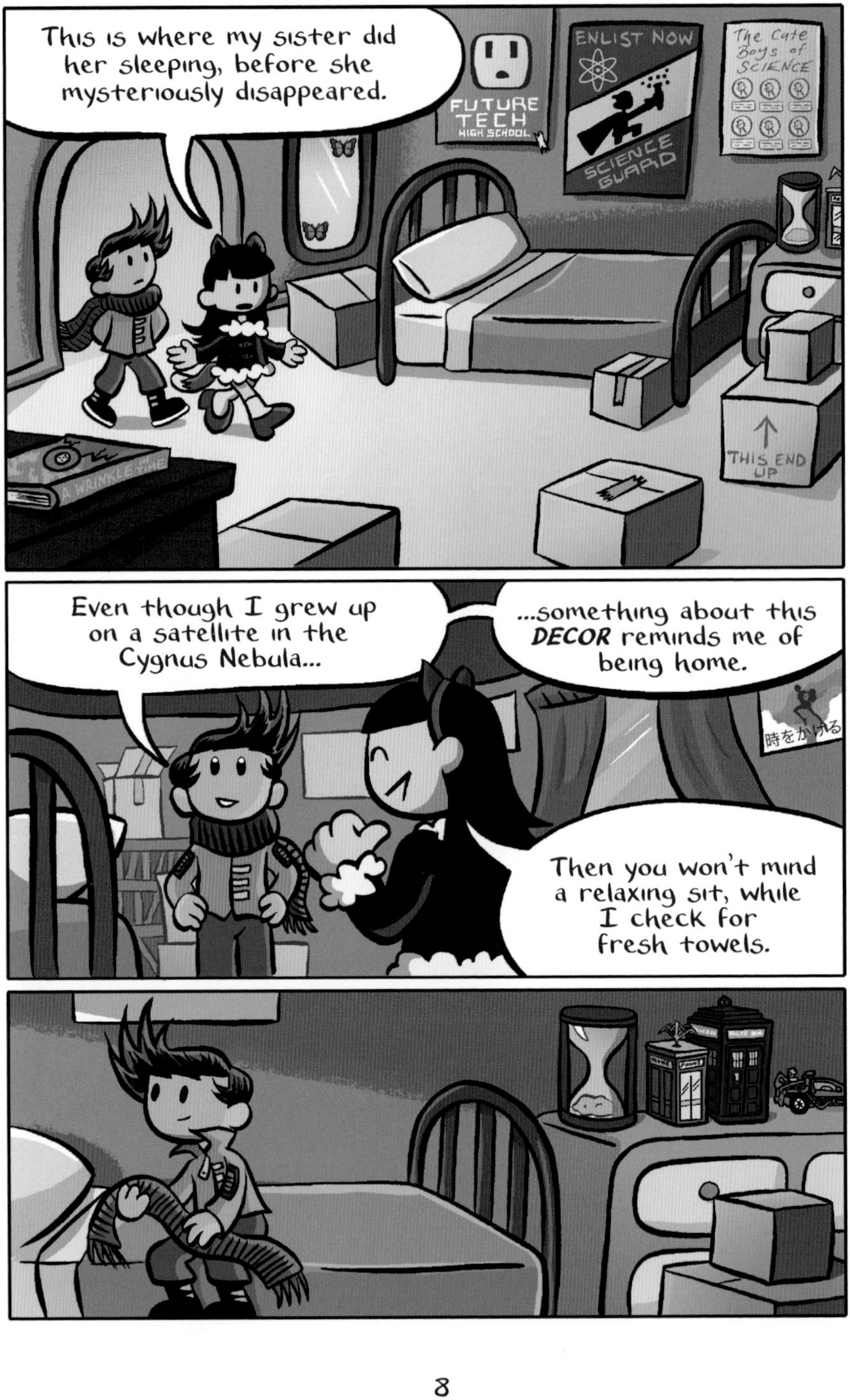
This is where my sister did her sleeping, before she mysteriously disappeared.
FUTURE TECH HIGH SCHOOL
ENLIST NOW
SCIENCE GUARD
The Cute Boys of SCIENCE
A WRINKLE IN TIME
THIS END UP
Even though I grew up on a satellite in the Cygnus Nebula...
...something about this DECOR reminds me of being home.
時をかける
Then you won't mind a relaxing sit, while I check for fresh towels.

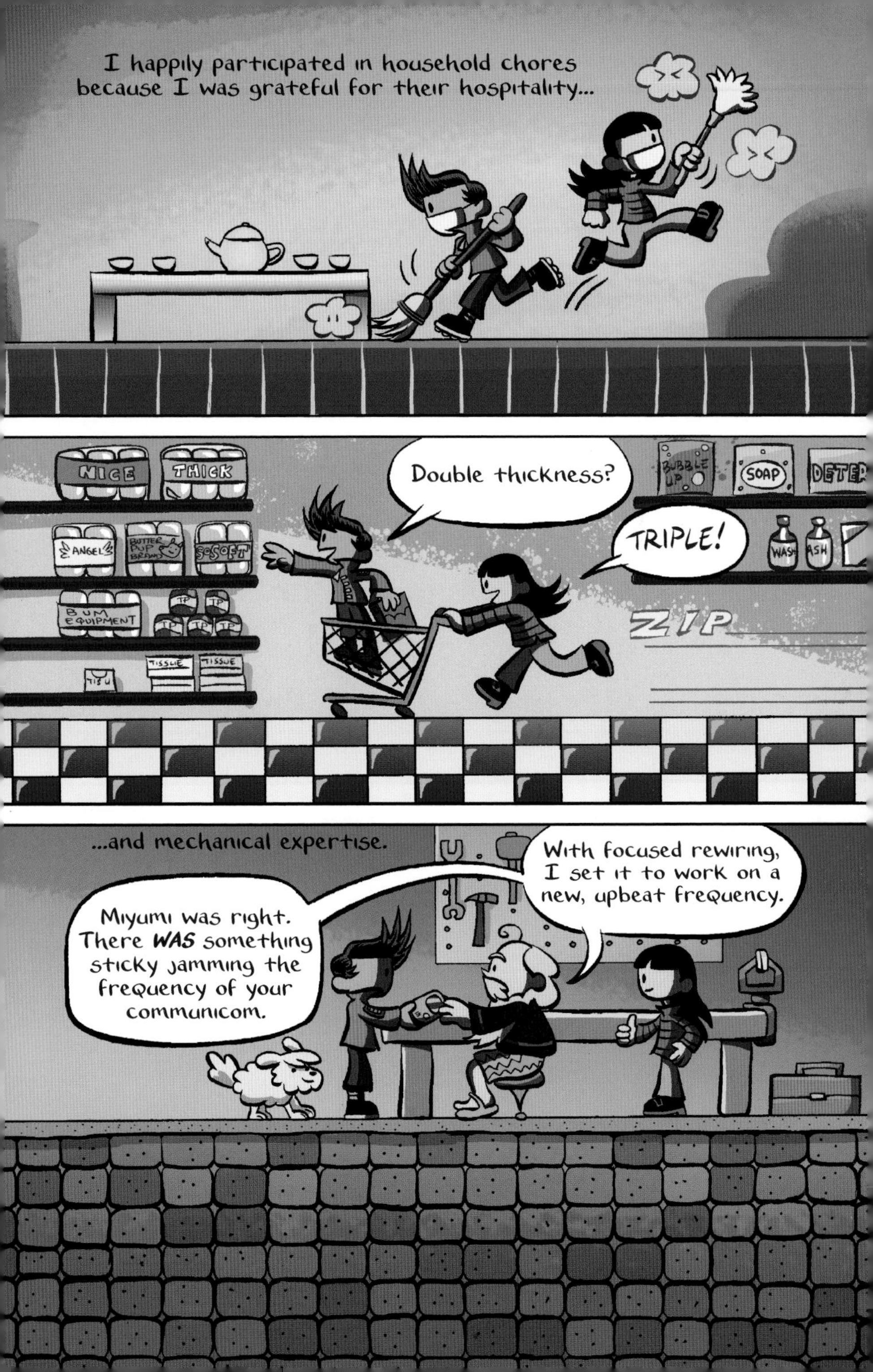

I happily participated in household chores because I was grateful for their hospitality...
NICE
THICK
ANGEL
BUTTER PUP BRAND
SoSOFT
BUM EQUIPMENT
TP
TISSUE
TISSUE
Double thickness?
BUBBLE UP
SOAP
DETER
TRIPLE!
WASH
ASH
ZIP
...and mechanical expertise.
Miyumi was right. There *WAS* something sticky jamming the frequency of your communicom.
With focused rewiring, I set it to work on a new, upbeat frequency.

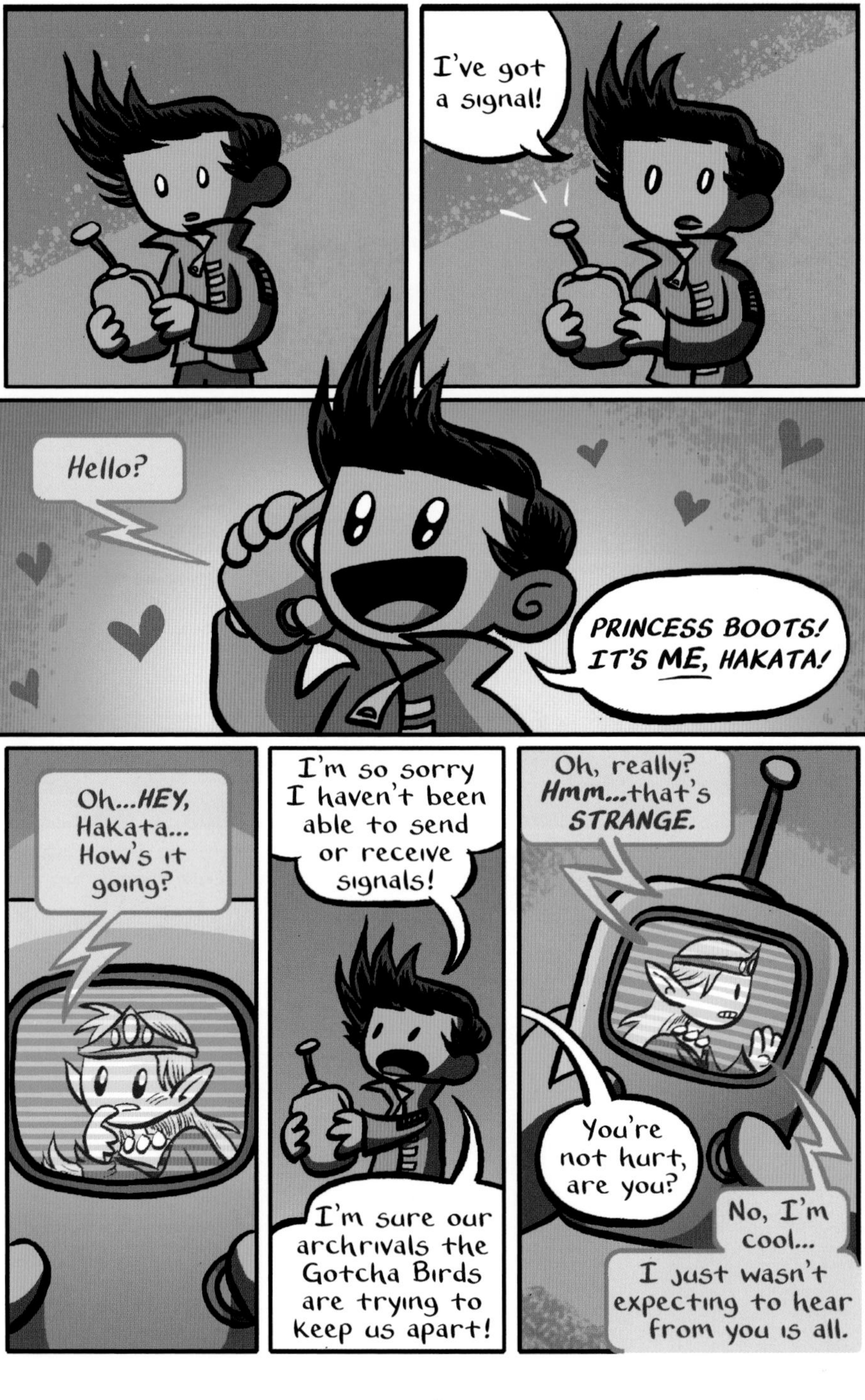
I've got a signal!
Hello?
PRINCESS BOOTS! IT'S ME, HAKATA!
Oh...HEY, Hakata... How's it going?
I'm so sorry I haven't been able to send or receive signals!
I'm sure our archrivals the Gotcha Birds are trying to keep us apart!
Oh, really? Hmm...that's STRANGE.
You're not hurt, are you?
No, I'm cool... I just wasn't expecting to hear from you is all.

I've wanted nothing more than to talk to you these past few months!

I *DID* give you one of my hearts, after all.

Right. About that...

The thing is, Hakata... I always liked you the way I like *ALL* the members of the Meta-Team.

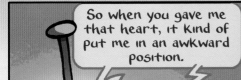

So when you gave me that heart, it kind of put me in an awkward position.

I figured since Gadget is your best friend, I'd give it to him for safe-keeping.

You gave my heart away?

Yeah...and since I've got you on the line, I should probably *ALSO* tell you--

NO, WAIT! Let *ME* tell him!

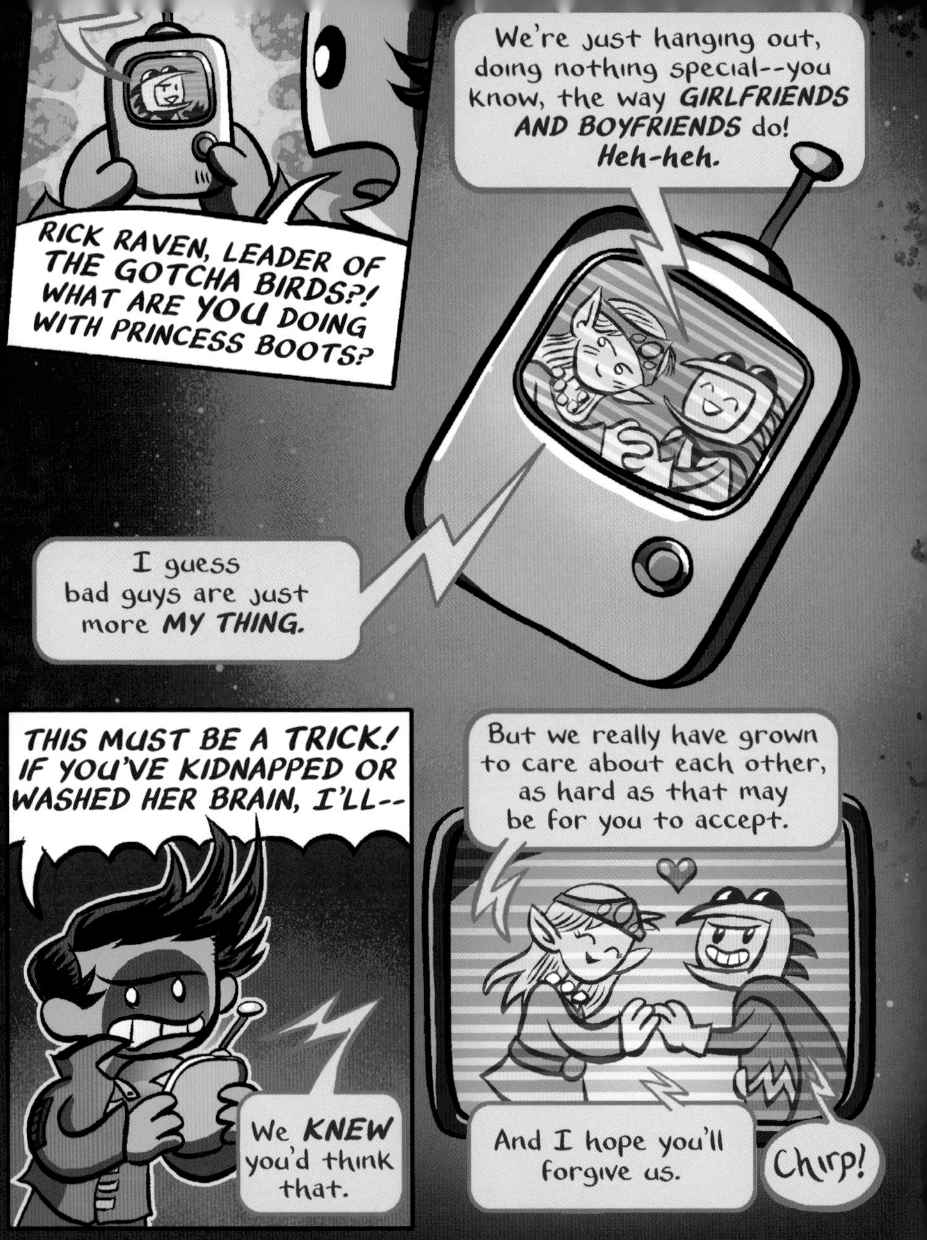

RICK RAVEN, LEADER OF THE GOTCHA BIRDS?! WHAT ARE YOU DOING WITH PRINCESS BOOTS?
We're just hanging out, doing nothing special--you know, the way GIRLFRIENDS AND BOYFRIENDS do! Heh-heh.
I guess bad guys are just more MY THING.
THIS MUST BE A TRICK! IF YOU'VE KIDNAPPED OR WASHED HER BRAIN, I'LL--
We KNEW you'd think that.
But we really have grown to care about each other, as hard as that may be for you to accept.
And I hope you'll forgive us.
Chirp!

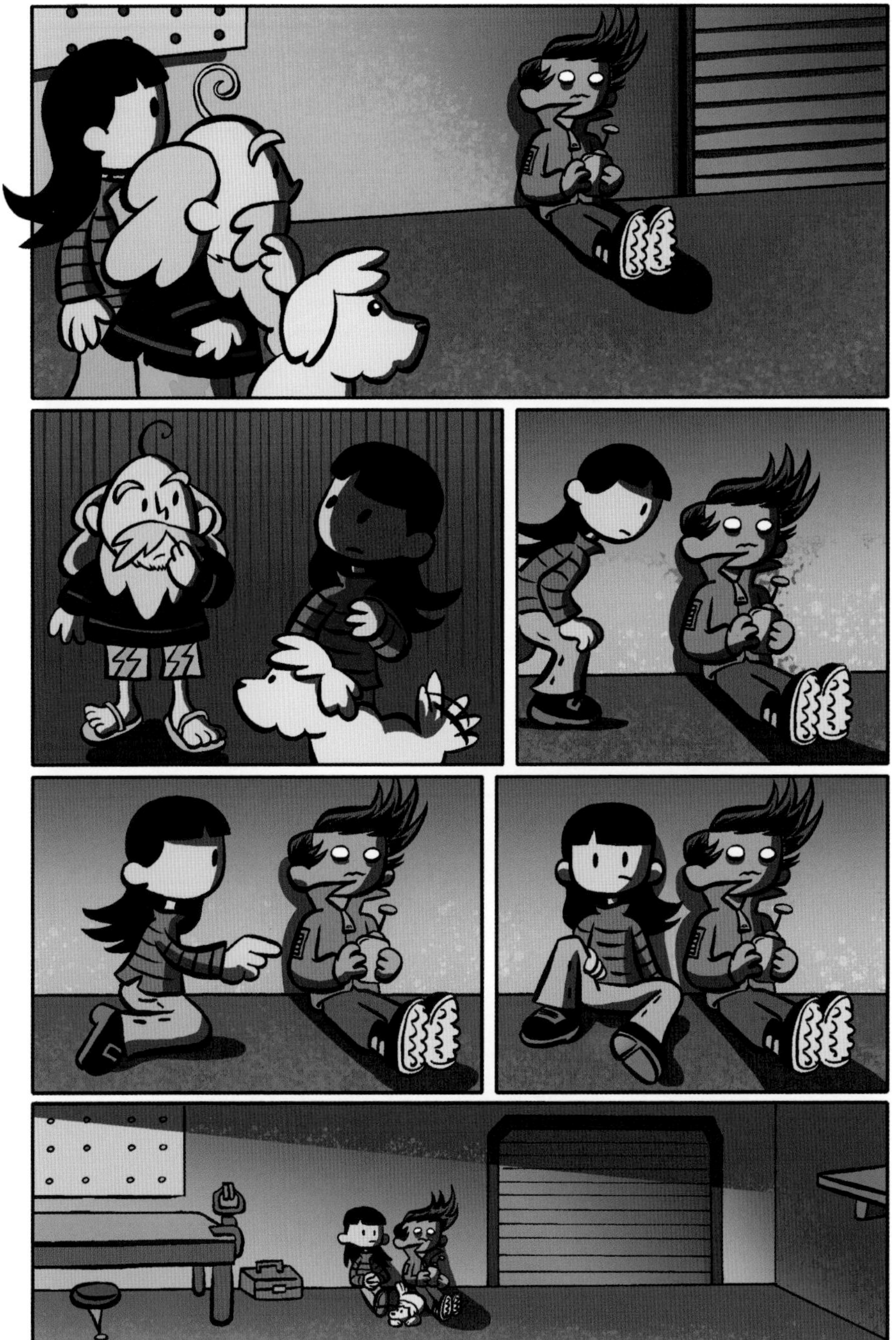

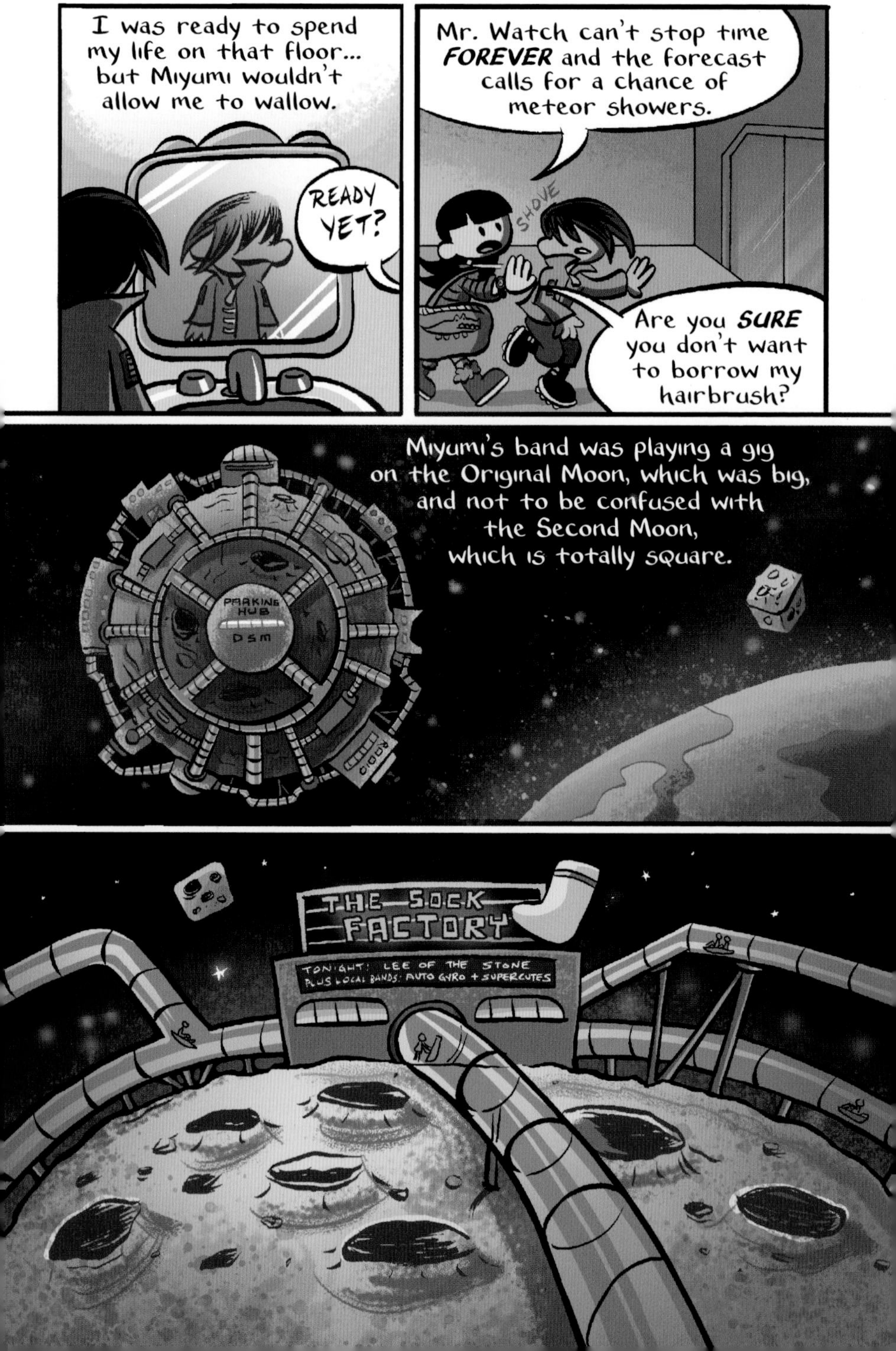
I was ready to spend my life on that floor... but Miyumi wouldn't allow me to wallow.
READY YET?
Mr. Watch can't stop time **FOREVER** and the forecast calls for a chance of meteor showers.
SHOVE
Are you **SURE** you don't want to borrow my hairbrush?
Miyumi's band was playing a gig on the Original Moon, which was big, and not to be confused with the Second Moon, which is totally square.
PARKING HUB
DSM
THE SOCK FACTORY
TONIGHT: LEE OF THE STONE
PLUS LOCAL BANDS: AUTO GYRO + SUPERCUTES

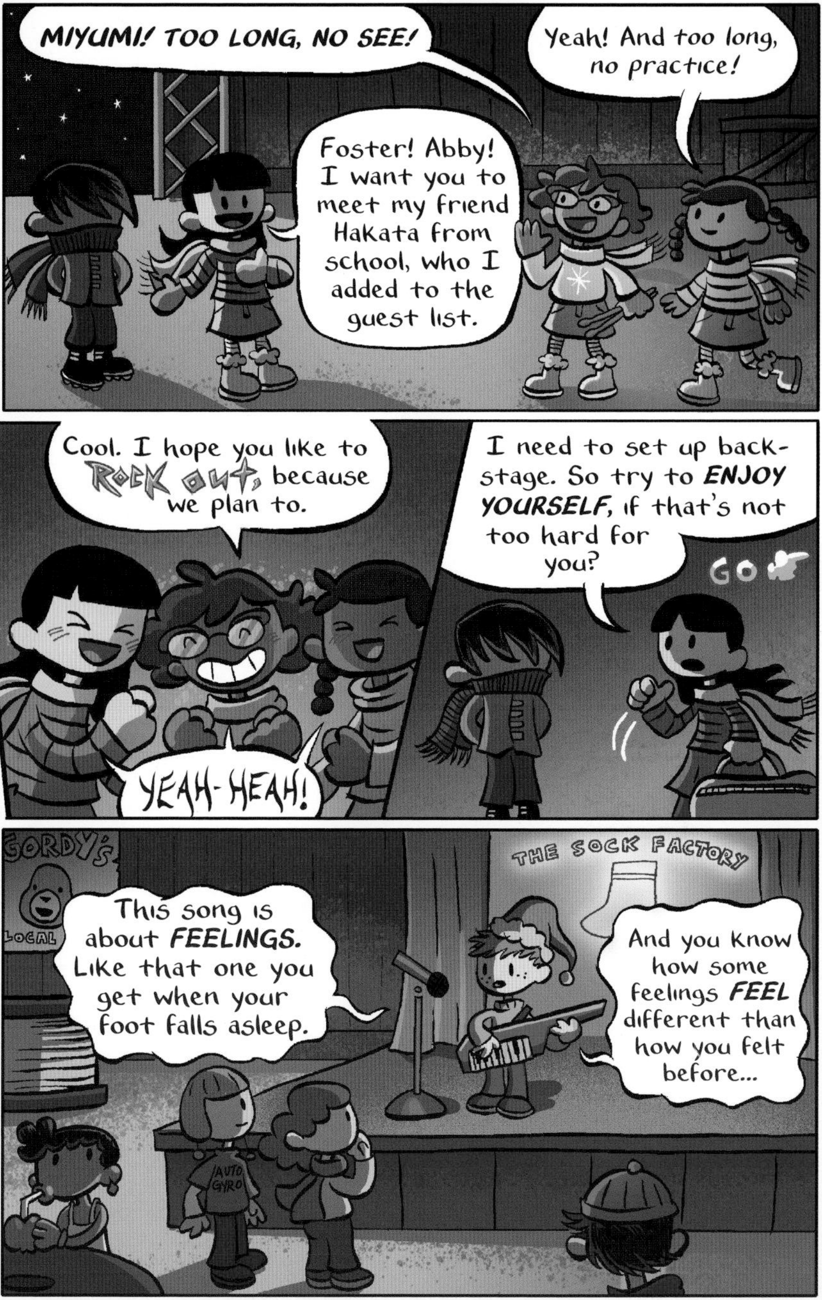
MIYUMI! TOO LONG, NO SEE!
Yeah! And too long, no practice!
Foster! Abby! I want you to meet my friend Hakata from school, who I added to the guest list.
Cool. I hope you like to ROCK OUT, because we plan to.
YEAH-HEAH!
I need to set up back-stage. So try to ENJOY YOURSELF, if that's not too hard for you?
GO
GORDY'S
LOCAL
THE SOCK FACTORY
This song is about FEELINGS. Like that one you get when your foot falls asleep.
And you know how some feelings FEEL different than how you felt before...
AUTO GYRO

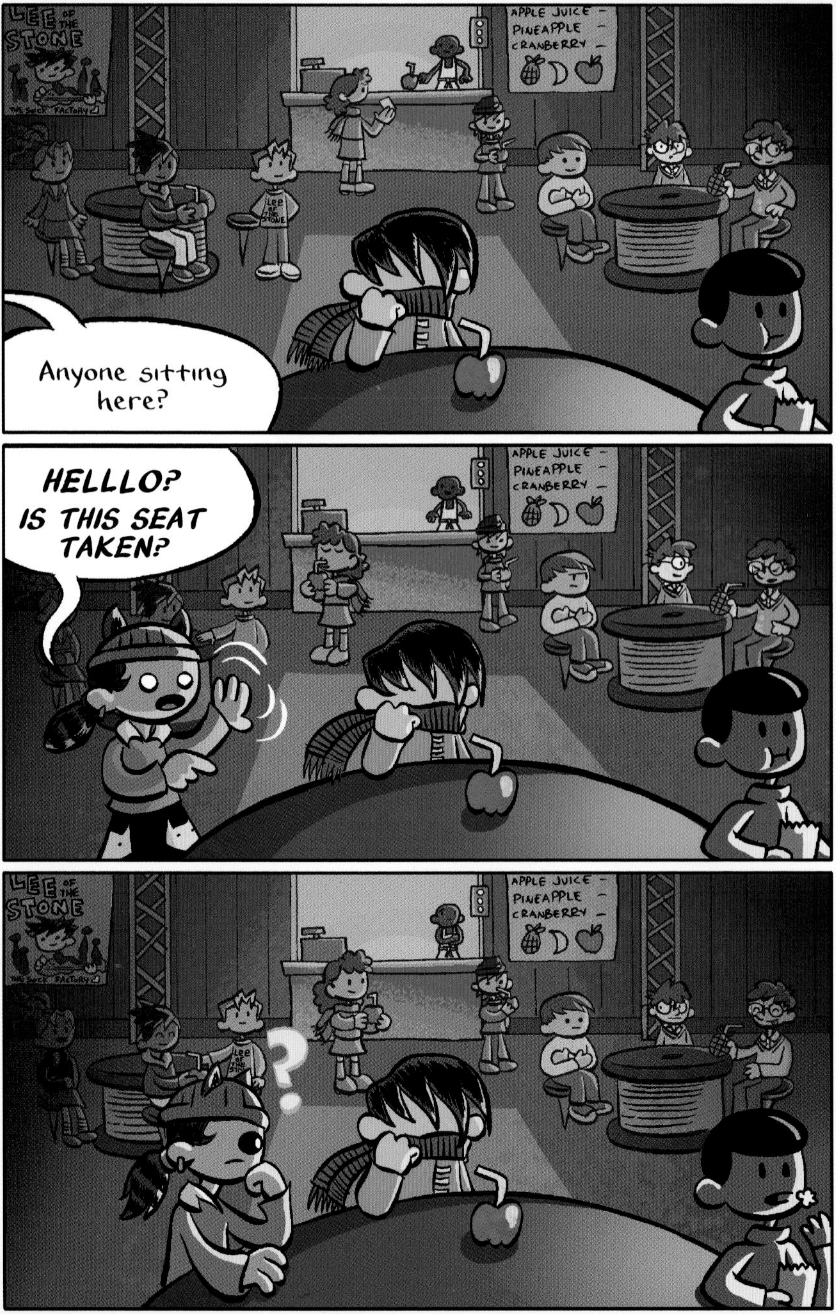
LEE OF THE STONE
THE SOCK FACTORY
APPLE JUICE -
PINEAPPLE -
CRANBERRY -
Anyone sitting here?
HELLLO? IS THIS SEAT TAKEN?
?

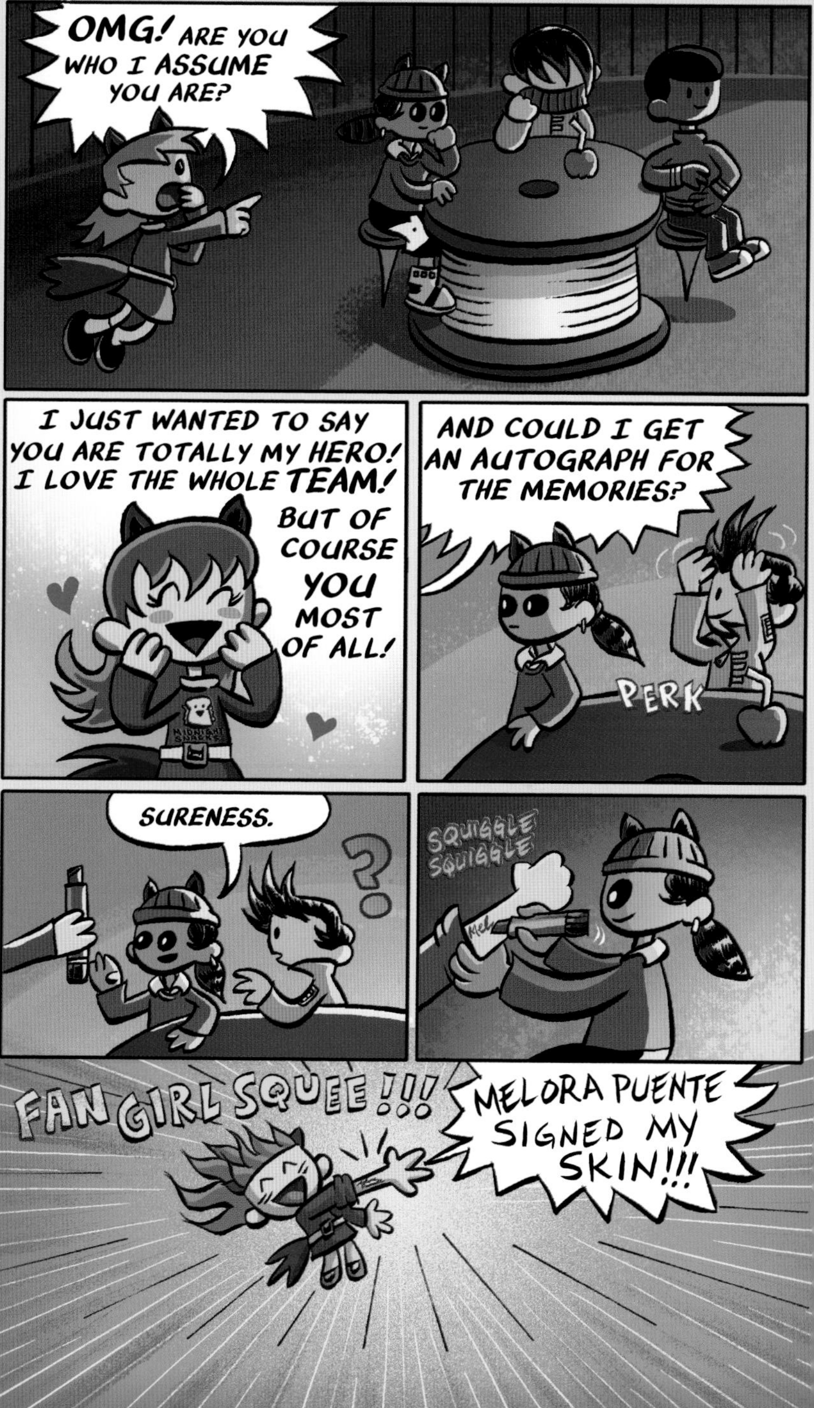
OMG! ARE YOU WHO I ASSUME YOU ARE?
I JUST WANTED TO SAY YOU ARE TOTALLY MY HERO! I LOVE THE WHOLE TEAM!
BUT OF COURSE YOU MOST OF ALL!
AND COULD I GET AN AUTOGRAPH FOR THE MEMORIES?
PERK
SURENESS.
?
SQUIGGLE SQUIGGLE
FAN GIRL SQUEE!!!
MELORA PUENTE SIGNED MY SKIN!!!

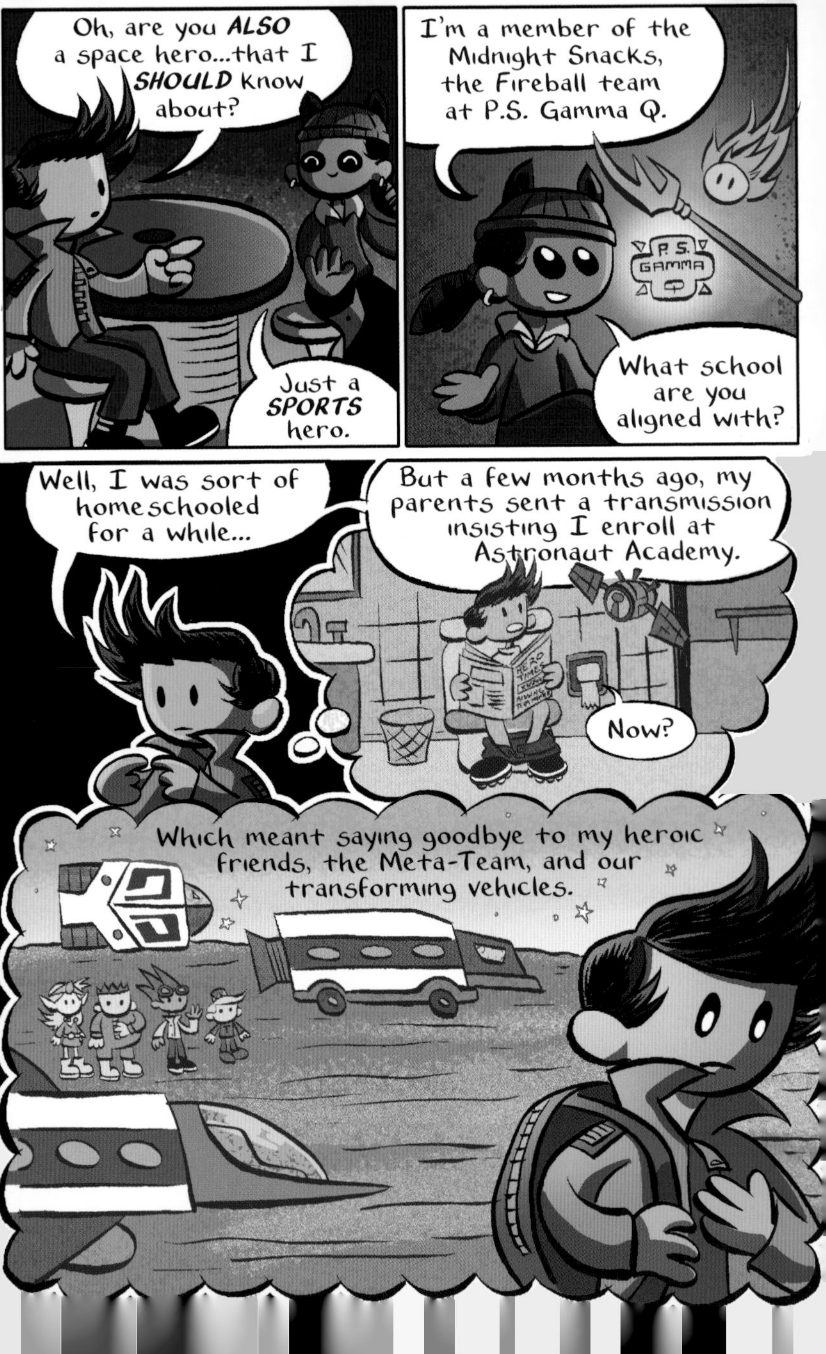
Oh, are you ALSO a space hero...that I SHOULD know about?
Just a SPORTS hero.
I'm a member of the Midnight Snacks, the Fireball team at P.S. Gamma Q.
P.S. GAMMA Q
What school are you aligned with?
Well, I was sort of homeschooled for a while...
But a few months ago, my parents sent a transmission insisting I enroll at Astronaut Academy.
HERO TIMES
Now?
Which meant saying goodbye to my heroic friends, the Meta-Team, and our transforming vehicles.

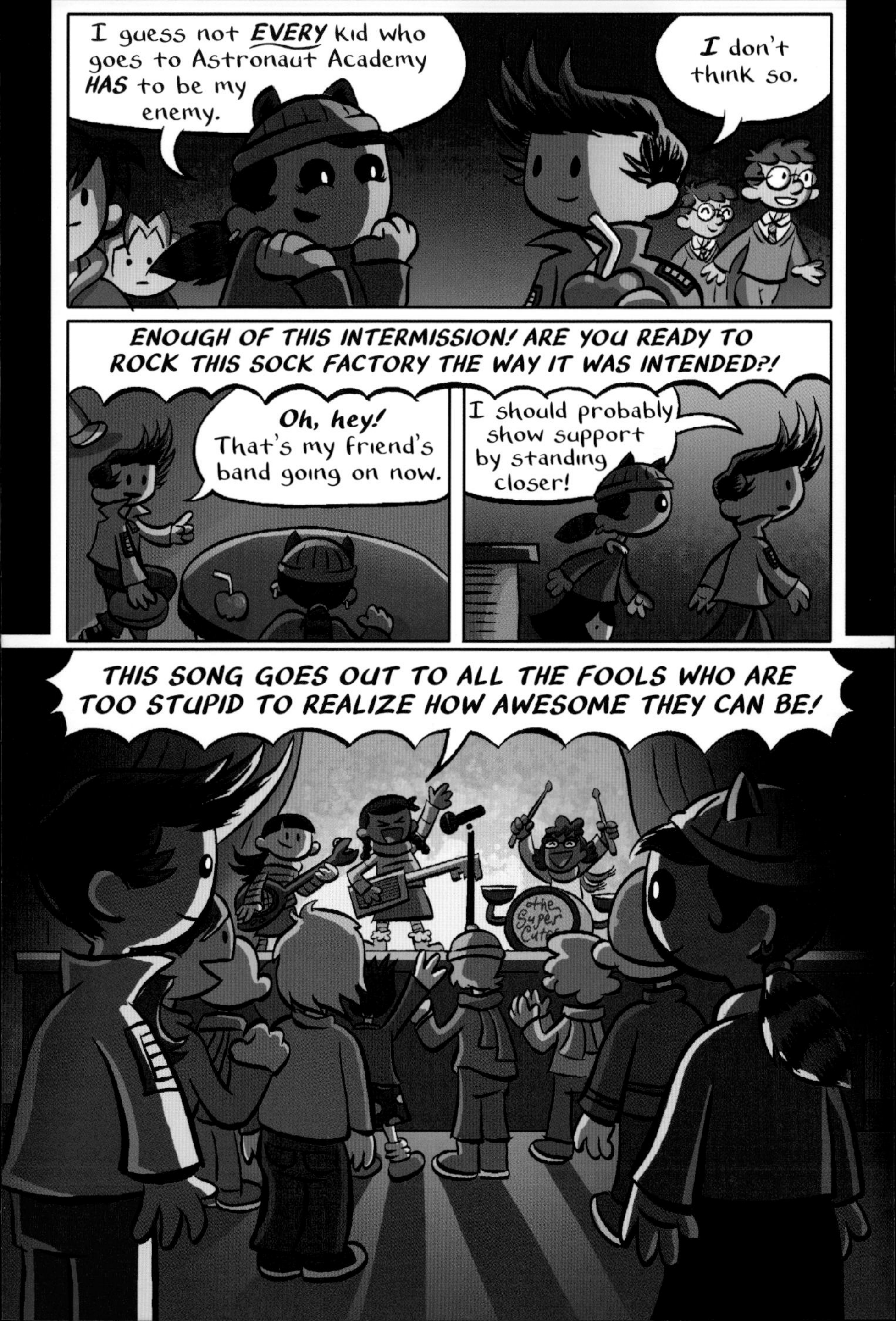
I guess not EVERY kid who goes to Astronaut Academy HAS to be my enemy.
I don't think so.
ENOUGH OF THIS INTERMISSION! ARE YOU READY TO ROCK THIS SOCK FACTORY THE WAY IT WAS INTENDED?!
Oh, hey! That's my friend's band going on now.
I should probably show support by standing closer!
THIS SONG GOES OUT TO ALL THE FOOLS WHO ARE TOO STUPID TO REALIZE HOW AWESOME THEY CAN BE!
the Super Cutes

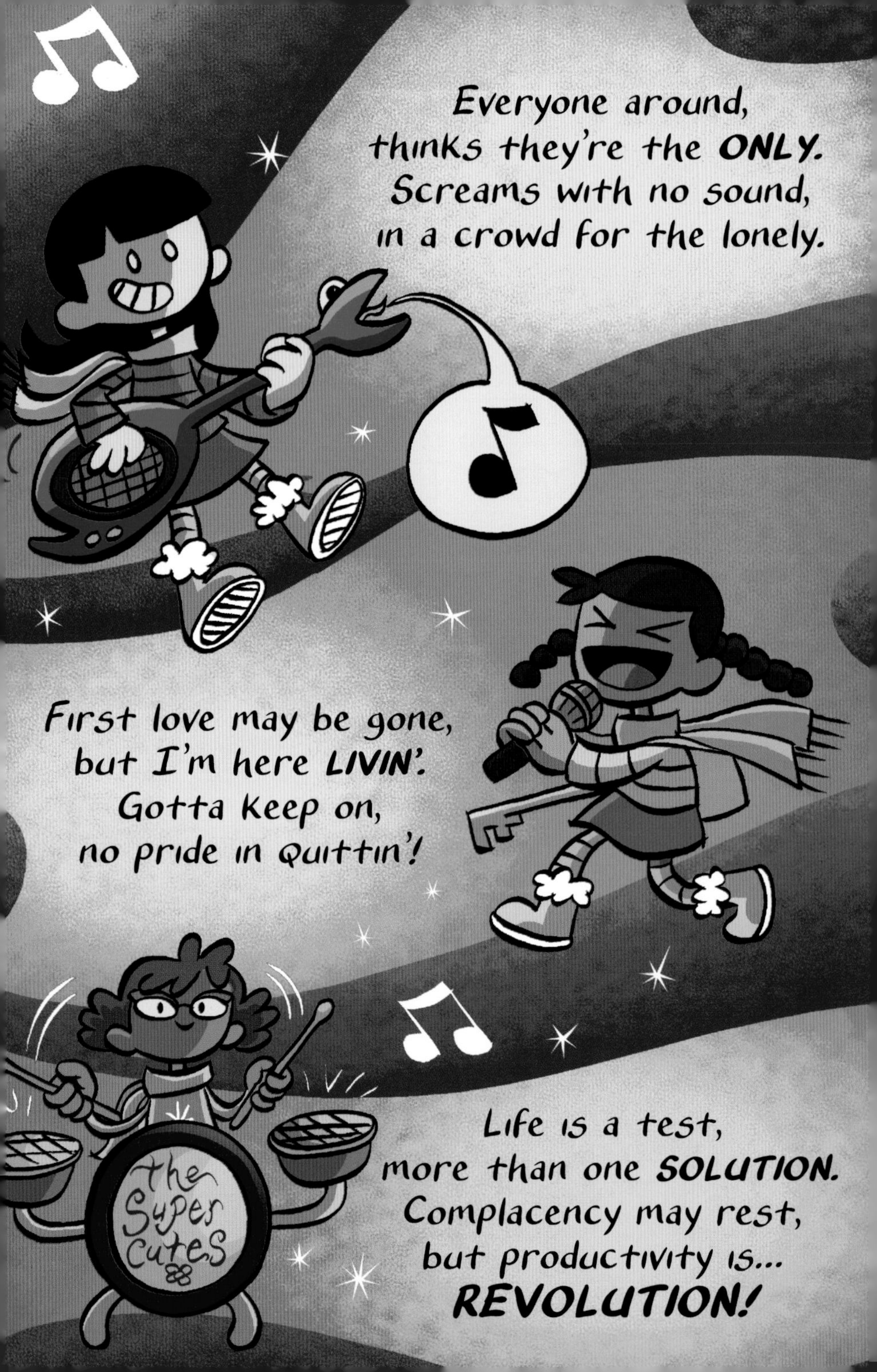
Everyone around, thinks they're the ONLY. Screams with no sound, in a crowd for the lonely.
First love may be gone, but I'm here LIVIN'. Gotta keep on, no pride in quittin'!
the Super Cutes
Life is a test, more than one SOLUTION. Complacency may rest, but productivity is... REVOLUTION!

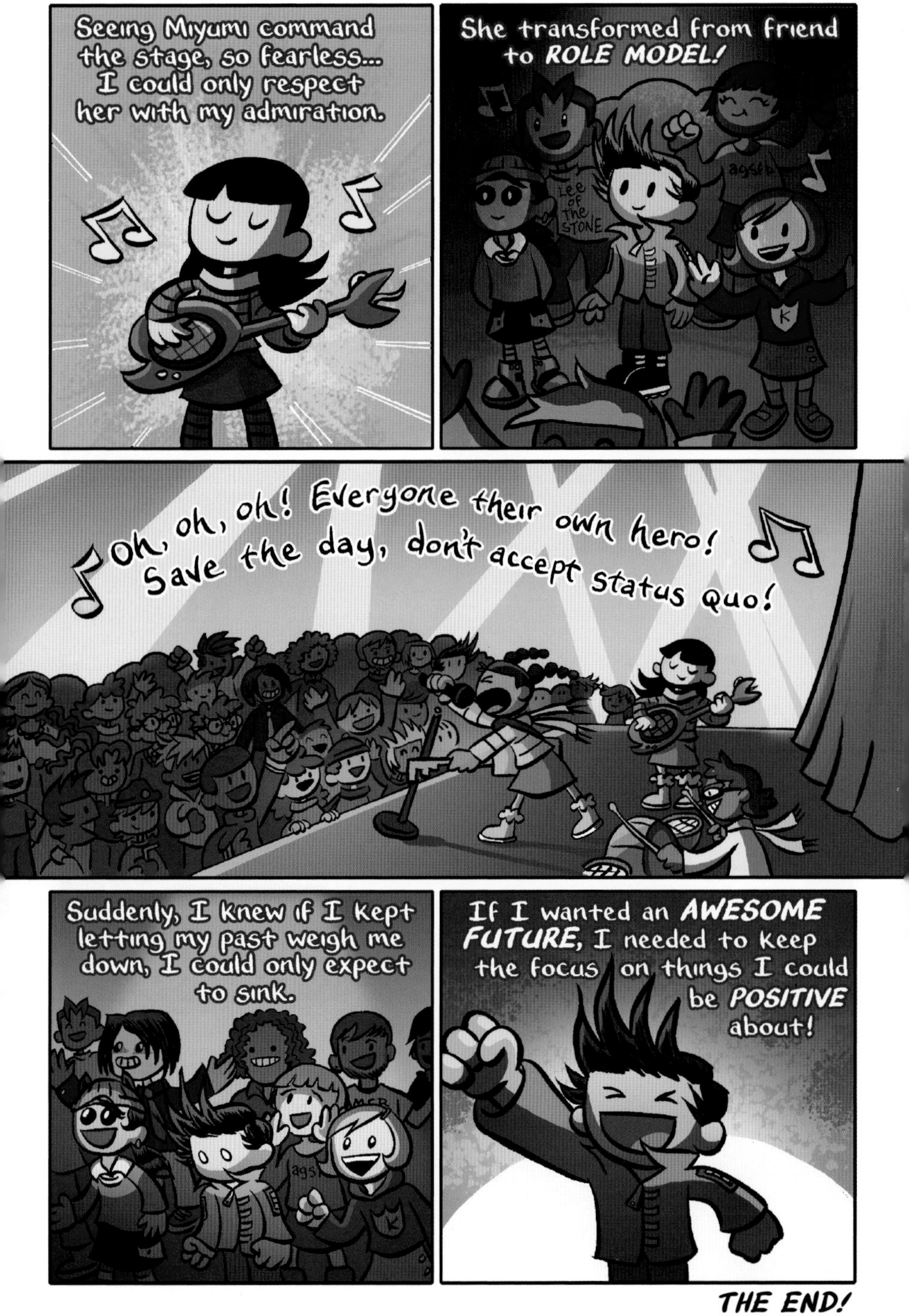
Seeing Miyumi command the stage, so fearless... I could only respect her with my admiration.
She transformed from friend to ROLE MODEL!
Lee of the STONE
agsb
K
Oh, oh, oh! Everyone their own hero! Save the day, don't accept status quo!
Suddenly, I knew if I kept letting my past weigh me down, I could only expect to sink.
MCR
agsb
K
If I wanted an AWESOME FUTURE, I needed to keep the focus on things I could be POSITIVE about!

THE END!

It Pay$ to be the Be$t

My name is: MARIBELLE MELLONBELLY

And I am the richest and most pretty girl in all of:

ASTRONAUT ACADEMY

What did I do over my holiday break?

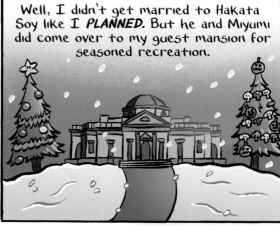

Well, I didn't get married to Hakata Soy like I *PLANNED.* But he and Miyumi did come over to my guest mansion for seasoned recreation.

Miyumi and I tried to relive our glory days but some things just don't bounce like they used to.

Hoot!

Ha!

Heh.

FSSS

FFPH

But before all that...

22

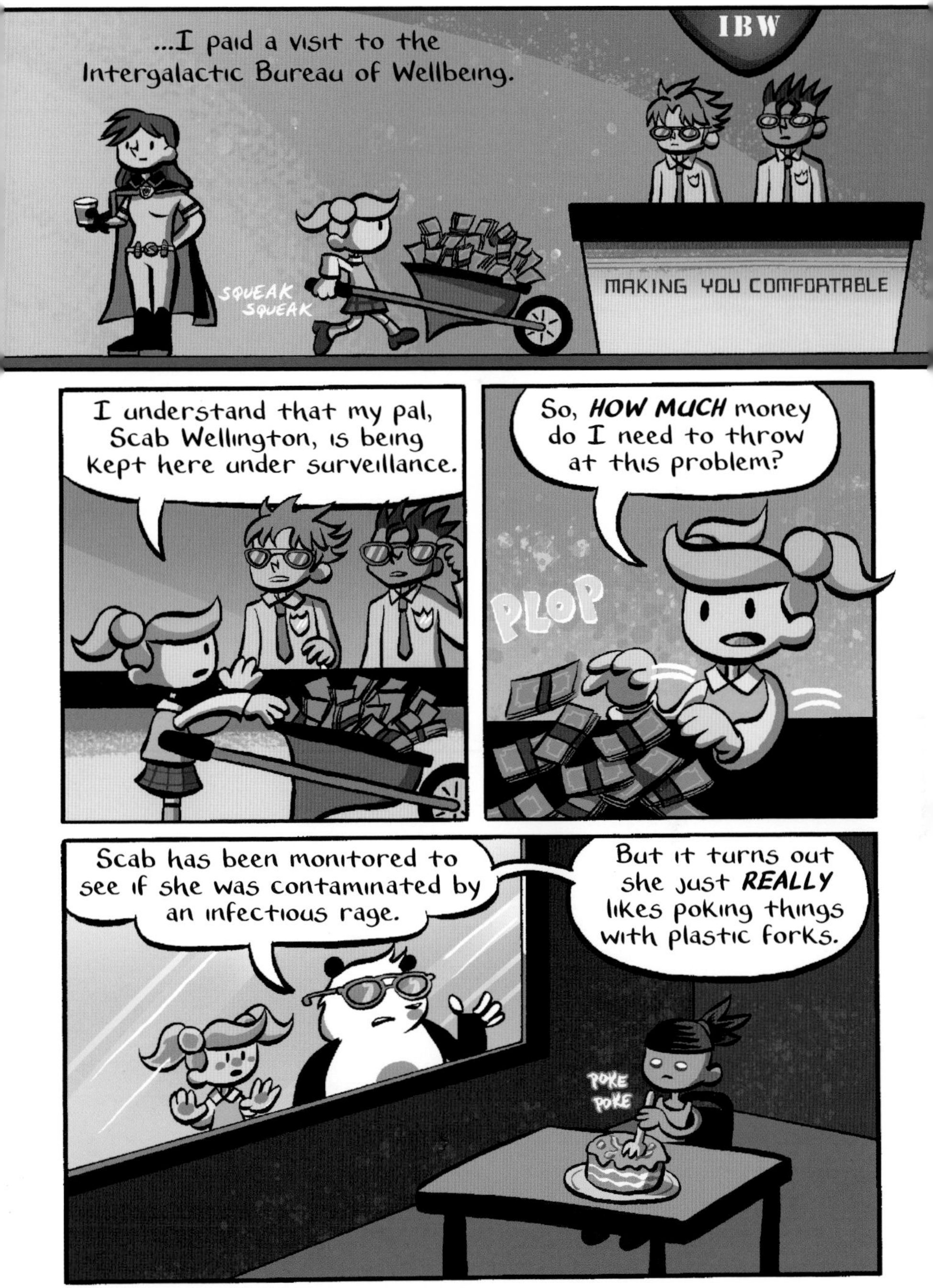
...I paid a visit to the Intergalactic Bureau of Wellbeing.
IBW
SQUEAK SQUEAK
MAKING YOU COMFORTABLE
I understand that my pal, Scab Wellington, is being kept here under surveillance.
So, HOW MUCH money do I need to throw at this problem?
PLOP
Scab has been monitored to see if she was contaminated by an infectious rage.
But it turns out she just REALLY likes poking things with plastic forks.
POKE POKE

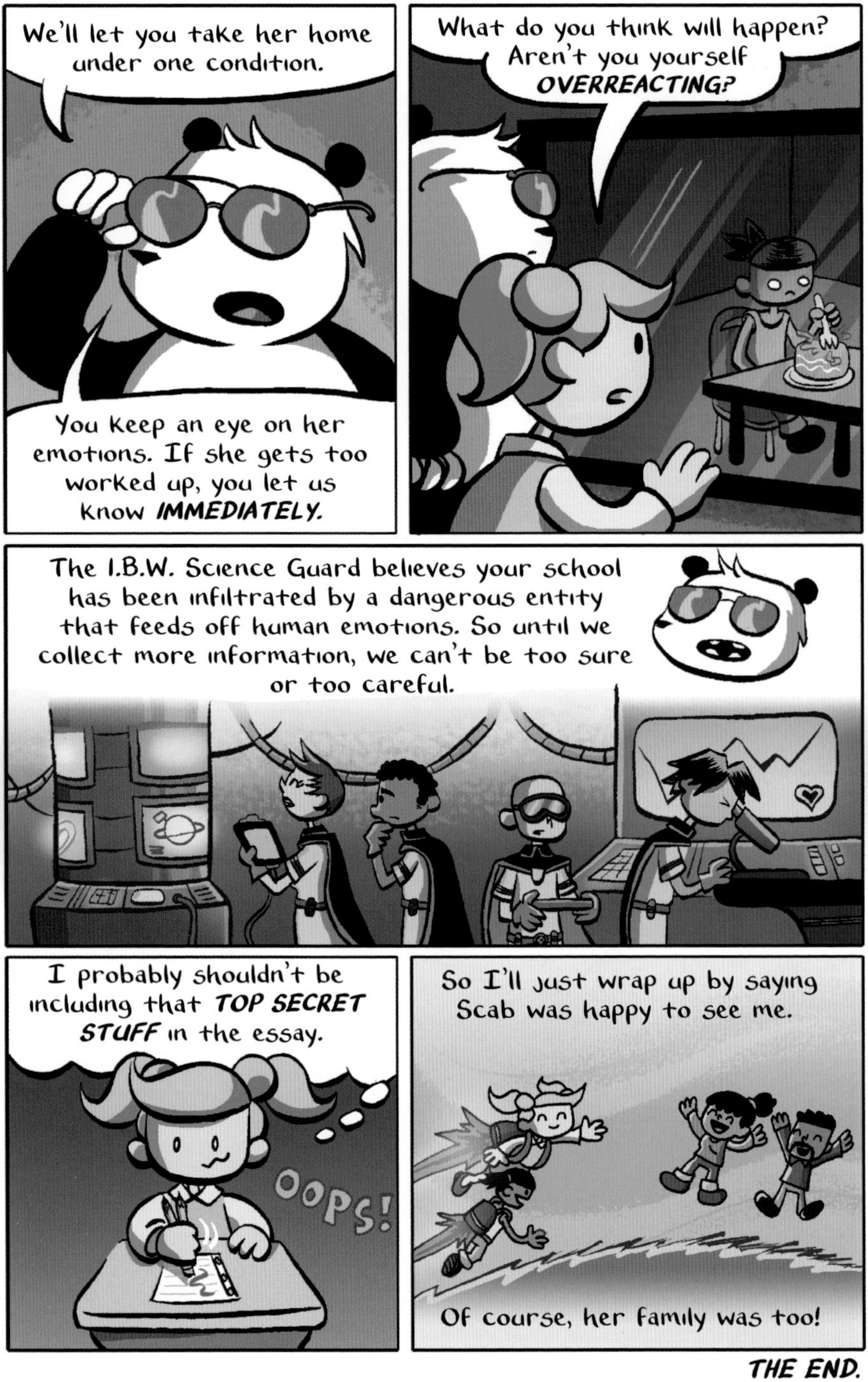
We'll let you take her home under one condition.
You keep an eye on her emotions. If she gets too worked up, you let us know IMMEDIATELY.
What do you think will happen? Aren't you yourself OVERREACTING?
The I.B.W. Science Guard believes your school has been infiltrated by a dangerous entity that feeds off human emotions. So until we collect more information, we can't be too sure or too careful.
I probably shouldn't be including that TOP SECRET STUFF in the essay.
OOPS!
So I'll just wrap up by saying Scab was happy to see me.
Of course, her family was too!
THE END.

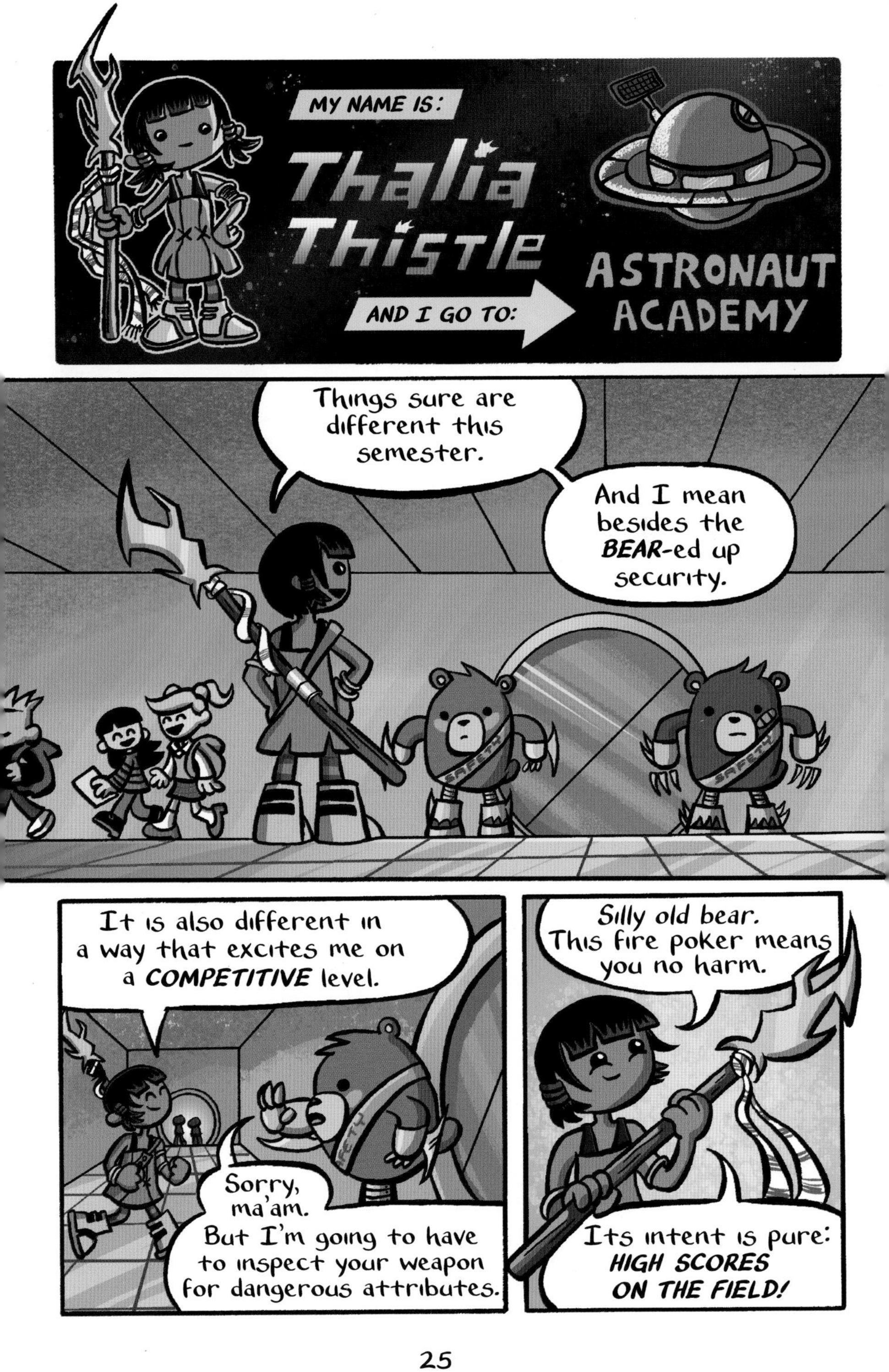
MY NAME IS:
Thalia Thistle
AND I GO TO:
ASTRONAUT ACADEMY
Things sure are different this semester.
And I mean besides the BEAR-ed up security.
SAFETY
SAFETY
It is also different in a way that excites me on a COMPETITIVE level.
Sorry, ma'am. But I'm going to have to inspect your weapon for dangerous attributes.
Silly old bear. This fire poker means you no harm.
Its intent is pure: HIGH SCORES ON THE FIELD!

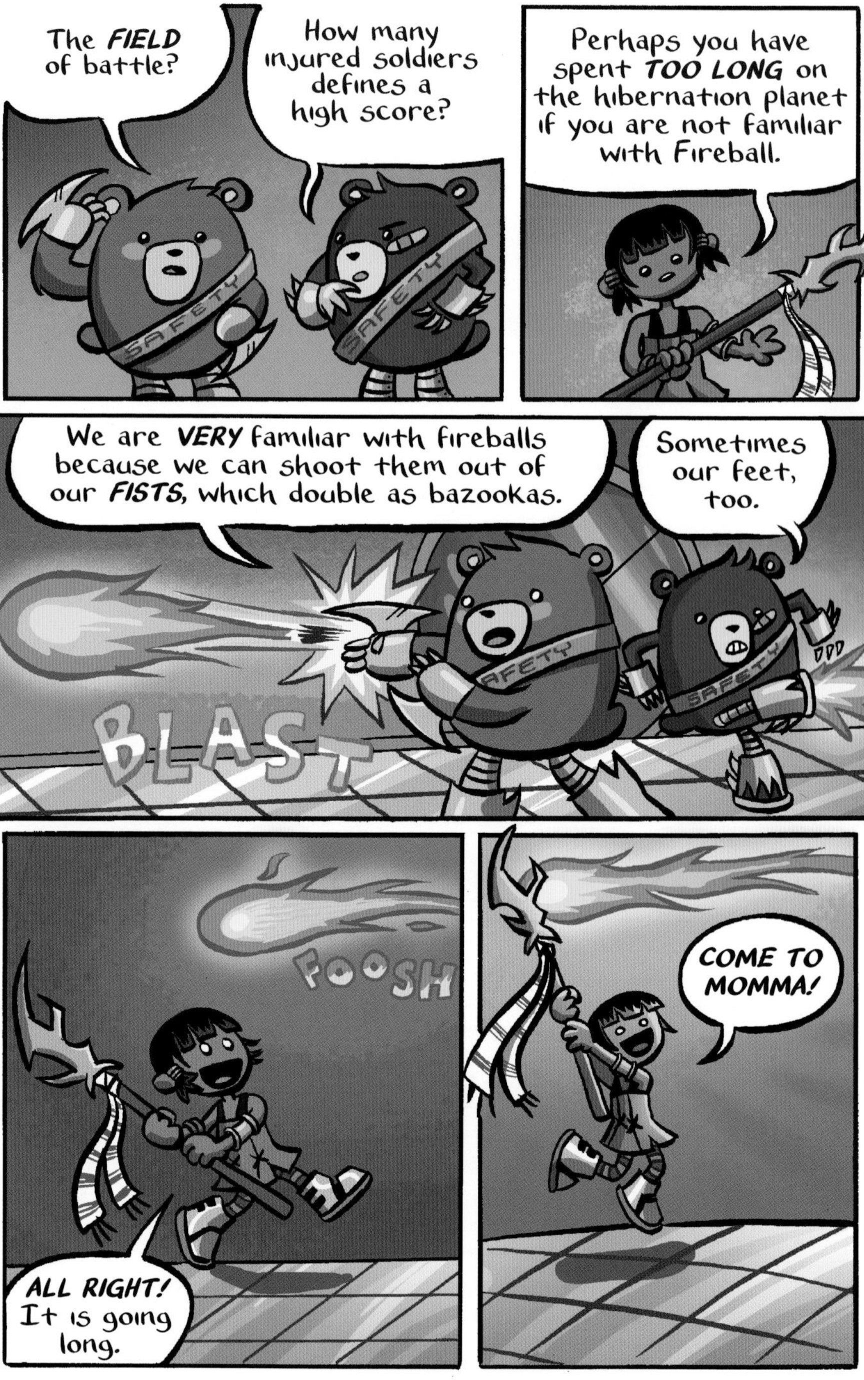

The FIELD of battle?
How many injured soldiers defines a high score?
Perhaps you have spent TOO LONG on the hibernation planet if you are not familiar with Fireball.
We are VERY familiar with fireballs because we can shoot them out of our FISTS, which double as bazookas.
Sometimes our feet, too.
SAFETY
SAFETY
SAFETY
SAFETY
BLAST
FOOSH
ALL RIGHT! It is going long.
COME TO MOMMA!

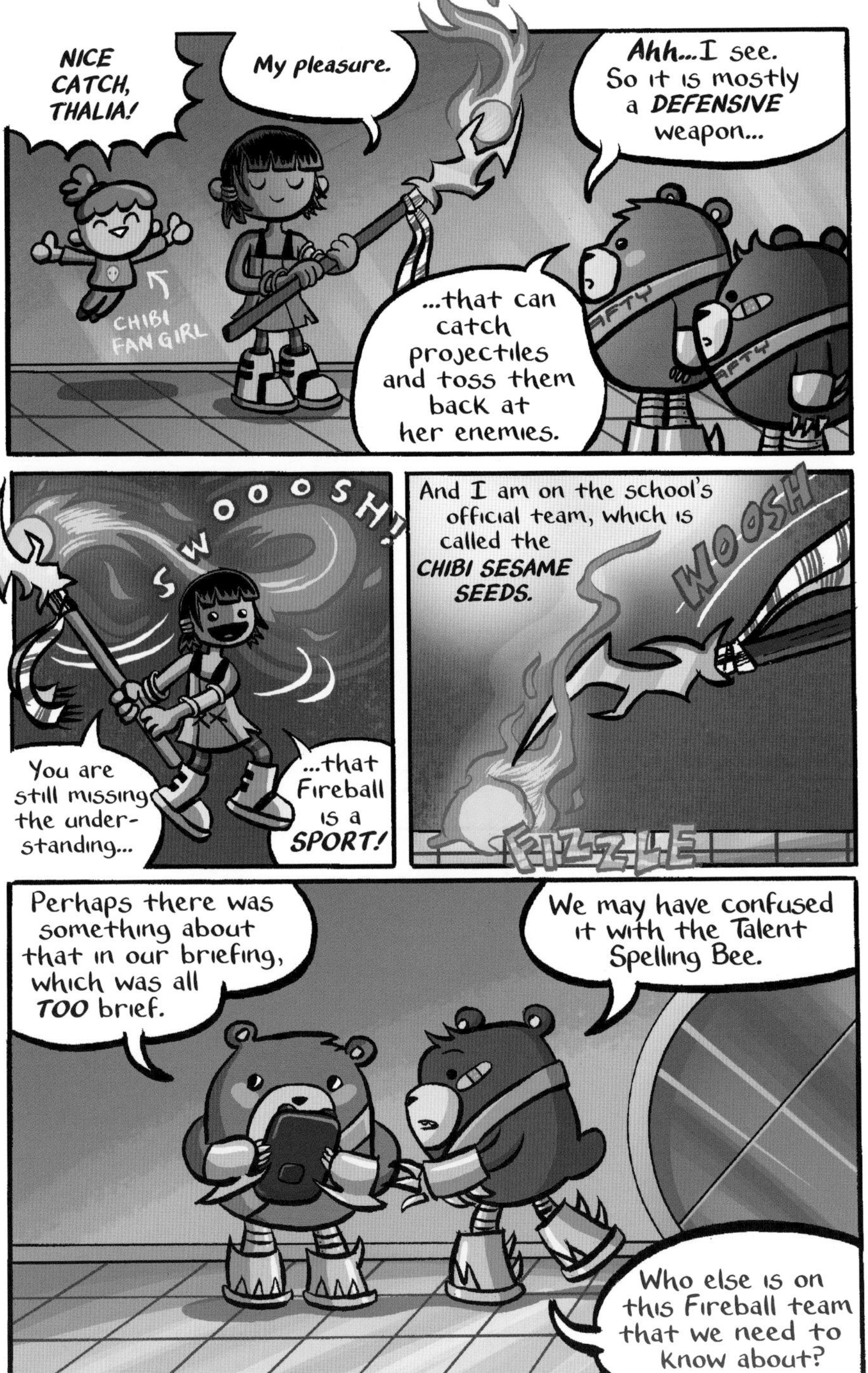
NICE CATCH, THALIA!
My pleasure.
Ahh...I see. So it is mostly a DEFENSIVE weapon...
CHIBI FAN GIRL
...that can catch projectiles and toss them back at her enemies.
SWOOOOSH!
You are still missing the under-standing...
...that Fireball is a SPORT!
And I am on the school's official team, which is called the CHIBI SESAME SEEDS.
WOOSH
FIZZLE
Perhaps there was something about that in our briefing, which was all TOO brief.
We may have confused it with the Talent Spelling Bee.
Who else is on this Fireball team that we need to know about?

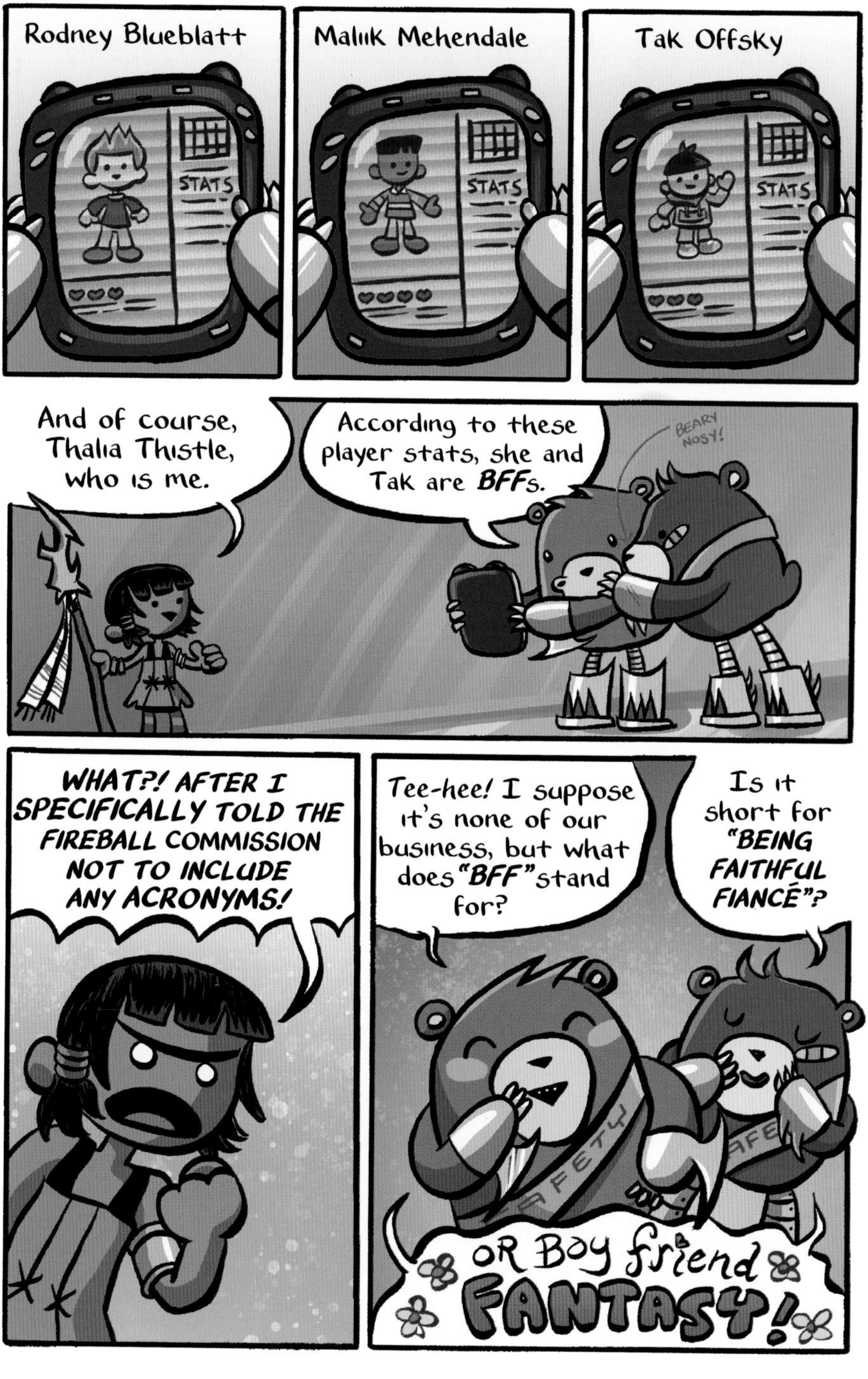

Rodney Blueblatt
STATS
Malik Mehendale
STATS
Tak Offsky
STATS
And of course, Thalia Thistle, who is me.
According to these player stats, she and Tak are BFFs.
BEARY NOSY!
WHAT?! AFTER I SPECIFICALLY TOLD THE FIREBALL COMMISSION NOT TO INCLUDE ANY ACRONYMS!
Tee-hee! I suppose it's none of our business, but what does "BFF" stand for?
Is it short for "BEING FAITHFUL FIANCÉ"?
OR Boy friend FANTASY!

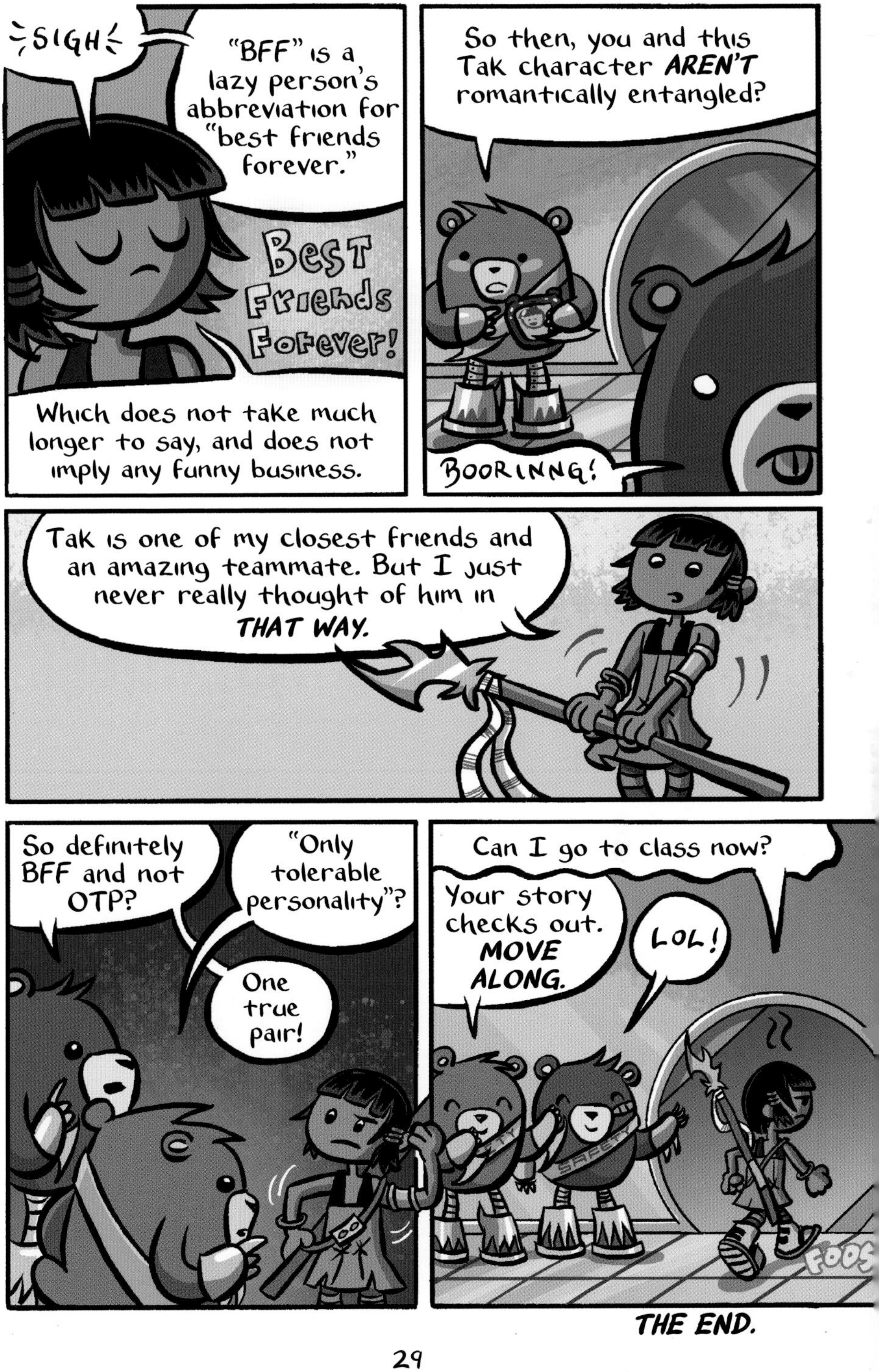
SIGH
"BFF" is a lazy person's abbreviation for "best friends forever."
Best Friends Forever!
Which does not take much longer to say, and does not imply any funny business.
So then, you and this Tak character AREN'T romantically entangled?
BOORINNG!
Tak is one of my closest friends and an amazing teammate. But I just never really thought of him in THAT WAY.
So definitely BFF and not OTP?
"Only tolerable personality"?
One true pair!
Can I go to class now?
Your story checks out. MOVE ALONG.
LOL!
SAFETY
FOOS

THE END.

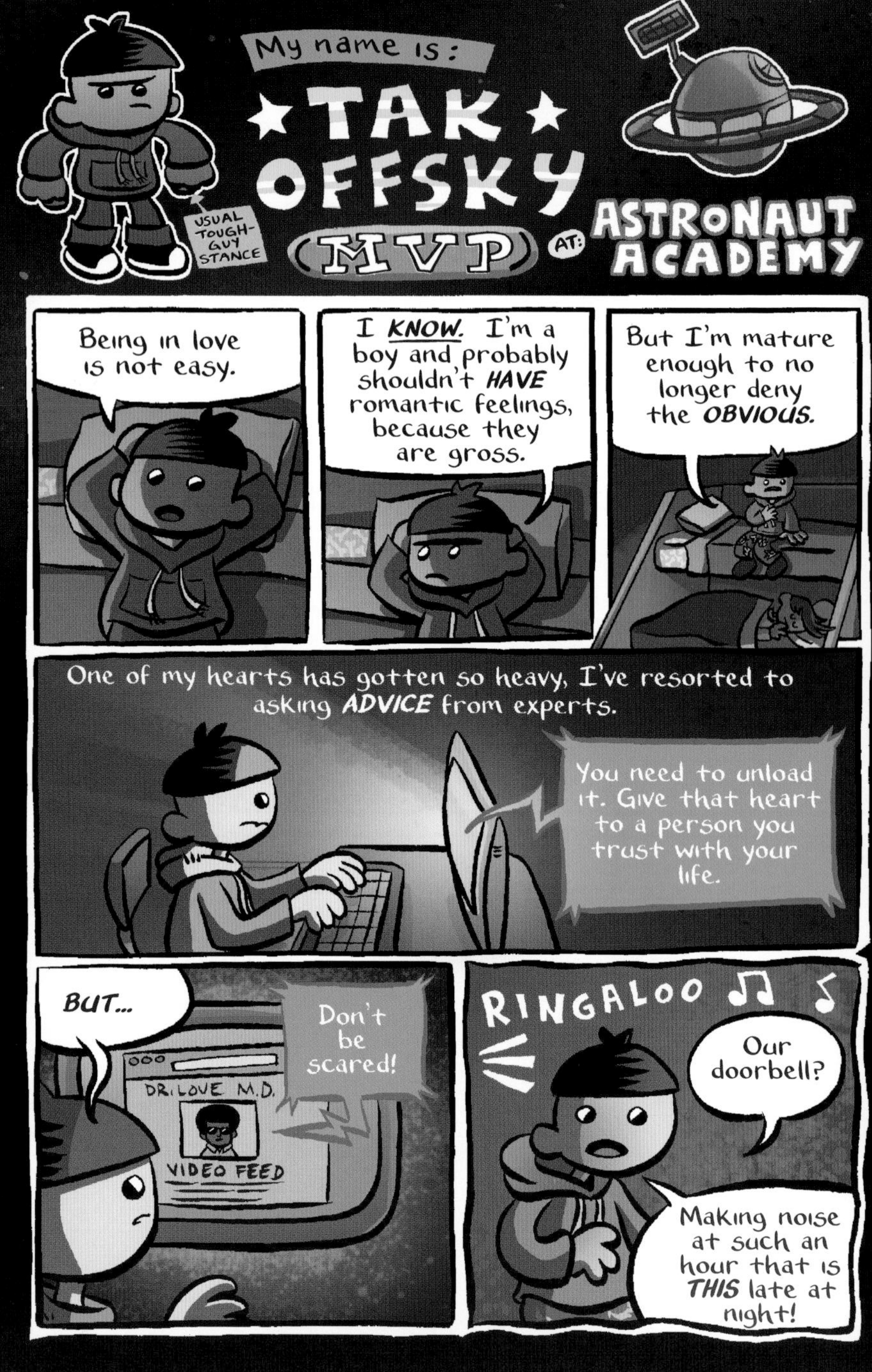
My name is:
TAK OFFSKY
USUAL TOUGH-GUY STANCE
MVP
AT:
ASTRONAUT ACADEMY
Being in love is not easy.
I KNOW. I'm a boy and probably shouldn't HAVE romantic feelings, because they are gross.
But I'm mature enough to no longer deny the OBVIOUS.
One of my hearts has gotten so heavy, I've resorted to asking ADVICE from experts.
You need to unload it. Give that heart to a person you trust with your life.
BUT...
Don't be scared!
DR. LOVE M.D.
VIDEO FEED
RINGALOO
Our doorbell?
Making noise at such an hour that is THIS late at night!

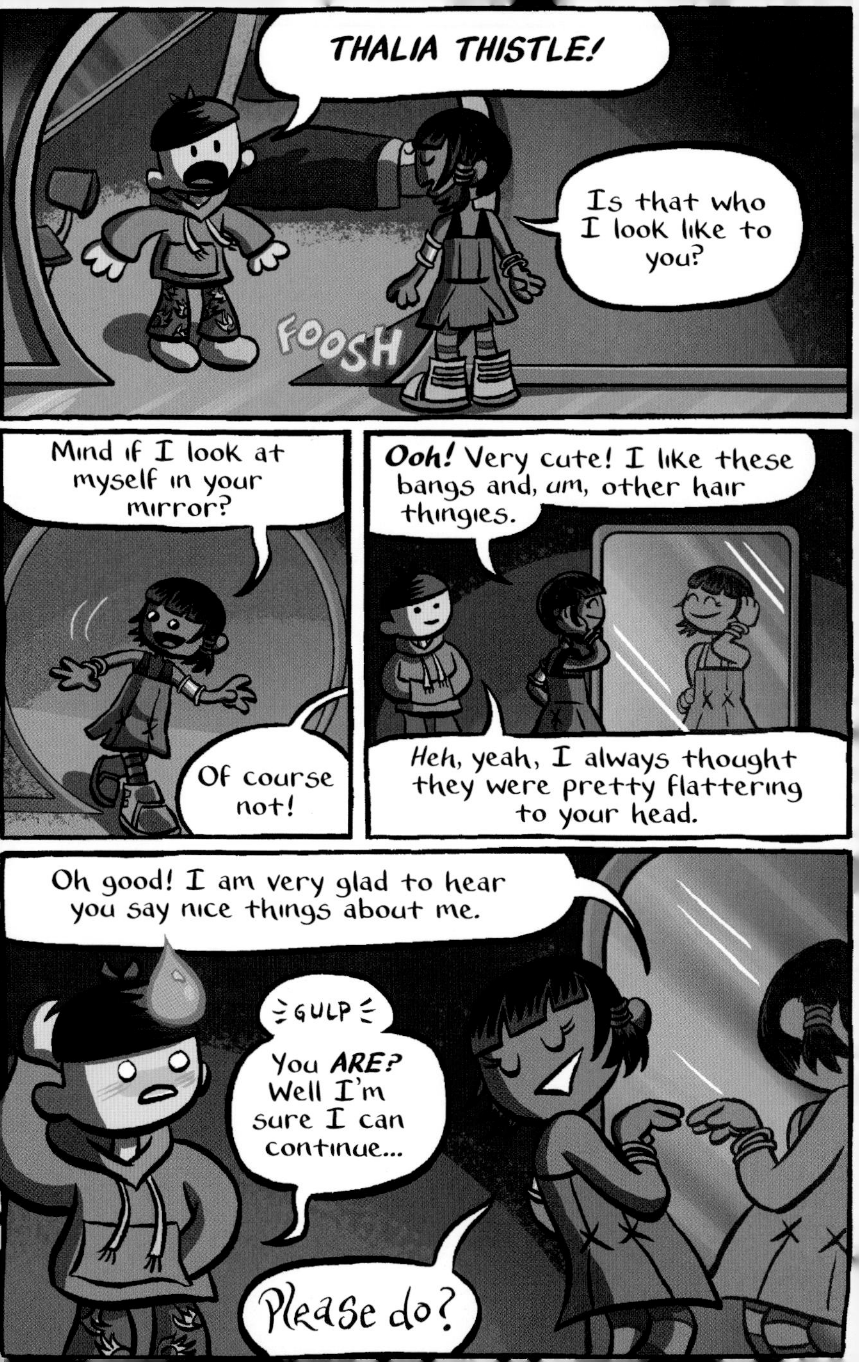
THALIA THISTLE!
Is that who I look like to you?
FOOSH
Mind if I look at myself in your mirror?
Of course not!
Ooh! Very cute! I like these bangs and, um, other hair thingies.
Heh, yeah, I always thought they were pretty flattering to your head.
Oh good! I am very glad to hear you say nice things about me.
GULP
You ARE? Well I'm sure I can continue...
Please do?

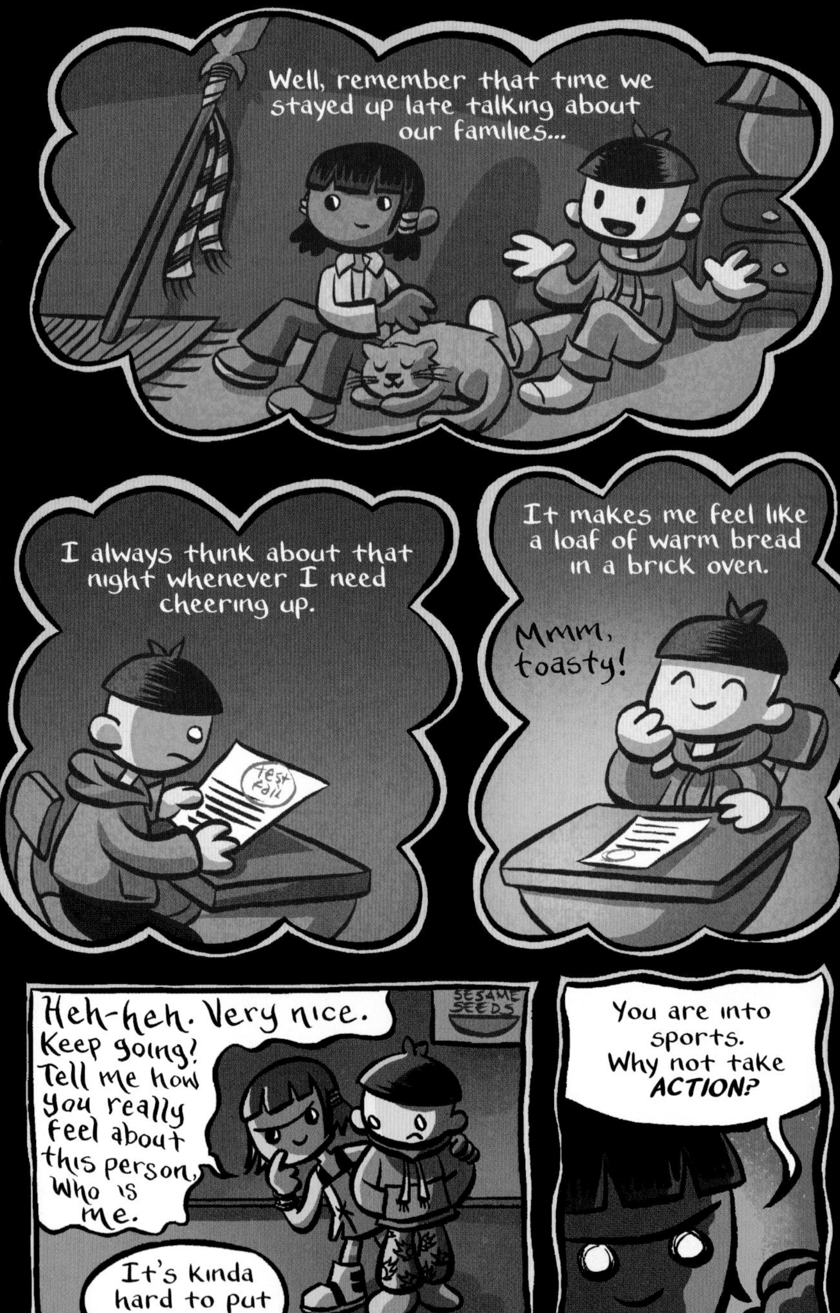
Well, remember that time we stayed up late talking about our families...
I always think about that night whenever I need cheering up.
TEST FAIL
It makes me feel like a loaf of warm bread in a brick oven.
Mmm, toasty!
SESAME SEEDS
Heh-heh. Very nice. Keep going! Tell me how you really feel about this person, who is me.
It's kinda hard to put into words.
You are into sports. Why not take ACTION?

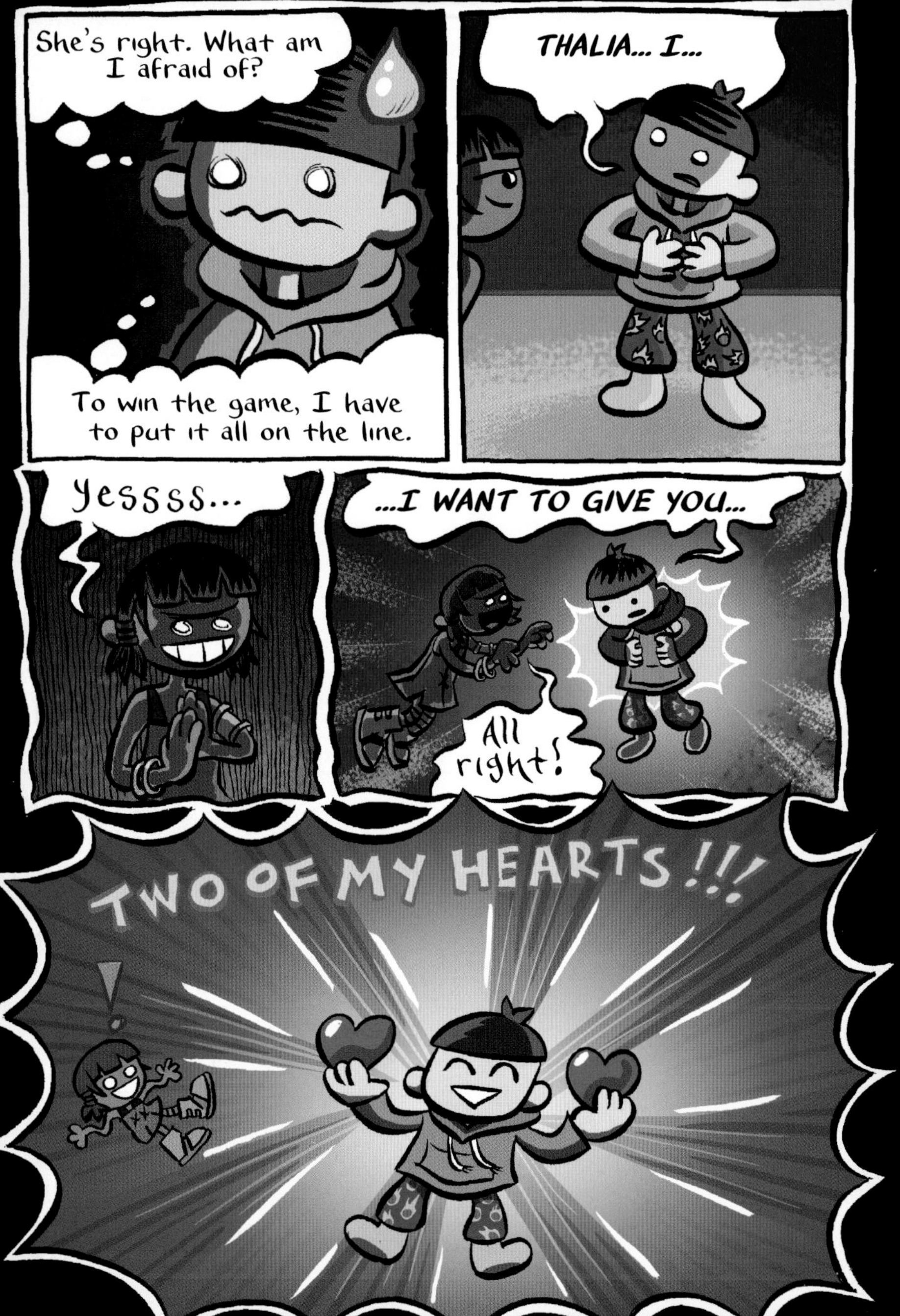
She's right. What am I afraid of?
To win the game, I have to put it all on the line.
THALIA... I...
Yessss...
...I WANT TO GIVE YOU...
All right!
TWO OF MY HEARTS!!!
!

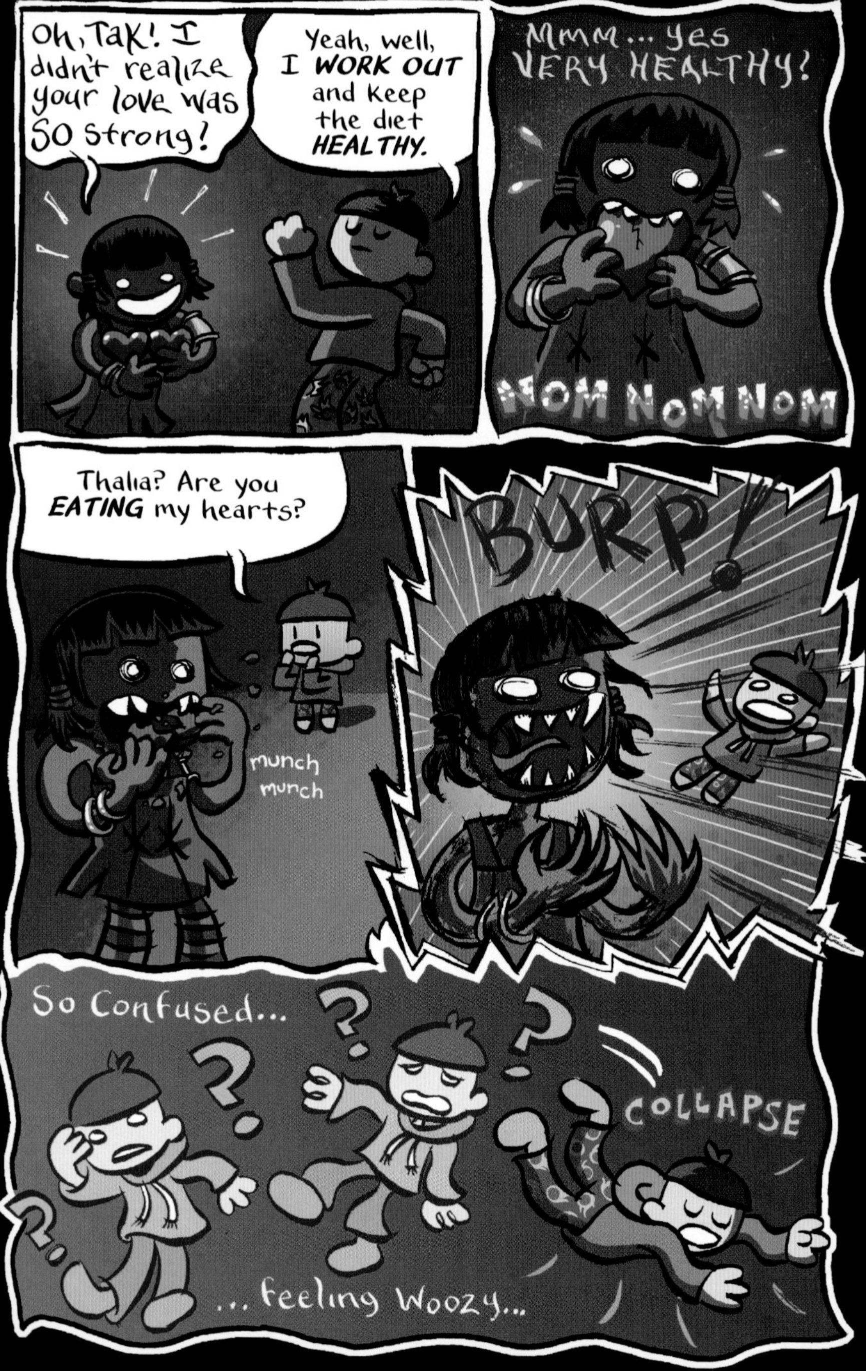
Oh, TAK! I didn't realize your love was SO Strong!
Yeah, well, I **WORK OUT** and keep the diet ***HEALTHY.***
Mmm... yes VERY HEALTHY?
NOM NOM NOM
Thalia? Are you ***EATING*** my hearts?
munch munch
BURP!
So Confused...
COLLAPSE
... feeling Woozy...

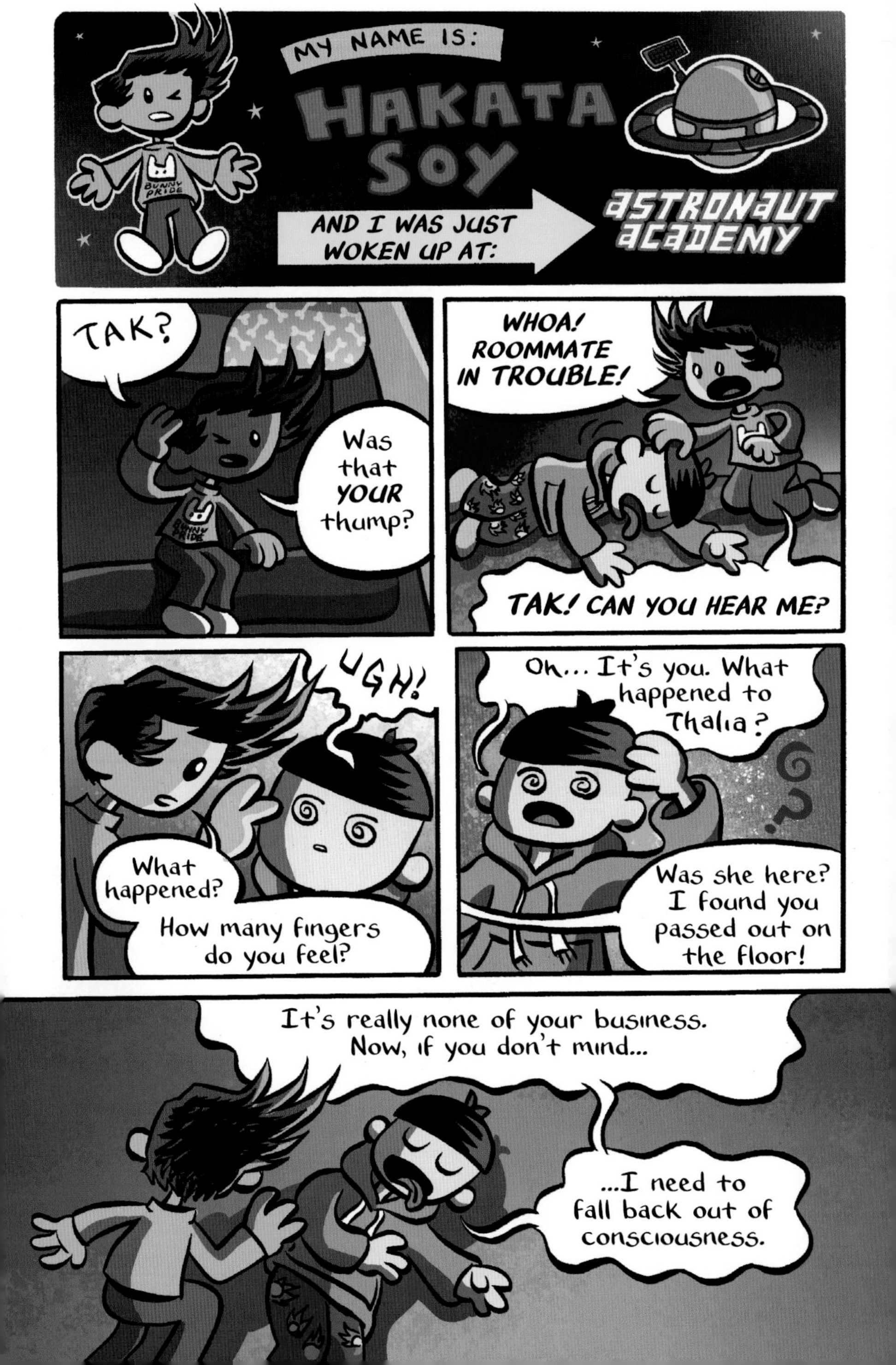
MY NAME IS:
HAKATA SOY
AND I WAS JUST WOKEN UP AT:
ASTRONAUT ACADEMY
TAK?
Was that YOUR thump?
WHOA! ROOMMATE IN TROUBLE!
TAK! CAN YOU HEAR ME?
UGH!
What happened?
How many fingers do you feel?
Oh... It's you. What happened to Thalia?
Was she here? I found you passed out on the floor!
It's really none of your business. Now, if you don't mind...
...I need to fall back out of consciousness.

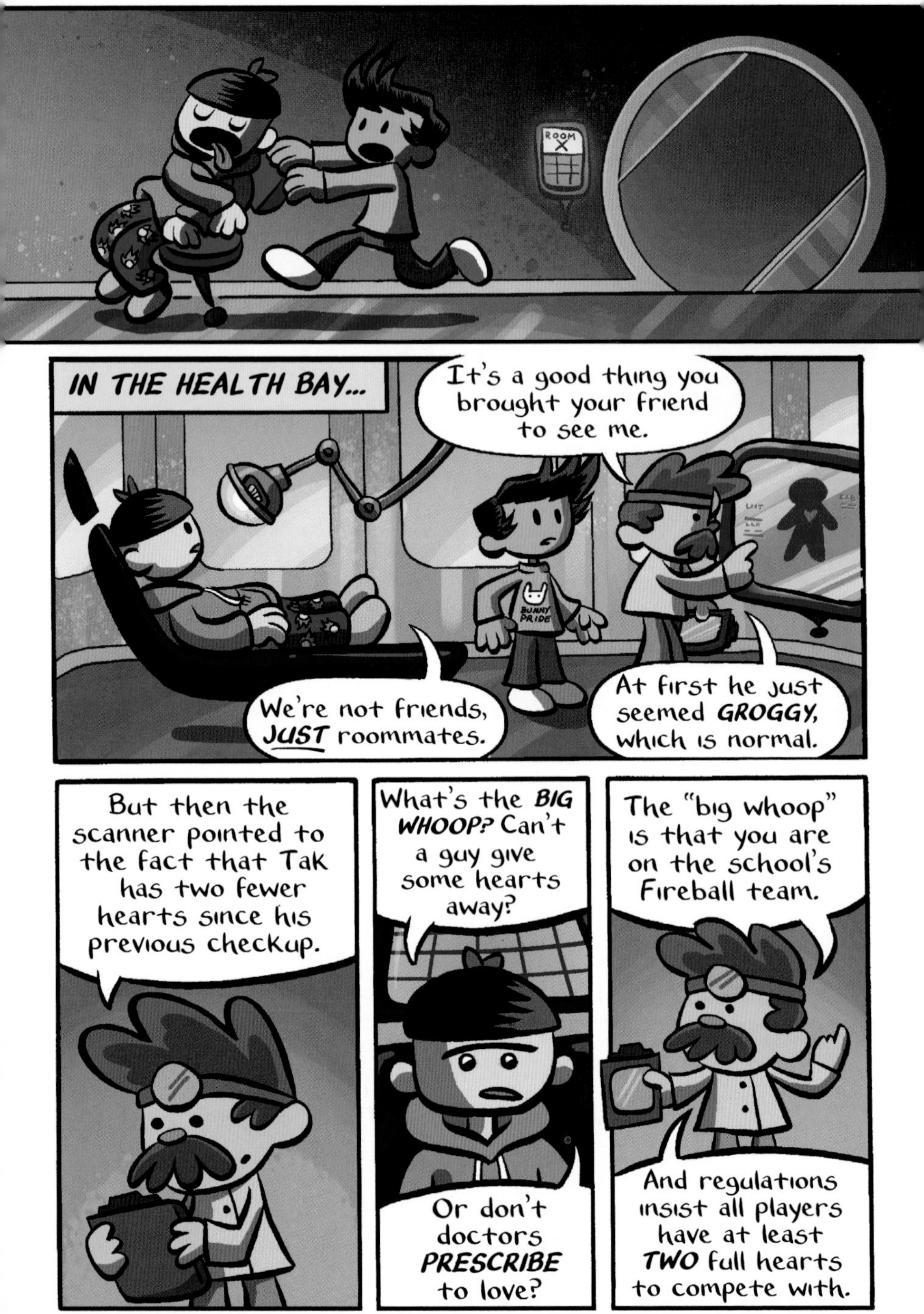
IN THE HEALTH BAY...
It's a good thing you brought your friend to see me.
We're not friends, JUST roommates.
At first he just seemed GROGGY, which is normal.
But then the scanner pointed to the fact that Tak has two fewer hearts since his previous checkup.
What's the BIG WHOOP? Can't a guy give some hearts away?
Or don't doctors PRESCRIBE to love?
The "big whoop" is that you are on the school's Fireball team.
And regulations insist all players have at least TWO full hearts to compete with.

I'm going to ignore what you just said because I didn't like the way it **SOUNDED.**

Then you better look into finding an additional heart before the first official game or else you'll be in denial on the sidelines.

THIS IS ALL YOUR FAULT!

WHAT? HOW?

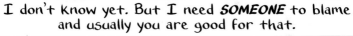

I don't know yet. But I need **SOMEONE** to blame and usually you are good for that.

What about Thalia Thistle? **SHE'S** the one you gave your hearts to, right?

I'm sure she'll give them back if she knows it's going to affect the team.

Don't think that's going to happen. They're probably **DIGESTED** by now.

37

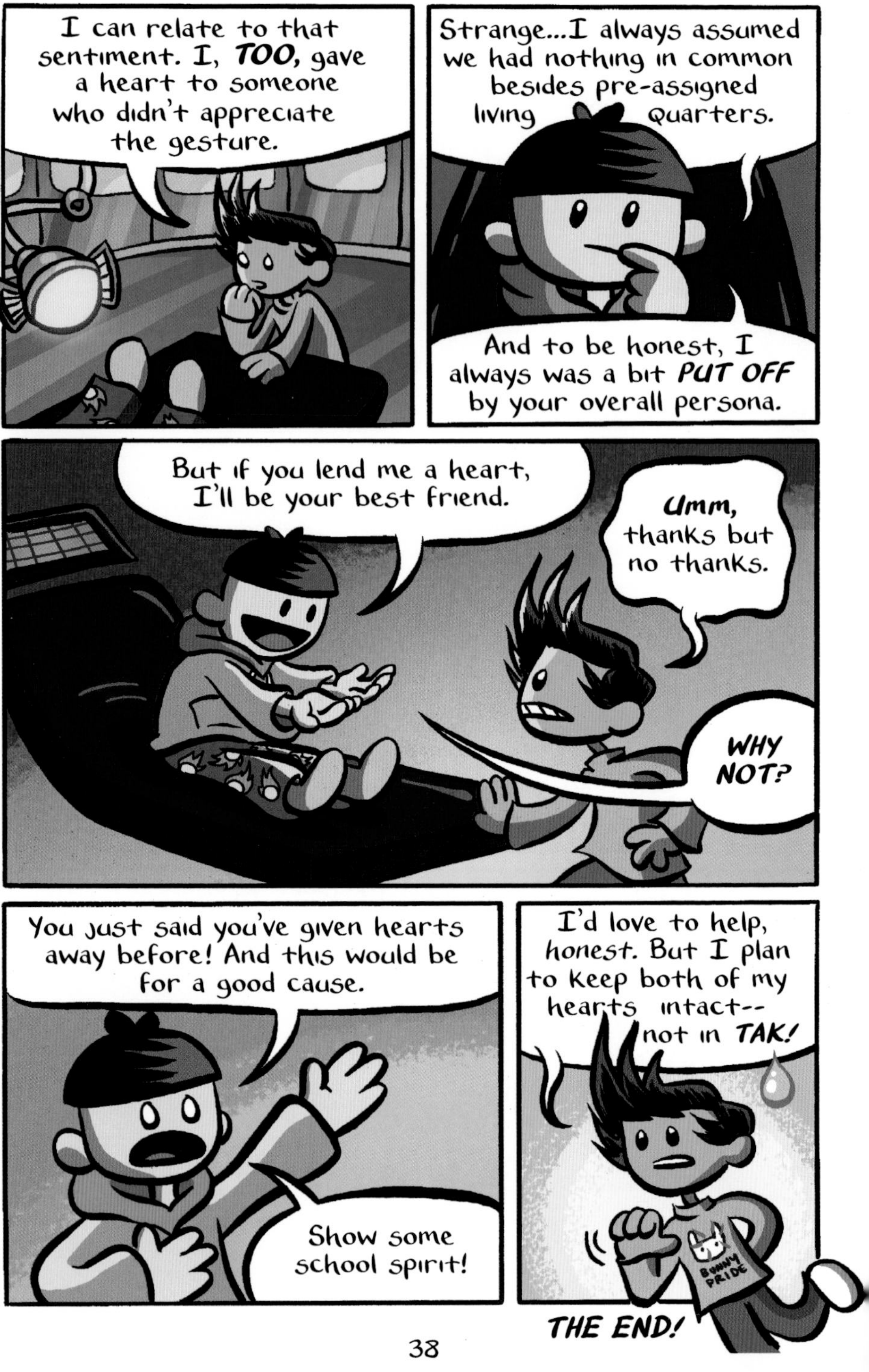
I can relate to that sentiment. I, TOO, gave a heart to someone who didn't appreciate the gesture.
Strange...I always assumed we had nothing in common besides pre-assigned living quarters.
And to be honest, I always was a bit PUT OFF by your overall persona.
But if you lend me a heart, I'll be your best friend.
Umm, thanks but no thanks.
WHY NOT?
You just said you've given hearts away before! And this would be for a good cause.
Show some school spirit!
I'd love to help, honest. But I plan to keep both of my hearts intact--not in TAK!
BUNNY PRIDE
THE END!

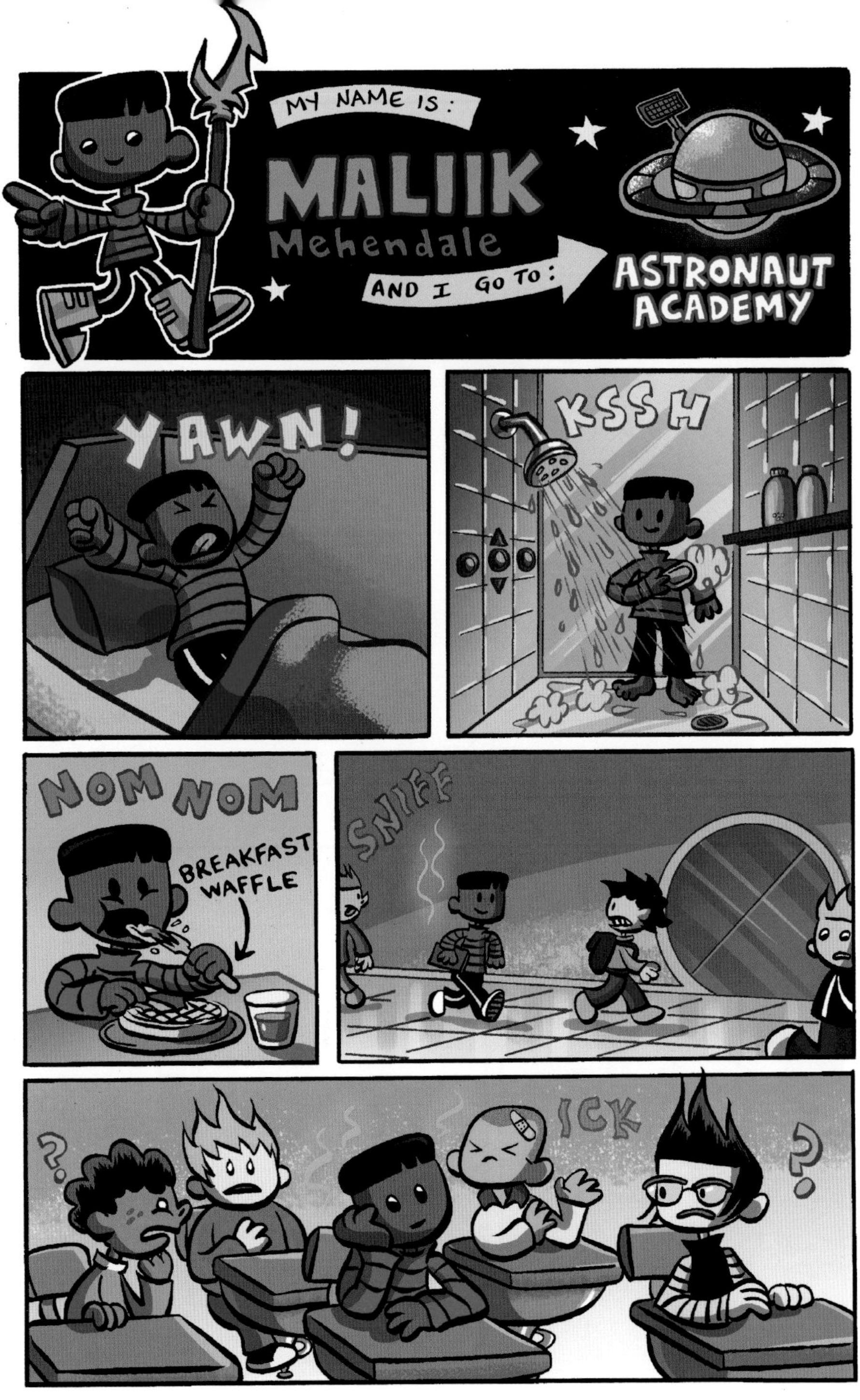

MY NAME IS:
MALIIK
Mehendale
AND I GO TO:
ASTRONAUT ACADEMY
YAWN!
KSSH
NOM NOM
BREAKFAST WAFFLE
SNIFF
ICK
?
?

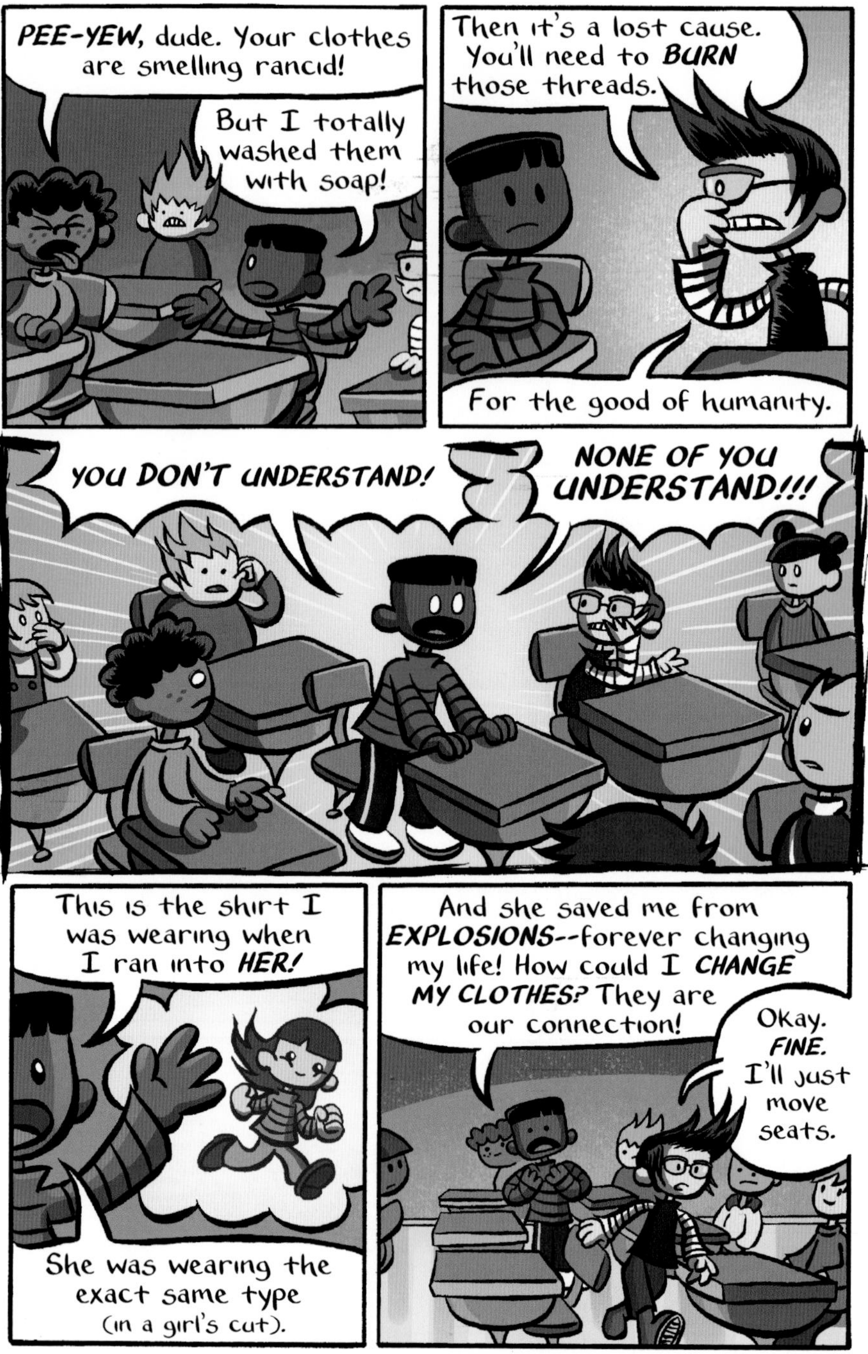
PEE-YEW, dude. Your clothes are smelling rancid!
But I totally washed them with soap!
Then it's a lost cause. You'll need to BURN those threads.
For the good of humanity.
YOU DON'T UNDERSTAND!
NONE OF YOU UNDERSTAND!!!
This is the shirt I was wearing when I ran into HER!
She was wearing the exact same type (in a girl's cut).
And she saved me from EXPLOSIONS--forever changing my life! How could I CHANGE MY CLOTHES? They are our connection!
Okay. FINE. I'll just move seats.

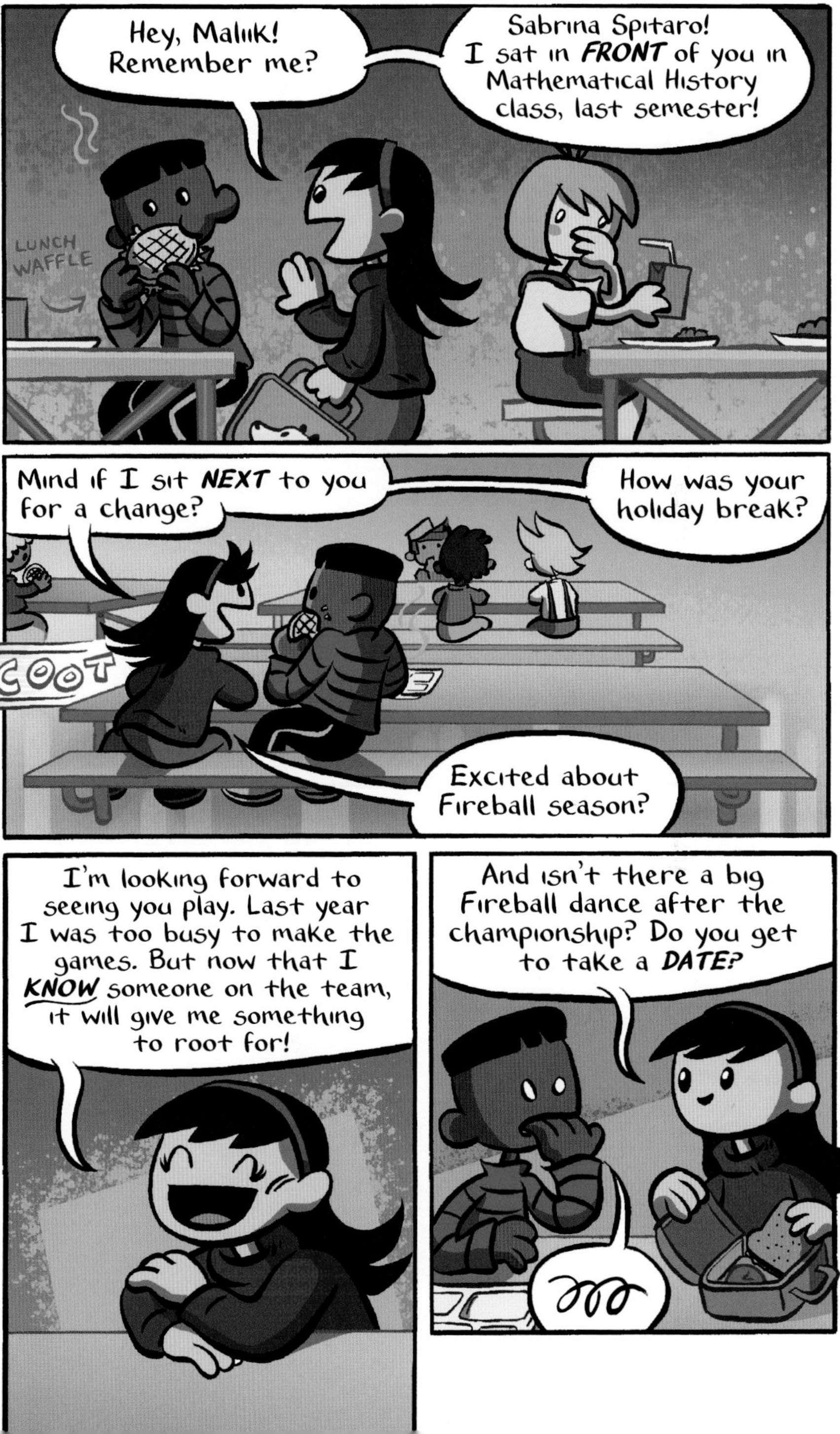
Hey, Malik! Remember me?
Sabrina Spitaro! I sat in FRONT of you in Mathematical History class, last semester!
LUNCH WAFFLE
Mind if I sit NEXT to you for a change?
How was your holiday break?
SCOOT
Excited about Fireball season?
I'm looking forward to seeing you play. Last year I was too busy to make the games. But now that I KNOW someone on the team, it will give me something to root for!
And isn't there a big Fireball dance after the championship? Do you get to take a DATE?

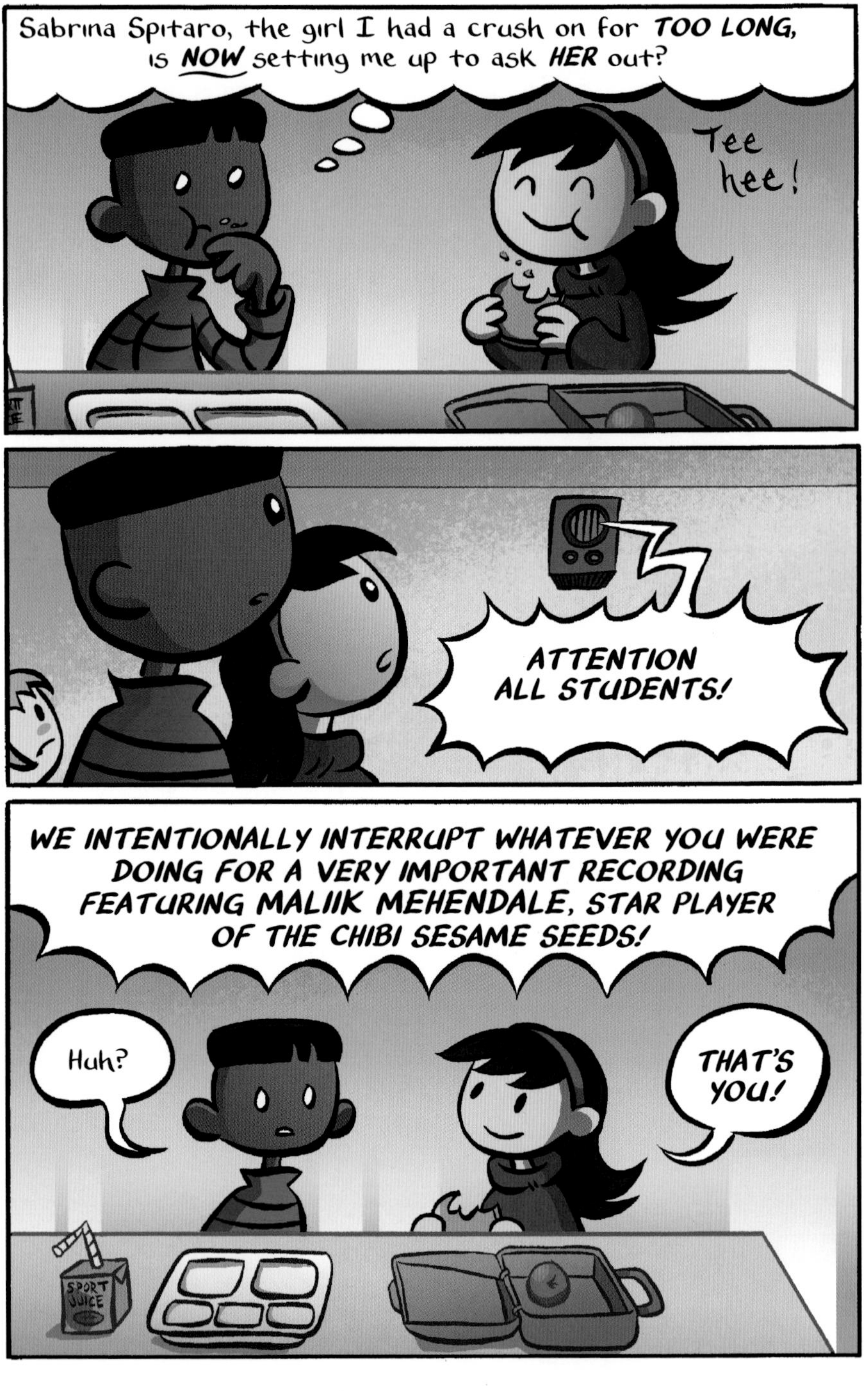
Sabrina Spitaro, the girl I had a crush on for TOO LONG, is NOW setting me up to ask HER out?
Tee hee!
ATTENTION ALL STUDENTS!
WE INTENTIONALLY INTERRUPT WHATEVER YOU WERE DOING FOR A VERY IMPORTANT RECORDING FEATURING MALIIK MEHENDALE, STAR PLAYER OF THE CHIBI SESAME SEEDS!
Huh?
THAT'S YOU!
SPORT JUICE

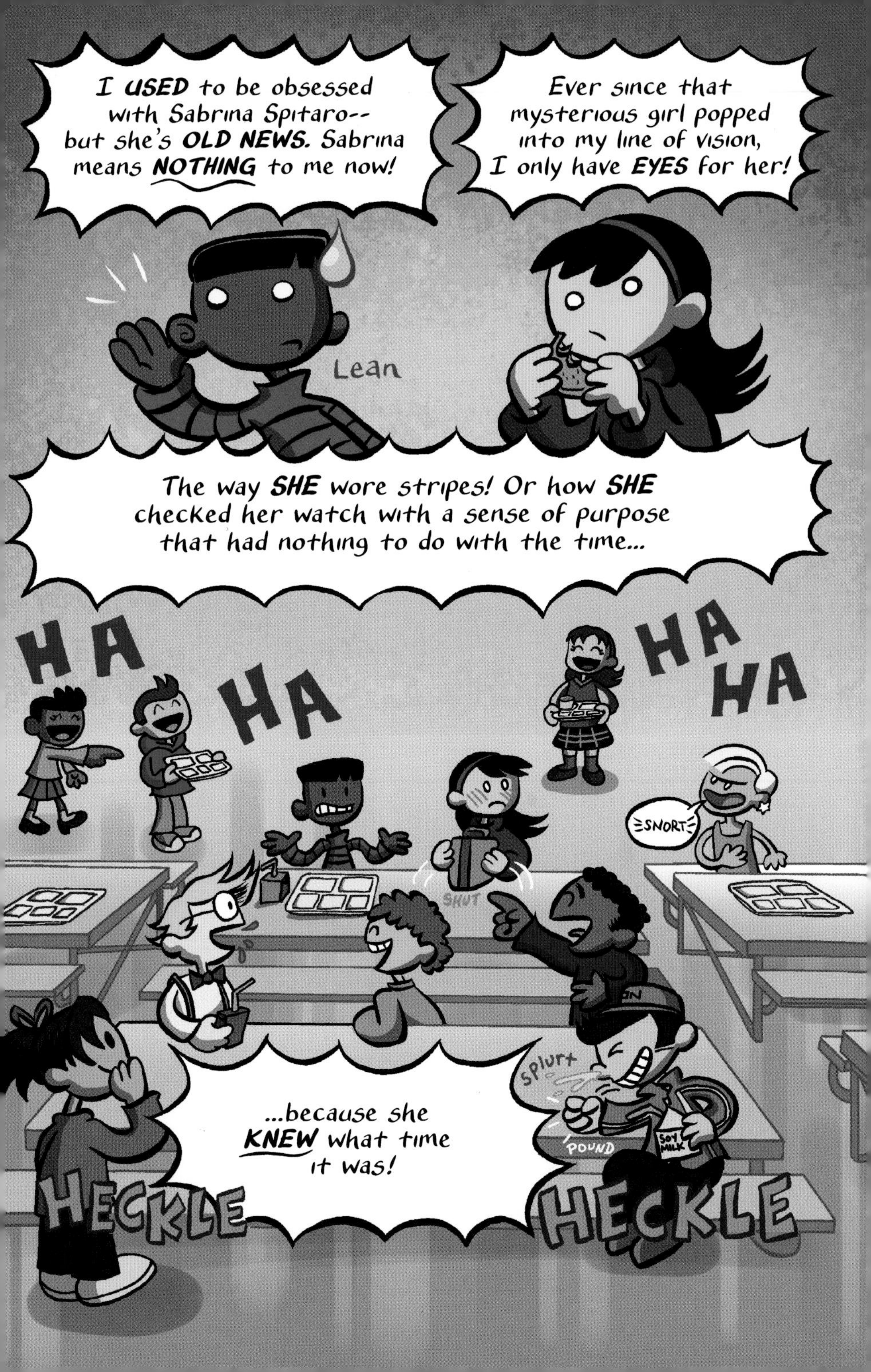
I USED to be obsessed with Sabrina Spitaro--but she's OLD NEWS. Sabrina means NOTHING to me now!
Ever since that mysterious girl popped into my line of vision, I only have EYES for her!
Lean
The way SHE wore stripes! Or how SHE checked her watch with a sense of purpose that had nothing to do with the time...
HA HA
HA HA
HA HA
SNORT
SHUT
splurt
POUND
SOY MILK
...because she KNEW what time it was!
HECKLE
HECKLE

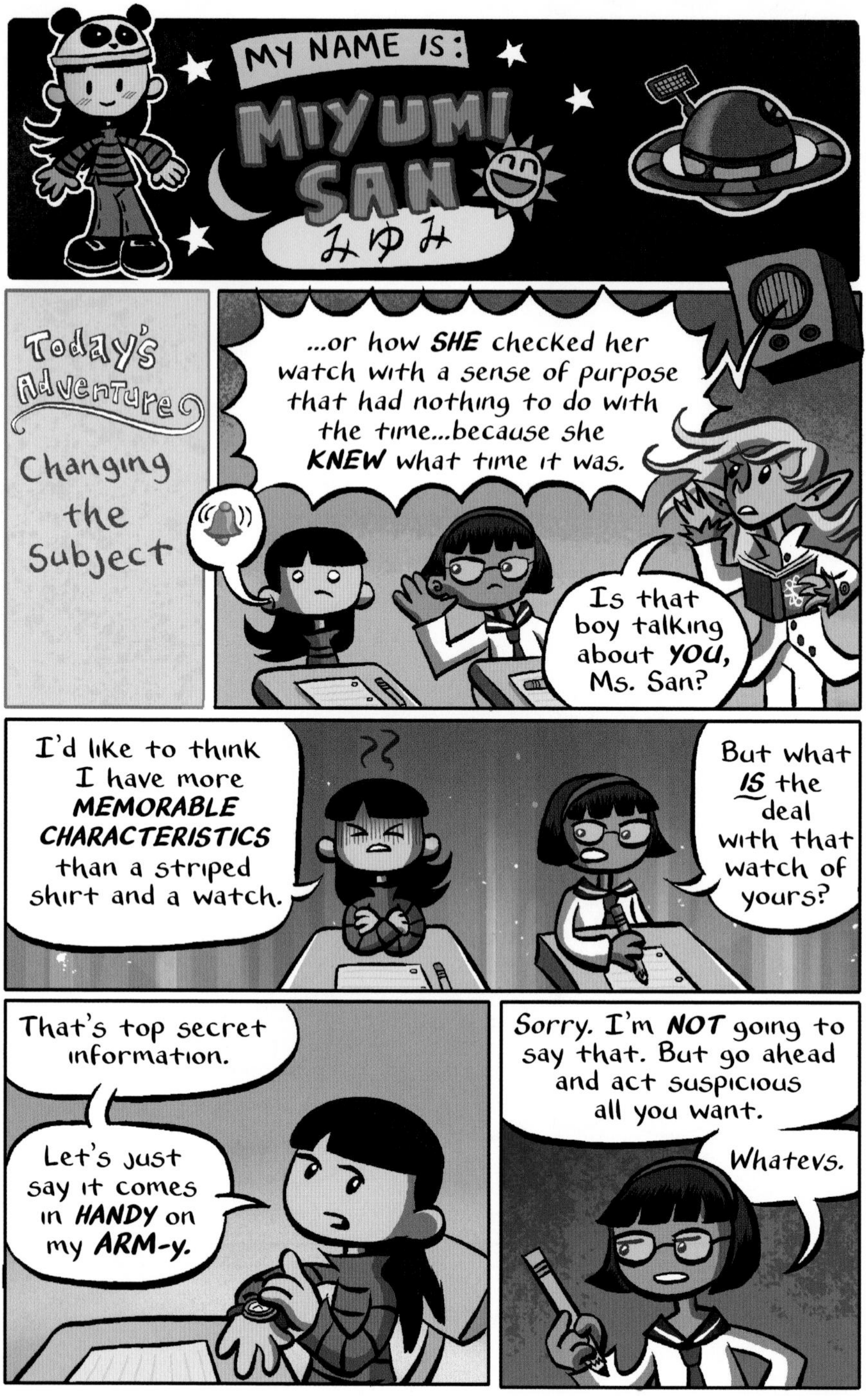
MY NAME IS:
MIYUMI SAN
みゆみ
Today's Adventure
Changing the Subject
...or how SHE checked her watch with a sense of purpose that had nothing to do with the time...because she KNEW what time it was.
Is that boy talking about YOU, Ms. San?
I'd like to think I have more MEMORABLE CHARACTERISTICS than a striped shirt and a watch.
But what IS the deal with that watch of yours?
That's top secret information.
Let's just say it comes in HANDY on my ARM-y.
Sorry. I'm NOT going to say that. But go ahead and act suspicious all you want.
Whatevs.

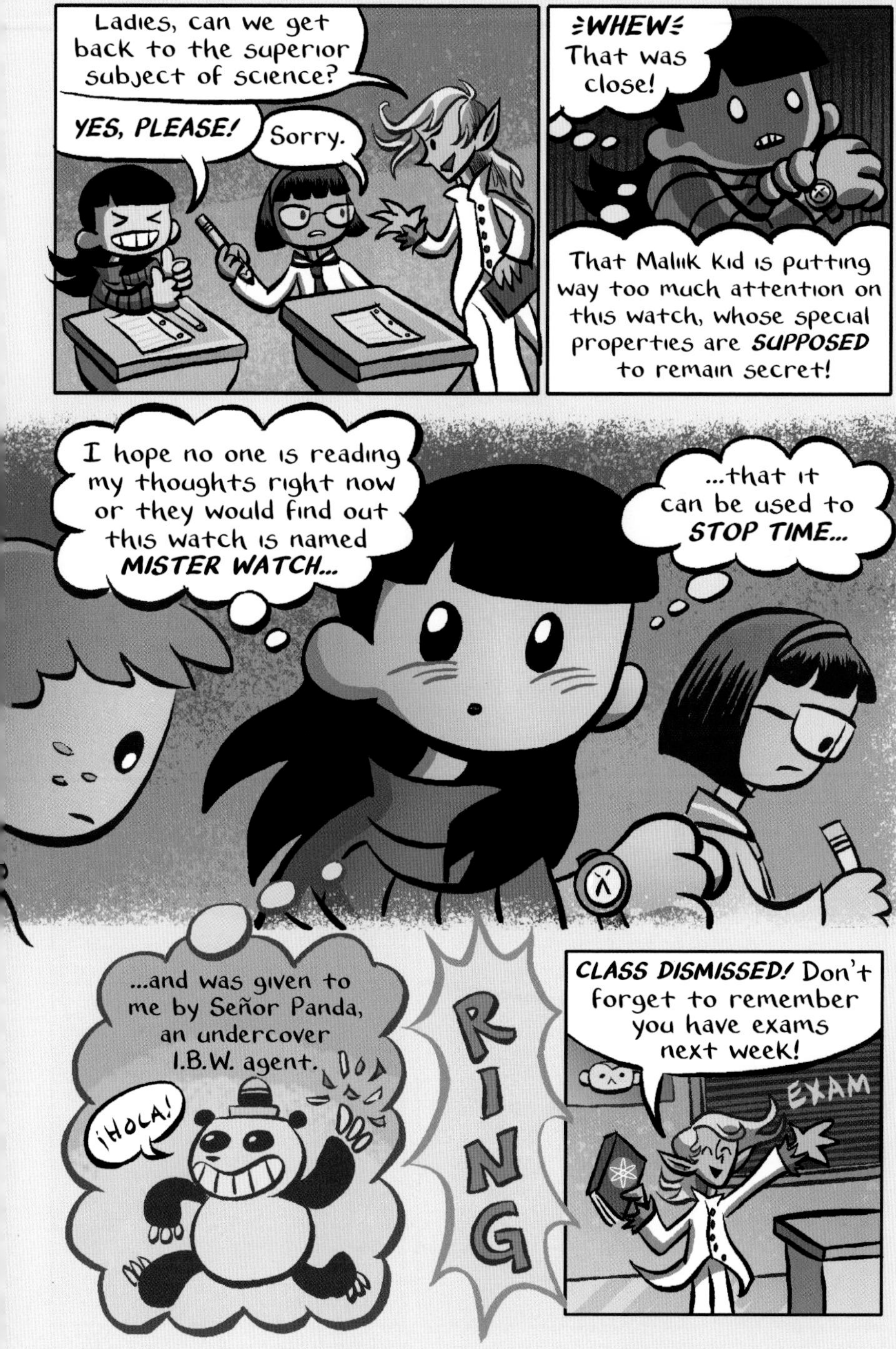
Ladies, can we get back to the superior subject of science?
YES, PLEASE!
Sorry.
WHEW That was close!
That Malik kid is putting way too much attention on this watch, whose special properties are SUPPOSED to remain secret!
I hope no one is reading my thoughts right now or they would find out this watch is named MISTER WATCH...
...that it can be used to STOP TIME...
...and was given to me by Señor Panda, an undercover I.B.W. agent.
¡HOLA!
RING
CLASS DISMISSED! Don't forget to remember you have exams next week!
EXAM

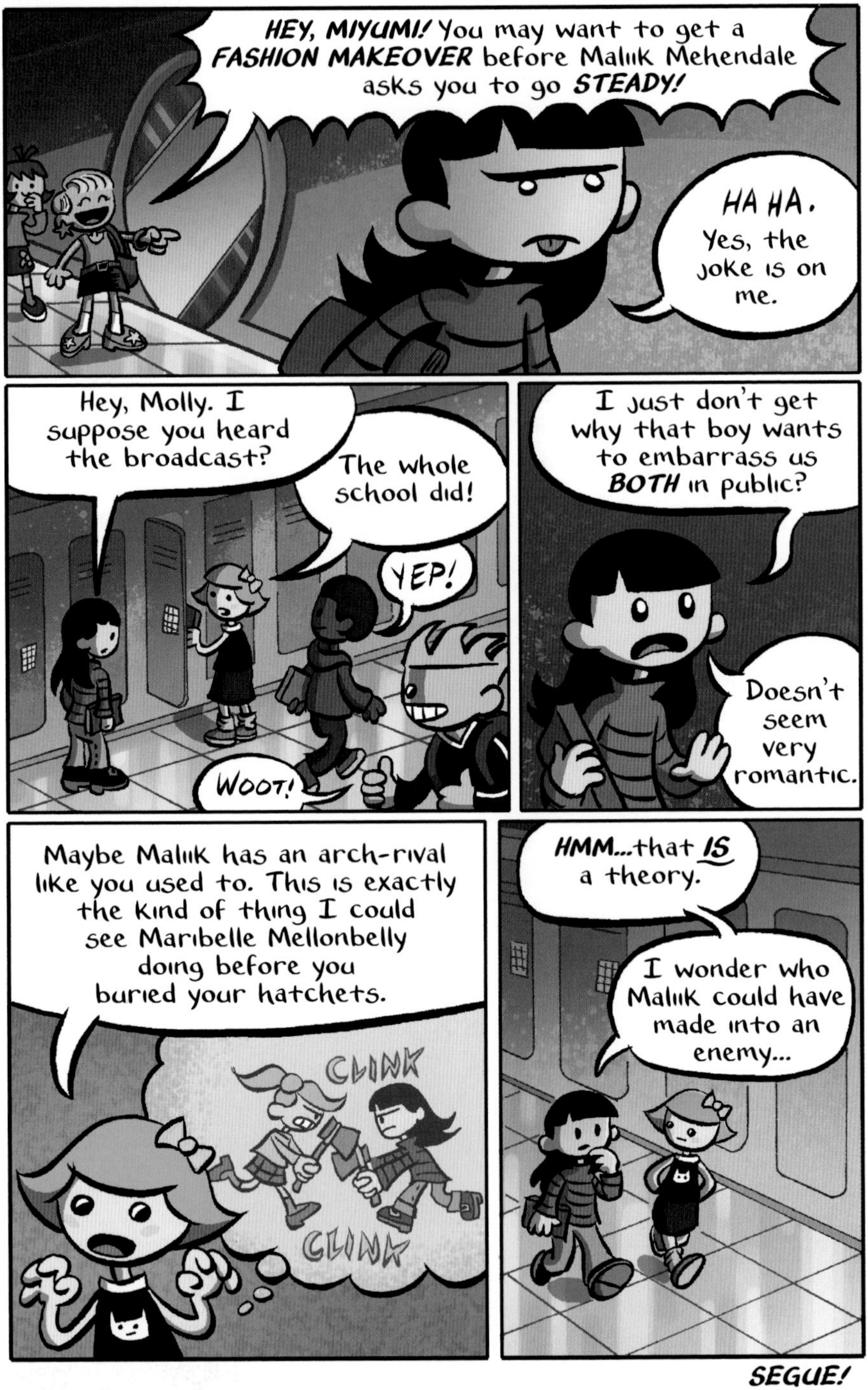
HEY, MIYUMI! You may want to get a FASHION MAKEOVER before Malik Mehendale asks you to go STEADY!
HA HA. Yes, the joke is on me.
Hey, Molly. I suppose you heard the broadcast?
The whole school did!
YEP!
WOOT!
I just don't get why that boy wants to embarrass us BOTH in public?
Doesn't seem very romantic.
Maybe Malik has an arch-rival like you used to. This is exactly the kind of thing I could see Maribelle Mellonbelly doing before you buried your hatchets.
CLINK
CLINK
HMM...that IS a theory.
I wonder who Malik could have made into an enemy...
SEGUE!

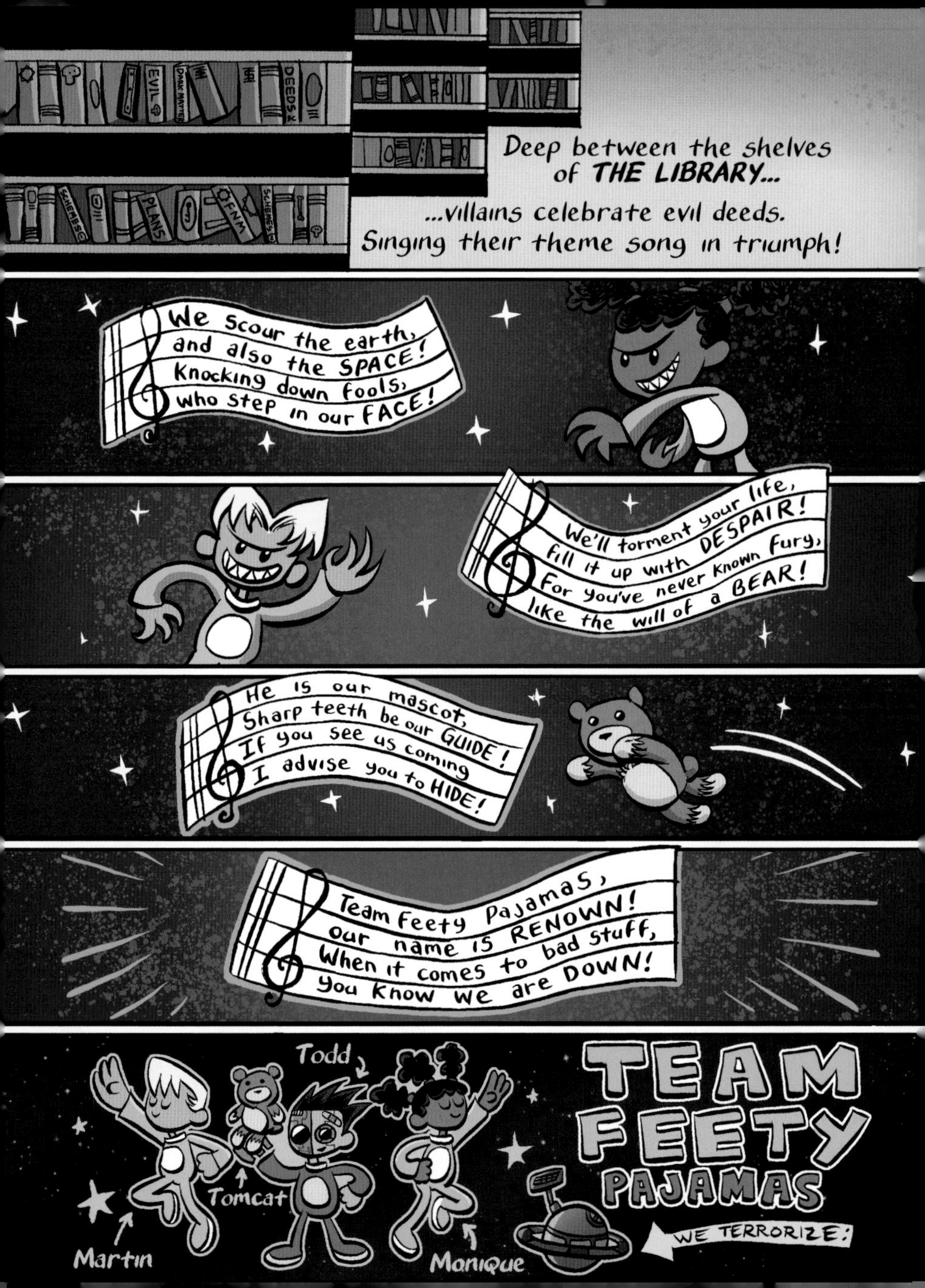

EVIL
DARK MATTER
DEEDS
SCHEMES
PLANS
FNM
SCHEMES
Deep between the shelves of THE LIBRARY...
...villains celebrate evil deeds. Singing their theme song in triumph!
We scour the earth, and also the SPACE! Knocking down fools, who step in our FACE!
We'll torment your life, fill it up with DESPAIR! For you've never known fury, like the will of a BEAR!
He is our mascot, Sharp teeth be our GUIDE! If you see us coming I advise you to HIDE!
Team Feety Pajamas, our name is RENOWN! When it comes to bad stuff, You know we are DOWN!
Todd
Tomcat
Martin
Monique
TEAM FEETY PAJAMAS
WE TERRORIZE:

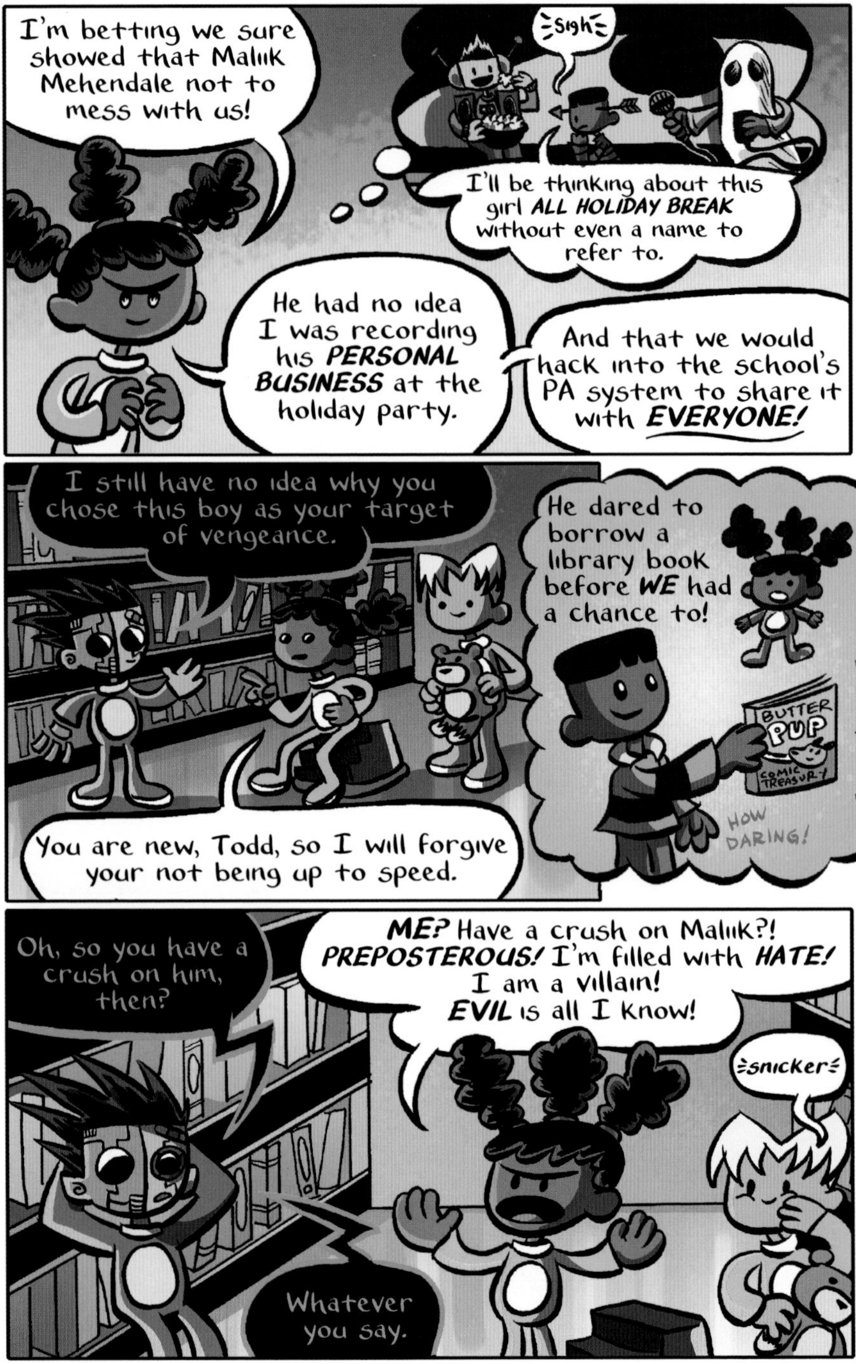
I'm betting we sure showed that Malik Mehendale not to mess with us!
Sigh
I'll be thinking about this girl ALL HOLIDAY BREAK without even a name to refer to.
He had no idea I was recording his PERSONAL BUSINESS at the holiday party.
And that we would hack into the school's PA system to share it with EVERYONE!
I still have no idea why you chose this boy as your target of vengeance.
He dared to borrow a library book before WE had a chance to!
BUTTER PUP COMIC TREASURY
HOW DARING!
You are new, Todd, so I will forgive your not being up to speed.
Oh, so you have a crush on him, then?
ME? Have a crush on Malik?! PREPOSTEROUS! I'm filled with HATE! I am a villain! EVIL is all I know!
snicker
Whatever you say.

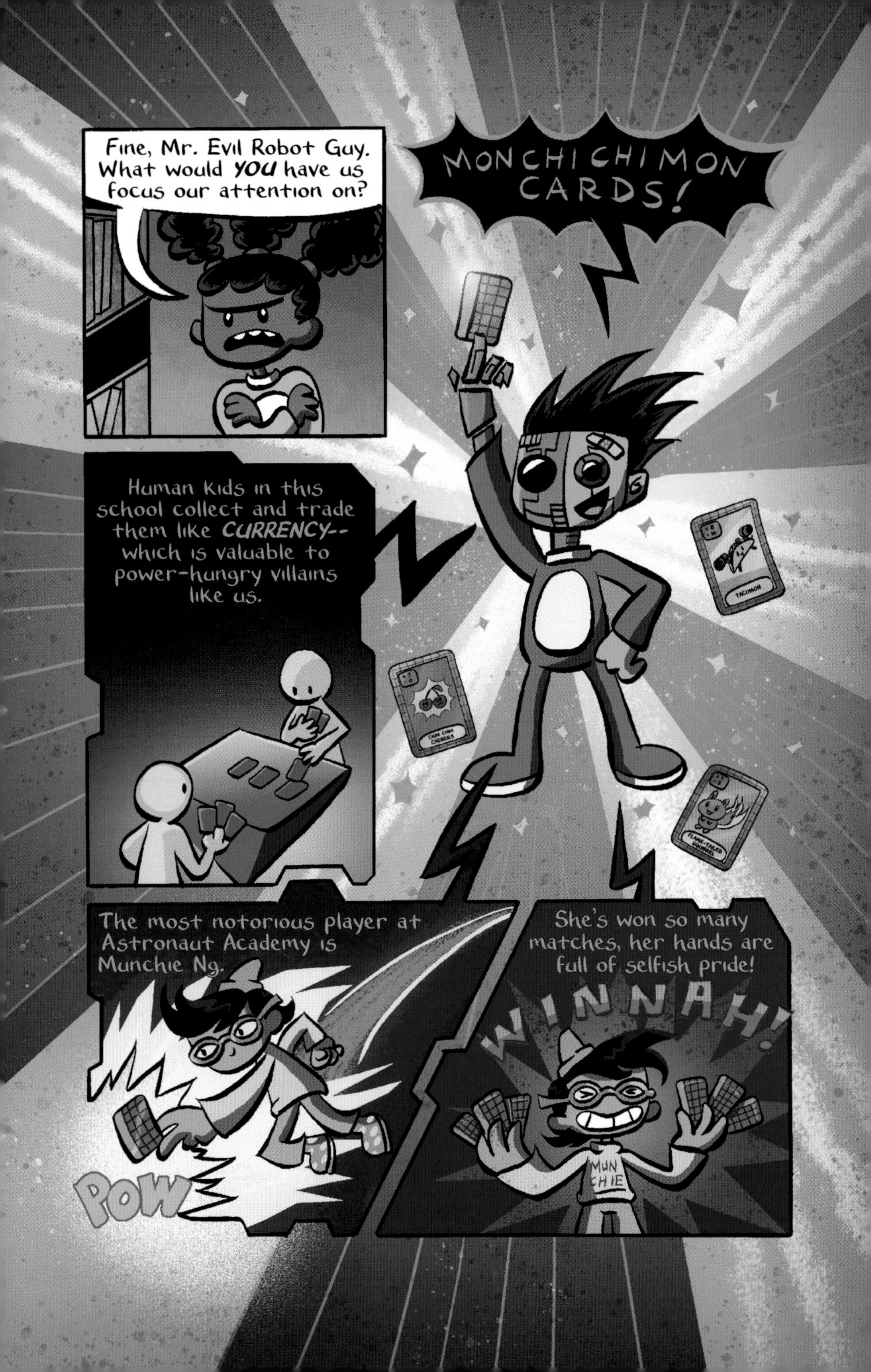
Fine, Mr. Evil Robot Guy. What would YOU have us focus our attention on?
MONCHICHIMON CARDS!
Human kids in this school collect and trade them like CURRENCY-- which is valuable to power-hungry villains like us.
TACOMON
CHIM CHIM CHERRIES
FLAME-TAILED SQUIRREL
The most notorious player at Astronaut Academy is Munchie Ng.
POW
She's won so many matches, her hands are full of selfish pride!
WINNAH!
MUNCHIE

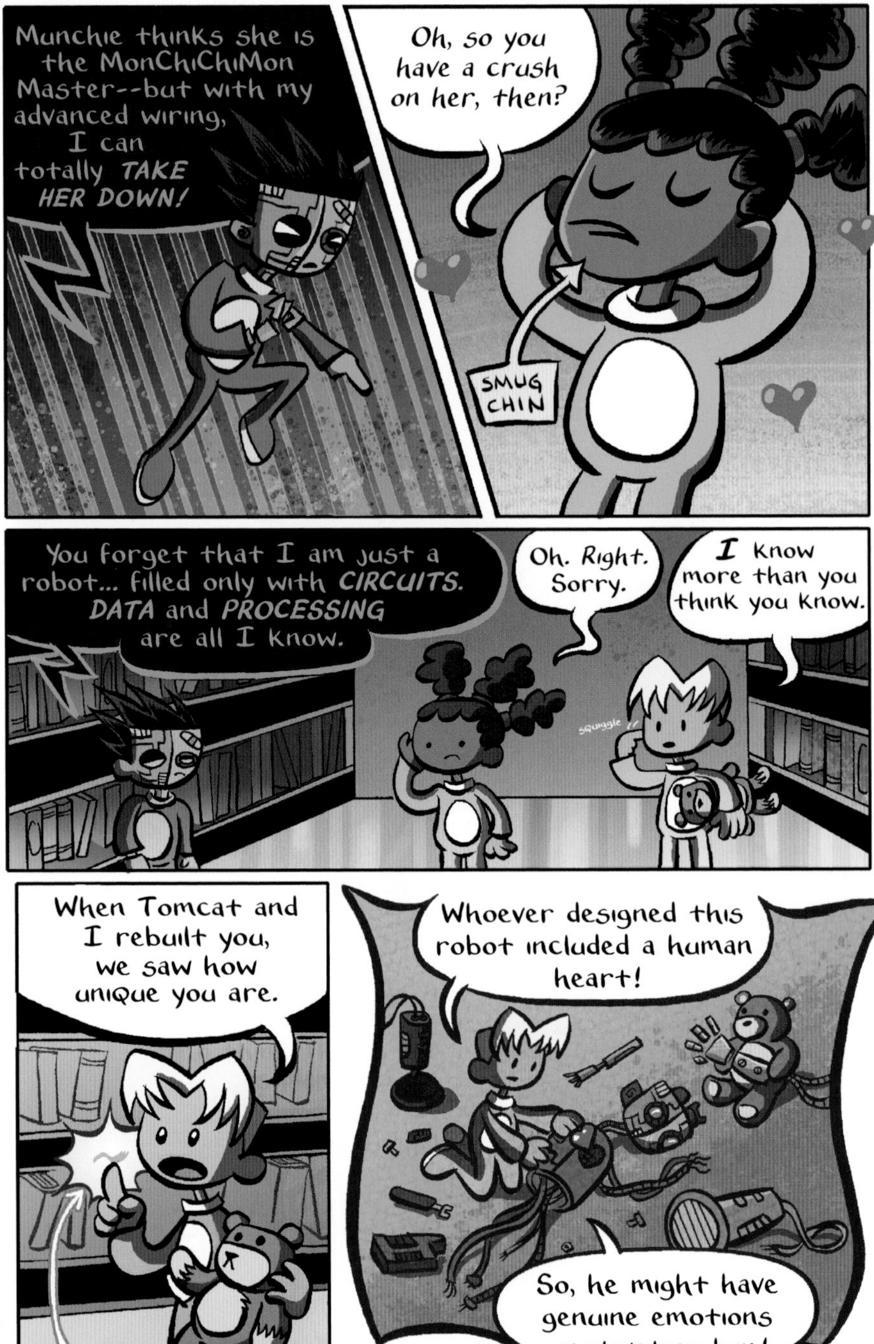
Munchie thinks she is the MonChiChiMon Master--but with my advanced wiring, I can totally TAKE HER DOWN!
Oh, so you have a crush on her, then?
SMUG CHIN
You forget that I am just a robot... filled only with CIRCUITS. DATA and PROCESSING are all I know.
Oh. Right. Sorry.
I know more than you think you know.
squiggle
When Tomcat and I rebuilt you, we saw how unique you are.
FLASHBACK
Whoever designed this robot included a human heart!
So, he might have genuine emotions motivating him!

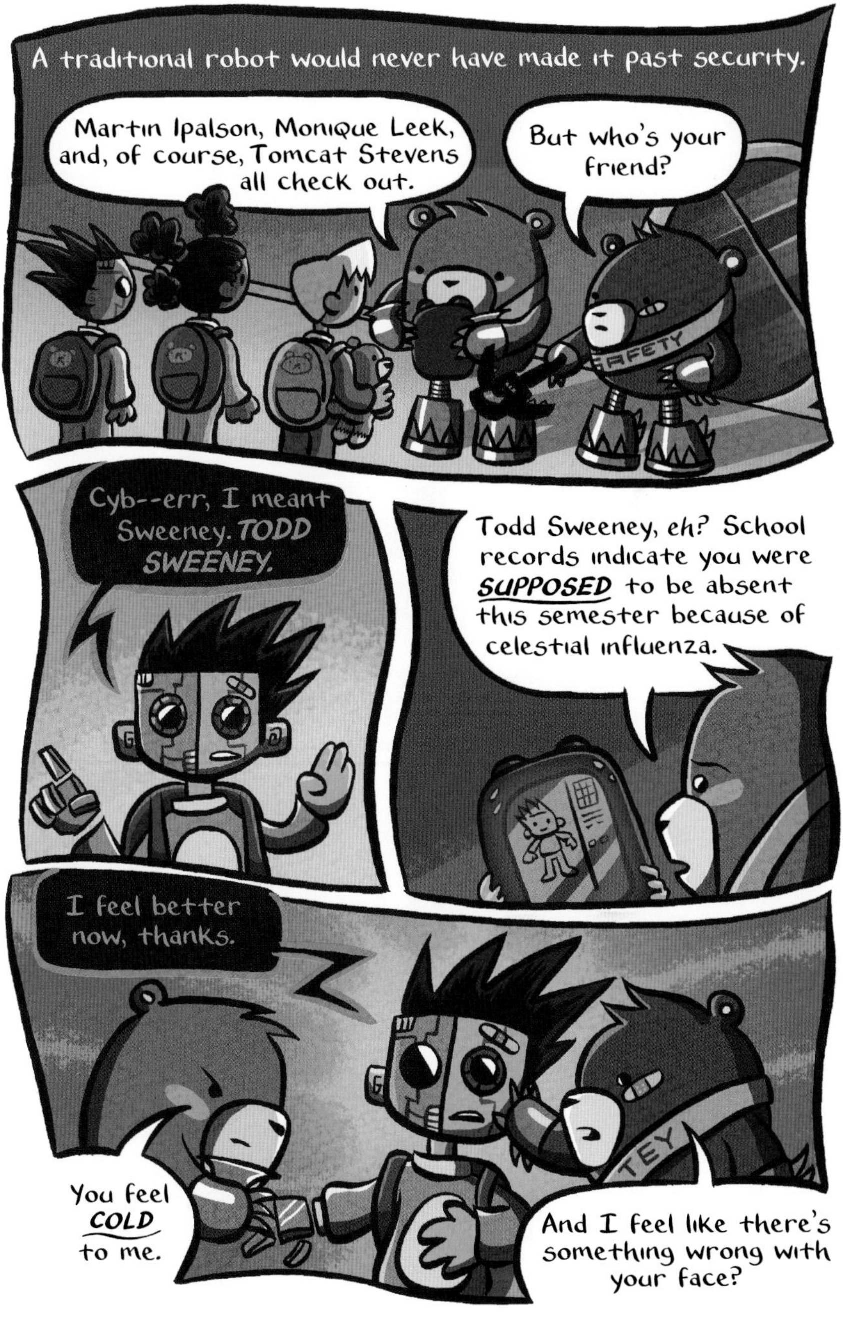
A traditional robot would never have made it past security.
Martin Ipalson, Monique Leek, and, of course, Tomcat Stevens all check out.
But who's your friend?
RFETY
Cyb--err, I meant Sweeney. TODD SWEENEY.
Todd Sweeney, eh? School records indicate you were SUPPOSED to be absent this semester because of celestial influenza.
I feel better now, thanks.
You feel COLD to me.
And I feel like there's something wrong with your face?
TEY

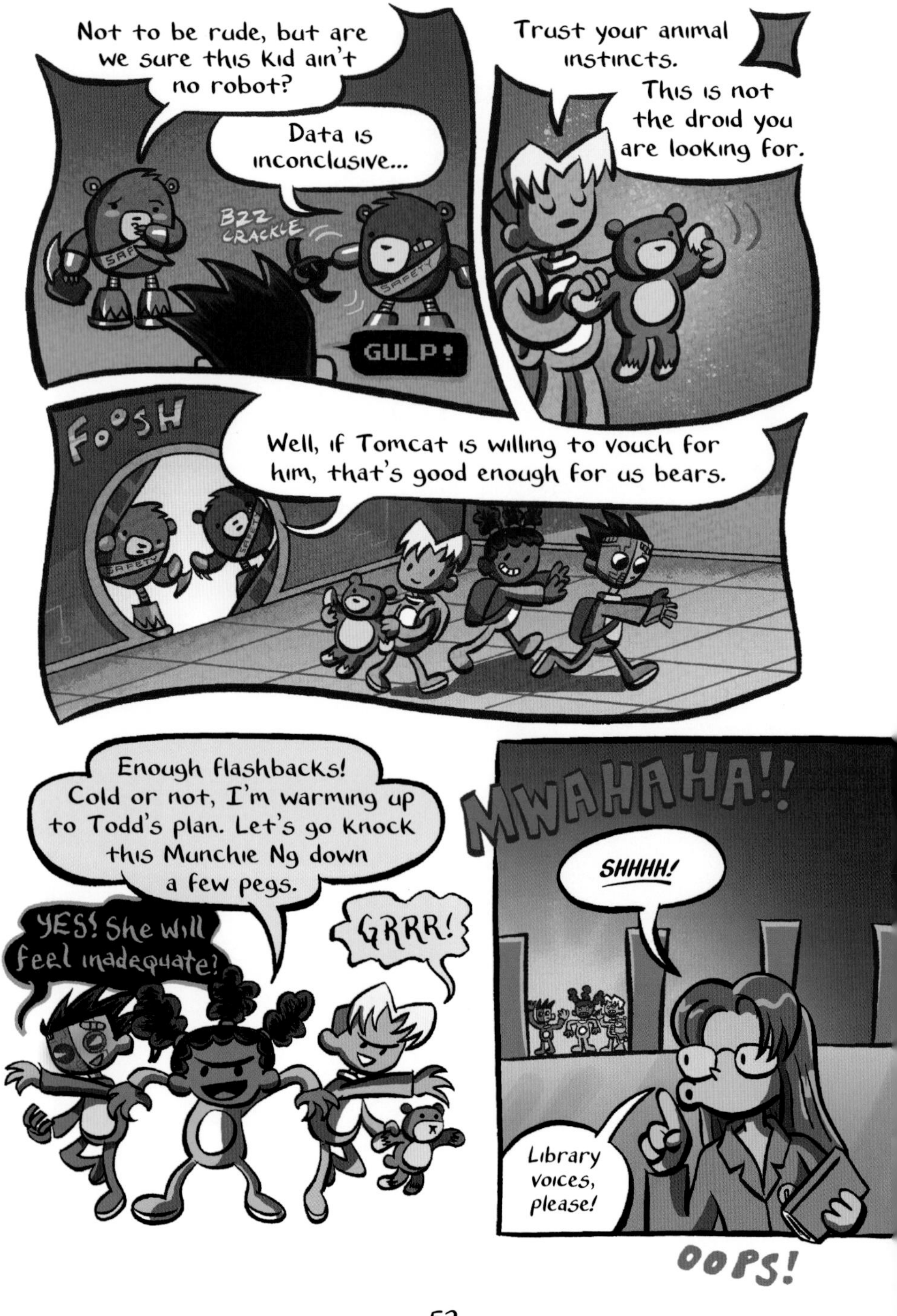
Not to be rude, but are we sure this kid ain't no robot?
Data is inconclusive...
BZZ CRACKLE
SAFETY
GULP!
Trust your animal instincts.
This is not the droid you are looking for.
FOOSH
Well, if Tomcat is willing to vouch for him, that's good enough for us bears.
SAFETY
Enough flashbacks! Cold or not, I'm warming up to Todd's plan. Let's go knock this Munchie Ng down a few pegs.
YES! She will feel inadequate!
GRRR!
MWAHAHA!!
SHHHH!
Library voices, please!
OOPS!

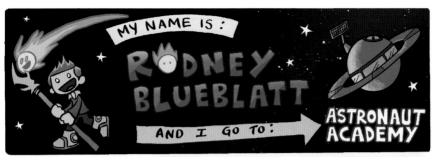

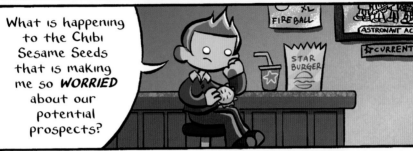

MY NAME IS :
RODNEY BLUEBLATT
AND I GO TO :
ASTRONAUT ACADEMY
XL FIREBALL
ASTRONAUT AC
CURRENT
STAR BURGER
What is happening to the Chibi Sesame Seeds that is making me so WORRIED about our potential prospects?
As team captain, it is my job to make sure everyone is FOCUSED on not being distracted.
Prepared to practice?!
What?
Oops. Yeah. Sorry.
Of course!
020
06
01
12
To make sure they haven't gone crazy.
Malik, please concentrate on the sport at hand!
Do I have to concentrate with my HEARTS...
...as well as brains?

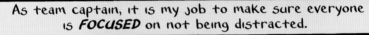

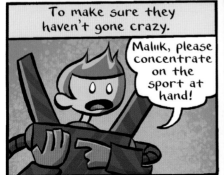

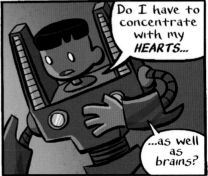

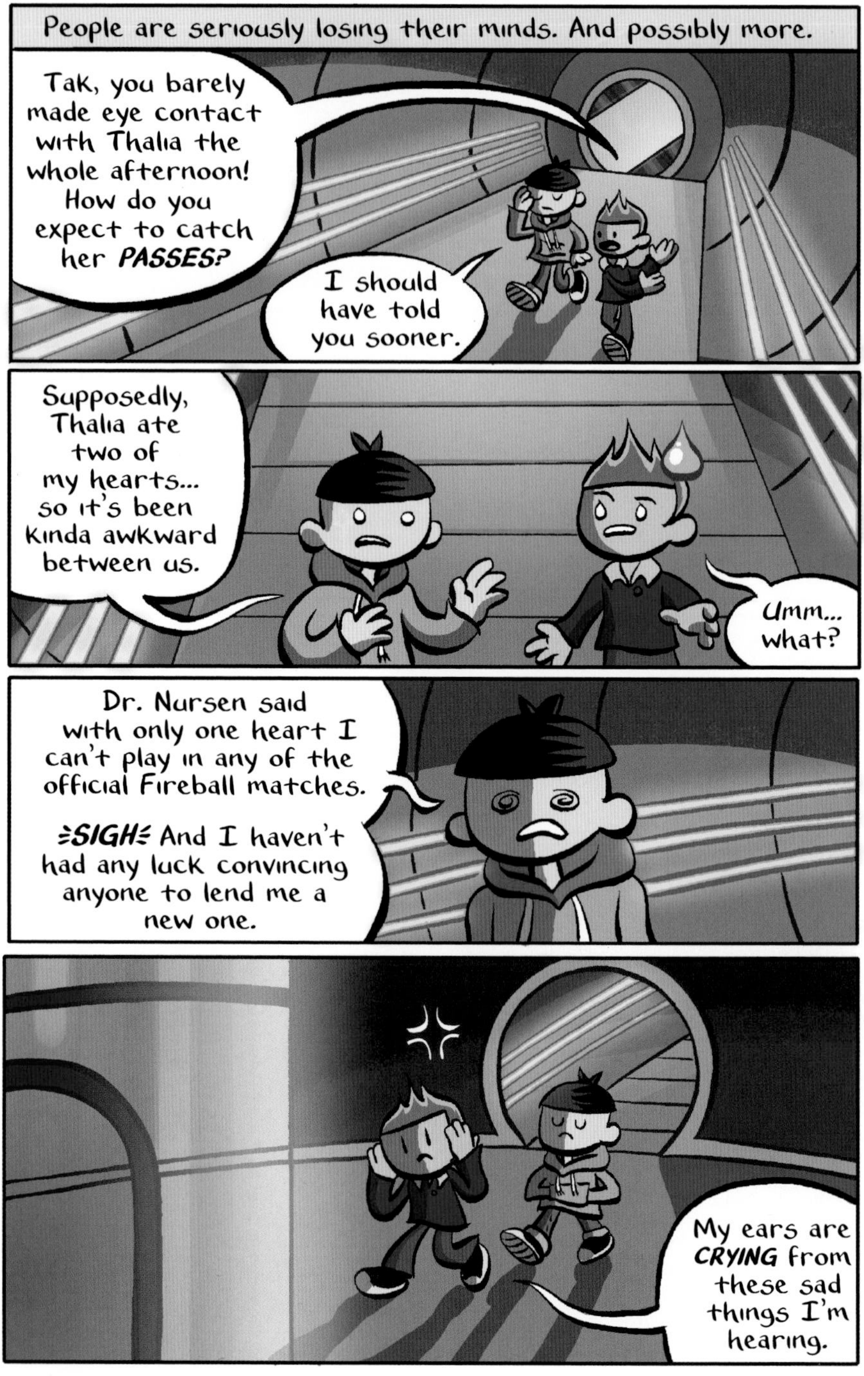
People are seriously losing their minds. And possibly more.
Tak, you barely made eye contact with Thalia the whole afternoon! How do you expect to catch her PASSES?
I should have told you sooner.
Supposedly, Thalia ate two of my hearts... so it's been kinda awkward between us.
Umm... what?
Dr. Nursen said with only one heart I can't play in any of the official Fireball matches.
SIGH And I haven't had any luck convincing anyone to lend me a new one.
My ears are CRYING from these sad things I'm hearing.

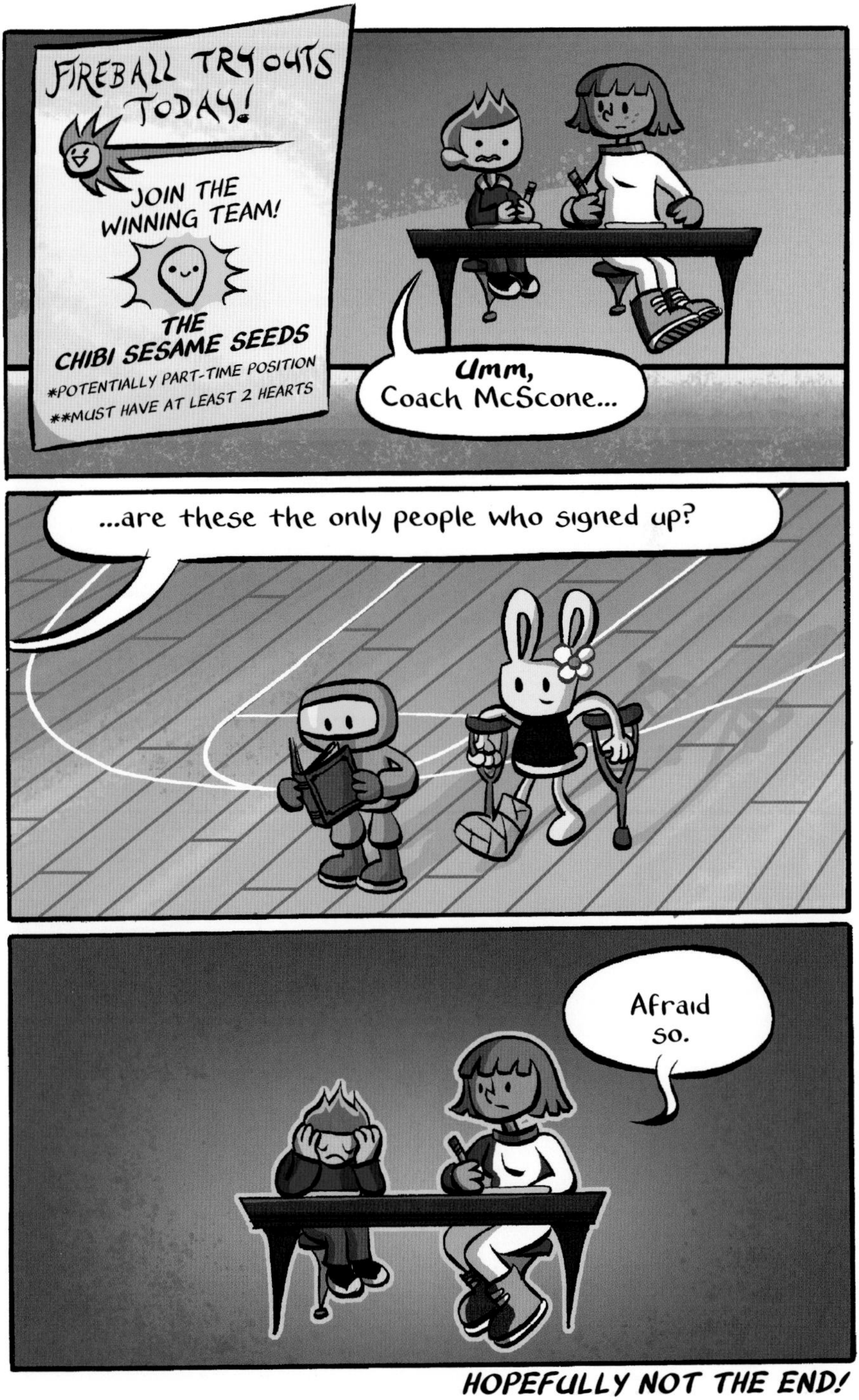
FIREBALL TRYOUTS TODAY!
JOIN THE WINNING TEAM!
THE CHIBI SESAME SEEDS
*POTENTIALLY PART-TIME POSITION
**MUST HAVE AT LEAST 2 HEARTS
Umm, Coach McScone...
...are these the only people who signed up?
Afraid so.
HOPEFULLY NOT THE END!

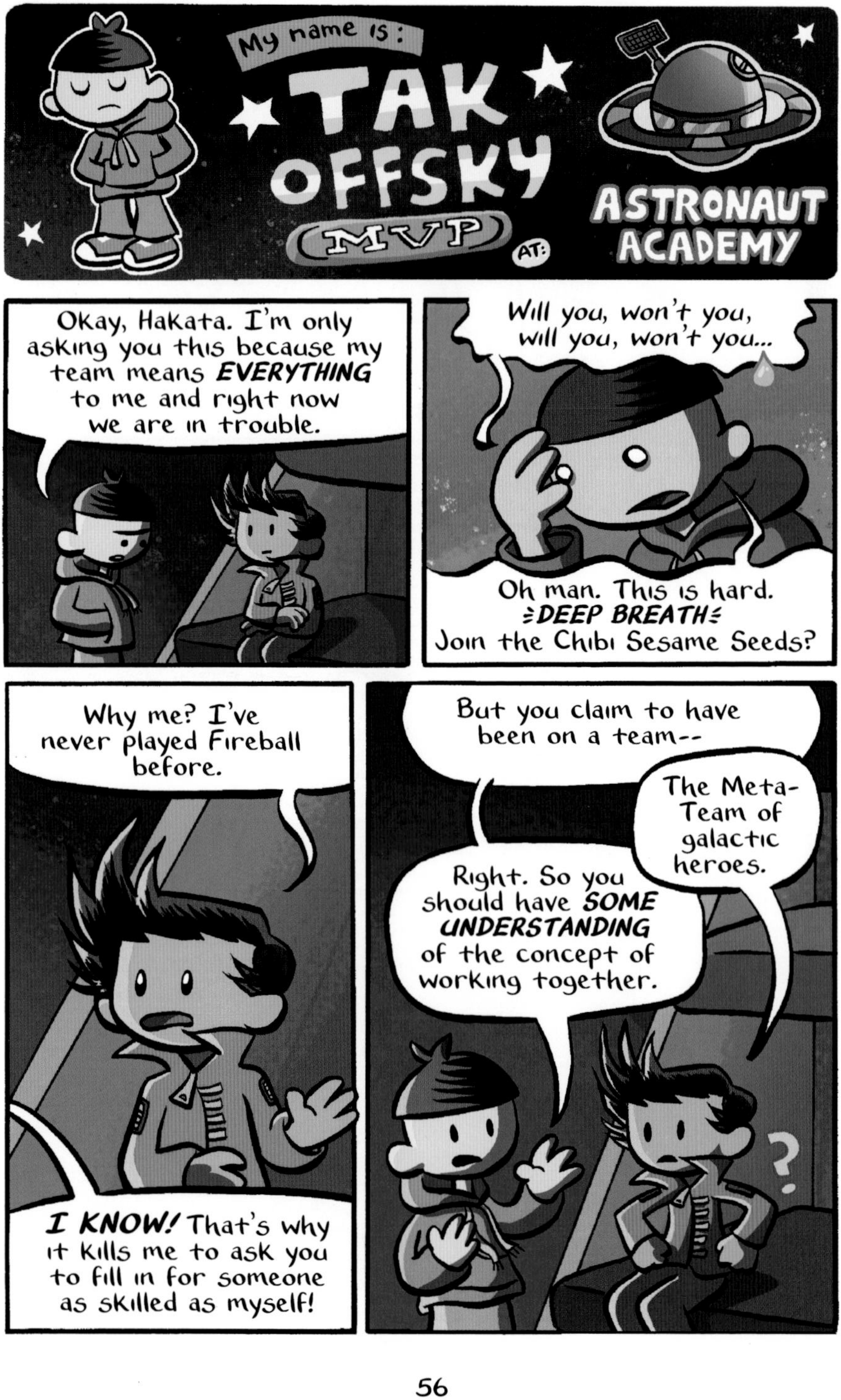
My name is:
TAK OFFSKY
(MVP)
AT:
ASTRONAUT ACADEMY
Okay, Hakata. I'm only asking you this because my team means EVERYTHING to me and right now we are in trouble.
Will you, won't you, will you, won't you...
Oh man. This is hard. ≑DEEP BREATH≑ Join the Chibi Sesame Seeds?
Why me? I've never played Fireball before.
I KNOW! That's why it kills me to ask you to fill in for someone as skilled as myself!
But you claim to have been on a team--
The Meta-Team of galactic heroes.
Right. So you should have SOME UNDERSTANDING of the concept of working together.
?

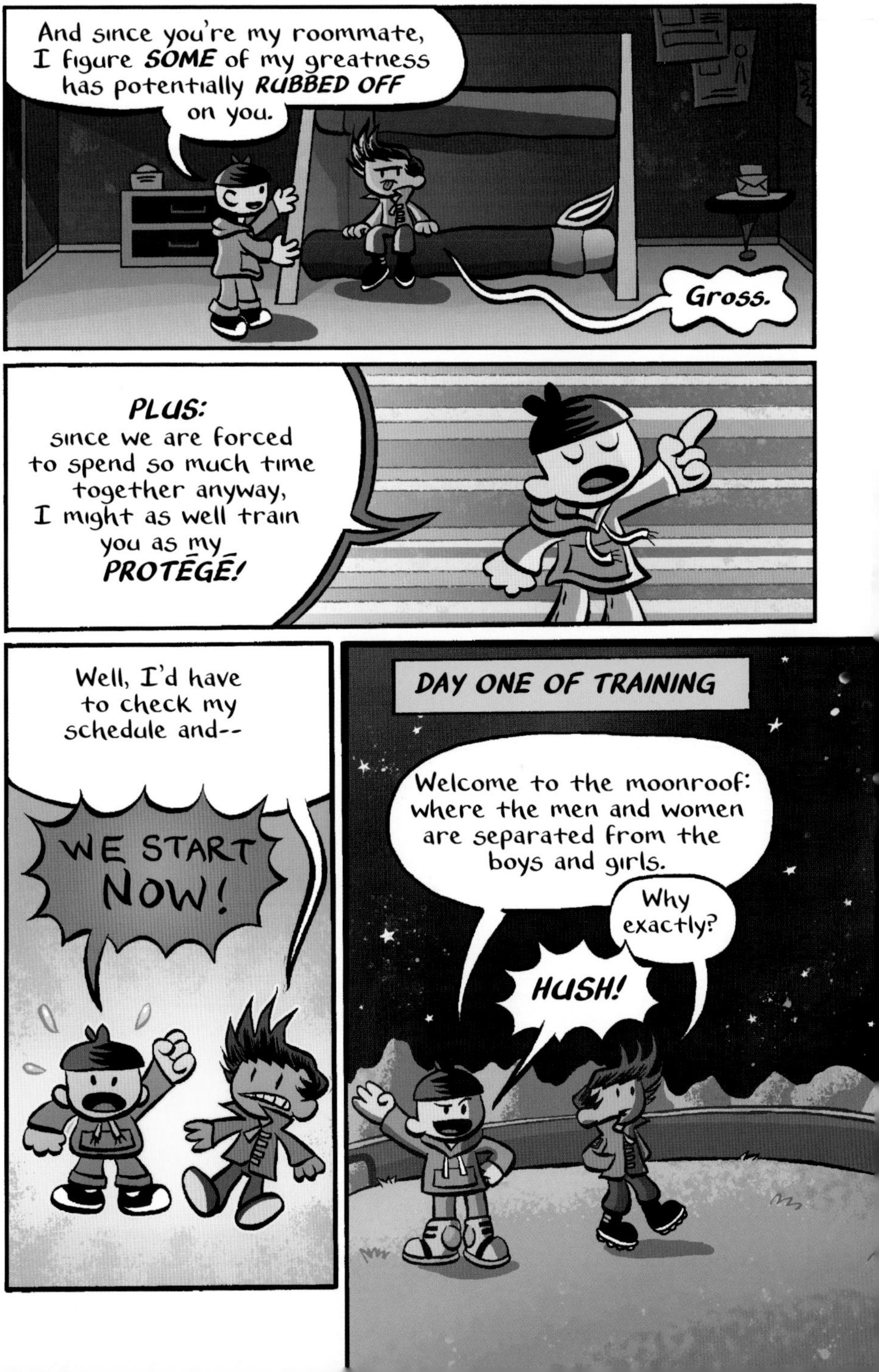
And since you're my roommate, I figure SOME of my greatness has potentially RUBBED OFF on you.
Gross.
PLUS: since we are forced to spend so much time together anyway, I might as well train you as my PROTÉGÉ!
Well, I'd have to check my schedule and--
WE START NOW!
DAY ONE OF TRAINING
Welcome to the moonroof: where the men and women are separated from the boys and girls.
Why exactly?
HUSH!

This is the Fireball field. Each team has a fortress on their designated side.

Behind each fortress is the team's trophy.

Each piece of the opponents' fortress destroyed gains *YOUR* team some points. The side with the higher score at the end of the countdown wins!

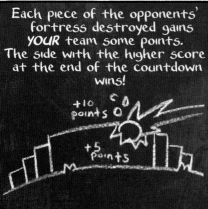

+10 points

+5 points

If you manage to get a fireball into the other team's trophy you win *INSTANTLY!*

Last year, I got a *HOLE IN ONE* in under three minutes!

But don't worry. I won't set your expectations that high.

PAT PAT

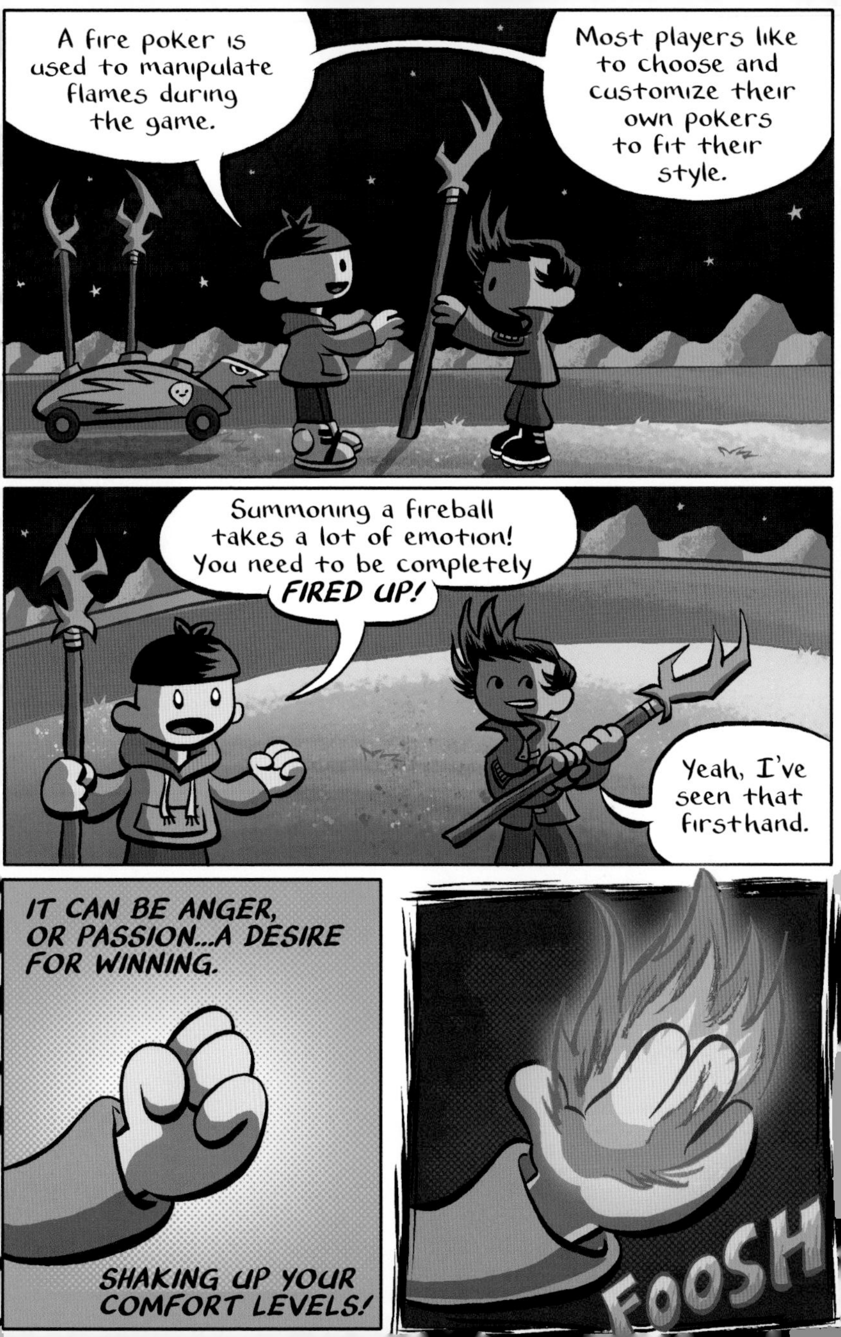
A fire poker is used to manipulate flames during the game.
Most players like to choose and customize their own pokers to fit their style.
Summoning a fireball takes a lot of emotion! You need to be completely FIRED UP!
Yeah, I've seen that firsthand.
IT CAN BE ANGER, OR PASSION...A DESIRE FOR WINNING.
SHAKING UP YOUR COMFORT LEVELS!
FOOSH

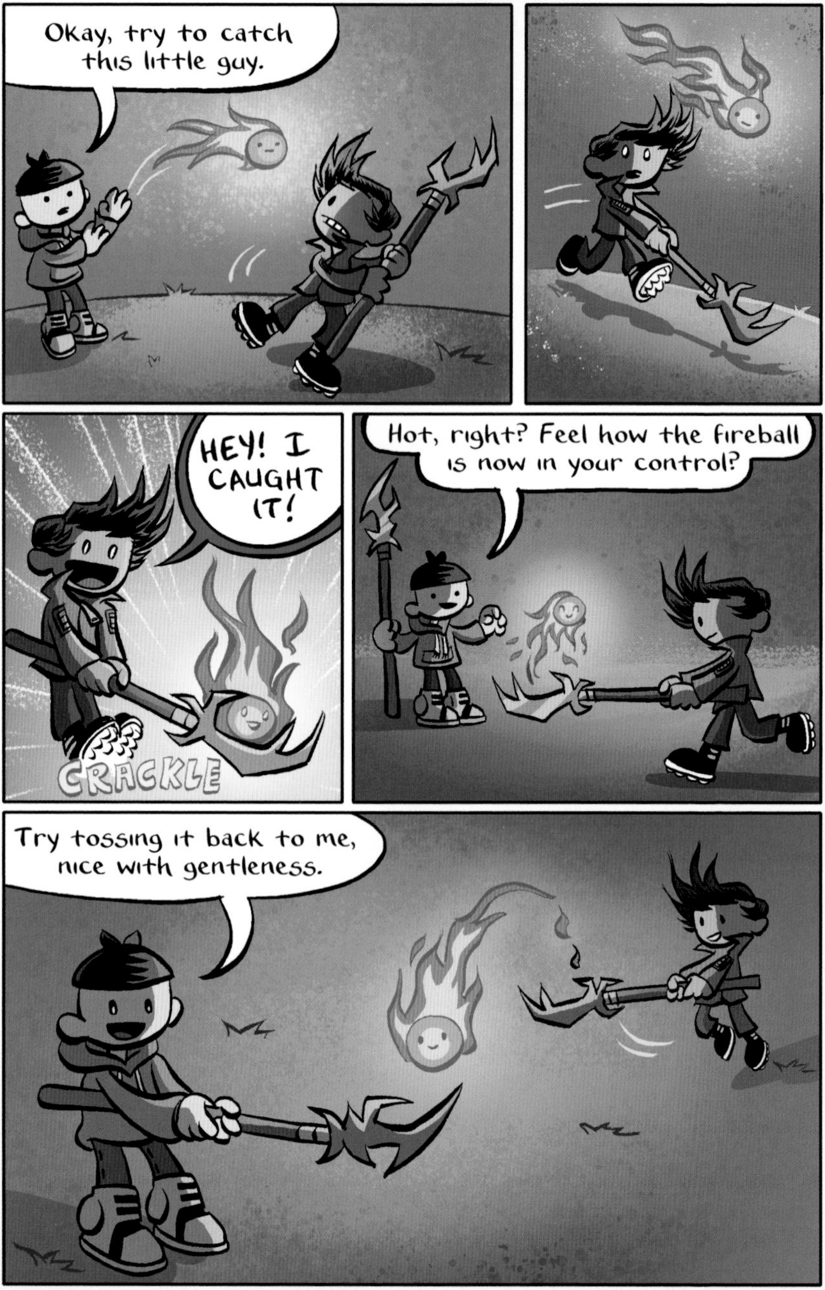

Okay, try to catch this little guy.
HEY! I CAUGHT IT!
CRACKLE
Hot, right? Feel how the fireball is now in your control?
Try tossing it back to me, nice with gentleness.

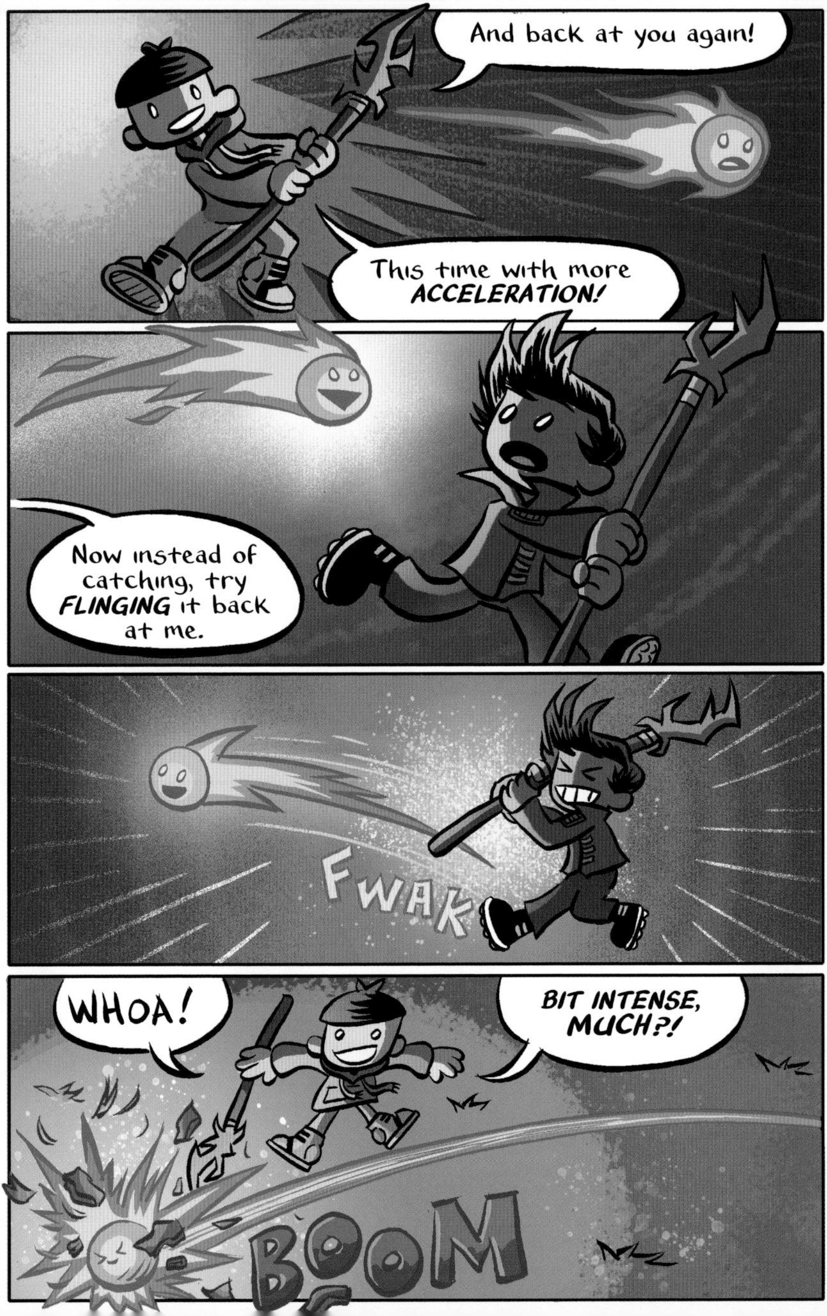
And back at you again!
This time with more ACCELERATION!
Now instead of catching, try FLINGING it back at me.
FWAK
WHOA!
BIT INTENSE, MUCH?!
BOOM

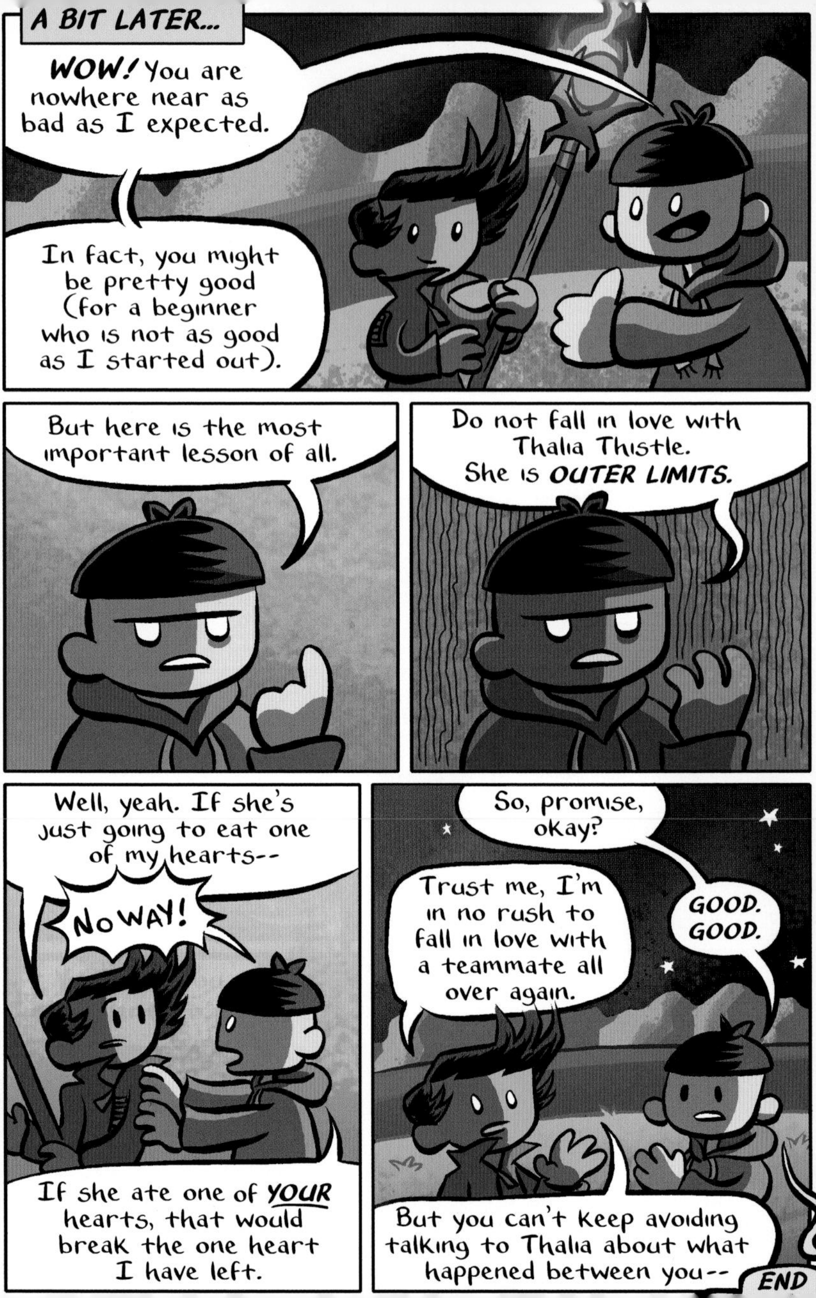
A BIT LATER...
WOW! You are nowhere near as bad as I expected.
In fact, you might be pretty good (for a beginner who is not as good as I started out).
But here is the most important lesson of all.
Do not fall in love with Thalia Thistle. She is OUTER LIMITS.
Well, yeah. If she's just going to eat one of my hearts--
No WAY!
If she ate one of YOUR hearts, that would break the one heart I have left.
So, promise, okay?
Trust me, I'm in no rush to fall in love with a teammate all over again.
GOOD. GOOD.
But you can't keep avoiding talking to Thalia about what happened between you--
END

SO WHAT HAS

DOUG HIRO

BEEN UP TO AT:

ASTRONAUT ACADEMY?

I know I'm mostly known for floating in space...

...and wearing my helmet in class.

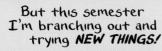

But this semester I'm branching out and trying **NEW THINGS!**

Why, you ask?

You know, Doug, you should really branch out and try new things.

Okay, Mrs. Cupcake.

But only because I love you.

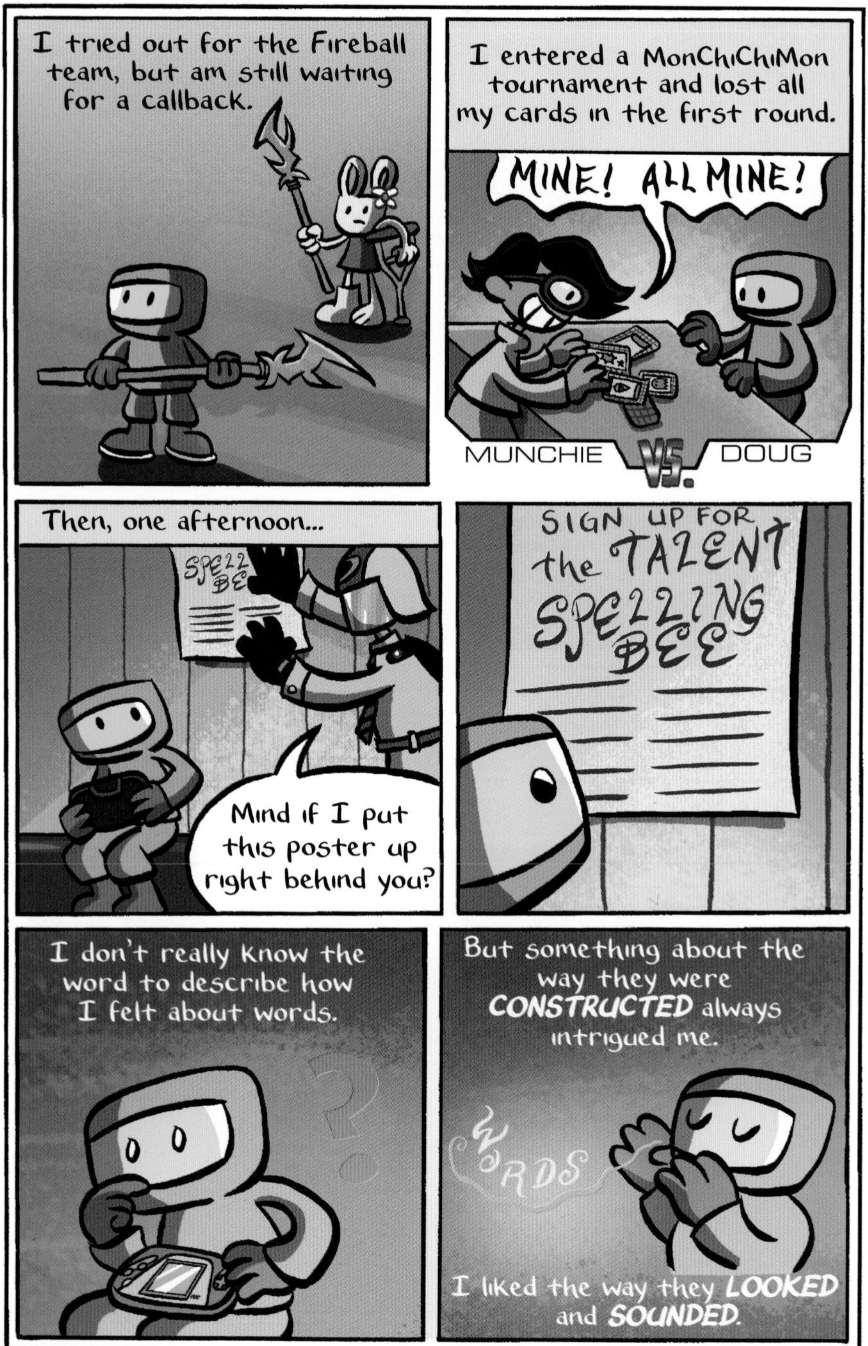

I tried out for the Fireball team, but am still waiting for a callback.
I entered a MonChiChiMon tournament and lost all my cards in the first round.
MINE! ALL MINE!
MUNCHIE VS. DOUG
Then, one afternoon...
Mind if I put this poster up right behind you?
SIGN UP FOR the TALENT SPELLING BEE
I don't really know the word to describe how I felt about words.
But something about the way they were CONSTRUCTED always intrigued me.
WORDS
I liked the way they LOOKED and SOUNDED.

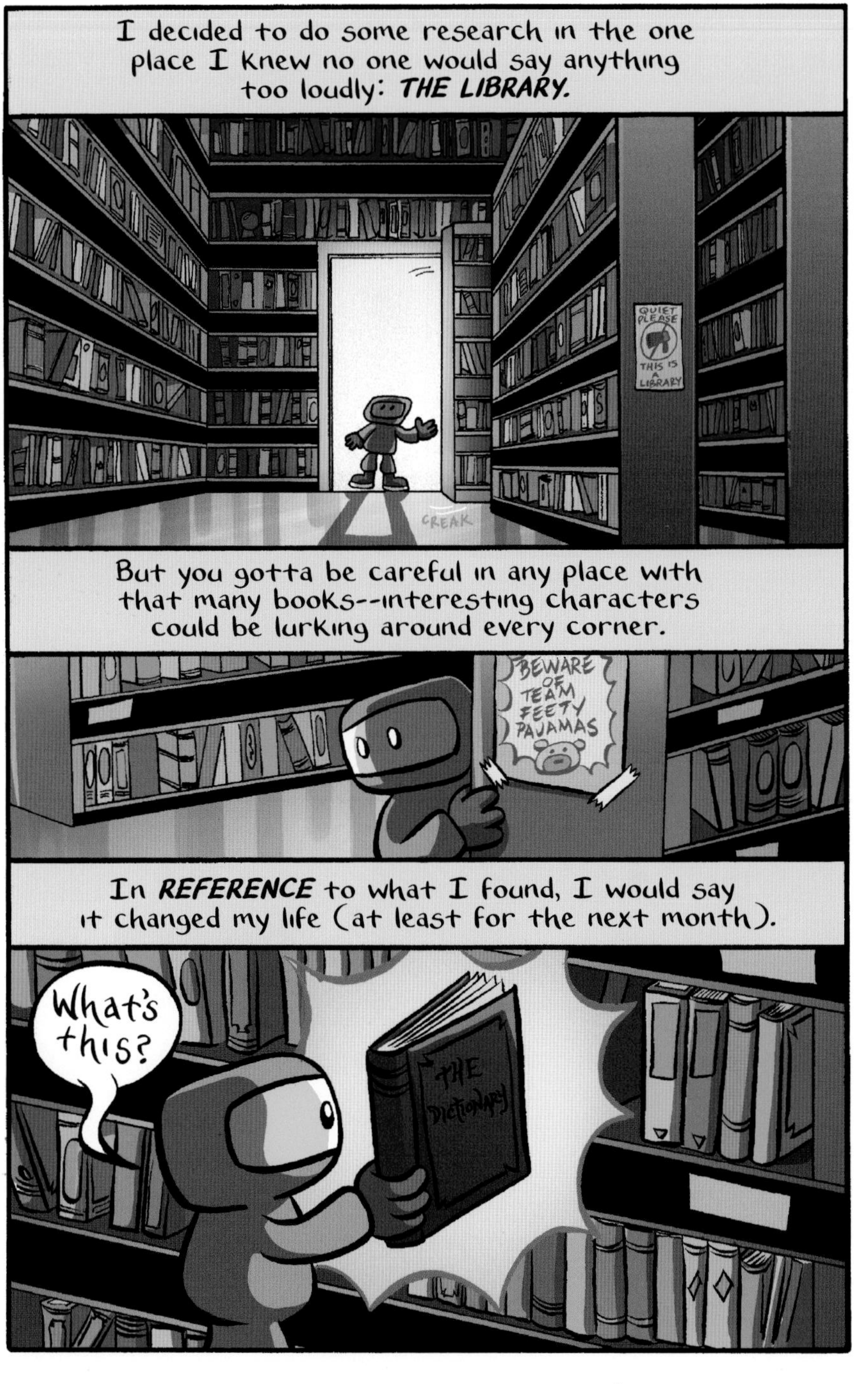
I decided to do some research in the one place I knew no one would say anything too loudly: THE LIBRARY.
QUIET PLEASE THIS IS A LIBRARY
CREAK
But you gotta be careful in any place with that many books--interesting characters could be lurking around every corner.
BEWARE OF TEAM FEETY PAJAMAS
In REFERENCE to what I found, I would say it changed my life (at least for the next month).
What's this?
THE DICTIONARY

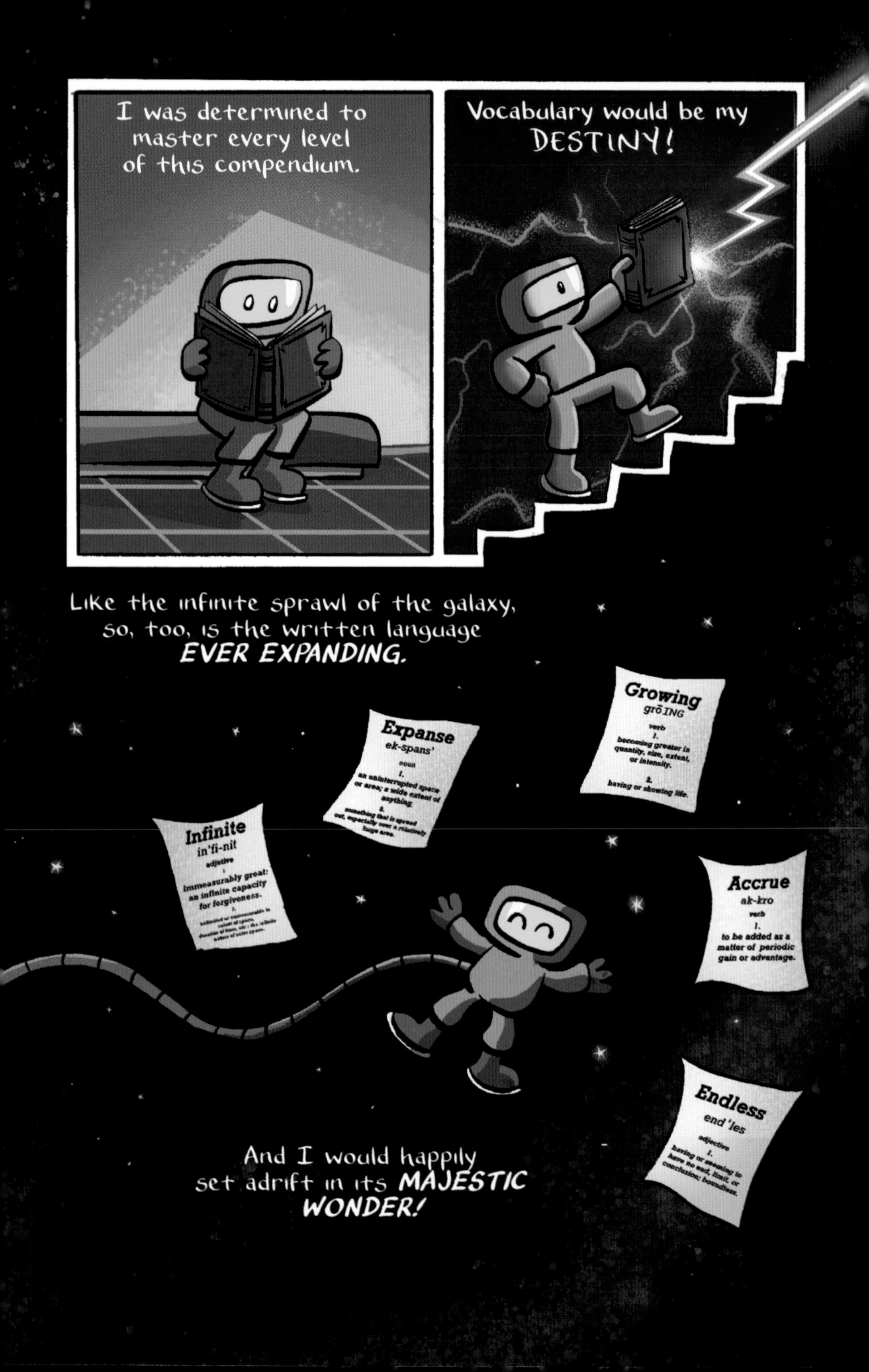
I was determined to master every level of this compendium.
Vocabulary would be my DESTINY!
Like the infinite sprawl of the galaxy, so, too, is the written language EVER EXPANDING.
Expanse
ek-spans'
noun
1.
an uninterrupted space or area; a wide extent of anything.
2.
something that is spread out, especially over a relatively large area.
Growing
grōING
verb
1.
becoming greater in quantity, size, extent, or intensity.
2.
having or showing life.
Infinite
in'fi-nit
adjective
1.
immeasurably great: an infinite capacity for forgiveness.
Accrue
ak-kro
verb
1.
to be added as a matter of periodic gain or advantage.
Endless
end'les
adjective
1.
having or seeming to have no end, limit, or conclusion; boundless.
And I would happily set adrift in its MAJESTIC WONDER!

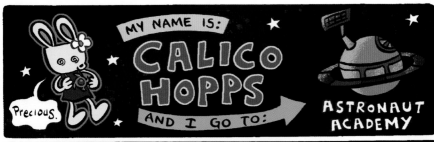

My name is: **CALICO HOPPS** and I go to: → **ASTRONAUT ACADEMY**

Precious.

I heard you are getting your cast off today.

Yep.

Think I could have it when you are done?

It's got all those signatures, so it might be a collector's item someday.

I'd always thought bunnies were made of marshmallow and unable to "break a leg" even during a semester break.

So, what happened?

I needed to get with the **SERIOUS BUSINESS** if I wanted to be like my space hero, Hakata Soy.

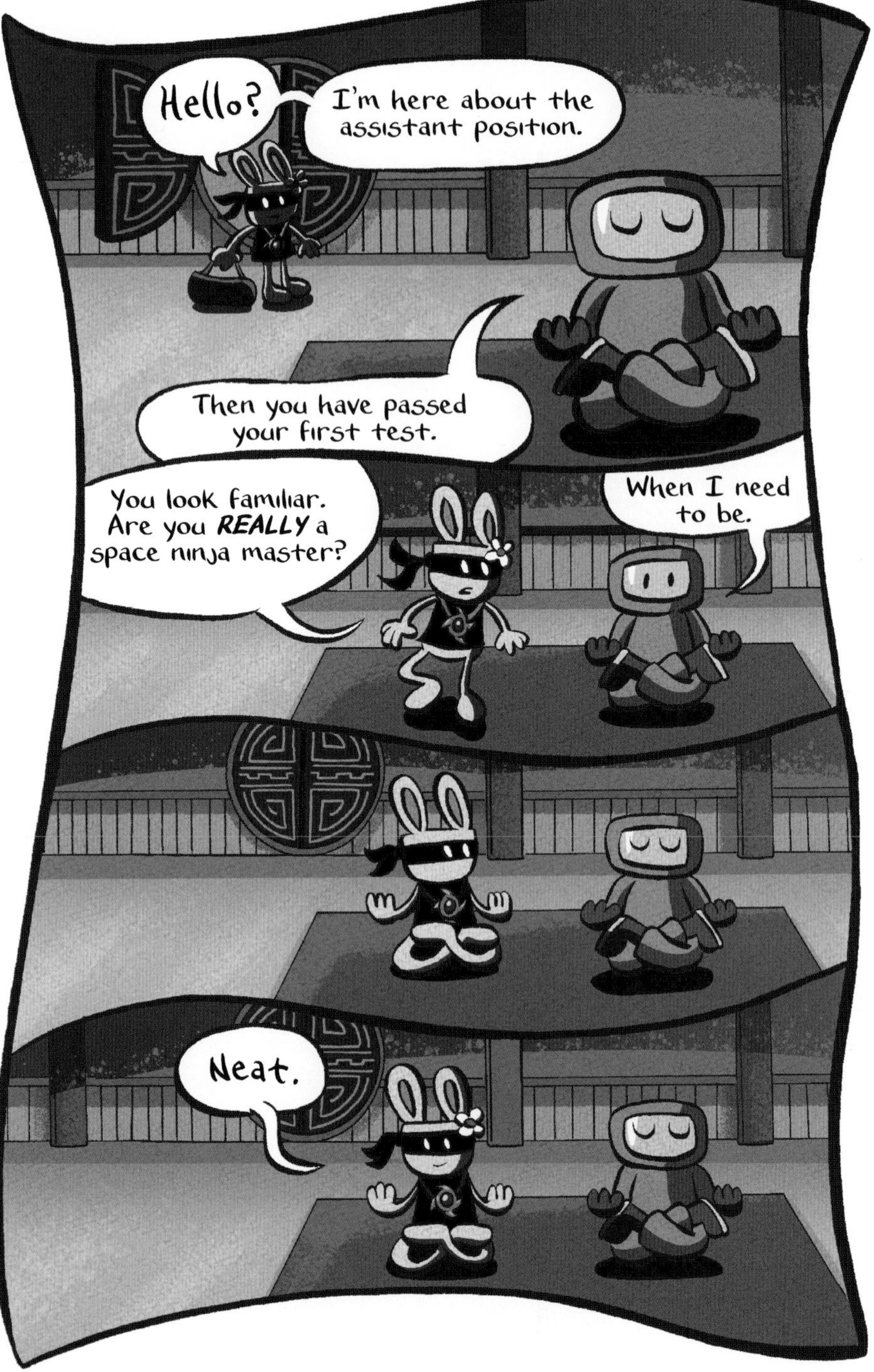
Hello?
I'm here about the assistant position.
Then you have passed your first test.
You look familiar. Are you REALLY a space ninja master?
When I need to be.
Neat.

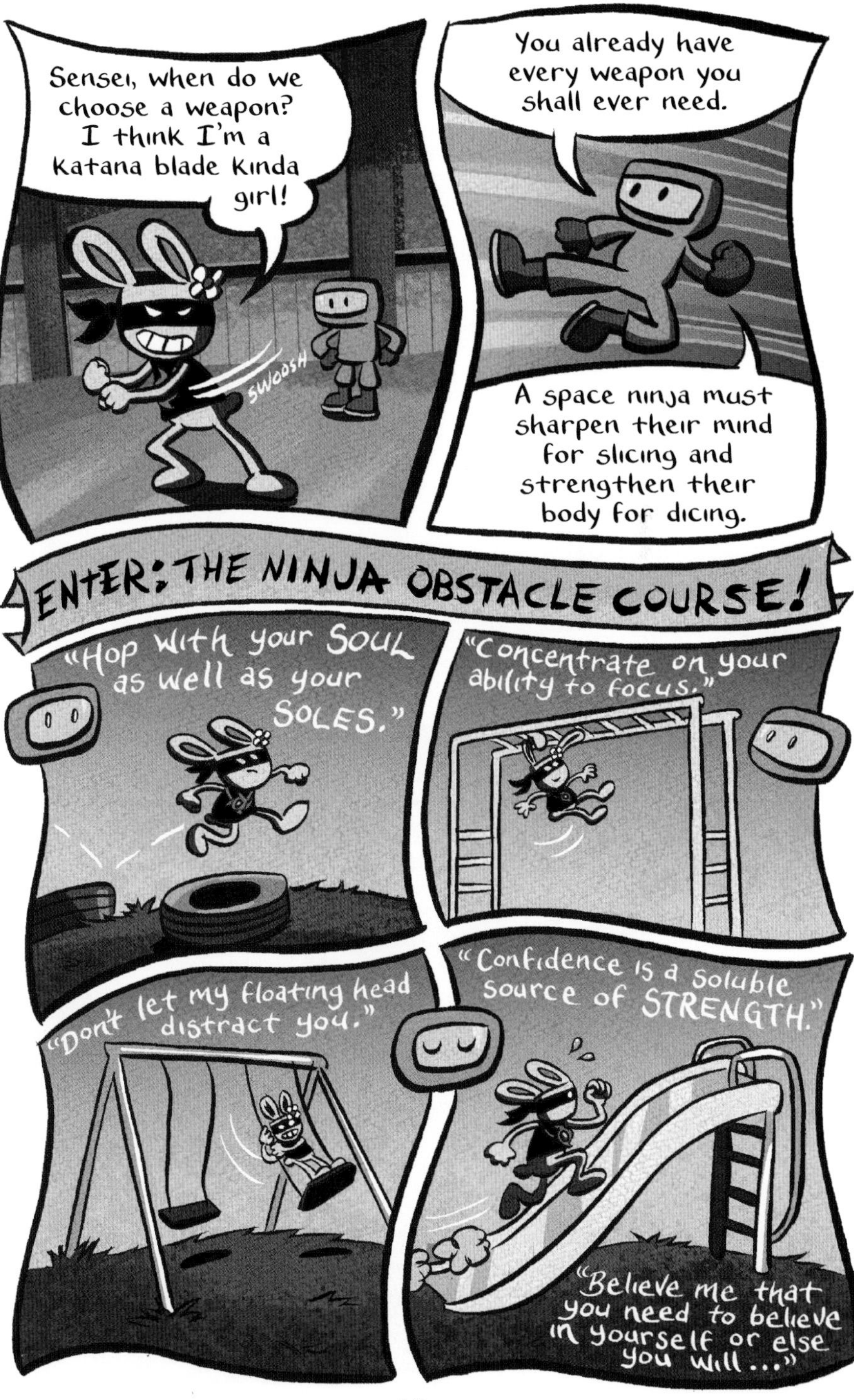
Sensei, when do we choose a weapon? I think I'm a Katana blade Kinda girl!
SWOOSH
You already have every weapon you shall ever need.
A space ninja must sharpen their mind for slicing and strengthen their body for dicing.
ENTER: THE NINJA OBSTACLE COURSE!
"Hop with your SOUL as well as your SOLES."
"Concentrate on your ability to focus."
"Don't let my floating head distract you."
"Confidence is a soluble source of STRENGTH."
"Believe me that you need to believe in yourself or else you will..."

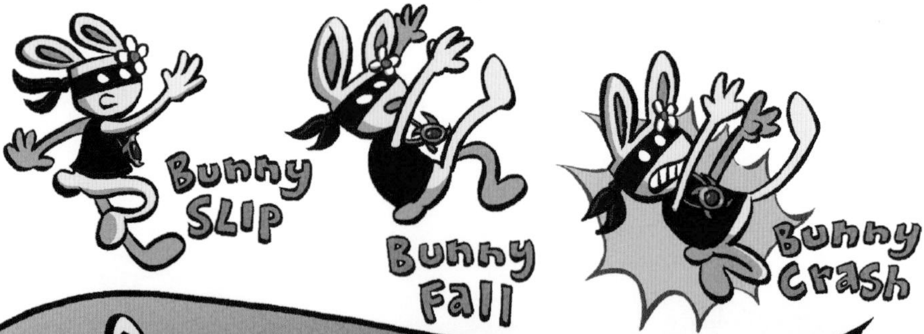
Bunny SLIP
Bunny Fall
Bunny Crash

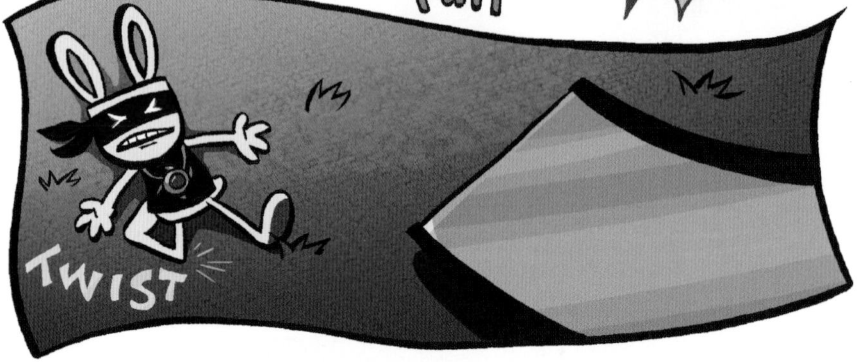
TWIST

I debated using my medallion to call Hakata Soy.

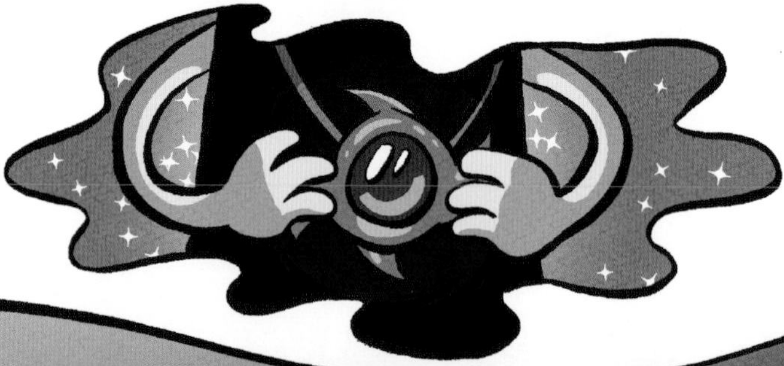

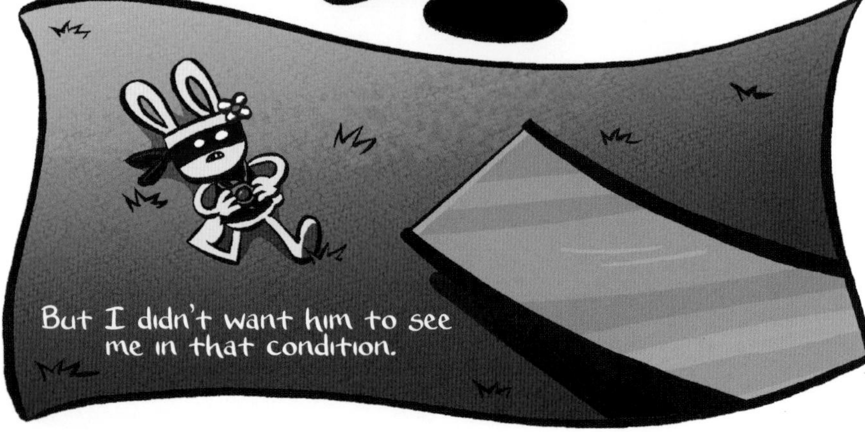
But I didn't want him to see me in that condition.

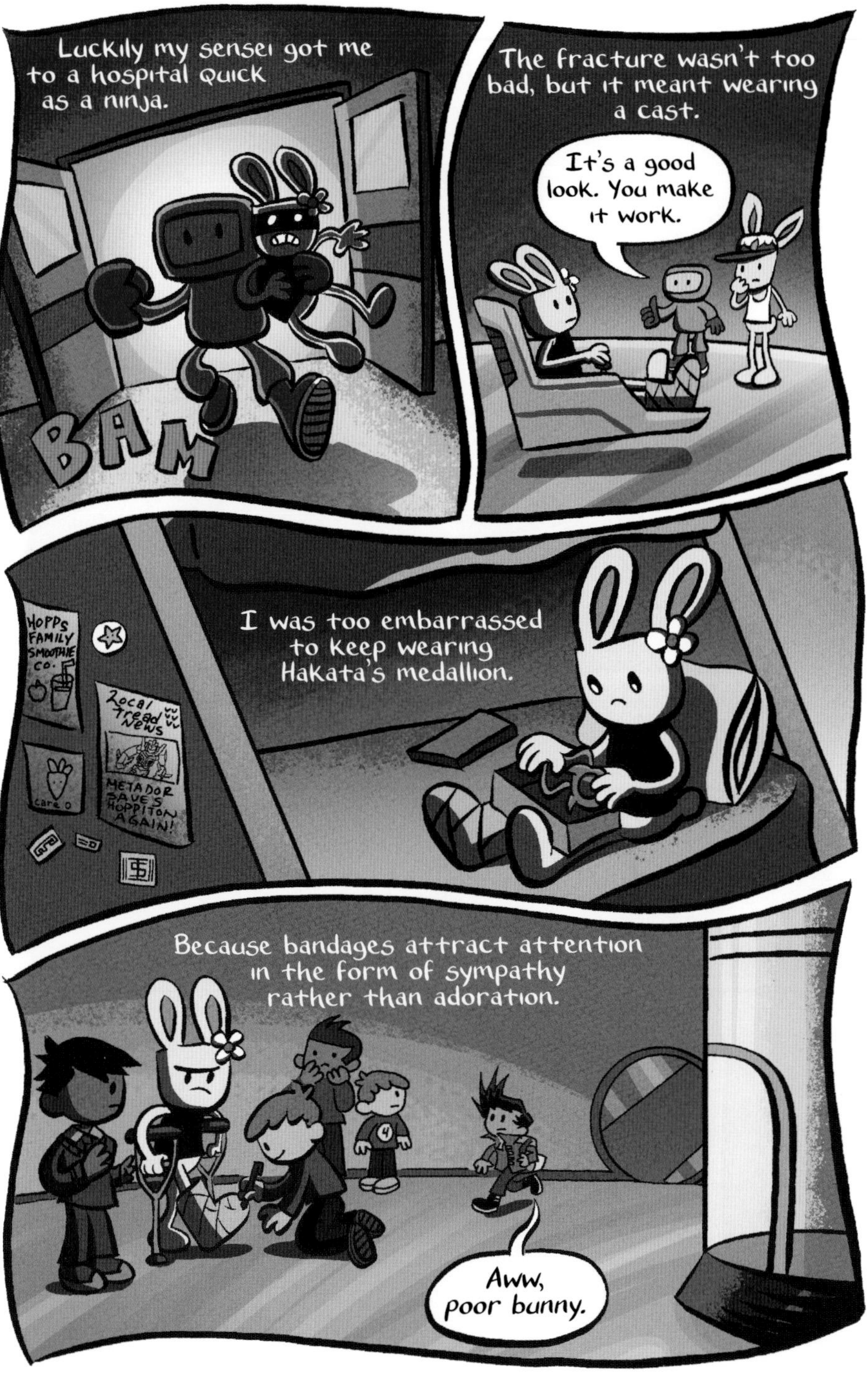
Luckily my sensei got me to a hospital quick as a ninja.
BAM
The fracture wasn't too bad, but it meant wearing a cast.
It's a good look. You make it work.
I was too embarrassed to keep wearing Hakata's medallion.
HOPPS FAMILY SMOOTHIE CO.
METADOR SAVES HOPPITON AGAIN!
Because bandages attract attention in the form of sympathy rather than adoration.
Aww, poor bunny.

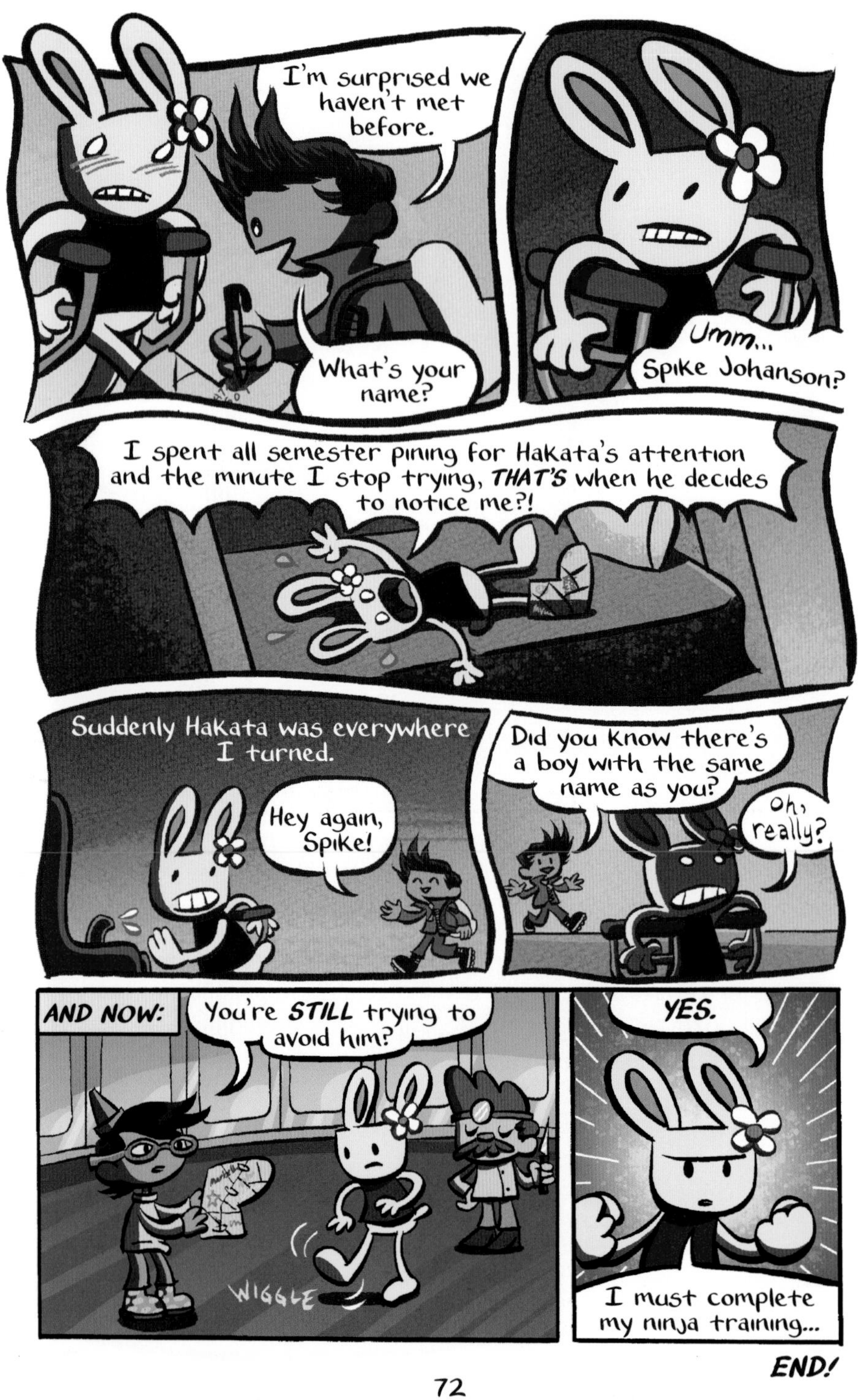
I'm surprised we haven't met before.
What's your name?
Umm... Spike Johanson?
I spent all semester pining for Hakata's attention and the minute I stop trying, THAT'S when he decides to notice me?!
Suddenly Hakata was everywhere I turned.
Hey again, Spike!
Did you know there's a boy with the same name as you?
Oh, really?
AND NOW:
You're STILL trying to avoid him?
WIGGLE
YES.
I must complete my ninja training...
END!

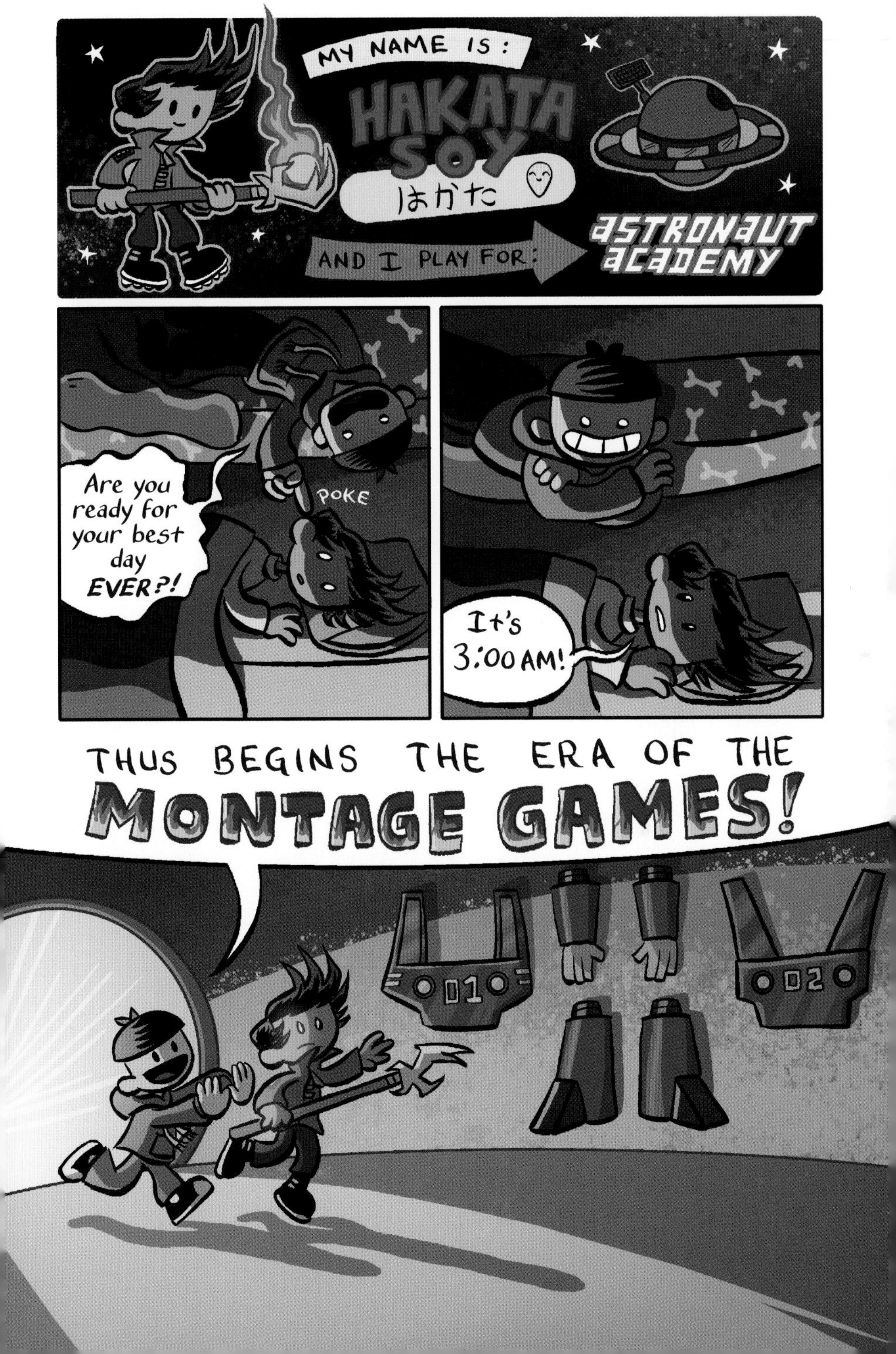
MY NAME IS:
HAKATA SOY
はかた
AND I PLAY FOR:
astronaut academy
Are you ready for your best day EVER?!
POKE
It's 3:00 AM!
THUS BEGINS THE ERA OF THE
MONTAGE GAMES!
01
02

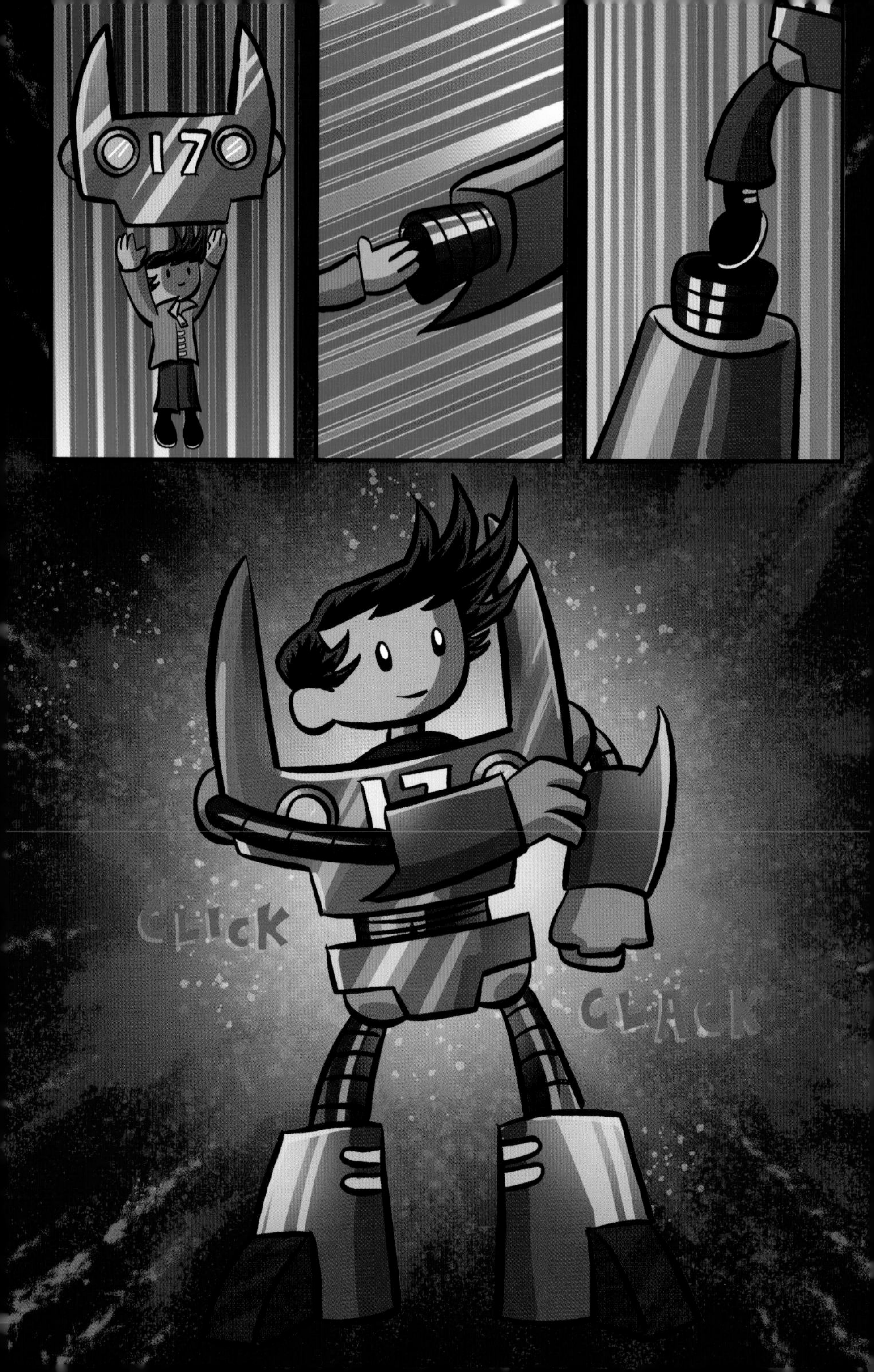
CLICK
CLACK

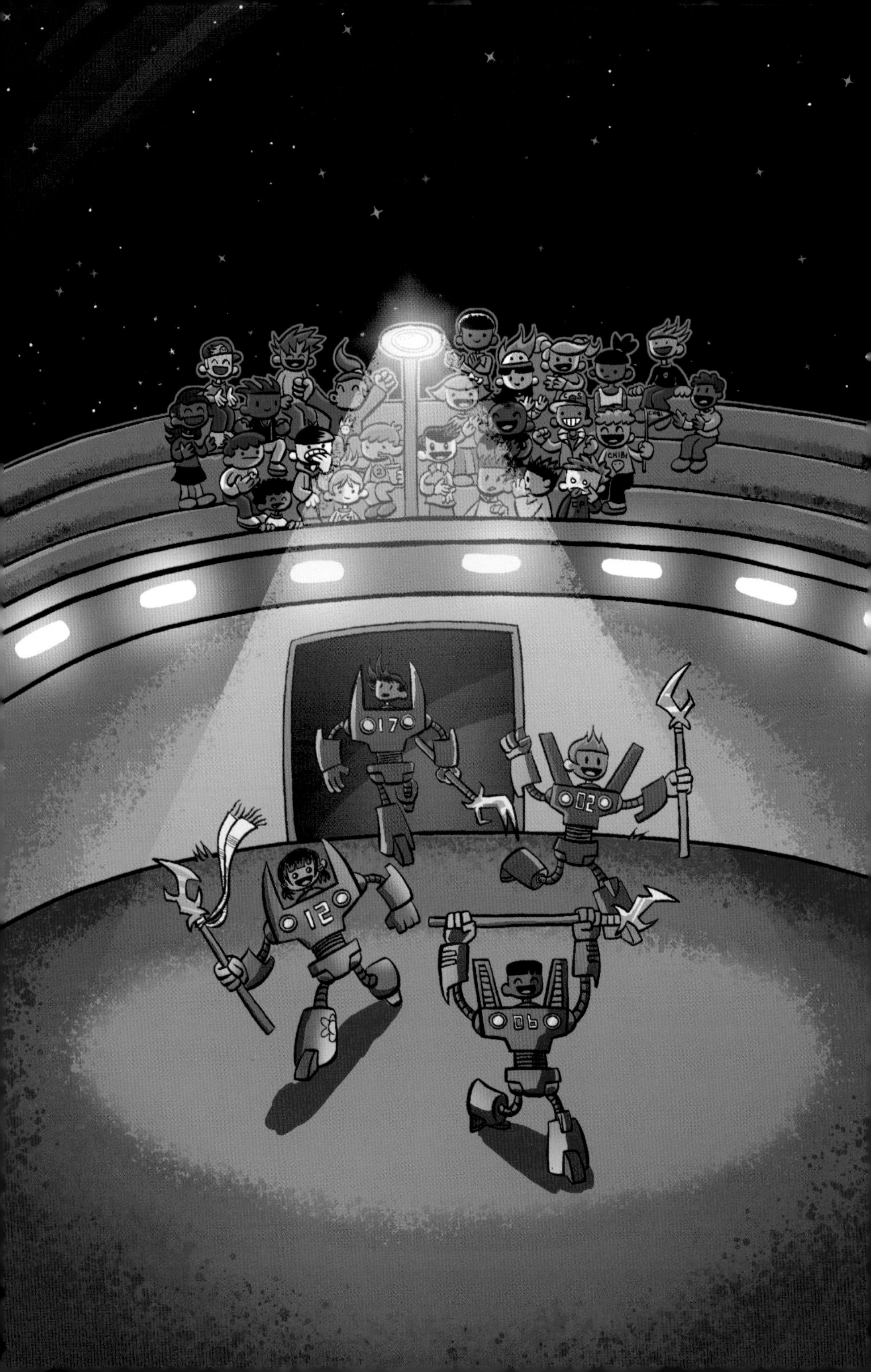
CHIBI
17
02
12
06

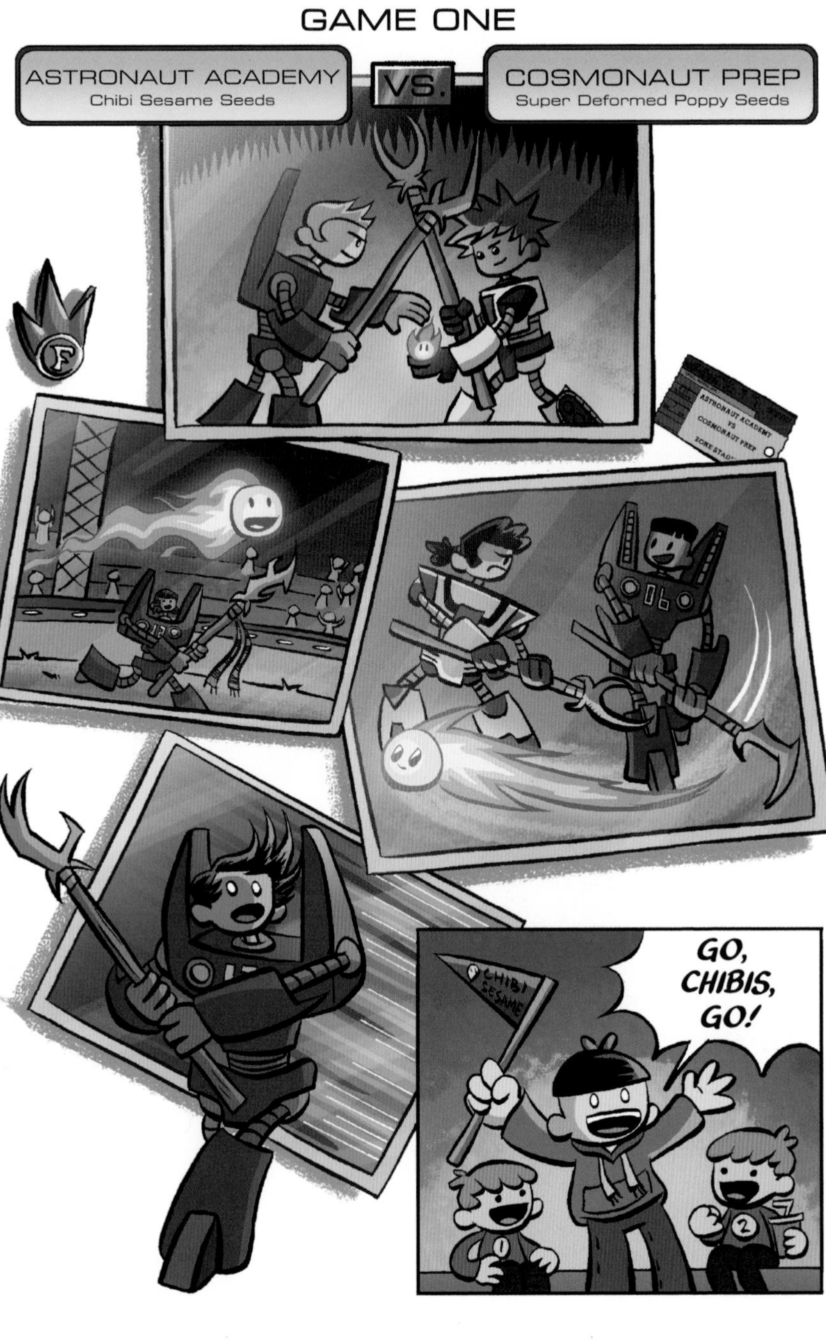
GAME ONE
ASTRONAUT ACADEMY
Chibi Sesame Seeds
VS.
COSMONAUT PREP
Super Deformed Poppy Seeds
CHIBI SESAME
GO, CHIBIS, GO!

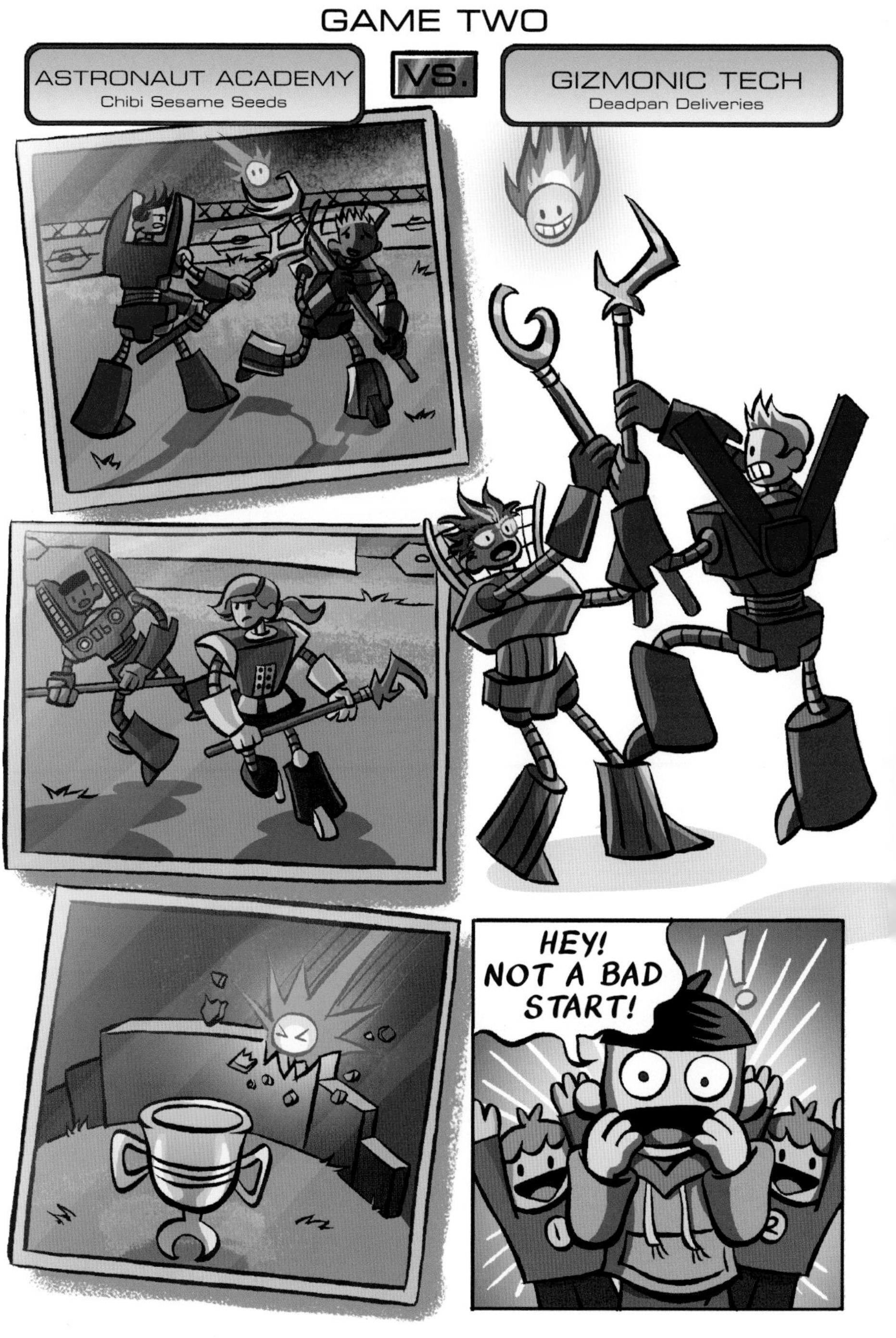
GAME TWO
ASTRONAUT ACADEMY
Chibi Sesame Seeds
VS.
GIZMONIC TECH
Deadpan Deliveries
HEY! NOT A BAD START!

GAME THREE

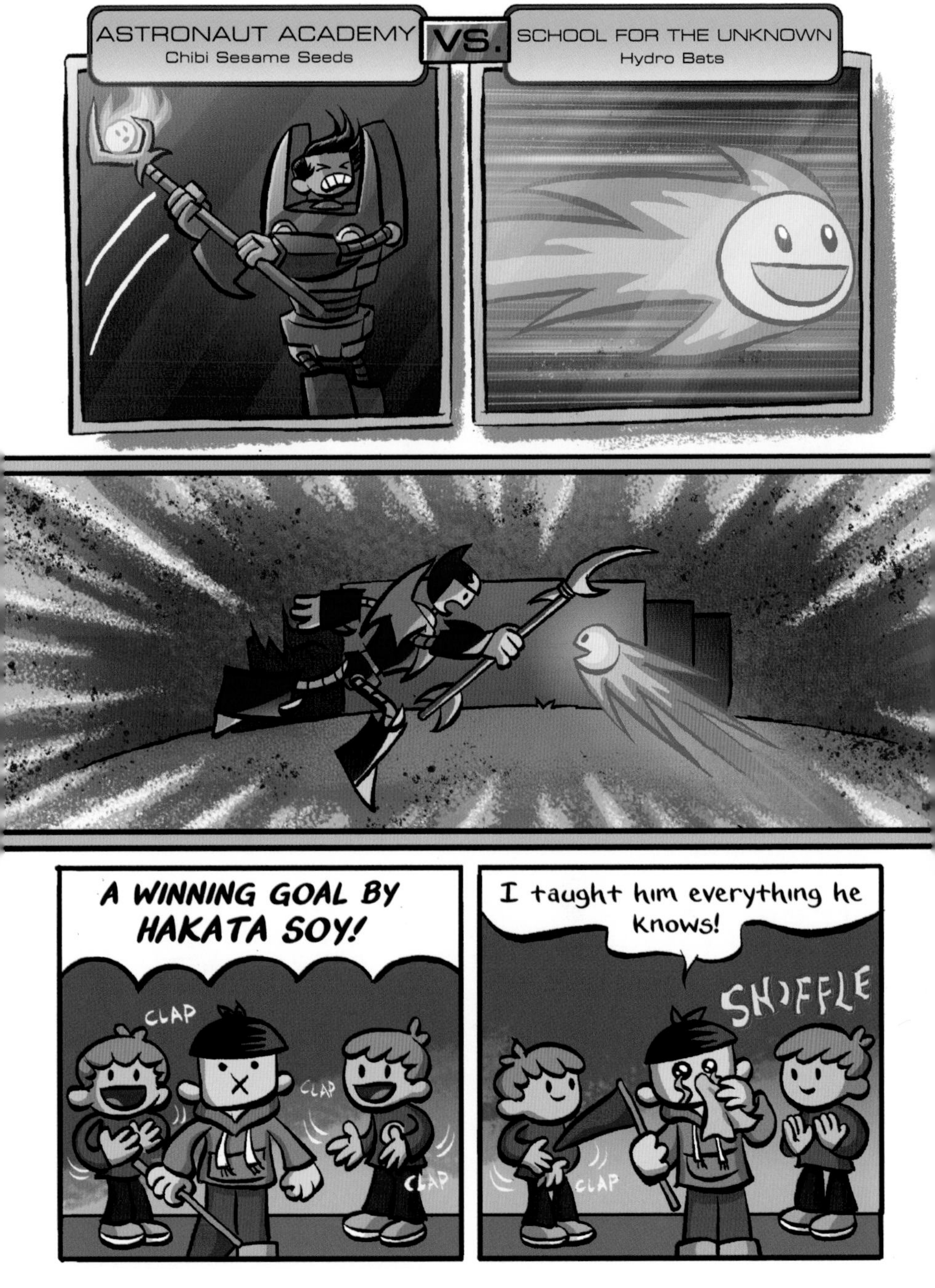

ASTRONAUT ACADEMY
Chibi Sesame Seeds
VS.
SCHOOL FOR THE UNKNOWN
Hydro Bats
A WINNING GOAL BY HAKATA SOY!
CLAP
CLAP
CLAP
I taught him everything he knows!
SNIFFLE
CLAP

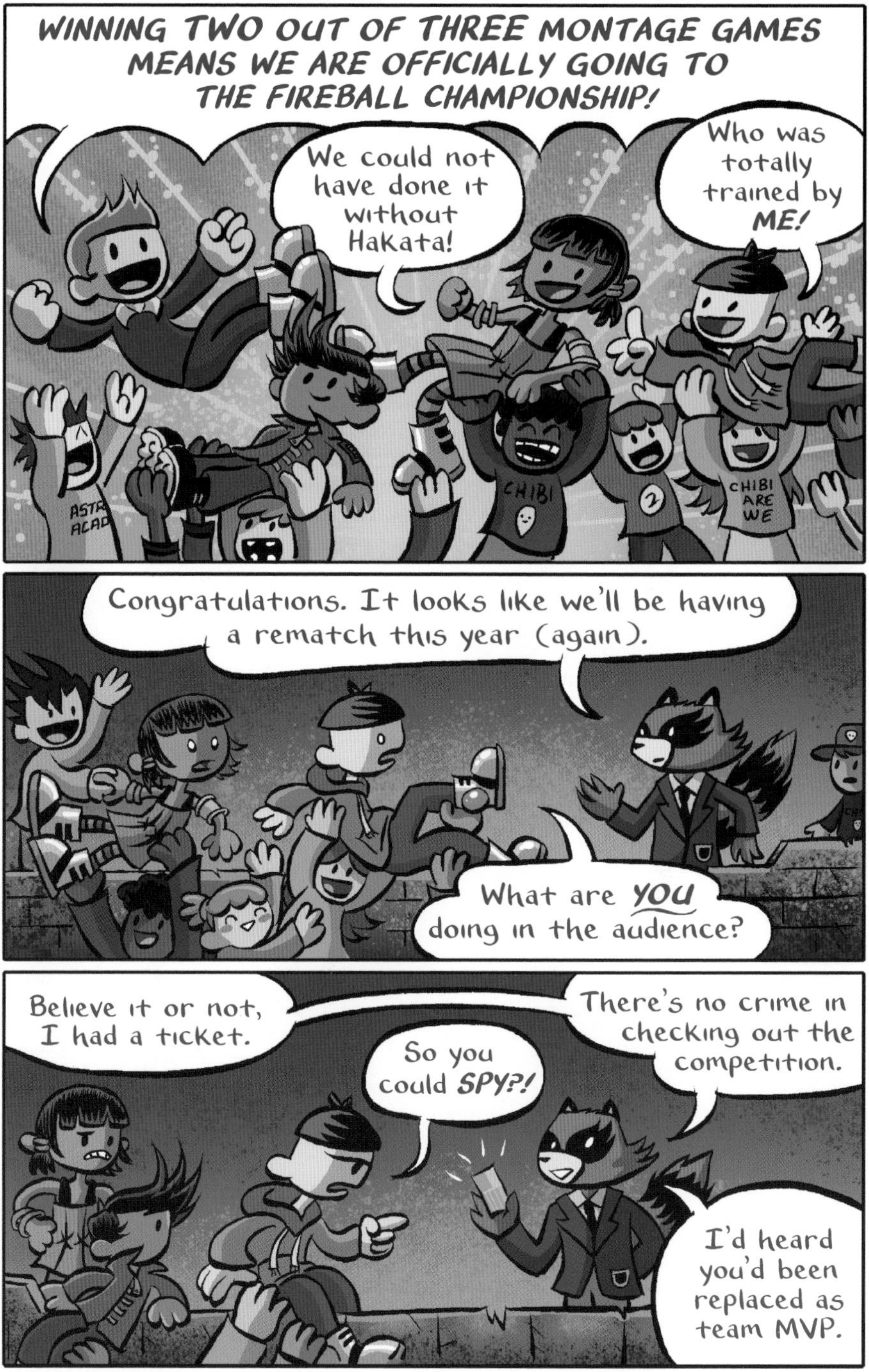
WINNING TWO OUT OF THREE MONTAGE GAMES MEANS WE ARE OFFICIALLY GOING TO THE FIREBALL CHAMPIONSHIP!
We could not have done it without Hakata!
Who was totally trained by ME!
CHIBI
CHIBI ARE WE
Congratulations. It looks like we'll be having a rematch this year (again).
What are YOU doing in the audience?
Believe it or not, I had a ticket.
There's no crime in checking out the competition.
So you could SPY?!
I'd heard you'd been replaced as team MVP.

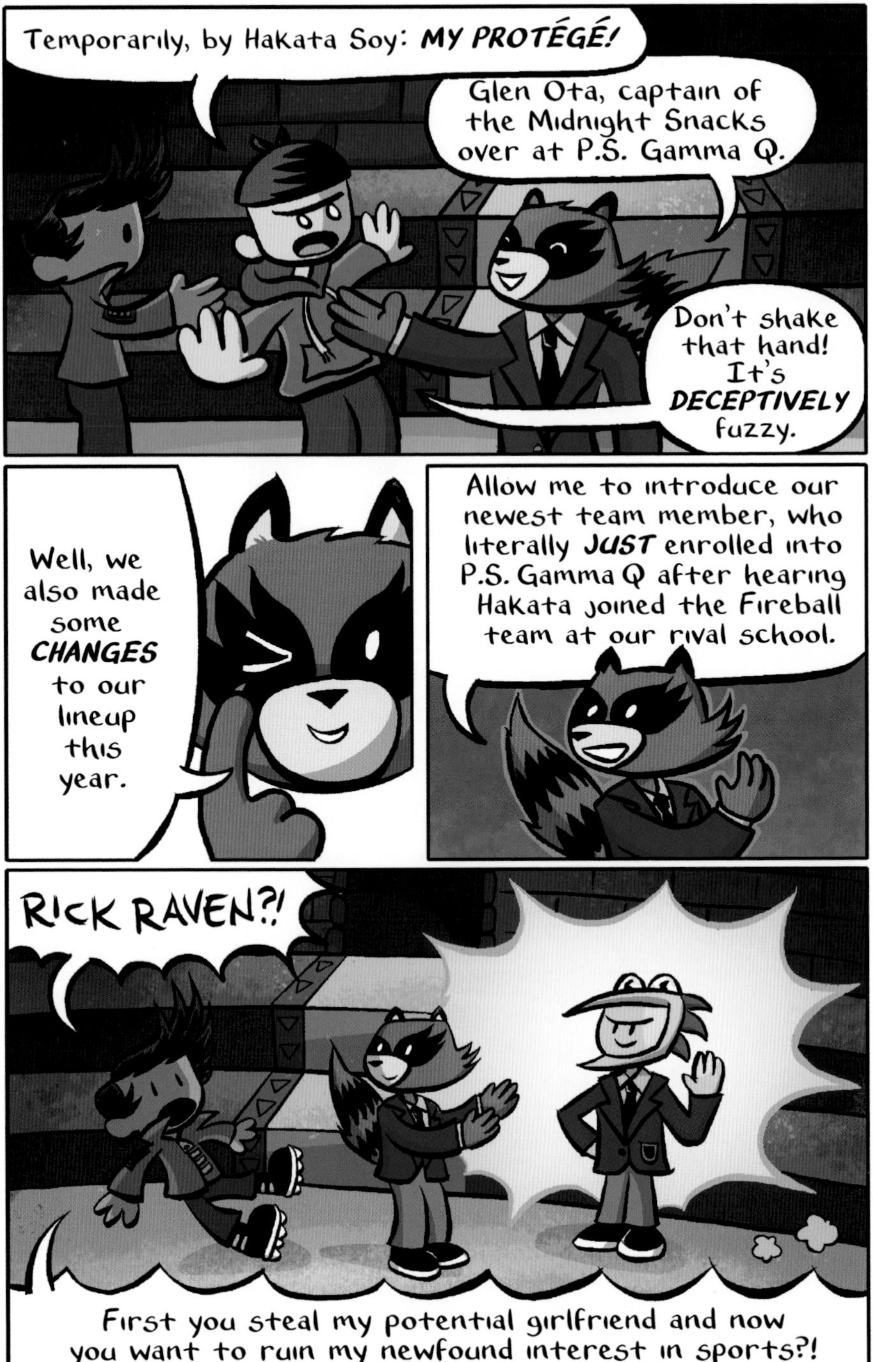
Temporarily, by Hakata Soy: MY PROTÉGÉ!
Glen Ota, captain of the Midnight Snacks over at P.S. Gamma Q.
Don't shake that hand! It's DECEPTIVELY fuzzy.
Well, we also made some CHANGES to our lineup this year.
Allow me to introduce our newest team member, who literally JUST enrolled into P.S. Gamma Q after hearing Hakata joined the Fireball team at our rival school.
RICK RAVEN?!
First you steal my potential girlfriend and now you want to ruin my newfound interest in sports?!

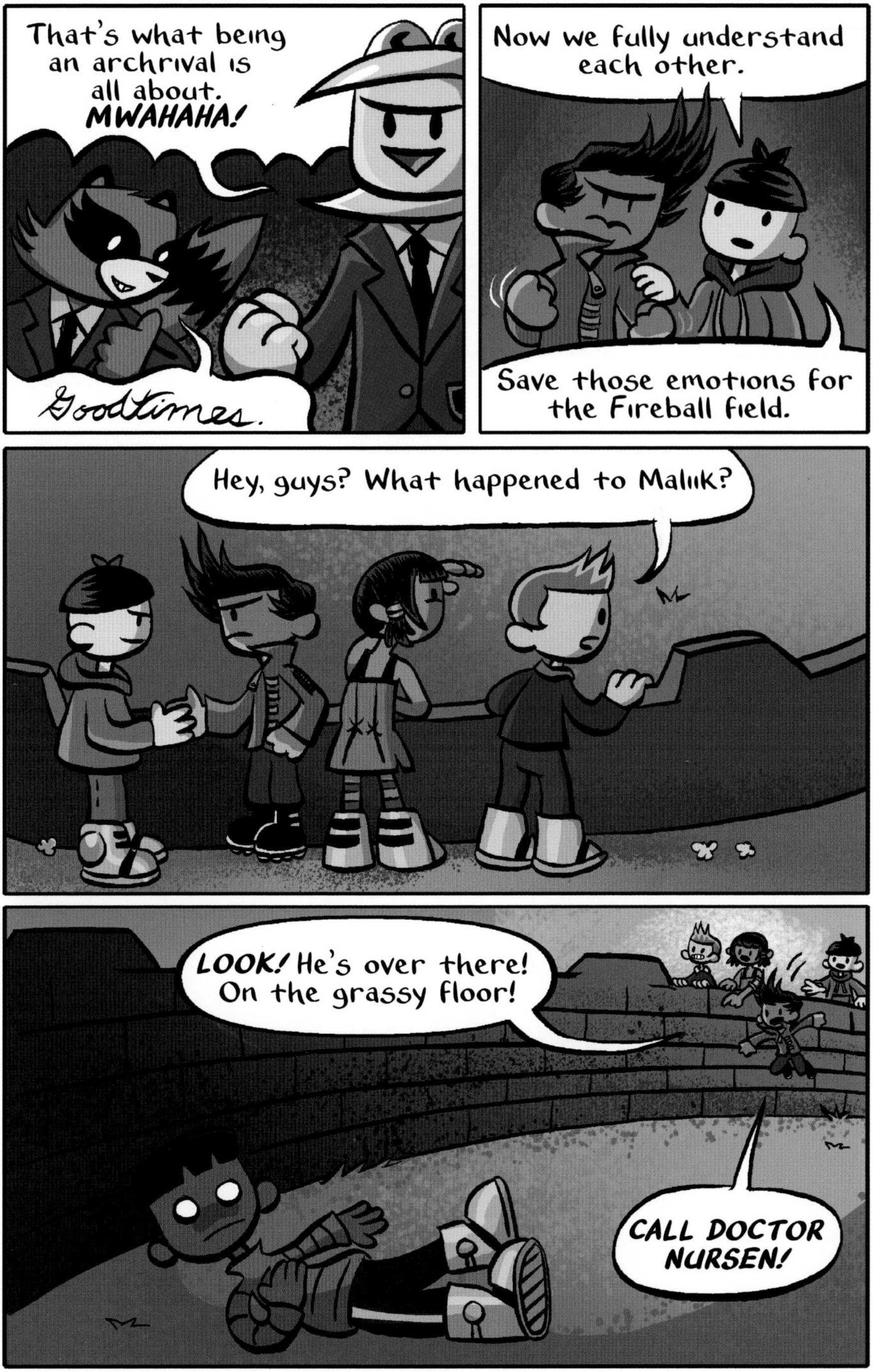

That's what being an archrival is all about. MWAHAHA!
Goodtimes.
Now we fully understand each other.
Save those emotions for the Fireball field.
Hey, guys? What happened to Maliik?
LOOK! He's over there! On the grassy floor!
CALL DOCTOR NURSEN!

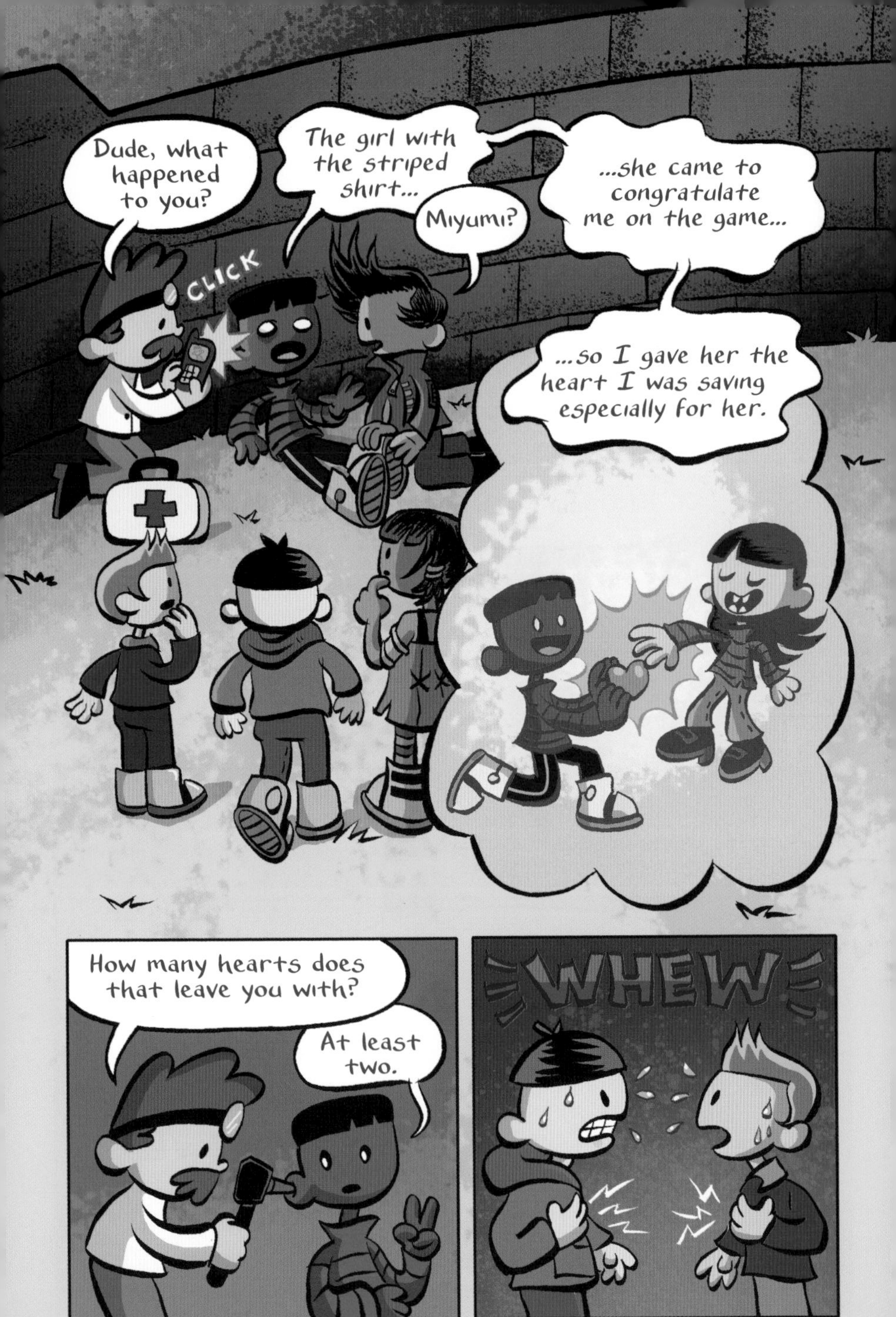
Dude, what happened to you?
CLICK
The girl with the striped shirt...
Miyumi?
...she came to congratulate me on the game...
...so I gave her the heart I was saving especially for her.
How many hearts does that leave you with?
At least two.
WHEW
THAT WAS CLOSE!

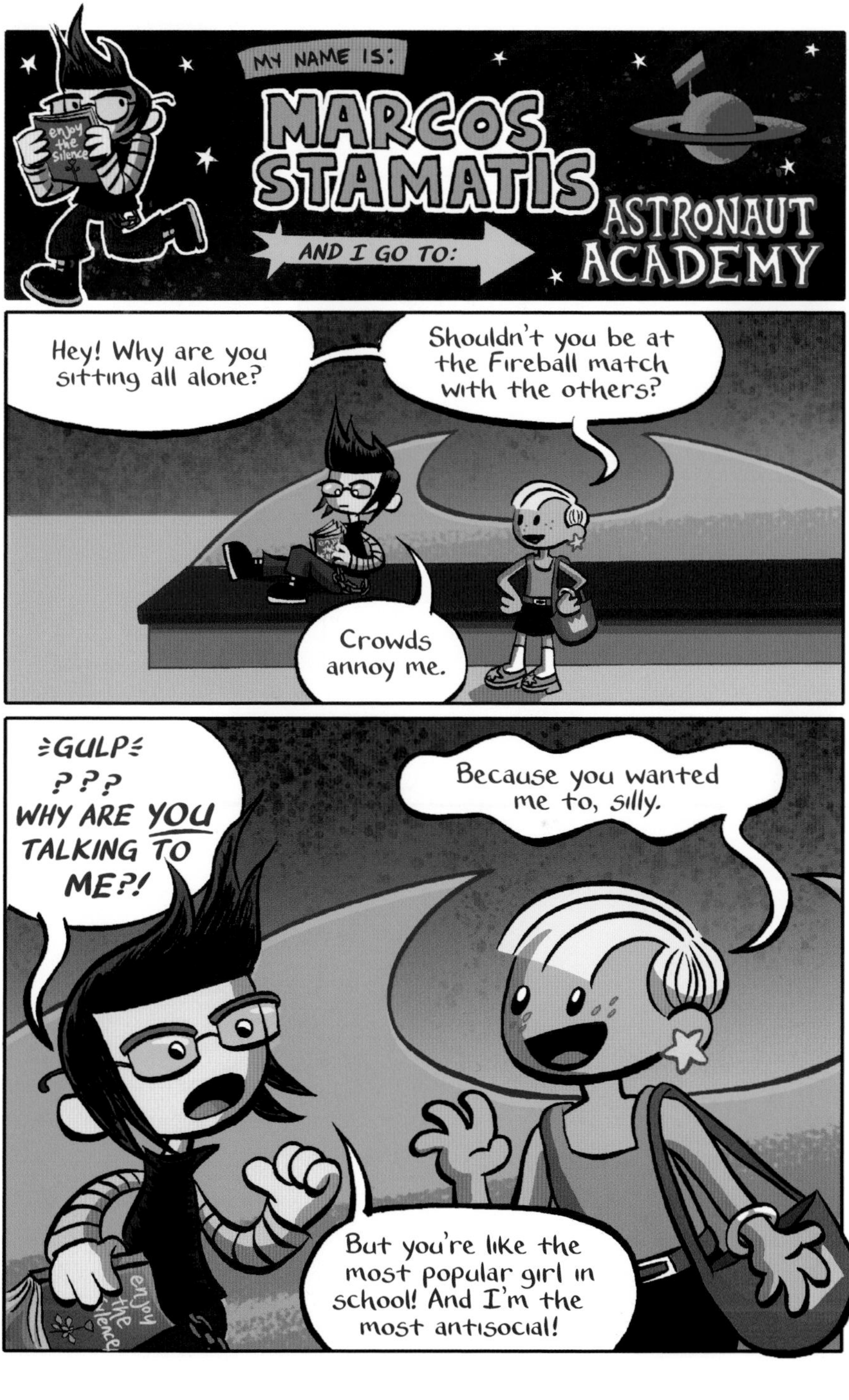
MY NAME IS:
MARCOS STAMATIS
AND I GO TO:
ASTRONAUT ACADEMY
enjoy the silence
Hey! Why are you sitting all alone?
Shouldn't you be at the Fireball match with the others?
Crowds annoy me.
≶GULP≶
???
WHY ARE YOU TALKING TO ME?!
Because you wanted me to, silly.
But you're like the most popular girl in school! And I'm the most antisocial!
enjoy the silence

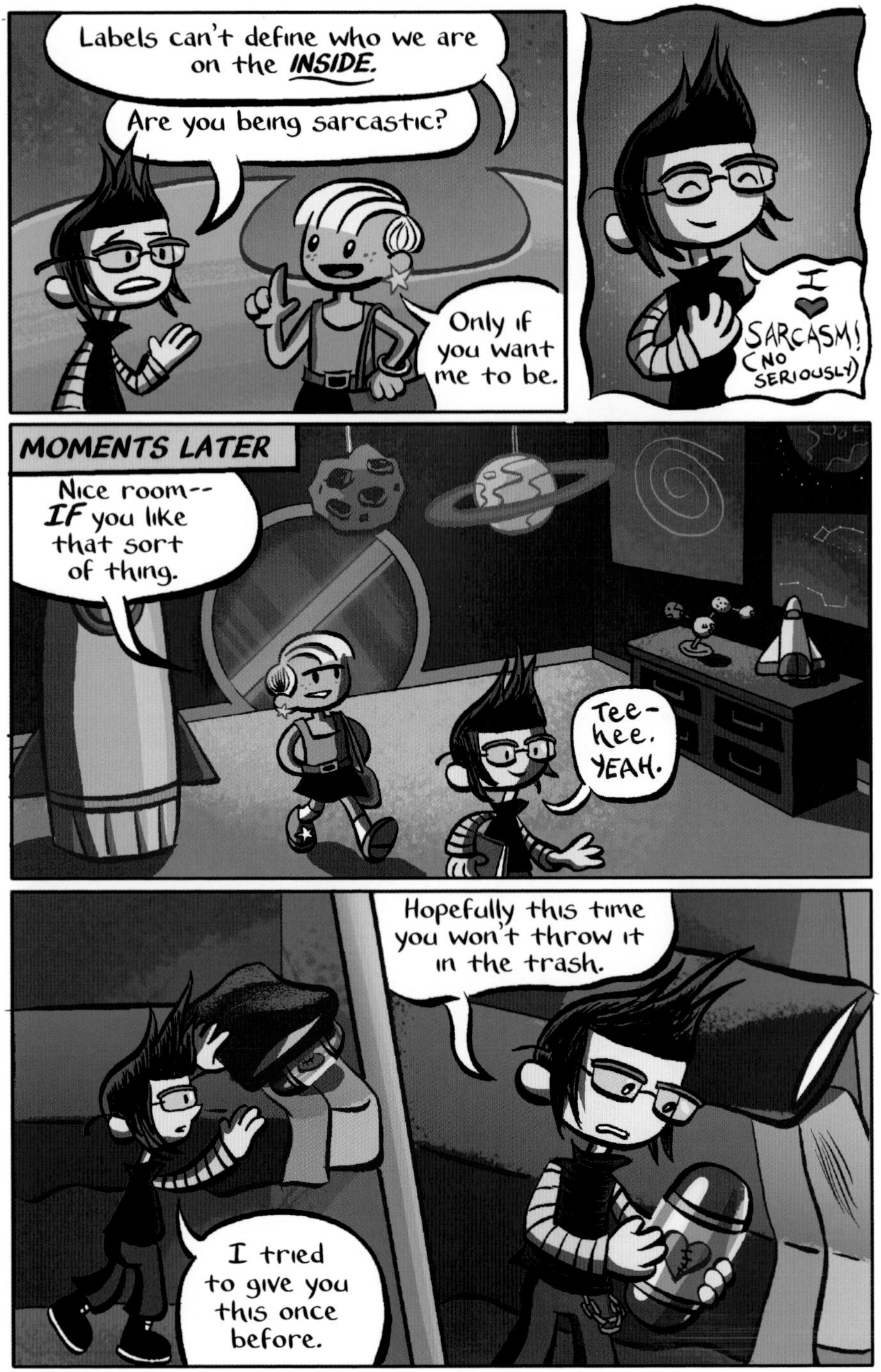

Labels can't define who we are on the INSIDE.
Are you being sarcastic?
Only if you want me to be.
I ♥ SARCASM! (NO SERIOUSLY)
MOMENTS LATER
Nice room-- IF you like that sort of thing.
Tee-hee. YEAH.
Hopefully this time you won't throw it in the trash.
I tried to give you this once before.

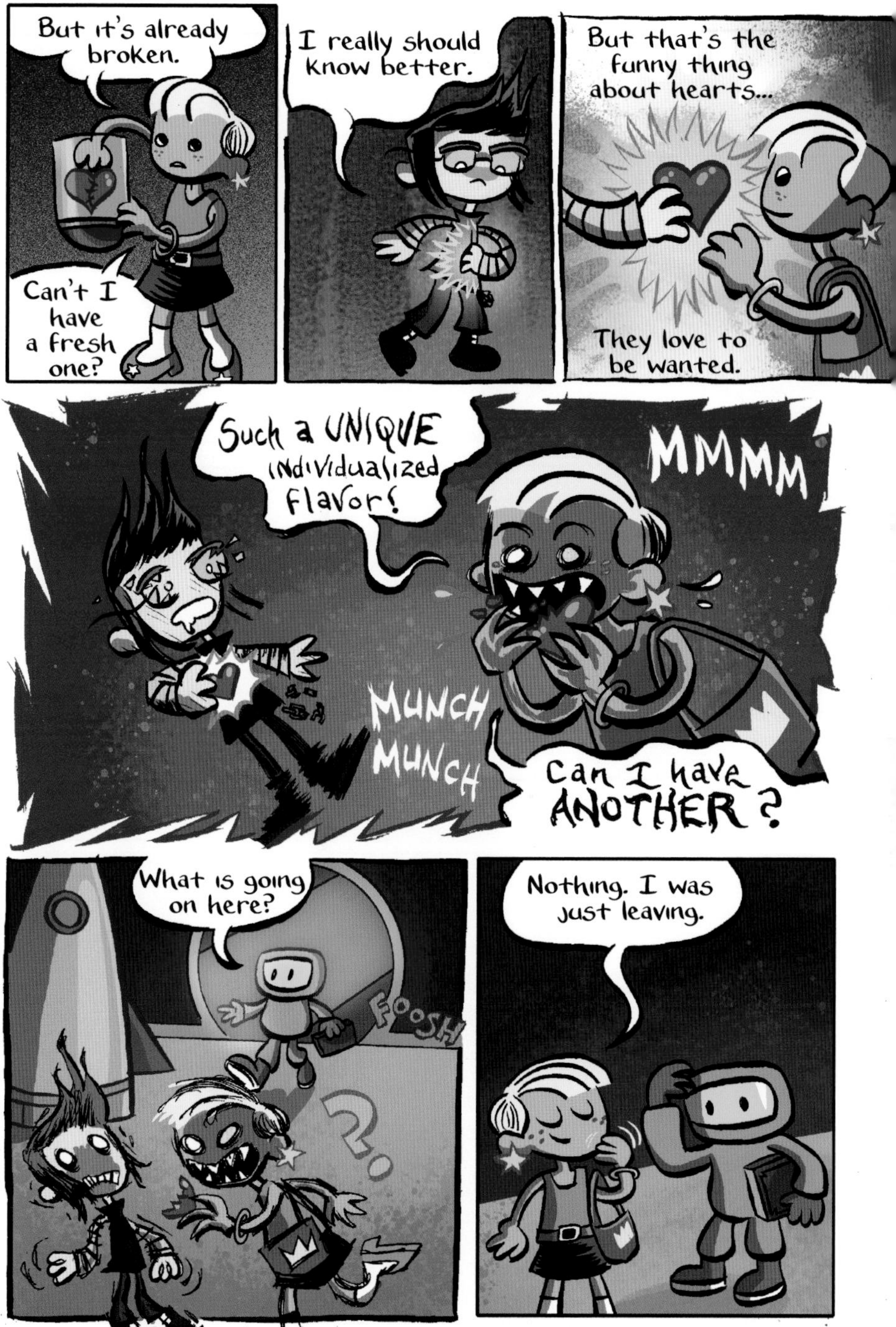

But it's already broken.
Can't I have a fresh one?
I really should know better.
But that's the funny thing about hearts...
They love to be wanted.
Such a UNIQUE individualized flavor!
MMMM
MUNCH MUNCH
Can I have ANOTHER ?
What is going on here?
FOOSH
Nothing. I was just leaving.

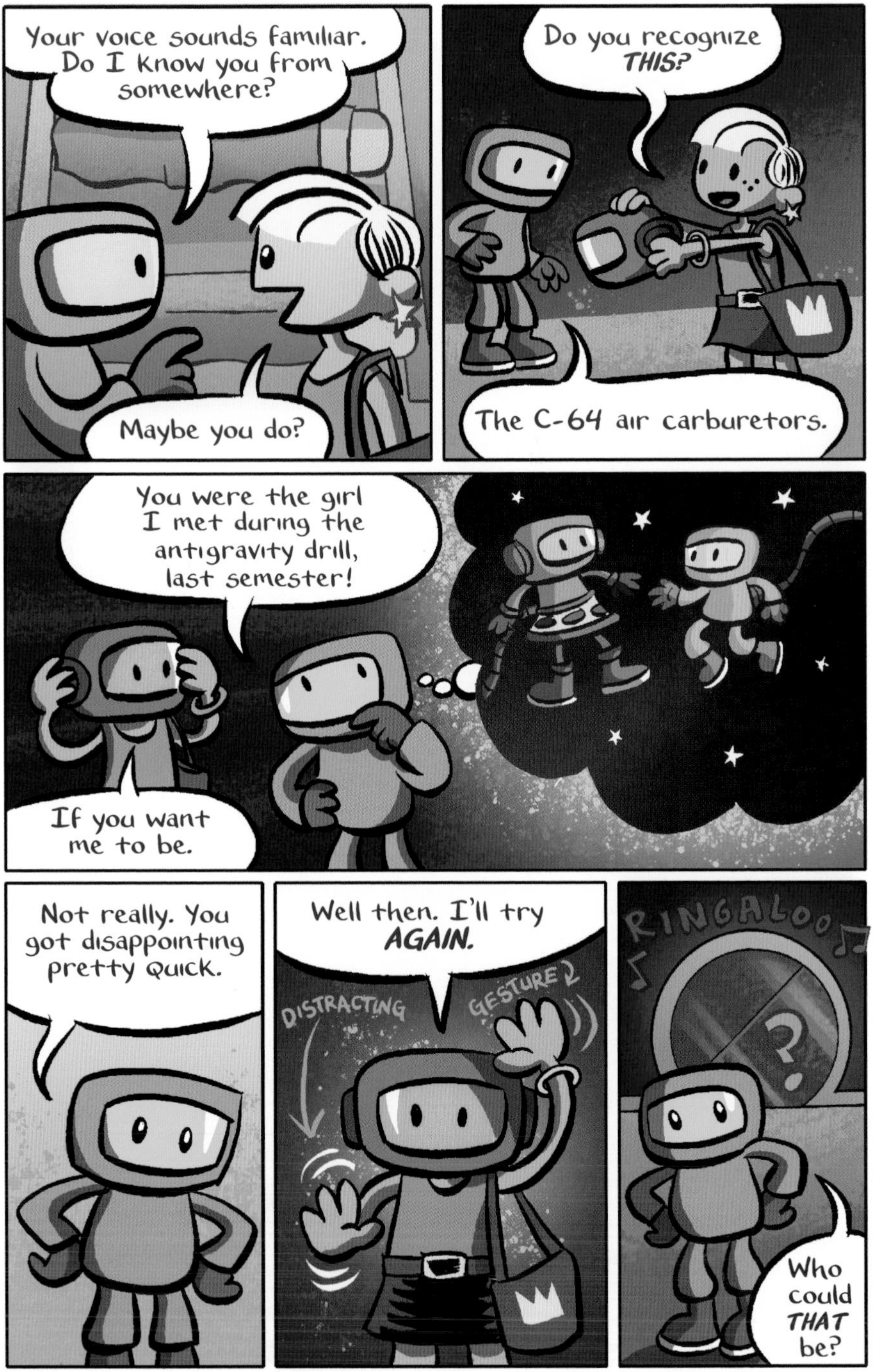
Your voice sounds familiar. Do I know you from somewhere?
Maybe you do?
Do you recognize THIS?
The C-64 air carburetors.
You were the girl I met during the antigravity drill, last semester!
If you want me to be.
Not really. You got disappointing pretty quick.
Well then. I'll try AGAIN.
DISTRACTING
GESTURE
RINGALOO
Who could THAT be?

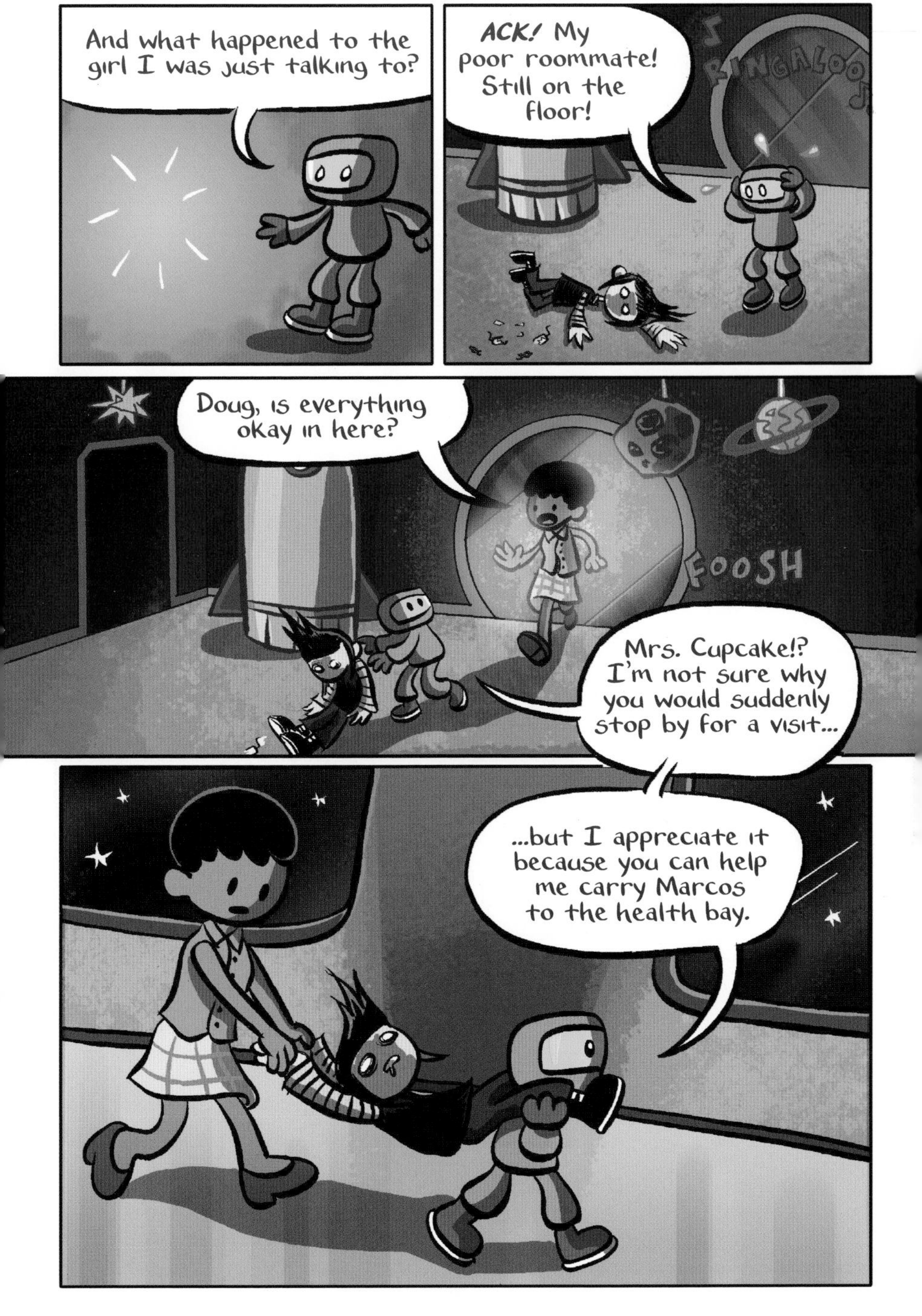
And what happened to the girl I was just talking to?
ACK! My poor roommate! Still on the floor!
Doug, is everything okay in here?
FOOSH
Mrs. Cupcake!? I'm not sure why you would suddenly stop by for a visit...
...but I appreciate it because you can help me carry Marcos to the health bay.

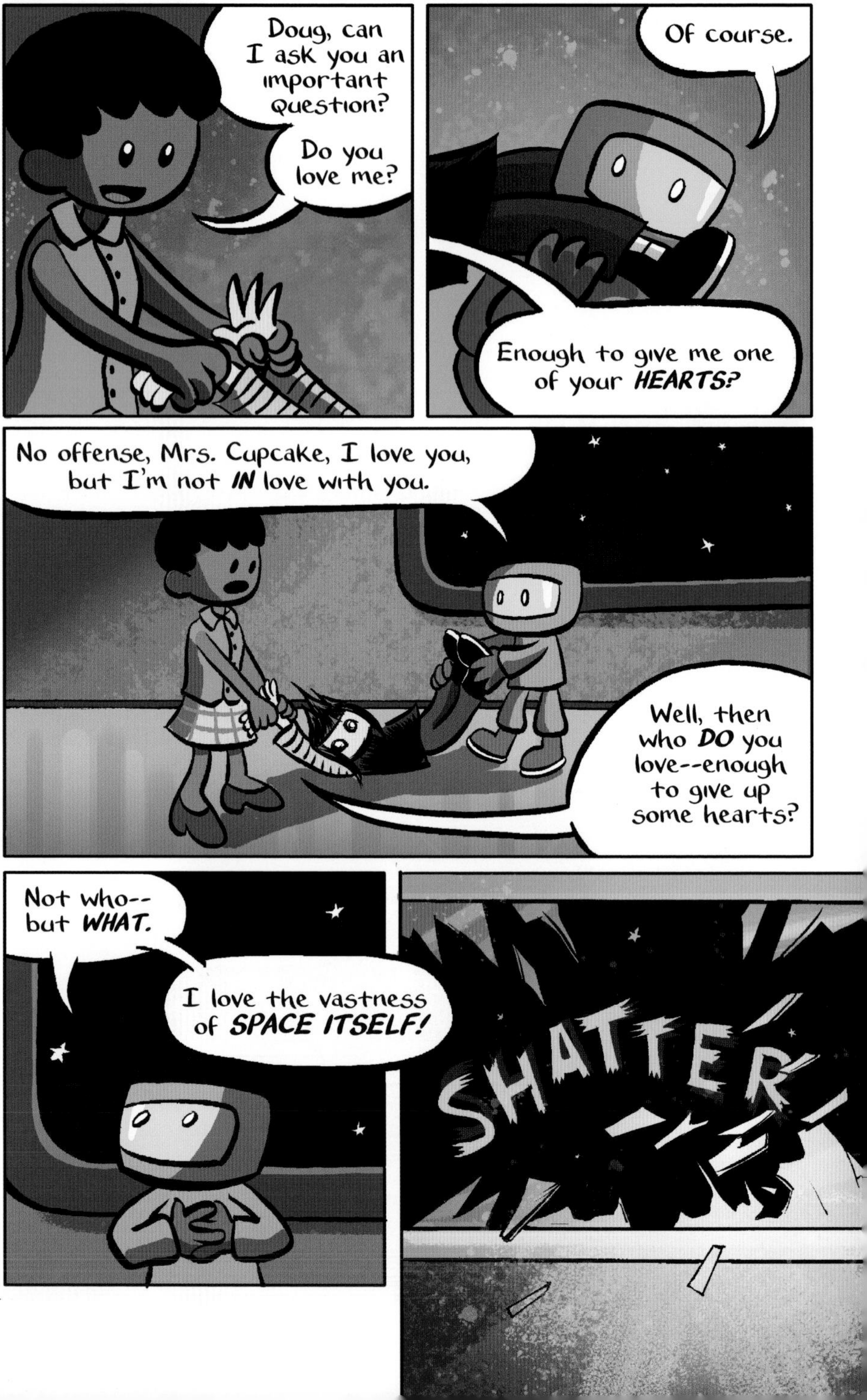
Doug, can I ask you an important question?
Do you love me?
Of course.
Enough to give me one of your HEARTS?
No offense, Mrs. Cupcake, I love you, but I'm not IN love with you.
Well, then who DO you love--enough to give up some hearts?
Not who--but WHAT.
I love the vastness of SPACE ITSELF!
SHATTER

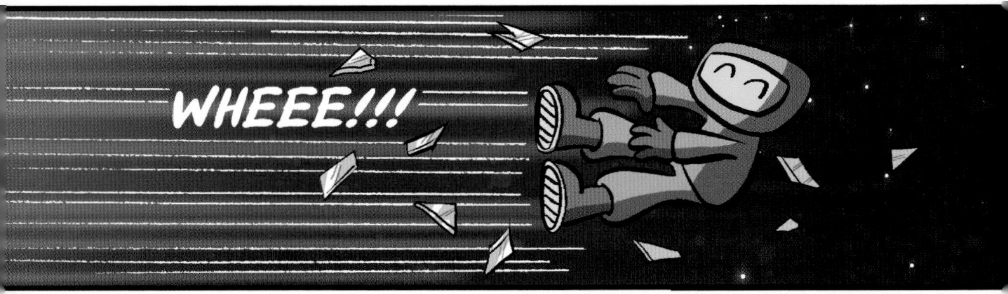
WHEEE!!!

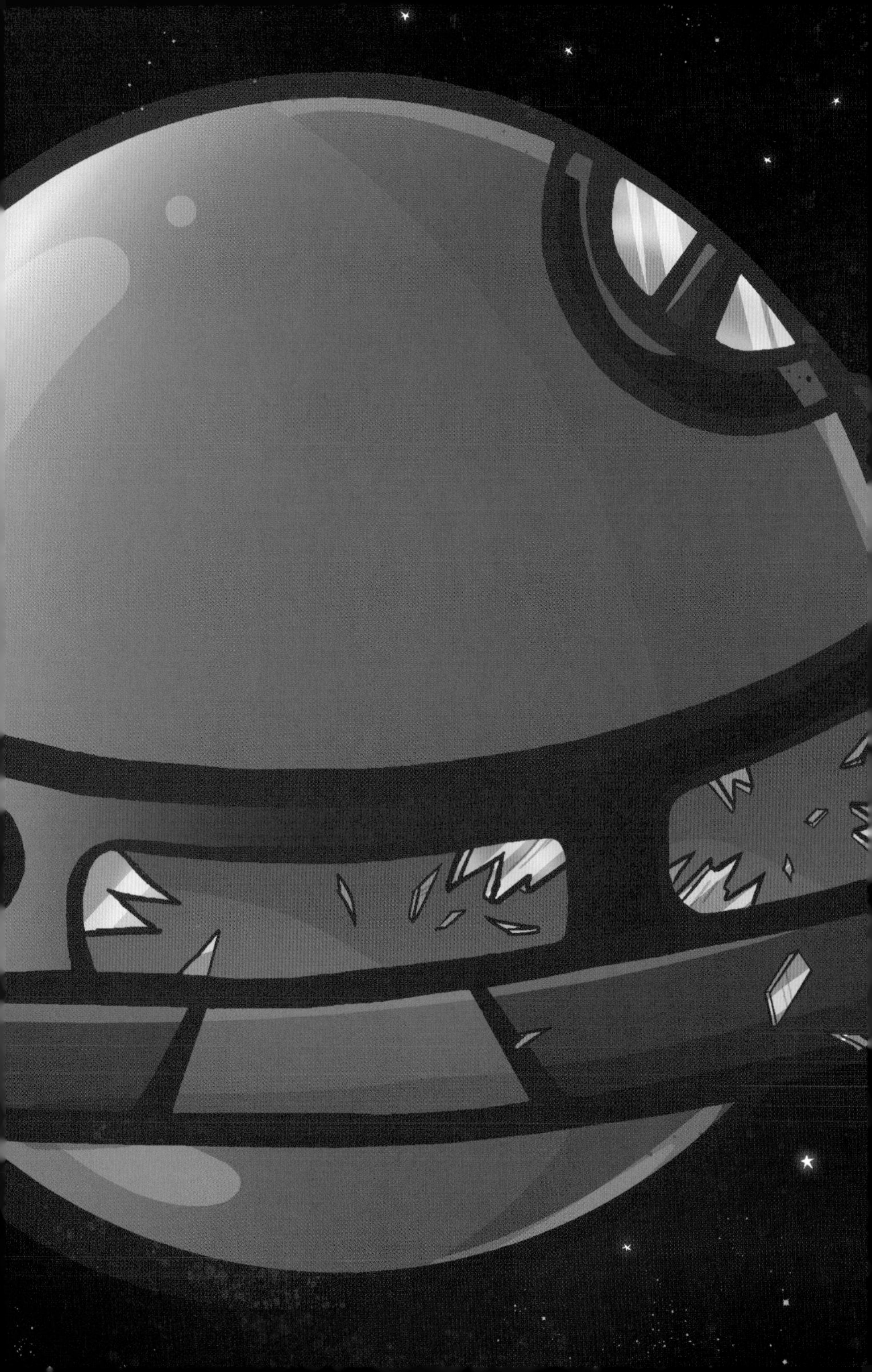

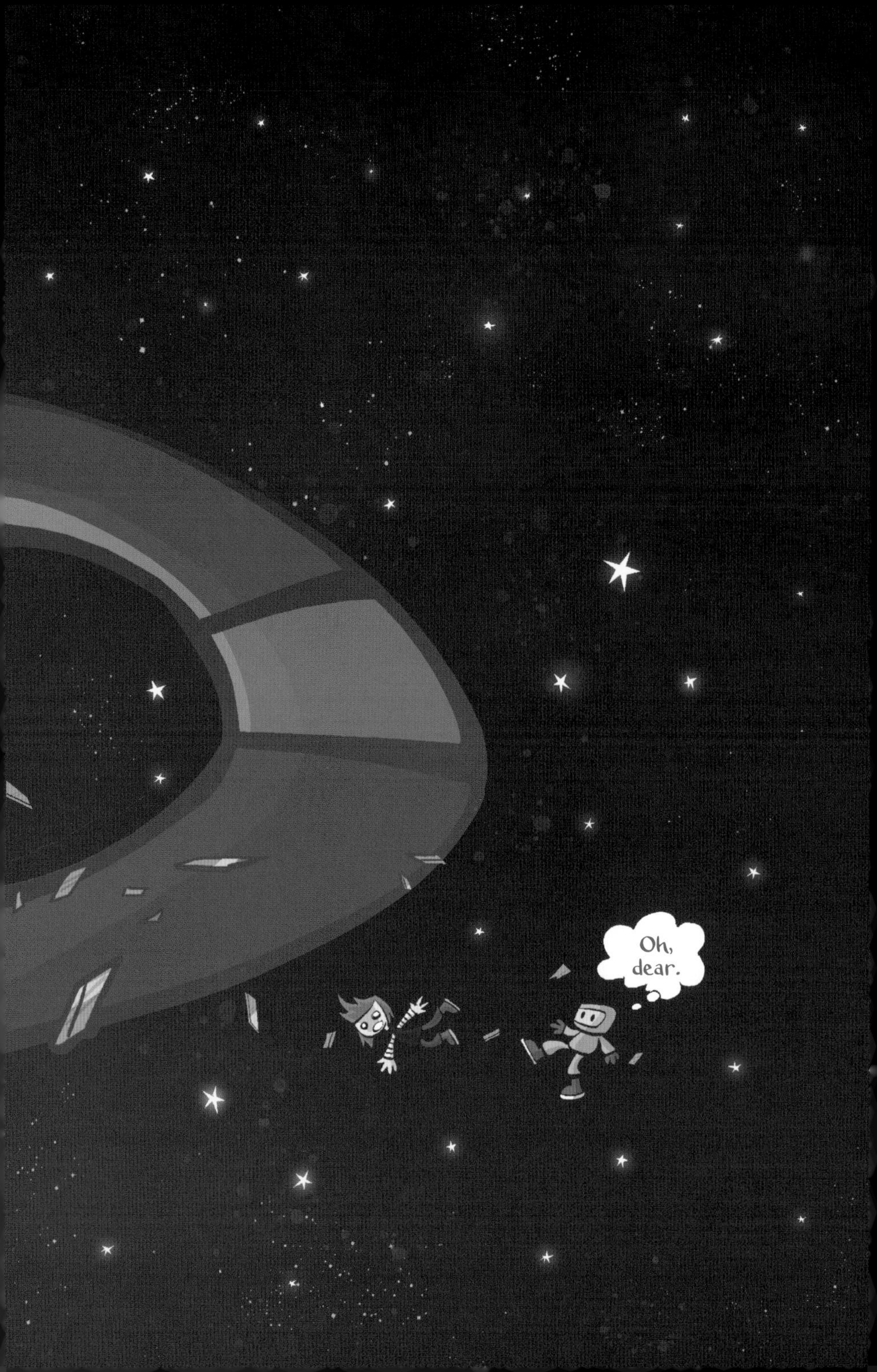
Oh, dear.

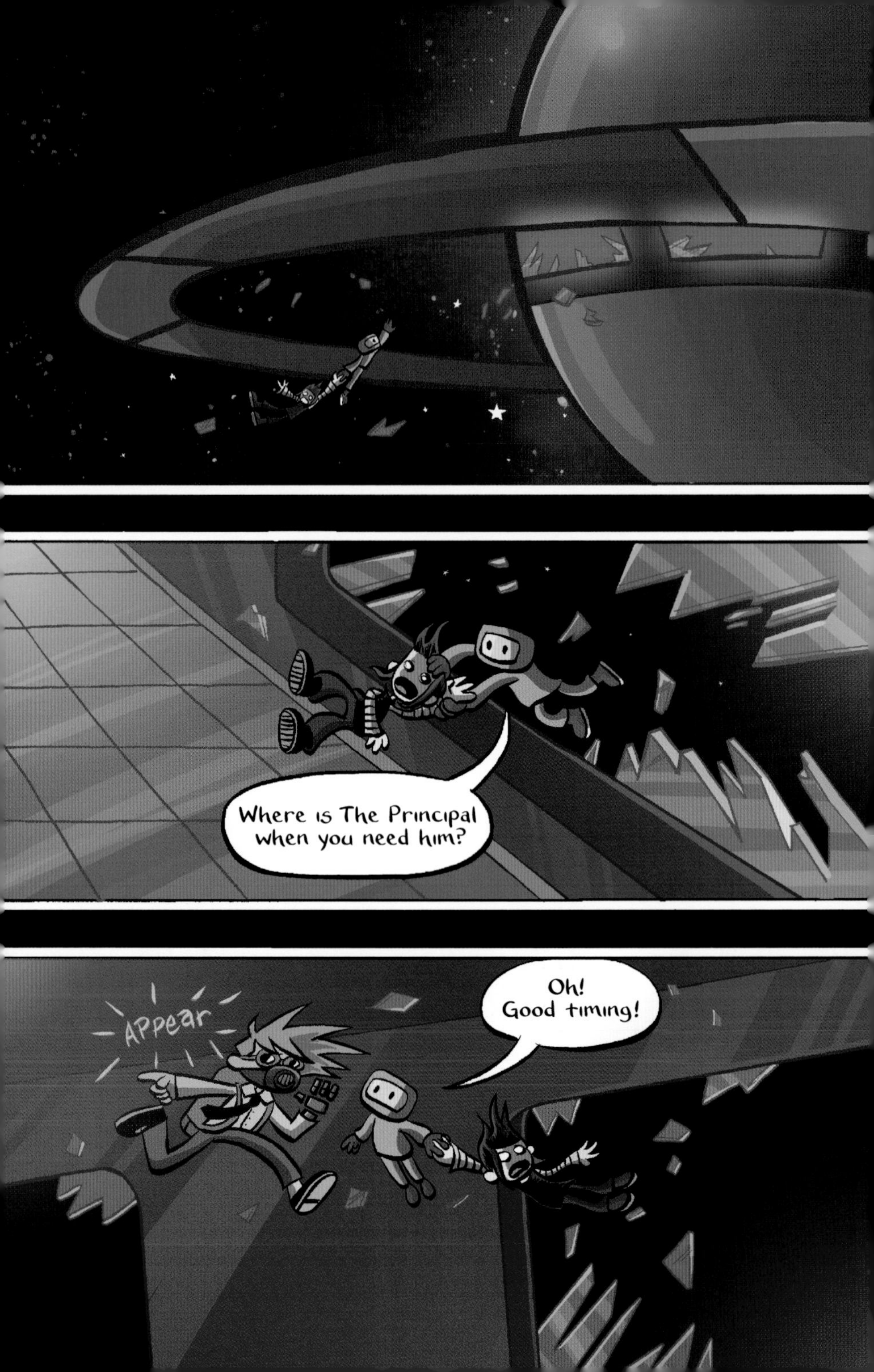
Where is The Principal when you need him?
APPEAR
Oh! Good timing!

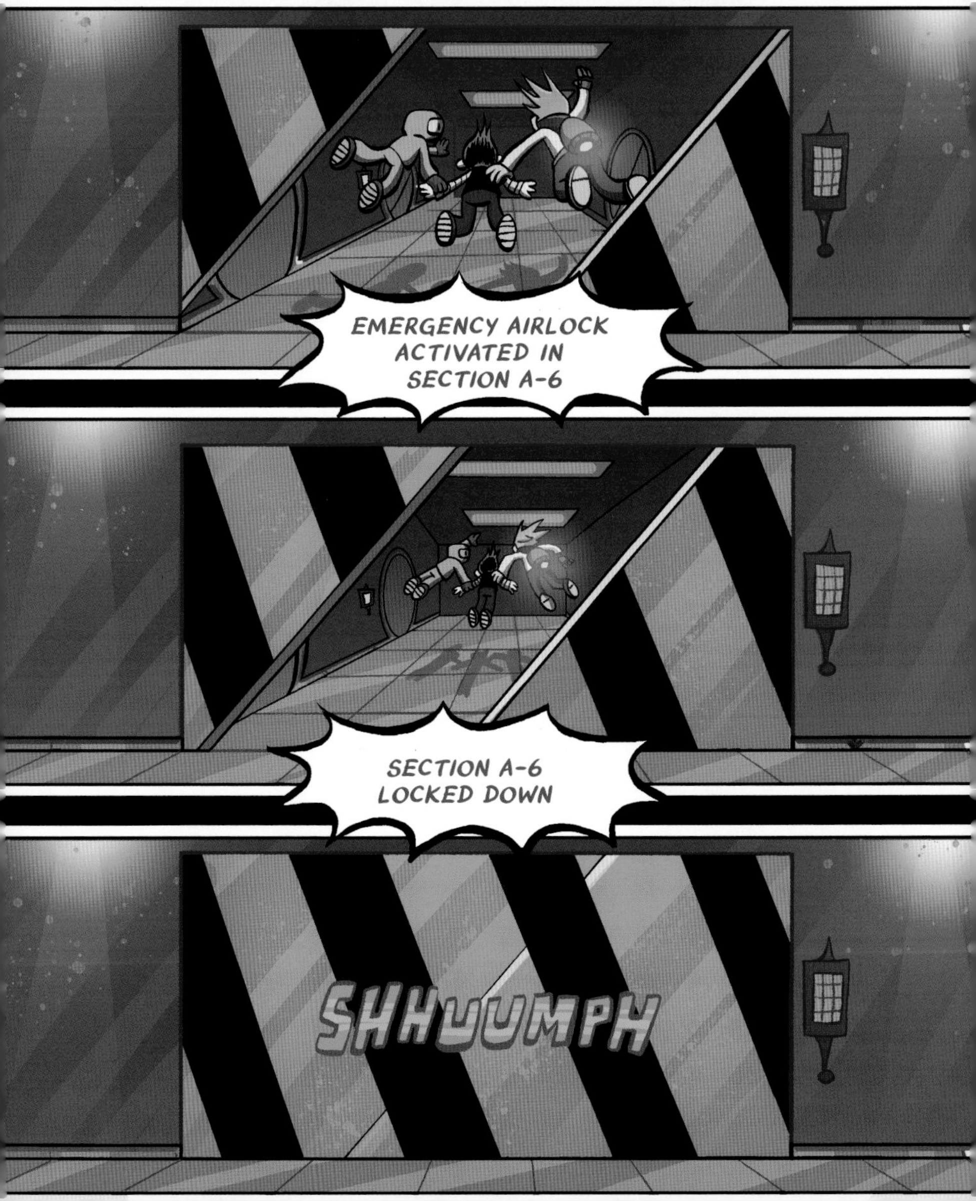
EMERGENCY AIRLOCK ACTIVATED IN SECTION A-6
SECTION A-6 LOCKED DOWN
SHHUUMPH

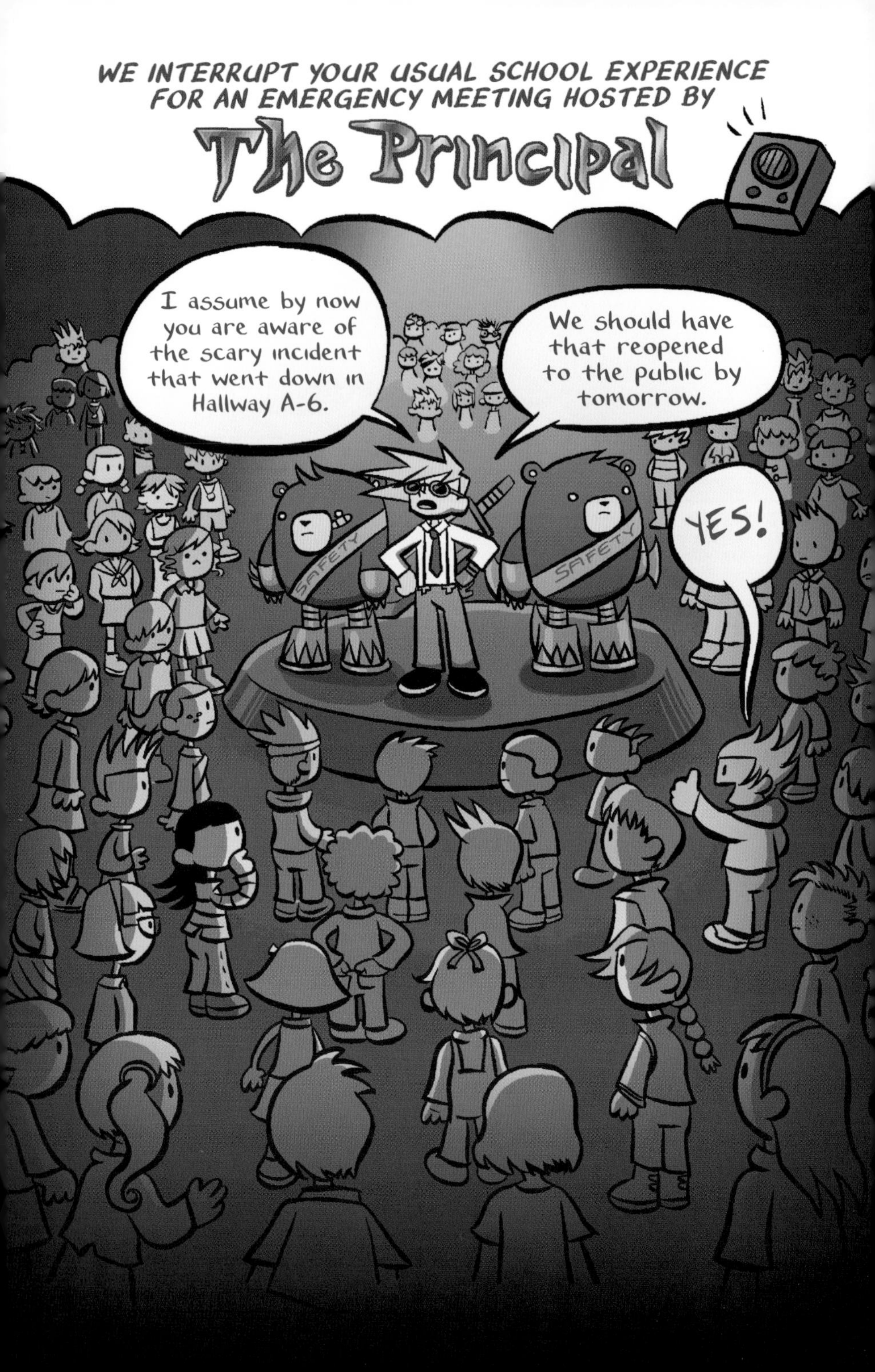
WE INTERRUPT YOUR USUAL SCHOOL EXPERIENCE FOR AN EMERGENCY MEETING HOSTED BY
The Principal
I assume by now you are aware of the scary incident that went down in Hallway A-6.
We should have that reopened to the public by tomorrow.
YES!
SAFETY
SAFETY

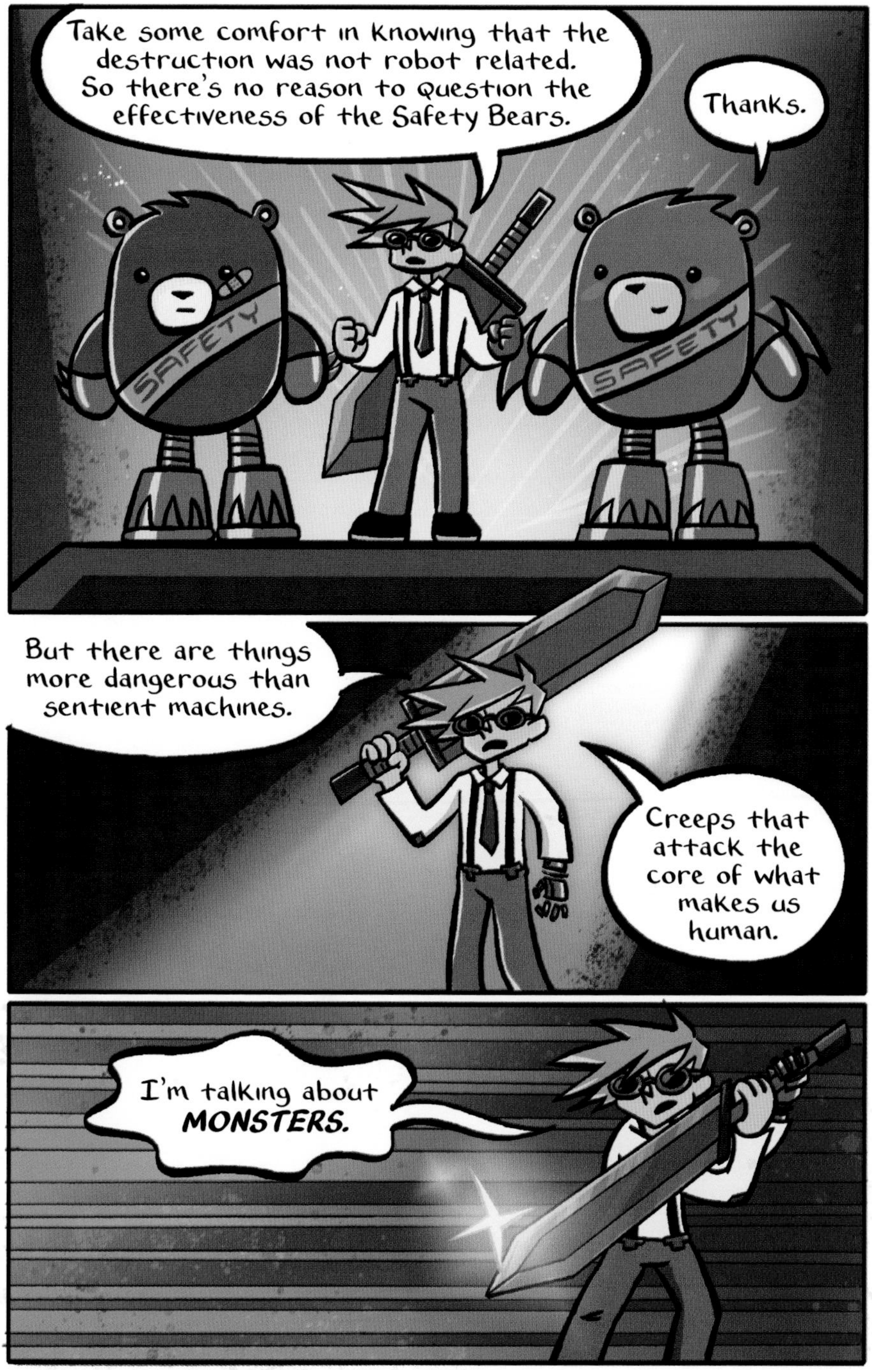
Take some comfort in knowing that the destruction was not robot related. So there's no reason to question the effectiveness of the Safety Bears.
Thanks.
SAFETY
SAFETY
But there are things more dangerous than sentient machines.
Creeps that attack the core of what makes us human.
I'm talking about ***MONSTERS.***

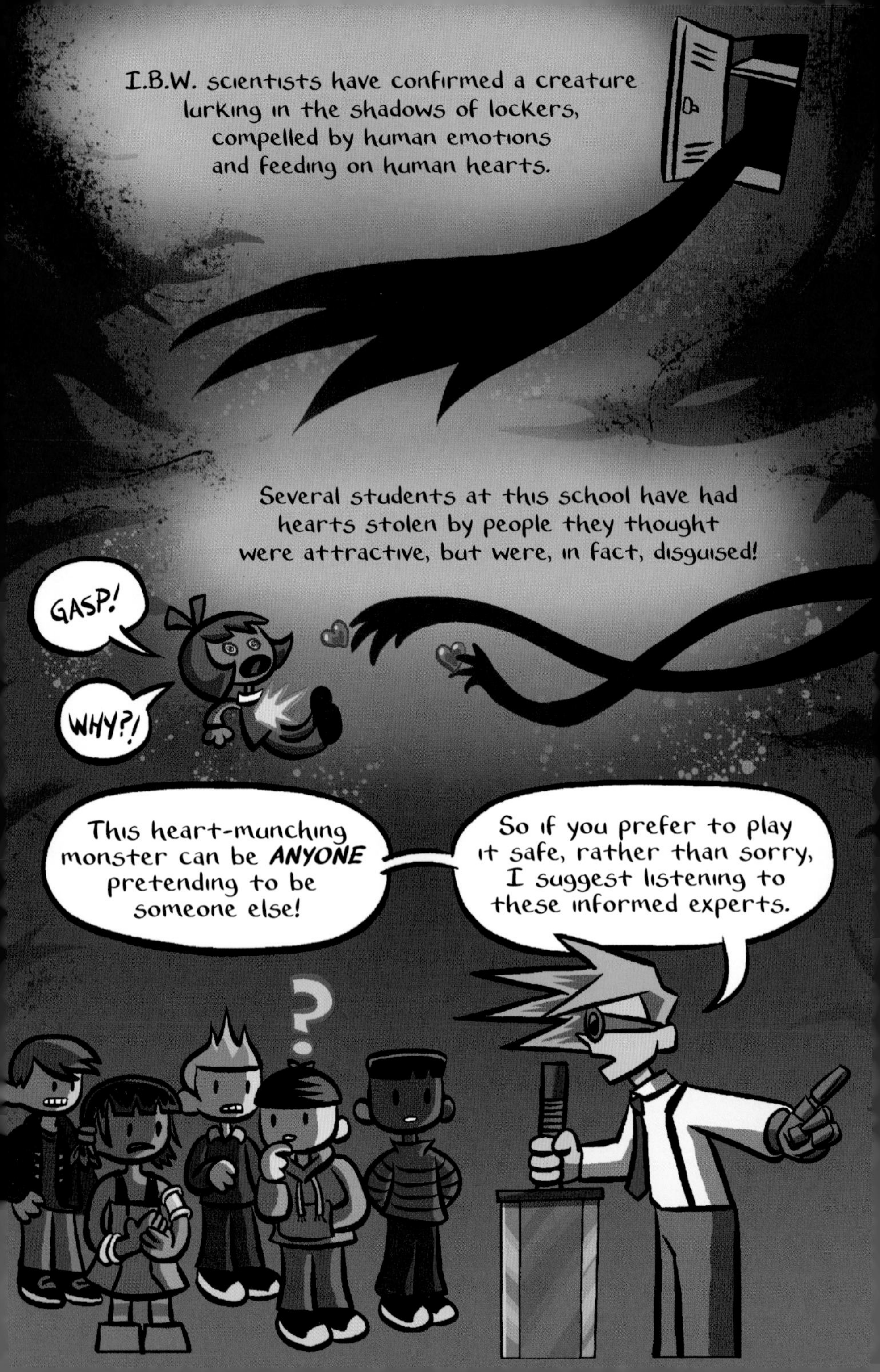
I.B.W. scientists have confirmed a creature lurking in the shadows of lockers, compelled by human emotions and feeding on human hearts.
Several students at this school have had hearts stolen by people they thought were attractive, but were, in fact, disguised!
GASP!
WHY?!
This heart-munching monster can be ANYONE pretending to be someone else!
So if you prefer to play it safe, rather than sorry, I suggest listening to these informed experts.
?

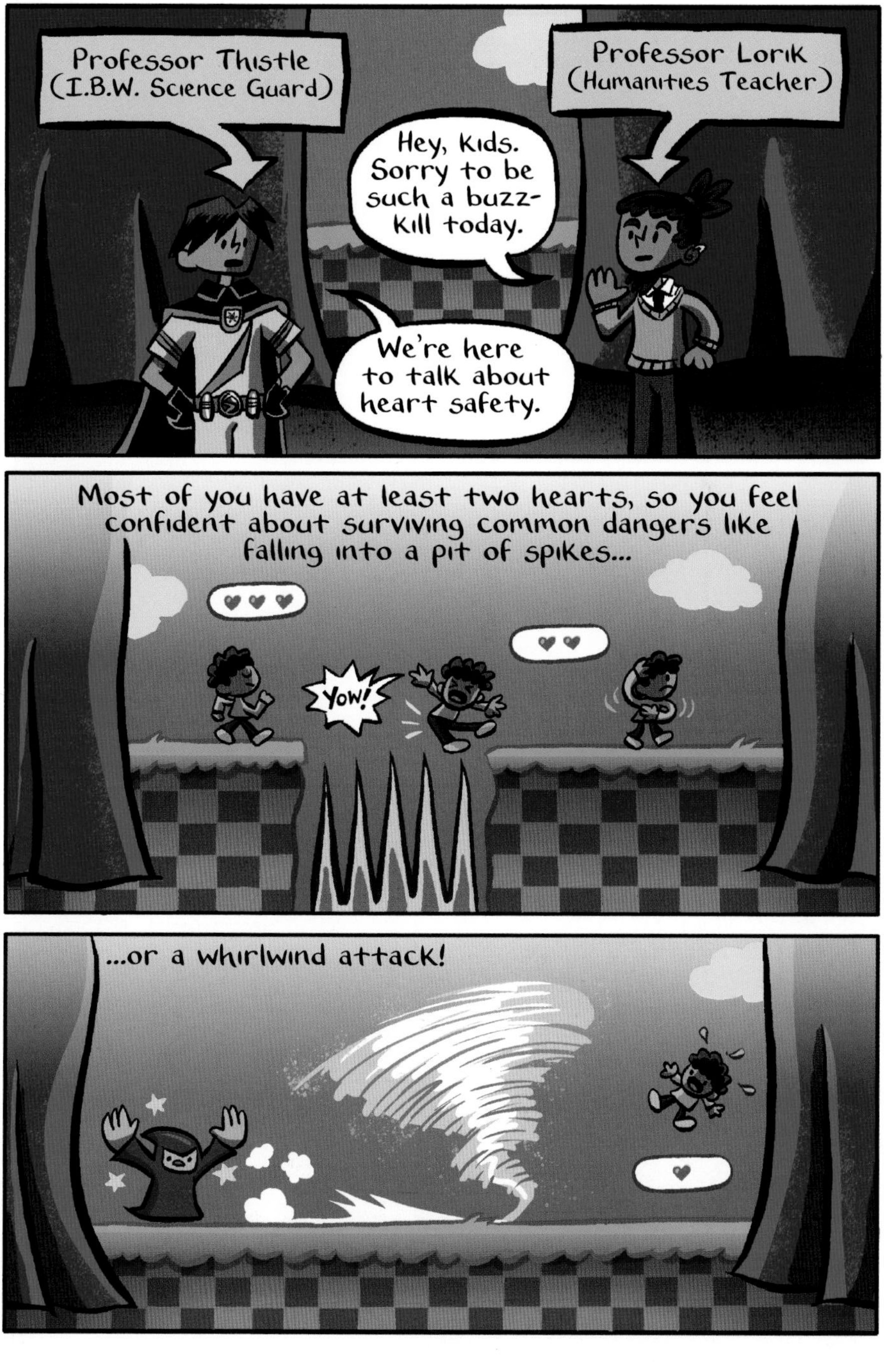
Professor Thistle (I.B.W. Science Guard)
Professor Lorik (Humanities Teacher)
Hey, kids. Sorry to be such a buzz-kill today.
We're here to talk about heart safety.
Most of you have at least two hearts, so you feel confident about surviving common dangers like falling into a pit of spikes...
YOW!
...or a whirlwind attack!

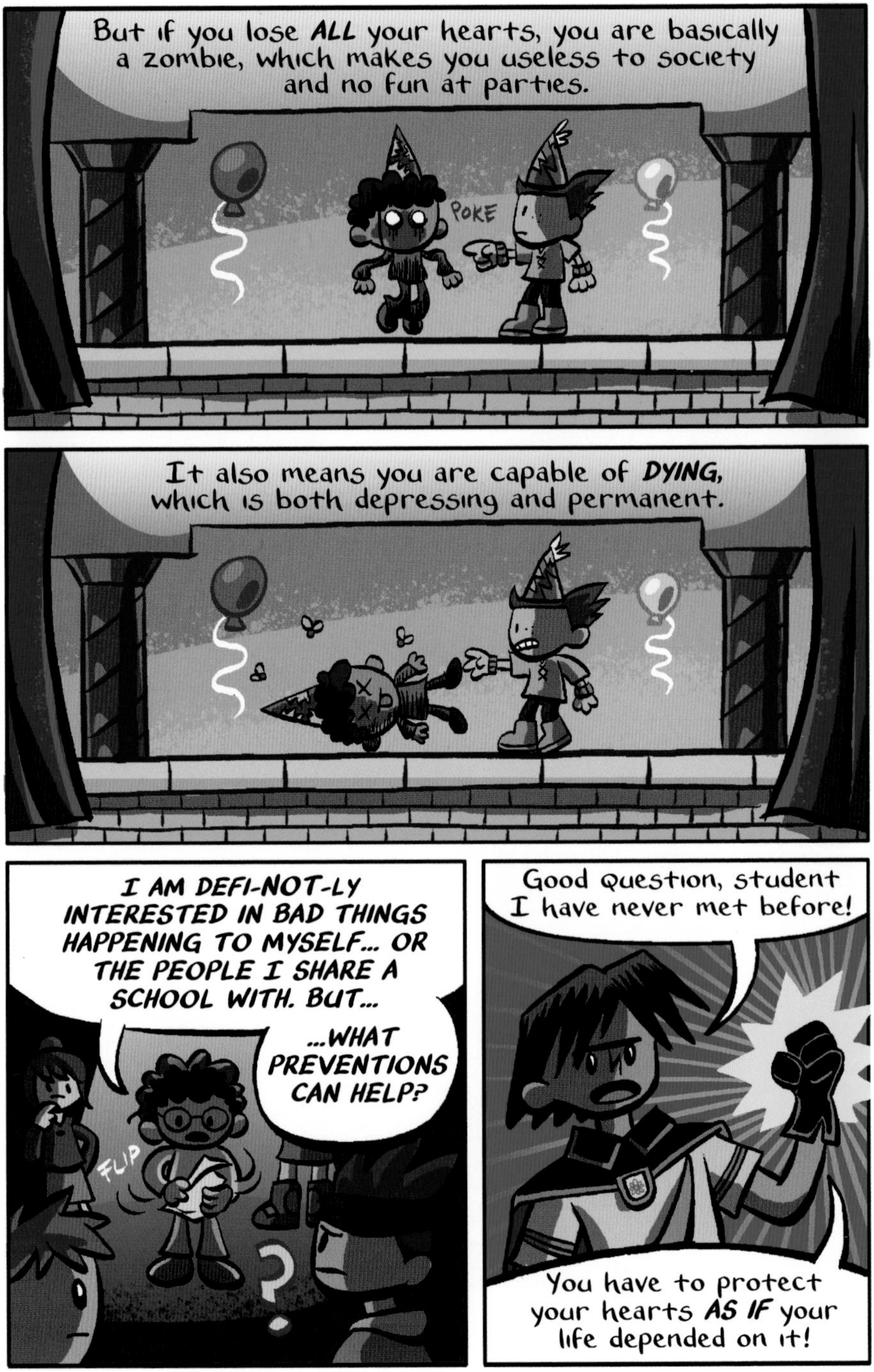
But if you lose ALL your hearts, you are basically a zombie, which makes you useless to society and no fun at parties.
POKE
It also means you are capable of DYING, which is both depressing and permanent.
I AM DEFI-NOT-LY INTERESTED IN BAD THINGS HAPPENING TO MYSELF... OR THE PEOPLE I SHARE A SCHOOL WITH. BUT...
...WHAT PREVENTIONS CAN HELP?
FLIP
Good question, student I have never met before!
You have to protect your hearts AS IF your life depended on it!

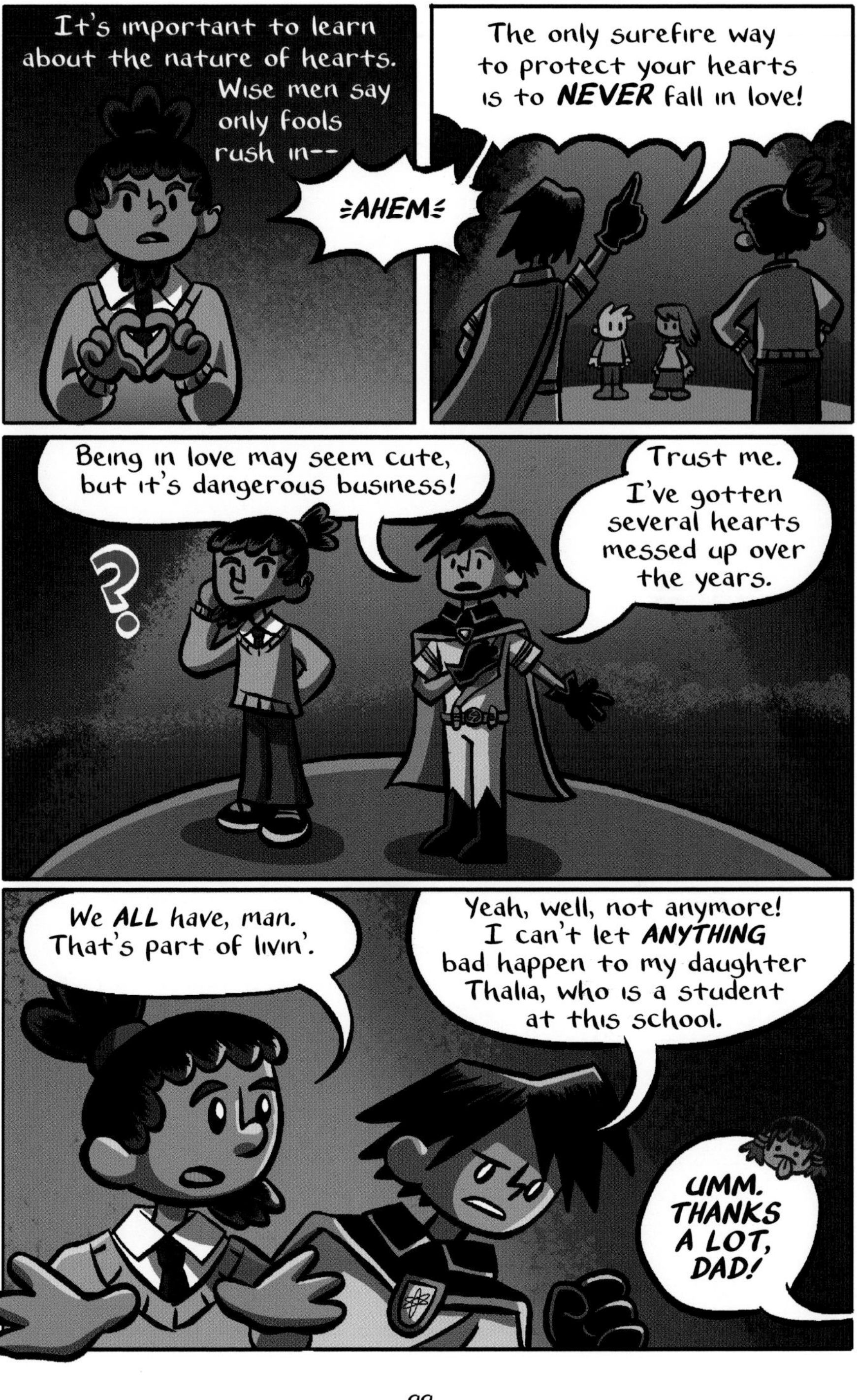
It's important to learn about the nature of hearts.
Wise men say only fools rush in--
AHEM
The only surefire way to protect your hearts is to NEVER fall in love!
Being in love may seem cute, but it's dangerous business!
Trust me.
I've gotten several hearts messed up over the years.
We ALL have, man. That's part of livin'.
Yeah, well, not anymore! I can't let ANYTHING bad happen to my daughter Thalia, who is a student at this school.
UMM. THANKS A LOT, DAD!

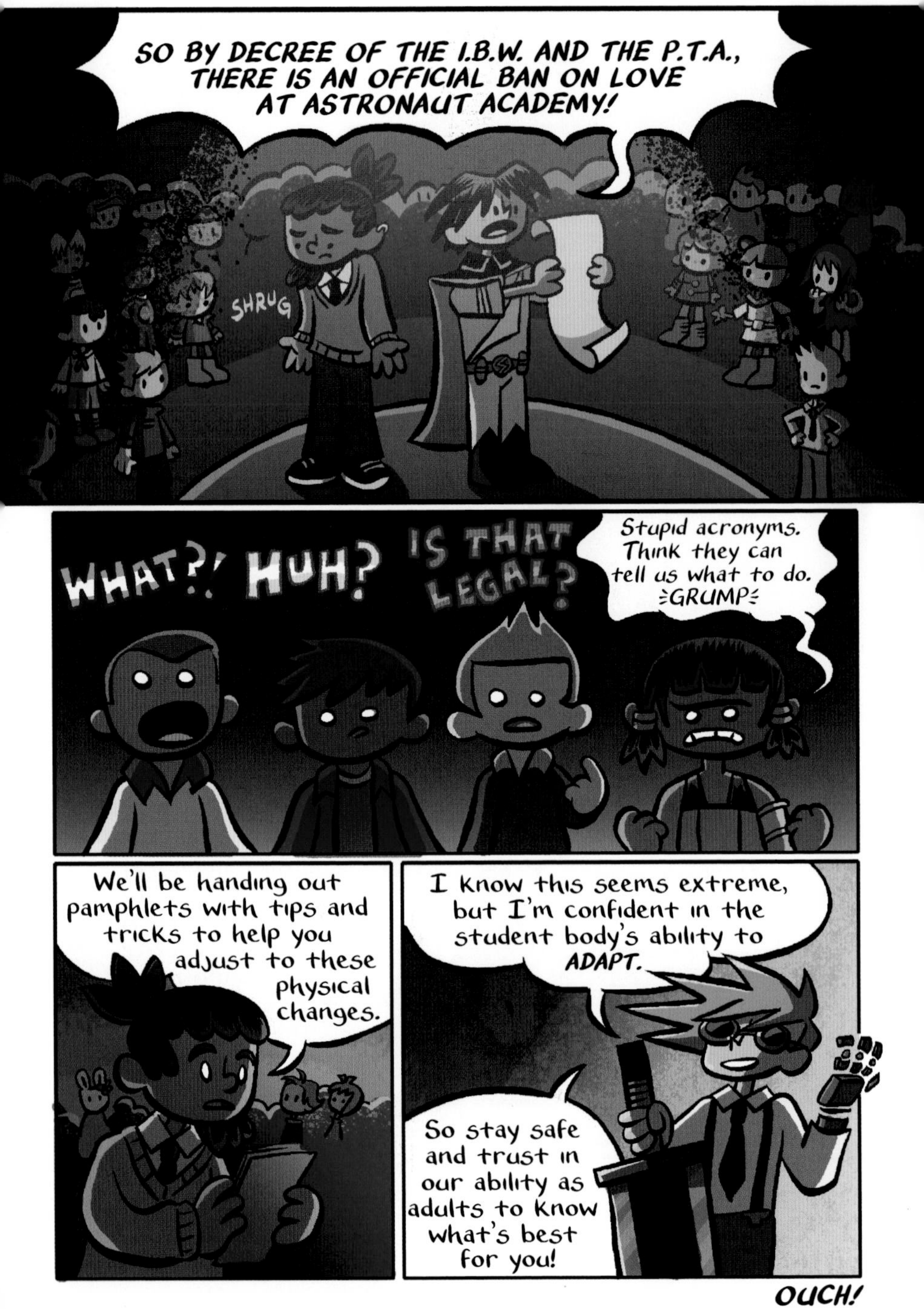
SO BY DECREE OF THE I.B.W. AND THE P.T.A., THERE IS AN OFFICIAL BAN ON LOVE AT ASTRONAUT ACADEMY!
SHRUG
WHAT?!
HUH?
IS THAT LEGAL?
Stupid acronyms. Think they can tell us what to do. GRUMP
We'll be handing out pamphlets with tips and tricks to help you adjust to these physical changes.
I know this seems extreme, but I'm confident in the student body's ability to ADAPT.
So stay safe and trust in our ability as adults to know what's best for you!
OUCH!

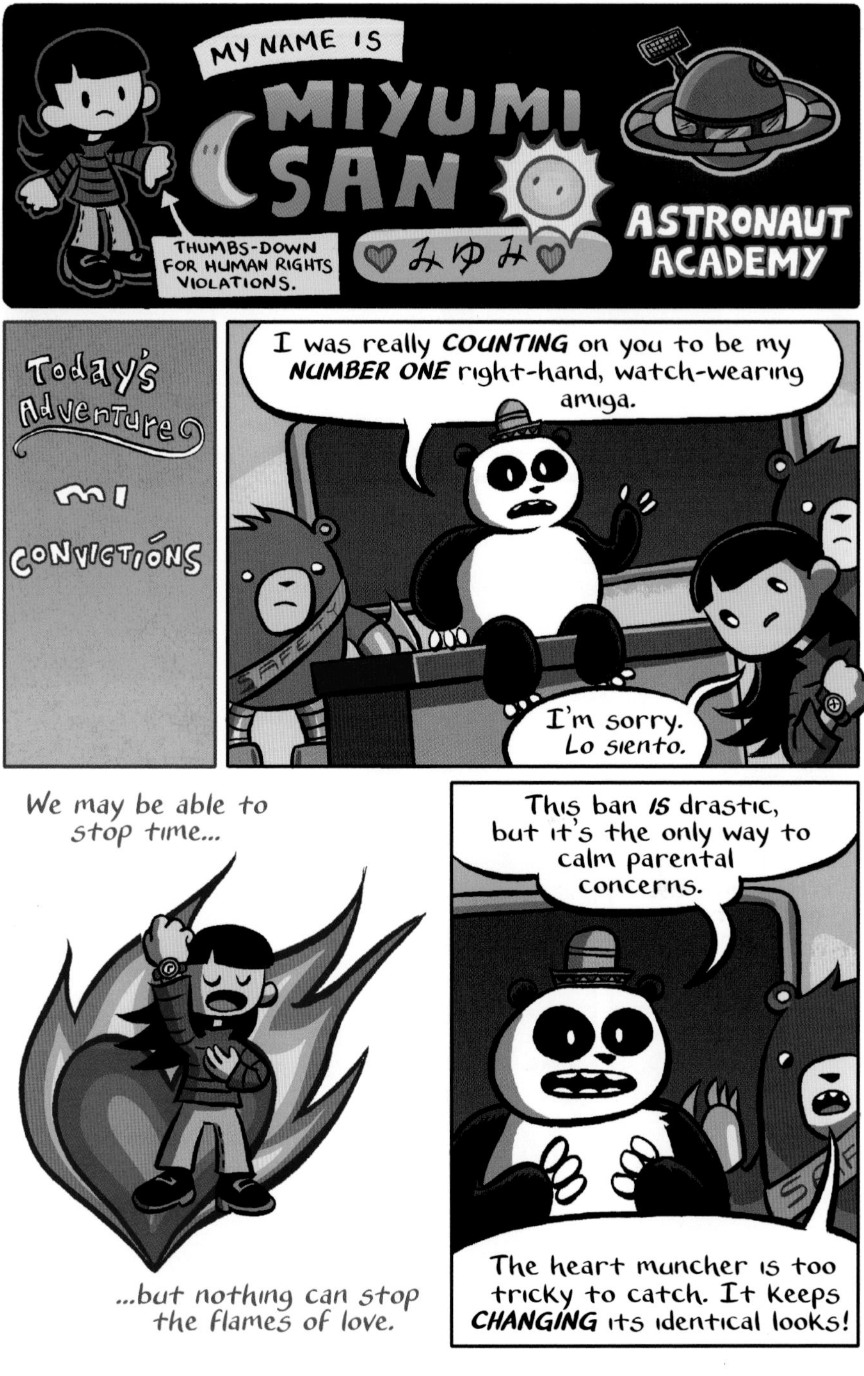
MY NAME IS
MIYUMI SAN
THUMBS-DOWN FOR HUMAN RIGHTS VIOLATIONS.
みゆみ
ASTRONAUT ACADEMY
Today's Adventure
mi convictións
I was really COUNTING on you to be my NUMBER ONE right-hand, watch-wearing amiga.
SAFETY
I'm sorry. Lo siento.
We may be able to stop time...
...but nothing can stop the flames of love.
This ban IS drastic, but it's the only way to calm parental concerns.
The heart muncher is too tricky to catch. It keeps CHANGING its identical looks!

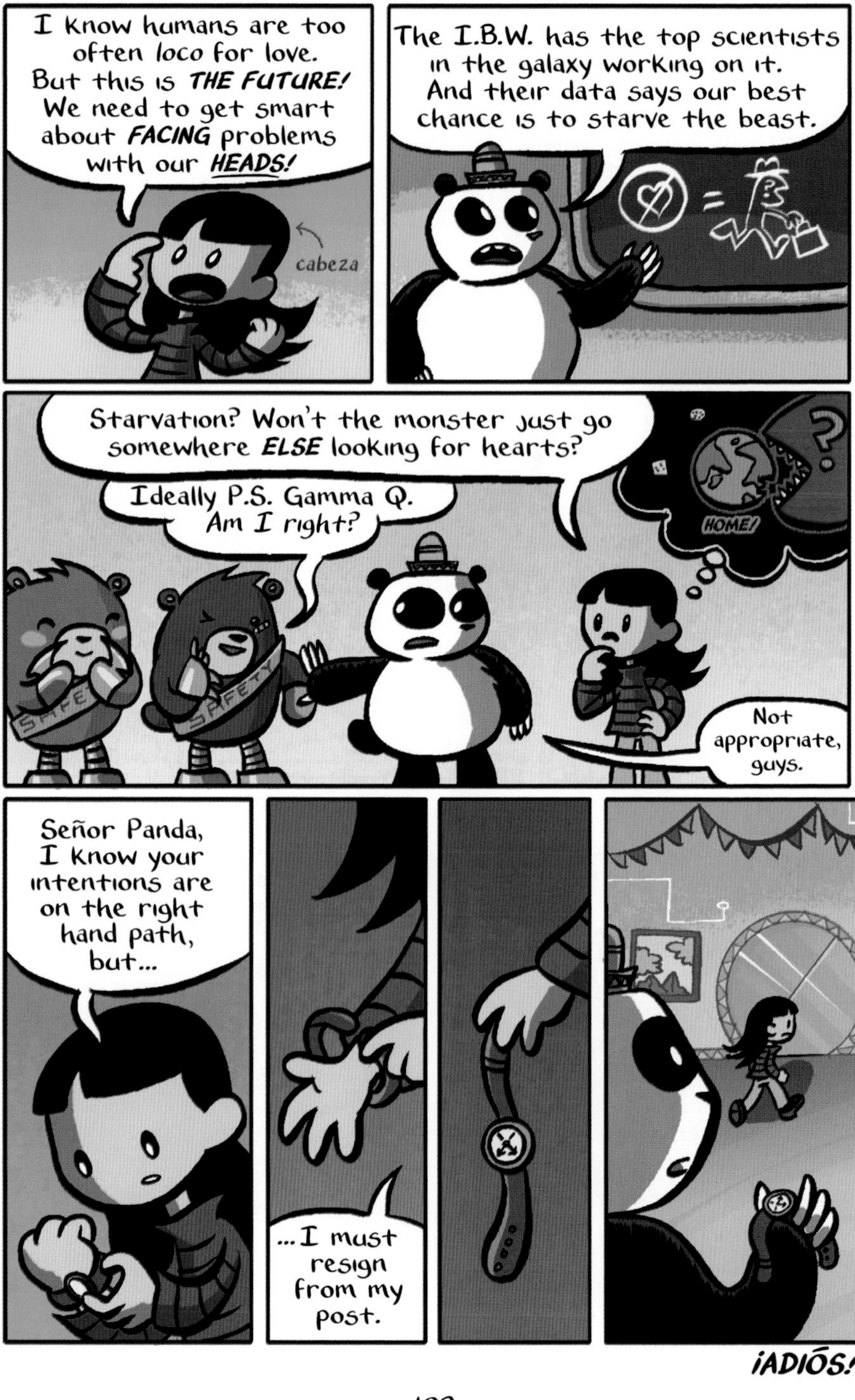
I know humans are too often loco for love. But this is THE FUTURE! We need to get smart about FACING problems with our HEADS!
cabeza
The I.B.W. has the top scientists in the galaxy working on it. And their data says our best chance is to starve the beast.
Starvation? Won't the monster just go somewhere ELSE looking for hearts?
Ideally P.S. Gamma Q. Am I right?
HOME!
SAFETY
SAFETY
Not appropriate, guys.
Señor Panda, I know your intentions are on the right hand path, but...
...I must resign from my post.
¡ADIÓS!

MY NAME IS:

BILLY LEE

AND I GO TO:

ASTRONAUT ACADEMY

Personally, I think the ban on love is the best thing to happen to this school.

I thought you were a fan of love?

I WAS...

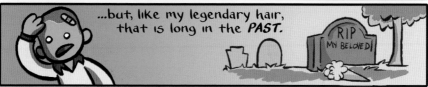

...but, like my legendary hair, that is long in the *PAST*.

RIP MY BELOVED!

Back then, I was **CONTENT** to passively watch the content of Maribelle and Miyumi's seemingly endless feud.

I'M NOT LOOKING AT YOU!

ME NEITHER!

But I became **TOO CAPTIVATED!** My vision grew cloudy! I had to see what it felt like to be a spectator who got **INVOLVED**.

Hey, baby!

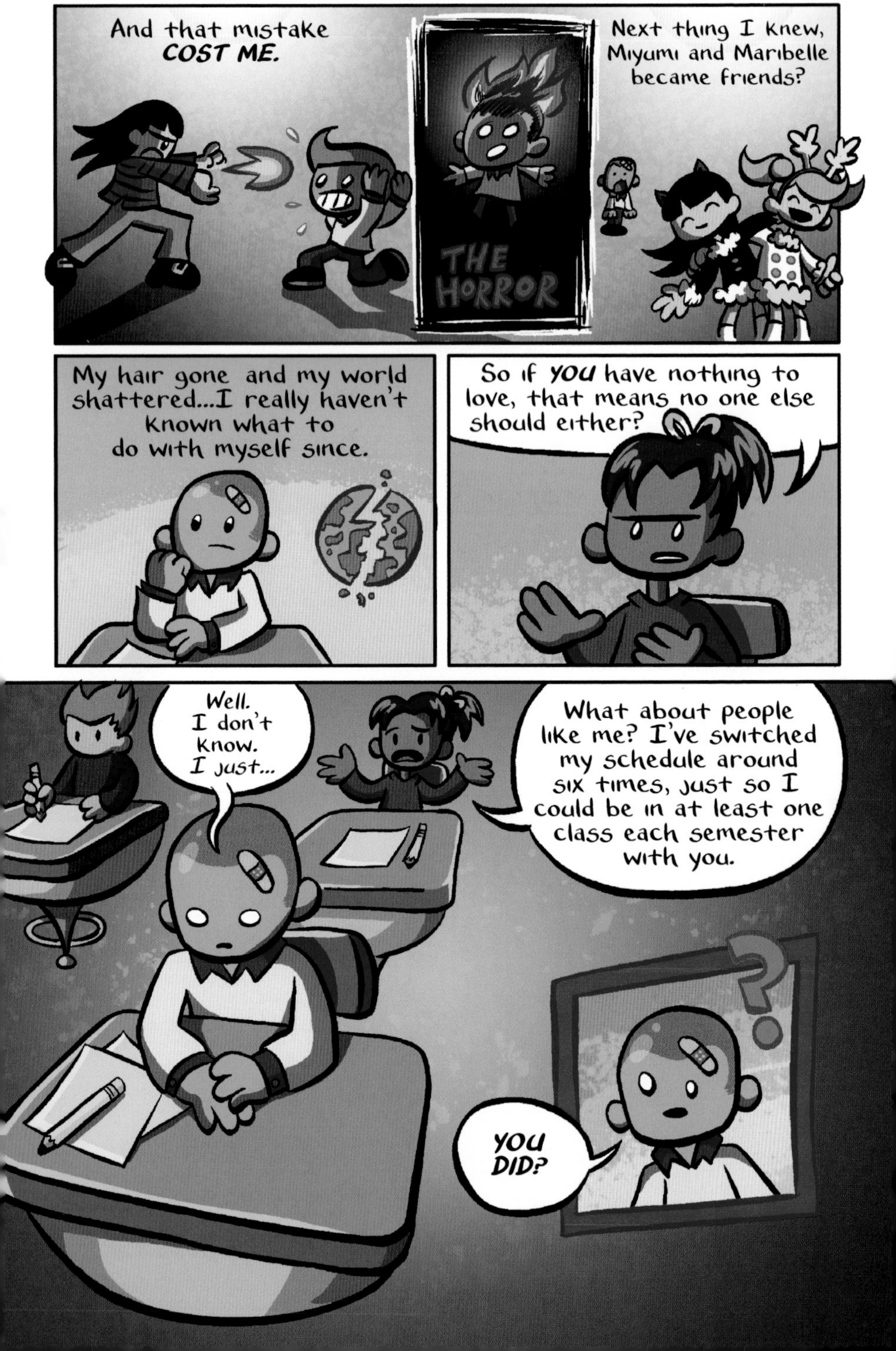
And that mistake COST ME.
THE HORROR
Next thing I knew, Miyumi and Maribelle became friends?
My hair gone and my world shattered...I really haven't known what to do with myself since.
So if YOU have nothing to love, that means no one else should either?
Well. I don't know. I just...
What about people like me? I've switched my schedule around six times, just so I could be in at least one class each semester with you.
YOU DID?

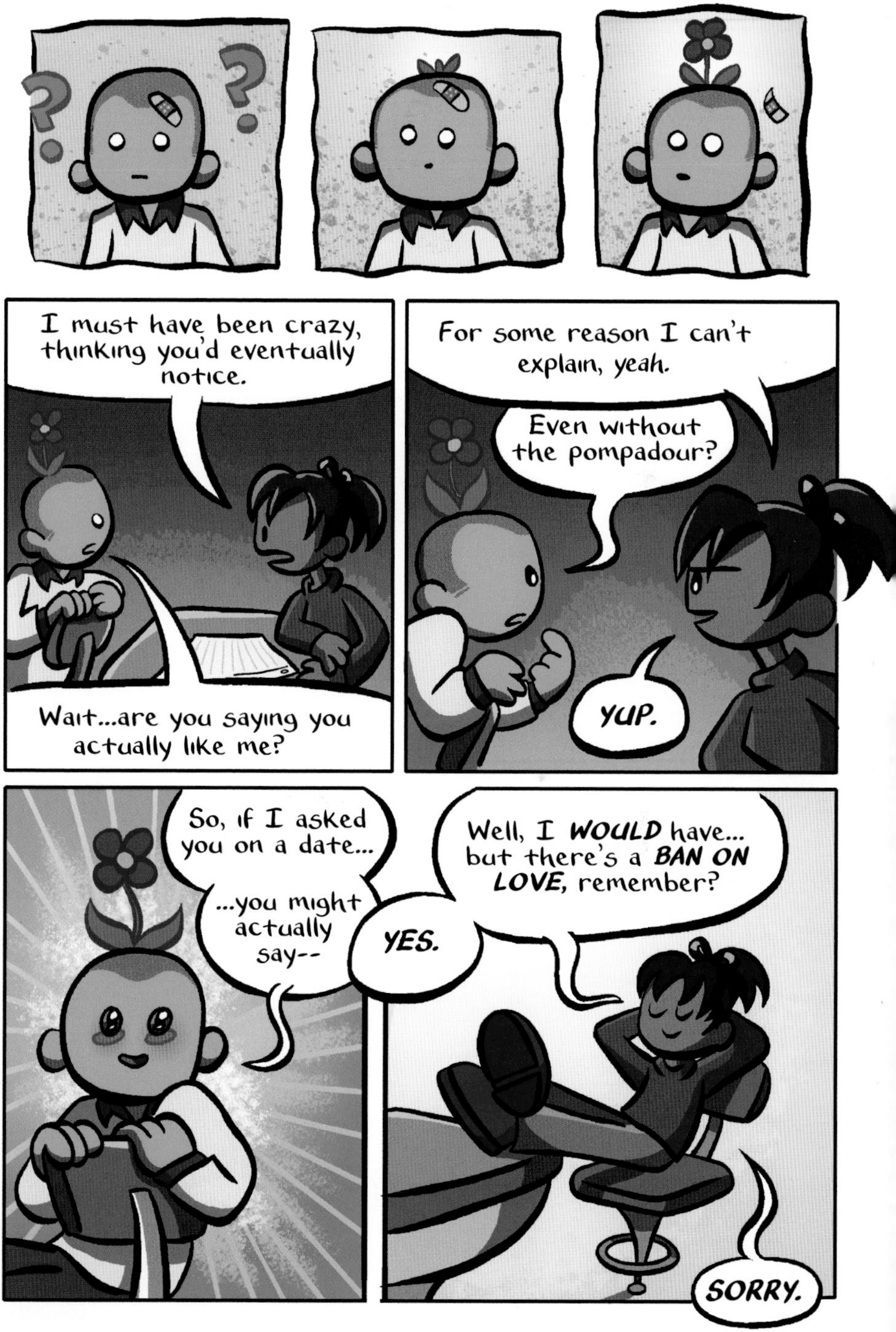
I must have been crazy, thinking you'd eventually notice.
Wait...are you saying you actually like me?
For some reason I can't explain, yeah.
Even without the pompadour?
YUP.
So, if I asked you on a date...
...you might actually say--
YES.
Well, I WOULD have... but there's a BAN ON LOVE, remember?
SORRY.

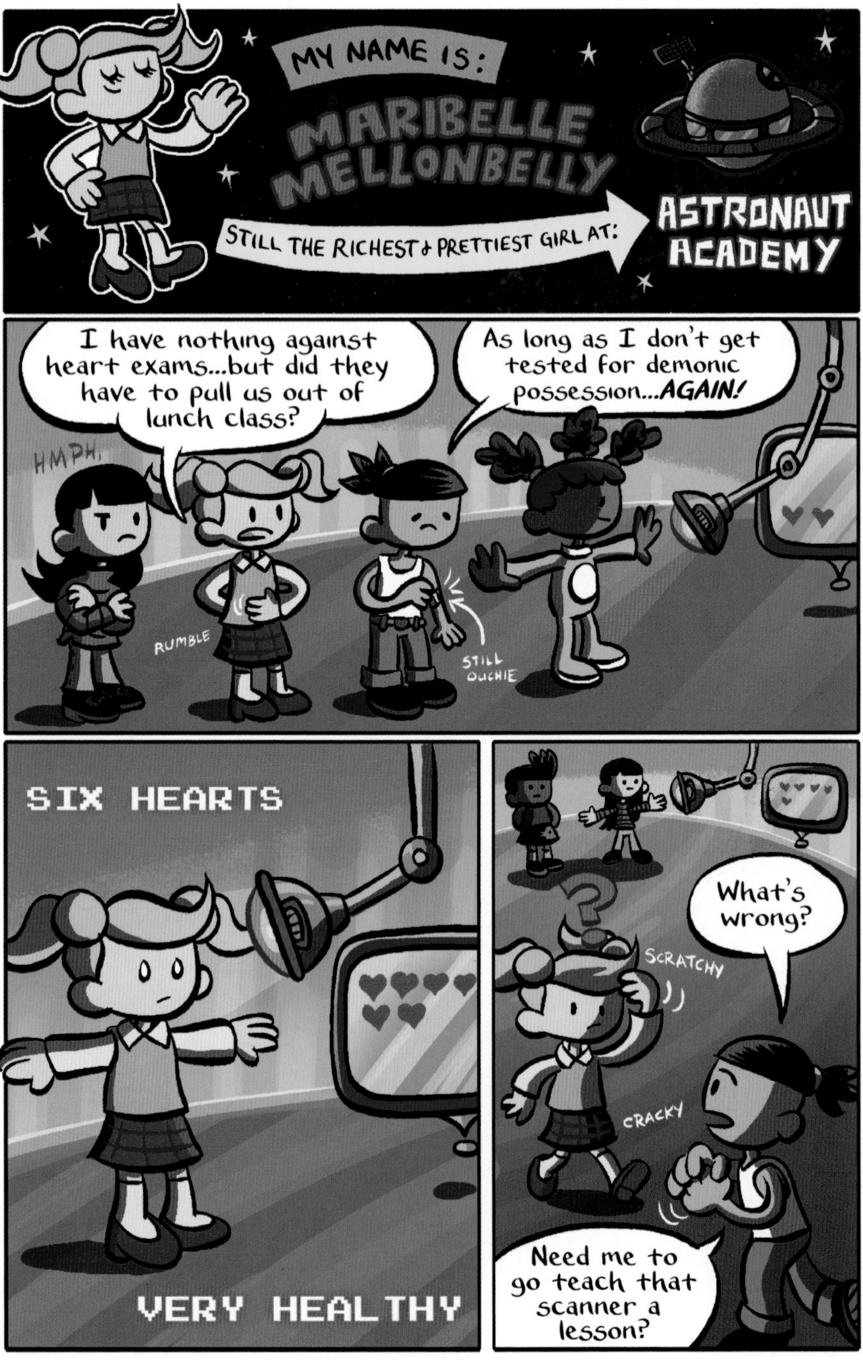
MY NAME IS:
MARIBELLE MELLONBELLY
STILL THE RICHEST & PRETTIEST GIRL AT:
ASTRONAUT ACADEMY
I have nothing against heart exams...but did they have to pull us out of lunch class?
As long as I don't get tested for demonic possession...AGAIN!
HMPH.
RUMBLE
STILL OUCHIE
SIX HEARTS
VERY HEALTHY
What's wrong?
SCRATCHY
CRACKY
Need me to go teach that scanner a lesson?

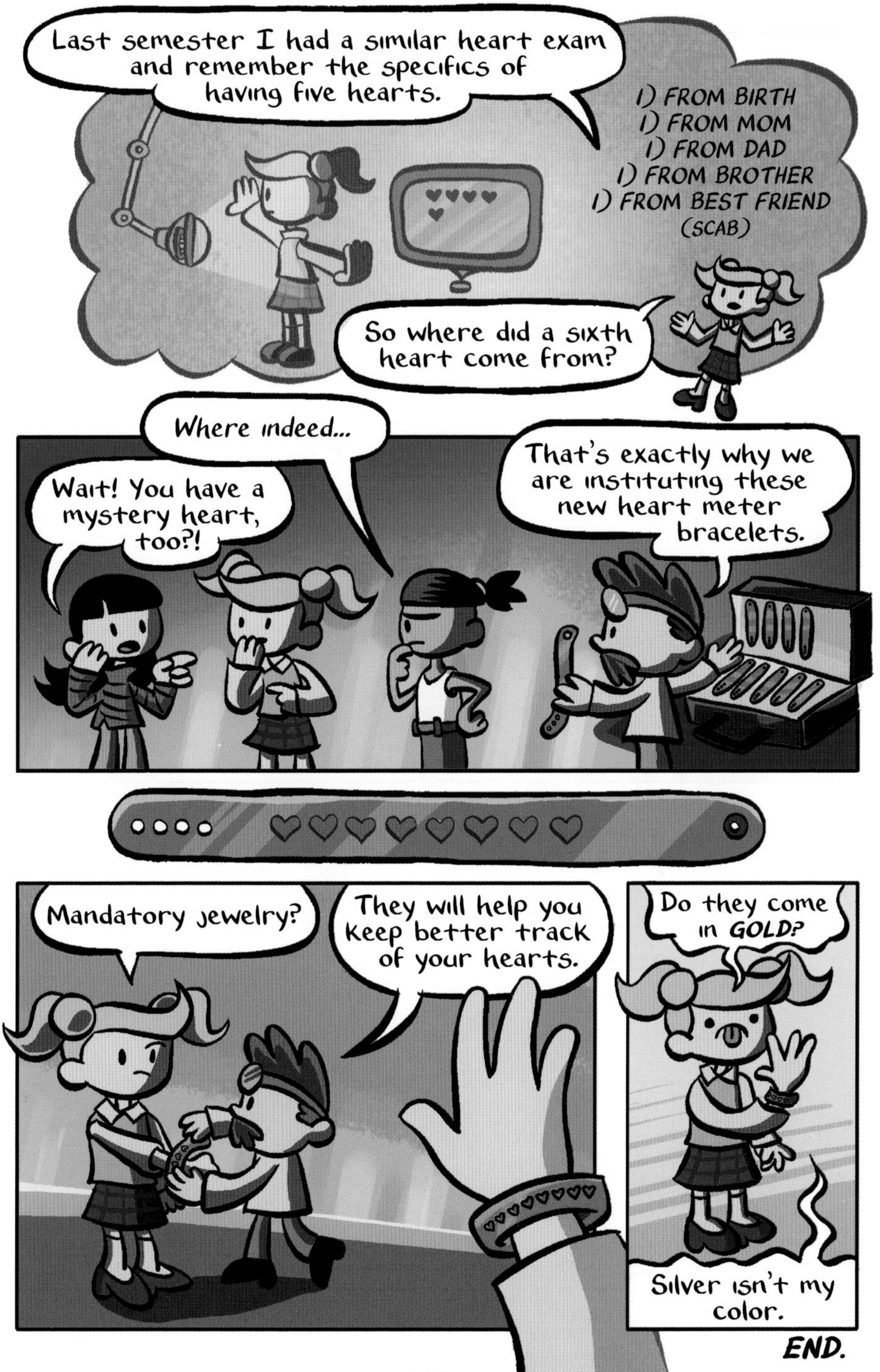
Last semester I had a similar heart exam and remember the specifics of having five hearts.
1) FROM BIRTH
1) FROM MOM
1) FROM DAD
1) FROM BROTHER
1) FROM BEST FRIEND
(SCAB)
So where did a sixth heart come from?
Where indeed...
Wait! You have a mystery heart, too?!
That's exactly why we are instituting these new heart meter bracelets.
Mandatory jewelry?
They will help you keep better track of your hearts.
Do they come in GOLD?
Silver isn't my color.
END.

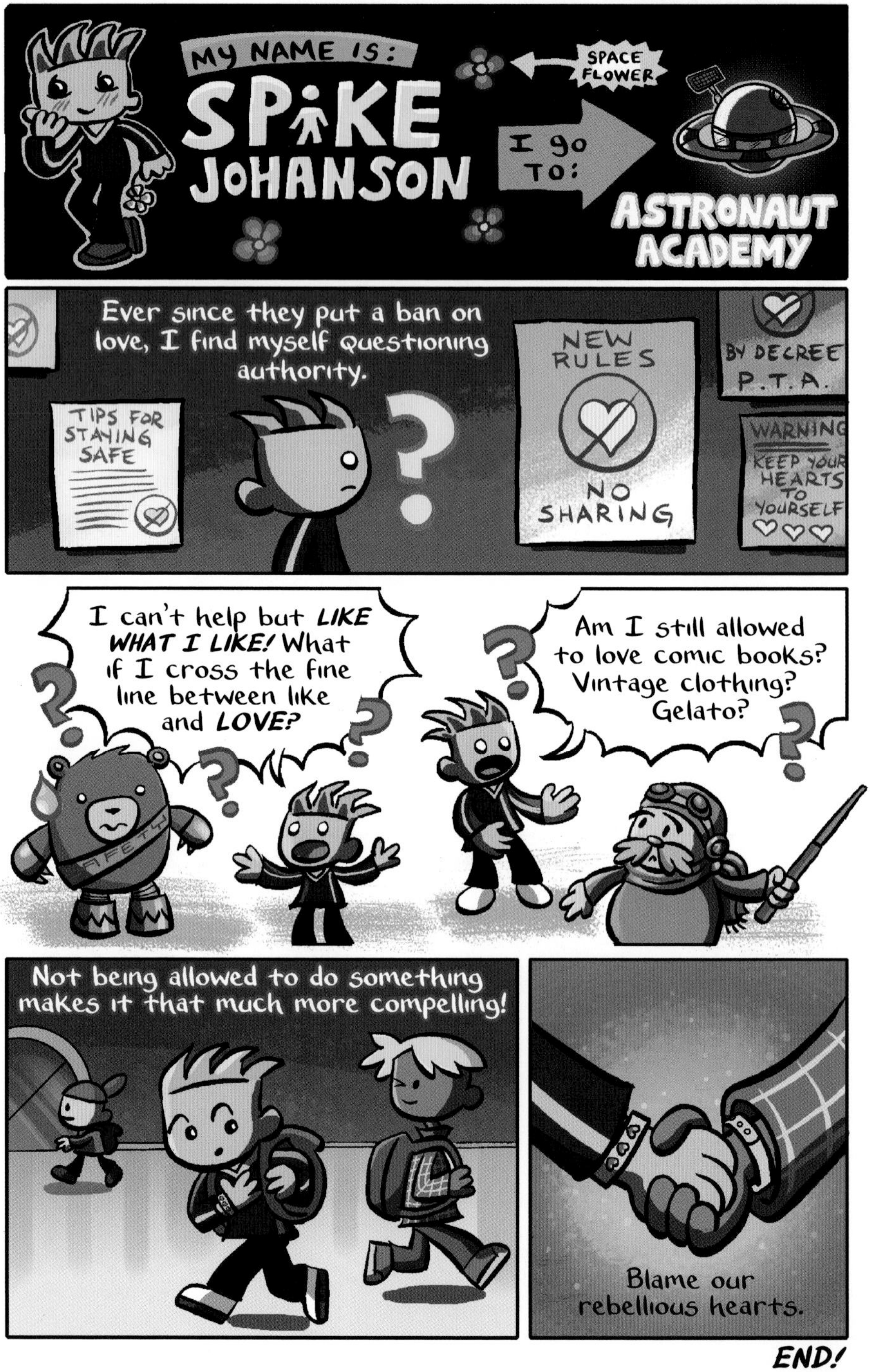
MY NAME IS:
SPIKE JOHANSON
SPACE FLOWER
I go TO:
ASTRONAUT ACADEMY
Ever since they put a ban on love, I find myself questioning authority.
TIPS FOR STAYING SAFE
NEW RULES
NO SHARING
BY DECREE P.T.A.
WARNING
KEEP YOUR HEARTS TO YOURSELF
I can't help but LIKE WHAT I LIKE! What if I cross the fine line between like and LOVE?
Am I still allowed to love comic books? Vintage clothing? Gelato?
Not being allowed to do something makes it that much more compelling!
Blame our rebellious hearts.
END!

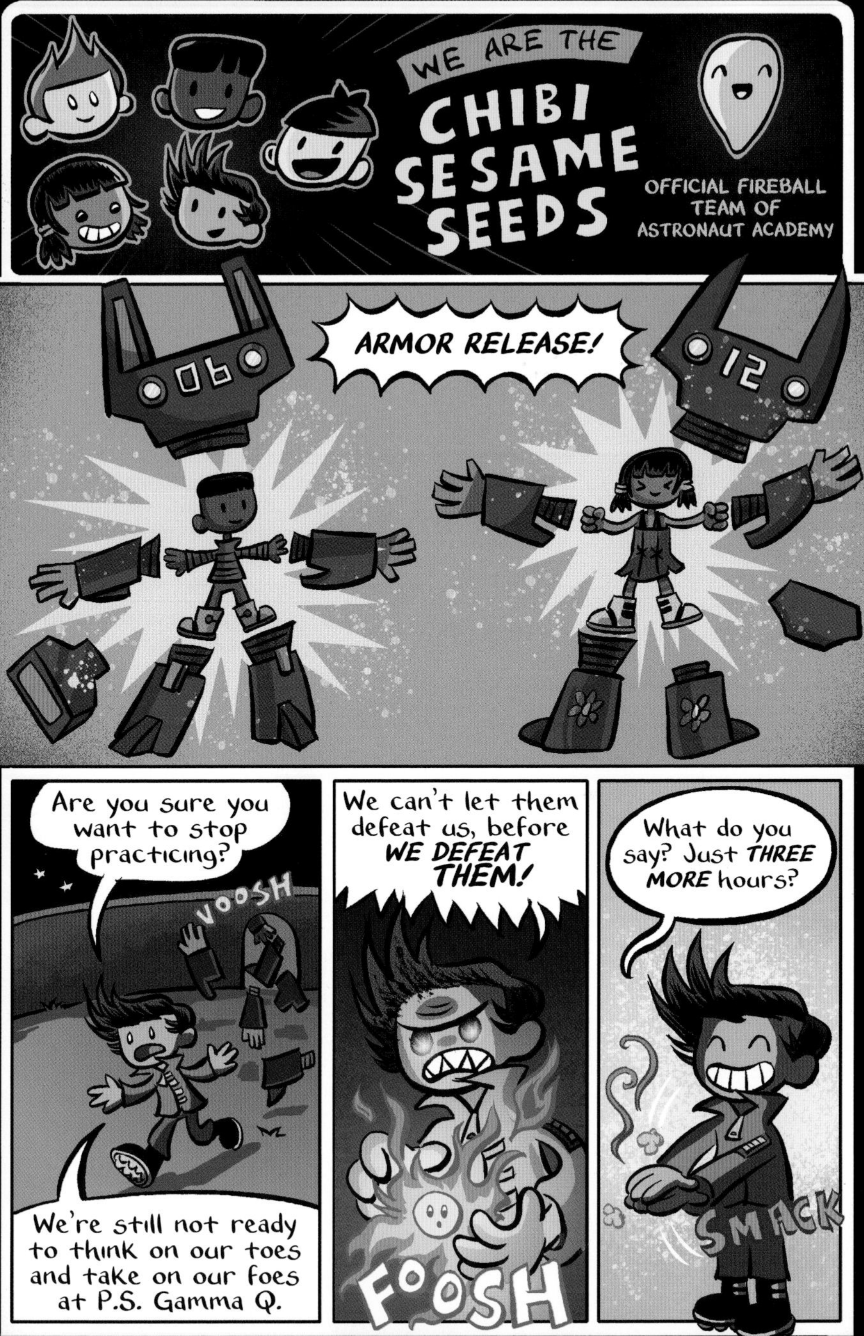

WE ARE THE
CHIBI SESAME SEEDS
OFFICIAL FIREBALL TEAM OF ASTRONAUT ACADEMY
ARMOR RELEASE!
06
12
Are you sure you want to stop practicing?
VOOSH
We're still not ready to think on our toes and take on our foes at P.S. Gamma Q.
We can't let them defeat us, before WE DEFEAT THEM!
FOOSH
What do you say? Just THREE MORE hours?
SMACK

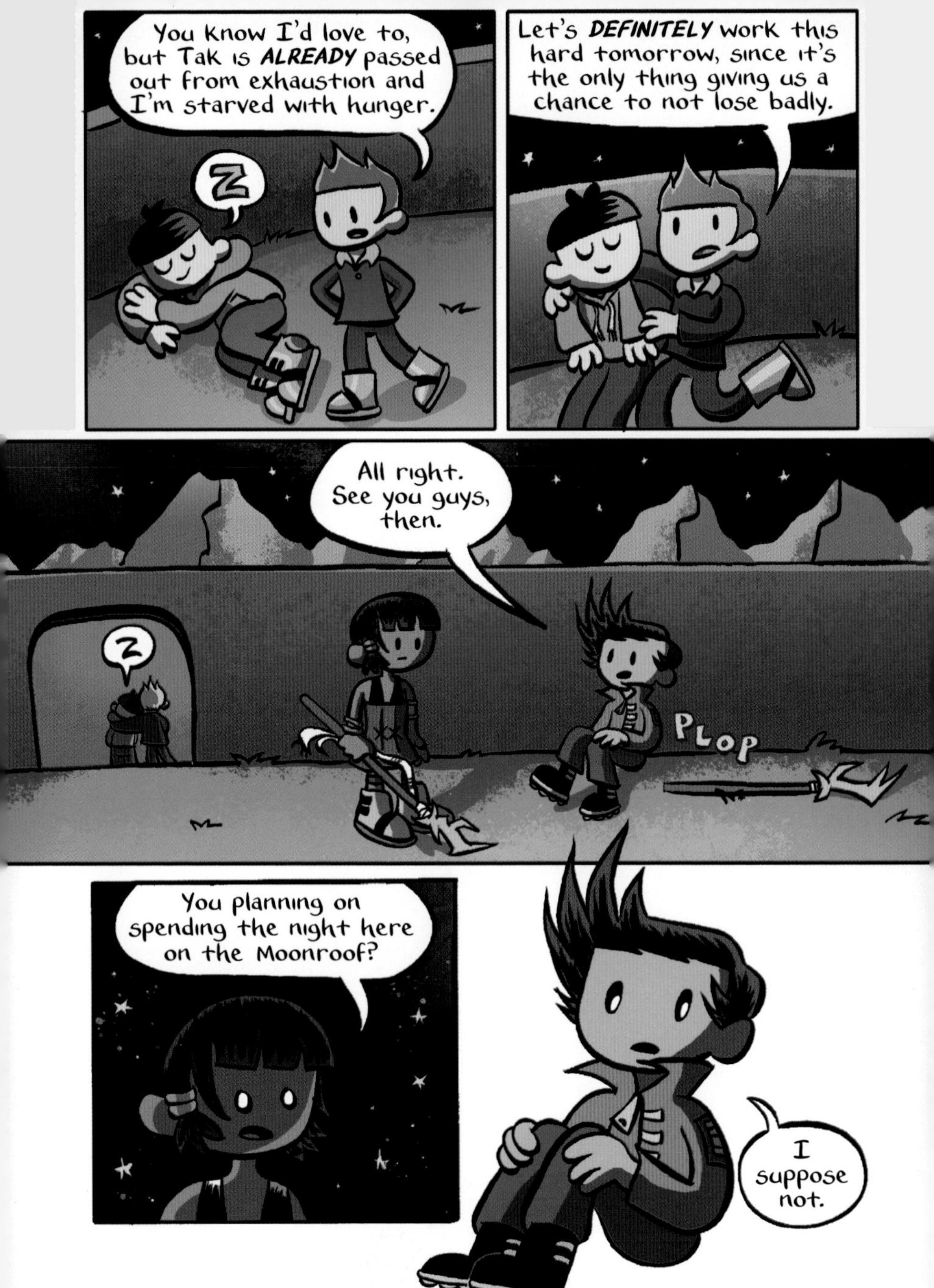
You know I'd love to, but Tak is ALREADY passed out from exhaustion and I'm starved with hunger.
Z
Let's DEFINITELY work this hard tomorrow, since it's the only thing giving us a chance to not lose badly.
All right. See you guys, then.
Z
PLOP
You planning on spending the night here on the Moonroof?
I suppose not.

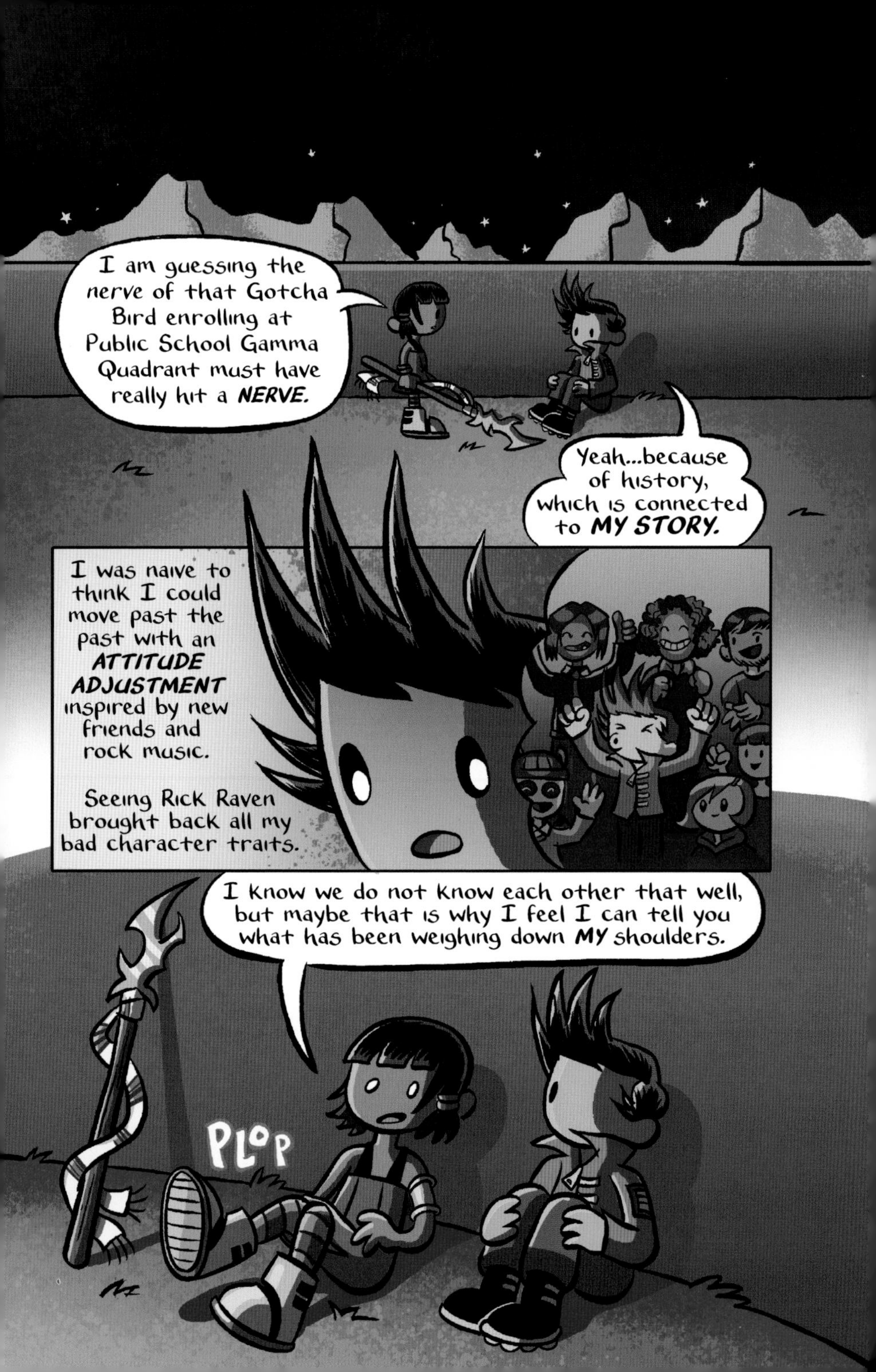

I am guessing the nerve of that Gotcha Bird enrolling at Public School Gamma Quadrant must have really hit a NERVE.
Yeah...because of history, which is connected to MY STORY.
I was naive to think I could move past the past with an ATTITUDE ADJUSTMENT inspired by new friends and rock music.
Seeing Rick Raven brought back all my bad character traits.
I know we do not know each other that well, but maybe that is why I feel I can tell you what has been weighing down MY shoulders.
PLOP

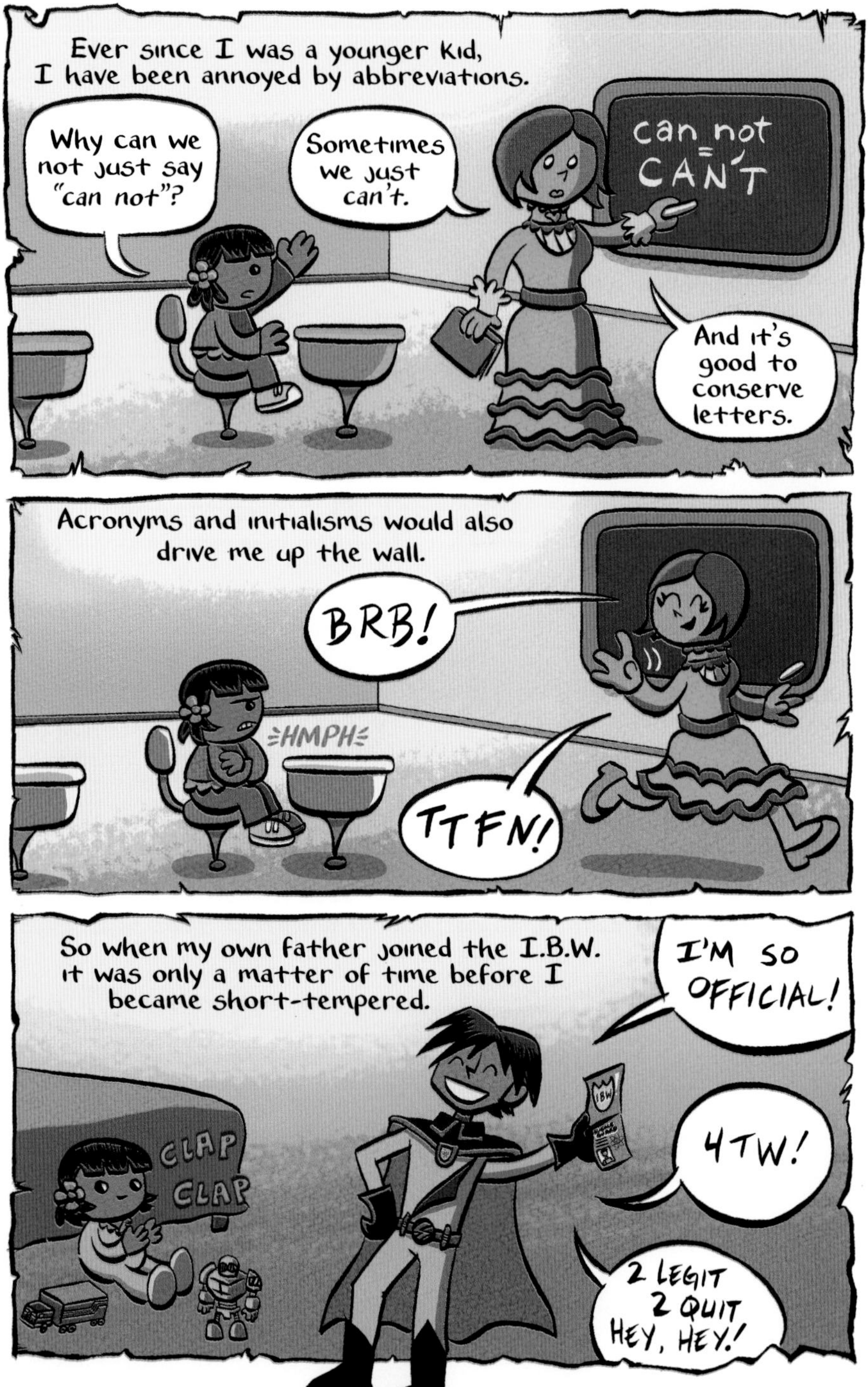
Ever since I was a younger kid, I have been annoyed by abbreviations.
Why can we not just say "can not"?
Sometimes we just can't.
can not = CAN'T
And it's good to conserve letters.
Acronyms and initialisms would also drive me up the wall.
BRB!
HMPH
TTFN!
So when my own father joined the I.B.W. it was only a matter of time before I became short-tempered.
I'M SO OFFICIAL!
CLAP CLAP
4TW!
2 LEGIT 2 QUIT HEY, HEY!

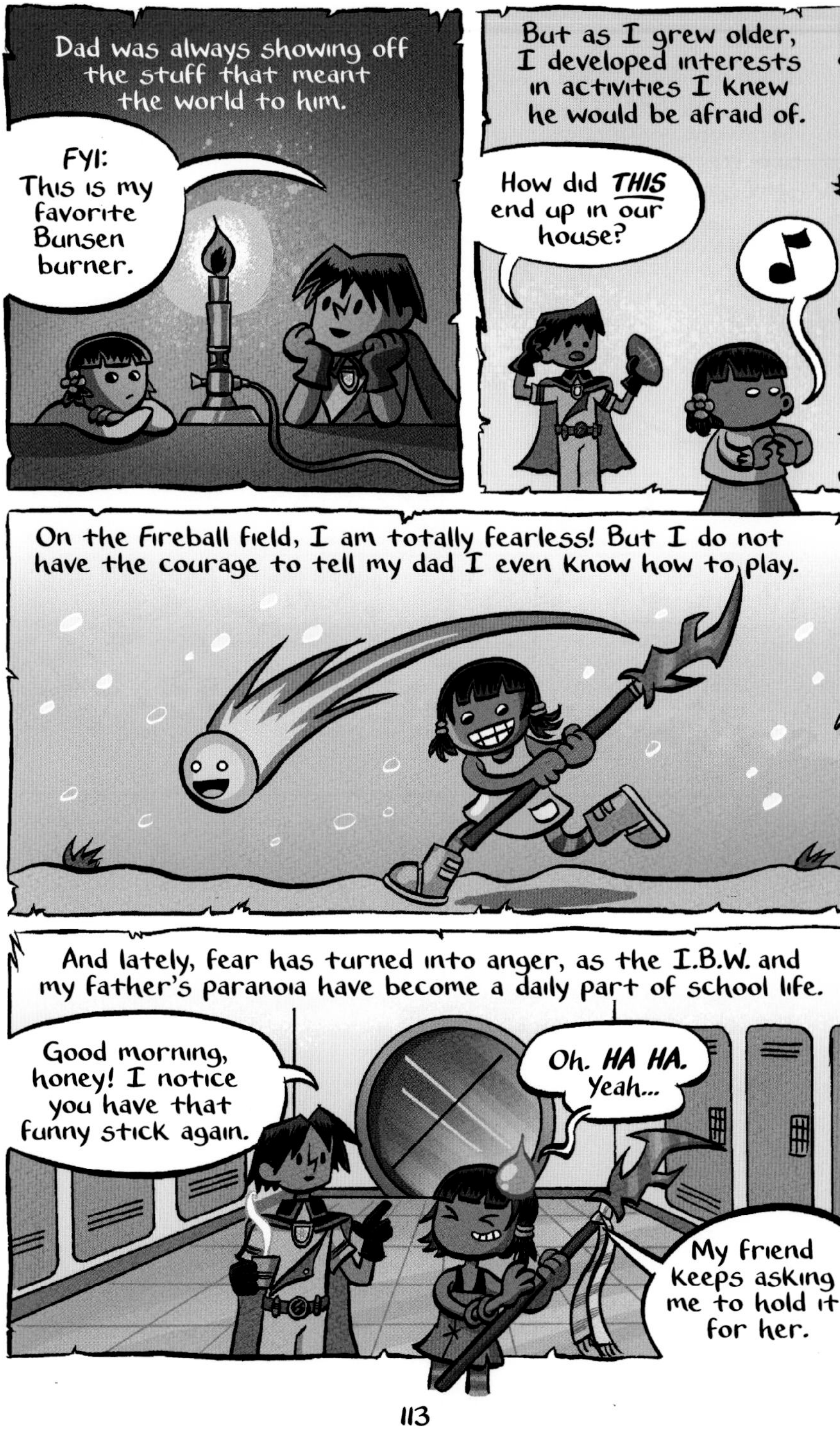
Dad was always showing off the stuff that meant the world to him.
FYI: This is my favorite Bunsen burner.
But as I grew older, I developed interests in activities I knew he would be afraid of.
How did ***THIS*** end up in our house?
On the Fireball field, I am totally fearless! But I do not have the courage to tell my dad I even know how to play.
And lately, fear has turned into anger, as the I.B.W. and my father's paranoia have become a daily part of school life.
Good morning, honey! I notice you have that funny stick again.
Oh. **HA HA.** Yeah...
My friend keeps asking me to hold it for her.

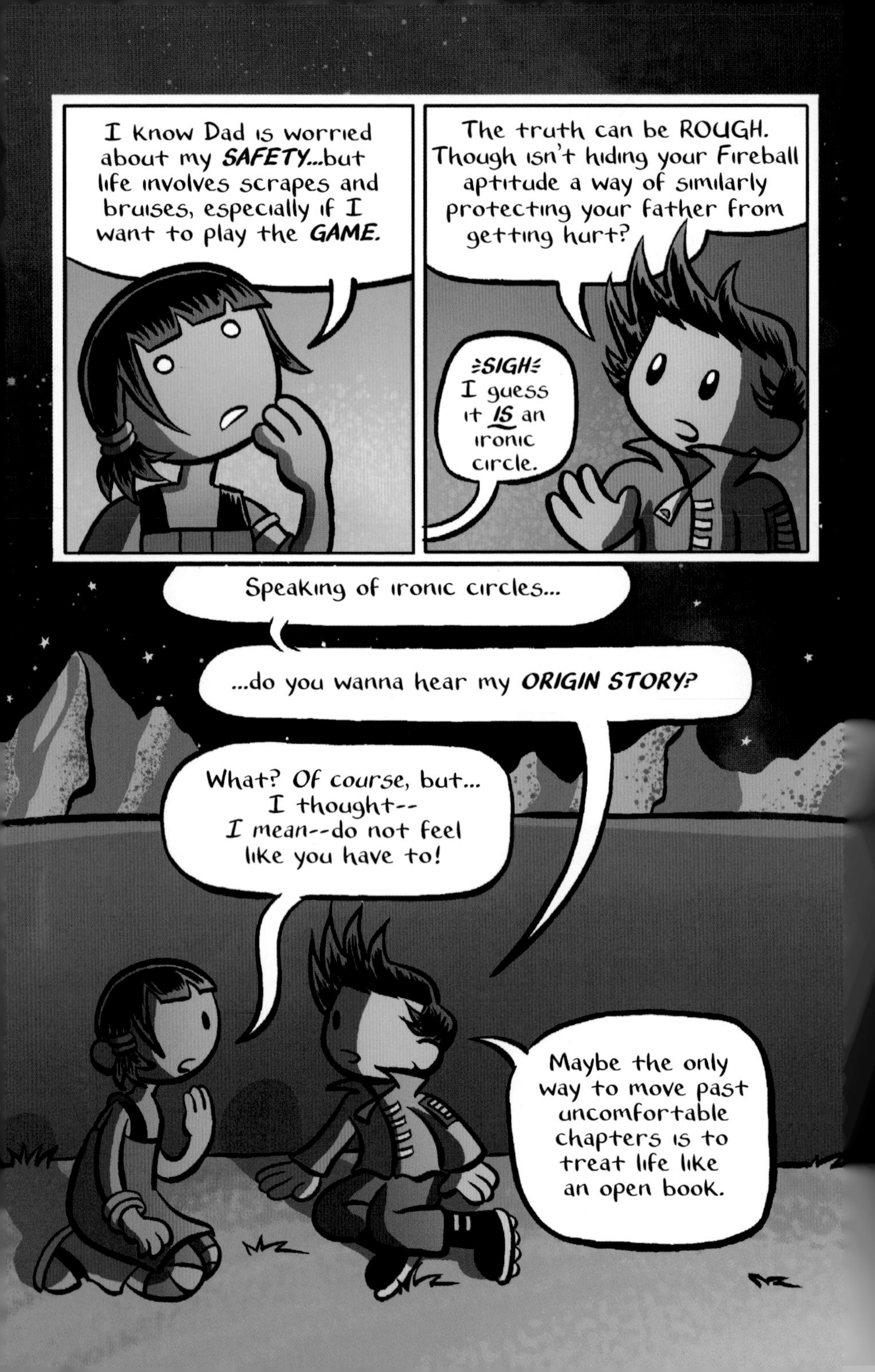
I know Dad is worried about my SAFETY...but life involves scrapes and bruises, especially if I want to play the GAME.
The truth can be ROUGH. Though isn't hiding your Fireball aptitude a way of similarly protecting your father from getting hurt?
SIGH I guess it IS an ironic circle.
Speaking of ironic circles...
...do you wanna hear my ORIGIN STORY?
What? Of course, but... I thought-- I mean--do not feel like you have to!
Maybe the only way to move past uncomfortable chapters is to treat life like an open book.

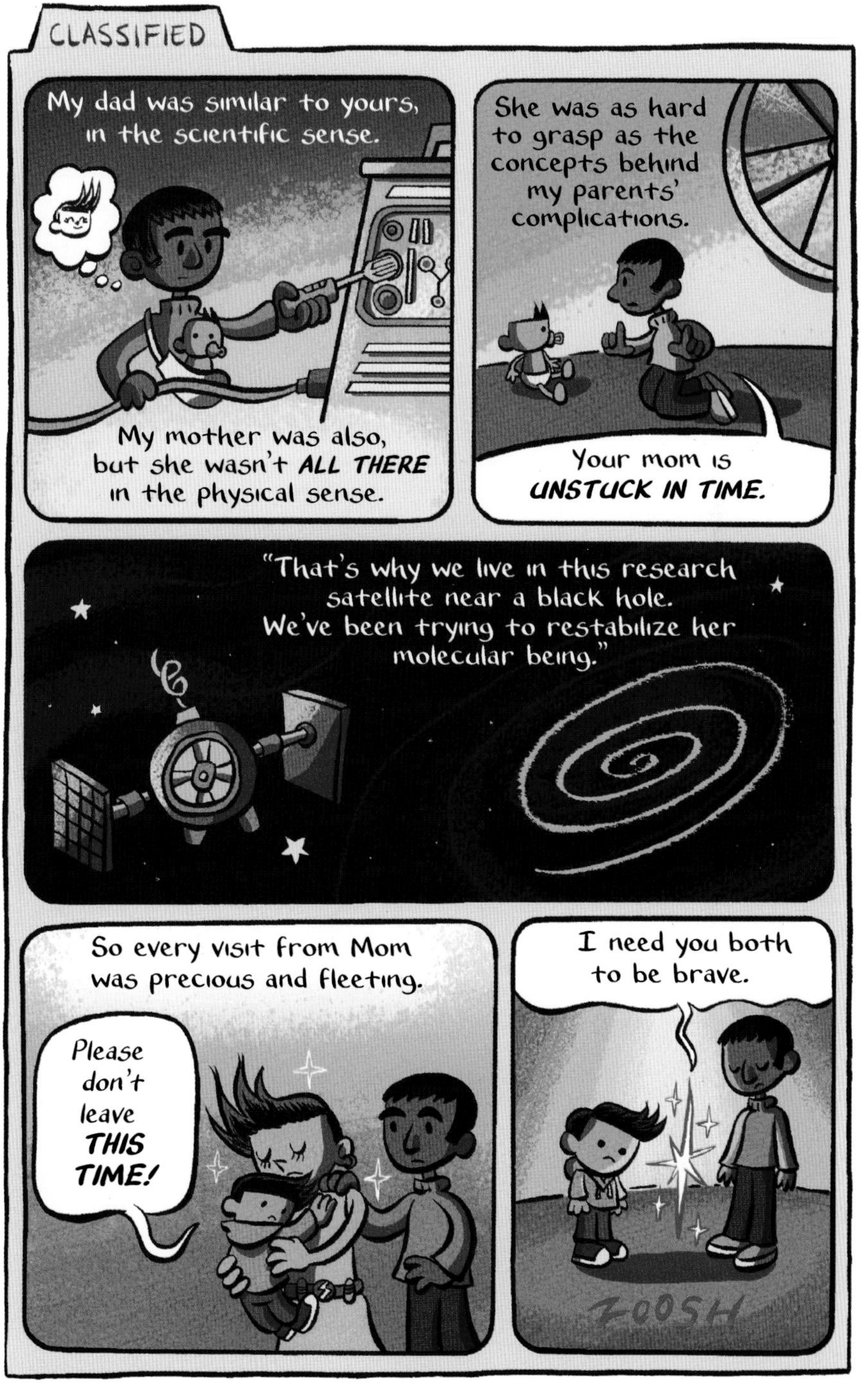
CLASSIFIED
My dad was similar to yours, in the scientific sense.
My mother was also, but she wasn't ALL THERE in the physical sense.
She was as hard to grasp as the concepts behind my parents' complications.
Your mom is UNSTUCK IN TIME.
"That's why we live in this research satellite near a black hole. We've been trying to restabilize her molecular being."
So every visit from Mom was precious and fleeting.
Please don't leave THIS TIME!
I need you both to be brave.
ZOOSH

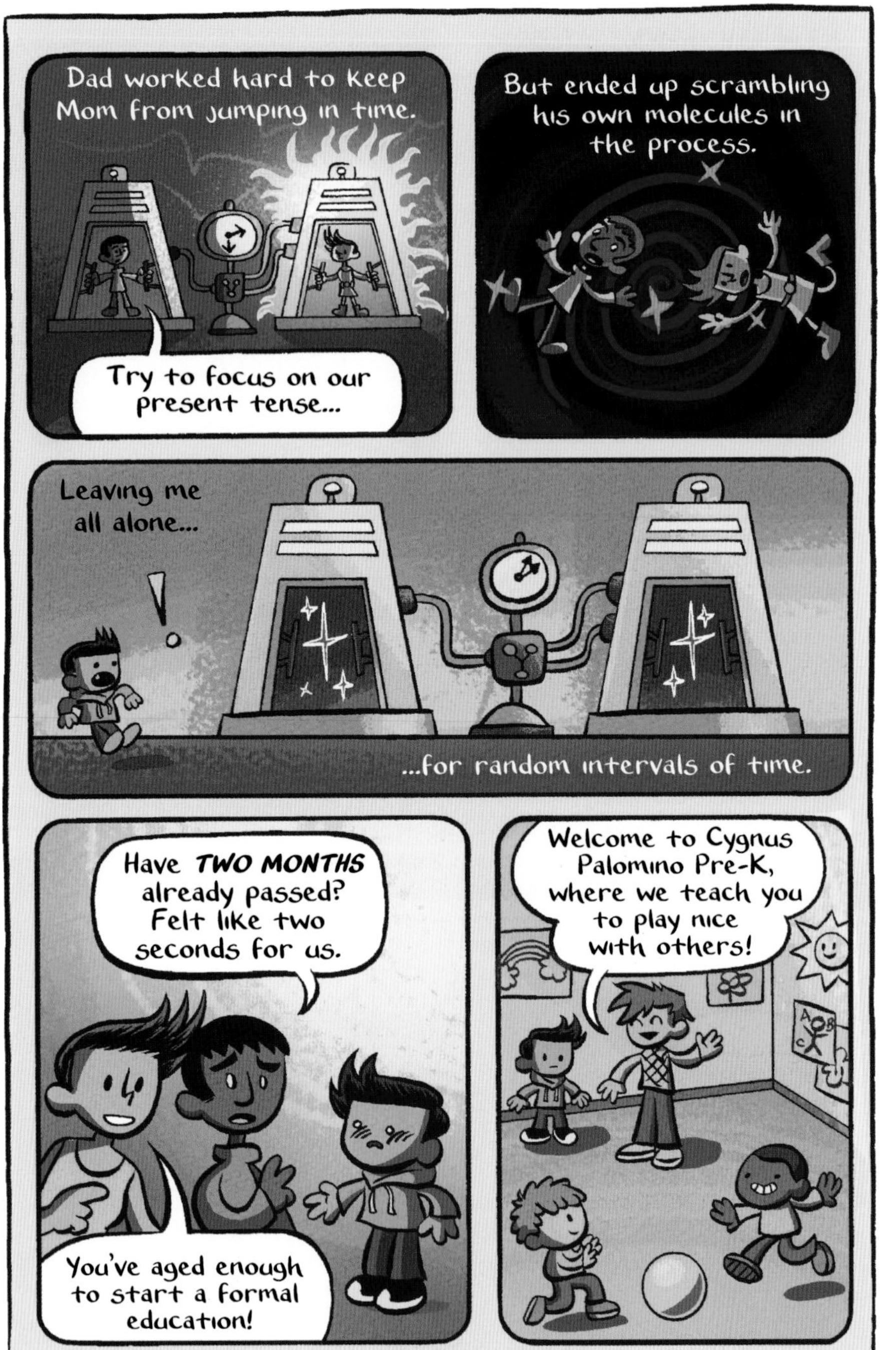
Dad worked hard to keep Mom from jumping in time.
Try to focus on our present tense...
But ended up scrambling his own molecules in the process.
Leaving me all alone...
!
...for random intervals of time.
Have **TWO MONTHS** already passed? Felt like two seconds for us.
You've aged enough to start a formal education!
Welcome to Cygnus Palomino Pre-K, where we teach you to play nice with others!

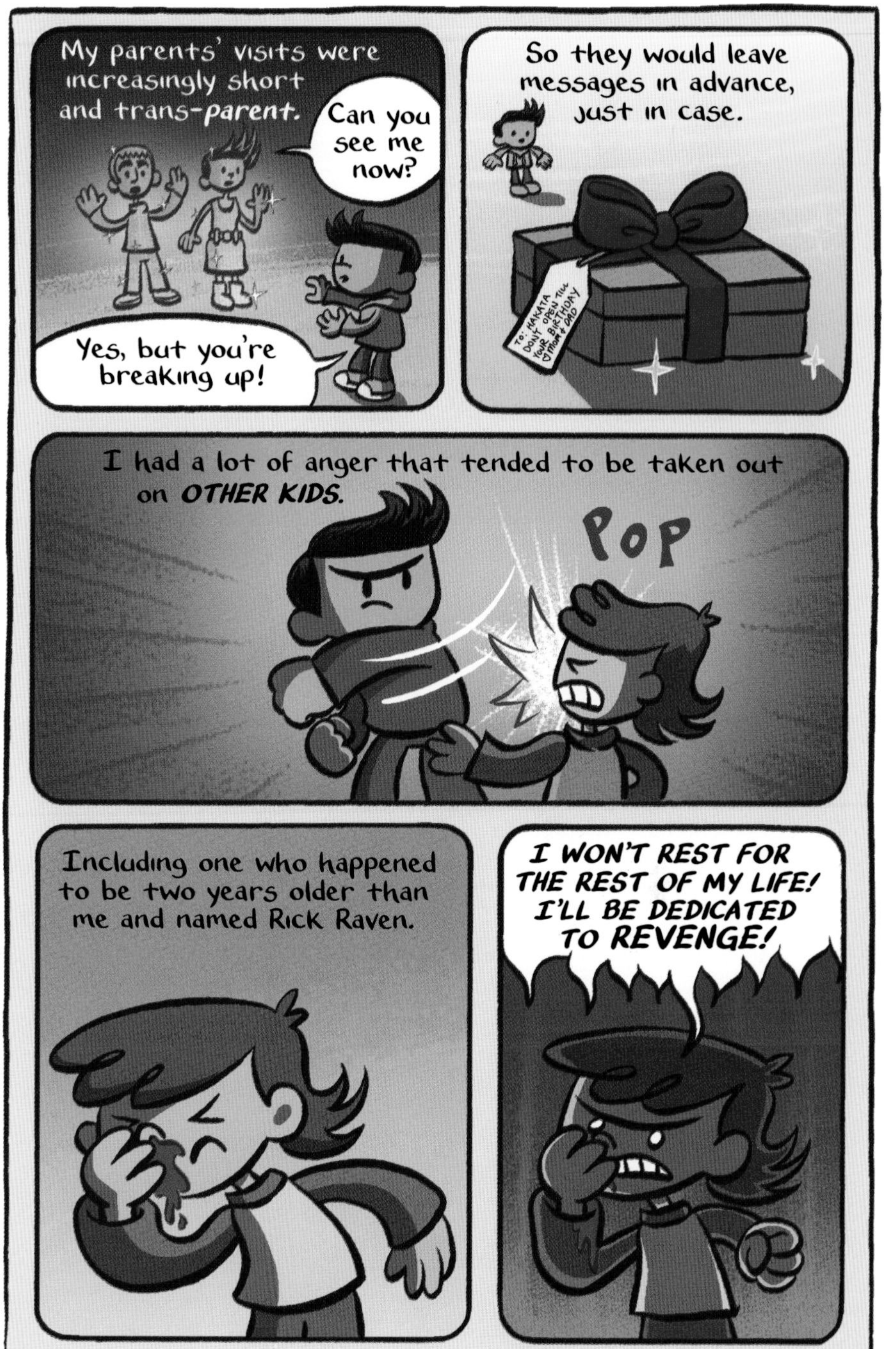
My parents' visits were increasingly short and trans-*parent*.
Can you see me now?
Yes, but you're breaking up!
So they would leave messages in advance, just in case.
TO: HAKATA DON'T OPEN TILL YOUR BIRTHDAY MOM & DAD
I had a lot of anger that tended to be taken out on *OTHER KIDS*.
POP
Including one who happened to be two years older than me and named Rick Raven.
I WON'T REST FOR THE REST OF MY LIFE! I'LL BE DEDICATED TO REVENGE!

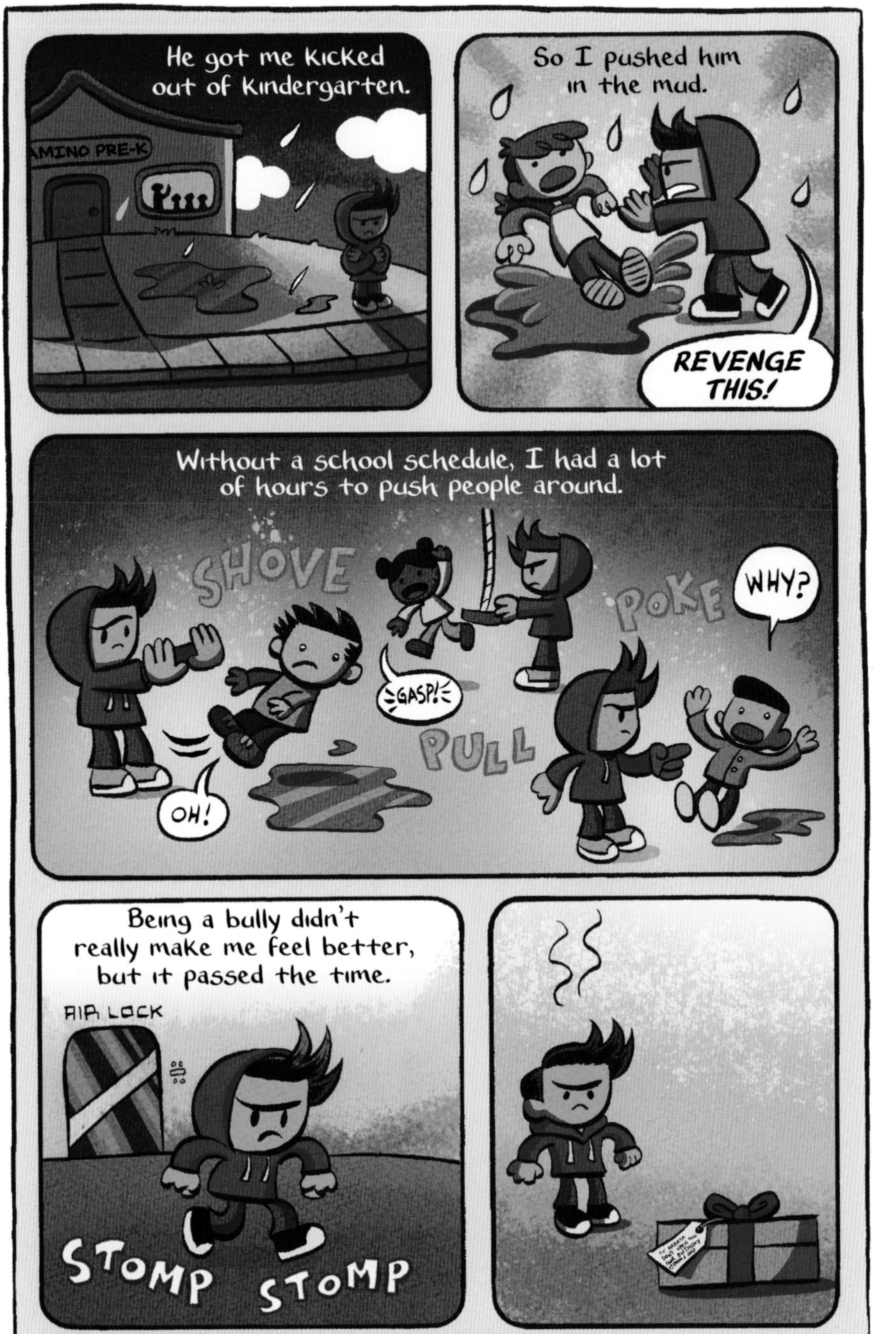
He got me kicked out of kindergarten.
AMINO PRE-K
So I pushed him in the mud.
REVENGE THIS!
Without a school schedule, I had a lot of hours to push people around.
SHOVE
OH!
GASP!
POKE
WHY?
PULL
Being a bully didn't really make me feel better, but it passed the time.
AIR LOCK
STOMP STOMP

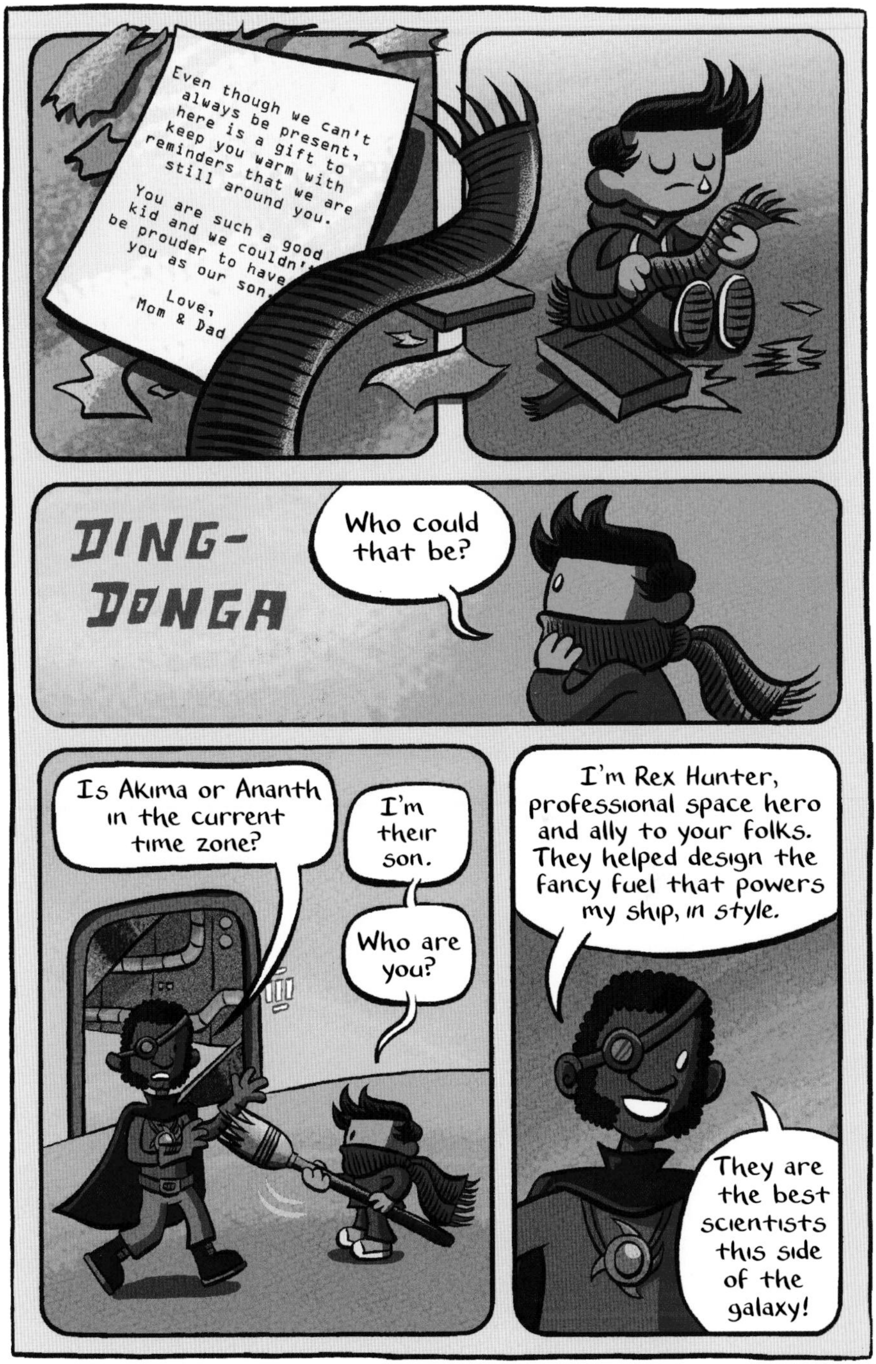

Even though we can't always be present, here is a gift to keep you warm with reminders that we are still around you.
You are such a good kid and we couldn't be prouder to have you as our son.
Love,
Mom & Dad
DING-DONGA
Who could that be?
Is Akima or Ananth in the current time zone?
I'm their son.
Who are you?
I'm Rex Hunter, professional space hero and ally to your folks. They helped design the fancy fuel that powers my ship, in *style.*
They are the best scientists this side of the galaxy!

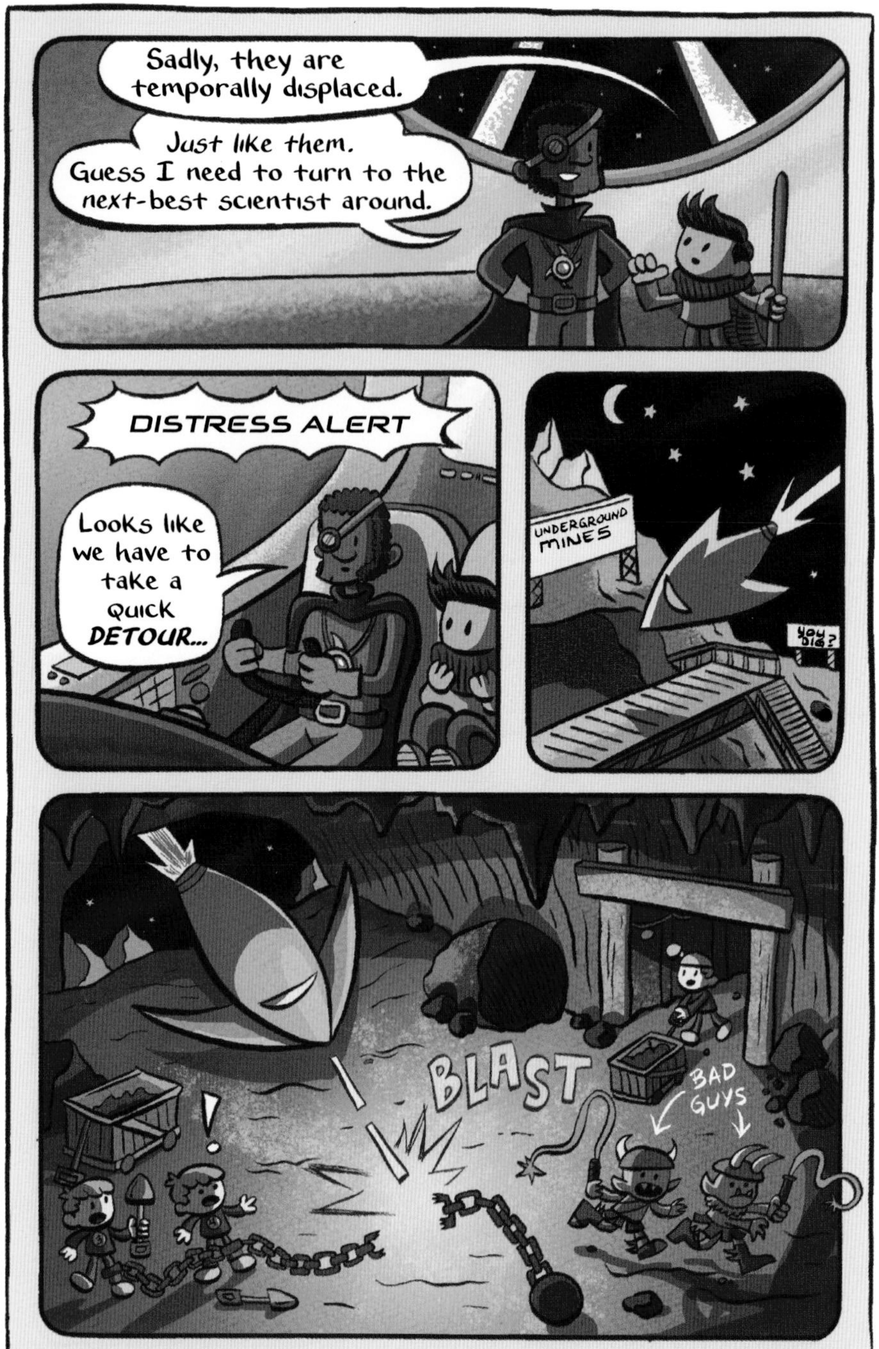
Sadly, they are temporally displaced.
Just like them. Guess I need to turn to the next-best scientist around.
DISTRESS ALERT
Looks like we have to take a quick DETOUR...
UNDERGROUND MINES
YOU DIG?
BLAST
BAD GUYS
!

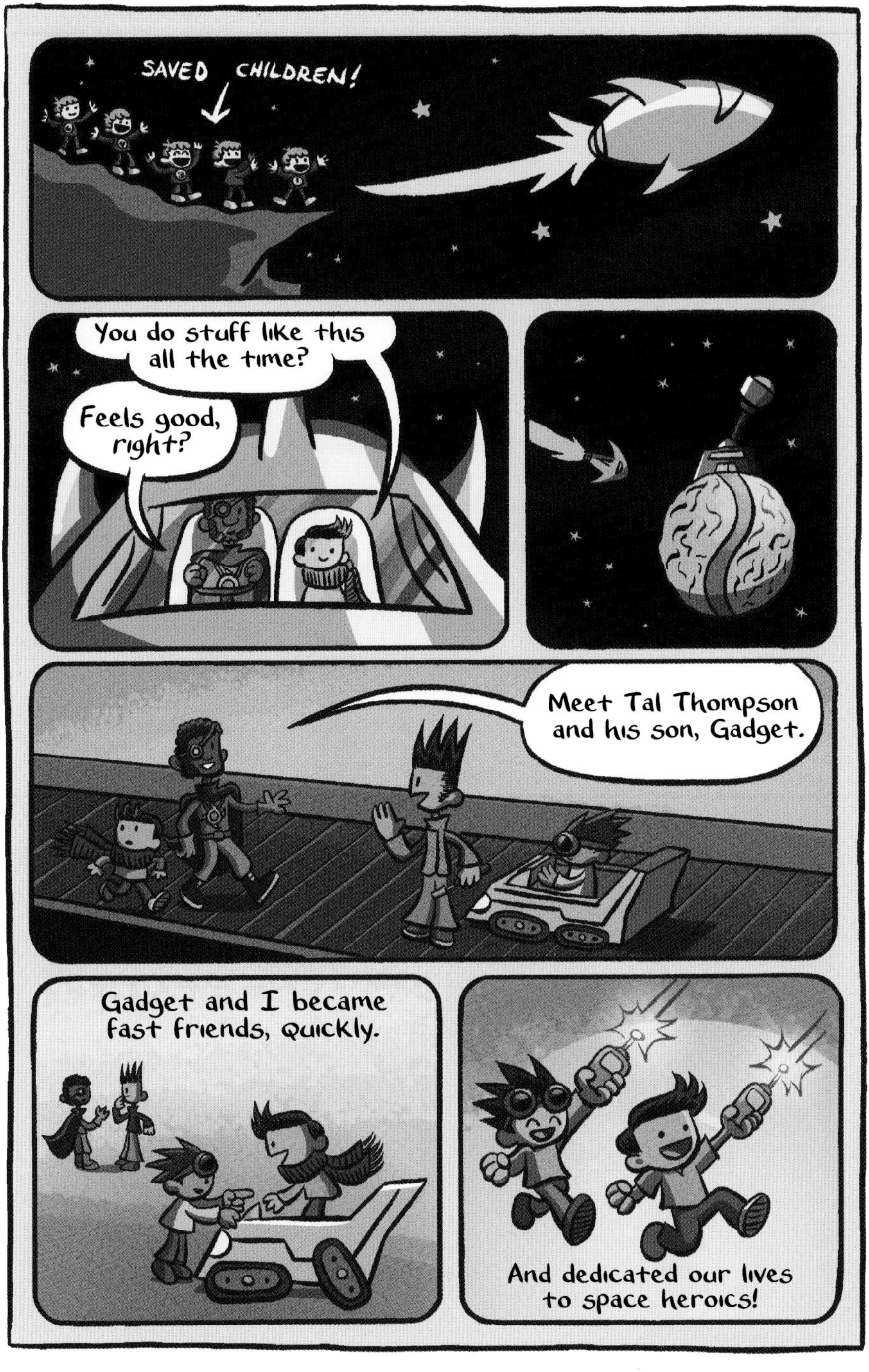
SAVED CHILDREN!
You do stuff like this all the time?
Feels good, right?
Meet Tal Thompson and his son, Gadget.
Gadget and I became fast friends, quickly.
And dedicated our lives to space heroics!

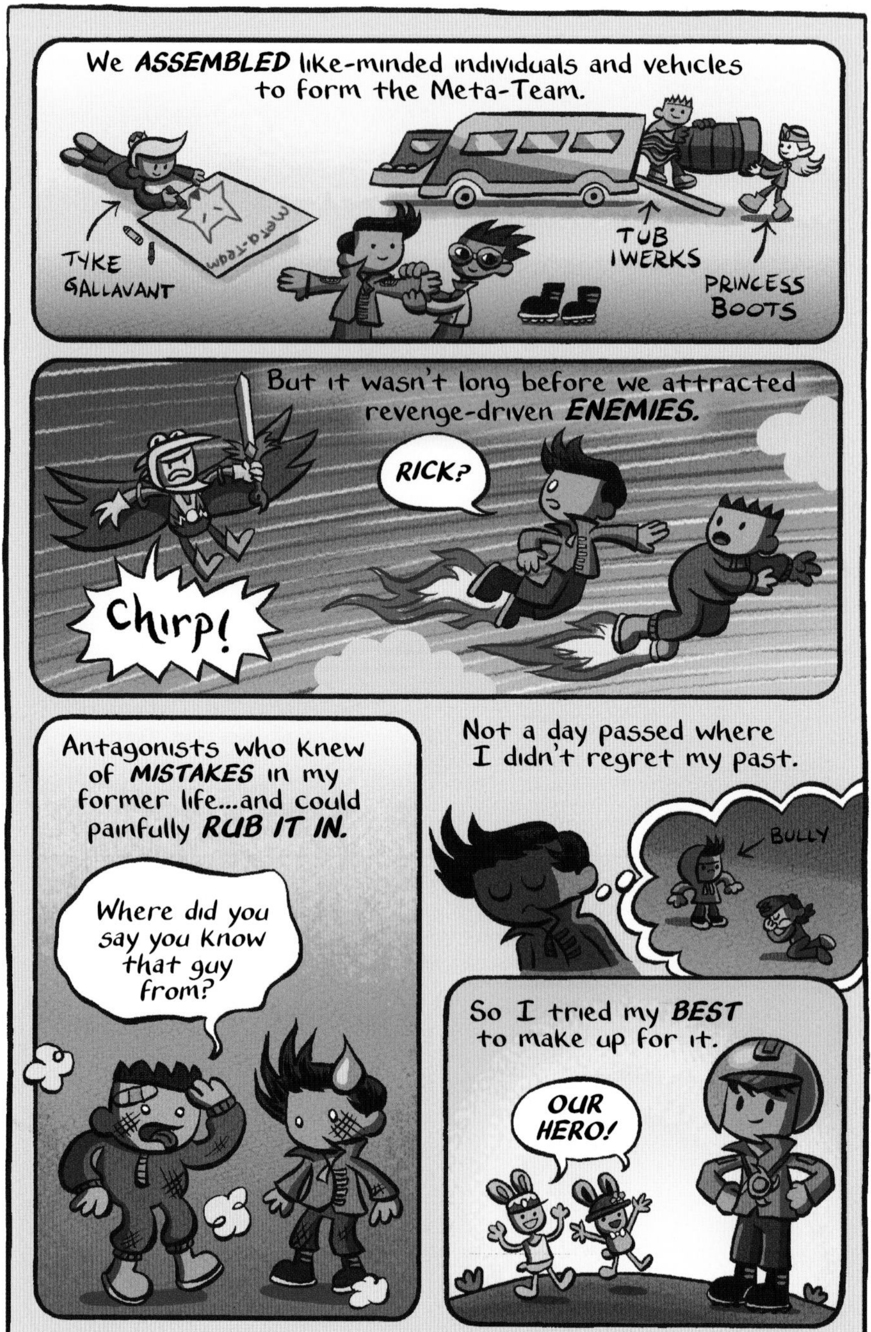
We ASSEMBLED like-minded individuals and vehicles to form the Meta-Team.
TYKE GALLAVANT
META-TEAM
TUB IWERKS
PRINCESS BOOTS
But it wasn't long before we attracted revenge-driven ENEMIES.
RICK?
Chirp!
Antagonists who knew of MISTAKES in my former life...and could painfully RUB IT IN.
Where did you say you know that guy from?
Not a day passed where I didn't regret my past.
BULLY
So I tried my BEST to make up for it.
OUR HERO!

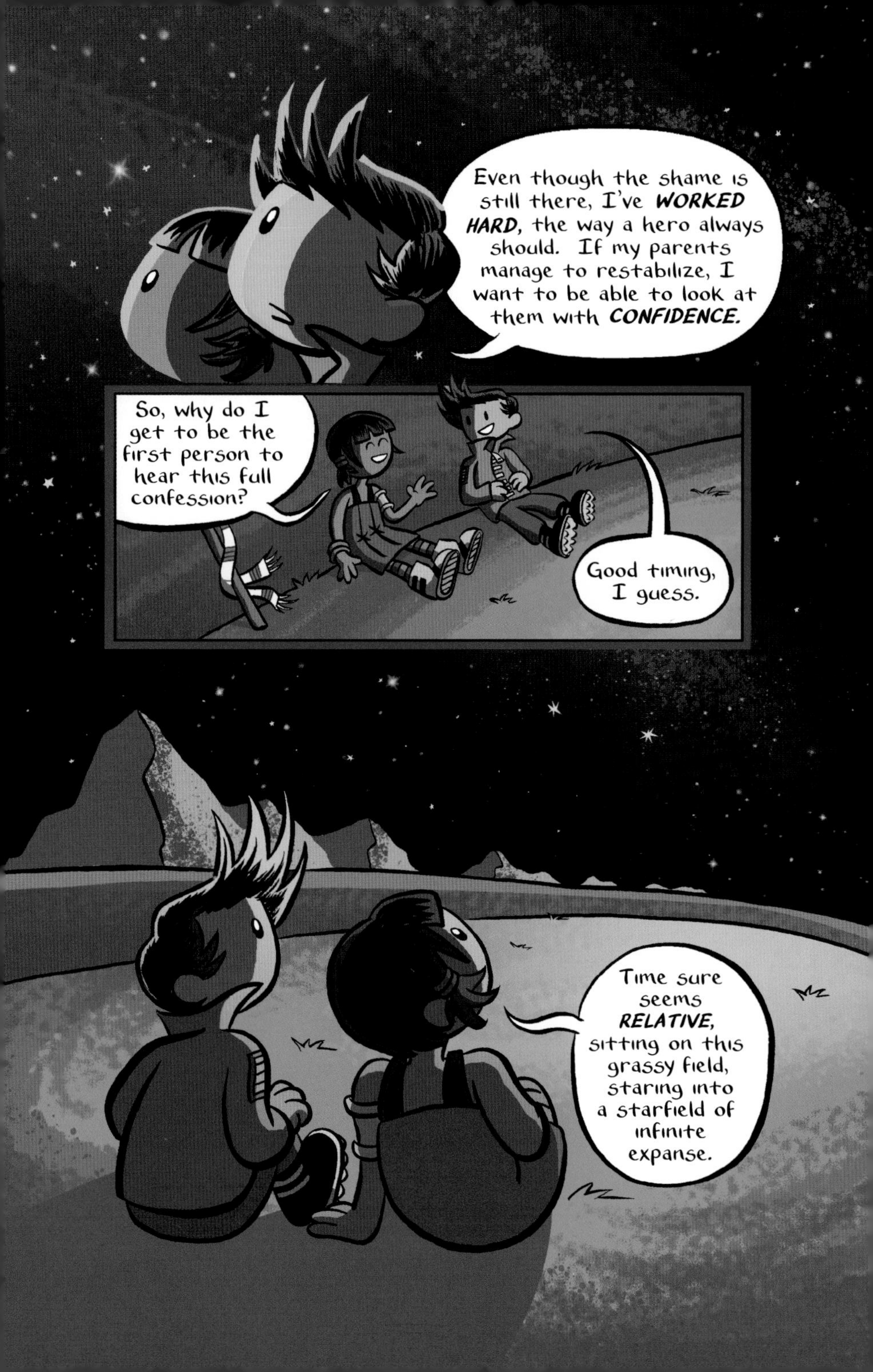
Even though the shame is still there, I've **WORKED HARD,** the way a hero always should. If my parents manage to restabilize, I want to be able to look at them with **CONFIDENCE.**
So, why do I get to be the first person to hear this full confession?
Good timing, I guess.
Time sure seems **RELATIVE,** sitting on this grassy field, staring into a starfield of infinite expanse.

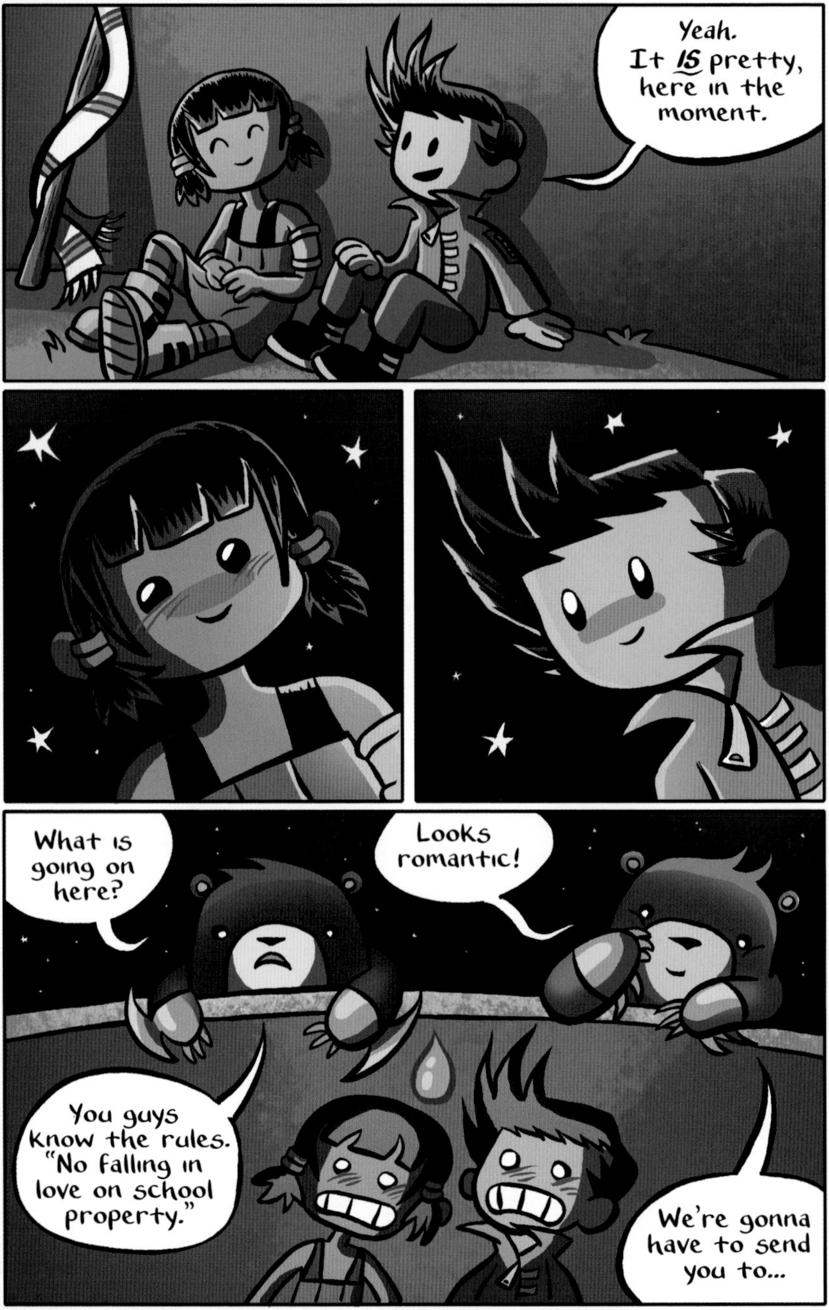

Yeah. It IS pretty, here in the moment.
What is going on here?
Looks romantic!
You guys know the rules. "No falling in love on school property."
We're gonna have to send you to...

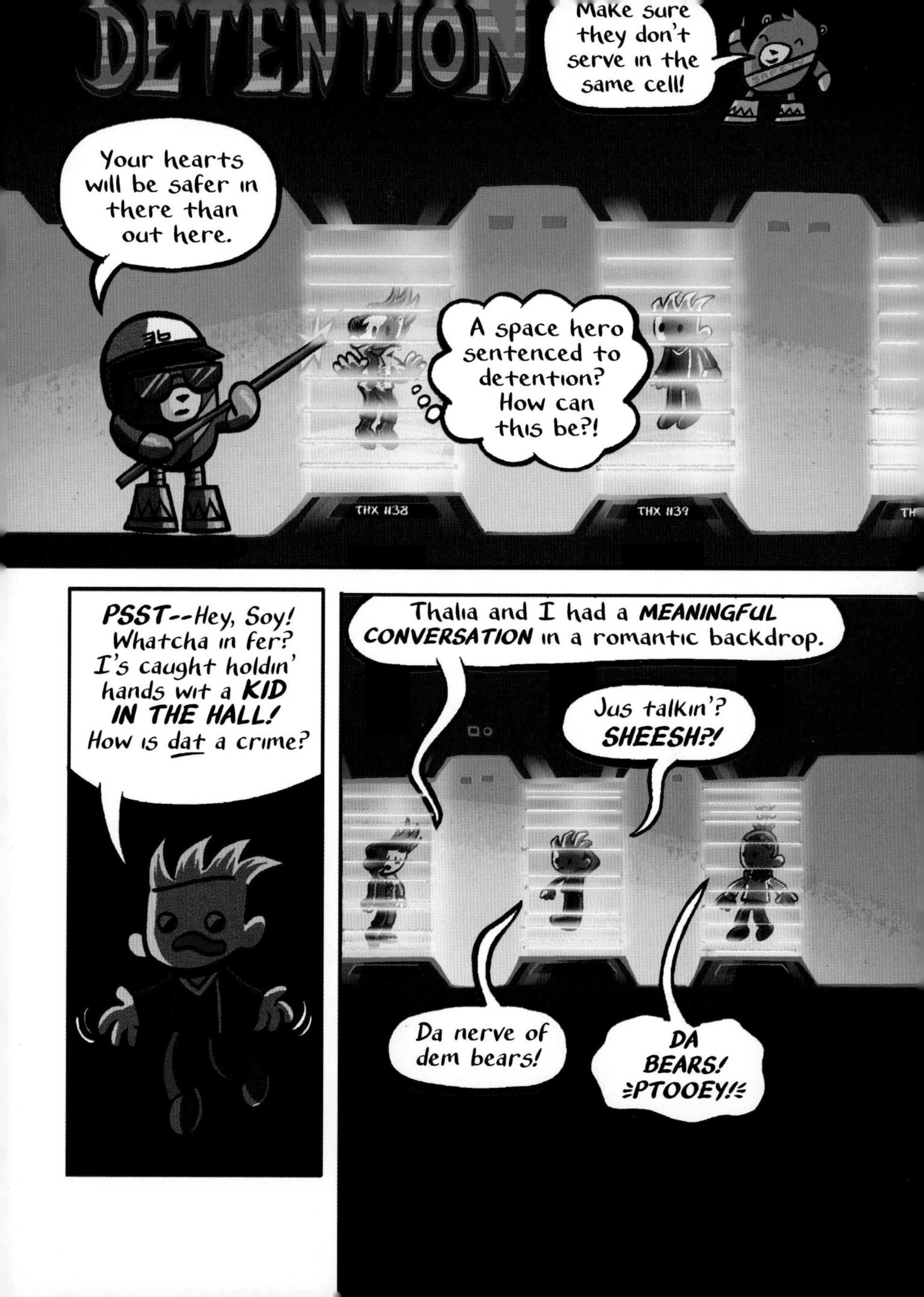
DETENTION
Make sure they don't serve in the same cell!
Your hearts will be safer in there than out here.
A space hero sentenced to detention? How can this be?!
THX 1138
THX 1139
PSST--Hey, Soy! Whatcha in fer? I's caught holdin' hands wit a KID IN THE HALL! How is dat a crime?
Thalia and I had a MEANINGFUL CONVERSATION in a romantic backdrop.
Jus talkin'? SHEESH?!
Da nerve of dem bears!
DA BEARS! PTOOEY!

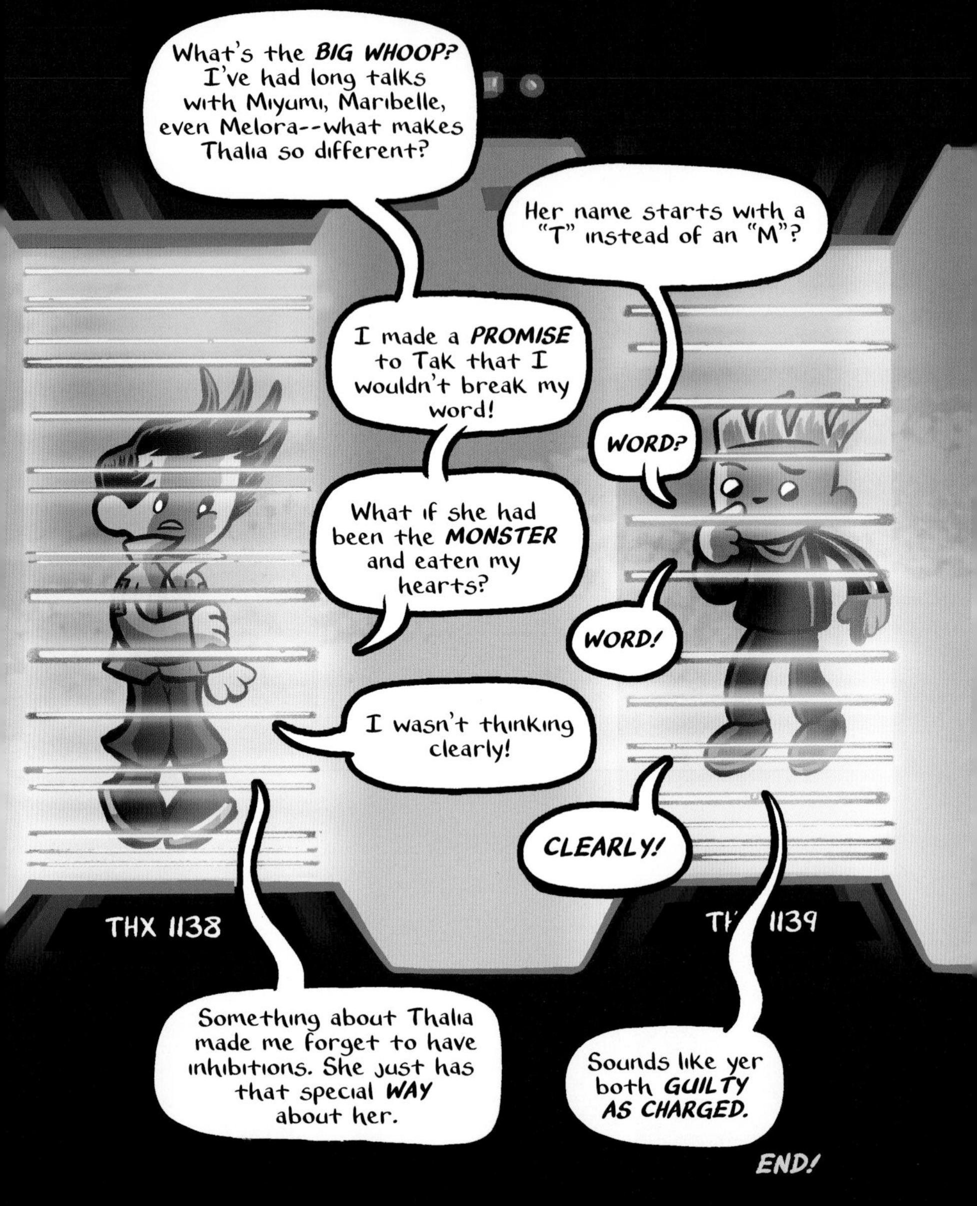
What's the BIG WHOOP? I've had long talks with Miyumi, Maribelle, even Melora--what makes Thalia so different?
Her name starts with a "T" instead of an "M"?
I made a PROMISE to Tak that I wouldn't break my word!
WORD?
What if she had been the MONSTER and eaten my hearts?
WORD!
I wasn't thinking clearly!
CLEARLY!
THX 1138
1139
Something about Thalia made me forget to have inhibitions. She just has that special WAY about her.
Sounds like yer both GUILTY AS CHARGED.
END!

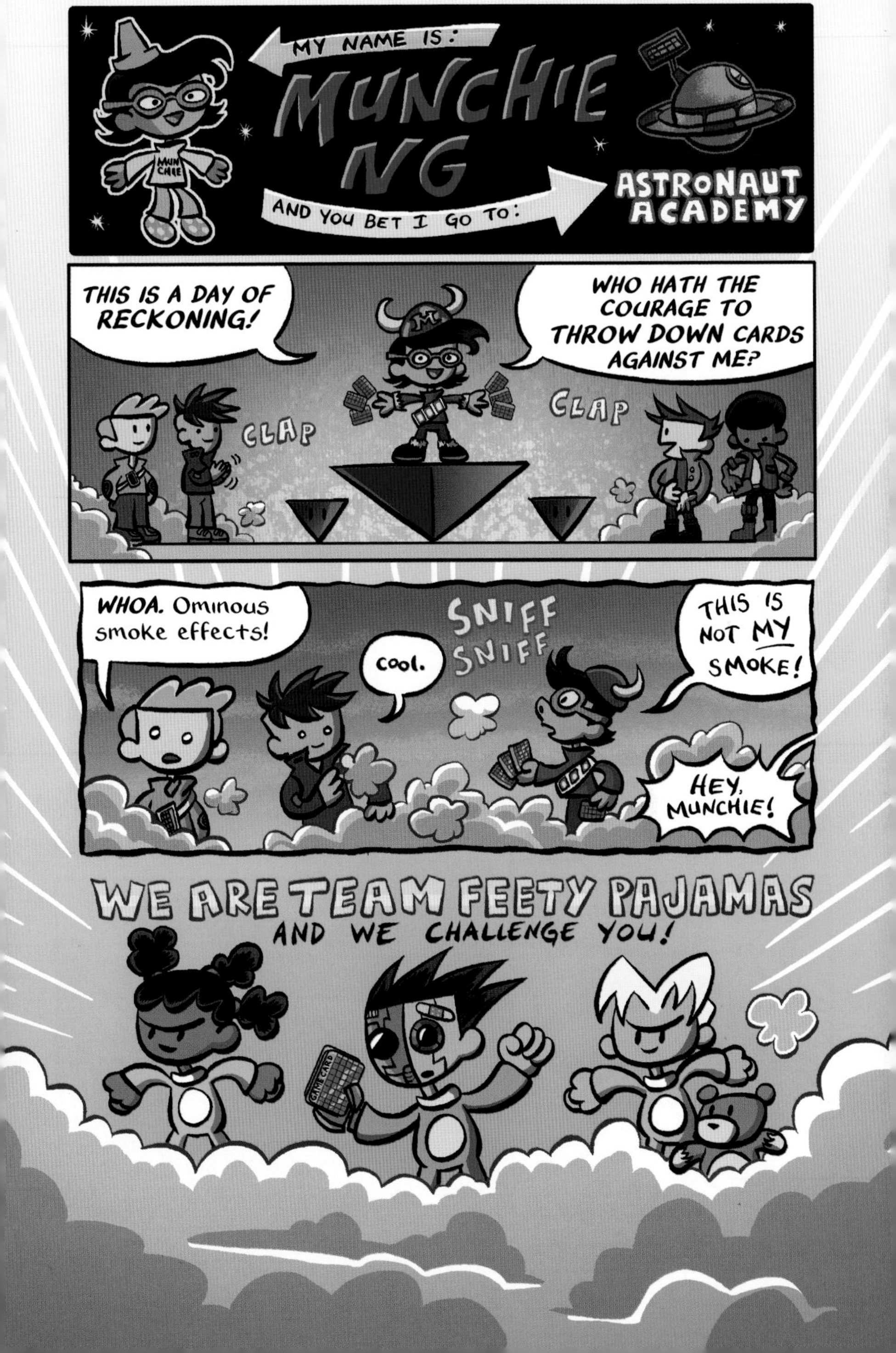
MY NAME IS:
MUNCHIE NG
AND YOU BET I GO TO:
ASTRONAUT ACADEMY
MUN CHIE
THIS IS A DAY OF RECKONING!
WHO HATH THE COURAGE TO THROW DOWN CARDS AGAINST ME?
CLAP
CLAP
WHOA. Ominous smoke effects!
cool.
SNIFF SNIFF
THIS IS NOT MY SMOKE!
HEY, MUNCHIE!
WE ARE TEAM FEETY PAJAMAS
AND WE CHALLENGE YOU!
GAME CARD

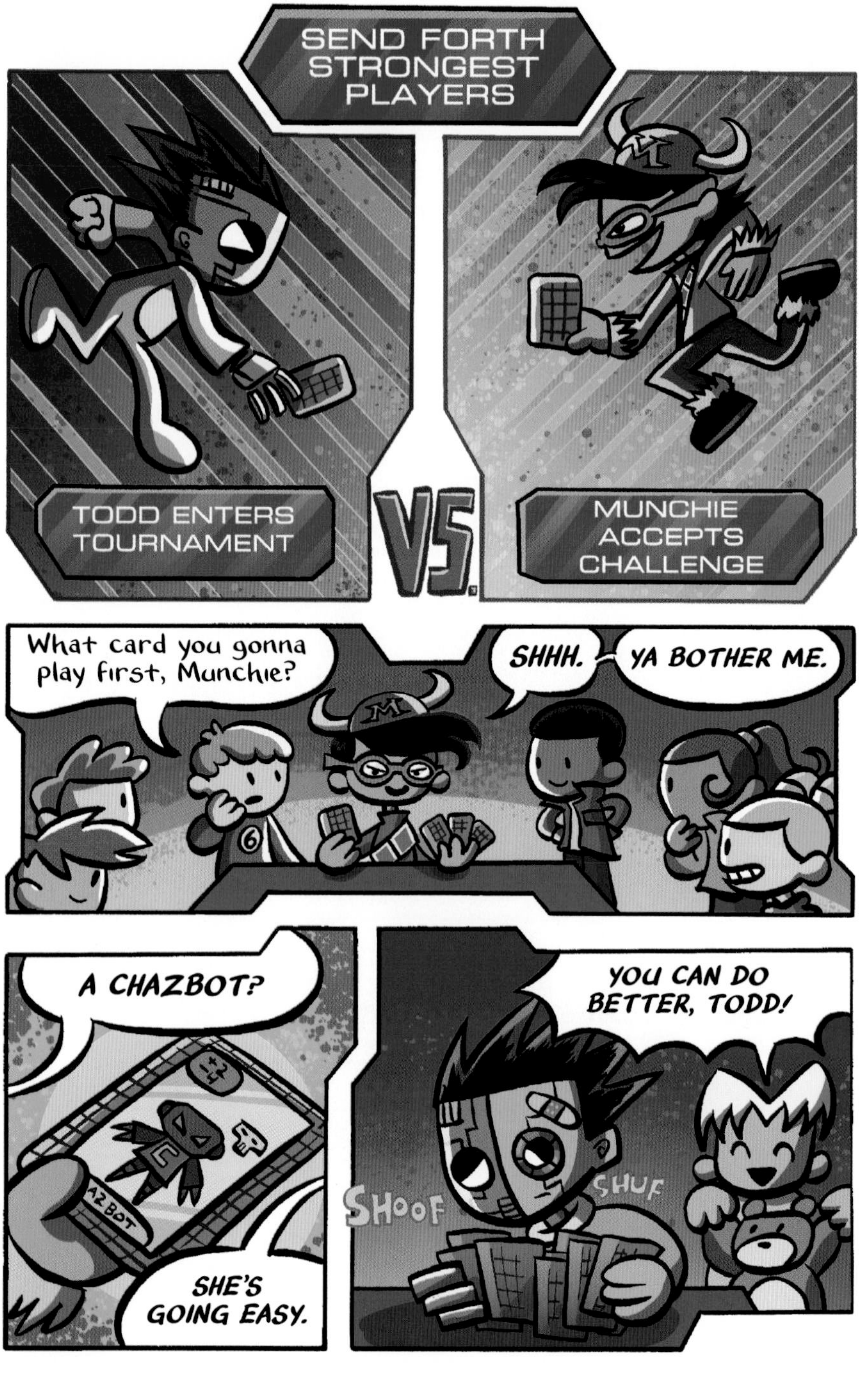
SEND FORTH STRONGEST PLAYERS
TODD ENTERS TOURNAMENT
VS.
MUNCHIE ACCEPTS CHALLENGE
What card you gonna play first, Munchie?
SHHH.
YA BOTHER ME.
A CHAZBOT?
SHE'S GOING EASY.
YOU CAN DO BETTER, TODD!
SHOOF
SHUF

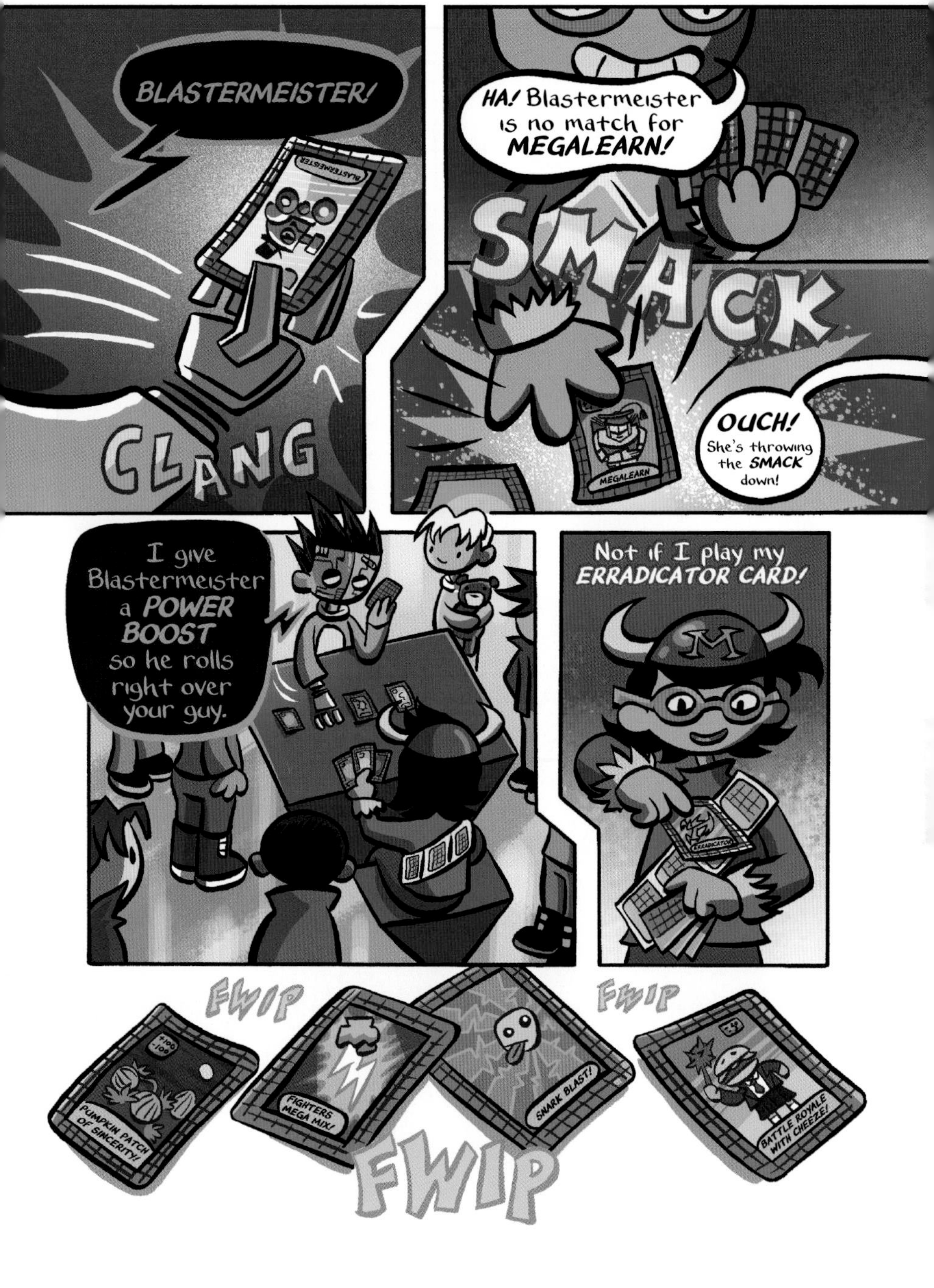
BLASTERMEISTER!
BLASTERMEISTER
CLANG
HA! Blastermeister is no match for MEGALEARN!
SMACK
MEGALEARN
OUCH! She's throwing the SMACK down!
I give Blastermeister a POWER BOOST so he rolls right over your guy.
Not if I play my ERRADICATOR CARD!
ERRADICATOR
FWIP
FWIP
+100 -100
PUMPKIN PATCH OF SINCERITY!
FIGHTERS MEGA MIX!
SNARK BLAST!
BATTLE ROYALE WITH CHEEZE!
FWIP

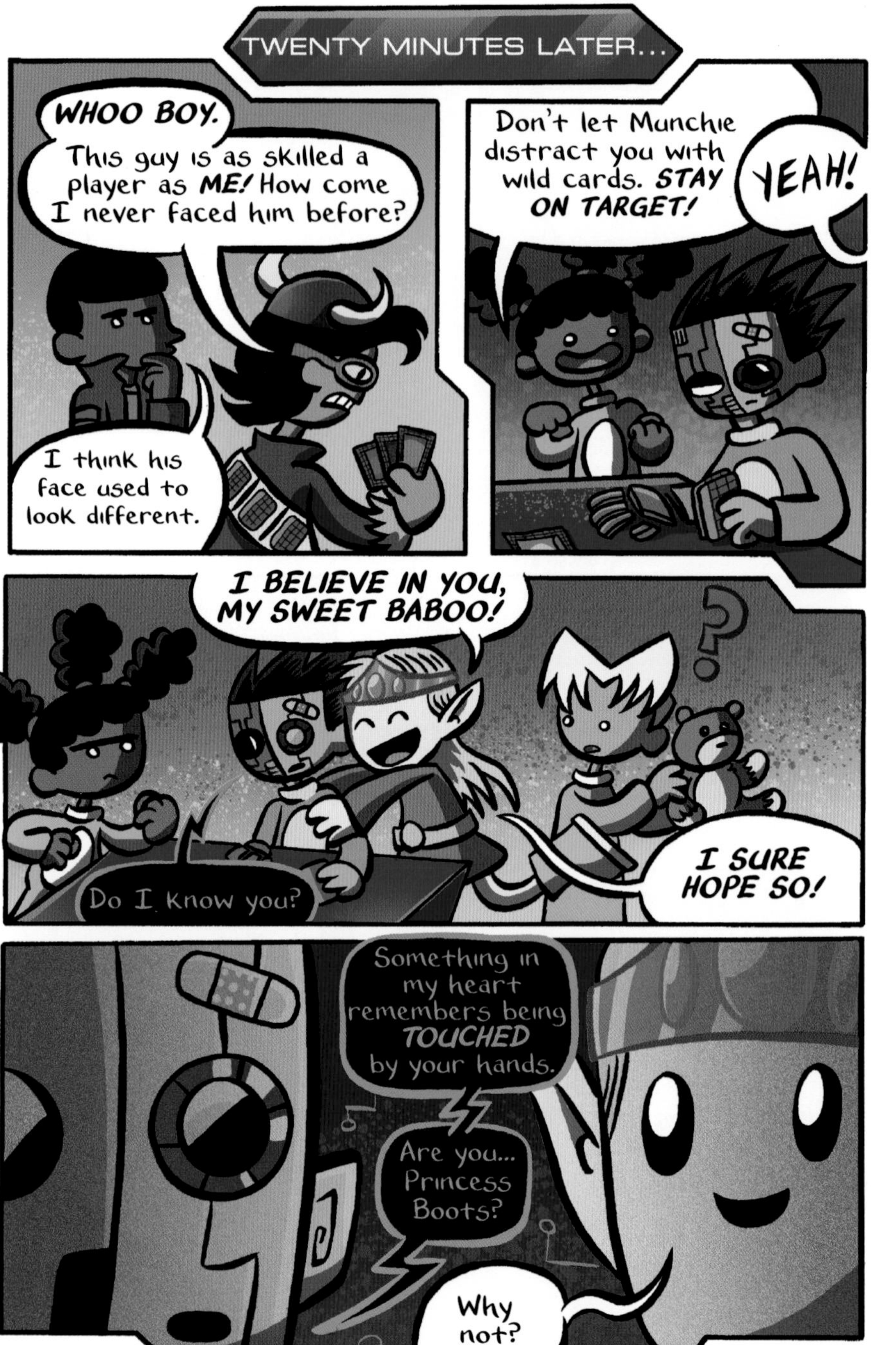

TWENTY MINUTES LATER...
WHOO BOY.
This guy is as skilled a player as ME! How come I never faced him before?
I think his face used to look different.
Don't let Munchie distract you with wild cards. STAY ON TARGET!
YEAH!
I BELIEVE IN YOU, MY SWEET BABOO!
?
Do I know you?
I SURE HOPE SO!
Something in my heart remembers being TOUCHED by your hands.
Are you... Princess Boots?
Why not?

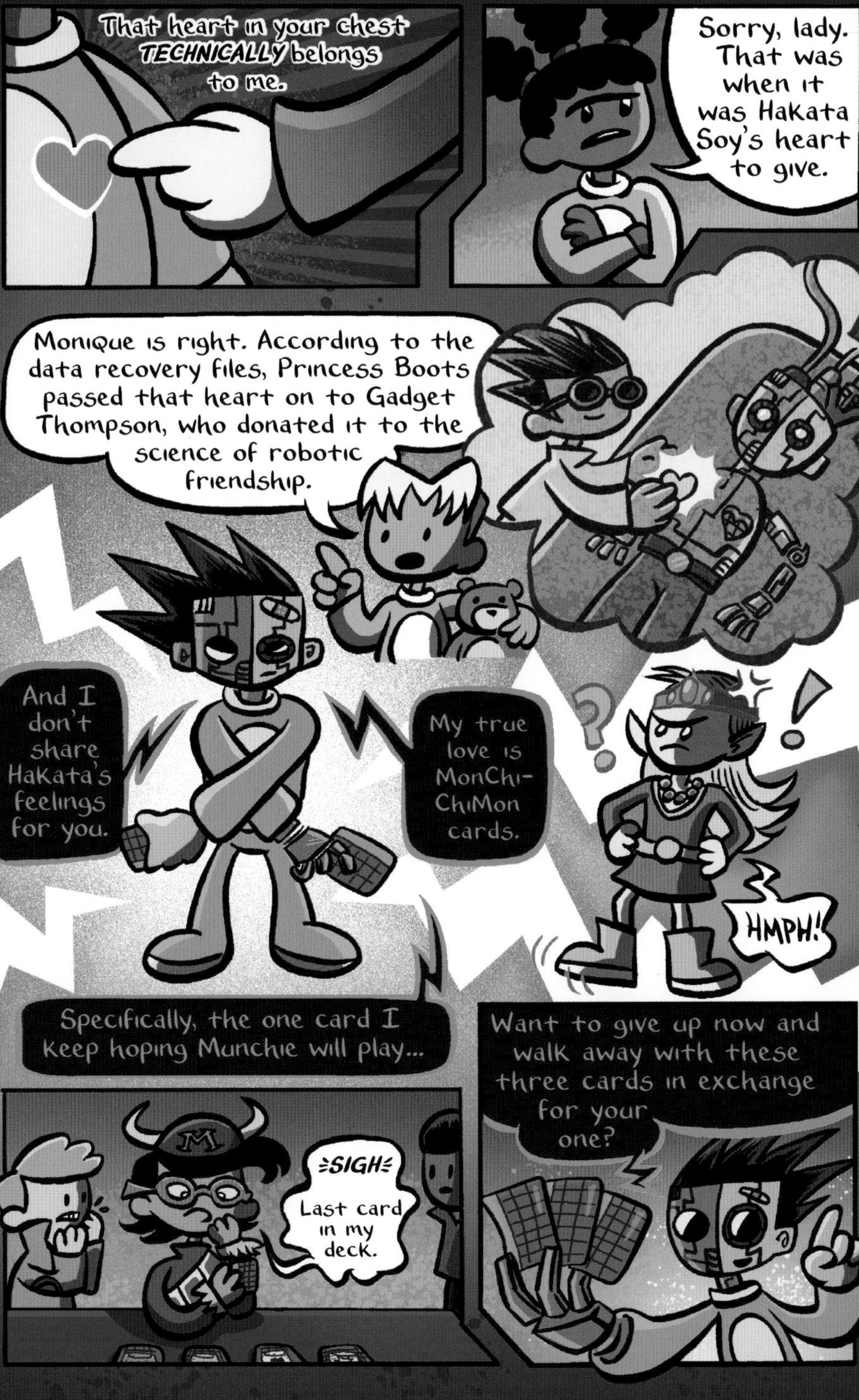
That heart in your chest TECHNICALLY belongs to me.
Sorry, lady. That was when it was Hakata Soy's heart to give.
Monique is right. According to the data recovery files, Princess Boots passed that heart on to Gadget Thompson, who donated it to the science of robotic friendship.
And I don't share Hakata's feelings for you.
My true love is MonChi-ChiMon cards.
?
!
HMPH!
Specifically, the one card I keep hoping Munchie will play...
SIGH
Last card in my deck.
Want to give up now and walk away with these three cards in exchange for your one?

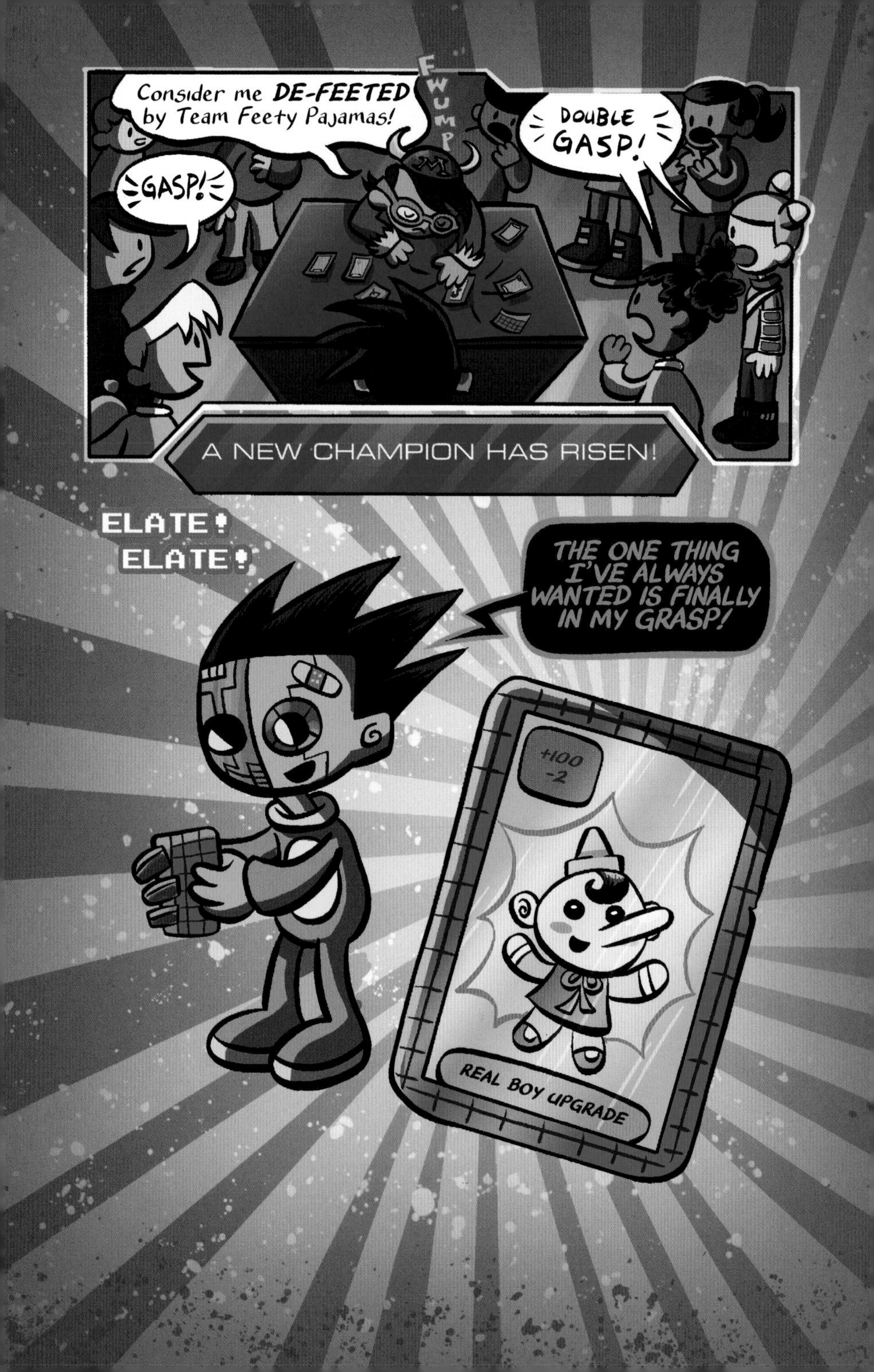

Consider me DE-FEETED by Team Feety Pajamas!
FWUMP
GASP!
DOUBLE GASP!
A NEW CHAMPION HAS RISEN!
ELATE!
ELATE!
THE ONE THING I'VE ALWAYS WANTED IS FINALLY IN MY GRASP!
+100
-2
REAL BOY UPGRADE

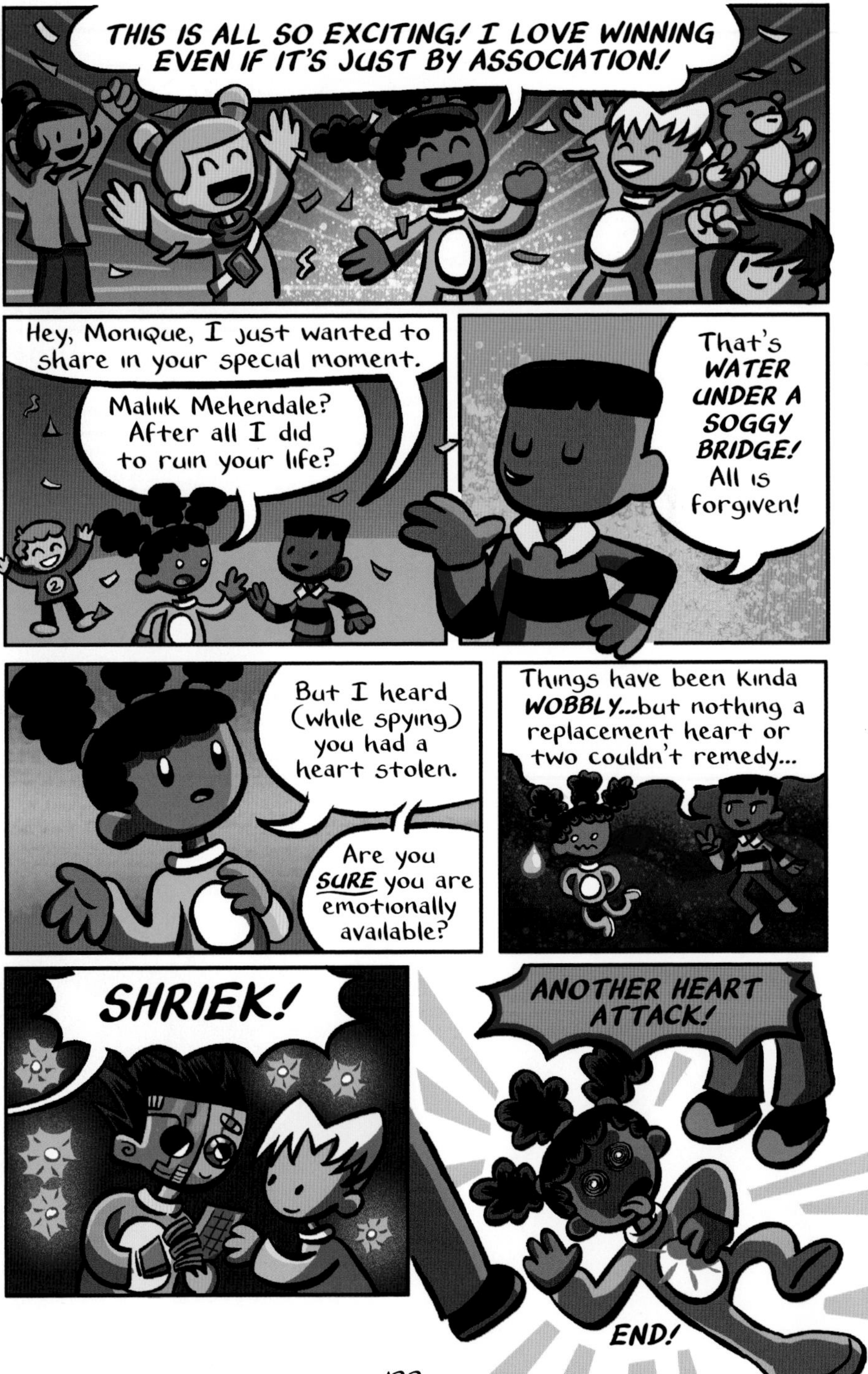
THIS IS ALL SO EXCITING! I LOVE WINNING EVEN IF IT'S JUST BY ASSOCIATION!
Hey, Monique, I just wanted to share in your special moment.
Malik Mehendale? After all I did to ruin your life?
That's WATER UNDER A SOGGY BRIDGE! All is forgiven!
But I heard (while spying) you had a heart stolen.
Are you SURE you are emotionally available?
Things have been kinda WOBBLY...but nothing a replacement heart or two couldn't remedy...
SHRIEK!
ANOTHER HEART ATTACK!
END!

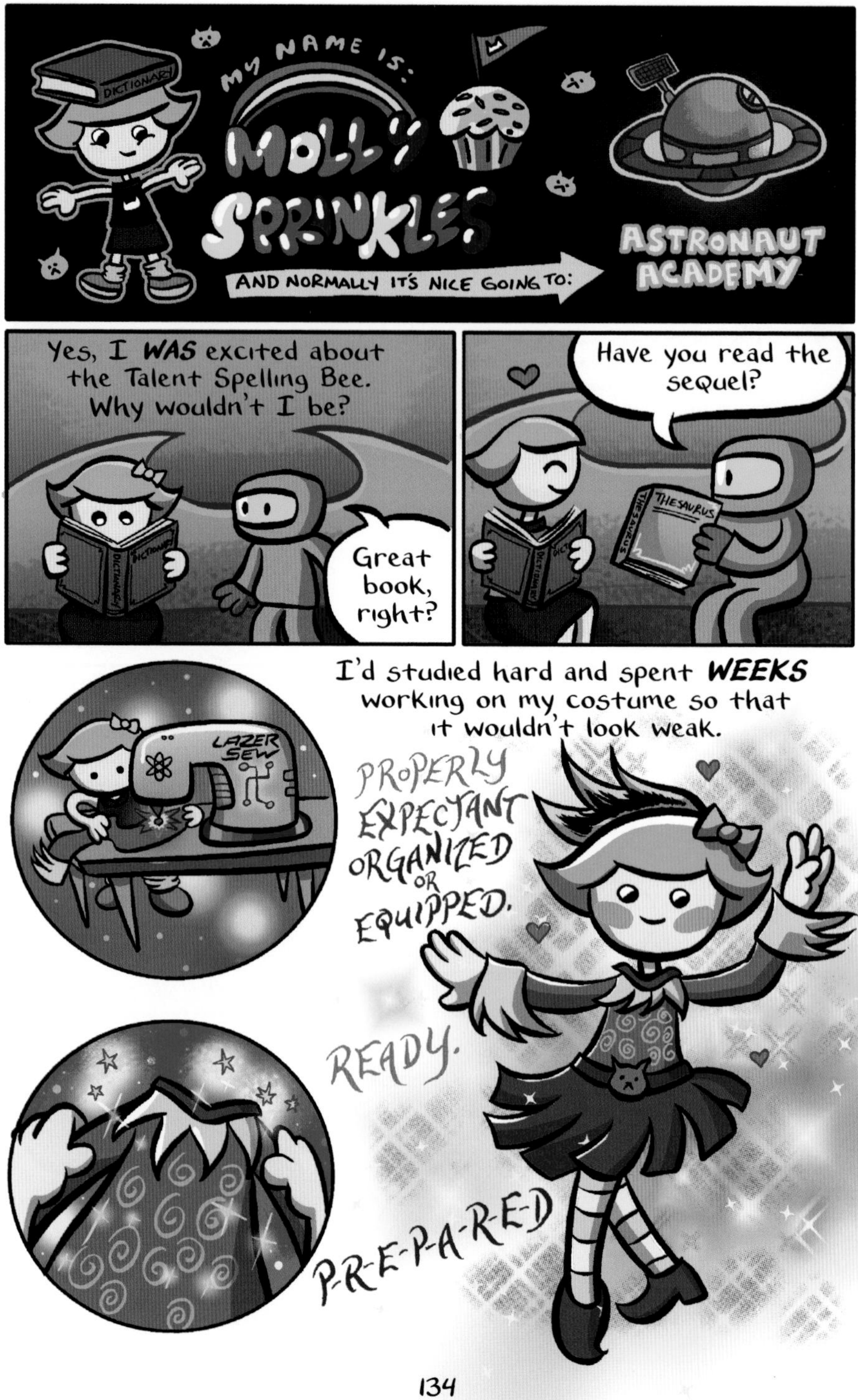

MY NAME IS:
MOLLY SPRINKLES
DICTIONARY
AND NORMALLY IT'S NICE GOING TO:
ASTRONAUT ACADEMY
Yes, I WAS excited about the Talent Spelling Bee. Why wouldn't I be?
Great book, right?
Have you read the sequel?
THESAURUS
I'd studied hard and spent WEEKS working on my costume so that it wouldn't look weak.
LAZER SEW
PROPERLY EXPECTANT ORGANIZED OR EQUIPPED.
READY.
P-R-E-P-A-R-E-D

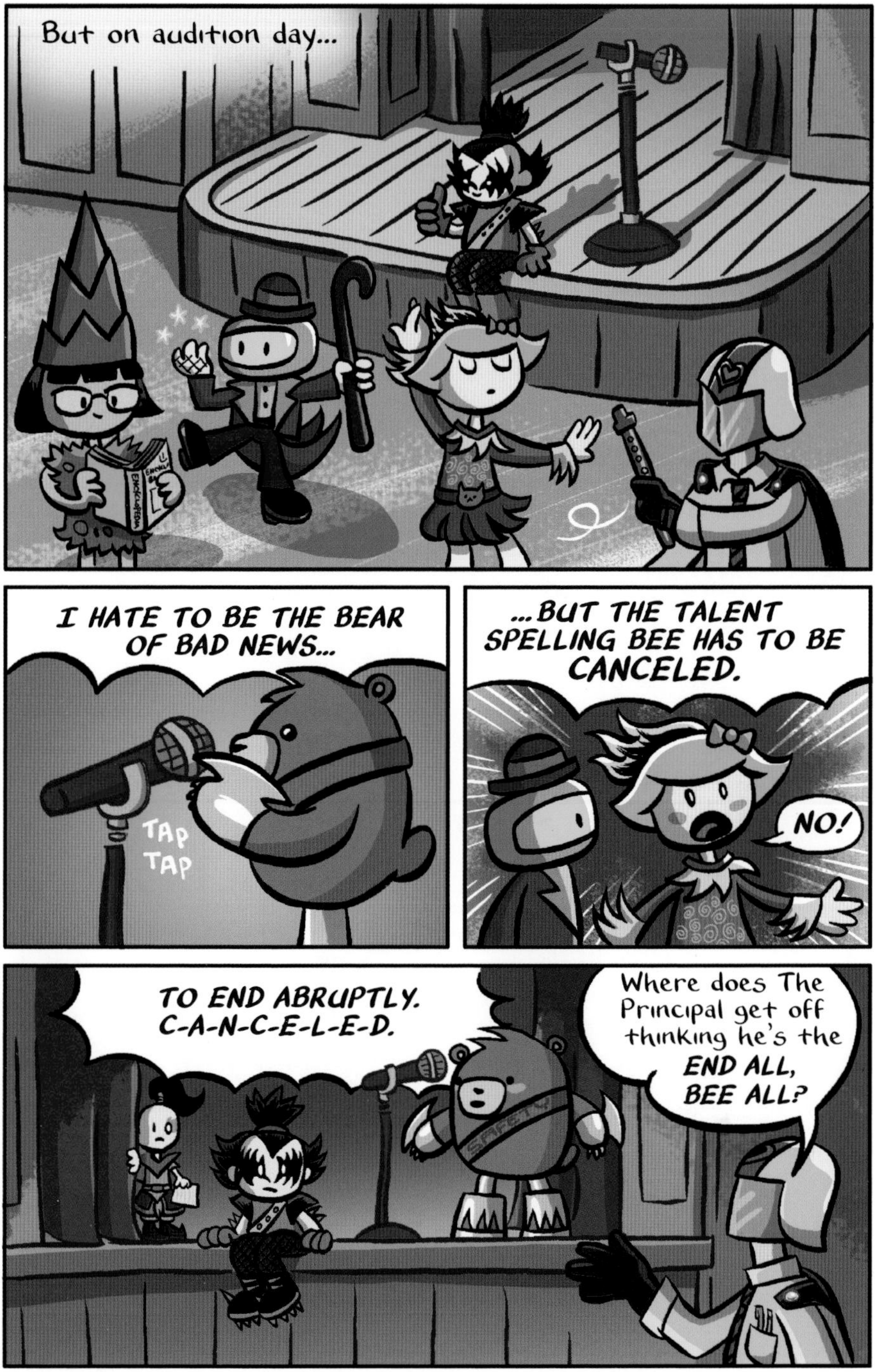
But on audition day...
I HATE TO BE THE BEAR OF BAD NEWS...
TAP TAP
...BUT THE TALENT SPELLING BEE HAS TO BE CANCELED.
NO!
TO END ABRUPTLY. C-A-N-C-E-L-E-D.
Where does The Principal get off thinking he's the END ALL, BEE ALL?

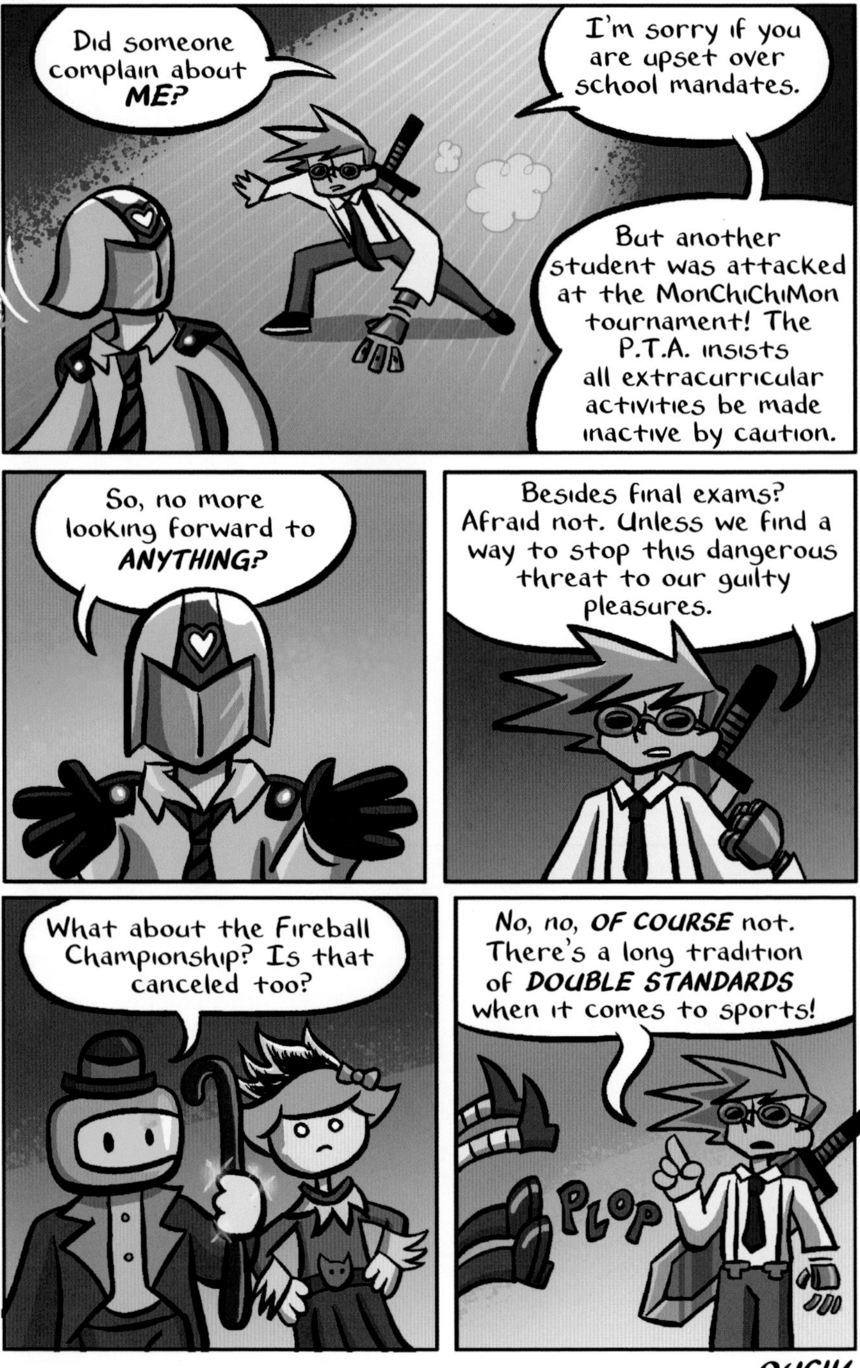
Did someone complain about ME?
I'm sorry if you are upset over school mandates.
But another student was attacked at the MonChiChiMon tournament! The P.T.A. insists all extracurricular activities be made inactive by caution.
SWN
So, no more looking forward to ANYTHING?
Besides final exams? Afraid not. Unless we find a way to stop this dangerous threat to our guilty pleasures.
What about the Fireball Championship? Is that canceled too?
No, no, OF COURSE not. There's a long tradition of DOUBLE STANDARDS when it comes to sports!
PLOP
OUCH!

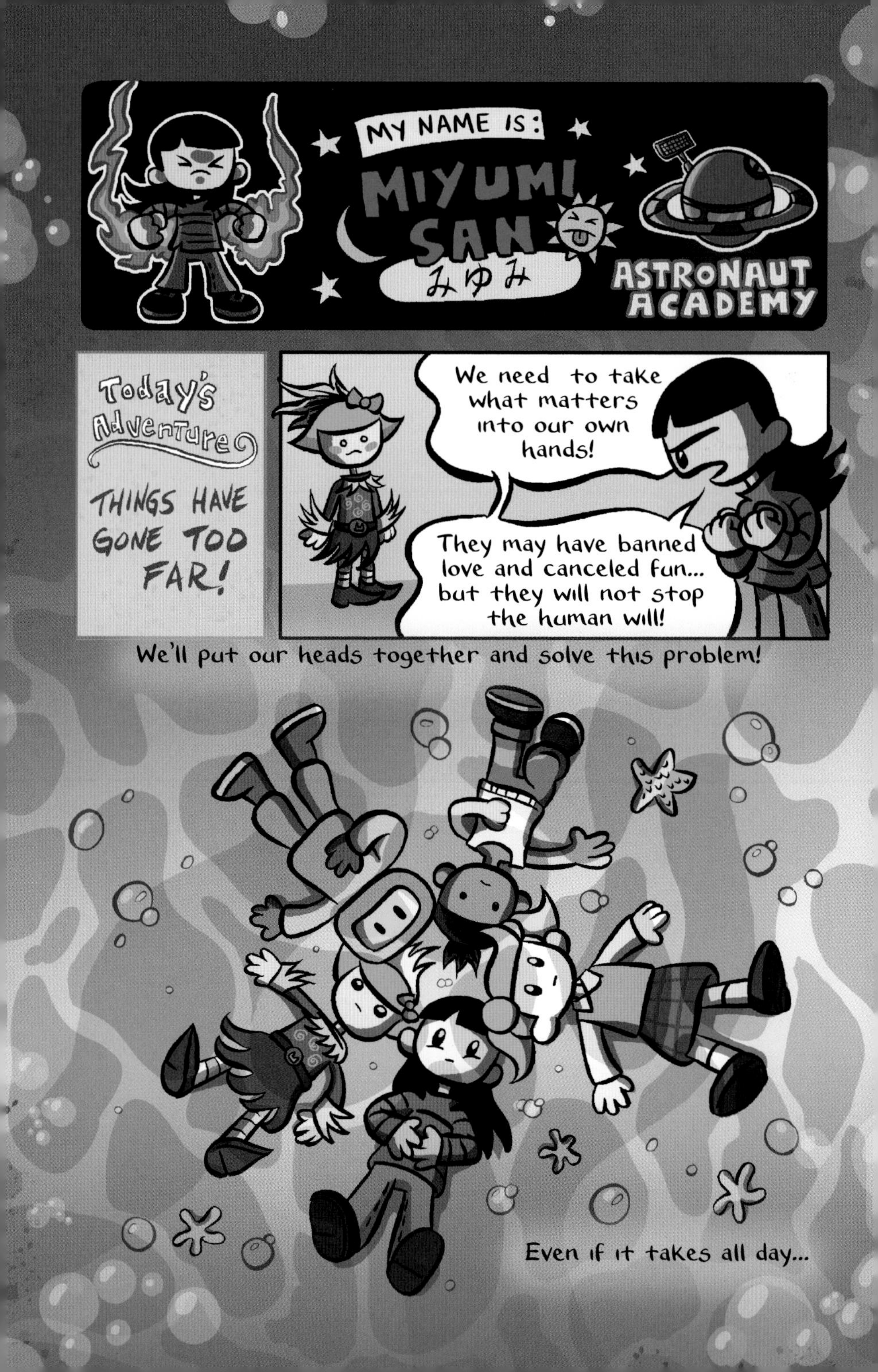
MY NAME IS:
MIYUMI SAN
みゆみ
ASTRONAUT ACADEMY
Today's Adventure
THINGS HAVE GONE TOO FAR!
We need to take what matters into our own hands!
They may have banned love and canceled fun... but they will not stop the human will!
We'll put our heads together and solve this problem!
Even if it takes all day...

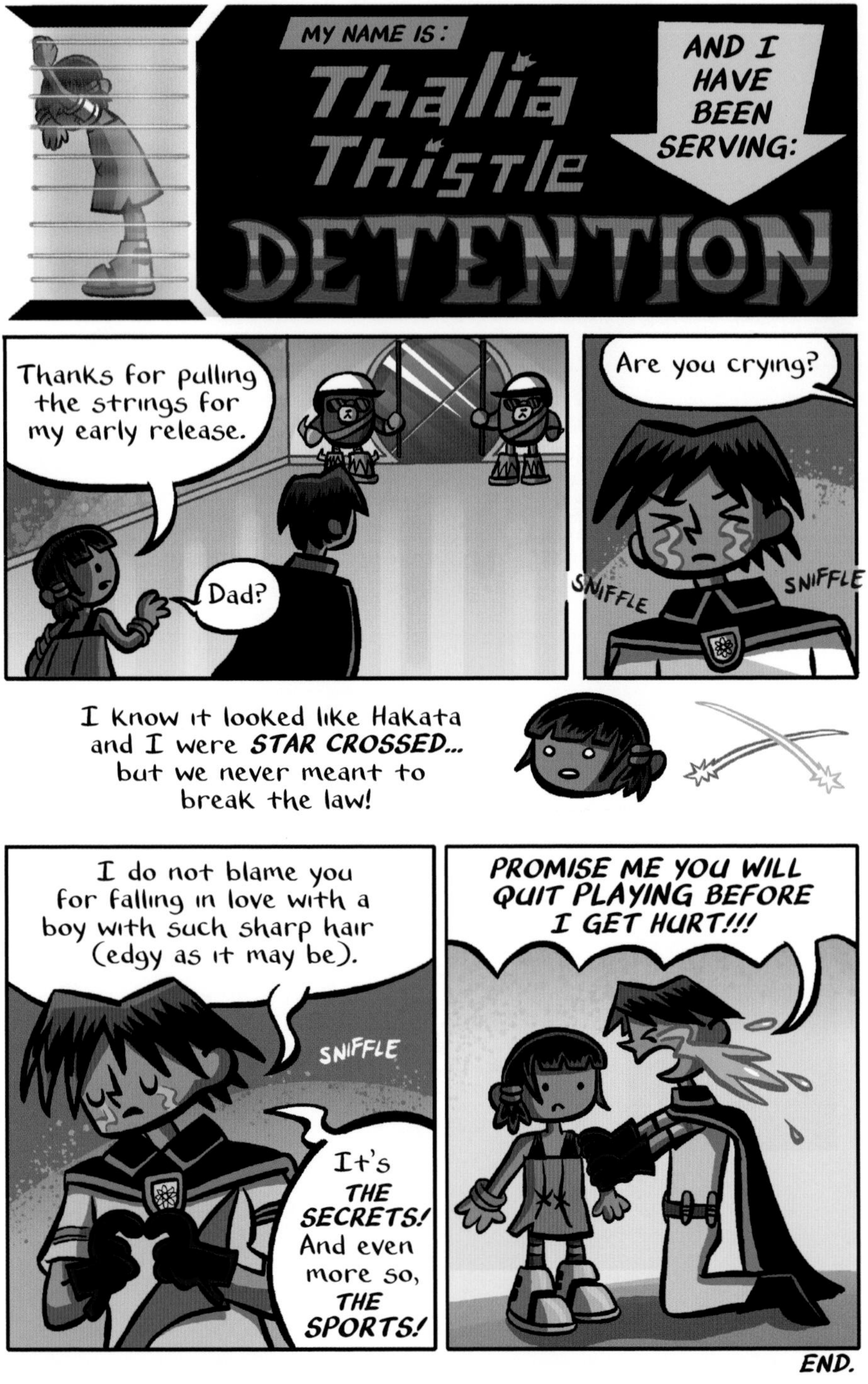
MY NAME IS:
Thalia Thistle
AND I HAVE BEEN SERVING:
DETENTION
Thanks for pulling the strings for my early release.
Dad?
Are you crying?
SNIFFLE
SNIFFLE
I know it looked like Hakata and I were STAR CROSSED... but we never meant to break the law!
I do not blame you for falling in love with a boy with such sharp hair (edgy as it may be).
SNIFFLE
It's THE SECRETS! And even more so, THE SPORTS!
PROMISE ME YOU WILL QUIT PLAYING BEFORE I GET HURT!!!
END.

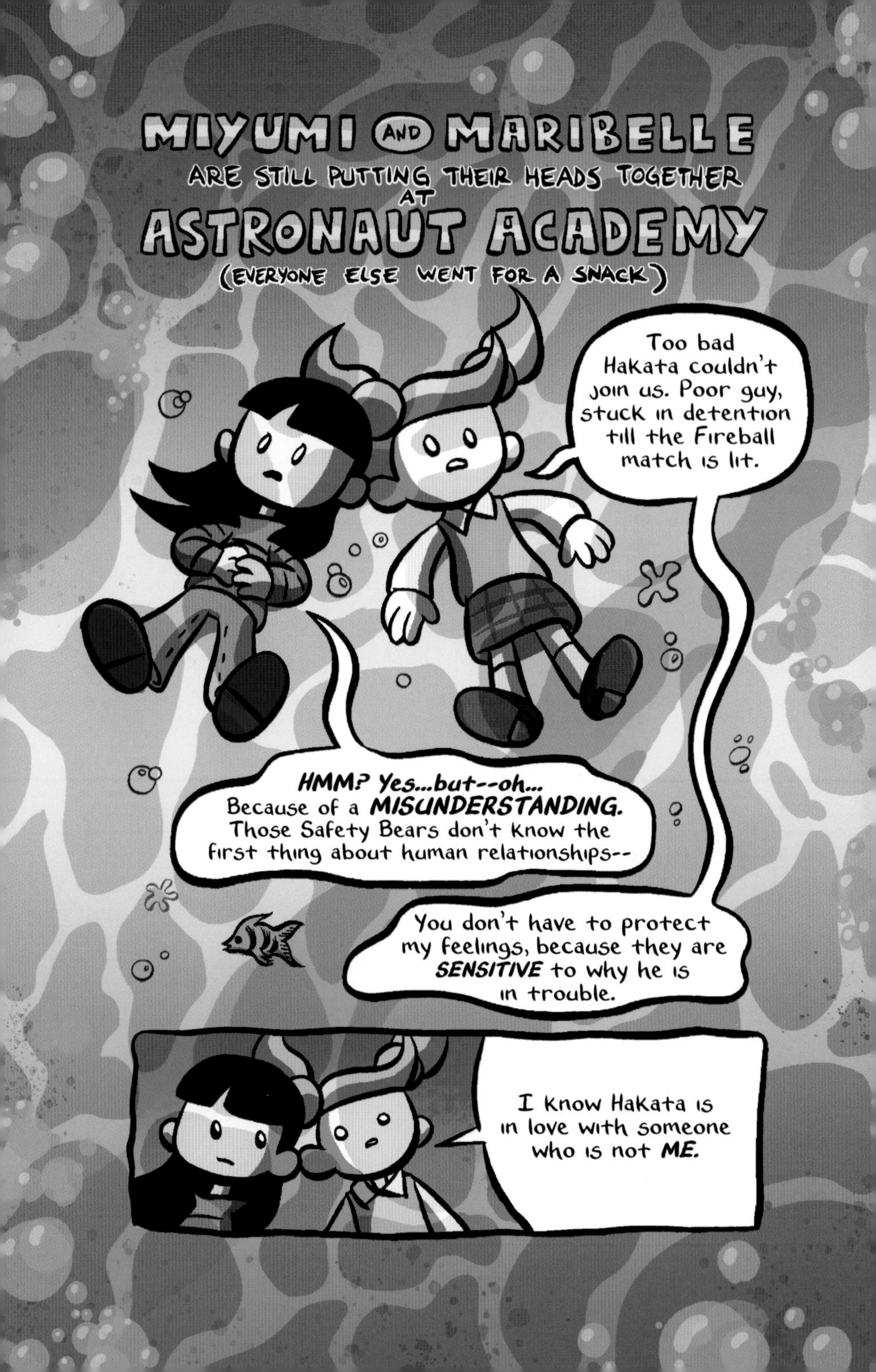
MIYUMI AND MARIBELLE
ARE STILL PUTTING THEIR HEADS TOGETHER
AT
ASTRONAUT ACADEMY
(EVERYONE ELSE WENT FOR A SNACK)
Too bad Hakata couldn't join us. Poor guy, stuck in detention till the Fireball match is lit.
HMM? Yes...but--oh... Because of a MISUNDERSTANDING. Those Safety Bears don't know the first thing about human relationships--
You don't have to protect my feelings, because they are SENSITIVE to why he is in trouble.
I know Hakata is in love with someone who is not ME.

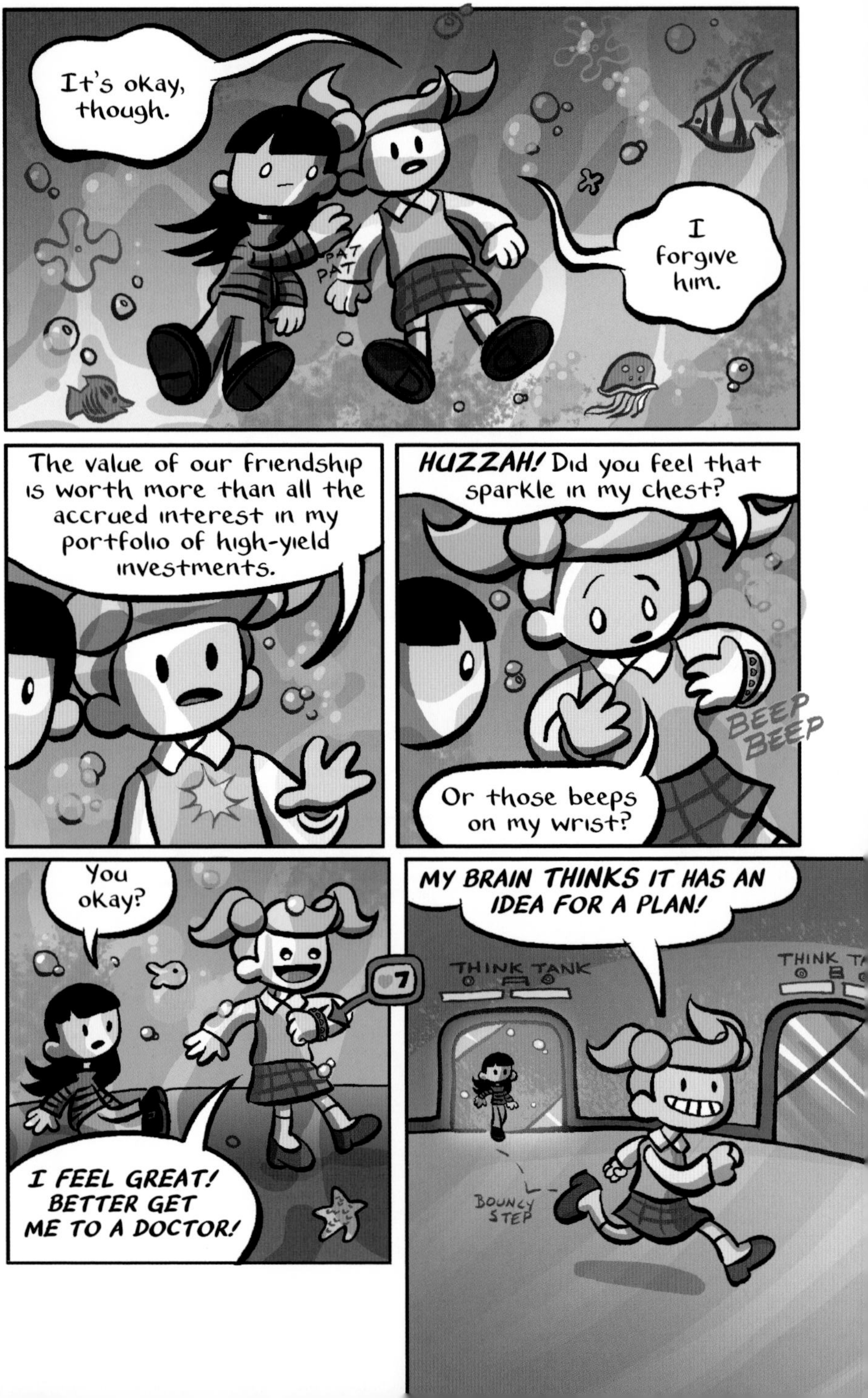
It's okay, though.
PAT PAT
I forgive him.
The value of our friendship is worth more than all the accrued interest in my portfolio of high-yield investments.
HUZZAH! Did you feel that sparkle in my chest?
BEEP BEEP
Or those beeps on my wrist?
You okay?
7
I FEEL GREAT! BETTER GET ME TO A DOCTOR!
MY BRAIN THINKS IT HAS AN IDEA FOR A PLAN!
THINK TANK
A
THINK TA
B
BOUNCY STEP

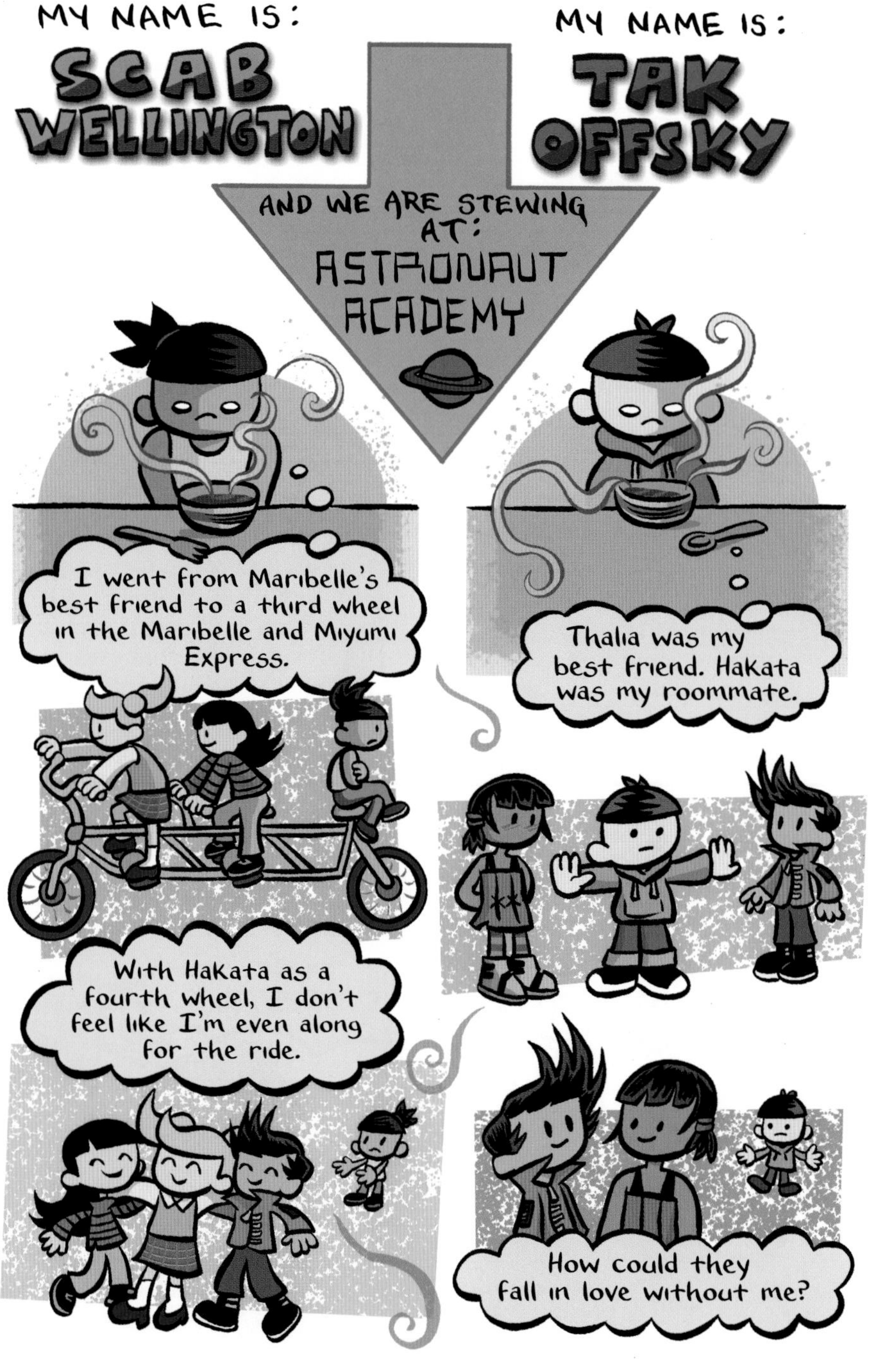
MY NAME IS:
SCAB WELLINGTON
MY NAME IS:
TAK OFFSKY
AND WE ARE STEWING AT:
ASTRONAUT ACADEMY
I went from Maribelle's best friend to a third wheel in the Maribelle and Miyumi Express.
Thalia was my best friend. Hakata was my roommate.
With Hakata as a fourth wheel, I don't feel like I'm even along for the ride.
How could they fall in love without me?

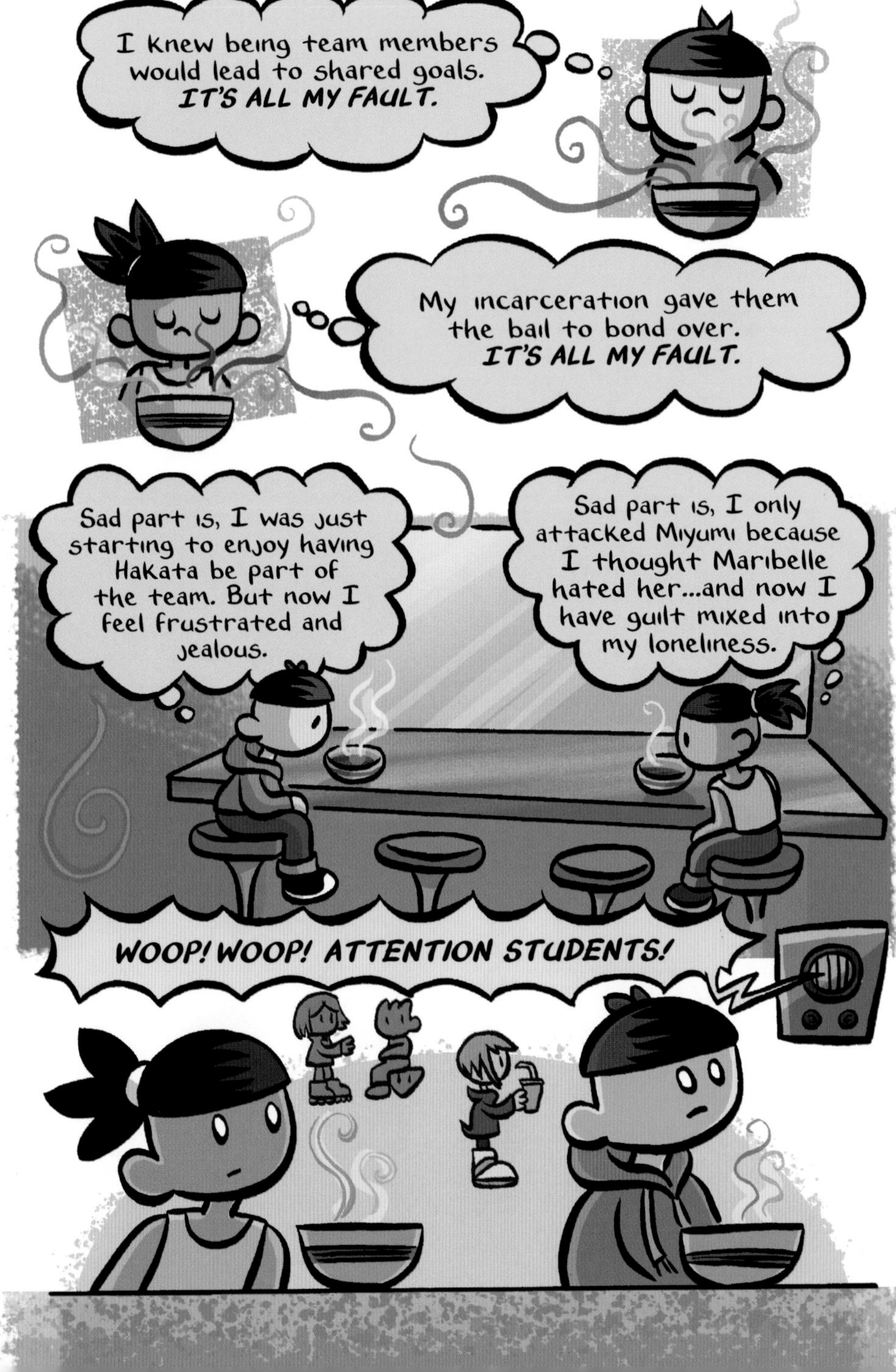
I knew being team members would lead to shared goals. IT'S ALL MY FAULT.
My incarceration gave them the bail to bond over. IT'S ALL MY FAULT.
Sad part is, I was just starting to enjoy having Hakata be part of the team. But now I feel frustrated and jealous.
Sad part is, I only attacked Miyumi because I thought Maribelle hated her...and now I have guilt mixed into my loneliness.
WOOP! WOOP! ATTENTION STUDENTS!

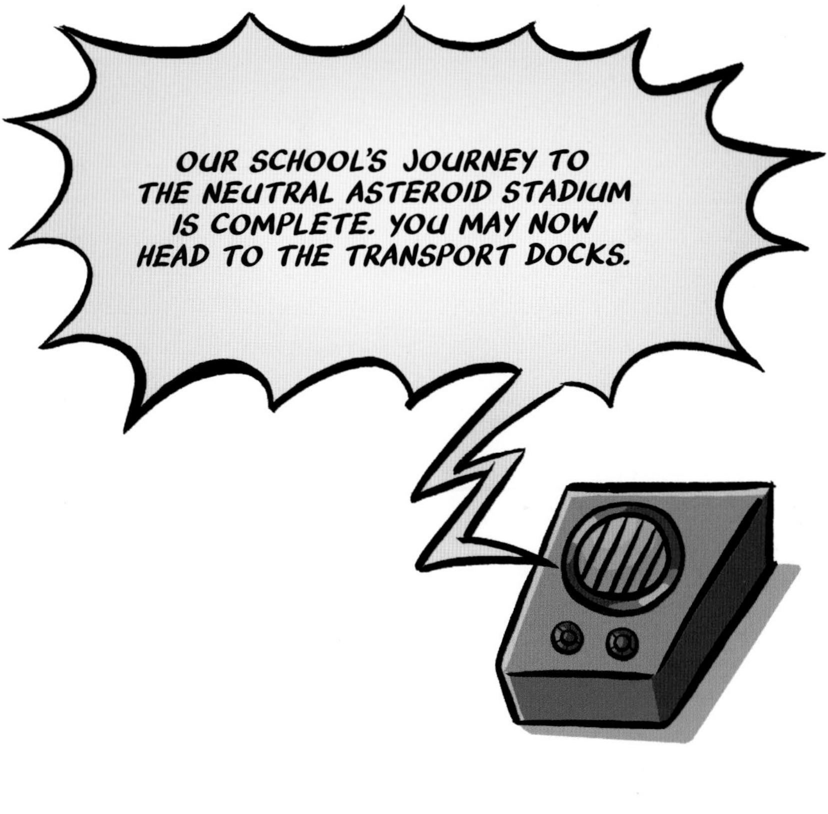
OUR SCHOOL'S JOURNEY TO THE NEUTRAL ASTEROID STADIUM IS COMPLETE. YOU MAY NOW HEAD TO THE TRANSPORT DOCKS.

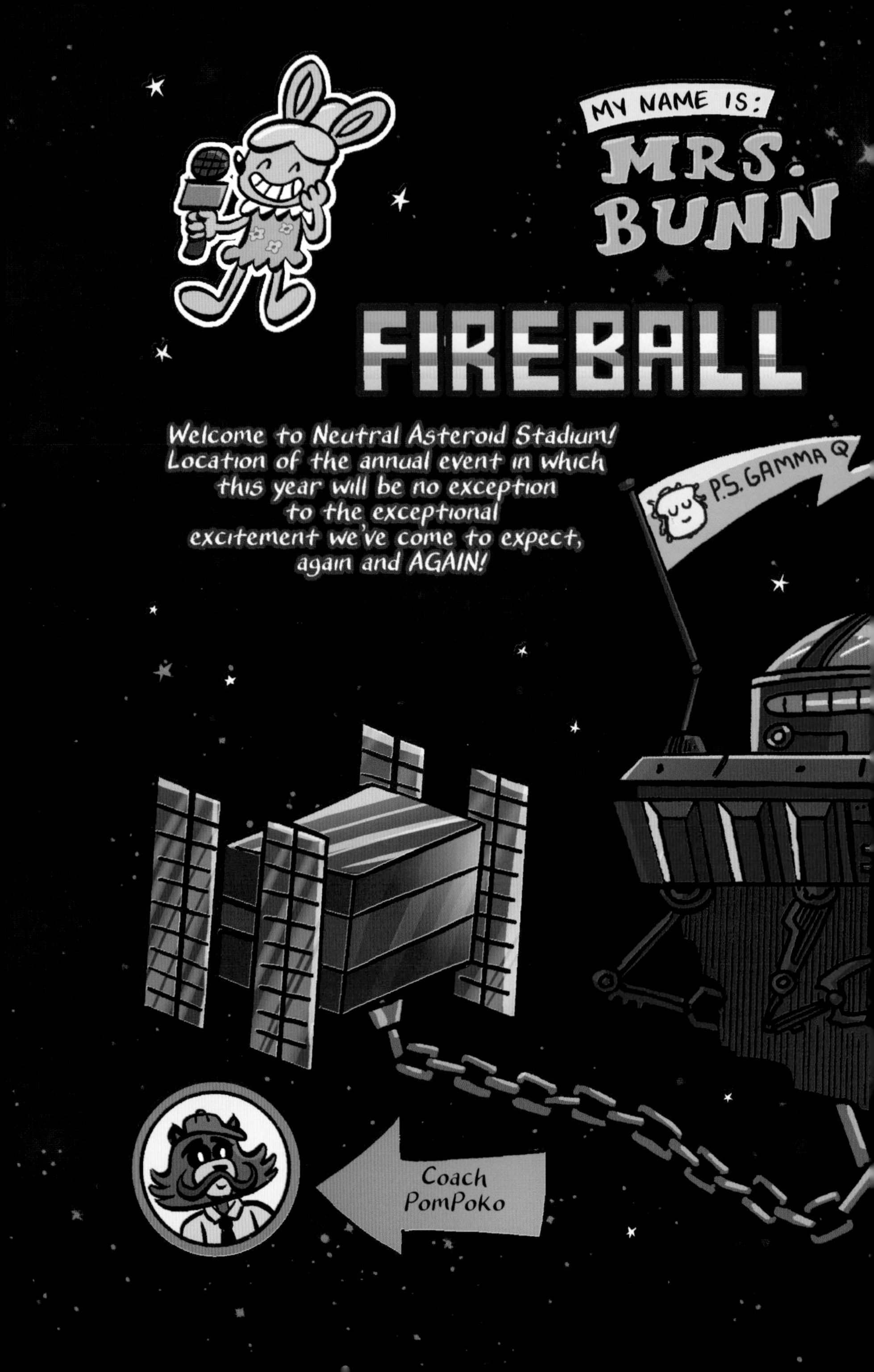
MY NAME IS:
MRS. BUNN
FIREBALL
Welcome to Neutral Asteroid Stadium! Location of the annual event in which this year will be no exception to the exceptional excitement we've come to expect, again and AGAIN!
P.S. GAMMA Q
Coach PomPoko

And I'll be your color commentator for this year's:

CHAMPIONSHIP

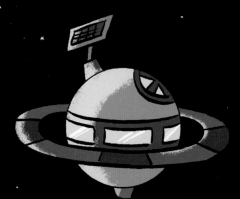

A.A.

Competitions are fun
IF you like to take sides...
and this game will have two of them!

Coach McScone

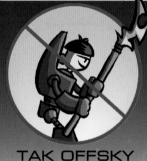

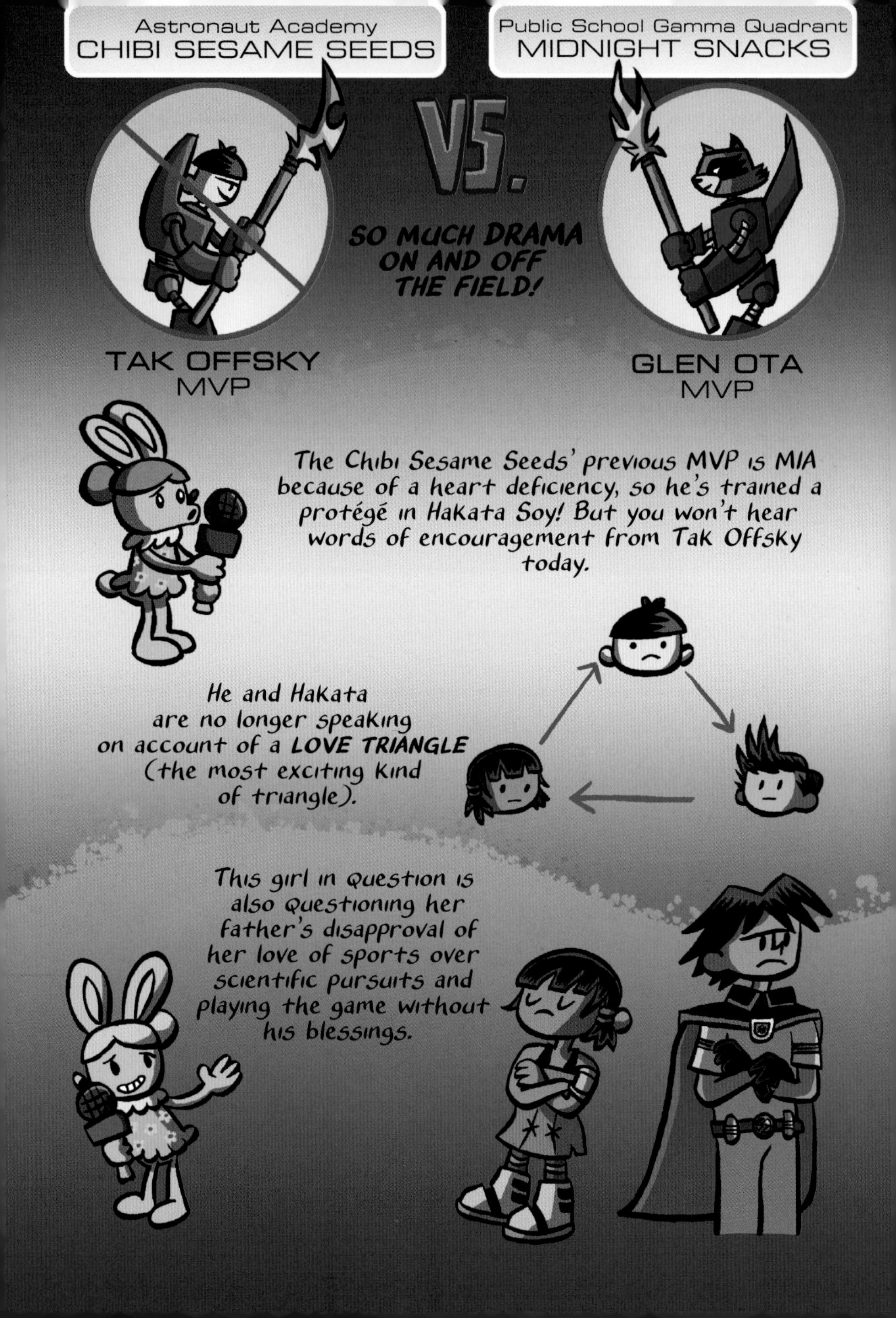

Astronaut Academy
CHIBI SESAME SEEDS
Public School Gamma Quadrant
MIDNIGHT SNACKS
VS.
SO MUCH DRAMA ON AND OFF THE FIELD!
TAK OFFSKY
MVP
GLEN OTA
MVP
The Chibi Sesame Seeds' previous MVP is MIA because of a heart deficiency, so he's trained a protégé in Hakata Soy! But you won't hear words of encouragement from Tak Offsky today.
He and Hakata are no longer speaking on account of a LOVE TRIANGLE (the most exciting kind of triangle).
This girl in question is also questioning her father's disapproval of her love of sports over scientific pursuits and playing the game without his blessings.

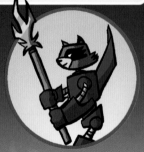

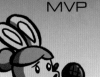

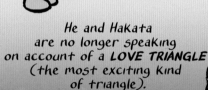

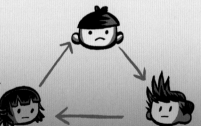

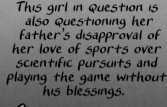

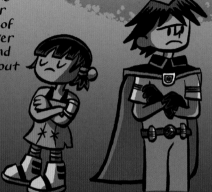

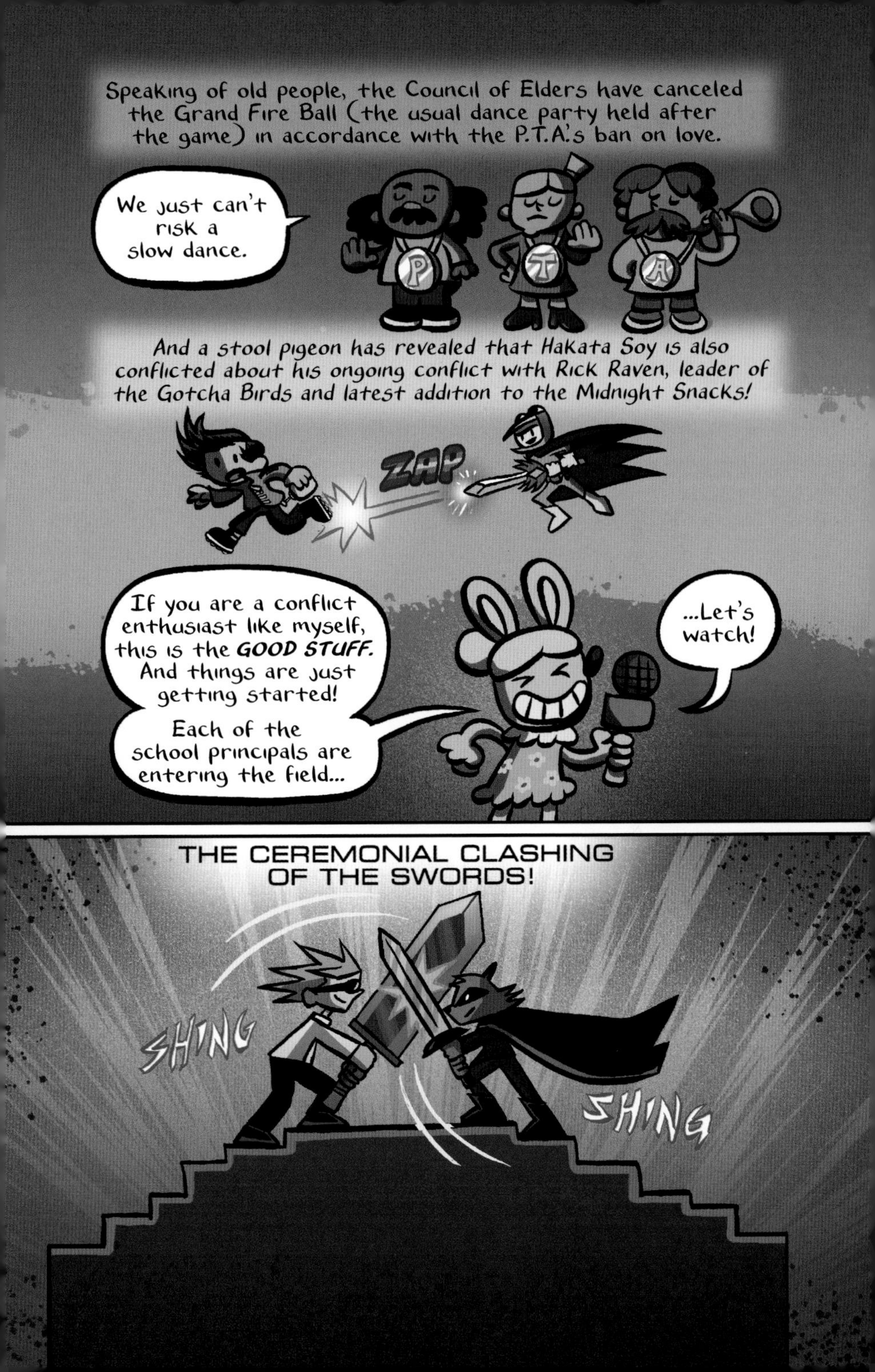
Speaking of old people, the Council of Elders have canceled the Grand Fire Ball (the usual dance party held after the game) in accordance with the P.T.A.'s ban on love.
We just can't risk a slow dance.
P
T
A
And a stool pigeon has revealed that Hakata Soy is also conflicted about his ongoing conflict with Rick Raven, leader of the Gotcha Birds and latest addition to the Midnight Snacks!
ZAP
If you are a conflict enthusiast like myself, this is the GOOD STUFF. And things are just getting started!
Each of the school principals are entering the field...
...Let's watch!
THE CEREMONIAL CLASHING OF THE SWORDS!
SHING
SHING

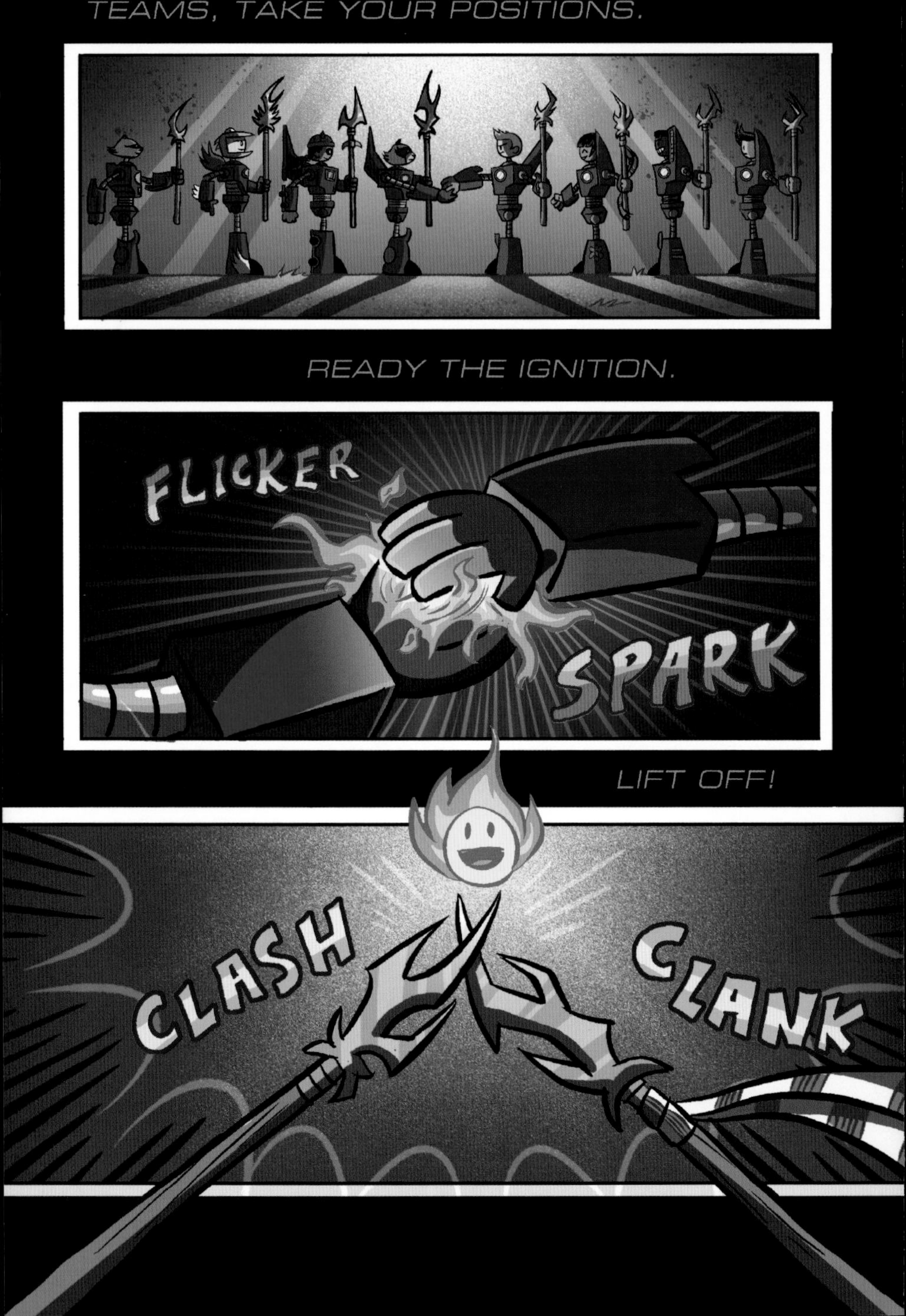
TEAMS, TAKE YOUR POSITIONS.
READY THE IGNITION.
FLICKER
SPARK
LIFT OFF!
CLASH
CLANK

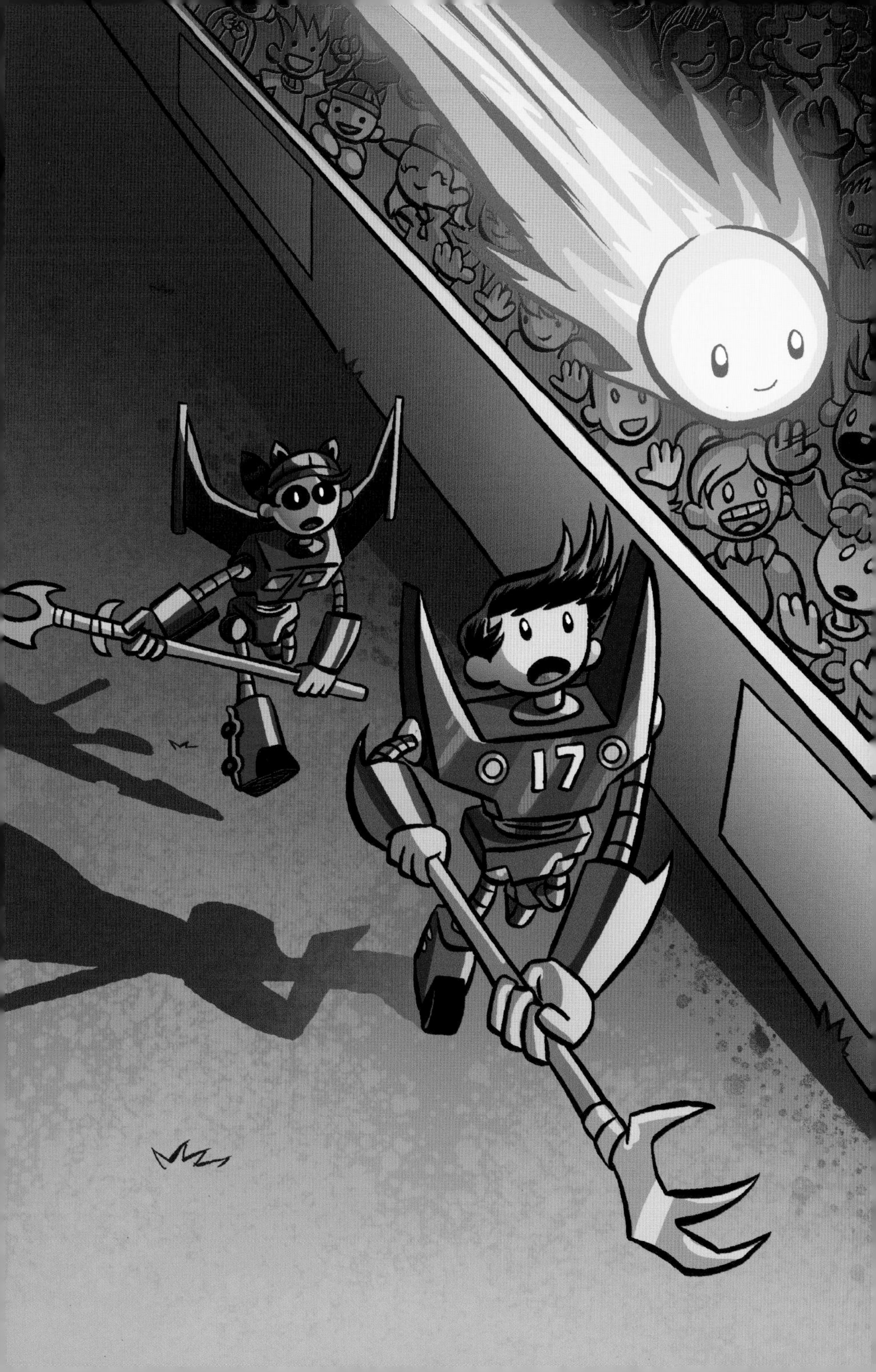
17

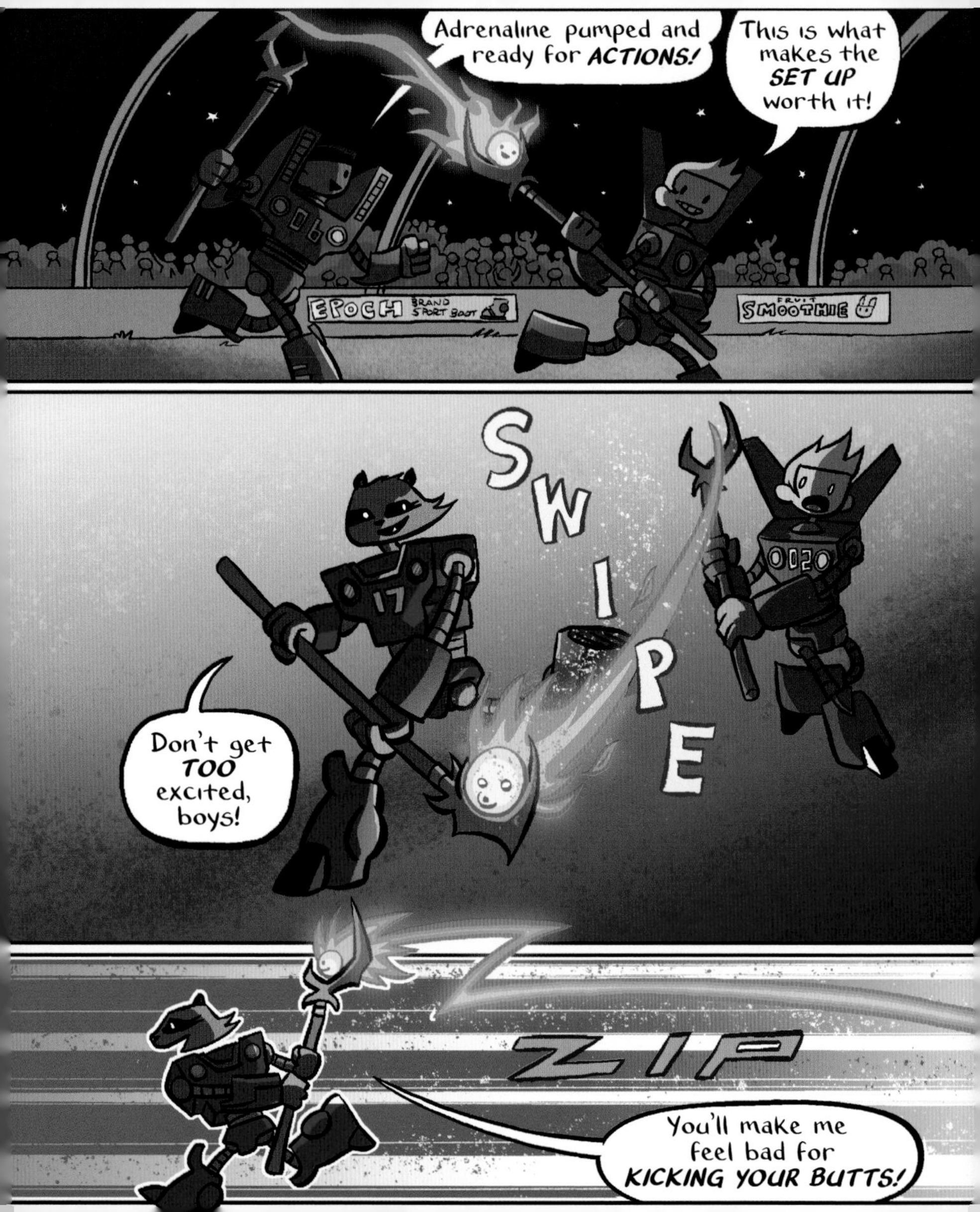
Adrenaline pumped and ready for ACTIONS!
This is what makes the SET UP worth it!
EPOCH BRAND SPORT BOOT
SMOOTHIE
SWIPE
Don't get TOO excited, boys!
ZIP
You'll make me feel bad for KICKING YOUR BUTTS!

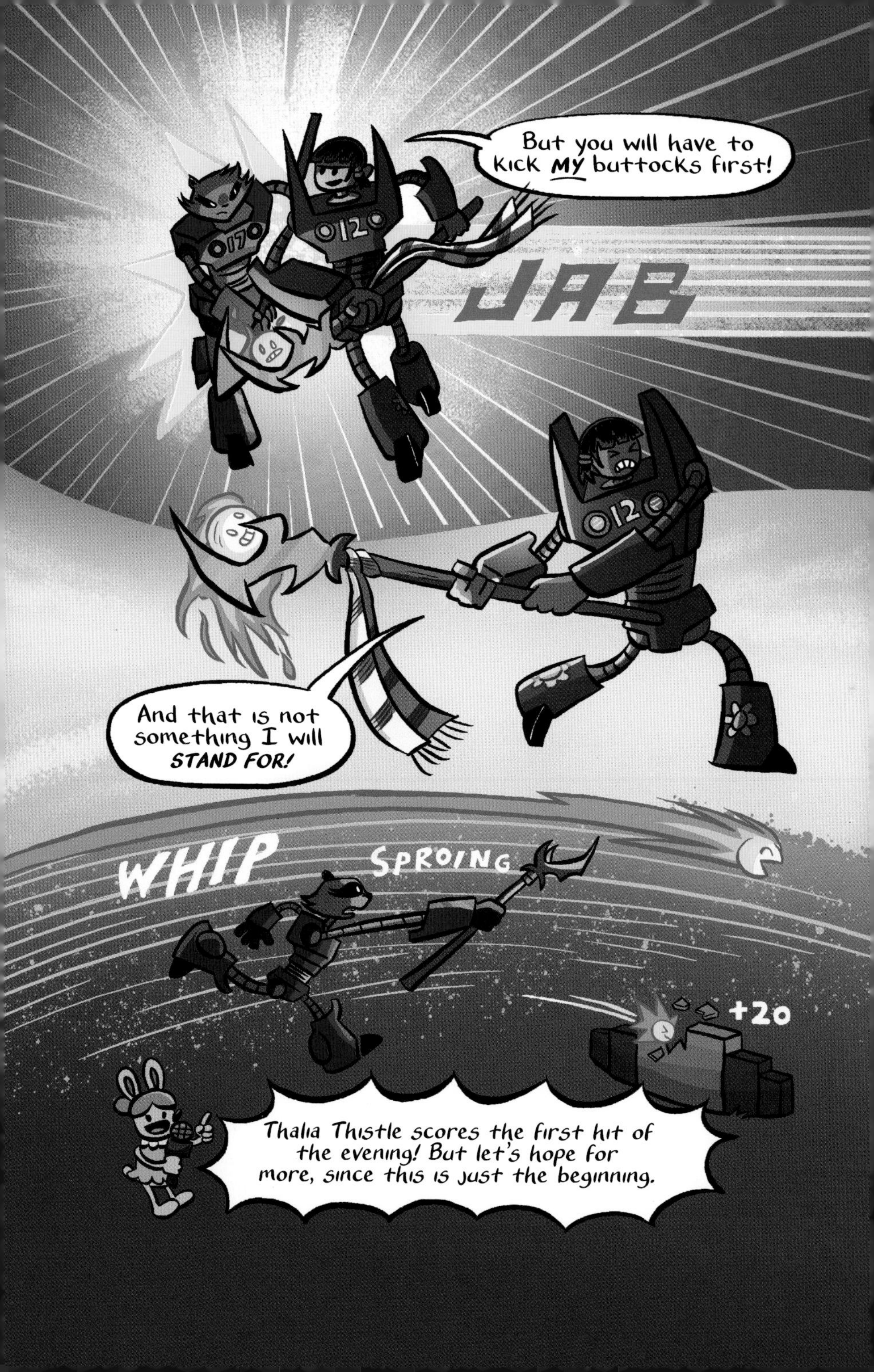
But you will have to kick MY buttocks first!
JAB
And that is not something I will STAND FOR!
WHIP
SPROING
+20
Thalia Thistle scores the first hit of the evening! But let's hope for more, since this is just the beginning.

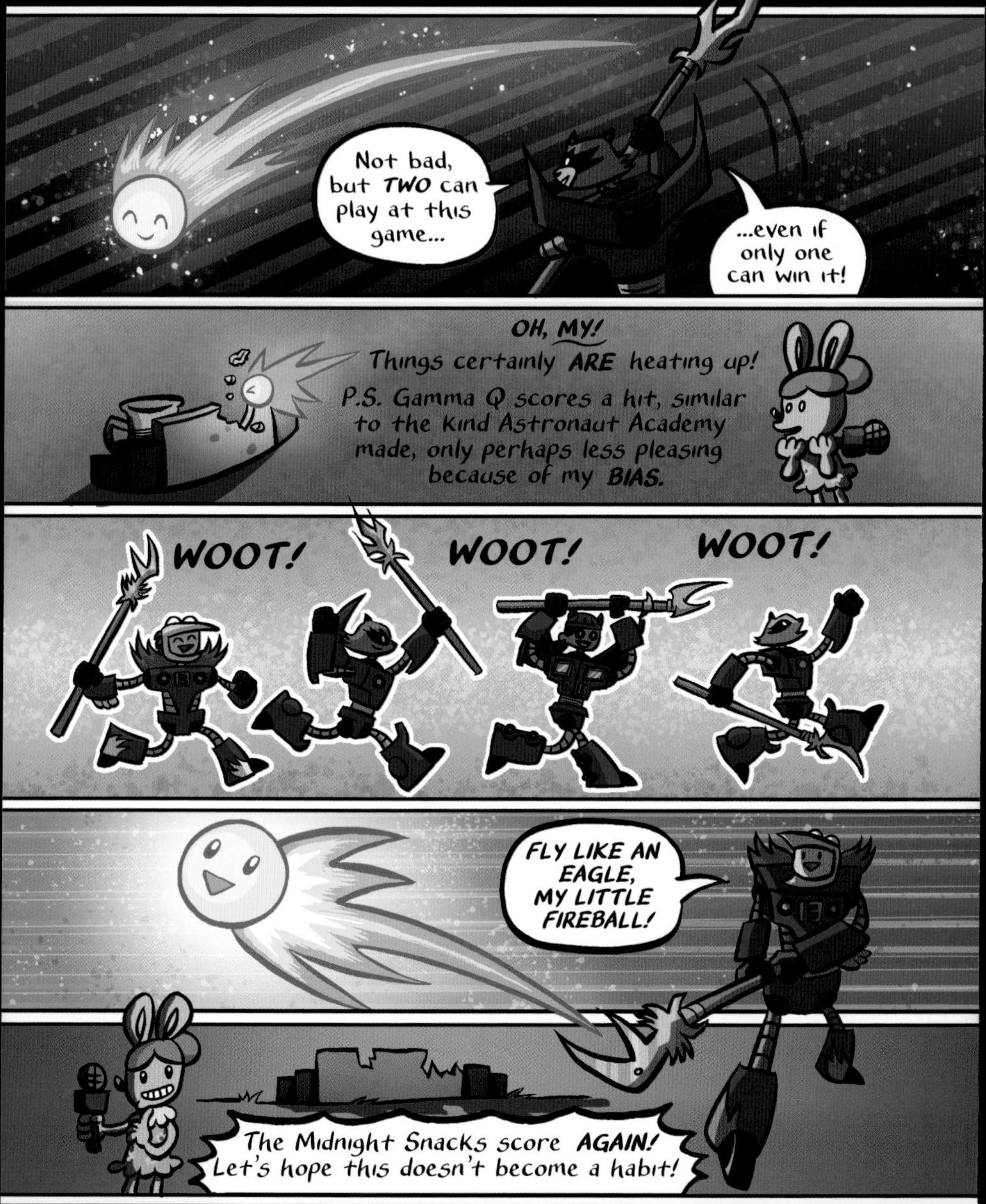
Not bad, but TWO can play at this game...
...even if only one can win it!
OH, MY! Things certainly ARE heating up!
P.S. Gamma Q scores a hit, similar to the kind Astronaut Academy made, only perhaps less pleasing because of my BIAS.
WOOT!
WOOT!
WOOT!
FLY LIKE AN EAGLE, MY LITTLE FIREBALL!
The Midnight Snacks score AGAIN! Let's hope this doesn't become a habit!

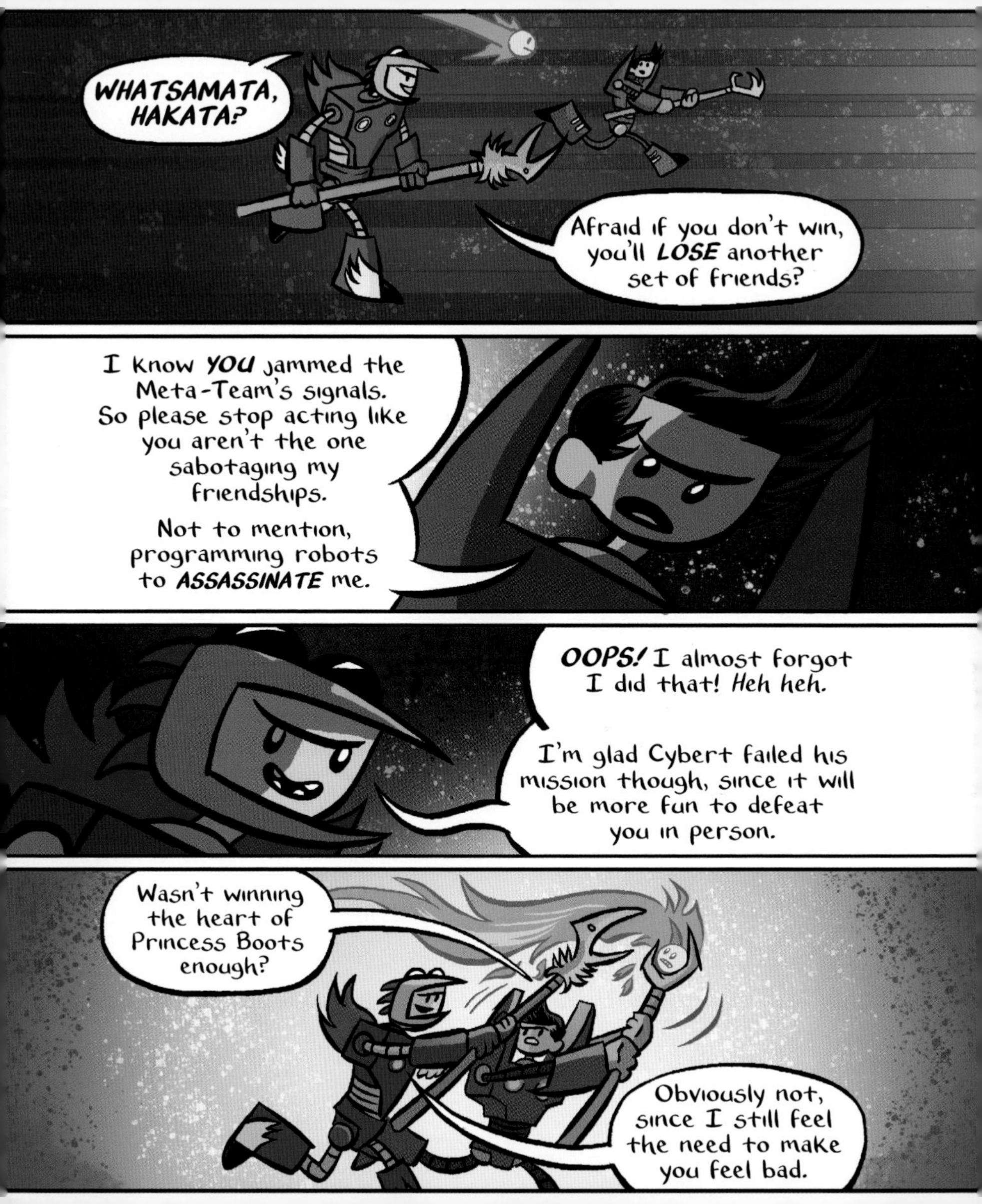
WHATSAMATA, HAKATA?
Afraid if you don't win, you'll LOSE another set of friends?
I know YOU jammed the Meta-Team's signals. So please stop acting like you aren't the one sabotaging my friendships.
Not to mention, programming robots to ASSASSINATE me.
OOPS! I almost forgot I did that! Heh heh.
I'm glad Cybert failed his mission though, since it will be more fun to defeat you in person.
Wasn't winning the heart of Princess Boots enough?
Obviously not, since I still feel the need to make you feel bad.

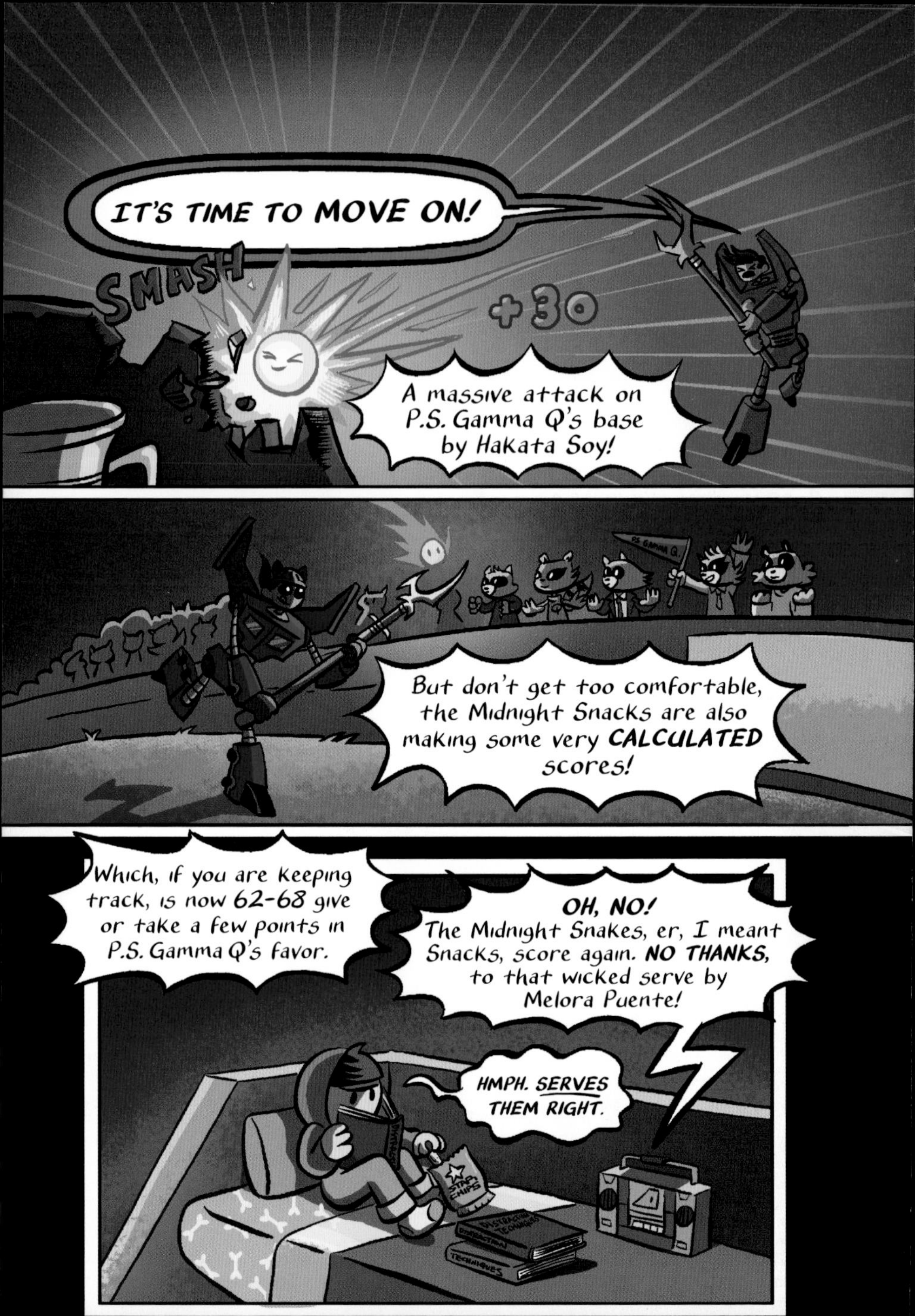
IT'S TIME TO MOVE ON!
SMASH
+30
A massive attack on P.S. Gamma Q's base by Hakata Soy!
But don't get too comfortable, the Midnight Snacks are also making some very **CALCULATED** scores!
Which, if you are keeping track, is now 62-68 give or take a few points in P.S. Gamma Q's favor.
OH, NO! The Midnight Snakes, er, I meant Snacks, score again. **NO THANKS,** to that wicked serve by Melora Puente!
HMPH. SERVES THEM RIGHT.

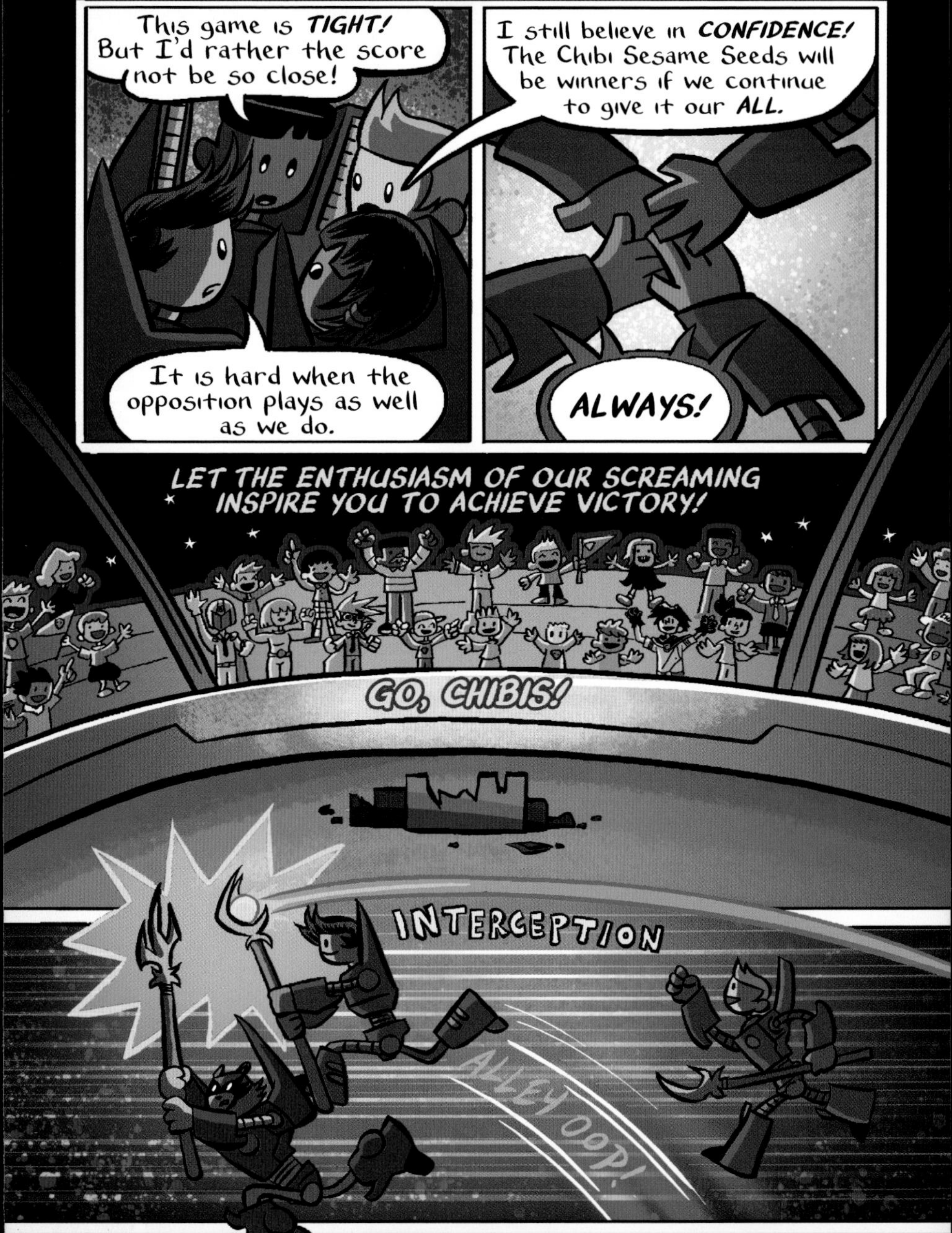
This game is TIGHT! But I'd rather the score not be so close!
It is hard when the opposition plays as well as we do.
I still believe in CONFIDENCE! The Chibi Sesame Seeds will be winners if we continue to give it our ALL.
ALWAYS!
LET THE ENTHUSIASM OF OUR SCREAMING INSPIRE YOU TO ACHIEVE VICTORY!
GO, CHIBIS!
INTERCEPTION
ALLEY OOP!

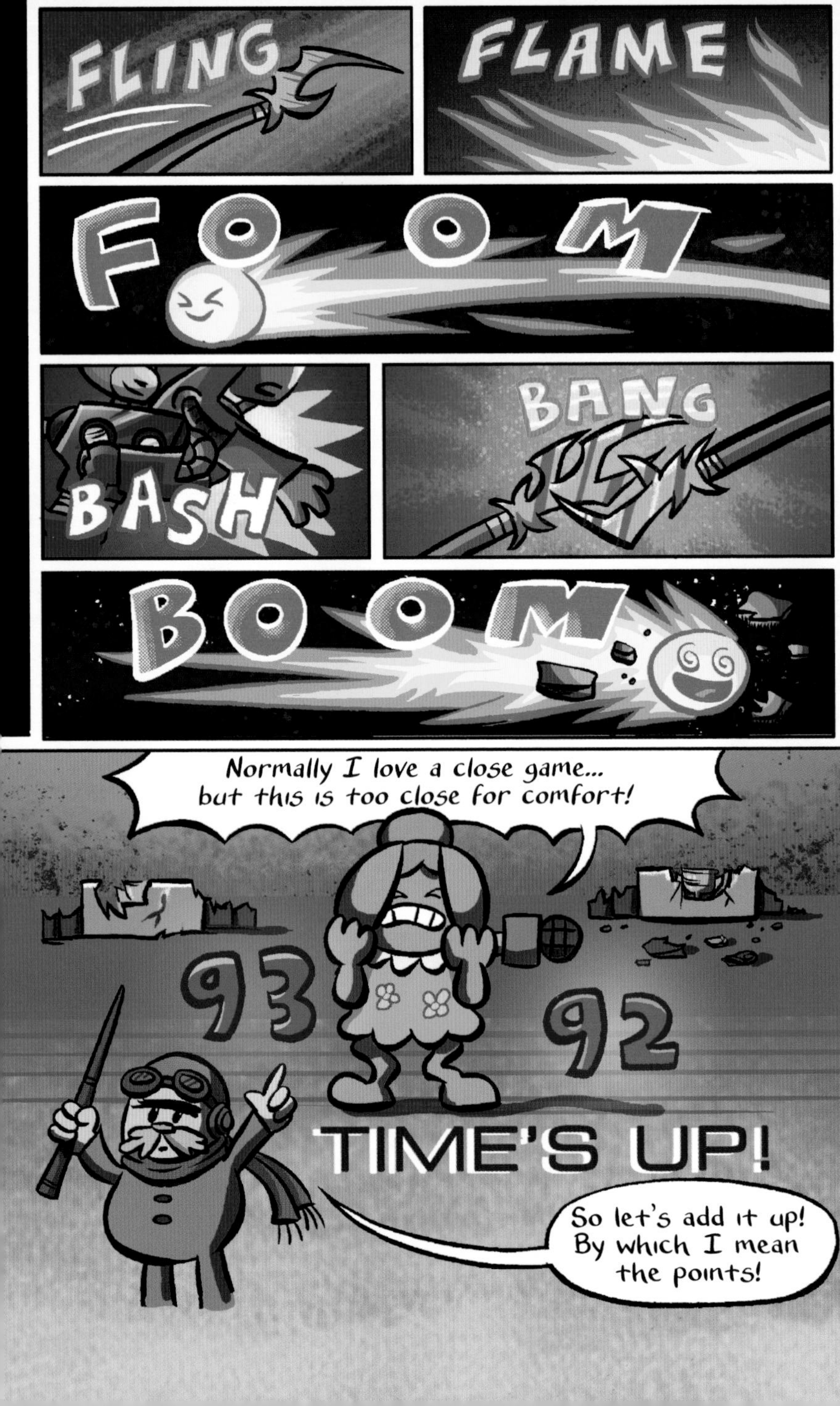
FLING
FLAME
FOOM
BASH
BANG
BOOM
Normally I love a close game... but this is too close for comfort!
93
92
TIME'S UP!
So let's add it up! By which I mean the points!

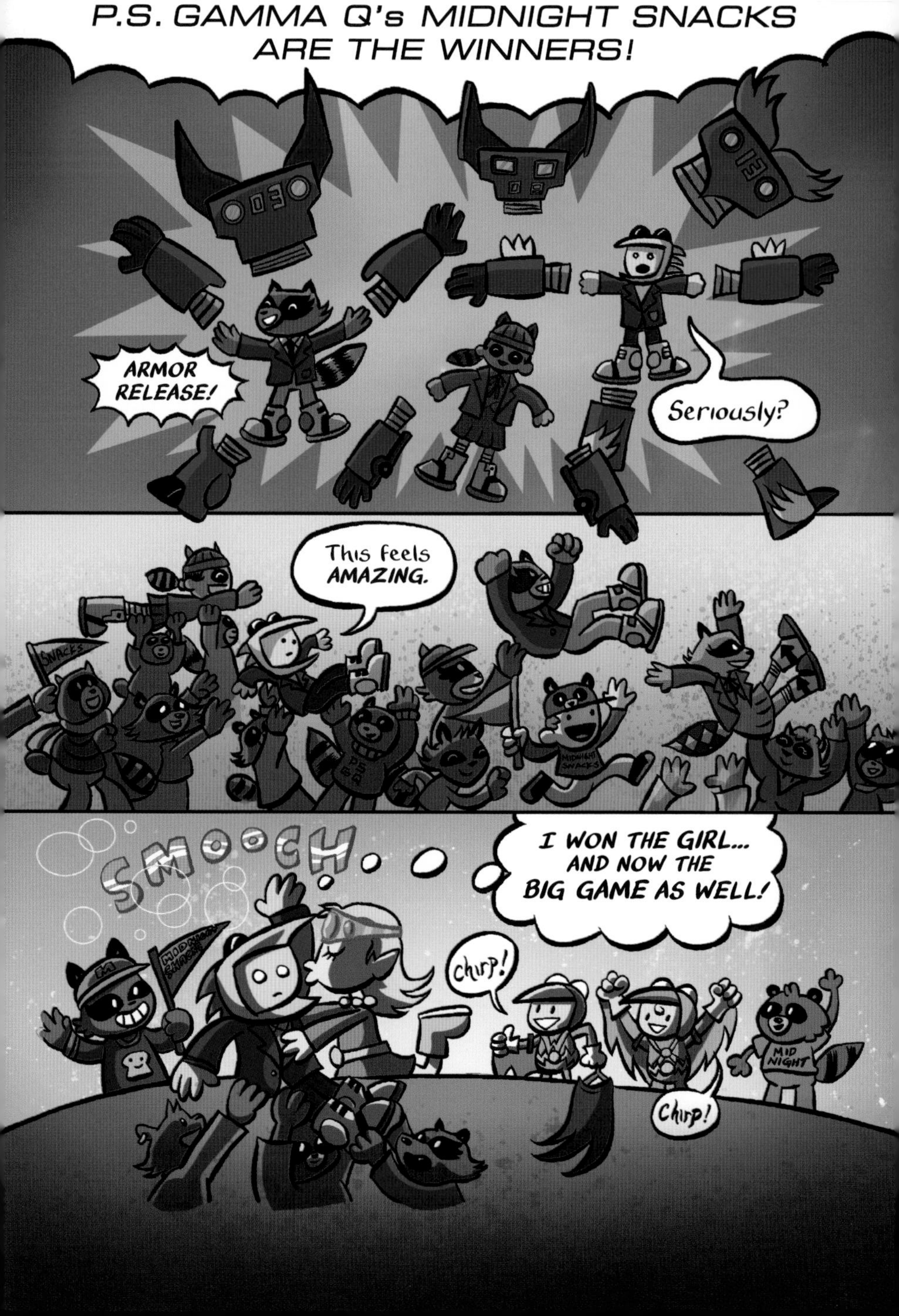

P.S. GAMMA Q's MIDNIGHT SNACKS ARE THE WINNERS!
ARMOR RELEASE!
Seriously?
This feels AMAZING.
SNACKS
MIDNIGHT SNACKS
SMOOCH
I WON THE GIRL... AND NOW THE BIG GAME AS WELL!
Chirp!
Chirp!
MID NIGHT

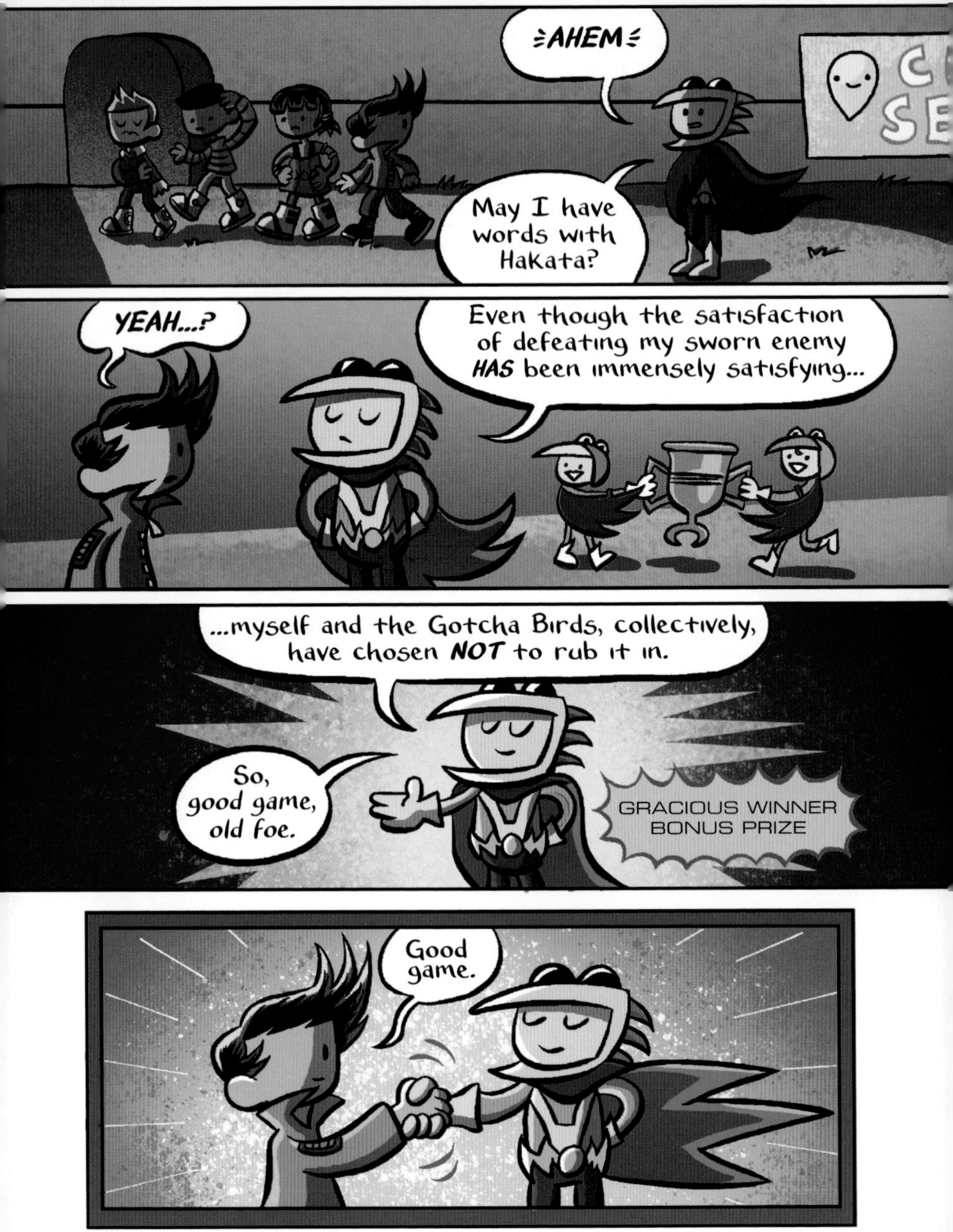
AHEM
May I have words with Hakata?
YEAH...?
Even though the satisfaction of defeating my sworn enemy HAS been immensely satisfying...
...myself and the Gotcha Birds, collectively, have chosen NOT to rub it in.
So, good game, old foe.
GRACIOUS WINNER BONUS PRIZE
Good game.

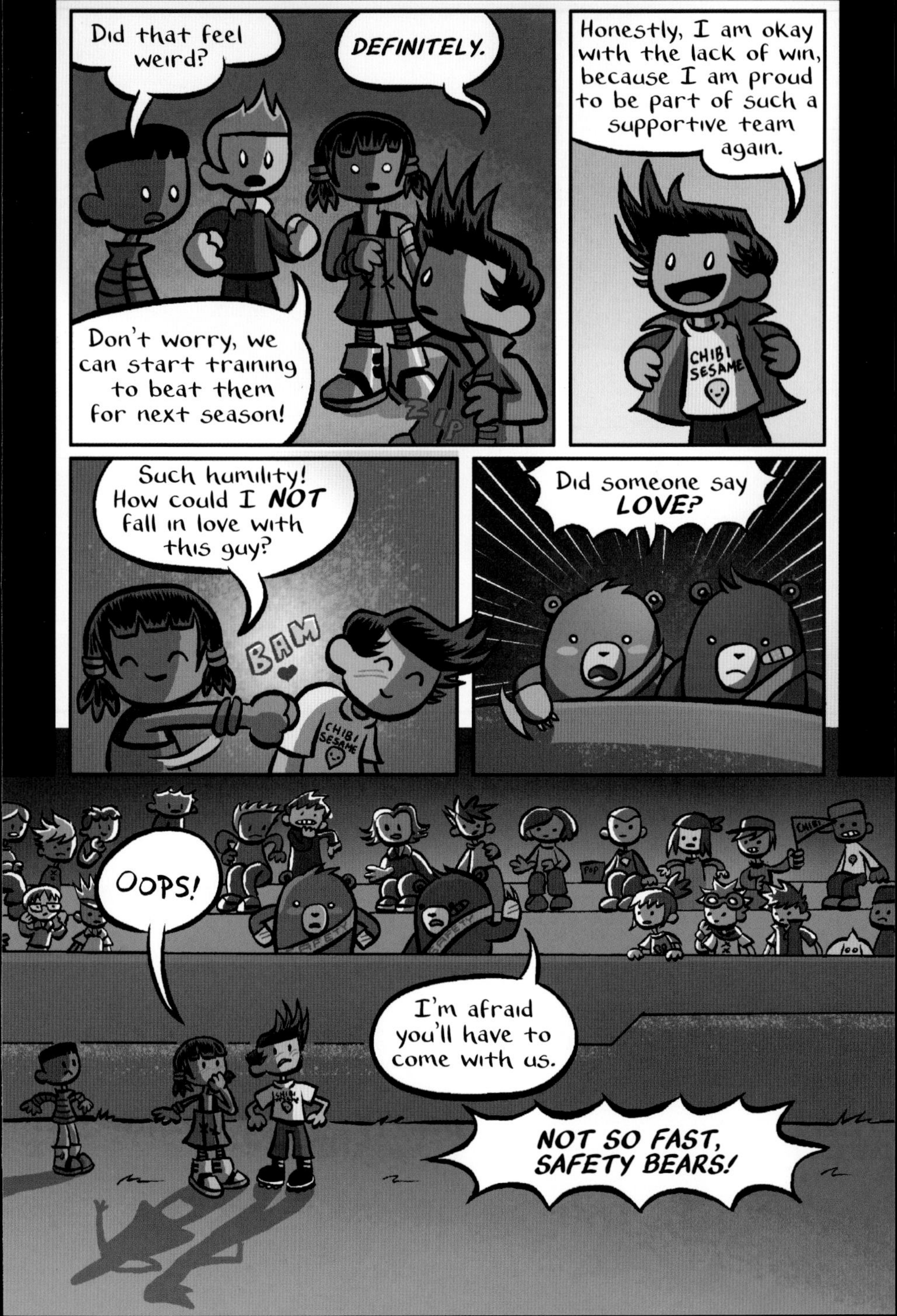
Did that feel weird?
DEFINITELY.
Don't worry, we can start training to beat them for next season!
ZIP
Honestly, I am okay with the lack of win, because I am proud to be part of such a supportive team again.
CHIBI SESAME
Such humility! How could I NOT fall in love with this guy?
BAM
CHIBI SESAME
Did someone say LOVE?
OOPS!
I'm afraid you'll have to come with us.
NOT SO FAST, SAFETY BEARS!

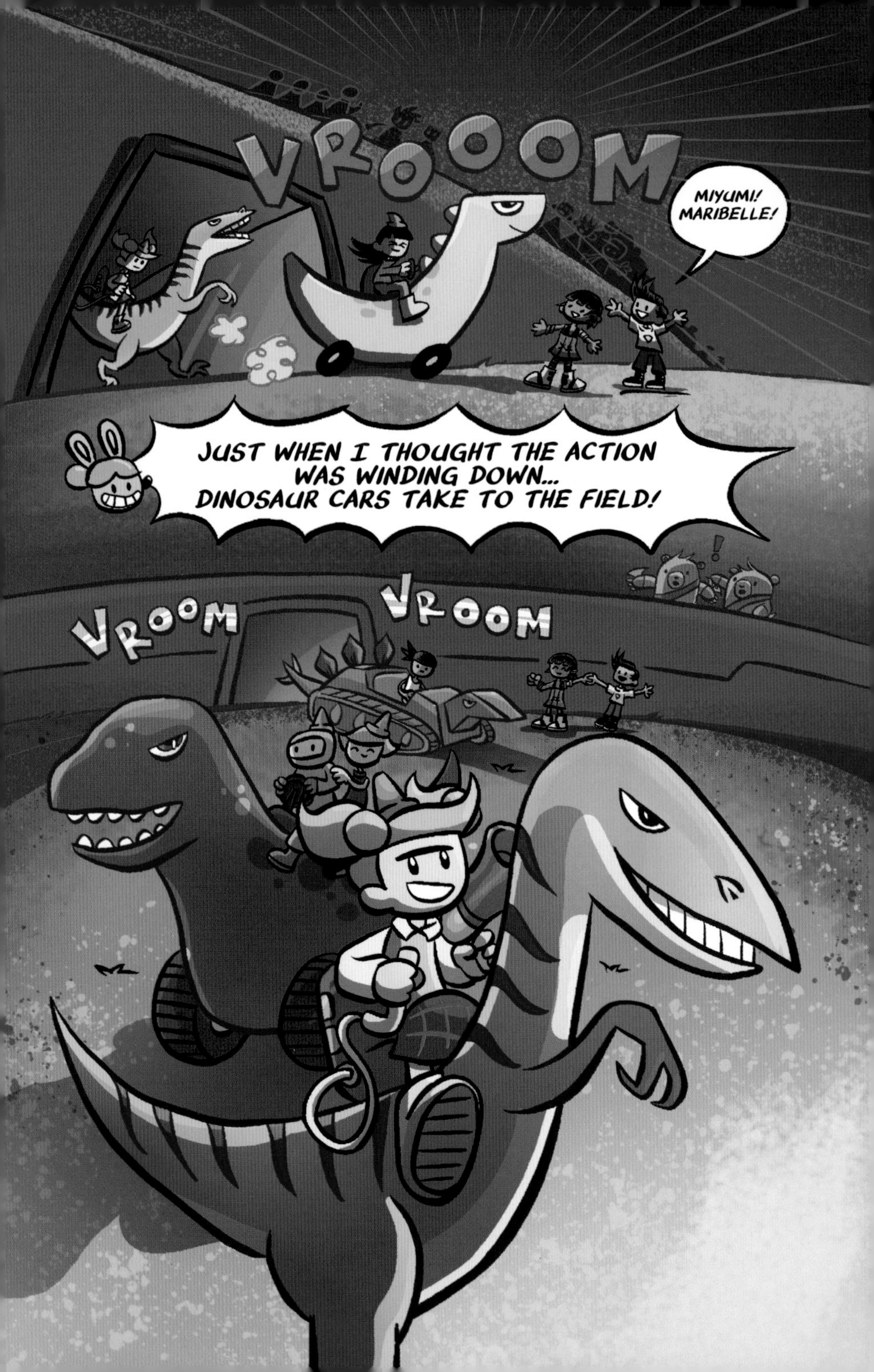
VROOOOM
MIYUMI! MARIBELLE!
JUST WHEN I THOUGHT THE ACTION WAS WINDING DOWN... DINOSAUR CARS TAKE TO THE FIELD!
!
VROOM
VROOM

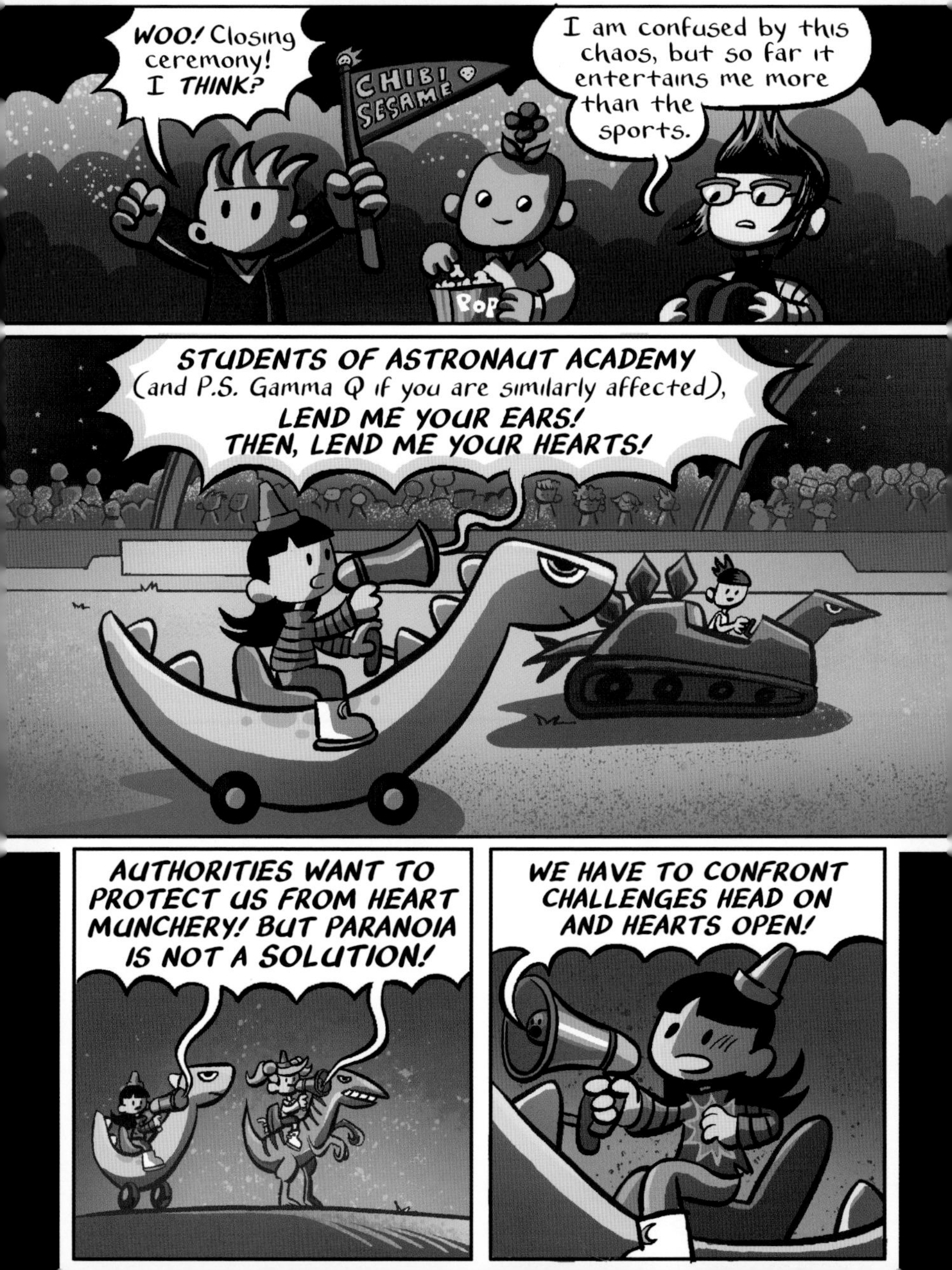
WOO! Closing ceremony! I THINK?
CHIBI SESAME
I am confused by this chaos, but so far it entertains me more than the sports.
POP
STUDENTS OF ASTRONAUT ACADEMY (and P.S. Gamma Q if you are similarly affected), LEND ME YOUR EARS! THEN, LEND ME YOUR HEARTS!
AUTHORITIES WANT TO PROTECT US FROM HEART MUNCHERY! BUT PARANOIA IS NOT A SOLUTION!
WE HAVE TO CONFRONT CHALLENGES HEAD ON AND HEARTS OPEN!

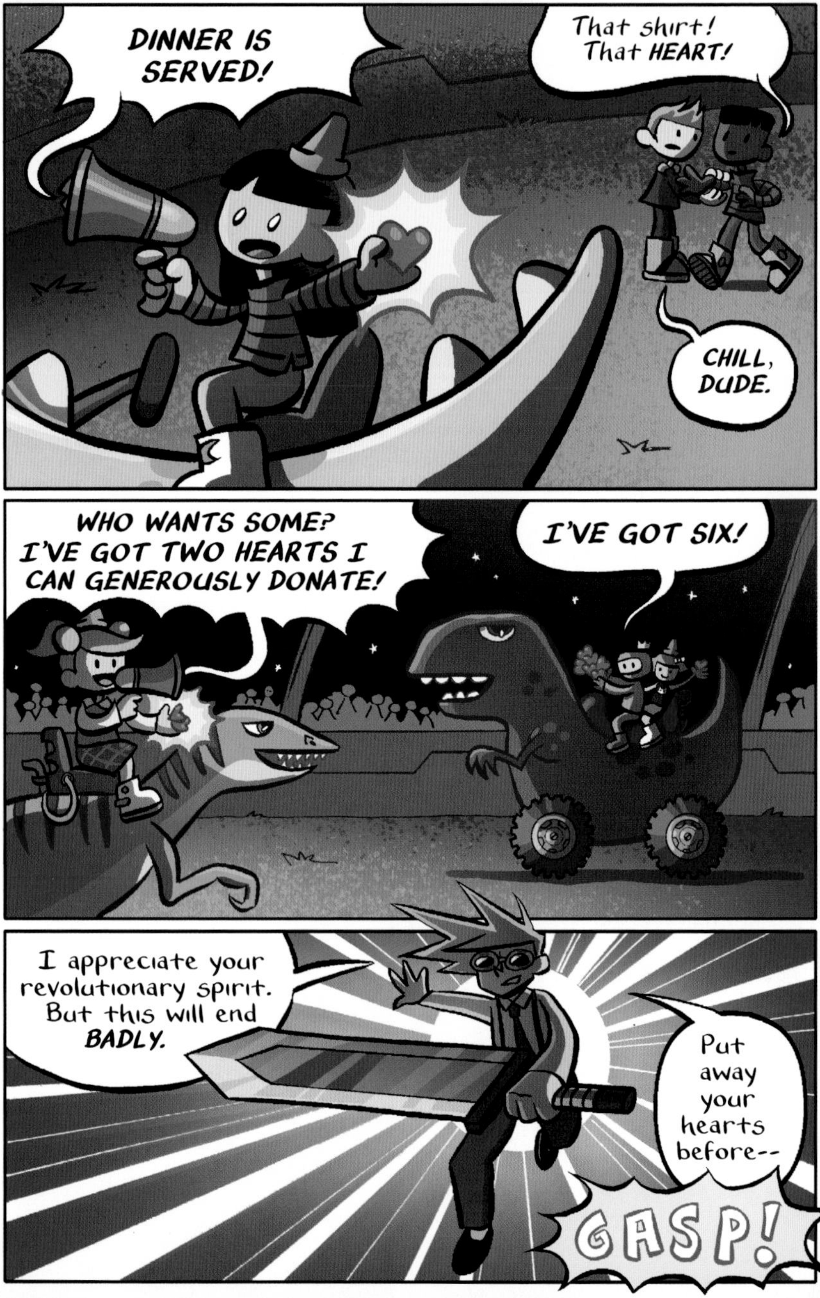
DINNER IS SERVED!
That shirt! That HEART!
CHILL, DUDE.
WHO WANTS SOME? I'VE GOT TWO HEARTS I CAN GENEROUSLY DONATE!
I'VE GOT SIX!
I appreciate your revolutionary spirit. But this will end BADLY.
Put away your hearts before--
GASP!

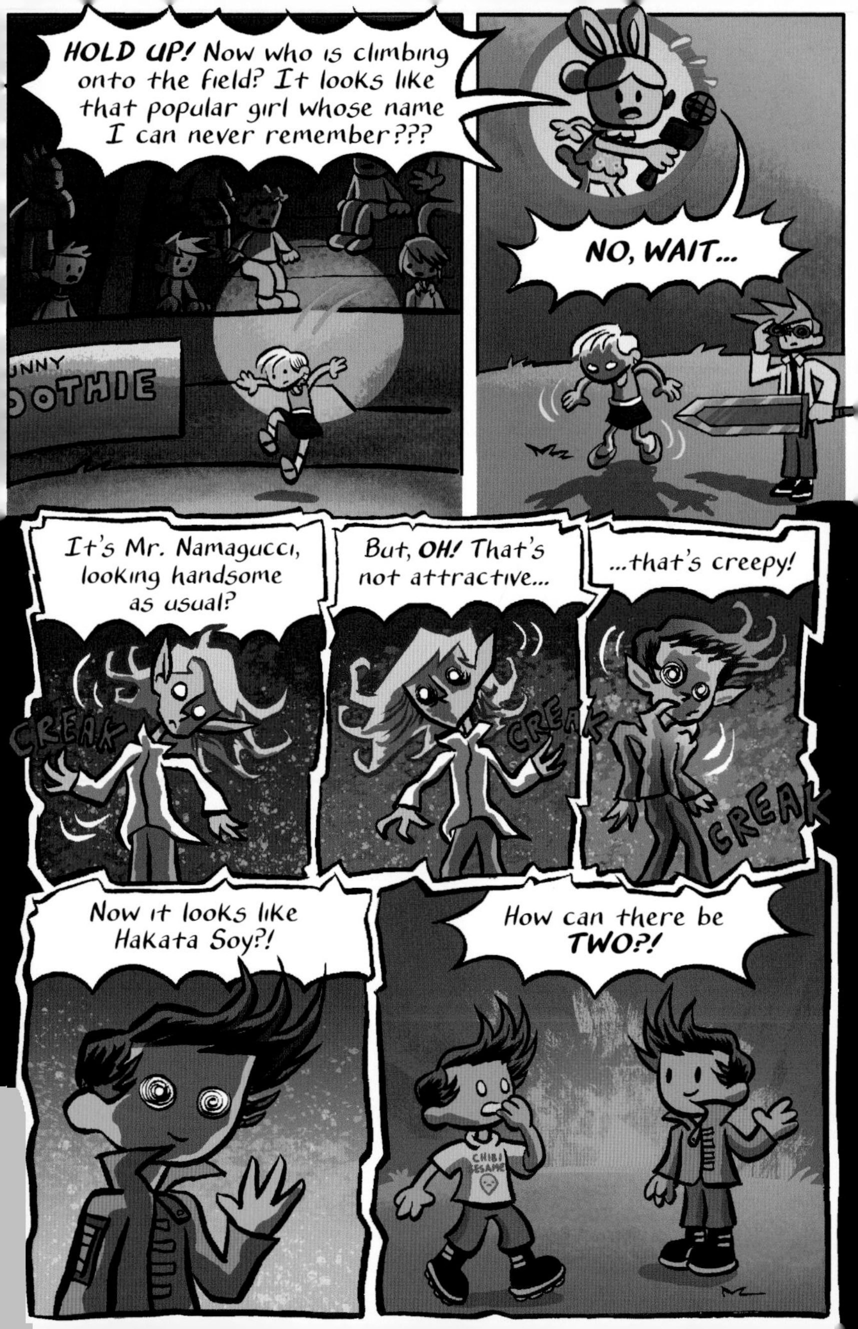
HOLD UP! Now who is climbing onto the field? It looks like that popular girl whose name I can never remember???
UNNY
OOTHIE
NO, WAIT...
It's Mr. Namagucci, looking handsome as usual?
CREAK
But, OH! That's not attractive...
CREAK
...that's creepy!
CREAK
Now it looks like Hakata Soy?!
How can there be TWO?!
CHIBI SESAME

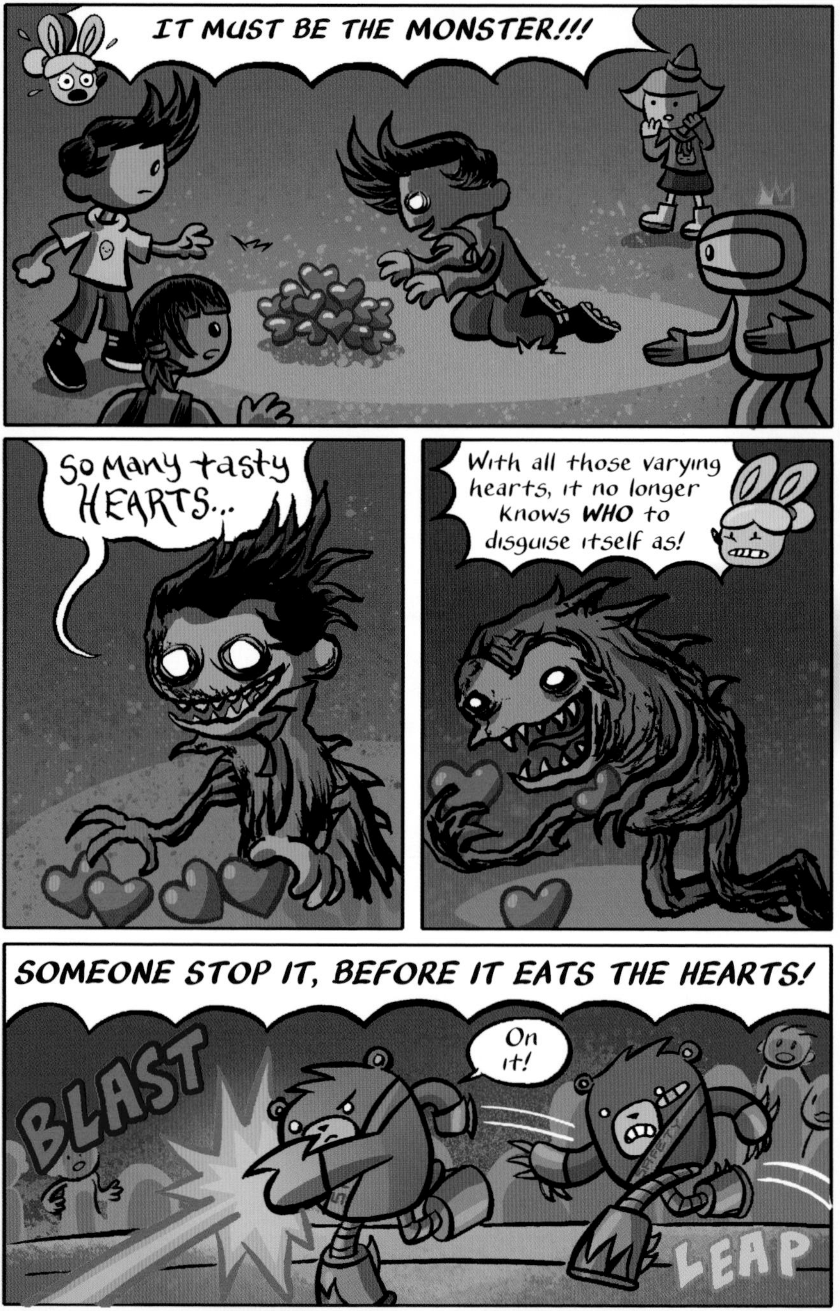
IT MUST BE THE MONSTER!!!
So Many tasty HEARTS...
With all those varying hearts, it no longer knows WHO to disguise itself as!
SOMEONE STOP IT, BEFORE IT EATS THE HEARTS!
BLAST
On it!
LEAP

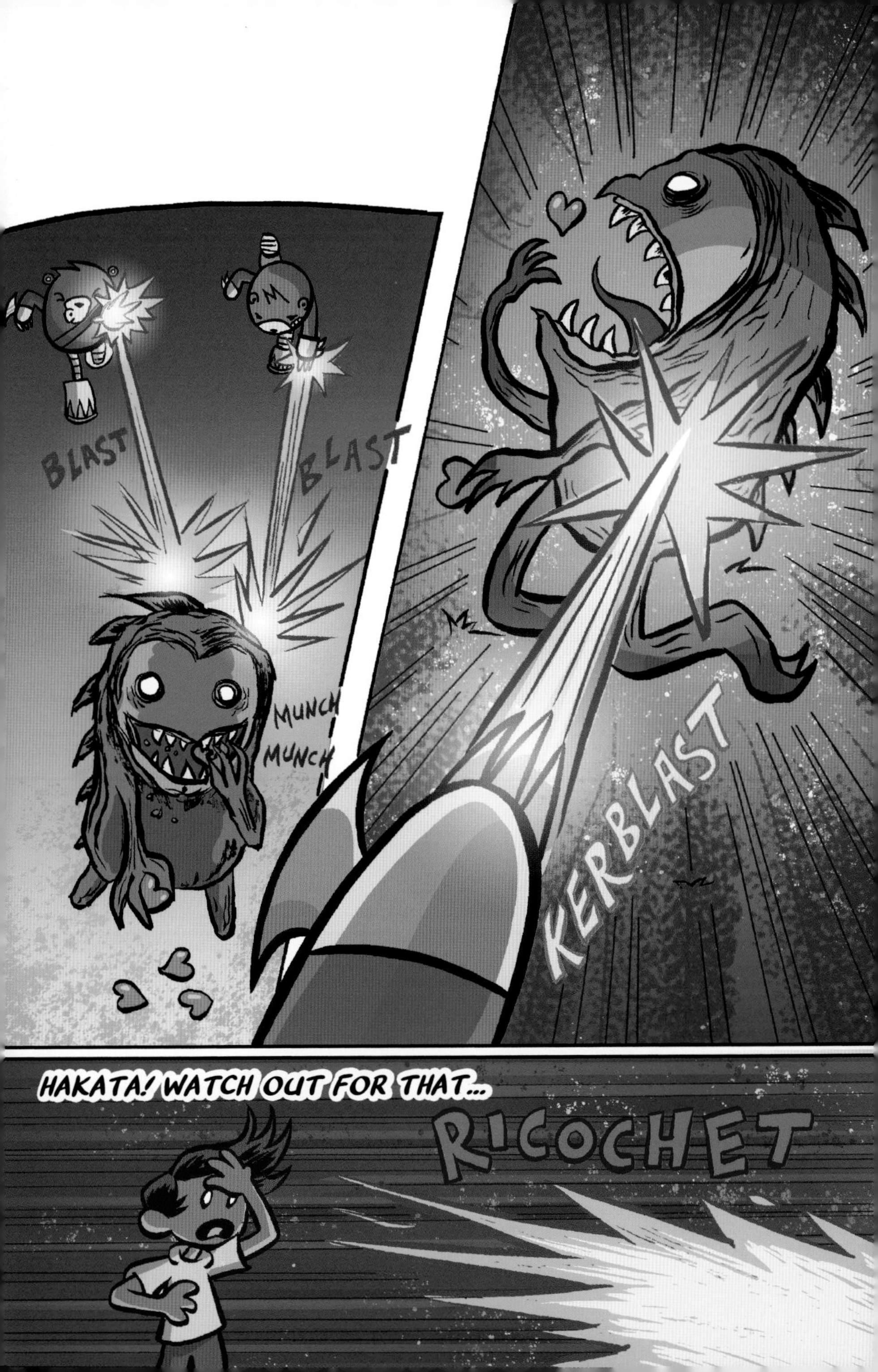
BLAST
BLAST
MUNCH
MUNCH
KERBLAST
HAKATA! WATCH OUT FOR THAT...
RICOCHET

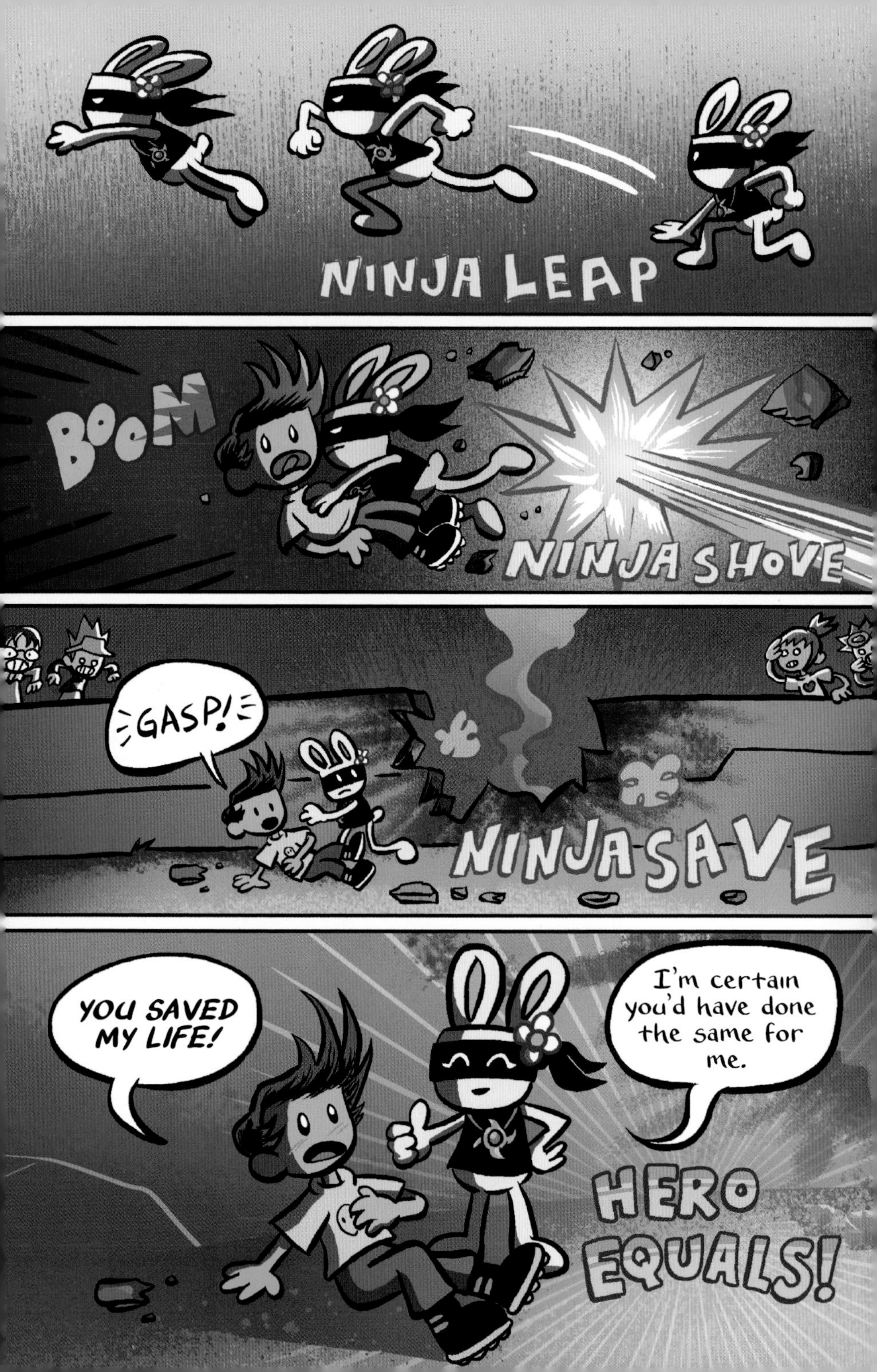
NINJA LEAP
BOOM
NINJA SHOVE
GASP!
NINJA SAVE
YOU SAVED MY LIFE!
I'm certain you'd have done the same for me.
HERO EQUALS!

Eating all those hearts has made the monster *SO CHUNKY!*

SWOOSH

RICOCHET

POP

Even *MY SWORD* has no effect!

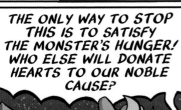

THE ONLY WAY TO STOP THIS IS TO SATISFY THE MONSTER'S HUNGER! WHO ELSE WILL DONATE HEARTS TO OUR NOBLE CAUSE?

No offense, but that's kind of asking a lot.

Can't I just donate my naturally curly hair?

At least that tends to *GROW BACK!*

THAT'S OUR POINT! MARIBELLE HERE DISCOVERED YOUR HEARTS CAN--

Um, Maribelle?

HEY! Who turned off the time?

POKE POKE

TOTALLY FROZEN

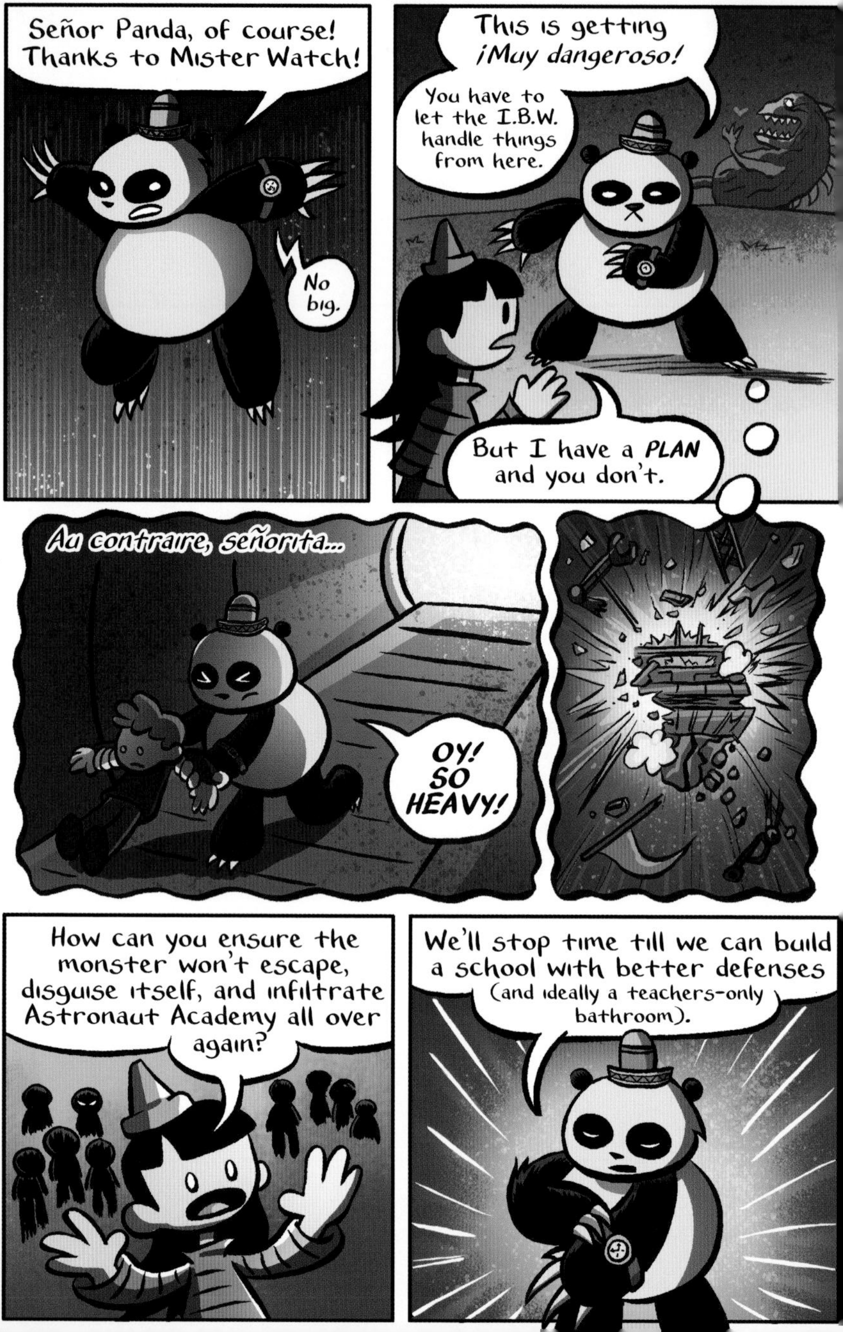
Señor Panda, of course! Thanks to Mister Watch!
No big.
This is getting ¡Muy dangeroso!
You have to let the I.B.W. handle things from here.
But I have a PLAN and you don't.
Au contraire, señorita...
OY! SO HEAVY!
How can you ensure the monster won't escape, disguise itself, and infiltrate Astronaut Academy all over again?
We'll stop time till we can build a school with better defenses (and ideally a teachers-only bathroom).

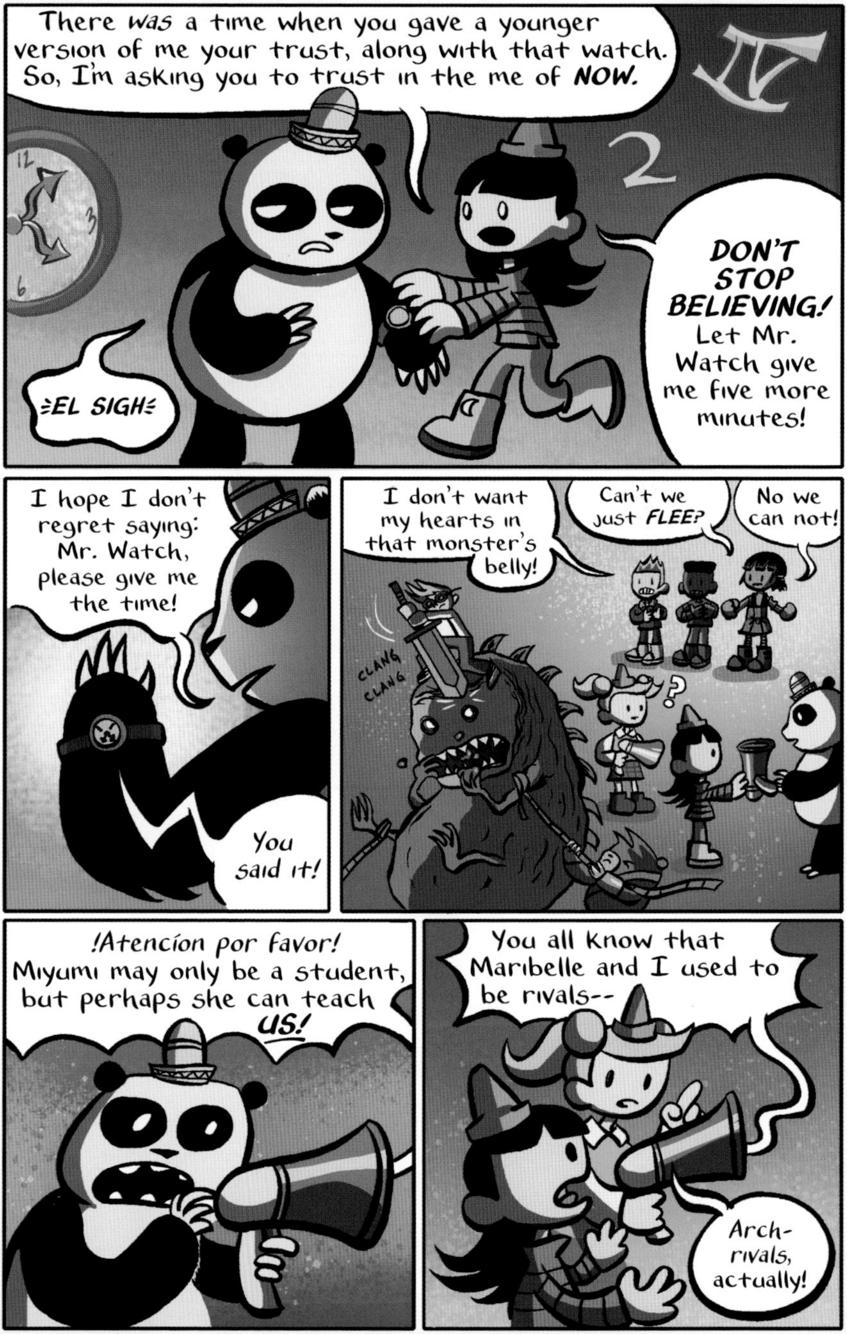
There *was* a time when you gave a younger version of me your trust, along with that watch. So, I'm asking you to trust in the me of **NOW.**
DON'T STOP BELIEVING! Let Mr. Watch give me five more minutes!
EL SIGH
I hope I don't regret saying: Mr. Watch, please give me the time!
You said it!
I don't want my hearts in that monster's belly!
Can't we just **FLEE?**
No we can not!
CLANG CLANG
!Atencíon por favor! Miyumi may only be a student, but perhaps she can teach **US!**
You all know that Maribelle and I used to be rivals--
Arch-rivals, actually!

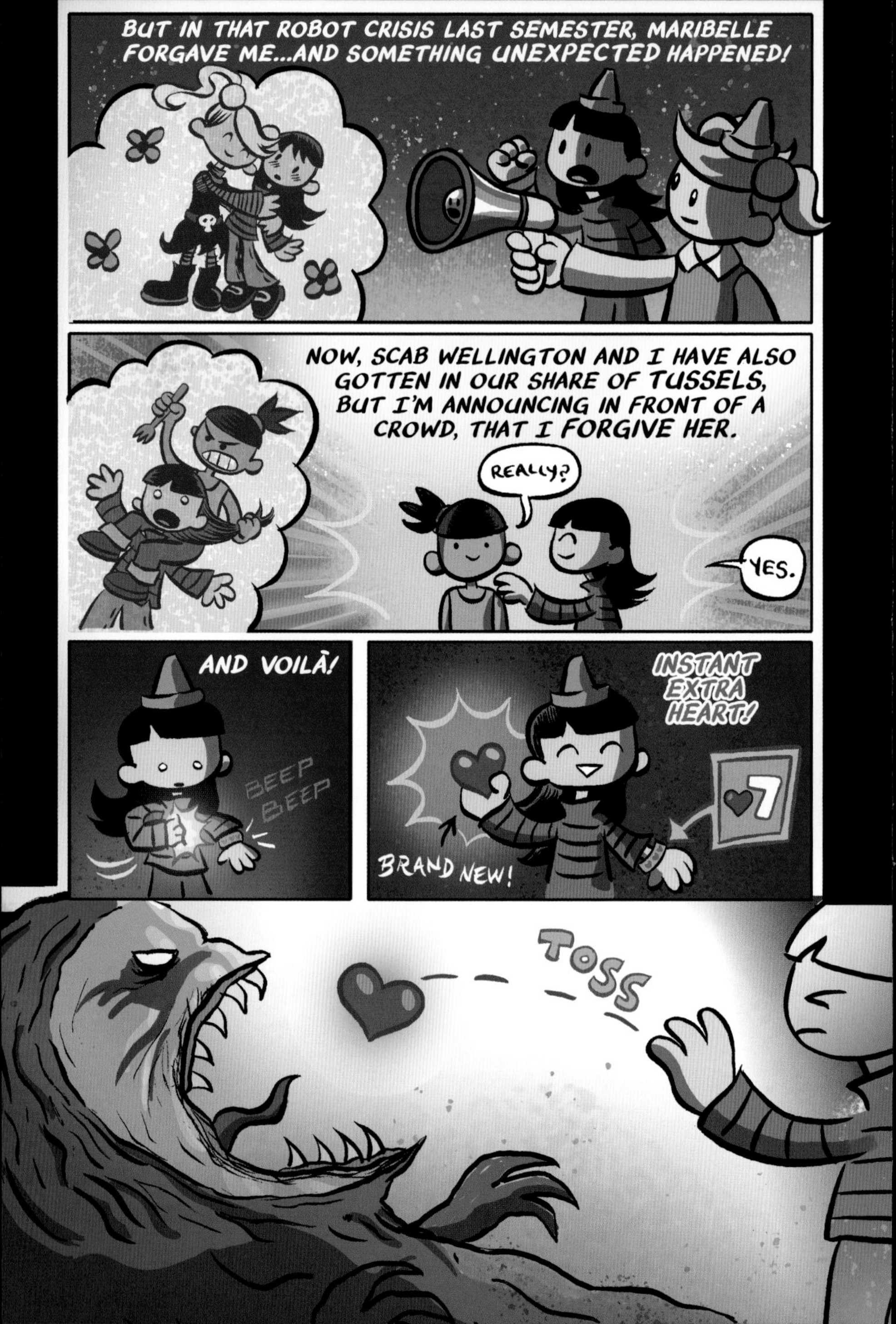
BUT IN THAT ROBOT CRISIS LAST SEMESTER, MARIBELLE FORGAVE ME...AND SOMETHING UNEXPECTED HAPPENED!
NOW, SCAB WELLINGTON AND I HAVE ALSO GOTTEN IN OUR SHARE OF TUSSELS, BUT I'M ANNOUNCING IN FRONT OF A CROWD, THAT I FORGIVE HER.
REALLY?
YES.
AND VOILÀ!
BEEP BEEP
INSTANT EXTRA HEART!
7
BRAND NEW!
TOSS

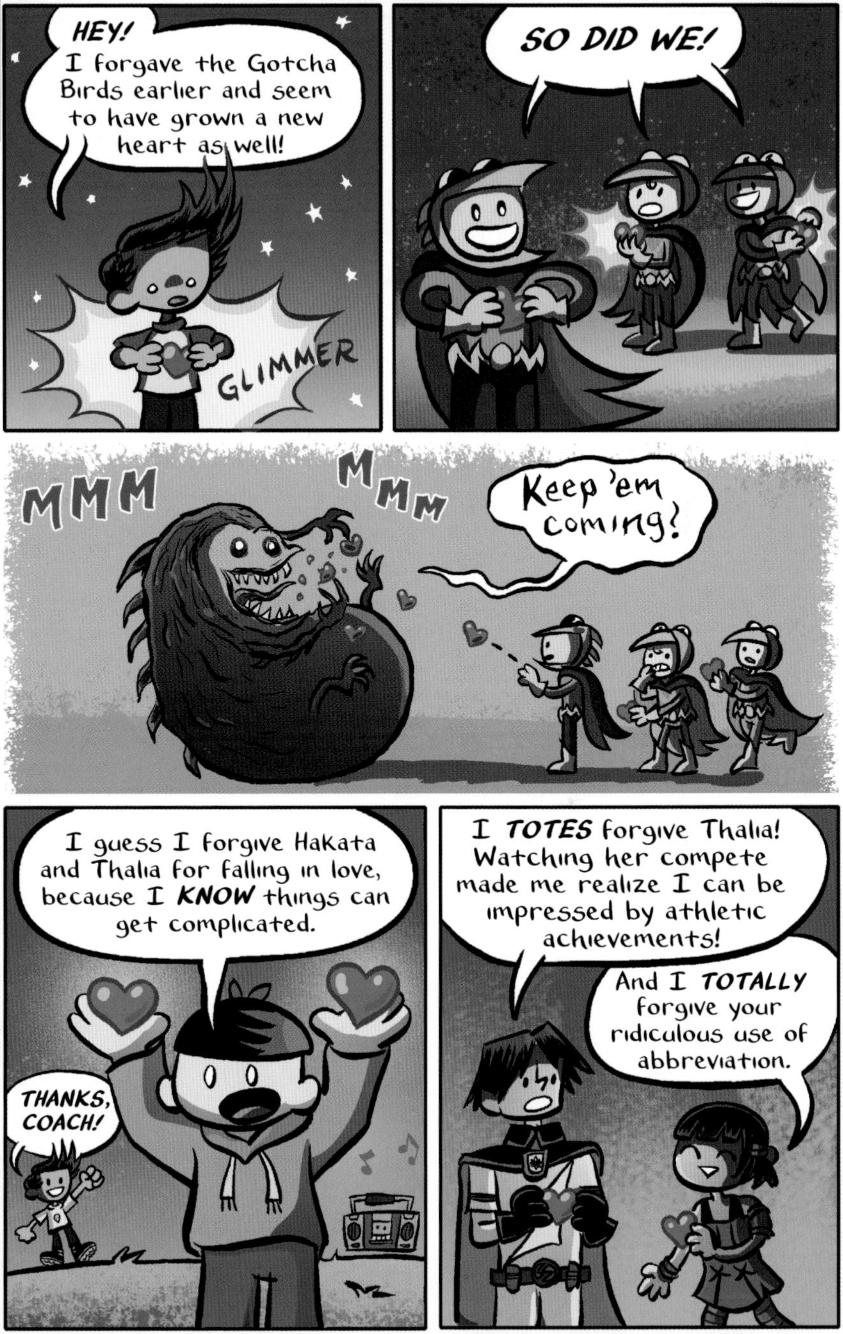
HEY!
I forgave the Gotcha Birds earlier and seem to have grown a new heart as well!
GLIMMER
SO DID WE!
MMM
MMM
Keep 'em coming?
I guess I forgive Hakata and Thalia for falling in love, because I KNOW things can get complicated.
THANKS, COACH!
I TOTES forgive Thalia! Watching her compete made me realize I can be impressed by athletic achievements!
And I TOTALLY forgive your ridiculous use of abbreviation.

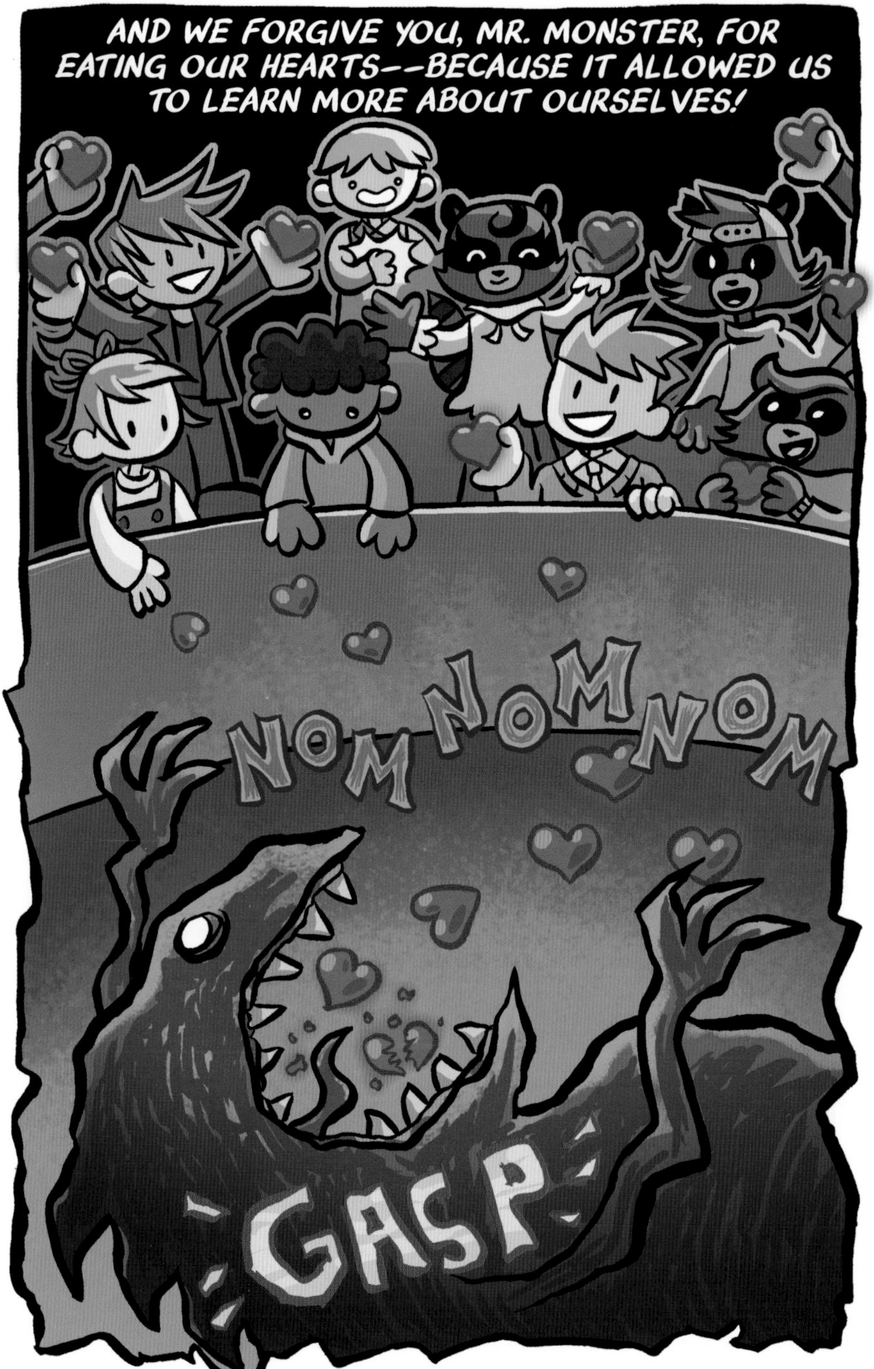
AND WE FORGIVE YOU, MR. MONSTER, FOR EATING OUR HEARTS--BECAUSE IT ALLOWED US TO LEARN MORE ABOUT OURSELVES!
NOM NOM NOM NOM
GASP

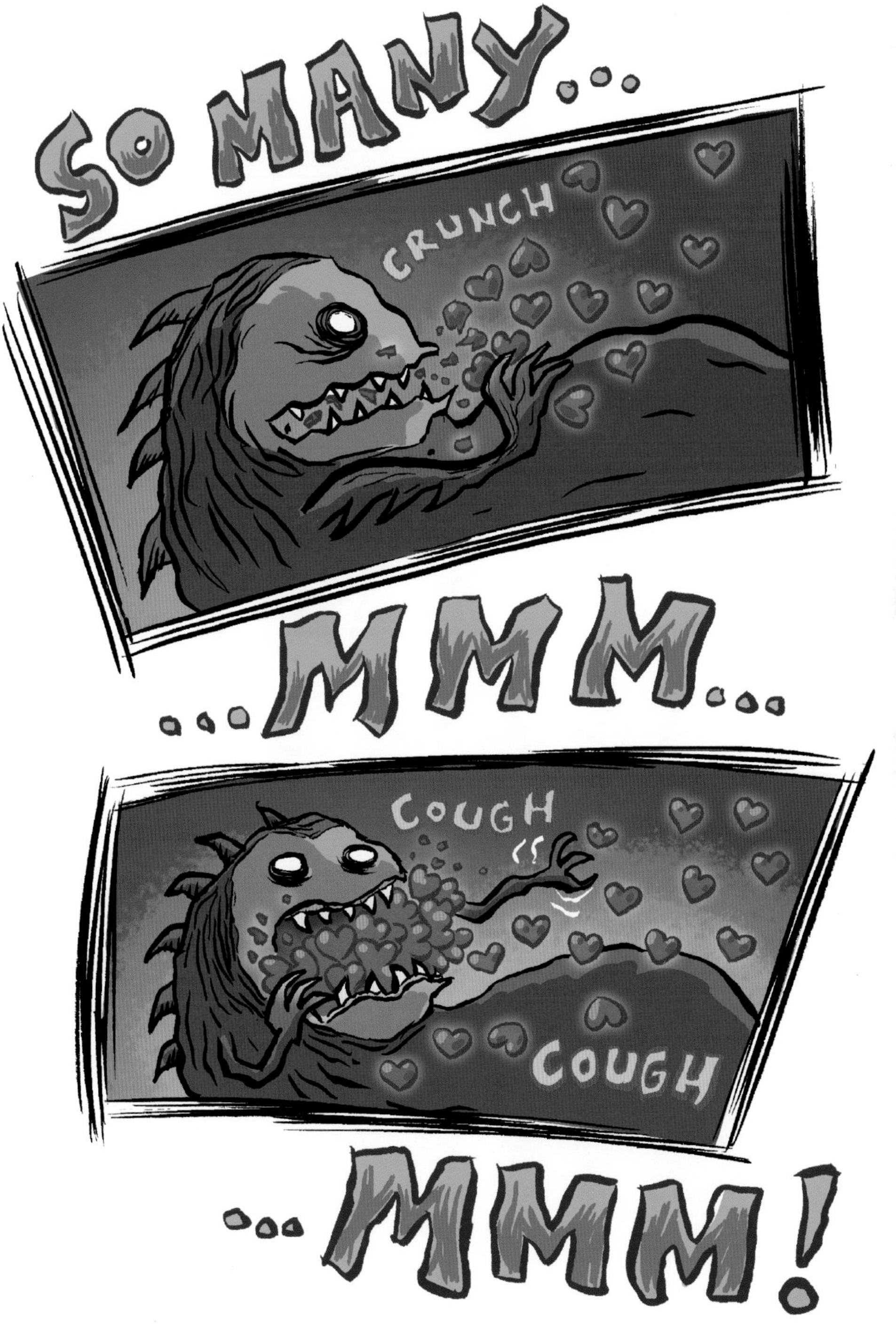
SO MANY...
CRUNCH
...MMM...
COUGH
COUGH
...MMM!

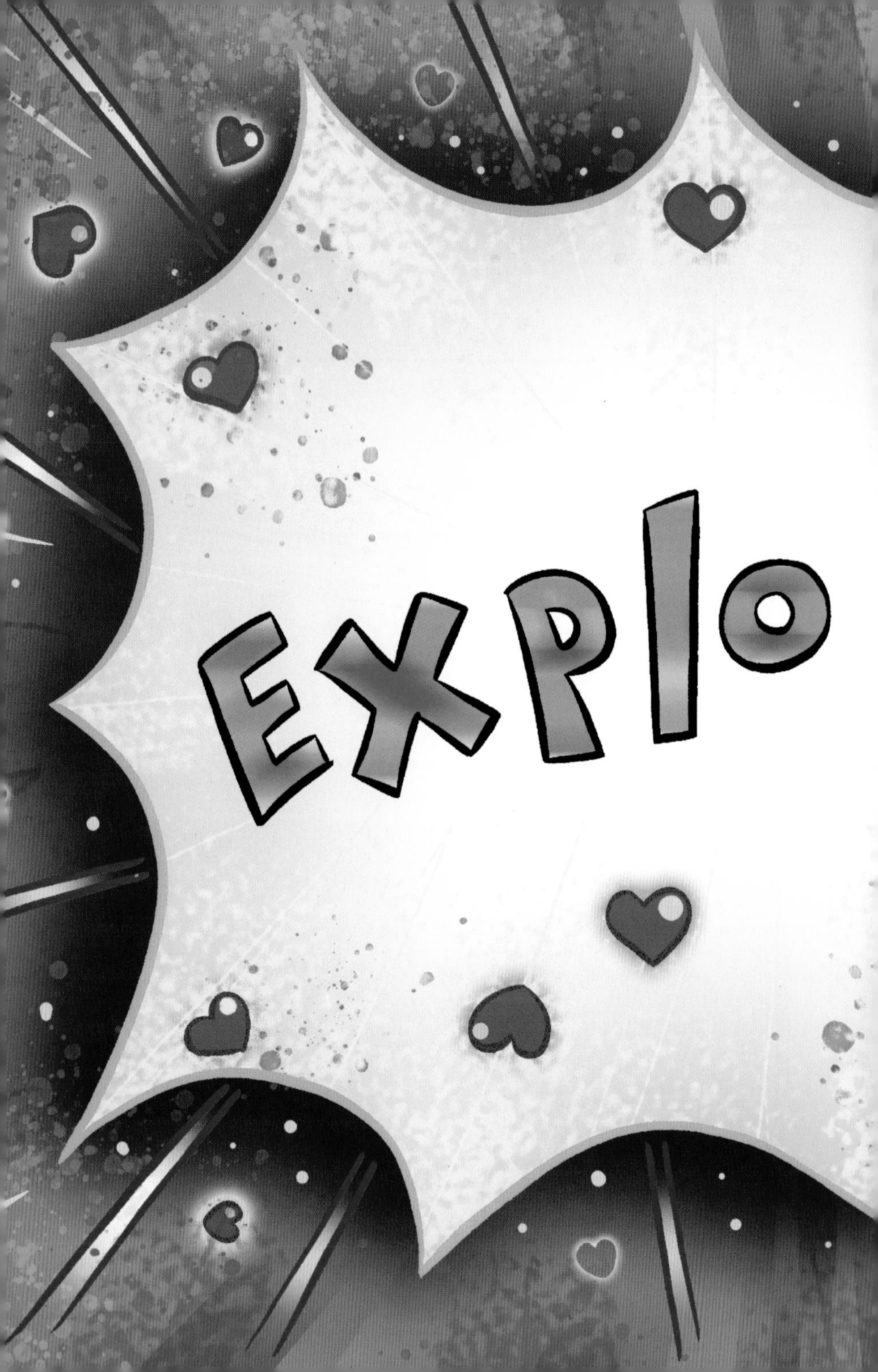
Explo

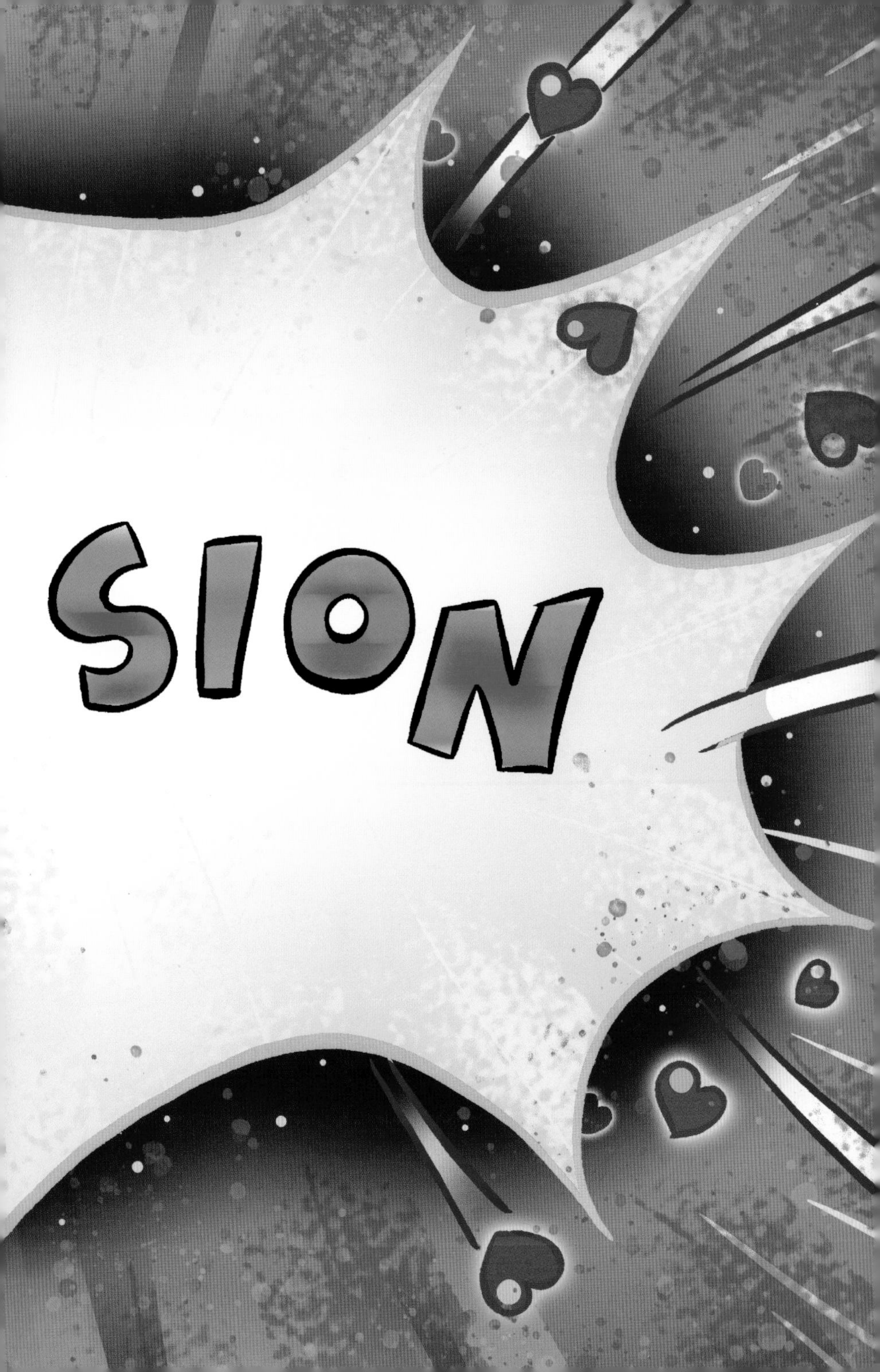
SION

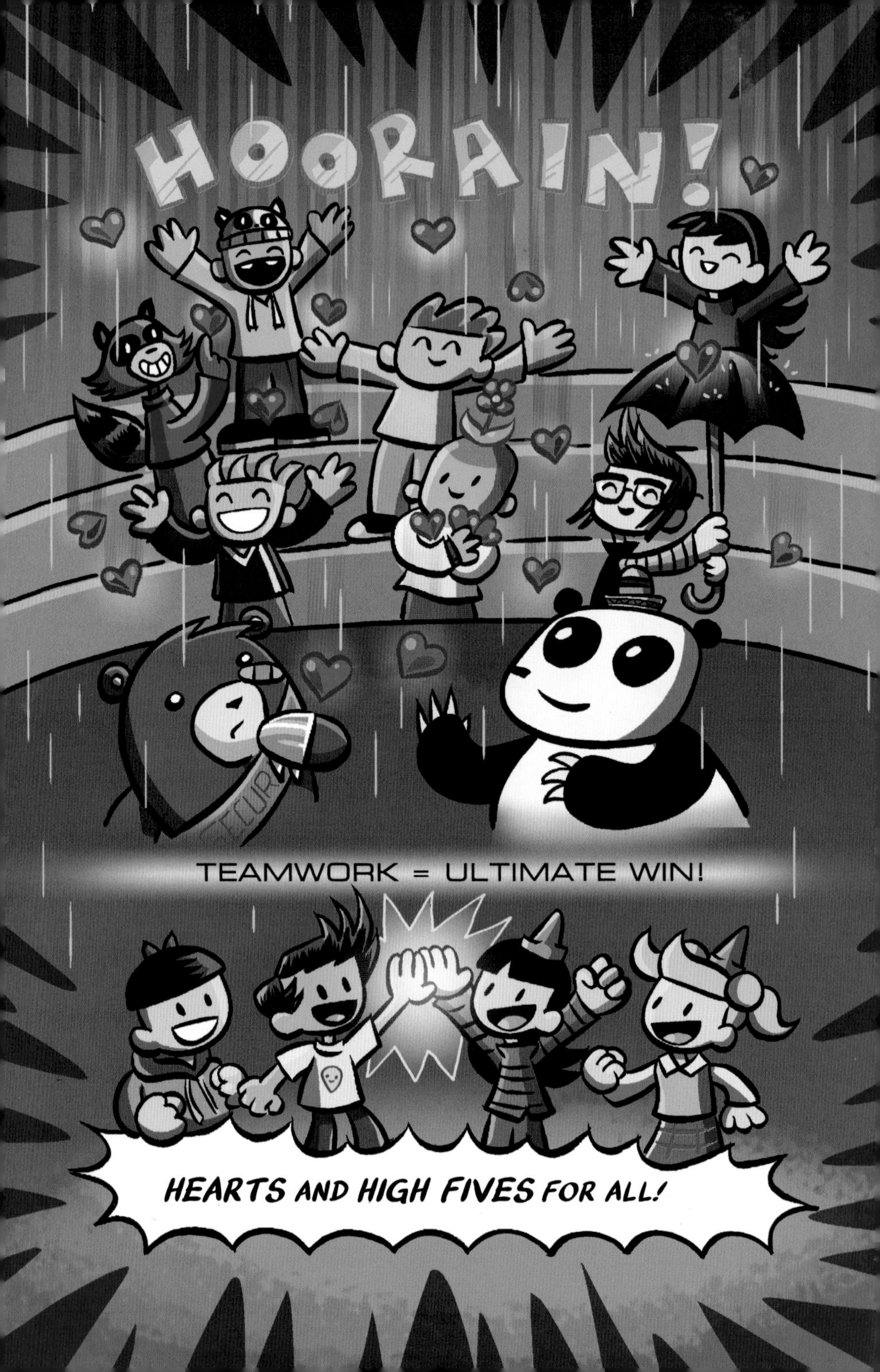
HOORAIN!
TEAMWORK = ULTIMATE WIN!
HEARTS AND HIGH FIVES FOR ALL!

AND SO...

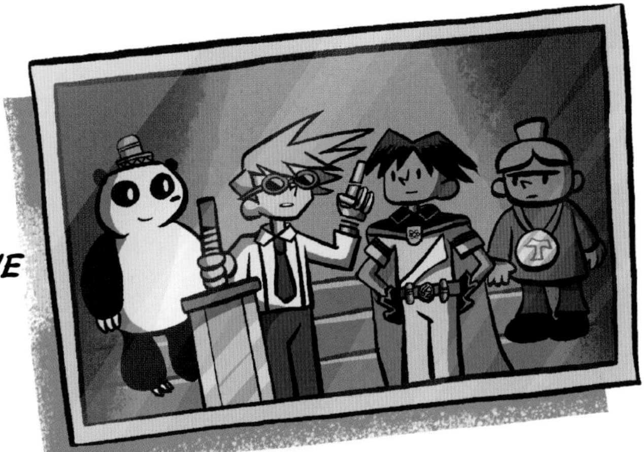

THE BAN ON LOVE
WAS LIFTED.

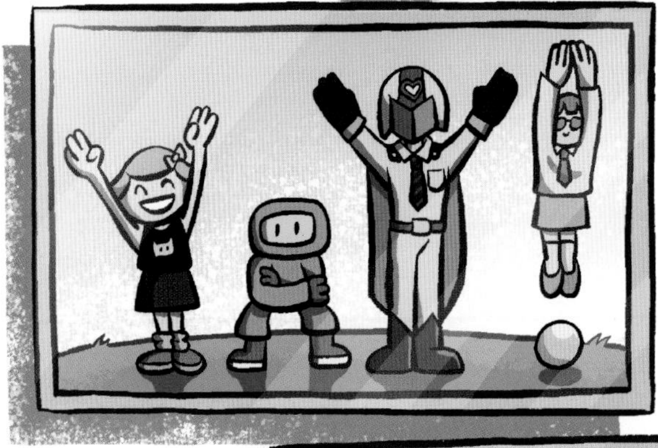

THE TALENT
SPELLING
BEE WAS
RESCHEDULED.

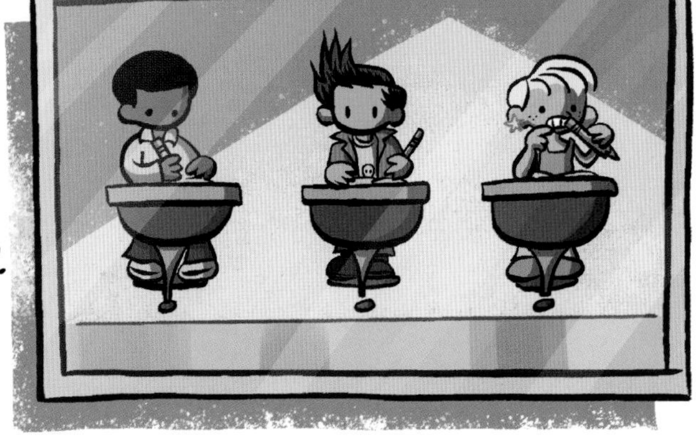

EVENTUALLY
FINAL EXAMS
WERE TAKEN.

BUT FIRST...
THERE WAS A DANCE PARTY!
(As is customary for the end
of dramatic conflicts.)

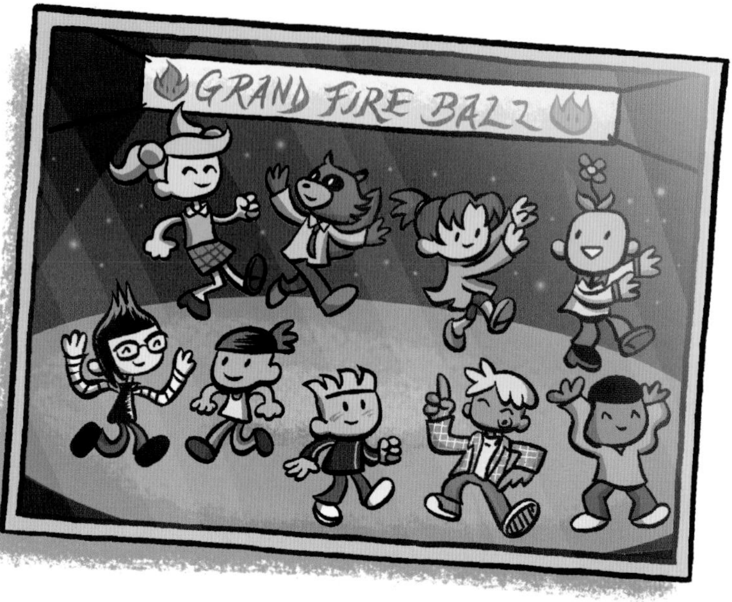
GRAND FIRE BALL

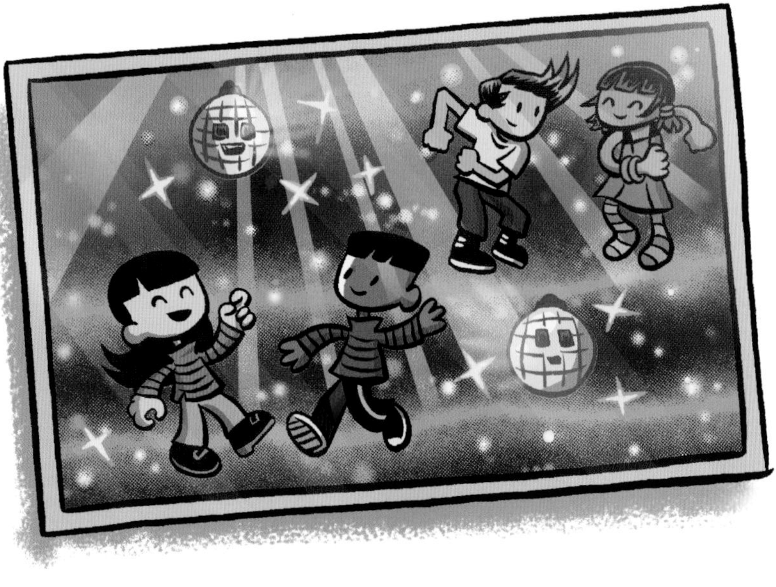

EVEN THOUGH A LOT OF RIVALRIES ENDED...

...NOT EVERYONE WAS READY FOR
FRIEND REQUESTS.

BUT NO ONE KNOWS WHO OR WHAT
THE FUTURE CAN HOLD!

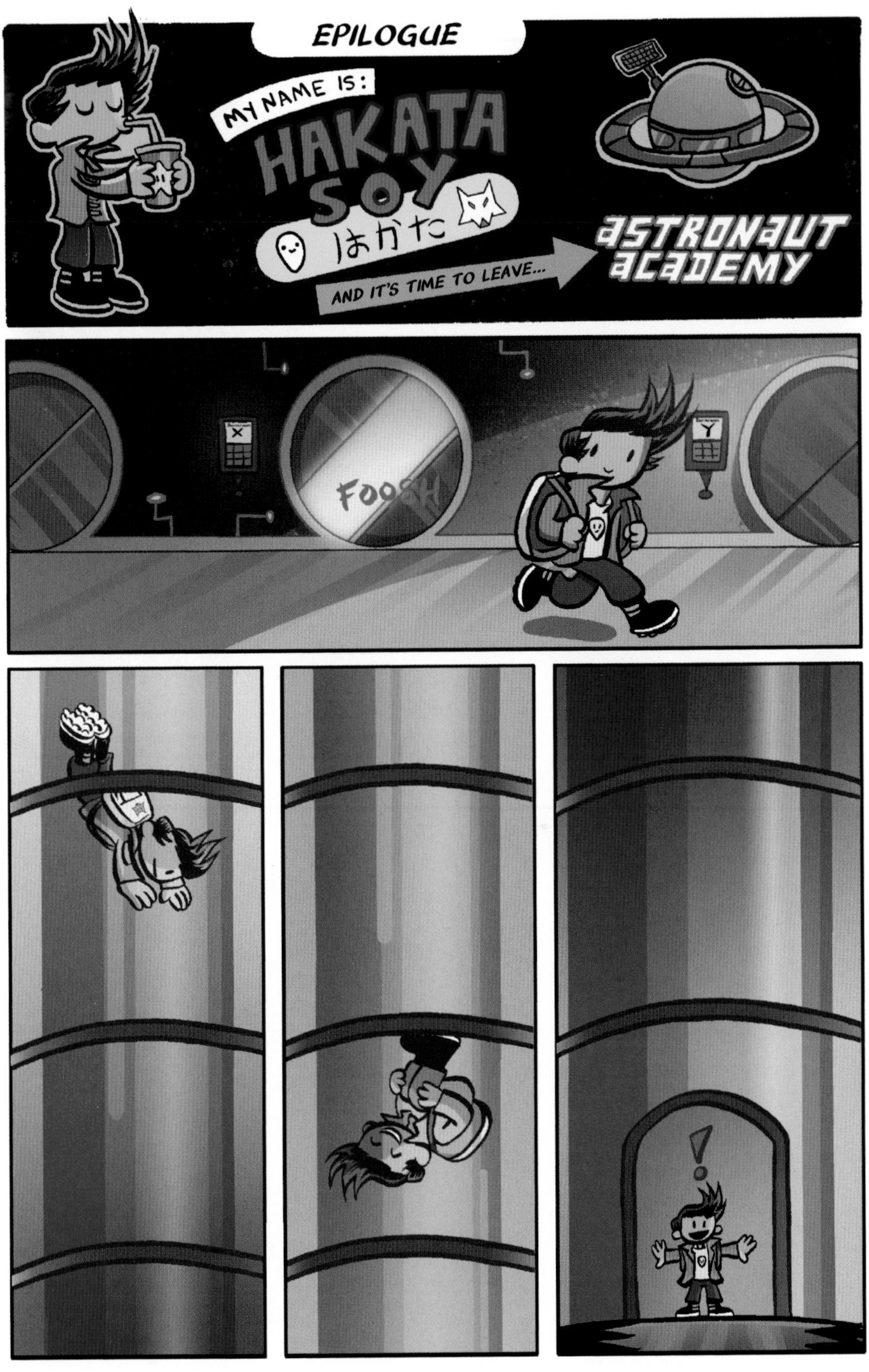
EPILOGUE
MY NAME IS:
HAKATA SOY
はかた
AND IT'S TIME TO LEAVE...
ASTRONAUT ACADEMY
FOOSH

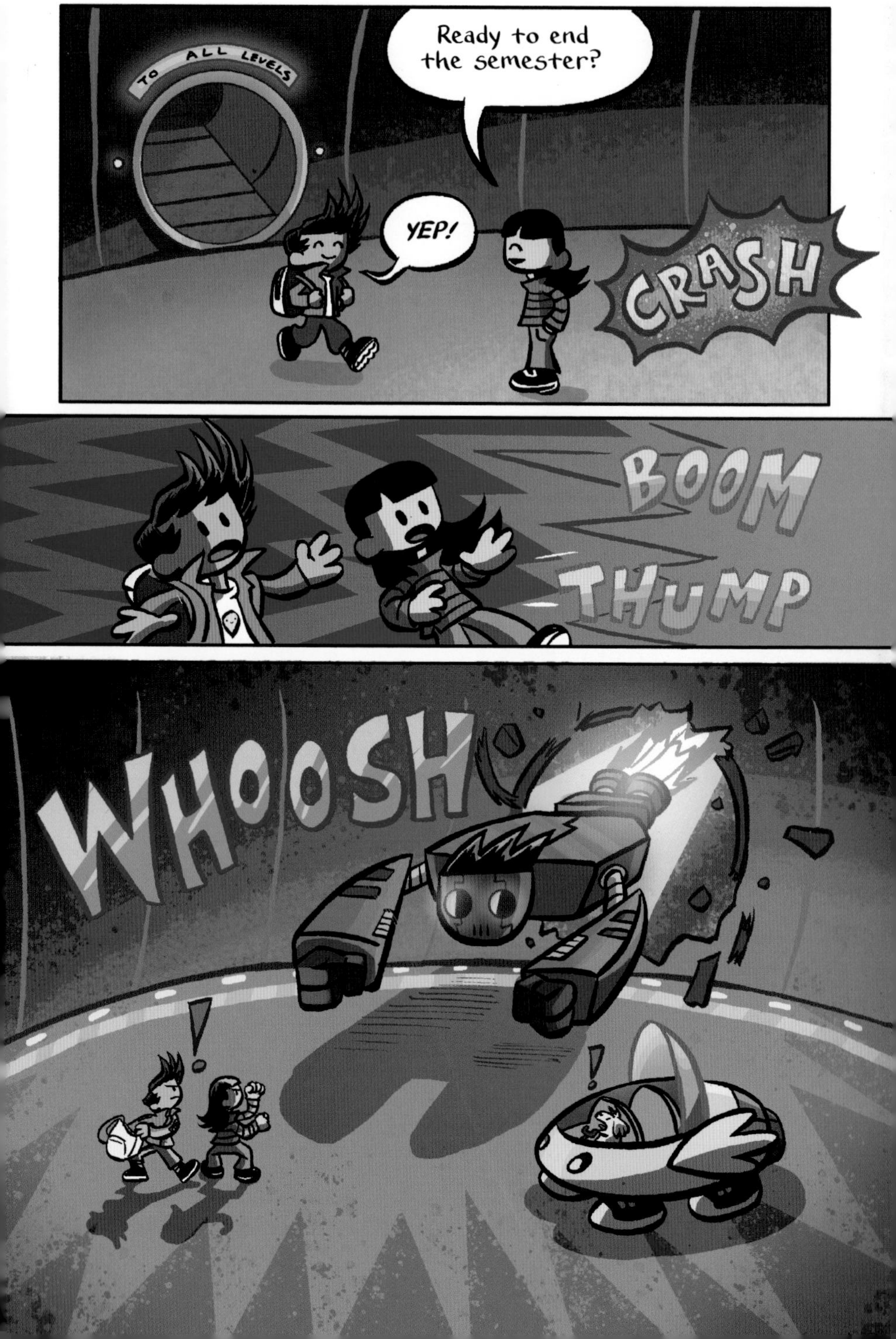

TO ALL LEVELS
Ready to end the semester?
YEP!
CRASH
BOOM
THUMP
WHOOSH
!
!

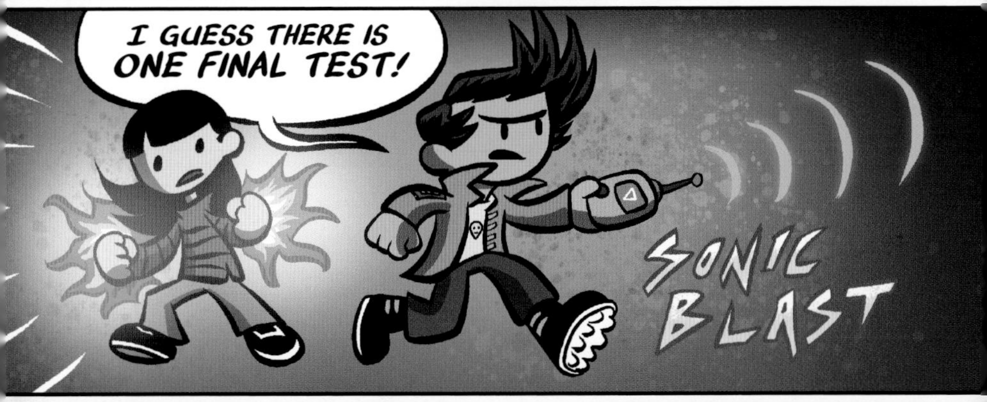
I GUESS THERE IS ONE FINAL TEST!
SONIC BLAST

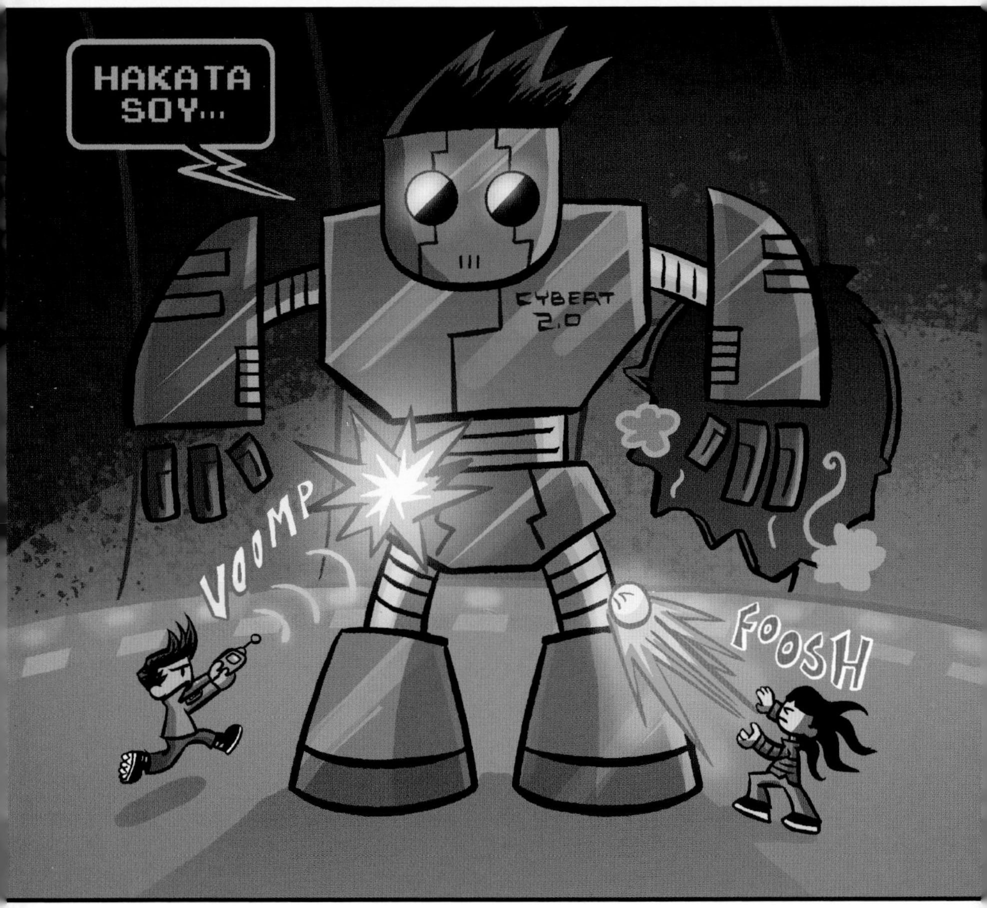
HAKATA SOY...
CYBERT 2.0
VOOMP
FOOSH

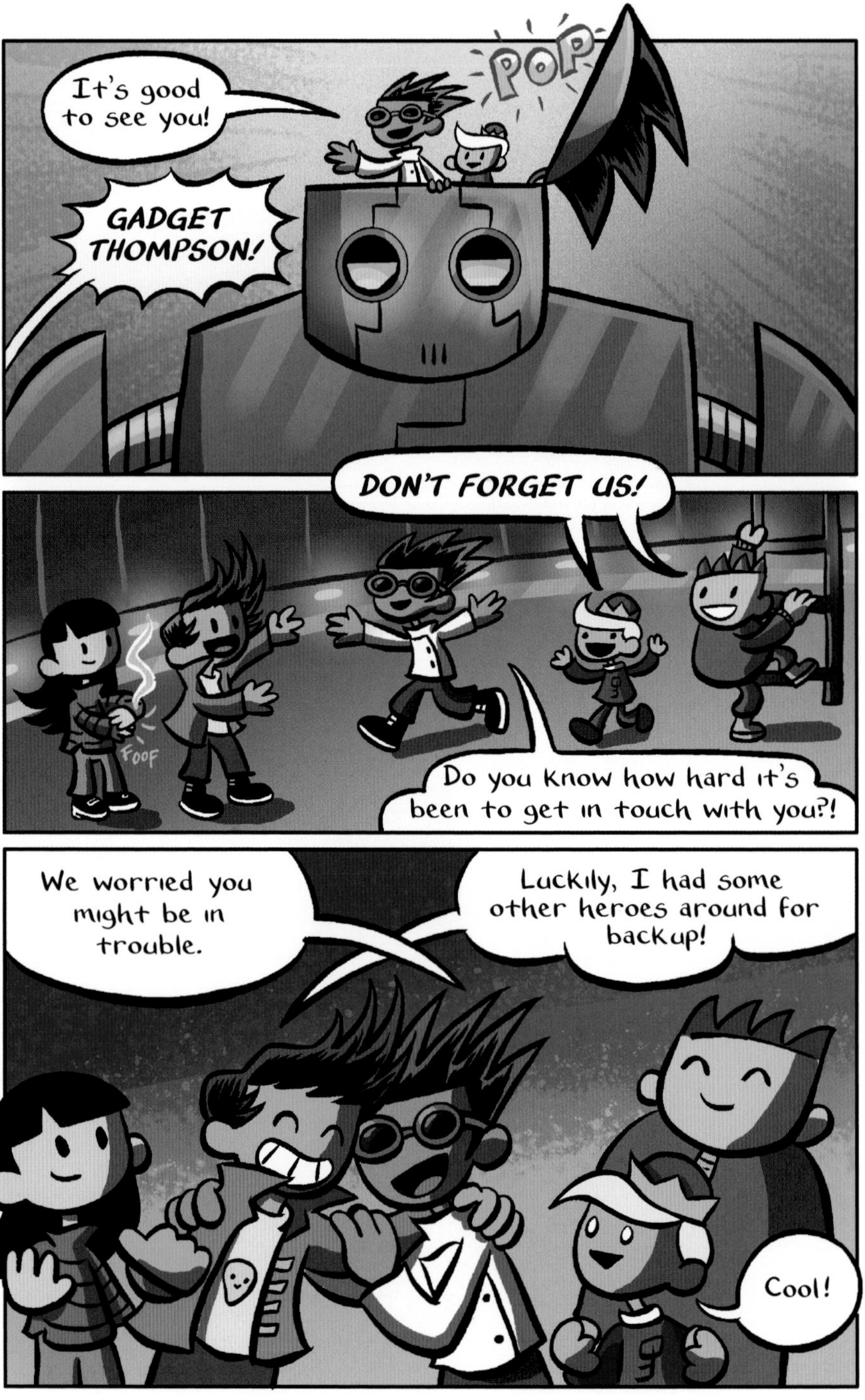
POP
It's good to see you!
GADGET THOMPSON!
DON'T FORGET US!
FOOF
Do you know how hard it's been to get in touch with you?!
We worried you might be in trouble.
Luckily, I had some other heroes around for backup!
Cool!

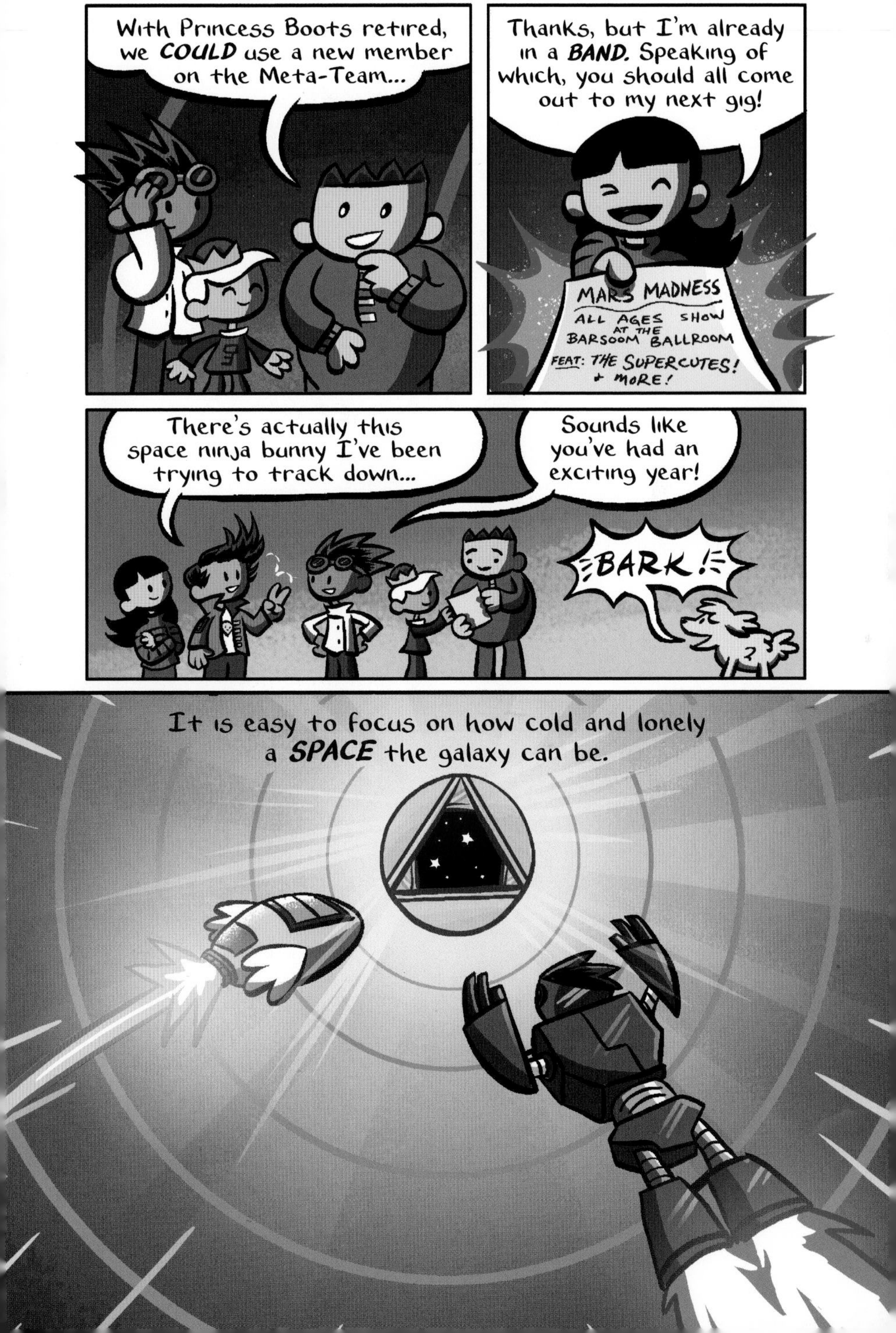
With Princess Boots retired, we COULD use a new member on the Meta-Team...
Thanks, but I'm already in a BAND. Speaking of which, you should all come out to my next gig!
MARS MADNESS
ALL AGES SHOW AT THE BARSOOM BALLROOM
FEAT: THE SUPERCUTES! + MORE!
There's actually this space ninja bunny I've been trying to track down...
Sounds like you've had an exciting year!
BARK!
It is easy to focus on how cold and lonely a SPACE the galaxy can be.

But with the transformative power of
old and new friends combined...

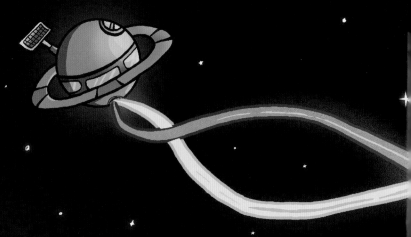

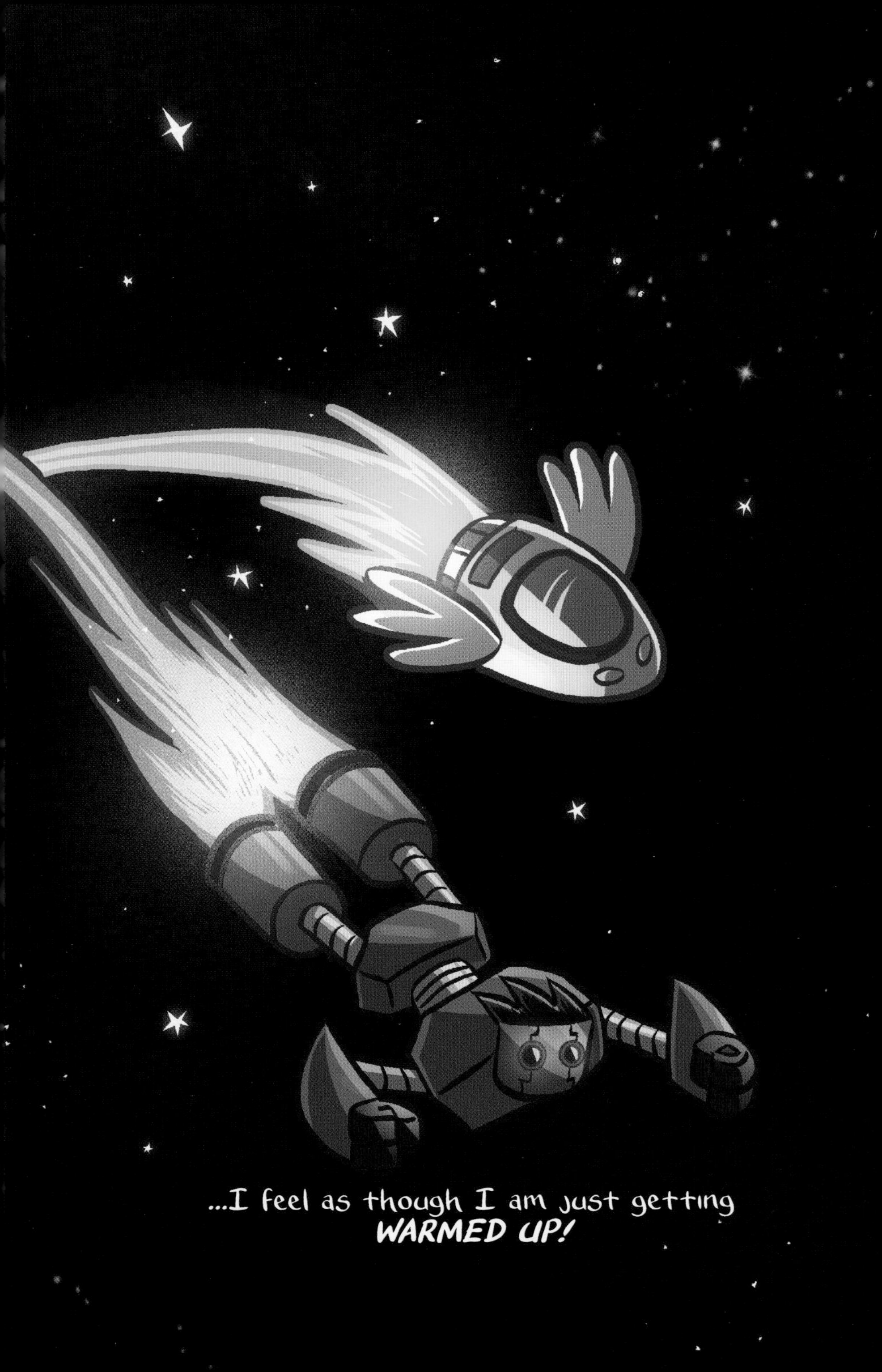
...I feel as though I am just getting
WARMED UP!

making astronaut academy

by dave roman

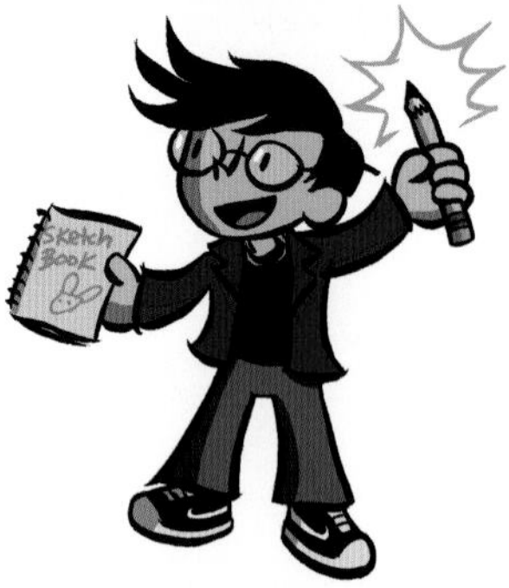
Sketch Book

Ideas can come at any time, so I always keep a sketchbook and pencil close by.

I love designing new characters and imagining how they might interact with each other.

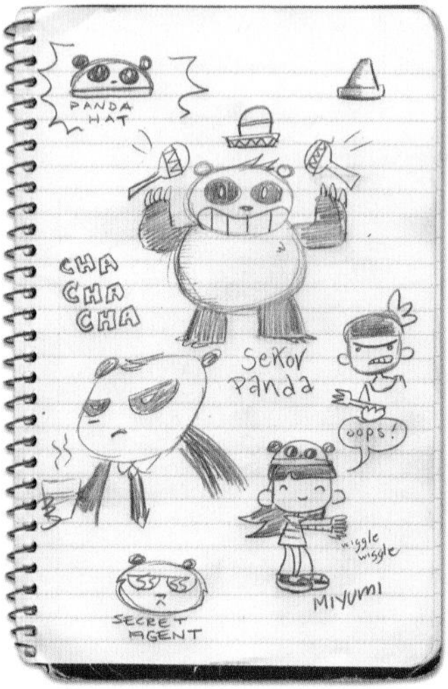
PANDA HAT
CHA CHA CHA
Señor Panda
oops!
wiggle wiggle
SECRET AGENT
MIYUMI

prelude ??

1) Middle
2) Beginning
3) END!
4) Epilogue

SHOULD THIS GO FIRST?

I organize my various ideas by making lists and a story outline.

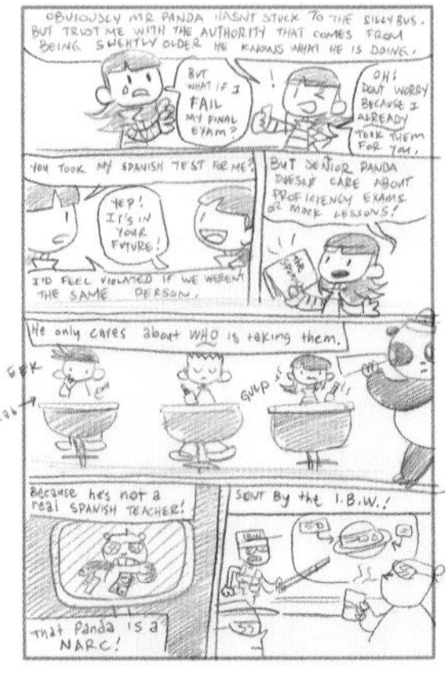
OBVIOUSLY MR PANDA HASN'T STUCK TO THE SILLYBUS. BUT TRUST ME WITH THE AUTHORITY THAT COMES FROM BEING SLIGHTLY OLDER HE KNOWS WHAT HE IS DOING.
BUT WHAT IF I FAIL MY FINAL EXAM?
OH! DON'T WORRY BECAUSE I ALREADY TOOK THEM FOR YOU.
YOU TOOK MY SPANISH TEST FOR ME?!
YEP! IT'S IN YOUR FUTURE!
I'D FEEL VIOLATED IF WE WEREN'T THE SAME PERSON.
BUT SEÑOR PANDA DOESN'T CARE ABOUT PROFICIENCY EXAMS OR MOCK LESSONS!
He only cares about WHO is taking them.
Because he's not a real SPANISH TEACHER!
Sent By the I.B.W.!
That Panda is a NARC!

I write the "script" as a series of rough layouts called thumbnails.

My editor will read the early draft to give feedback and request revisions before I move on to the final art.

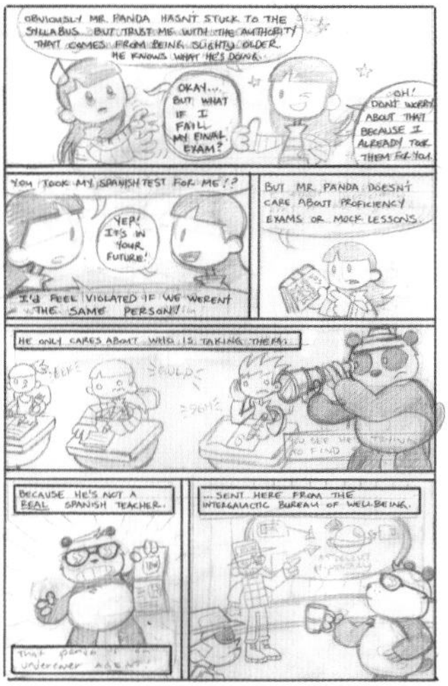
OBVIOUSLY MR. PANDA HASN'T STUCK TO THE SYLLABUS... BUT TRUST ME WITH THE AUTHORITY THAT COMES FROM BEING SLIGHTLY OLDER. HE KNOWS WHAT HE'S DOING.
OKAY... BUT WHAT IF I FAIL MY FINAL EXAM?
OH! DON'T WORRY ABOUT THAT BECAUSE I ALREADY TOOK THEM FOR YOU.
YOU TOOK MY SPANISH TEST FOR ME!?
YEP! IT'S IN YOUR FUTURE!
I'D FEEL VIOLATED IF WE WERENT THE SAME PERSON!
BUT MR. PANDA DOESN'T CARE ABOUT PROFICIENCY EXAMS OR MOCK LESSONS.
HE ONLY CARES ABOUT WHO IS TAKING THEM.
EEK
GULP
SIGH
BECAUSE HE'S NOT A REAL SPANISH TEACHER.
...SENT HERE FROM THE INTERGALACTIC BUREAU OF WELL-BEING.

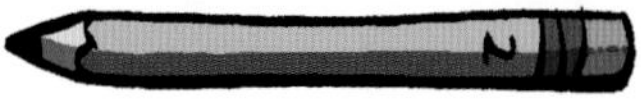

The pencil art is drawn on thick Bristol board, which can handle lots of erasing!

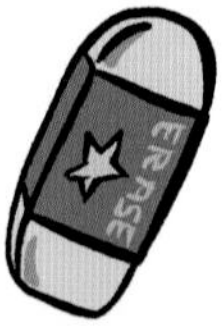
ERASE

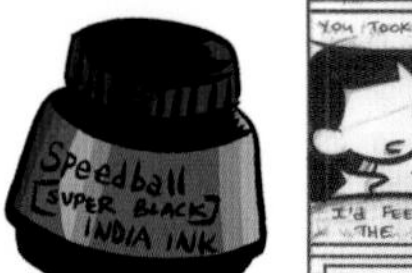
Speedball
SUPER BLACK
INDIA INK

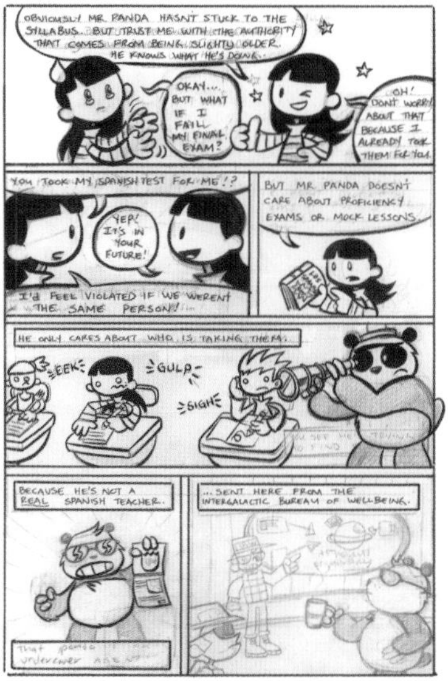
OBVIOUSLY MR. PANDA HASN'T STUCK TO THE SYLLABUS... BUT TRUST ME WITH THE AUTHORITY THAT COMES FROM BEING SLIGHTLY OLDER. HE KNOWS WHAT HE'S DOING.
OKAY... BUT WHAT IF I FAIL MY FINAL EXAM?
OH! DON'T WORRY ABOUT THAT BECAUSE I ALREADY TOOK THEM FOR YOU.
YOU TOOK MY SPANISH TEST FOR ME!?
YEP! IT'S IN YOUR FUTURE!
I'D FEEL VIOLATED IF WE WERENT THE SAME PERSON!
BUT MR. PANDA DOESN'T CARE ABOUT PROFICIENCY EXAMS OR MOCK LESSONS.
HE ONLY CARES ABOUT WHO IS TAKING THEM.
EEK
GULP
SIGH
BECAUSE HE'S NOT A REAL SPANISH TEACHER.
...SENT HERE FROM THE INTERGALACTIC BUREAU OF WELL-BEING.

India ink is used to create dark, permanent lines. I apply it with a watercolor brush capable of various line weights.

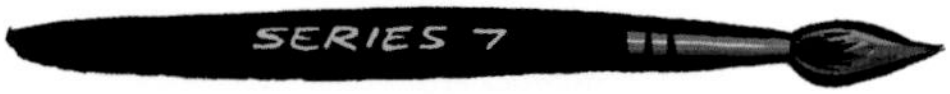
SERIES 7

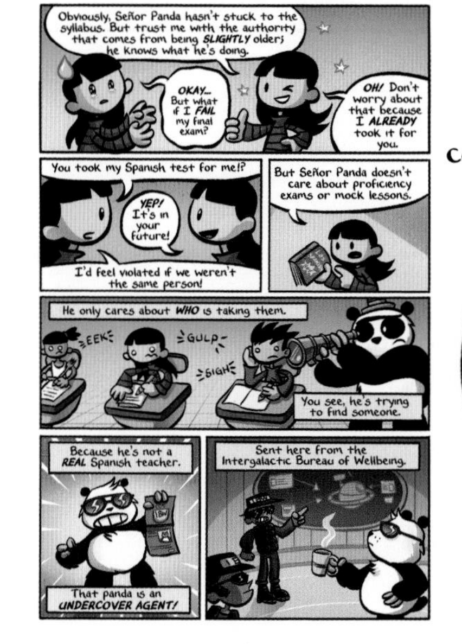
Obviously, Señor Panda hasn't stuck to the syllabus. But trust me with the authority that comes from being SLIGHTLY older; he knows what he's doing.
OKAY... But what if I FAIL my final exam?
OH! Don't worry about that because I ALREADY took it for you.
You took my Spanish test for me!?
YEP! It's in your future!
I'd feel violated if we weren't the same person!
But Señor Panda doesn't care about proficiency exams or mock lessons.
He only cares about WHO is taking them.
EEK
GULP
SIGH
You see, he's trying to find someone.
Because he's not a REAL Spanish teacher.
Sent here from the Intergalactic Bureau of Wellbeing.
That panda is an UNDERCOVER AGENT!

The inked pages are scanned into a computer for cleaning up and lettering then shared with the colorist so they can create their magic.

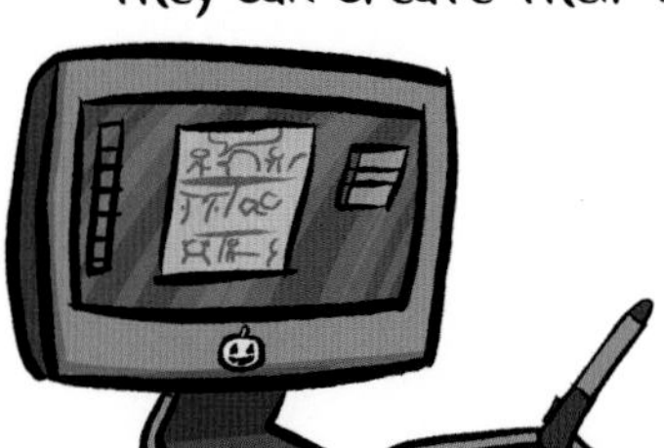

The final files are sent to the publisher and we start the process all over again!

First Second
New York

Text and illustrations copyright © 2013 by Dave Roman
Published by First Second
First Second is an imprint of Roaring Brook Press,
a division of Holtzbrinck Publishing Holdings Limited Partnership
120 Broadway, New York, NY 10271

Don't miss your next favorite book from First Second!
For the latest updates go to firstsecondnewsletter.com and
sign up for our enewsletter.

Library of Congress Control Number: 2020911251
Paperback ISBN: 978-1-250-22593-1
Hardcover ISBN: 978-1-250-22594-8

Our books may be purchased in bulk for promotional, educational,
or business use. Please contact your local bookseller or the Macmillan
Corporate and Premium Sales Department at (800) 221-7945
ext. 5442 or by email at MacmillanSpecialMarkets@macmillan.com.

Edited by Calista Brill and Rachel Stark
2021 cover design by Kirk Benshoff
2021 interior design by Rob Steen
2021 color by Fred C. Stresing
2013 cover design by Colleen AF Venable
2013 interior book design by John Green
2013 production assistants: Gale Williams and Megan Brennan
2013 gray color assists: Ma. Victoria Robado (Shouri),
Charles Eubanks, and Craig Arndt
2013 technical support: John Green
2013 life support: Raina Telgemeier

Printed in China by RR Donnelley Asia Printing Solutions Ltd.,
Dongguan City, Guangdong Province

First edition, 2013
Revised edition, 2021

Drawn with Staedtler graphite pencils on Strathmore 500 series Bristol paper.
Inked with Winsor & Newton Series 7 sable brushes and Speedball India ink.
Lettered with a combination of Speedball Hunt 107 crow quill nib and Yaytime font.
Colored with Photoshop.

Paperback: 10 9 8 7 6 5 4 3 2 1
Hardcover: 10 9 8 7 6 5 4 3 2 1

DAVE ROMAN is the author/illustrator of the Astronaut Academy series (winner of Maryland's Black-Eyed Susan Book Award) and writer of the graphic novels *Teen Boat! The Race for Boatlantis* (with John Patrick Green) and *Agnes Quill: An Anthology of Mystery*. He has contributed stories and art to Goosebumps Graphix's *Slappy's Tales of Horror, Nursery Rhyme Comics*, and the Flight anthology series. Roman is a graduate of the School of Visual Arts, a former editor at *Nickelodeon Magazine*, and is currently the editor for First Second's Science Comics and History Comics ongoing series of nonfiction graphic novels. He lives in NYC and draws a webcomic called *Starbunny, Inc.* You can find him online at yaytime.com and on Twitter and Instagram @yaytime.